THE
ANGEL'S
PROMISE

Frédéric Lenoir
&
Violette Cabesos

PEGASUS BOOKS
NEW YORK

THE ANGEL'S PROMISE

Pegasus Books LLC
45 Wall Street, Suite 1021
New York, NY 10005

Copyright © 2005 by Editions Albin Michel

Translation copyright © 2006 by Lauren Yoder

First Pegasus Books edition 2006

Library of Congress Cataloging-in-Publication Data is available.

ISBN: 1-933648-06-6

10 9 8 7 8 6 5 4 3 2 1

Printed in the United States of America

Distributed by Consortium

I

W ITH A CLASH OF CYMBALS, THE SYMPHONY CAME TO AN END. Johanna's head was pounding, and she had to strain to hear the notes from the next selection. Insidiously the melody filled the space in the car around her, and its sweet sadness brought a lump to her throat. The music's haunting lament—slow, simple, fatal, like life itself—kept returning insistently.

She recognized Ravel's *Pavane pour une infante défunte* and turned her head toward her window so the driver couldn't see the tears that welled up in her eyes whenever she heard that music.

In spite of September's sunshine, the countryside took on a lugubrious tone. The music washed over Johanna; tears drowned her eyes.

"Pierrot, my little brother," she thought, "this is your song, the song of your too-brief existence. It's free from anger, and its tenderness lets sadness show through."

Like Pierre, Ravel's infanta was letting herself be carried off without resistance into a world of dreams where she's welcomed by the angelic sparkling of flutes, by grave horns, and by nostalgic strings. The composer's conclusion was upsetting. After a caressing surge, it continued on resignedly without combat until the breath of the music died away delicately, almost peacefully, to leave the listener hoping in vain to hear the refrain one more time. It was over, but Johanna still waited, half expecting to hear the notes toll once again with their hope of resurrection.

Overwhelmed by her feelings, she turned off the radio.

"Well, I see we've passed the turnoff for Le Havre," she noted, her voice resonant with emotion. "We must be going toward Caen and lower Normandy. I hope you're not taking me to Deauville. I don't want to run into crowds from Paris."

"I know," François answered calmly. "Don't worry, we're not going to Deauville. Trust me, you won't be disappointed; it'll be just the kind of mysterious romantic weekend you like."

"Cabourg?" she asked. "You're not so decadent that you'd take me to your house in Cabourg?"

François blushed. He already felt guilty enough about his relationship with Johanna; he would never have the audacity to take her to the house in Cabourg that his wife Marianne owned. Johanna realized that her words had made him uncomfortable.

"I'm sorry, François. How clumsy of me. I'm not jealous of your wife and children, only interested in everything about you. You've just spent a month's vacation with them and haven't said a word about it."

"I'm interested in everything about you, too, Johanna," François answered. He wasn't keen on talking about his family. "But unlike you, I am jealous!"

"Really?" she said, feigning surprise.

"Yes. Another man occupies your mind, your actions, all the time."

Johanna frowned.

"You wouldn't take any vacation time this summer so you could stay with him," François continued. "Well, maybe not with him, but at least with his ghost. You spend all your time looking for him, but for the time being he stays out of sight."

Johanna understood what François meant and, bursting into laughter, caressed his large hands.

"Some rival! You're jealous of Hugh de Semur, father superior of the Cluny abbey. But he died in 1109! And don't forget that you're the reason my life is centered upon him in the first place."

"Yes, and if I'd known that he would take so much of your time. . . . Maybe he did die in the twelfth century, but his whitened carcass seems to fascinate you more than mine!"

"I've been working in Cluny for only two years," Johanna answered. "But I'm still going strong, and the tomb must be there somewhere. I'll find it if it's the last thing I do. But that doesn't keep me from admiring the way you look."

"But you're spending your life in Cluny, in a hole with dead people. You'll end up just like that Hugh fellow you adore so much!"

Johanna let François take her hand.

"Go ahead and make fun of me! But what if we do manage to get our hands, or shovels, on his tomb?" she went on. "Do you realize what that would mean, for you as well? A tomb lost for centuries. Nobody knows where it is, or even if it still exists. The tomb of the abbot who led the monastery when it was at the height of its glory. He was as powerful as a king. A medieval King Tut! Can you imagine what treasures must be in his grave? If we find it, we could learn so much about those days."

"Now she thinks she's Howard Carter in the Valley of the Kings, and she's dreaming of glory!"

"I don't give a damn about glory, just like Carter," she answered sharply. "And furthermore, don't forget that I'm just an assistant, not the director of the dig. So I won't be the discoverer of the tomb even if we do find it, and I couldn't care less. All I want is to dig, dig, dig."

"Just what I was saying. Some day you'll turn into a mole!"

Johanna grew thoughtful. Her career as an archeologist had become second nature to her. No matter where she was, she couldn't help listening to the messages conveyed in stones shaped by men. For stones did send her messages. Sections of fallen-down or buried walls told her magical stories, and she worked hard to give them new life. But it hurt François to see how she lived, how she gave priority not to relationships with the living but rather to her love for the dead.

"François," she said, lifting his fingers to her lips. "This mole promises to give you its full attention, at least for this weekend. With its little brush, it'll caress you as if you were a twelfth-century stone, and it won't use a pickax."

He leaned over and, taking his eyes of the highway, tried to kiss her.

"Careful!" she shouted.

He straightened back up, grumbling.

Laughing, Johanna watched the countryside slide by. They were nearing Caen.

"So, François, what story did you come up with to explain this weekend?"

"I didn't have to come up with a story," he said sharply. "I don't lie to Marianne. I told her I had a complicated project to check on, that it might be tricky, and that I needed to meet the administrator from Historical Monuments. And that's the truth, whether you happen to be with me or not."

Johanna removed her tiny glasses and began to nibble suspiciously on one of the earpieces.

"Historical Monuments? What are you talking about?"

François turned off the toll road away from Caen and took the highway toward Saint-Lô and then, leaving the town behind, he continued on toward the southwest.

"So it's not Normandy, but Brittany," Johanna observed. "Historical Monuments . . . Saint-Malo?"

François flashed his lovely smile.

"I want it to be a surprise. I won't tell you until we're there."

"Well, in that case, I'm going to take a nap. This poor digger with no vacation needs to rest up for later."

"I can't wait!"

Leaning back in her seat, she closed her eyes and wondered what their destination could be. She was a little annoyed to see François trying once again to mix work and pleasure, but she knew, given his guilty feelings, that it was the only way they could go on seeing each other. Suddenly she felt exhausted. She probably should indeed have taken some vacation, some real vacation. She had plenty of vacation days coming to her. But her friends hadn't been available and she didn't enjoy traveling alone. And then there was that grave she was looking for. She could feel it was there, but somehow it managed to stay hidden is spite of all her efforts. What if she was mistaken? What if the grave was somewhere else? There she was again, thinking only about her work! No, she wouldn't do that this weekend; she was with François, not excavating in her trench. She dozed off, her hand on his leg.

From the very beginning, two years earlier in a muddy hole in Cluny, she had been attracted by François's brilliance and tenderness. A historian with degrees from both the École Normale Supérieure and the École Nationale d'Administration, François was now the associate director of archeology in the Ministry of Culture.

Preceded by his pedigree, he had come to Cluny to inspect a new project his administration had initiated and financed. This wasn't his usual role. Normally, he had the enviable task of staying in his office and making decisions in the name of the minister, authorizing or refusing archeological digs at sites of national interest. But he enjoyed the company of old stones and thought it important to talk with the people at work on the ground.

One day he had been strolling along, alone, through what little was left of the monastery in Burgundy. Paul, the director of the dig, happened to be absent, and it was Johanna who climbed out of the hole along with her fellow workers to greet the important government representative. She recalled how much his height, his clothes, and his official position had impressed her. She was ashamed of her filthy clothing as she stood timidly before him, as she looked more like a worker in the Metro than the medieval archeologist she really was. But he shook her hand firmly and gently, and his amber eyes were warm and direct. She had relaxed, and, as she showed him around the site, they talked about her driving passion, Romanesque art, which gave meaning to her life.

François also loved Romanesque art, but it had taken him more than a year to win Johanna over. It wasn't so much that she resisted, because she was attracted to him immediately. It was more that, in spite of his charm, he wasn't a predatory kind of man and was truly terror-stricken at the idea of destroying his own marriage. Not that he was a slave to bourgeois conventions, but in fact he truly loved his wife and didn't want to see her suffer. Rather than its discouraging her, Johanna found his attachment to his wife comforting. Johanna was just getting over a tumultuous relationship with a colleague, and she longed for something more peaceful. She could accept sharing this man with another woman if that was the price she had to pay for a peaceful relationship that didn't interfere with what gave her life meaning: her work. Slowly, carefully, she had managed to convince François that she loved him and that she wouldn't endanger his marriage.

Lovers for ten months now, they had been careful to meet only in secret. For Johanna there was nothing discordant about a love triangle, and
seeing François only occasionally allowed her to devote herself to the
dig—and that, after all, was what was most important.

When she opened her eyes, she noticed a road sign and suddenly grew
pale. She hurriedly put her glasses back on to be sure. And sure enough,
she hadn't been dreaming.

"Oh, you're back," said François. "We're almost there. Sleep well?"

Johanna didn't say a word. Her face was white, and she tried to hide
how shaken she was.

"Still too sleepy to talk?" he asked. "You noticed the signs, so now I
guess you know where we're going."

Johanna knew only too well. With her hands clenched tightly, unable
to make a sound, she looked straight ahead through the windshield.

"What's wrong?" François asked worriedly, looking over toward her.
"Are you all right? You look really pale. Say something!"

"I'm fine," she forced herself to say. "It must be motion sickness, the
train from Mâcon, then the highway. I shouldn't have tried to sleep. I still
feel groggy."

François took some travel towelettes out of the glove compartment
and gave them to her.

"Here, my dear, these will help you cool down and feel better. Fortunately, we're just about there, and a lovely hotel room awaits us. Oh, look
there!" he said, enthusiastically.

As they came around a turn with dusk falling, off in the distance an incredible shape stood out above a field of violet flowers. They drove along
the field for several kilometers, and the stone pyramid kept growing
larger. François was speechless with admiration, and Johanna with fear.
Suddenly the earth seemed to disappear from the base of the giant totem
and give way to moving water. Several seconds later, the car started across
the causeway.

"'A fairy castle set in the sea,'" François recited. "'A gray shadow against
a hazy sky. As the sun set, the huge expanse of sand was red and the entire bay seemed reddish. Planted upright there far from shore like a fantastic manor, as stupefying as a dream palace, improbably strange and

beautiful, the abbey was almost black in the purple shadows of the dying day!' Maupassant, of course. Now, with the high tides of the equinox, may I present *Mons Sancti Michaelis de Periculo Maris*: Mont-Saint-Michel in peril of the sea!"

A half hour later, Johanna was sitting on the edge of a double bed. François, on his knees, put his hands on her hips and began to kiss her neck. She lay back and looked up at the ceiling. He unbuttoned her blouse, uncovered her breasts. She moved her hands to his torso, to his skin that affected her so, his dark, smooth skin. A generous skin, a little like smooth silk polished by swarms of caresses. The white ceiling was so cold, so smooth! Slowly, images began to form. She looked at François so she wouldn't see them, and, holding his head tightly, clinging to his lips, she breathed in the scent of him. She loved his sweaty smell, warm like sugar, and his brown skin smelled like French toast. She dug her face into his neck and, quivering like a cat, inhaled memories of a childhood tea party. His body was tall and broad, agreeably plump but still firm, soft and enveloping. Her own body began to respond to the familiar irresistible feelings. He was talking to her. But her gaze again was fixed on the white vault above, where a human silhouette was moving. A dark form with hazy outlines. She closed her eyes when he entered her. He kept talking, but she wasn't listening. Other words were pounding in her head, another sentence was forming painful furrows on her forehead and her neck, was mixing her body's pleasure with her spirit's pain. The ceiling was replaced by dark stones, a staircase climbing toward nothingness. Her eyes moved up the stairs and bumped against a dark profile that slowly turned toward her. François's gasp of pleasure brought her spirit back to her body. Staring vacantly, she realized where she was. Then he pulled away.

"Johanna," he murmured as he got his breath back. "Johanna," he repeated, holding her tightly. "You seemed a little distant. Was it good for you?"

"Of course, my dear," she answered, snuggling up against him. "You must have been dreaming. I swear, I'm fine. But don't let me go. Hold me tight."

He held her with infinite tenderness, happy just to be with her. He remembered that first meeting when he had seen her in her muddy work shoes, her jeans faded like the blue in her eyes behind her tiny glasses, her proud chin, her high forehead smudged with clay, the charming freckles on her nose, her long dark hair tied back and topped with a baseball cap. Archeology was a tough elitist career, a little misogynistic, and few women chose it, especially not women as attractive as she was, he thought.

His surprise had turned to intense attraction when Johanna, her eyes sparkling, had begun to talk about Romanesque art. She was barely thirty-one years old, but she had already finished her dissertation on Cluny III and won a job with the Centre National de Recherche Scientifique. It was unusual to meet someone who could talk with such feeling about the development of the tunnel vault and of the semicircular arch. The young woman exuded a powerful passion for her art, and her passion appealed to him. Later he had been afraid, deathly afraid of falling in love with her and of the disastrous consequences that would bring to his family, his source of energy and the point of stability that gave his life meaning. He had struggled against his feelings, as much to protect himself as to protect his wife Marianne, but Johanna had been too strong. Each time they met, he experienced desire like he never had before, even for his wife. Filled with such a strong appetite for both her mind and her body, he finally threw himself into her arms. Living a love triangle was hard for him, but keeping his liaison with Johanna secret allowed him to keep his family life intact.

They left the hotel, and before dinner François took her on a walk along the ramparts built during the Hundred Years' War. For her it seemed like real guard duty. She had changed from her usual tight pants and soft blouse into a short silk dress and red pumps, but although her clothing allowed her to move more freely, anxiety oppressed her like an iron corset.

"How lovely you are," François whispered. "As captivating as this place. But I haven't given you time to tell me what you think of my surprise. I imagine you probably already know the Mount by heart, but now we can yield to its charm together."

Johanna made herself breathe deeply before answering:

"Now it's my turn to surprise you. To tell you the truth, early on I focused on Cluny and Vézelay, and since Mont-Saint-Michel isn't a Cluniac monastery, I'm a long way from knowing it by heart."

François looked surprised, then pleased.

"It's unbelievable that you've never been interested in the Mount! But how marvelous. Because now I can be the one introduce you to its mythology. It's fascinated me since I was a kid, and I could go on forever talking about it."

Johanna felt that her psyche had fallen under attack as she stood watching the gray waves as they crashed against the causeway, swallowed up the parking lot, and began to lap at the towers.

"Take the bay, for example. The tides used to move at prodigious speeds. A meter per second and up to fifteen meters in amplitude. I say they used to, because, back in the year 1000, this was a true island. No causeway and no land reclamation, and both have contributed to silt buildup. Fortunately, they'll soon clean all this up and get rid of that crazy link to the mainland. Before long, if all goes well, we'll need to come on foot like all good pilgrims should. Damn the world of cars! Soon we'll have to leave our motorcars behind and walk across a footbridge."

Johanna said nothing. François took her silence for disapproval.

"You're right, my dear, I'm a lousy guide. I'm doing things backwards. I need to start at the beginning, and for that we need to climb the steps and go back in time."

He grabbed her hand excitedly and pulled her up along through the village with its narrow cobblestone streets and steep steps. On both sides, the wrought-iron signs in front of the tourist shops all looked pretty much alike. The half-timbered houses had been nicely restored, and most had evocative names like "The Artichoke House," "Typhaine Manor," "Du Guesclin," or "House of the Running Sow." As they made their way up the stone steps, they were welcomed by little gardens and hundred-year-old trees. At the top, far above ground level, with its golden steeple rising in the air, the imposing abbey stood in majesty, and their mouths gaped in wonder.

"There," said François, trying to catch his breath, "that's where it all began, thirteen centuries ago. Let's not go in yet, all right? Maybe later, after dinner. But for now, just follow me."

They continued up other stairways and, panting heavily, finally came out on the square in front of the abbey church, their legs wobbly. Many visitors, particularly couples, had gathered there to take in the extraordinary panorama. Water now covered the base of the Mount, still linked, however, to the mainland by that unfortunate causeway.

At the horizon, water and sky met, and pink streaks appeared in the deepening blue sky. Johanna sat on the parapet and marveled at the red setting sun. François cleared his throat and, putting his hands on her shoulders, looked out over the sea.

"Once upon a time, at the edge of a sandy, watery desert filled with fog and storms that were the stuff of legends, there was a granite rock called Mont Tombe. Like a stone statue reaching toward the sky, the mountain had been prey to nature's chaos since the time in the eighth century when the Scissy Forest that surrounded it, extending all the way to Brocéliande, had been swallowed up by a fiendish tempest. After that, twice a day, at the beck and call of the sun and the moon, the tides would rise as fast as a galloping horse and surround the rock with their foamy rage, cutting it off from the rest of the world."

Johanna smiled and seemed to relax a little. François was not only a good historian; he also knew how to tell stories that could make you dream.

"Here at the borders of celestial clouds and earthly shores," he continued, "between the earth and the great beyond, this strange 'Island of the Dead' had already been chosen by the divine Archangel as his dwelling place. The most important person in the celestial kingdom after Christ, the great organizer of passage to the other world, Saint Michael had appeared in a vision to Aubert, the bishop of Avranches, enjoining him to build a sanctuary on Mont Tombe. The prelate saw the archangel three times in his visions, and finally, after the third time, he resolved to carry out the order given by God's messenger."

"When was that?" asked Johanna, entranced by his words.

"Still back in the eighth century, my dear. On October 16, 709, Aubert consecrated an oratory dedicated to Saint Michael, and he built it with stones from the mountain, tight against the rock. From that moment on, in spite of all the dangers awaiting them—quicksand, tides, storms, brigands—pilgrims flocked to the sanctuary. Twelve Breton canons guarded it, and they lived off charity provided by the pilgrims, fish that washed up on shore, food from their garden watered by a miraculous spring Saint Michael had opened in the rock. It's called Saint Aubert's spring—and look, there it is right there!"

Johanna risked a quick, dizzying look down but felt more comfortable looking out over the sea.

François leaned forward and brushed his lips against her hair. "In the ninth century, the king of France gave the Mount to the Bretons. But the peace in Brittany didn't last long, for in those troubled times there was a new peril from the sea threatening the region. Hordes of barbarian Vikings were arriving from the north in their strange drakkars, and the king of France had to cede to a Scandinavian pirate named Rollon a region that later became . . . "

"Normandy!" Johanna exclaimed.

"Yes, and you know what happened next. In 933, the Vikings led their troops against the Bretons and crushed them. The king of France gave the Cotentin region to Guillaume-Longue-Epée, son of Rollon, and that's how Mont-Saint-Michel became Norman, to the Bretons' great chagrin. The boundary between these two neighboring enemy territories—yes, they were enemies for centuries—is right there before your eyes. At low tide, the Couesnon River, flowing at the foot of this rock, still marks the line between Brittany and Normandy. The Vikings were bloodthirsty barbarian pirates, but they converted to Christianity and became Norman lords. The dukes of Normandy gave generously to the monks on Mont-Saint-Michel: money, land, and villages."

"But weren't the first canons in the eighth century from Brittany?" asked Johanna.

"Right. In fact, Richard I, Duke of Normandy, appropriately called Richard the Fearless, soon began to suspect the canons' loyalty. According to Norman legends, they had lost their discipline and were more inclined to celebrate with other inhabitants on the Mount than to shower their devotions on Saint Michael.

"And so in 966, with the pope's blessing, Richard threw out the canons and entrusted the holy site to twelve Benedictine monks from Norman abbeys. And that's how the golden legend of Mont-Saint-Michel began, a legend molded over the centuries by Benedictines who tried unflaggingly to bring renown to the place as they built this immense abbey, ultimately the richest of the region, into a place of worship and a pilgrim site recognized throughout all Christendom."

Dressed as she was in a summer dress with thin shoulder straps, and in spite of her hair hanging down on her shoulders, Johanna couldn't keep from shivering when she heard François's words.

"You're shivering!" said François worriedly. "Is that because I'm talking about Benedictine monks without referring to your dear Hugh de Semur or to Cluny?"

Johanna looked away, out into the falling darkness.

"Oh, I'm sorry. I didn't mean to offend you," he murmured. "Here, put this on," he said, wrapping his coat around her. "That's a lovely dress, but it's a little light for this sea breeze. What's the matter? Don't you feel well?"

"No, not really. Your tale was captivating, but I haven't eaten anything since this morning, and I'm about to collapse. Let's go have dinner," she answered.

Their table was waiting on a terrace back off the street, and it had a great view over the ink-black bay. Johanna came back from the restroom and dropped weakly to her chair. She was very pale.

"Let's order right away," François said. "We need to get your blood sugar level back up," he said, touching her thigh.

Twenty minutes later, part of her face hidden by a huge seafood platter topped with large prawns, Johanna was concentrating on a crab and François on a large Cancale oyster.

"Could I have a little more wine?" she asked.

"Of course. Tell me, Johanna," he began. "We've known each other for nearly two years now and have been together for almost a year. And I've never seen you like this. Usually you are so strong and have so much energy. But now you can hardly speak, you're pale, and you're off somewhere else when we make love. You even have trouble walking, and you're drinking more than usual. Aren't you pleased to see me again? Do you have something to tell me? If so, I. . . . "

Johanna looked up and kept eating, as she gazed straight into his eyes. "It has nothing to do with you," she said.

"Nothing to do with me? Then who?" he asked, blood rising to his face. "Your work? Or perhaps you've met someone else?"

"Yes, I did meet someone else. A long time ago. Right here. And that meeting shattered my life."

François began to cough, as much out of relief as embarrassment. "Tell me," he said, reaching for her.

"It's a crazy story. I've never told anyone," she began, blushing a little. "But here goes. Once upon a time, when I was seven years old—or rather, when I was going to turn seven on August 15—my parents and I were spending our summer vacation in the little town of Agon-Coutainville up in the Cotentin, where we had rented a lovely cottage. What a change from the Drôme and the cold mistral wind! Anyway, my mother, like a good devout Catholic, wanted us to go the mass in Mont-Saint-Michel on August 15. In case you've forgotten your catechism, I remind you that the fifteenth is Ascension Day, the day the Virgin Mary ascended to heaven. It's my birthday, too, and a very painful day for my parents and me, because it was also my twin brother Pierre's birthday. He died three months after we were born, from sudden infant death syndrome. Yes, I know. I've never told you about it. But really I never talk about it because I don't really remember anything about him. In short, there we were, all three of us, at Mont-Saint-Michel. It was the first time we had been here, and like the thousands of other tourists who were here at the same time, we were awed by the abbey's beauty. Up above, in the abbey church, there was a strange atmosphere. High mass, the cool walls, the incense, the weight of history, the fervor of the chants of pilgrims who had come from the shore. It was as if time had stopped. So much so that we didn't feel like going back to Coutainville."

"Yes, the magic of old stones," François said, still surprised to learn that Johanna had had a twin brother.

"Yes. Finally, after the mass, while my mother was alone in one of the little chapels in the choir to pray in remembrance of my brother, my father and I went down into the village to find an inexpensive room where we could spend the night. I can still remember that my father bought me a big red lollipop shaped like Saint Michael. We did find a room."

She poured herself a little more of the Sancerre wine before continuing: "I had trouble falling asleep. It was so warm, and I was suffocating under the pink duvet. Finally, I drifted off, and I saw . . . "

Johanna looked around her like a frightened animal.

"I saw . . . a tall stone structure with a lot of ropes hanging from it. A bell tower, probably. There was a monk standing motionless by a dark opening. And then he fell. His fall was broken suddenly, and I could hear the sound of bones cracking. Down below, I moved toward the tower. It was dark and the wind was howling, but I could hear the waves lapping against the shore. I was beside an abbey near the sea, probably at Mont-Saint-Michel, but perhaps not, because things were not exactly as they are now. But one thing I do know is that up on the tower I could see the poor monk's body hanging, swinging in the wind like a marionette. I couldn't see his face, only his frock held by a long rope swaying against the tower. A hanging! Yes, a hanging! I lowered my eyes in horror, and suddenly I was somewhere else, a place I had never seen before, a dark chapel, with rough building stones exposed. Dark, stone, vaulted ceilings. There was a large candle burning on an altar with an arch above it, and an endless stairway. And a monk dressed just like the hanged man was slowly climbing the stairs. Suddenly he turned toward me!"

Johanna closed her eyes for a moment. François was hanging on her every word.

"And then I realized that he . . . that he didn't have a head. There was just a dark empty hole in the hood of his robe. He raised his arms, clasped his hands as if in prayer, and then in a grave, solemn voice he spoke, pronouncing each syllable as if it were the Last Judgment: 'Ad accedendum ad caelum, terram fodere opportet.' The chapel's stones echoed with the strange words."

François caught the meaning of the sentence, but didn't say anything. Johanna gave a sigh. A sigh of relief.

"The next morning, it was raining. The raindrops formed bars on the windows. Fog covered the bay. I didn't say a word. Papa paid the bill and we went back to Coutainville. I made sure to write the words down in a notebook. I wrote them phonetically, having no idea what they meant. I didn't even know what language it was. I thought it was the language of the dream fairies.

"Three years later, my father was able to get transferred to the Seine-et-Marne, because mother couldn't stand living in the Drôme. The mistral gave her too many migraines. I found myself in a classy school in Fontainebleau where they taught Latin. When I heard how Latin sounded, I knew it was the fairy language I had heard in my nightmare. It was the language of that mysterious sentence, and people called it a dead language. So, without delay, I showed the notebook to my Latin teacher after class one day. I said I had heard the sentence during mass in a monastery. He smiled when he saw my spelling mistakes. Then he whispered the sentence, his eyes grew bright, and he made some corrections. Afterwards he said that it was 'very beautiful and quite true, a lesson for life,' and that I should keep studying Latin. *Ad accedendum ad caelum, terram fodere opportet*: 'You must dig in the earth to reach heaven. . . .'"

"And you became an archeologist," François whispered.

"Yes," she answered softly. "I know. It's not by chance. I spend my life digging in the ground, but I've never again seen the headless monk. And I had never come back to Mont-Saint-Michel. Before today."

With tears in her eyes, her throat dry, she finished her wine.

"Well!" François said with emotion. "Really, Johanna. You are full of surprises! And I thought I'd be surprising you by bringing you here? You're quite an unusual person, and I'm pleased to understand you better. Johanna, brilliant medievalist, expert in Romanesque art, archeologist, who digs in the earth at Cluny—"

"So?" she cut in angrily.

"So? You're fulfilling a childhood dream. Your magnificent vocation as an archeologist, your devouring passion, is the result of a dream, my dear, the product of a child's nightmare. Your imagination has blown it all out of proportion, exacerbated by repressed guilt from the death of your twin brother."

Johanna's body stiffened. She was so angry that her face grew red and her voice cut like a razor.

"Oh, please! Spare me your dime-store psychology! Whether you believe it or not, I've always felt that the dream was communicating something very real. Something so real that I shiver whenever I think of it, as if I had witnessed some tragedy far back in history. Such a powerful tragedy that it had to reappear centuries later in a little girl's dream. And who knows? Perhaps over the centuries other people have had the same dream. After all, don't stones have memory?"

2

THE BLACK SKY IS HEAVY AND OPAQUE, ALMOST AS IF IT WERE carved from the wall itself, and it looks like a heavy, homespun monk's robe through the curved, flat-brick window. Stung by invisible forces, the silence and the mountain are buffeted by bitter whips of wind and water. Down below, waves are crashing against the shore, and higher up, the echo of their efforts to come ashore joins the powerful winds battering the church.

"Michael archangele . . . gloriam predicamus in terris."

As vibrant as the flame of candles burning on the altar, the glowing refrain rises from a column of monks the color of night.

"Eius precibus adiuvemur in caelis."

Impervious to the impetuous wind gusting through the openings in the wall, a second column of monks, parallel to the first, answers in harmony. For two long hours, standing in the shadows, facing the choir, the dark army watches, chants, its language of the spirit opposing the clamor of the terrestrial elements, its prayer shield forged in the world of heavenly angels. The priest's hebdomadary prayer marks the end of Matins.

Two by two, the monks bow before a little old man with blue eyes. He blesses each of his sons before they slowly file out of the abbey church. Outside, the monks, still in columns, pull their hoods up and silently disappear into the stormy darkness. The sharp gusts can't alter their pace; guided by a swaying lantern, they hold to their path. Wood and stone buildings arranged in the shape of a horseshoe surround the church like a protective belt. The temple guards file into the dormitory, a damp space separated into cells by lengths of hanging cloth. Each of the Archangel's servants moves toward his bed, a serge-covered mat and a pillow stuffed with hay. The bed will also serve as his shroud when the precious moment of death arrives.

The monks first remove their knives, then the waxed wooden tablets and the styluses hanging at their sides. Finally they take off their hooded scapulars and lie down in their robes.

On this night at the beginning of autumn, the cold isn't yet penetrating. But in this hidden corner of Normandy, much more than the snow, which is uncommon, and much more than the cold, which you can get used to, men fear the sea, the brutal sea that cuts the mountain off from the world of the living, that allies itself with the breath of the Evil One to crush boats or make them disappear in the thick fog, to seize pilgrims and drown them in its currents or swallow them up in its quicksand. The sea, whose briny breath eats at the hearts of clerics and lay brothers and leads them into the worst of sins, into acedia and despair. All the brothers but one go back to sleep after Matins, for one of them always keeps watch. In the middle of the dormitory, the *significator horarum,* sentinel of passing time, has just lit the third and last candle of the night. When it dies, the shadows will also disappear and the villagers, workmen, and lords can again come back to life and take up their place in the order of this world.

The last candle is still burning, radiating soft light in the midst of human silence and nature's anger. When it is about half consumed, the master of the hours rings a bell that hangs in the corner of the room. Then the army surges into wakefulness, dons its hoods, and again walks toward the abbey church. The columns reform, and immediately the chants of the office of Lauds rise up against the wind. As psalms and chants resonate, the dark sky begins to weaken and lose its matte blackness. A veil of light turns it gray as furtively as the flame on the altar eats away at the candle. The thick walls, their massive stones joined with sand and lime, become visible as the darkness recedes. The ceremony of Lauds proceeds. The *significator horarum* gathers the last breath of the third candle. Dawn has come, gray and starless, but certain. The struggle between the forces of light and darkness is over, and the brothers have completed their mission. The earthly world is still sleeping, but here, at the border between heaven and earth, they have kept watch over the souls of those who slept while, during the twelve hours of night, demons prowled. Their Lauds done, monks return once more to their dormitory and doze until the office of Prime, when the sun rises victorious and they all, clerics and lay people alike, can rise to live according to the measure of that pure symbol of divine light.

In their thatch-roofed huts, the villagers emerge naked from their family beds and cross themselves three times before they pray. They pull on their shirts and breeches or stockings and dresses while, up above them, the monks put their scapulars back on and reattach their knives and writing instruments. Then they all wash their hands and faces. The peasants noisily eat their bacon, soup, and bread along with garlic, mustard, and Norman wine. The silent monks meanwhile go back to church to celebrate Prime, which will be followed by morning mass. They won't break their own fast until midday, at the sixth hour, when the sun is at its zenith.

After morning mass, one of the clerics pulls his black hood back up over his head. His fine features concealed, he hurries out the monastery door and through the wooden palisade built by Richard I when the Benedictines arrived. Lost in thought, the cleric marches quickly down to the village, really only a few little huts with stone walls, thatched roofs, and oiled paper for windows. He looks up at the sun that has begun to burn away the fog banks and walks still faster down the muddy path. Worriedly, he studies the sea while returning the deferential greetings of the villagers busily carrying water from the spring, feeding their chickens and geese, or digging in their little gardens where beans, cabbage, and peas grow.

Brother Roman, twenty-nine years old, finally reaches the shore, where a small sailboat and a fisherman await him. As soon as the monk is aboard, they sail off toward the deep. Roman looks out over the waves, their color the same anthracite gray as his eyes. In spite of his youth, his thin lips and nose, along with his high forehead, give him a thoughtful look. His pale skin and the refined hands of a scholar betray his aristocratic origins, common among monastery priests. As the office of Terce begins in the monastery, the boat has already reached Granville and continues toward the west.

Roman kneels in the bottom of the boat and prays in silence, according to the rule of Saint Benedict. Soon thereafter, land is in sight. "Land" is really just a series of small windswept islands, the Chausey Islands, many of which aren't even visible at high tide. The boat pulls up onto the largest island. Roman signals the fisherman to wait, then walks out over the rocky expanse. Deserted. Sand beaches alternate with rocky cliffs, and gray, bare rocks lie everywhere, as if sown randomly by a giant's hand, their rough surfaces corroded by the sky's salty breath. The wind is strong, and Roman has to hold his hood over his tonsured skull. He comes out onto a strange area that looks like a Roman amphitheater with an ancient colossus as an audience. On the huge steps, workmen have set mortises in the rock's seams. Wood wedges, hammered into the cracks and then soaked with water, swell up and split the granite in layers, so the stonecutters can trim them right there in the quarry. When he sees Roman, Master Jehan leaps out of a trench. Brother Roman follows the master stonecutter down into the quarry. Consulting his parchments, the sketches drawn by Pierre de Nevers, a Cluny monk who drew up the plans for the new abbey church, he checks the quality of the material and the size of the stones.

Roman was fourteen when he first met Pierre de Nevers, the famous monk from Burgundy who had come to Bavaria to build the Bamberg cathedral. The monk was a friend of his father, Siegfried of Marburg, an important local nobleman, and so he stayed in the family's castle. For three years Roman, whose given name was Jean, got to know the scholar and grew passionate about his art. He followed the monk to the construction site; he learned about arithmetic and building materials; and he became utterly fascinated by the way Pierre de Nevers could transfer secret ideas to paper and make them grow. However, because he was the second son and therefore destined to give his life in service to God, Jean de Marburg had to leave his family and abandon his dreams of becoming a builder. As a novice, he began his theological studies in a Benedictine monastery in Cologne when he was seventeen. When he was ordained, he took the name of Roman; just after that, Pierre de Nevers wrote to his abbot to ask if he could take the young brother as his assistant and train him for a career in architecture. With the blessing of Father Romuald, the head of the order, Roman followed his master across Europe.

They were working on a project in Italy when, in 1017, the abbot of Mont-Saint-Michel called upon the famous architect to plan and construct the new abbey. The abbot, helped by his most erudite monks, set ambitious terms and conditions for Pierre de Nevers, and for five years he worked hard to transfer their ideas and symbols into architectural concepts. Roman was Pierre de Nevers's primary assistant during those days, and with much study he completed his apprenticeship. He was aided by Brother Bernard, an older monk who illuminated manuscripts. Once the drawings were finished, Pierre de Nevers left his assistant in charge of supervising the construction work. He went back to Cluny, his home monastery, where he was to complete the construction of Saint-Pierre-le-Vieil, a church started in 955. His good friend Odilon, the abbot, had given him the charge, and he had been working on it for sixteen years.

On the Mount, before the long construction process can get under way, Roman has to look after numerous details, especially the granite from the Chausey Islands. A stonecutter is the most important workman on a building site, and Roman has to be able to count on Master Jehan. Fortunately, Master Jehan is a reliable man at the head of a lodge of workmen whose reputation extends beyond Normandy and Brittany. The master can read, write, and speak Latin, so has no problem understanding the architect's notes and sketches. The stone is of excellent quality and there's an unlimited quantity on the islands, though there's none on the Mount itself. And the stones the team has cut are exactly what Pierre de Nevers was hoping for. The major difficulty lies in getting them to Mont-Saint-Michel. Once again, the fickle but powerful sea can help them, but they need to be wary of storms. Riding the tide, wooden barges will move the stones from Chausey to the Archangel's mountain. Brother Roman and Master Jehan are seeing to the details when the position of the sun indicates the sixth hour. The stonecutters put down their tools and pull knives, chunks of black bread, eggs, bacon, cheese, and flasks of wine from their bags.

Faithful to the Rule of Saint Benedict that forbids a monk to eat outside of the convent if he is absent for only one day, Brother Roman eats nothing. He leaves Master Jehan and his stonecutters and, following the path the stones will later take, returns to where the fisherman is waiting to take him back to more hospitable lands. When it's time for Nones, they get to the little port of Genêts. There, the quiet waters spread out in sinuous paths. Nearby, between the Dol and Tombelaine mountains, the silhouette of the sacred mountain stands tall with its round peak and its almost bare flanks, like Mount Ararat where Noah's ark came aground.

"A new ark will soon see the day up there, and pilgrims will flock here in fervent waves in search of salvation," Brother Roman dreams. A peasant on foot, leading a horse, calls out a humble greeting that brings the builder back to earth.

"Master," says the peasant in the local dialect, "here's your horse."

In 966, Duke Richard I had given the Benedictines not only the Mount and the surrounding lands but also the people who lived there, and the abbot held temporal and spiritual power over them. His vassals were not unhappy with their ecclesiastical lord, for he encouraged them to cultivate the rich soil as well as to raise sheep and pigs and thus guarantee their own subsistence as well as the abbey's opulence. Brother Roman nods to the man, climbs on the horse, and gallops toward the forest. He's a fine horseman, and he rides through a clearing where greedy pigs are eating acorns and beechnuts.

Whenever he gallops through these woods, he remembers the Bavarian forest where, hunting with his father, he rode after deer or hunted with falcons or hawks, as was the privilege of noblemen. He remembers Otton, the falcon he raised, trained, and then sadly had to give to his brother when he entered the monastery. Monks do not hunt, except sometimes for demons. When he does reflect on his past life, he feels neither emotion nor regret. His fervor is authentic and grows more intense daily, especially since he has discovered architecture as a way to express his faith. A smile comes to his face when he spots Master Roger, the future abbey church's carpenter. He's a solid forty-five-year-old with long hair and heavy muscles, his face tanned by the open air. Although the man is not without wit and learning, the young man is attracted to him primarily because of his friendly demeanor. And there's something quite curious about Roger. He has the same eyes as Roman's older, princely brother, who's so elegant yet strong. Large eyes, unusually gray, with flecks of green, as if they were painted by a great artist. When Roman looks Roger in the eyes, he often thinks for a moment that he's talking to his brother. But then he sees the carpenter's thick, blond beard and heavy shoulders, and he hears his booming voice. Roman takes pleasure in imagining that Roger is his brother's double and that he might appear in a knight's garb. Monks are not allowed to write to their families or receive any direct communication from them. When they join God's family, the brothers break with their own. So Roman hasn't seen his brother or any of his clan for twelve years. Although the carpenter is unaware of it, he has become a link with Roman's childhood and brings a little joy to his heart.

"Good day, Brother Roman!" says Master Roger.

Around him, woodsmen are chopping down oak and chestnut trees— oak is strong and chestnut protects from lightning—in a section of the forest used exclusively for the needs of the monastery. Off to one side, under shelter, mountains of logs are already drying. They were cut in the winter when the moon was waning, then debarked, rough hewn, and soaked in water for a year to remove all sap and salt and thus prevent rotting. Roman gets down off his horse and tethers it to a tree. A big smile on his face, he goes over to the carpenter.

"My greetings, Master Roger," he says, throwing his arms around him and looking into his eyes. "How are you and your family?"

"Quite well, except for little Brigitte, my fourth daughter, who's barely ten. For the last two days she hasn't been herself. She can't swallow even a spoonful of soup without vomiting."

"Have you called the doctor?" Roman asks, saddened by the news.

"He came yesterday just before Compline," answers Roger, wringing his hands. "He bled her, but she still vomited up her soup last night and this morning. She's very weak and getting weaker all the time."

The carpenter grows quiet, but his eyes seem to want to add something. Roman is used to the language of silence and waits patiently. Roger continues: "I'm—I'm not sure what to do, but my wife says that if Brigitte is still sick this evening, she'll go get the healer from Beauvoir village."

Master Roger pauses again. He's watching to see what Roman's reaction might be. Roman, being a scholar monk, probably mistrusts folk healers (people in the region call them *toucheurs*). Roman understands Roger's fear and says nothing, but his face remains encouraging.

"I know what you must think," the carpenter finally says. "Some people say that she has commerce with the devil, but in the village we all know her. She's a good Christian, and with her plants she healed little Andelme. The doctor didn't give him more than two days; he had the fever, and she saved him. And old Herold couldn't even walk any more, and she fixed up his leg."

Roman knows that he must say something.

"I've heard about the woman's good deeds, as have we all in the monastery," he says, interrupting Roger. "The devil doesn't heal sick bodies; he tries to seize souls. If the woman is able to heal the sick without causing harm to their souls, why not call her to your daughter's bedside?"

The monk's words bring a smile of relief to Roger's face.

"But don't forget," Roman adds: "Prayer is the best remedy, and Christ is the greatest healer. And now I place Brigitte in the hands of our Lord."

"Thank you, Brother Roman. May our Lord hear you."

"He hears all prayers, Master Roger, and the destiny of all men is in his hands."

Roman turns toward an apprentice, who lays down his ax. He allows the monk to examine the beam he's hewing. Roger and Roman spend the afternoon choosing timbers for building the granite barges, and set aside as well the very best one, which will be cured under shelter for years and eventually used to crown the Ark. Then the priest climbs back on his horse so that he can be back at the abbey before the tide turns and Vespers begins.

The bells are already ringing on the mountain as he walks up. He leaves his horse with the lay brother in charge of the stable and joins the monks already forming two columns in the church near the altar. The right column passes along the wall with open windows, but the left column walks along the two large stone arcades separating the church from another sanctuary. Indeed, beside the oratory where the brothers praise the Lord, there's another oratory; and just as the two lines of monks mirror each other, so do the oratories, in that they have the same layout and covering, the same square nave ending in a small choir with a barrel vault where the altar stands along with a staircase that rises up to meet the stone vault.

One detail alone differentiates the twin sanctuaries: The altar lit with candles and chants during the office is dedicated to the Holy Trinity, whereas, beyond the arcades, its double holds a wooden statue of Mary holding the Child Jesus to her bosom. The statue is a Black Virgin with narrow eyes, her face darkened by smoke from candles and incense, her presence invoked to protect travelers and to make women fertile.

"De Angelis, fetivis diebus ad Vesperus . . . "

"Our good Richard of Normandy is right," Roman thinks. "This double sanctuary is an aberration. When I think about his marriage with Judith of Brittany and about all those noblemen from Brittany and Normandy who couldn't get into the church because it was too small . . . "

"Te Deus omnipotens rogamus . . . Hic est prepositus paradisi archangelus . . . "

"All this Carolingian masonry copied from Roman times, built by those canons, long-haired savages dressed in goatskins. How barbarous!"

"Sancte Michael archangele defende nos in prelio . . . "

"These stones drowned in mortar, these naked walls with no attempt at rhythm . . . "

"Deus qui miro ordine . . . "

"It would have been better to preserve Saint-Aubert's oratory as it was—circular, modeled after the oratory on Mount Gargano, rather than replacing it with this square twin temple to the west, facing the setting sun, facing shadows and darkness."

"Deus cuius claritatis."

"Glory to you, our Lord. With the help of your divine Archangel, this temple, now so unworthy of you, will soon exist no longer, and a New Jerusalem will rise up to meet you!"

"Amen."

A few moments later, Roman washes his hands, the obligatory ritual before each meal. The abbot, Christ's vicar according to Saint Benedict, is washing the feet of his guests, a small group of pilgrims, as Jesus washed his apostles' feet. In the refectory, they all wait silently in order at their seats for the abbot to go with the pilgrims to the superior's table. In this year of 1022, the abbey doesn't yet have a hostel, but it does offer hospitality to those who request it. This year, as every year, the growing flood of pilgrims for Saint Michael's Day, at the end of the month, will bring its share of problems. Most of the pilgrims can find lodging in nearby villages if they have a little money, but the abbey needs to provide room and board for the indigent and for those who have given large gifts to the Angel for building the new church.

The abbot offers a prayer, and, after the *De verbo Dei,* the brothers are seated.

The lector begins to read a passage from the Rule. Those designated as servants for the week carry in the bread and the *pulmentum,* a meatless fava bean soup. After the soup, they bring in vegetables cooked in whale oil and garlic. Roman nods to thank the brother who serves him. Without knowing that monastery sign language will one day be helpful to those who have no voice, he imitates the gesture of a cook stirring a sauce; thus he is able to get mustard without saying a word. With another sign, he asks for a second serving. Saint Benedict, always concerned with *moderatio,* wanted his monks to have enough food "for the weakness of each," and each person, when fast was broken, to have enough to satisfy his hunger. Roman eats half a plate of herring and shares the other half with one of his brothers. Picking up his cup with both hands, he drinks some Gascon wine the cellarer brought in from Bordeaux. The local Brion wine is weak, and the brothers hate it, leaving it for the peasants. Only during grape harvest do they allow a few bunches of fresh grapes on the abbey tables for dessert. Wine is an important part of the lives of men of God, and Saint Benedict learned that at his own expense. He believed that the value of wine was purely symbolic and that it should be used only in celebrating mass, so he tried to limit its use to inside the church. But his monks had a greater vision of its virtues, and they wanted to extend them to the refectory. When the monks mutinied, Saint Benedict wisely gave in. In his Rule, he set limits to the amount of wine consumed by each brother during meals. Benedictine monasticism wasn't imperiled when a secular priest, envious of the growing order, brought in naked girls and had them dance outside the walls of the Subiaco monastery to tempt the monks (Benedict preserved his monks' chastity by exiling them to Mount Cassino). And it was hardly shaken during the times of pillaging barbarian hordes. It was endangered by only one thing: the love Saint Benedict's sons had for the blood of grapes.

Roman listens absentmindedly to the reading while he enjoys the cheese, called *angelo,* invented by a monk trying to find ways to preserve milk. And then he shows honor to the lovely autumn fruits and to the *oublies,* little pastries stacked up on the table. Finally he returns to his empty glass, covers it with a corner of the tablecloth, and waits for the abbot to signal the end of supper. He rises with his brothers, gives thanks, and moves with the monks toward the church as they chant to the sound of the bells. The day's last office, Compline, marks the end of words, for afterward speaking is forbidden. The office also marks the return to the rock of high tide, night, and the monks' battle against the shadows. Roman doesn't forget to entrust little Brigitte to the Archangel's care.

While the sacristan and the cantor sprinkle water and incense on the church's twin altars and then join their brothers to rest until Matins, Roman goes to the abbot's cell. Attached to the church, this is a vestige of life on the Mount before the 992 fire and is the only private cell that didn't burn. Roman follows the old abbot, who hobbles into the wooden hut. The cell is sparsely furnished: a table, two chairs, and a modest bed like that of the other monks. The only special privilege the abbot enjoys is the fireplace, but he rarely uses it, even during the winter.

A tapestry hanging above the table demonstrates his position of power in the monastic hierarchy. It represents Saint Michael with a sword in his right hand and scales in his left, weighing the souls of humans who have fallen asleep for the last time. It's a reproduction of a sculpture standing in the first European sanctuary dedicated to Saint Michael and consecrated in Italy in the fifth century, on Mount Gargano. Father Hildebert is the son of a noble knight from Rotoloi, in the Cotentin. He is totally devoted to the Duke of Normandy and has been father superior in the abbey for twelve years. In the year 1009, Abbot Maynard II, weakened by age and malady, asked his protector, Richard

II, to relieve him of his duties. Upon the request of the monastic community and the counsel of bishops and the nobles, the duke passed the pastoral staff to Hildebert, who was then the abbey's prior. According to Richard, the venerable monk was "in youthful bloom but already remarkable for his lively subtle intelligence and for his mature actions." The monks agreed with this judgment and tolerated the intervention by the prince and by the secular clergy in the choice of their new abbot, although that was contrary to the Rule of Saint Benedict. But they were pleased with the choice, as was the duke, because Hildebert proved to be a very effective abbot, perfectly managing the abbey's fields, forests, and men. He led the monastery into prosperity, and the monks loved him. He treated them strictly, but he always kept in mind Benedictine moderation and equity. As far as the construction of the large abbey was concerned— a project decided upon in 1017 by Richard II, after his marriage with Judith of Brittany in the narrow little Carolingian church—it has rejuvenated Hildebert, and he devotes all his efforts to the task. It has become his life's work. Little does it matter to him that he'll never set eyes on the completed building; it's enough that he has set in motion the building of this splendid homage to the Angel: Mont-Saint-Michel will be the most amazing abbey in Western Christendom! Hildebert spent years, months, days, and nights with Pierre de Nevers in calculating the symbolic weight of each stone. Today, before the work gets under way, he insists on checking every minute detail. Roman's visits to see the stonecutter and the carpenter are important details. Hildebert himself has been to the Chausey Islands, but he's interested now in knowing what Roman thinks about Master Jehan's work.

This evening, facing the young master builder, Hildebert's eyes gleam so ardently that if he were not the abbot, and if they weren't talking about an abbey, one might wonder where the gleam came from.

"Well, my son," he begins softly with his firm voice. "What do you think? You may speak."

Roman doesn't dare sit down and hurries through the day's events. He spreads out his master's sketches on the table, then, removing his stylus and tablet from his belt, reads some notes that he has taken.

"Fine," the abbot agrees. "When do you think we can begin?"

"We can start the foundations for the choir in the spring, as planned, Father, once we've gathered together the necessary cranes and the various teams of porters."

"Will we have enough men? Or should I send messengers south to recruit more hands?"

"There's nothing to fear, Father," Roman says reassuringly. "We have enough men."

"Good. And how about boats, Brother Roman? Have you planned for enough barges to move the stones? It would be a catastrophe if we had to stop working because we didn't have enough granite."

"Relax, Father," Roman humbly replies. "We have chosen the trees, and they are abundant. Today, Master Jehan began building the boats. He has a large, efficient team and should be able to finish them by mid-Lent. However, I intend to check on their progress regularly; if I think there aren't enough men, we may need to requisition some of our peasants to help in the forest."

"If necessary, they will be requisitioned," Hildebert says in his authoritative voice, "and they'll accept with joy, glad to contribute to the construction of the Archangel's dwelling place."

"I'm sure they will, Father. In fact," he continues, "I'm not worried about our men, nor about the stone and wood, because these are things that vigorous human hands can control. My fear comes from the sea, for it can upset boats loaded with granite and even swallow them up forever in its belly."

"Son, you've been living here with your brothers on this rock for five years, and I had almost forgotten that you come from a country of forests and fields. It is presumptuous and vain to expect to master the unmasterable, and foolish to be afraid. Let us praise the Lord. He is just and good to his servants. The Lord will help us as he has always done, for he alone holds the power of nature's forces."

"Yes, Father," Roman answers, lowering his head. "With the help of God and his Archangel, we will succeed."

Hildebert looks tenderly at the young priest and smiles. He knows the brother's passion for his art and knows he does his work well. Indeed, his ardor will help him reach a sacred goal; but, like any strong feeling, it needs to be restrained appropriately for a monk. The abbot's comment has no other purpose than to remind Roman of what's appropriate, because his passion has become almost an obsession since his master left. At the thought, Hildebert's smile disappears from his wrinkled face. He leans down and picks up a letter lying on his desk.

"My son, I have something important to tell you before you sleep. I'll be telling your brothers tomorrow morning during chapter meeting, but I wanted to inform you first, and in private, because it has to do with you. I've received this missive from my good friend Odilon, father superior at Cluny. Two weeks ago, Pierre de Nevers had an accident on the building site. His bones were crushed when he fell from the scaffolding. Since that time, he's been struggling for his life with his typical courage, but the infirmarer knows that his suffering, given his advanced age. . . . "

Roman is overwhelmed by the news. All those years he spent with the architect had turned Pierre de Nevers into a kind of father, with a stature not unlike that of an abbot, his spiritual shepherd. Pierre de Nevers is even closer than his own father. If his master were to die, Roman would lose his family a second time.

"Tomorrow, I'll entrust Pierre de Nevers to the whole community's prayers," Hildebert adds. "Believe me, my son, I'm as affected as you by this sad event."

Pale, Roman picks up his sketches, says good-bye to Hildebert, and withdraws. He walks mechanically toward the dormitory. He goes into the common room. His brothers are already lying quietly. The *significator horarum* is murmuring psalms and watching the first candle burn down. To help Pierre de Nevers, Roman has better things to do than sleep. He picks up a lantern, lights it, and walks out into the shadows. The wind, the eternal wind, has begun its combat with the mountain; the waters have begun their inevitable rise. Roman needs to keep struggling with himself so as not to give in to the relentless elements. He walks around the Carolingian church. At this time of the night, it is forbidden to enter. This prohibition to enter doesn't come from the Rule, but rather it's a practice passed down from the early canons. It is said that those who have entered the church between Compline and Matins have all experienced angelic or demonic apparitions; and they all died when dawn broke. Before

Roman stands Saint Martin's Chapel, below the rock's summit and against its southern slope. He pushes open the door. All is dark inside. He raises up the lantern to light the chapel's three naves, then walks down the central nave with its high open windows, lined on both sides with lower, barrel-vaulted lateral naves. The masonry, made with stone taken directly from the rock, is rough and archaic, identical to the masonry in the church. The chapel also dates from Carolingian times, but unlike the church, which will be destroyed, the chapel will be preserved, even though the site will require much transformation.

The chapel is a sanctuary for the dead. Even though Roman can't sense any trace of a living human presence, he knows that he's surrounded by the illustrious dead lying under the stones of the choir floor: Breton lords who died in combat; Norgod, the bishop of Avranches, who in 1007, thanks to an angelic miracle, watched the Mount be devoured by flames like Mount Sinai and then gave up the staff and miter to finish his days as a humble monk devoted to the Archangel; the wife of Richard II, Judith of Brittany, who died shortly after she was married in the Carolingian church. The Normans' desire to raze the canons' church, Hildebert's wish to build a grand abbey, and their common goal of preserving the sepulchers in Saint Martin's Chapel explain why the chapel had been chosen to be one of the crypts supporting the future abbey church. But this evening Roman isn't thinking about construction. He sets down his lamp, lights the altar candles, and falls on his knees at the foot of the cross to implore Christ to save Pierre de Nevers.

Suddenly, a slight noise, like a cloth brushing against stone, arouses him from his prayers. He turns around but sees nothing. Mechanically, his eyes inspect the chapel and instantly open wide. The stone slabs marking the tombs are decorated with flowers: freshly picked Scotch broom, their color like the sun undulating with the candles' flames. Annoyed, Roman stands up and grabs his lantern. Shining it around, he opens his mouth to ask if anyone is there, but then refrains from speaking out of respect for the Rule. Again he kneels and addresses his supplication to the Lord. And then, once more, he thinks he hears a suspicious noise in a corner of one of the side naves.

"It sounds like the wake of a moving ghost," he thinks.

Might it be that the spirits of the night have deserted the church and come to Saint Martin's Chapel? Quaking, Roman gets back to his feet. Brandishing his lantern like a lance or a shield, he hurries over to the place where he thinks the sound is coming from. The candle's yellowish halo drowns his facial features. The brown crown of his tonsured hair, like a horizontal shadow, stands in contrast to the pallor of his skin. His eyes, the color of evening and outlined with delicate lashes, stare straight ahead. Roman moves forward, pale, preparing himself for a supernatural confrontation, placing his soul in the Archangel's hands. And then he sees, behind a column, a shadow that's darker than the gray of the stones. Still trembling, he resolutely raises the lantern and his mouth drops open. He's unable to utter a sound, not out of respect for the Rule but be-cause he's so totally surprised. The shadow, standing motionless, watches him. Transparent, almond-shaped green eyes set in a woman's virginal face shrouded by a veil, and then a slender, white neck where he can see veins throbbing as if the pulsation of her heart is coursing throughout her body. . . .

A long, flared dress of an unusual color, the color of the forest, of the seasons, of time. Her emerald eyes gleam with life, and myriads of freckles on her cheeks and nose add to their golden glow. Blood, the elixir of existence, rushes up into her diaphanous face and colors it pink. There, before the monk standing transfixed and mute, her lips begin to tremble like an autumn leaf, and then suddenly all her features break into a smile!

3

D O STONES HAVE MEMORY?" FRANÇOIS REPEATED, BRUSHING A strand of hair back from her face. "Yes, they remember people and things people have forgotten in the course of time. They pass information to those who can understand them, historians, archeologists, people with passion, like you. But you know, I have trouble believing that one night the walls of the abbey on Mont-Saint-Michel could send you a dream message about strange events that no one has ever mentioned in any book. I'm not saying that your story is made up. It's real enough, you're right about that, but I think it's more likely a message to you from your own building blocks, from your personal earth, your unconscious, if you will. . . . "

"Does that mean that what I saw might simply be telling me my own personal family story on a symbolic level, unconnected with anything else?"

"Unless you're the reincarnation of some old Mont-Saint-Michel monk, and I don't believe that for a second," he continued with a smile. "So that's probably what it is."

Johanna looked down, stared dreamily at her glass.

"For me it's simply a childhood memory. Lifelike and macabre, but still a memory."

"If I had known, Johanna, I swear I'd have taken you somewhere else. I could kick myself for bringing all that back."

"Oh, no, François, don't feel guilty. I'm a big girl. And in any case, it's done me good to tell you about it. Seriously, I feel like a weight has lifted."

He leaned over and planted a kiss on her mouth.

"Thanks for believing in me. Say, since a weight's been lifted, do you have room for some dessert?"

Later the couple was climbing back up the steps to the abbey to take in the sound-and-light show presented every night during peak tourist season. Although she wasn't totally relaxed, Johanna looked forward to being lulled by the words emanating from the monastery's stones; their words carried the force and splendor of the centuries. Saltpeter-gray moss, like drops of time, was eating away at the walls. Near the stained-glass windows, pigeons and gulls were greeting visitors. Johanna was moved by the ancient poetry of a Gothic garden—eight small squares, bordered with neatly trimmed boxwood, arrayed strawberries, green tomatoes, some squash, and a little ripe rhubarb. In the middle of the vegetable garden, a rosebush entwined with a hawthorn seemed to rise from deep down in the well to wrap itself around a rusty crucifix. They walked into the heart of the abbey, and when Johanna closed her eyes, she could identify the stones by their smell—granite. She shivered slightly because of the change in temperature, then reopened her eyes.

"François!" she exclaimed. "It's extraordinary! We could be in Egypt, at Karnak! Here everything is more austere, of course."

They were surrounded by a forest of cylindrical pillars supporting the sumptuous vaulted ceiling.

"Six meters in circumference, my dear. The 'big-pillar crypt.'"

"Flamboyant Gothic!" Johanna couldn't help saying.

"Right," he said. "It was built in the fifteenth century to support the flamboyant choir of the abbey church, located just above. The Romanesque choir collapsed during the Hundred Years' War."

"What a pity!" she sighed. "Yes, I remember the Gothic choir, but I had never seen this crypt. It's spectacular."

"You haven't seen anything yet."

They came out on the esplanade, where a huge wooden treadmill stood near an opening through which they could see the night stars.

"There's the old nag!" Johanna shouted joyously.

The machine was really called a colt. The monks used it to lift supplies up to the abbey: Several men would climb inside it, and, walking in place, they turned the wheel, which wound up a rope and pulled up their supplies.

"That's how they got the granite up here for building the abbey, using machines like that," François explained.

Accompanied by lugubrious music from hidden loudspeakers, they followed corridors where shadows played on the walls. In a low voice François related how the abbey had served as a prison at the end of the Hundred Years' War, when the king of France sent his political opponents to the monastery. The conditions were horrible. Indeed, during the *ancien régime,* Mont-Saint-Michel was known as the Bastille of the Seas, and the monks served as jailers. The Revolution kept the tradition alive but chased out the Benedictines and turned the abbey into a gigantic state prison that held as many as six hundred prisoners, including Barbès and Blanqui. What they were going to see now, however, did indeed date from the Middle Ages.

In the thirteenth century, at the height of the abbey's glory, Robert de Thorigny, one of the most famous abbots of the Mount, decided to reorganize the abbey as his power grew. Like a grand feudal lord, he had his own lodgings built, as well as a courtroom where he meted out justice to both his monks and those peasants who "belonged" to him because they lived on land owned by the Mount. To punish those who didn't follow the rules, he instituted what were called the "twins." Johanna and François entered a tiny room with low arches and an earthen floor. Pieces of protective glass covered two narrow openings in the rock. They looked in and could imagine the obvious horror the twins evoked: two dungeons, with chains still visible hanging down in the holes.

"How horrible and fascinating at the same time," Johanna remarked, clinging to François. "I think it's time to change scenery."

They next visited the Merveille, a masterpiece of Gothic architecture made up of several buildings constructed in the thirteenth century to replace the Romanesque buildings destroyed during the historic fire of 1204, which was set by Bretons trying to take the Mount back from their long-standing enemies, the Normans. But the Bretons weren't able to get into the citadel, so they set fire to the village, and the fire spread to the Romanesque abbey.

"What a surprise!" said Johanna from the center of the monks' refectory, where the walls were spouting Gregorian chants. "The space is laid out in Romanesque style, but the light is like the light we see in Gothic cathedrals. What a beautiful synthesis!"

François agreed. "This abbey is indeed built on disasters and astonishing reconstructions. And the Merveille is an architectural jewel."

He led her to the loveliest of the buildings forming the Merveille, the cloister. Around the large, square garden ran a gallery, its thin elegant columns decorated with plant motifs. From the north side, the view of the sea was wonderfully romantic, and in spite of the other tourists, they stood there a long time nestled against each other, looking out over the infinite bay. After a brief pause in the abbey church, where Johanna recalled her mother praying on that fateful August 15 in one of the little chapels in the choir, they headed toward the majestic common rooms of the Merveille: the knight's room, used in fact as a scriptorium by the monks, and the guest room. In the guest room, where one could imagine long-gone eras—whole oxen roasting in the gigantic fireplaces, while jugglers and acrobats diverted important pilgrims like the kings of France—now employees of the Historical Monuments Department welcomed their guests much more modestly with a cup of spiced tisane.

"You need to imagine this room furnished, of course," said François thoughtfully. "Imagine rich tapestries on the walls, the vaults painted yellow and ocher and decorated with geometric figures, the blue and red stained-glass windows and red and green floor tiles painted with the armories of the king of France and of Blanche de Castille: fleur de lys and Spanish castles. As usual, time has effaced the medieval colors. I often think what a pity it is that people today dream about the medieval past as it has become today—gray and bare, though it was really just the opposite. When we say that the churches were multicolored, people look at us as if we were idiots!"

"Forsooth, my handsome prince. I'm pleased to see that your dreams take you, too, back to the Middle Ages!"

"Indeed, my princess. But in my case, the monks stand praying in the church, not hanging in the tower. And their heads are screwed tight to their shoulders!"

The look in Johanna's eyes was as dark as a monk's black robe.

"Oh, come on," he said, giving her a kiss. "To gain forgiveness, I'm going to take you to a most magical place, the oldest spot in the whole abbey. It's where the Angel dwells, and afterward I'll show you what's left of the Romanesque structure."

They followed damp, resonant stairways. Johanna paused near an unusual sculpture on the wall: Dressed like a Roman soldier, a faceless, featureless Saint Michael was touching with an angry finger the forehead of a bishop kneeling at his feet.

"Saint Aubert!" François shouted. "The bishop of Avranches. Michael the archangel is angry because Aubert still hasn't carried out his order to build a sanctuary for him on the Mount, so he appears to him a third time, marking his forehead to make sure the prelate will finally agree. And Aubert quickly did build the sanctuary. Today we can still see a part of his original oratory. Thanks to Yves-Marie Froidevaux, chief architect with Historical Monuments, who in 1960 found part of the old sanctuary wall while restoring the crypt we're going to see now."

"Good for Historical Monuments!" she exclaimed. "Your knowledge about Mont-Saint-Michel is amazing, my dear François. You know it all by heart!"

"I'll never know as much as you," he answered, blushing, "but I'm touched by the compliment. What do you expect? A love affair of more than forty years with this mountain, so I've managed to learn a thing or two. . . . Careful on that step! Here we are."

It was dark in the underground crypt in spite of the lamps and the granite, still white after the restoration process. When they entered, a strange feeling, a mysterious, meditative feeling, caused their throats to tighten. Maybe because there were no windows or because they sensed the double nature of the dark chapel, which by a macabre association of ideas made them remember the twins they had seen a short time before—the twin dungeons. Separated by two stone arcades, two identical square naves extended out before them, each finished off by the same small tunnel-vaulted choir with a similar altar above which a platform and staircase rose to the vaulted stone ceiling.

"Notre-Dame-sous-Terre," François murmured. "The name itself sounds supernatural, and the atmosphere here is always magical, though I'm not sure why. Perhaps because of its age. It's Carolingian, built around 900, but no one has been able to date it with any exactness. We still don't know if it was built by the Breton canons or by the first Benedictine Normans. Historians carve each other up over the question. It was walled off in the eighteenth century and for a long time it was completely lost, forgotten. Look there," he added, showing her some rough stone blocks behind the two altars; "that's the Cyclopean wall of Saint-Aubert's oratory."

But Johanna wasn't listening. She'd turned as pale as the granite walls as she stared at the two flights of parallel twin staircases climbing toward nothingness. Suddenly wild tears welled up in her eyes and she burst into sobs.

"Johanna!" François exclaimed. "What's wrong?"

She looked at him wide-eyed, and though her lips moved, no sounds came out. François took her by the shoulders.

"My dear! What's the matter?"

"There!" she pointed toward one of the staircases, and other tourists turned to stare. "That's where he was, I'm absolutely sure! Here's where I saw him! Right here. He was climbing those stairs when he spoke to me. I was right, it wasn't a dream!"

"Who are you talking about?"

"About the monk! The monk without a head!" she cried.

Back in the hotel room, François tried to dissuade Johanna from thinking that her fateful childhood dream had any real historical connection to Mont-Saint-Michel's past. She was clearly in anguish over her discovery and kept pacing back and forth in the room while twisting her hands and muttering.

"I can't be mistaken. I can remember the slightest details—it's the same décor: the altar, stones, vault, platform, staircase. It can't be anywhere else. This is the crypt I saw in my dream! Yes, it had to be Notre-Dame-sous-Terre!"

François sat on the bed and looked directly into her eyes, as if to try to keep her from her pacing.

"Of course it was Notre-Dame-sous-Terre, and it's easy to explain what must have happened. When you visited the abbey with your parents on that memorable afternoon on the fifteenth of August, you surely came through the crypt. It naturally left its mark on you, because it leaves its mark on everyone, even adults. So, a few hours later, it was the place you saw in your nightmare."

She leaned back against the window and clenched her fists.

"No! You're wrong! That can't be right!" she answered. "I had never seen the crypt before this evening, except in my dream. I'm absolutely certain. When I was here with my parents, I didn't visit the abbey. All we did was go to mass in the abbey church. I can't have forgotten. I've always had a good memory—and I was seven years old, after all, not three!"

"Johanna," he said, standing up and joining her by the window. "Human memory is a complex and selective thing," he reasoned, trying to take her in his arms. "You've got to admit that's the obvious explanation. For some reason unknown to others, you've erased the visit from your conscious mind, but your unconscious mind had recorded all those images in the crypt and gave them back to you in a dream, along with that macabre stage setting— "

She jerked away.

"I know what I'm talking about. I'm neither crazy nor stupid!" she shouted. "How about the man I saw hanging? What can you say about him? He was surely murdered. And besides, we can verify something right now," she said, taking out her cell phone. "I'm going to call my parents and ask them if we went into Notre-Dame-sous-Terre or not, that day. You'll have to believe them and we'll see who's right."

François rushed over to her and took the phone from her hands. Somebody started pounding on the wall from the next room.

"Johanna, come on! That's enough!" he said, lowering his voice. "It's one thirty in the morning. We're already waking up everyone in the hotel. Do you really want to wake your parents up in the middle of the night?"

That's when Johanna fell apart and burst into a flood of tears. Her whole being was overwhelmed by a little girl's pain, by a child's fear her adult mind couldn't comprehend. She stood trembling in the middle of the room, pouring out her long-repressed pain. Quietly, François came over and held out his arms to envelop her, and she hid her face against his neck. Happy just to kiss her dark hair, he let time absorb her sobs.

"I'm sorry," she finally whispered. "I just can't take it any longer. I don't understand what's happening."

"Tomorrow." he answered. "Tomorrow, Johanna. Now you must lie down and try to sleep. Tomorrow you'll see. Okay?"

Unable to speak, she nodded. He helped her take off her clothes and splashed some water on her eyes. She squeezed up against his body for comfort, in the fetal position, and relaxed in the warmth of their bed.

"MICHAEL ARCHANGELE . . . GLORIAM *predicamus in terries . . .* "

The chant rises up into the shadowy sky. The moon weakly hangs above a pale hand pushing a monk from a high rock. The monk screams before disappearing into the dark sea.

" *. . . eius precibus adiuvemur in caelis . . .* "

The monk rises to the surface and struggles in the impetuous waves.

"Help! In the name of the Omnipotent One, help me!"

He calls for help as the bay's waters lap at his face. The watery immensity surrounds him. Behind him, the high tide has vanquished the rock. Like the petals of a black flower, the cloth of the Benedictine frock spreads out in the waves.

" *Te Deus omnipotens regamus . . . Hic est prepositus paradisi archangelus . . .* "

Latin chants waft from the Romanesque windows of the abbey planted on the rock's peak. The thick walls are singing Matins, are echoing with fervent antiphonal responses, but they remain deaf to the laments of the monk screaming at the mountain's base.

"My brothers, I beg you! Listen to me! I'm drowning!"

Alone against nature, the monk struggles. The more he moves his arms, the more water he swallows and the more he is buffeted by the angry waves. With all his strength he struggles. His old face, red from the desperate struggle, is frozen in effort. Soon it will be frozen in death. The waves hold him, then release him in a cruel cat-and-mouse game.

" *Sancte Michael archangele defende nos in prelio . . .* "

The monk tries to join his raucous voice to the solemn chant. His pale face streams with salt tears. The dark ocean plays with him, rocks him in its waves before swallowing him up, then spitting him back out. The monk begins to tremble. He clears his throat, but water creeps back into it.

"*Deus qui miro ordine . . .* "

The monk is still, exhausted. His eyelids close convulsively. And then, like a shroud, a wave covers his body. In one final effort to live, he raises his head to breathe. His tonsured cranium and his forehead appear; he gasps for air and fights against the waves.

"*Deus cuius claritatis,*" the abbey walls intone.

The waves storm the cranium's peak, the raging water splashing it with foam before covering it completely. A few final bubbles. And then it's all over. The ocean has won.

"*Amen,*" the thick church walls conclude in chorus.

Suddenly, the scene changes. To inside the abbey walls, like in a stone womb. Separated by arcades, the two twin naves end in similar, small, barrel-vaulted choirs, with their altars and staircases: Notre-Dame-sous-Terre. On the steps a monk stands waiting, head lowered. He raises it: The hood is empty! The headless brother raises his arms toward the underground heavens, then lowers them back toward the ground, and says with a hollow voice: "*Ad accedendum ad caelum, terram fodere opportet.*"

JOHANNA WOKE UP immediately. Feeling as if someone had struck her, she sat upright, panting and sweating, looking dully around her. In a panic she threw off the sheets and, unclothed, rushed to the window. She pulled open the curtains. The bay leaped up at her. The sun was shining brightly in the azure sky, and the sea was smooth and light blue around Mont-Saint-Michel. No clouds and no waves. The tide was out, and tongues of sand glistened like party streamers. In the distance, in fields reclaimed from the sea, sheep were grazing. Nearby, the roofs of the neighboring houses offered their ancestral slate up to the new morning. Nature was spread out in all its splendor and in reassuring calm, but the picture brought no joy to Johanna's heart still racked by those disturbing images. She couldn't see the abbey from her room, but the monastery walls were still real within her. She turned around, remembered François and their scene the evening before, and realized that she was alone. That brought her back to reality, back to the present, and dissipated the last fog of her violent nightmare.

"François," she called.

On his pillow she found a letter.

My love,

You are sleeping so soundly that I don't have the heart to wake you. I'm off to my meeting with the abbey administrator. Be back around noon.

Love.

She grabbed her watch: ten thirty. She couldn't bear staying inside those four walls alone for another hour and a half. She couldn't bear to spend another night beneath these abbey walls, the cause of her nightmares. It was impossible. She needed to get away, go back to Cluny or Paris, to her Paris apartment, yes, her own peaceful cavern, her own place! François would be furious. Too bad.

Fifteen minutes later, dressed in jeans and a T-shirt, her hair still wet and her travel bag packed, she slipped out of the room, left the hotel, and found temporary refuge in a café packed with tourists. It opened out onto the street, so she would be able see François coming back, although she couldn't see the monastery. The crowd, its noise, the bustling, the foreign languages, and breakfast made her feel better. She tried to read a newspaper lying on the table. But she couldn't concentrate. How long he was taking! What could François be cooking up with Historical Monuments? No, she didn't really want to know, didn't want to hear about archeological digs, about the past, about the history of the Mount. Didn't want to have any more visions. Wanted just to get away as quickly as possible, with nobody able to make any comments. But what should she tell François so that they could leave right away? She chewed on her nails as she thought. For once, she didn't mind lying, but she needed come up with a lie that worked. She had to preserve her sanity. Say that there was an emergency back at Cluny? No, that was too dangerous; it'd be too easy for him to check. That her mother had been in an accident? No, the superstition linked to her brother's death kept her from trying that. Isa? Maybe she could say that Isabelle, her best friend, was sick and needed her? Isa would never tell on her, but then she'd have to explain everything to her, and she didn't want to do that. She didn't want to talk about it to anybody! Never again! Just forget it all and leave the place! And anyhow, Isabelle didn't live alone, and François would never understand why her husband couldn't take care of her. Why keep worrying? Johanna decided to tell him she wanted to leave and that was all there was to it. If he couldn't accept that, well, she would just leave him there on that damned rock and take the train home alone. There. When she saw him coming down the street at a quarter till twelve, she was pumped up like a boxer before his match. He was just strolling along at his usual elegant gait, a little smile on his face, eyes hidden behind his sunglasses. Johanna stood up and waved from the edge of the terrace. His face brightened, and then his smile froze when he saw her tense expression. He quickly kissed her and, removing his sunglasses, sat down across from her. The evening before, she had shocked him, but he had hoped that today she would be herself again—funny, lively, and sensuous.

"Good morning, my dear! How are things this morning? How did you sleep?" he asked, already knowing what she would say.

"François, I can't stay here a second longer. I've decided to go back to Paris immediately, with or without you."

"What's wrong?" he wondered tiredly.

"Nothing, just relax!" she answered sarcastically. "Nothing's wrong, except that I want to go home."

"What is it now?" he exclaimed, taking her arm. "We haven't seen each other for a month, and you're just going to leave me here to go do whatever in Paris?"

"François," she sighed. "I'm worn out, I don't have the strength to argue. Either we go back together or I go back alone, but I'm not up for a long discussion. I'm sorry to act like this, believe me. I understand why you're upset, but it has nothing to do with you. I've got to go."

He sat thoughtfully for several moments.

"I've got an idea," he finally said with a smile, seeing that she was adamant. "How about going somewhere else for the rest of the weekend? How about a romantic evening in Saint-Malo or Honfleur and a boat ride tomorrow?"

"Sorry, François," she replied, truly sorry not to be able to accept, "but even in Honfleur or somewhere else I'd be lousy company this evening. What I need is an evening alone at home, absolutely alone."

At a quarter past twelve they were in his car leaving Mont-Saint-Michel. Johanna didn't even look back at the fairytale-like view. They hardly spoke during the drive back. François was upset, and Johanna was lost in thought. Late that Saturday afternoon, with the sun shining, the car turned from the boulevard de Pont-Royal onto the rue Henri-Barbusse, a short way from the Luxembourg Gardens, and stopped in front of an old apartment building. He turned off the motor and unfastened his seat belt.

"Wouldn't you like me to come up a minute?" he wondered. "So we can talk?"

"No, François," she said gently. "I'd prefer not. Thanks for being there. Don't worry, things will be fine now."

And it's true, her face did seem to be alive again, and she wasn't as tense as she had been.

"Johanna." he said, pulling her tight. "If you don't feel well, give me a call and I'll come right over."

"You're an angel, François, but I'll be fine, I promise."

He looked into her eyes. Such a deep sky blue. He caught a little flash of something, and he understood immediately.

"It's fear!" he exclaimed. "Fear in the presence of death."

She turned away, grabbed her bag, and opened the car door.

"Death, François? What are you talking about? Come on now, don't you get into it too. Or I'll need to be taken to the Sainte-Anne psychiatric hospital. I've got to go. Call you later."

She slammed the door and waved good-bye. Through the grainy glass window of the front door, he could watch her dark silhouette climb the stairway.

JOHANNA DOUBLE-LOCKED the door and pulled the living-room curtains shut because the sun was too bright. In her tiny bedroom she partially closed the shutters and left just a thin vertical opening for the light to come in. She knelt down beside her bedside table, really an old metal trunk, hard to tell any more what color it was. She took off the lamp and the magazines, books, and archeology journals that were piled haphazardly on top of it. Then she opened the trunk. She pulled out some letters, boxes full of photos taken when she had been a gangly adolescent, the complete collection of a history magazine, some gifts from old boyfriends, her grandfather's tobacco pouch that she had inherited, some stone sculptures, some old telescopes, an illustrated copy of the *Contes de la table ronde*, dried flowers, a graphology kit; and finally a little notebook with a yellowish-blue cover, on which were written her name and the words "elementary school, second grade."

On the first page was the sentence in Latin that she had carried away from her dream like a piece of music and had transcribed from memory, with the corrected version below it and finally the translation she had added three years later in black ink at the bottom of the page, as if at a respectful distance from the original language. She hadn't touched the notebook for years, and now the sentence would meet the eyes of an adult. Johanna remembered that those seven words had been enough to spark her childhood imagination, orient her adolescent longings, and nourish her adult quest. Seven words to fertilize a life. Her life. Who was the faceless man who had sowed them?

Ad accedendum ad caelum, terram fodere opportet.

4

THE YOUNG WOMAN STANDS THERE QUIETLY BEFORE ROMAN. Her smile disappears and she doesn't say a word. The monk sheds his initial fear. He looks at her without speaking either. Suddenly Roman breathes in a sweet smell of dry leaves, of ripe berries, of thick, rich grass in the rain, and the woman seems to him to be an embodiment of autumn. The veiled woman holds the monk's stare a long time, and he feels himself sinking into her eyes, which are bright, like dawn or late afternoon. Roman's forehead and cheeks begin tingling. Warmth rushes violently into his body when he notices a long strand of hair escape from beneath her veil. Quickly, she raises her gloved fingers to replace the strand, then lowers her gaze and flees.

Roman remains in Saint Martin's Chapel, alone with the dead. Slowly, he turns around and walks toward the altar, the lantern still in his hand. Who can this woman be? Perhaps someone from the village? No, he would surely have noticed her in the town or monastery, and he knows he hasn't seen her before. And furthermore, a local would never dare come here after Compline. A stranger? She hadn't been among the pilgrims who had supped with them. A lost sheep looking for shelter for the night? But she isn't dressed like some vagabond wandering through the countryside. The way she carries herself, she seems more like the daughter of a great lord. The only thing Roman can be sure of is that she isn't a ghost but a living, breathing person. As he nears the choir, his yellow lamplight again falls on the yellow Scotch broom strewn on the tombs.

"That's what this is about," he thinks. "The woman brought flowers to honor the dead and meditate in the Lord's presence . . . I interrupted her prayers and must have frightened her as much as she frightened me! And yet what a strange time to come pray."

With that, he remembers why he's here in this holy place: to pray for the salvation of Pierre de Nevers before his brothers awaken. At the thought of his master, of his accident at the Cluny construction site, he piously kneels down and tries to cast from his mind the turmoil this mysterious encounter has roused.

The next morning, after Prime, the thirty priests, novices, and lay brothers gather near the church in one of the monastery buildings furnished with benches and a central chair. Father Hildebert sits in the chair with a beautifully bound book in his hands. This day, September 7, is devoted to Saint Regina, the virgin martyr of Autun. The chapter meeting begins, as usual, by reading a passage from *The Mirror of Perfection,* the Rule of Benedict of Nursia, written in the sixth century.

"*Constituenda est ergo nobis Dominici scola servitii: in qua institutione nihil asperum, nihil grave nos constituros speramus,*" the abbot reads with conviction from the richly illuminated manuscript. "We are about to found therefore a school for the Lord's service, in the organization of which we trust that we shall ordain nothing severe and nothing burdensome. But even if, the demands of justice dictating it, something a little irksome shall be the result, for the purpose of amending vices or preserving charity, thou shalt not therefore, struck by fear, flee the way of salvation, which cannot be entered upon except through a narrow entrance. But as one's way of life and one's faith progresses, the heart becomes broadened, and, with the unutterable sweetness of love, the way of the mandates of the Lord is traversed. Thus, never departing from His guidance, continuing in the monastery in his teaching until death, through patience we are made partakers in Christ's passion, in order that we may merit to be companions in His kingdom . . . *ut et regno eius mereamur esse consortes. Amen.*"

"Amen," the monks respond in chorus.

"The holy Rule of our father Benedict is a guide on the way of the Lord, a torch on the path toward Man's fulfillment of God's love," says the abbot. "However, as our founder reminds us in this passage taken from the Rule, the Most High does not expect us to be his slaves, weighed down under the yoke of asceticism and mortification. We are not God's serfs, but rather his faithful servants, nurtured by his love, exemplary models of his love for the people of this earth. Furthermore, my sons, don't forget that although monastic life demands rigor and obedience, it must never be exempt of *moderatio,* of mildness and mansuetude toward oneself."

Silence. The abbot looks lovingly at the brothers as would a father.

"My sons," he continues in the same tone, "Saint Benedict has always invited us to celebrate our offices in the presence of angels and to live with them, for they carry all our actions up to God. We are surrounded by their love, here more than anywhere else, for this place was chosen by the one who vanquished the hosts of Hell. If we want to remain faithful to Aubert's work, we owe it to ourselves to build an edifice worthy of Heaven's Provost, an edifice that people won't keep comparing to the one on Mount Gargano! Today, I'm announcing that construction will begin during the New Year, after Easter festivities. Let us recall Saint John's Book of Revelations: 'One of the seven angels carried me in spirit to a tall mountain and showed me the holy city, Jerusalem, descending from heaven, from God, and with it the glory of God.' Jerusalem formed a cube of equal dimensions. Let us also remember the Book of Kings, describing Solomon's temple built on three levels, the third level holding the Ark of the Covenant, God's dwelling place. Finally, let's imagine Noah's Ark, described in the Book of Genesis as being three hundred cubits long, fifty cubits wide, and having 'compartments on three stories.'"

Like a good actor, Hildebert reaches into his cowl and pulls out Pierre de Nevers's drawings, which he displays to the astonished monks. At this moment Brother Roman is proud of his master's work, but he's also worried about the immensity of the task and the weight of his own responsibilities now that he's alone without his master, who will probably never return to the Mount.

"As you see, my sons," the abbot continues, pointing to a place on the parchment, "the edifice will be as long as the rock is high. Thus, the church will form a perfect square, all four sides equal, in keeping with the sacred number of the New Jerusalem and with the perfect world created by divine wisdom: the four winds, the four Evangelists, the four horizons, the four rivers of Paradise, the four elements. The structure will be built on three different levels: Our church's narthex will be the porch of Solomon's temple, the nave and the transept will be the Holy Place where the faithful will meet, and the choir will be the Holy of Holies. Pilgrims will climb from the setting sun toward the rising sun, from the darkness to light, and they will continue climbing toward their ultimate goal: the altar of Saint Michael the Archangel. The central space in our church will have the very proportions God dictated to Noah. As for the new monastery buildings, to be built on the north flank along the church's nave, they'll establish as a symbol, before the end of time, God's ultimate covenant with mankind, a new Noah's Ark! The Ark's lower level was for animals. Therefore, my sons, on the lower level we will build a hostel to welcome pilgrims. For they will be coming everywhere in search of salvation. The Ark's middle level was for food. That's where we'll build our refectory and the storeroom for our earthly sustenance. The upper story was reserved for Noah's family, so we'll make it our dormitory—"

"Father," Brother Drocus interrupts. "All that brings joy to our hearts. But when we raze the current church, won't the offices be perturbed?"

"My son, it will be several years before we destroy the old church, only after we've finished the nave of the grand abbey church. Then we can pray in the holy of holies or in the transept chapels, for they will have been completed. But until the choir is ready, our offices will continue in the present church. The construction work will be troubling to your souls, for decades will pass before the new church is erected, and most of us will have joined our Lord long before it's finished. But it will be born out of our love for God, and it will bear witness to that love forever!"

The brothers, touched by the abbot's words, sit quietly. Hildebert thinks about the construction process, and his face grows more serious. He waits until the moment of grace has passed and then says that unfortunately he is also the bearer of bad news. He announces the accident that befell Pierre de Nevers and entrusts the author of the drawings to the community's fervent prayers. The monks turn toward Roman, their eyes filled with compassion and hope. Their brother's heart aches. But material life reclaims its dues: The chapter meeting continues; they hear the abbey's financial report as it is presented by the cellarer, whose job it is to provide food, manage the fields and forests, and collect tolls and taxes. Things are going well, and famine seems distant.

"Oysters are fat and plentiful this year, especially the ones from our domains in Cancale," the steward says with satisfaction. "So the tithes the abbot receives on shellfish are substantial."

In the monks' minds, each penny is transformed into stone for the future church, and this morning the oysters become granite arches.

After a moment of silence, the abbot puts an end to his sons' grandiose dreams and begins the final part of the chapter meeting: time for repentance.

"*Nunc,*" the abbot intones with authority. "*Si aliquid sit loquendum, dicite.*"

This standard formula is the prelude to their public confession of sins, that is, of any breaches of the Rule. As the abbot speaks, a young priest, Brother Guillaume, stands up and prostrates himself at the father superior's feet.

"*Quae est causa, frater?*" the abbot asks.

Guillaume rises to his knees.

"*Mea culpa, domine* . . . Father, I sneaked a bowl of chicken bouillon from the kitchen. I ask God and my brothers for forgiveness," the monk says before lying down once more, face down, arms extended like a cross, while awaiting his penance.

At this moment the old abbot thinks about the Rule prohibiting meat, but even more about his vile predecessors on the rock, those Breton canons, known for the festive dinners they organized with the villagers. Their feasts certainly weren't limited to bowls of bouillon.

"Stand up, my son," the abbot tells him, "and bow your head. You'll fast two days and one night while you pray that God and your brothers will forgive you."

Bringing individual mistakes out into the open allows for collective forgiveness, and forgiveness is always granted. Religious life in community signifies a bringing together of pure souls, souls that have been cleansed of all sin before the office of Compline, before the sun sets and the world of shadows awakens. Guillaume takes his seat. In the High Middle Ages, the golden age of Benedictine monasticism when the Rule is still applied to the letter, the brothers eat no meat, for meat can awaken passion and lust. Only sick monks and those who have been bled are allowed to consume meat bouillon, on the condition that the meat not come from a quadruped. Fortunately, chickens have only two legs, so Guillaume's punishment is not severe.

No other candidate for public confession appears on this particular day, so the abbot closes the chapter meeting and everyone goes off to morning mass.

As they walk along, Brother Bernard, whom Pierre de Nevers and Hildebert have chosen from among the brothers to be Roman's assistant, comes up to him. Without a word, he puts his ink-stained hands on the young man's shoulder and gives him a slight squeeze of support before entering the church.

TWO WEEKS HAVE gone by, and still no news from Cluny has reached the mountain in Normandy. Hildebert has not allowed Roman to go to his master's hospital bed. Such a trip is long and perilous, and the prudent abbot doesn't want to risk losing the Burgundian scholar's heir, the one man who can replicate the great architect's knowledge. Roman faces the long wait by praying and by throwing himself completely into his work. His body has grown thin, but the demands on his mind have made it sharper still, so much so that instead of letting his assistant Bernard help, he's sent him back to the scriptorium. One morning, a few days before Saint Michael's Day, when he goes to the forest to check on Master Roger and his team of carpenters, Roman immediately notices the joy in the craftsman's eyes, a joy strong and simple like the man himself.

"Happiness shines in your eyes like the sun, Master Roger," Roman says. "Good news?"

"Oh, Brother Roman, it's the flame of gratitude!" the carpenter replies, wiping sweat from his forehead. "Gratitude to the Most High who in his infinite goodness has spared my little Brigitte. And gratitude to his earthly servant who healed her!"

"I rejoice with you at Brigitte's recovery, my friend! Tell me, this 'servant of God,' as you say, is this the healer from Beauvoir we spoke about?"

Master Roger lowers his gray-green eyes in regret for not having shown a little less enthusiasm for the healer when speaking to a man of God.

"Exactly, she's the one," he answers quietly. "Forgive me, Brother Roman, but her medicine did so much for my little girl, without even bleeding her. We ignorant sinners think it was a miracle!"

Roman breaks into a smile. He truly admires this man Roger, for he has the inner wisdom to love God, the saints, and his own flesh and blood with the same intensity.

"We are all ignorant sinners compared to the Most High," the monk answers. "Perhaps he has chosen the pure white hand of a virgin to accomplish one of his plans. You said she was quite pious."

With these words a warm smile comes to Roman's face, and a strange idea is born in his mind.

"Besides," he continues, "what's she like? I don't believe I've ever seen her at the monastery."

Master Roger, seeing no malice in his question, is eager to satisfy the monk's curiosity.

"Well, she is indeed beautiful and pure! She always comes on foot, because she says that a donkey or horse would have trouble getting through the swamps. When she appears with her little bags of herbs and flowers, she looks like a forest princess—or perhaps a fairy from olden days. Her mother died giving birth to her younger brother, a poor fellow who has never been able to speak or hear a single word. Her father died from a nasty fever not long ago. The poor girl was left alone with her brother, and his condition has never improved. People say that God gave her the gift of healing as consolation for not being able to heal her own family."

Roman grows thoughtful. The physical description is very imprecise, but that feeling he had about a magical creature born in the forest, about a sylvan aristocrat . . . might it be the same person?

That evening in the refectory, at the abbot's table, there is a guest Roman has never seen. During Compline, the unknown monk participates in the office, then disappears.

As night falls and Roman, motivated by a secret desire, hurries toward Saint Martin's Chapel, the abbot stops him and gently asks him to come to his cell. Standing beneath the tapestry showing Saint Michael weighing souls, the old man seems to sag under some burden, and Roman begins to worry. At first he's surprised to also see the mysterious visitor in Hildebert's room, but soon everything becomes clear.

"My son," says the abbot solemnly, "this is Brother Jotsald, whom Father Odilon has sent here from Cluny."

Jotsald rises and comes over to embrace Roman. Roman stares at the tapestry, in which Saint Michael weighs the deeds of dead people and then either guides their souls to Paradise or sends them to Hell.

"My poor brother," says the Cluny monk. "I bring you very sad news."

PROSTRATE BEFORE THE altar in Saint Martin's Chapel, just a few feet away from the dried-up Scotch broom, Roman feels like an orphan and lets his suffering pour out. Tears flow down, delicately, without violence. This has been a strange day. One father tells him about a little unknown girl's healing, and a man he doesn't know tells him about his own father's passing. Life with the rising sun, death when night falls. The death of a man who fades like these Scotch-broom flowers, their life completed, set against the life of a little girl still to blossom.

"There's no injustice," the monk thinks as he sobs. "It's the order of the cosmos, God's order. My master has been at rest for seven days in holy ground at Cluny, there where he took his vows. He reposes in the choir, along with the sleeping saints. Saint Michael Archangel, weigher of our sins and our soul's guide toward the Most High, take good care of Pierre de Nevers, my father. O Conqueror of the Devil, Angel of the Last Judgment, guardian of the gates of Paradise, walk along with this good soul toward the Heavenly Kingdom and defend it against any demons who may try to seize it on the way. My very dear father, I'm praying for your passage to the Other World."

A sound suddenly interrupts his prayers. His eyes bright, the cleric rises to his feet. The sound came from behind him. Without pausing to pick up his lamp, he hurries over to the nave in the penumbra. He bumps against a bench, and as he rubs his painful knee, he notices two small yellow phosphorescent circles. He hears a meow, and a feral cat runs off.

Feeling his way along the stones, Roman continues around the pillars, but his hope evaporates, as has the cat: He's alone in the chapel. The Scotch broom still lies there fading on the stone slabs above the tombs, dry plant corpses as hard as bone.

In September, Michaelmas had brought constant waves of pilgrims to the rock. They all, even the poorest among them, contributed something toward building the huge basilica. They all had either a favor to ask of the Angel or a miracle to thank him for. Master Roger paid for a private mass to be said to honor the Archangel. At the craftsman's request, Roman himself officiated at a private mass in Saint Martin's Chapel for Roger's family. As he said the mass, he couldn't take his eyes off little Brigitte. She had long blond hair like her father and brown eyes like her mother, a pious, courageous woman who was proud of her ten children and of the eleventh on the way. Roman had waited for the celebration impatiently, as he was hoping, without admitting it, for the appearance on that important day of someone who never did show up.

September's Michaelmas, dedicated to the patron saint of the mountain, has now come and gone, and the monks are already getting ready for October's Michaelmas. October's feast day celebrates the founding of Saint Aubert's sanctuary on the rock, the birth of the holy mountain. On that day the streets are always crammed with hawkers, street performers, and strolling acrobats. And of course with thieves as well, and sometimes with dangerous brigands. As he does each year, the Duke of Normandy, the abbey's protector and financial supporter, will watch the grand procession in person along with his mother, the Duchess Gonor, his knights, and his court. Then Richard II will go to meditate on the tomb of the princess Judith of Brittany, his wife, in Saint Martin's Chapel. But this year, 1022, won't be exactly like the others. High mass in the Carolingian church will be taking on the special luster that comes with the glory accompanying the end of one era and the beginning of another. In fact, a sign from heaven had predicted for the abbey a grand renewal. Soon after the wedding of Richard and Princess Judith, a strange event had occurred in Father Hildebert's cell, built, as was the church, by the Breton canons. One night, before Matins, unexplainable pounding could be heard upon the ceiling. Above the tapestry depicting the Archangel, a hand not human was knocking on the wood, as if some immortal spirit was trapped under the roof. The abbot woke up and called for the prior and the cellarer, a stout young man known for his great strength. The cellarer set a ladder against the wall, climbed up, and pulled off some of the lathes. He discovered a leather chest jammed there between roof and ceiling. What was in the chest cleared up a mystery no one had been able to solve, for inside it they found Saint Aubert's remains. They had disappeared along with the canons back in 966 when the Benedictines arrived. But here were an arm, the right arm, and especially the cranium (recognizable because of the hole in the forehead, the mark of the Angel's finger when he appeared the third time), and a parchment attesting to the bones' authenticity. The tale of the miraculous discovery of the treasure the despicable canons had hidden away from the prayers of the faithful began to circulate rapidly throughout Normandy and even throughout enemy Brittany.

As a good Christian and faithful guardian, Richard realized what Saint Michael's wishes were and, although he had been hesitating before, made the decision to build the great abbey church. He gave Hildebert additional land, mills, and large amounts of money for the basilica's construction, plus the Chausey Islands and their indispensable granite reserves. As for the relics that had so fortuitously resurfaced, they were placed in a gold-plated silver reliquary set with crystal and precious stones and became the pride and joy of the abbey's treasure. For those protecting the treasure, they were a guarantee not only of Richard's support but also of a constant flow of pilgrims.

Several days before Michaelmas in October, also Saint Aubert's feast day, when the reliquary will be displayed to the faithful to remind them of the Angel's power, the whole monastery is bubbling with mystical passion. Many pilgrims have already arrived and been welcomed by the villagers and the brothers. All the monks who are also ordained priests are needed to say masses, some of which are for the faithful who died on the journey as victims of the sea, of the quicksand, or of brigands. "Before you go to Mont-Saint-Michel, don't forget to make your will," says a Norman proverb. Only one priest is exempt from saying these private masses, and that is Brother Roman, who goes and comes freely, far from the cloister's constraints. Now that he is the master builder, he's burdened by the enormity of his task and by the honor of following in Pierre de Nevers's footsteps. Never has he directed the building of even the smallest chapel, the most modest oratory, and suddenly he bears the full responsibility for building the New Jerusalem! His master used to say, as he showed him his sketches, that they marked the culmination of his life's work, and at the age of sixty he was already unusually old. In fact, his drawings are his testament and Roman his only heir. Roman is also afraid. In spite of the confidence Hildebert has expressed in him, he's not sure he can see the same confidence in his brothers' eyes. So, taking no time for rest, he organizes the work site, recruits workers and craftsmen, keeps his eye on the stonecutting on the Chausey Islands, stores the first blocks, and often goes to visit Master Roger when he's working in the forest. Roger has felled a large number of oaks, in keeping with his reputation and Roman's confidence in him. The wood for the future church's structure won't be ready for several years, but barges for transporting granite are already taking shape in the clearings. The new master builder's anxieties are allayed somewhat when he sees the progress. Roman enjoys his ride back through the forest to give his report to Hildebert.

On this rainy autumn day, he notes that the sky is the same color as the carpenter's and his brother's eyes, a lovely gray tinged with green. He feels Pierre de Nevers must be sending encouragement from up there in his new dwelling place. As he slows his horse to wend his way through tall trees whose thick branches prevent the feeble sunshine from lighting the path, he thinks he hears shouts. He stops and listens. Yes, he's not mistaken, there are indeed shouts. He can hear men shouting, and women, too. He turns and hurries toward what sound to him like calls for help. Following the voices, he draws closer. Suddenly, at the edge of a salt marsh, he sees a family of pilgrims standing in the sticky mud. With the parents are five children, and the mother, holding an infant in her arms, is screaming. Four heavyset bearded men armed with clubs and cutlasses are shouting threats and stealing food and money from the terror-stricken pilgrims. Without even thinking how many thieves there are, Roman starts swinging the stick he uses as a whip and gallops forward to help the victims.

"In the name of the All-Powerful One!" he cries while still at a distance. "Leave these people alone!"

"Hey, monk!" yells one of brigands. "You're afraid we're stealing money you're counting on yourself! Come get it if you dare!"

"You scum!" Roman shouts from his saddle. "Infidels, pagans! What you're stealing is sacred bread that belongs to the Lord, not me! Stand in awe of the Most High, fear for your souls and fear divine punishment!" he adds, whacking at them with his stick.

"Oh, the Lord surely doesn't mind sharing," responds one of the bearded rascals, dodging Roman's blows. "Punishment? When God has everything and we have nothing at all? The Lord will surely forgive us. Hey, fellows," he shouts, grabbing the horse's reins. "This thief has been on stage long enough. It's time to shut him up!"

And right before the poor pilgrims' eyes the three thugs pull Roman down off his horse. While the first man takes his horse, they beat him with their clubs. Flat on his back, the monk catches a fleeting glimpse of the sky, gray like a good omen, and then the band's leader falls on him with his hunting knife. Unbearable pain in his side, in his abdomen. Villainous black eyes above him. Then nothingness, as black as a brigand's eyes.

HELL'S FIRE BURNS red. It glows with tints of bronze and gold, and the flames curl around each other like waves in a sea of brass. The waves glow, loop around each other, pour out like molten lava. Jade leaves shaped like linden blossoms are growing out of an alabaster statue. A tiny bird, beating its wings, bleeds on the statue. The bird is singing.

"Brother Roman? Can you hear me? Can you see me?"

He does hear, and he does see. He can see fire curling out of the jewel-eyed statue and he can hear the little bird singing in the springtime.

"Don't move! And don't try to talk."

Welcome coolness on his forehead, eyes, and neck. A damp cloth appeases the flames. And there's the creature, a virgin sent by the devil, with red flaming torches flying above her head, transparent green eyes shaped like almonds in the middle of her pure face, a golden sheen on her nose and cheeks, lips that open and break into smile. A slender, white neck where he can see veins throbbing as if the pulsebeat of her heart is spreading throughout her body . . . Roman is startled. He recognizes who it is.

"Y-you?" he manages to stammer.

"Oh, you're getting your memory back. That's good!" she says with a radiant smile. "But it's better not to try to talk just yet. Don't be afraid, the Lord has granted you life, and you'll survive. I'm Moira. We've already met, I believe. Five days ago a peasant, alerted by the pilgrims after your brave efforts, found you. He was afraid you'd die if he took you back to the monastery with the tide coming in, so he put you in his cart and brought you here to Beauvoir, our village in the plains. You had lost a lot of blood, and your eyes were closed like a dead man's. I bandaged your wounds, but your mind was already feverish. Four of your brothers came. Brother Hosmund, your infirmarer, said that you shouldn't be moved until God decided whether you'd live or die. Brother Hosmund knows me, and with Christ watching, he entrusted you to me. Each day after Nones he comes to check on you, along with a monk named Bernard, who trembles for you. Yesterday, two other monks came with them, including an old man with sky-blue eyes who seemed very upset."

"Hil—"

"Shhh," she interrupts him, placing her long fingers on his tense mouth. "You'll probably see your brothers before long. In the meantime, I'll be taking care of you."

She turns away to busy herself near the wide fireplace where a cauldron is bubbling. Her long red hair doesn't just hang down over her shoulders, but rather it tumbles from her head in ringlets. Her surcoat is simple, like peasant dress, but its purple cloth is as fine as a noblewoman's. She's wearing an expensive-looking belt made not of leather but of gold-plated metal. And yet the house's interior is a peasant interior—stone walls, an earthen floor spread with gladioli from the harvest and with verbena and mint. A washtub, some furniture, and medicine jars everywhere. She's Moira, the Beauvoir healer, the one with the "touch." Roman smiles at the thought that after mistaking her first for a ghost, he next confused her with an angel from Hell. And yet she had apparently brought him back from the flames to the earth!

He's in pain, has great pain in his side. His head is foggy, painfully heavy. Burning sweat drips into his eyes, and yet his body is as cold as a corpse. He tries to move one leg but can't manage to raise it. Five days and five nights. He remembers visiting Master Roger, and he remembers the brigands. Then he thinks about Father Hildebert, who came in person, once Michaelmas was over, to check on the work, on what was needed, on how much time would be needed. He watches Moira crushing herbs in a mortar. He looks at the sacks of flowers and roots spilling out over a large wooden table. As he watches the young woman work, he recalls their first meeting in Saint Martin's Chapel. He had never seen her hair, because that evening it had been tied up under her veil. But he remembers the strand that escaped and affected him so much. He would have recognized her face in the middle of a crowd; his memory has not erased it. Her eyes, her neck, her lips, the amazing hair she now makes no attempt to hide from him, the fire. . . . He is hot and feels a strange tingling in his broken body. He thinks about the yellow Scotch broom in the chapel, and the physical pain grows less intense. She walks over and lifts up his head so he can drink some bitter-tasting hot wine.

"Don't be afraid," she says softly. "But I do need to change your dressings."

In one motion she pulls the blanket away.

To be able to attend to his wounds, she has had to cut away his homespun robe from the bottom up to his thighs and also at his chest. And he's a horrible sight: his right leg, immobilized in a wooden splint, is black and blue; the left is covered with splotches of dried blood; the left side of his abdomen is enveloped in linen compresses the color of putrefaction; his arms are bandaged, and his hands, his poor hands, lie there, yellow and swollen. Inert. At the sight of his unfamiliar body, Roman is nauseated. He looks desperately up at his nurse and is able to hold back his tears only with great effort.

"I understand, Brother Roman," she says, her eyes caressing him. "But the fever you have will soon leave you. Your leg is broken; the knife grazed your heart but, thank God, didn't harm it. The wound is deep, to be sure, but time and my herbs will heal everything, with the Holy Mother's help, of course. Her will has been done, for you are alive. Now we have to prevent gangrene. Close your eyes. It's better not to watch."

He does as she asks. She's a strange person, first telling him the truth about his condition and then asking him not to watch. With his eyes closed, like a little child Roman suddenly is afraid of the dark, afraid he'll leave the earth again and never return. However, he forces himself to keep his eyelids closed and breathe deeply. He can smell the cloth she pulls away carefully from his infected abdomen and then a fresh, clean, warm cloth. He can smell her, too, when her hair brushes over his face. She takes the bandages off his arms and replaces them with others. A wave of pain; he breathes deeply. He can't remember his mother's skin, she the mother of four sons. He does remember his nannies' smell, the only women ever to have touched him. But that wasn't like what he is smelling now, Moira's smell—a perfume of autumn leaves, perhaps, of burning earth, of salt rain. She breathes the forest, she resembles a tree.

"There," she announces, pulling the wool blanket back over him. "You may open your eyes. I've finished, for now."

He opens his eyes and his childish terror evaporates. There she stands in all her beauty. But to him, it's not the beauty of a human being. She reflects a sacred essence, the essence of the Virgin Mary.

In silence, Roman thanks the Lord for having spared him, and he gives praises to the divine angel the Most High has sent him.

AS SHE PREDICTED, some monks come to visit Roman after Nones. Moira picks up her bag for gathering herbs and her knife, then leaves her patient with Hosmund, the lay brother in charge of the monastery's infirmary, and with Almodius, the subprior. Hosmund is short and stout, and his ruddy face wears a cheery smile. Like the other monks, he wears the homespun robe and is tonsured, but along with the other lay brothers, Hosmund wears a beard, an indicator that he is illiterate. Hair signifies lack of culture, or even barbarism, given the Vikings' long hair and large mustaches. Already older than most when he joined the monastery, Hosmund is not expected to participate in all the offices. And in the church, since he's not a priest, he may not enter the choir. But he is a true part of the community nonetheless. He spends his time in prayer, respect for the Rule, and devotion to manual tasks. His work permits his clean-shaven scholar brothers to devote themselves to copying and illuminating the old manuscripts that contribute to the abbey's great reputation. Hosmund, a descendant of the Viking invaders, had been the chief squire for a noble family in Caen. When he was twenty, a horse kicked him violently and ripped open his abdomen. On his bed of suffering he prayed that the transporter of souls would spare his soul and promised to dedicate the rest of his life to the Archangel if he didn't die. Once he recovered, Hosmund kept his vow, and a few months later knocked at the Saint-Michel abbey where the abbot welcomed him. Still wary of horses, he preferred instead to learn about medicinal plants rather than serve in the monastery stable. For twelve years he trained his eyes and his memory with the old infirmarer. The old monk died about two years ago, and now Hosmund himself supervises the infirmary and takes care of the monks, pilgrims, and sometimes the villagers.

"Brother Roman, praise be to the Omnipotent, you're back among the living!" he exclaims, raising his arms to heaven. "The Archangel has answered our prayers. Our father was greatly saddened by the news of the attack. You were very brave. Attacking a monk!" he continued, clenching his teeth and fists. "Not only do those brutish infidels rob the faithful, but now they try to kill the Lord's servants. What a country we live in! Yesterday," he adds in a calmer voice, "Hildebert himself came to give you the unction of the sick. You were off in another world. Asking forgiveness for your sins, he anointed you with holy oil and bade a priest to come along with me every day to give you confession if you should wake up."

"Are you able to speak, Brother Roman?" Almodius asks, drawing near. "The woman says not, but you must make an effort and give over your sins to God so you can depart in peace if he should call you to him."

Almodius is tall and thin, about the same age as Roman, but he seems older. Like black ink stains, his eyes shine brightly from behind his smooth skin, dry and yellowed like the parchments he so carefully copies. As a child oblate, he was entrusted to the monastery by his parents, rich noble Normans, and he poured all his strength into religious fervor and all his intelligence into study. From then on, for life, his universe would be circumscribed within the monastery, and his goal was to hold an important position. Gifted, fervent, and confident, the oblate became a novice and the novice an ordained priest. He was fast becoming the abbey's best copyist. Recently, Hildebert has chosen him to assist the prior.

"Yes, I . . . I need to confess my sins to you." Roman can scarcely speak. Brother Hosmund frowns.

He knows that Roman's body is too exhausted to bear the least bit of speaking but that his soul is demanding confession. Fever might still come back and carry him off, in which case his errant soul would be left bearing the weight of his sins. As Bernard had done some time before when the abbot announced the accident involving Pierre de Nevers, Hosmund places a comforting hand on Roman's shoulder. And then he goes out to ask Moira what she thinks about the patient's progress. She's talking to the monks' horses not far away. Almodius remains alone with Roman.

When Brother Hosmund and Moira return to the healer's hut, Roman appears to be lifeless. Almodius is kneeling in prayer on the flower-strewn ground beside him.

"What's happened?" Moira cries, rushing toward the bed.

Almodius stands up and with one look stops her in her tracks.

"He's only fainted," he answers, looking her up and down. "His body is worn out, but his purified soul is now free. If the Most High has so decided, now he can take him. With the Archangel as his guide, my brother will reach the kingdom of heaven."

Moira realizes that Roman has fainted because he was too weak to make confession. He might never regain consciousness. She doesn't dare scold the man of God standing there by his brother's bedside like a guard at the gates of Paradise. She notices the subprior's eyes: Dry and determined, they are staring hard at her.

"We'll leave you now," Hosmund decides. "Vespers is approaching, and the tide will soon be rising. Keep taking care of him, and we'll keep praying. We'll be back tomorrow. I'm sure he will be better. Accept our thanks for your selflessness and for all the help you're giving him."

When the monks have gone, Moira sits down on the edge of the bed and lays her hand on Roman's forehead. No fever. But God only knows where his mind is wandering. She stirs up the fire in the fireplace, busies herself a long time with her mortars and pots, then comes back to him. She removes the dried verbena from the purulent wound on his abdomen and replaces it with fresh verbena she has boiled. On his broken leg she applies a hot cataplasm of green mallow leaves cooked in a new pot with five times their weight of plantain roots. Over the smaller cuts and bruises she spreads an unpleasant-smelling paste made from lily bulbs crushed into pork grease. Finally, she wraps his chest with ground ivy, lays some sage on his forehead, opens his mouth and places some basil leaves under his tongue. She watches him a few moments; he seems to be sleeping peacefully. And then she gets up and goes to cook the evening soup for herself and her brother.

When Roman wakes up, night is about to sweep over the land, as the sea has done already. He blinks his eyes and notices the yellow flame of a candle. For a second he thinks he must be in the choir of the church or in Saint Martin's Chapel where two brothers are preparing the altar for the ceremony. But what he thinks is an altar is just a wooden table on which a strapping boy and Moira are sorting plants by the glimmer of the fireplace and a tallow candle. Roman smiles at his mistake. He tastes something strange in his mouth and a sharp pain brings a moan.

"Brother Roman!" Moira greets him, standing up. "You're awake, and I'm delighted. I was so frightened."

Roman tries to respond but the sounds are covered over by his loud breathing.

"Oh, no, I pray, don't talk!" she says with authority in her voice. "Words are bad for your body. You shouldn't try to speak but rather focus all your strength inward so your wounds might heal. Do you understand?" she asks gently, her lips barely moving.

Roman nods while Moira signals for the boy to come over. He is disturbingly beautiful and unusually tall. His hair, reddish blond, stands out in ringlets like his sister's, but his is longer and thicker. He has a high forehead, big eyes green like a mountain lake, smooth tanned skin on which a blond beard and mustache are just beginning to appear. His hands are long like a copyist's and strong like a knight's.

"This is Brewen, my little brother. He's thirteen. He has often taken his turn watching you while I slept. He's like you: He can't speak, but he understands everything. He can't hear, but he can read words on lips and thoughts in hearts. Don't be afraid. I put some basil under your tongue. It's considered a cool plant and will remove heat from your mouth so you'll be able to speak again."

To answer the questioning look in his eyes, she explains to him the medicinal properties of the plants while, with Brewen's help, she changes the cataplasms.

Like most monks, Roman has some knowledge of plants' Latin names, but, although Moira refers to them in the local language, she clearly has knowledge that far surpasses his, and maybe even Hosmund's, though the infirmarer grows herbs in the monastery garden. However, the medical theories the young woman expounds are so different from the theories espoused by the Church that Roman is sorry not to be strong enough to contradict her.

"No need to imitate doctors and bleed bodies to free them from bad humors," she says as she removes the verbena poultice. "Doctors are right about one thing. The body's harmony is like the harmony of the cosmos. It's composed of the four divine elements: fire, earth, air, and water, in different proportions. A disparity among these four elements brings about sickness. But removing blood as they do also risks removing one of the healthy elements, and that can block healing. God is present in every man, in every animal, in every thing—rock, tree, river, and also in plants; for plants, too, have a soul and contain both good and evil. They can carry off the evil in man and reestablish equilibrium among the four elements if you respect their own harmony by using them carefully and propitiously. If not, they can cast you into the abyss. For example, arum root boiled in pure wine and combined with metal heated in the same wine can reduce demonic fever, but the arum's flower and stem are violent poisons causing sudden death."

The idea that plants and animals might have souls like men makes the monk's eyes grow bright and brings rumbling noises from his powerless throat. What blasphemy to believe such things! And how impudent to tell them to a monk. He wonders where Moira gets such superstitions. It's like animism, unworthy of a good Christian.

"I can see from your eyes what you're thinking," she says. "You're wondering who taught me my science, a woman like me. My father did. He was a great healer and scholar. His own father had taught him for twenty years. Father naturally assumed he would pass along his knowledge to a son, but it wasn't easy for my mother to have children. Two children were stillborn, and then finally she had a healthy child, but it was a girl, me. A boy, Brewen, came at last six years later. My mother died in childbirth, and that was unfortunate. My father loved her so much that he wanted to follow her to the other world, but he refused to do so until he could transmit his knowledge to his son. When he realized that Brewen, already three, was permanently deaf and dumb, he nearly died of shame. He wouldn't remarry just to have another son. So he taught me, his daughter, for ten years. I can even read and write! And then last winter a sudden fever carried him off. I wasn't able to cure him, just as he had not been able to cure my brother. I think he didn't want to get better, just like Brewen, who has no desire to hear human words. He prefers the words of fairies and forest spirits."

If he were able, Roman would be screaming. He is moved by Moira's family tragedy and by her sad courage, but what dangerous naïveté! What had her late father taught her? Paganism? Fairies! She's completely unaware that she's sinning, but how could he have pictured her like Mary, like a pure, virginal, bucolic princess? Her beauty, probably . . . beauty of the Demon! It's true that life is difficult for her. She knows about plants and helps her fellow men by healing the sick, but she's mistaken about the world. He must speak to her, preach to her, save her soul, bring her back to God's reason! For the moment, the only thing he is capable of doing is to open his mouth, but no sounds emerge.

"That's quite right, Brother Roman," she deduces from his efforts, "we mustn't forget to nourish our bodies. So says Saint Benedict himself in his writings. You're hungry, and that's a good sign. You'll get well faster if you eat and if you drink this hot wine with my remedies. I've got some pea soup without fatback, and a plump pigeon. You have the right to eat meat since you are ill, and a pigeon is not a quadruped, so you can eat it without breaking the Rule!"

With a conniving smile, she gets up to heat the monk's supper. He is astounded. She is acquainted with the Benedictine Rule, and she even knows Latin! And her smile, her eyes full of innuendos. This woman is sharper than he thought. But why does she keep repeating her sacrilegious beliefs? For if she is really well read, she couldn't possibly believe such nonsense. And her mockery, is it just a perverse game? Roman can't imagine that Moira could be a dangerous criminal. While she feeds him as if he is as helpless as an infant, he examines her eyes, her features, in hopes of discovering what she's really after.

Now, the young woman appears to be obeying the rule of silence as well as the monks. She keeps her gentle smile but says not a word, and he has no idea what she's thinking. But the mystery surrounding her radiates over Roman and makes him forget the pain from his wounds. Later in the evening, plastered with strong-smelling herbs, he drifts into a strange sleep filled with strange, human-headed animals after she has placed some basil under his tongue, like the host.

For two days and nights, Roman is unable to speak. He watches Moira and Brewen with a mixture of curiosity and gratitude. The two young people shower their care on the monk. Moira continues with her monologues about her salves and brews, just like a doctor, citing names in Latin and giving prescriptions. Hosmund, Bernard, and Almodius come to visit him daily and announce that Duke Richard has just given to the monastery the Abbey of Saint-Pair, once devastated by the Vikings. As soon as Roman can be moved, they'll take him back to Mont-Saint-Michel where he'll be under Hosmund's care. Although his hostess has always been discreet enough to leave during the brothers' visits, Roman senses that the subprior distrusts her. Is that simply because of the compromising situation, a lay woman spending her days and nights with a monk in an isolated hut? Or had she been so unwise as to share her beliefs with him? Observing her attitude daily, he feels instinctively that she has no commerce with the devil. So it seems more likely that she's just too young to know what she's doing. But sometimes he's half afraid that she does, and he is surprised to find that he fears for her. Roman is also worried about plans for the construction. For the moment, Bernard slaves away alone with the help of Master Jehan and Master Roger, who came by the day before to encourage Roman. But what if he stays the way he is forever? What if he can never walk or speak again? However devoted Bernard might be, he isn't familiar with the ins and outs of building science, and not everything shows up on the parchments Pierre de Nevers prepared. The master builder had taught everything to Roman by word of mouth for eight long years. Because Roman's hands and tongue are now petrified, he can't write or explain the slightest mystery to his assistant! All that's left for him to do is pray. So, closed up within himself, Roman prays day and night. Not for himself, but for the construction of the new basilica.

He entreats the Archangel to come help him, either by carrying him off quickly if his hour has come or by healing him so that he might complete his earthly task in honor of his teacher. At dawn on the third day, words finally emerge from his throat. Roman shouts his thanks to Saint Michael and his tears give thanks to Moira the Holy Mother. All Saints' Day is drawing near.

"Moira," he says with a moan. "I hear the bells in Beauvoir. Are they for Matins or Lauds? I don't know what time it is any more."

"For Prime, Brother Roman. The sun is already up. I'm going to wake up Brewen, but first, drink this," she says, holding out some hot wine with honey and hart's-tongue fern.

"Thank you," he says, sipping the brew. "You have been very good to me. You must be tired of having a sick man in your house, demanding your entire attention and depriving you of sleep because he occupies your bed."

"You're not depriving me of anything, Brother Roman. It's my hereditary mission to heal the body's suffering, as it is the monks' mission to heal the soul. As far as sleeping is concerned, a trunk filled with hay is perfect. And in any case, I don't sleep much."

While she speaks, she makes a fire and sets bread, wine, and bacon in the middle of the table for breakfast. The flames begin to crackle beneath the soup pot. Today she has on the same dress she was wearing on the evening of their strange encounter in Saint Martin's Chapel, a robe with hints of autumn.

"It's true that while others are sleeping," Roman says, "you are haunting abbeys to frighten poor monks!"

She bursts out laughing as she cuts the bread. It's a child's laugh, bright and mischievous.

"I didn't intend to frighten you, you know. I had gone to the Mount to see little Brigitte, the carpenter's daughter, and I took advantage of my visit to meditate near some tombs that are close my heart. But I got to the chapel too late and the bells for Compline were ringing. I went in anyhow, and, when I heard you coming, I hid. And besides, why do you haunt chapels after Compline? To frighten poor girls?"

Roman laughs, too, and then his laugh turns to a sad smile.

"For the same reason as you: to pray. My master had just suffered an accident and I was praying for him. He died a few days later, at Cluny."

"Your master?" she repeated, raising her head, eyes bright.

"Yes. Pierre de Nevers, the greatest builder of all Christendom. Is it Judith's memory you cherish?" he asked after a short silence.

Moira lays down her knife and, turning toward the monk, looks him straight in the eye.

"Yes, Princess Judith, and Conan d'Armorique. We are of the same race. Father knew both of them, and I remember Judith, who came to consult him before she married Richard the Norman. How lovely she was. Father predicted, however, that their marriage would be doomed. He had seen that she wouldn't live very long. But she sacrificed herself so that peace might finally reign between Normans and Bretons."

Roman realizes she is inviting him to uncover her secret. She has chosen the moment; she provokes him with a glance. Her back to the hearth, motionless, she waits.

"Oh, because your father also did oracles?" he risks sarcastically. "But tell me, he must have been a saint or a prophet! With your brother's fairies and your own forest spirits, he could have founded a new church!"

Moira takes in the monk's words. She walks slowly over to him. There is no menace in her eyes, but infinite sadness. For the first time, she sits down on the bed with her hand near his. He can sense her trembling.

"But this church already does exist!" she finally says, her voice low. "It existed before yours, but it was sacked by the Roman invaders and then destroyed by Christian missionaries."

"What?" shouts the monk. "How can you cherish long-dead, barbarian, ungodly religions? How can you question the civilization of Christ?"

"But I am a Christian, Brother Roman!" she states. "I am a Christian. People like you haven't left us much choice. Either Christ or death! 'Civilization,' as you call it, was pounded into our heads centuries ago, and you sacked our religious sites, simply killing the druids, my ancestors, if they refused to convert! I'm like you. I venerate God, Christ, Mary, and the angels, but I still remember the gods of this earth, and I proudly honor them as my ancestors."

Roman's mouth hangs open. Celts, druids. He doesn't know much about druids, except that they were like priests, only they dressed in white, and they offered up human sacrifices to their gods and read the future in the entrails of those their warriors had vanquished. And that's the enigma Moira presents to him. She remains faithful to primitive superstitions. How can she be proud of such cruel, savage ancestors? And how long will she perpetuate their bloody rites? Suddenly this creature's presence terrifies and pains him even more than his wounds.

"Have you been baptized, Moira?" he asks.

She nods.

"Then you belong to God's kingdom, on earth and in heaven. God loves you with his infinite love. But there is only one God. You cannot love him and still maintain sinful relations with idols on the pretext that they were your ancestors' idols. Furthermore, it hasn't escaped you that I'm a servant of the Lord and that what you are telling me is very serious."

"I know full well whom I'm speaking to, Brother Roman. I'm speaking to you alone."

"Have you measured the consequences of such a confession?" he continues.

"Yes. You see my brother and me just as we are, and we hide nothing from you. We are neither dangerous magicians nor perfect Christians. We can't deny our roots, but we fear God and mistrust men. We know that you won't betray us, contrary to what some of your brothers might do."

At first, Roman finds her words reassuring. Moira's crime must surely be limited to worshiping some old images. She's not a witch or a murderess offering up human or animal viscera to pagan gods. However, she has betrayed the Lord, and she's asking a monk to be her accomplice in this crime against faith. Roman feels irritation rise within him, anger reinforced by Moira's latest words about his community.

"How presumptuous!" he exclaims, face reddening. "You're committing the sin of heresy right at the foot of the mountain where the leader of the celestial army vanquished the forces of evil. And I, in the Archangel's service, I shouldn't tell anyone?"

Moira lowers her eyes. This is not the way to gain Roman's confidence. She must try another tactic.

"Brother Roman," she says in a thin voice, stressing the word *brother*. "Tell me the history of Mont-Saint-Michel and about Saint Michael's combat with the dragon."

"You're surely joking," he says, getting angrier by the minute.

"Not at all. You have my word, Brother Roman."

He can't see any danger in explaining the spiritual foundations of the mountain. On the contrary, he sees that perhaps Moira might wisely repent as she listens to him, might establish within herself the source of true Christian spirituality. Who better than a Benedictine monk to lead her back to the straight and narrow path?

"John's Book of Revelations reveals," he begins, "that Satan became a horrible dragon. In the eighth century the monster rose out of the waters and terrorized the region. The warrior archangel, Saint Michael, was summoned to fight against that demon. The battle began on Mont Dol in Brittany, near Mont-Saint-Michel, then called Mont Tombe. The evil hordes fought furiously, and Saint Michael, in his divine armor, brandished his fine sharp sword. The war lasted for days, and it came to its climax on Mont Tombe, where the dragon had taken refuge. Saint Michael raised his sword and cut the beast's head off. The bishop of Avranches, Aubert, witnessed the combat and three times he received the order from Saint Michael, in dreams, to build a place of worship on the spot where the Archangel had brought down the Evil One. The holy site became Mont-Saint-Michel."

"Once upon a time," Moira replies, to Roman's great surprise, "long before the eighth century, long before Christ was born, an evil dragon would come from the sea every seven years and kill everyone unless a young virgin was bound up and delivered to it to devour. One particular year the fiery dragon had demanded the king's daughter herself to eat. They tied her up on Mont Dol in Brittany, where she waited for the beast to come devour her. The dragon rose up out of the water and stretched its disgusting jaws toward the girl. But a young, handsome shepherd wearing a magic belt and a long sword he had stolen from a giant stepped between them and fought the monster for three days. On the third day of the horrible battle the shepherd pursued the dragon all the way to Mont Tombe, where it tried to hide. There, he gave an order to his magic belt, and it leaped on the demon and squeezed its throat so hard that the young man was able to raise his sword and chop off its head. He freed the king's daughter, and their wedding celebration lasted three days and three nights."

Roman and Moira stare at each other.

"Both stories are equally beautiful," says the woman finally. "My people's legend and the Christian legend both serve the same goal, the victory of love over demonic forces. We simply need to remember that before Saint Michael's time, the rock was more than nothing, my people were more than nothing, and that Christians drew inspiration from my people. Today our souls have been converted, the combat is over, and we should be able to tell both stories without opposition."

"You're trying to put Saint Michael and the dragon on the same level!" Roman responds in anger, furious at having been tricked.

And on this morning an unspoken struggle begins between Roman and Moira. They watch each other like two enemies in a heavy silence haunted by Brewen as if he were a ghost from the past. The only moments of truce occur when Roman reverts back to being the patient and Moira the doctor.

"This is all that remains of the infinite power of my druid ancestors and my father," she explains bitterly as she removes the plant poultices. "The art of medicinal plants, and on top of it all, it's an art practiced by a woman!"

"That's all that remains, but what remains is everything," says Roman. "Binding up the wounds of children and strangers is everything. Because it's an evangelical act, a God-inspired act of love."

She pauses for a moment and then continues to work, her forehead and cheeks blushing. On this day, when Hosmund, Bernard, and Almodius come into the thatched-roof hut, Roman hesitates but, even though he feels a little guilty, doesn't say anything about Moira's secret. Something keeps him from speaking. Something that burns too bright in the infirmarer's eyes, or something too cold in the subprior's. Not to mention the distress and pain emanating from Bernard. The manuscript illuminator seems to be carrying, like a cross on his thin shoulders, the arches and frames of the whole church. Roman remains quiet also, out of pride, perhaps, pride arising from the task he's set himself, the task of converting Moira by reason, of leading her to accept Christian beliefs through intelligence rather than through brute force. Her mind is sharp and tough, but he'll logically prove to her that she's wrong. The idea occupies him so much that he only half listens to the colorless news from the work site.

On All Saints' Day, he asks Moira to pray with him, and he tells her edifying stories about Christian martyrs. The young woman seems fascinated by the mystic exploits of these heroes of faith and virtue.

"All Saints' Day is the feast of God's elect," he says, "of those who have reached the Kingdom and merit eternal glory. The good Odilon, abbot of Cluny, has in his wisdom just added a new feast day to the calendar. Indeed, to reestablish appropriate harmony with All Saints' Day, he also thought about those who aren't saints but to whom God, in his infinite mercy, offers the possibility of reaching heaven. Tomorrow we celebrate that feast day, the Day of the Dead. Thanks to our prayers, we the living can intercede with the Most High and help the dead whose souls, still fouled by sins, have not yet been presented to the Lord."

"My people have never known Odilon or Cluny," she replies, "but tomorrow is also our day of the dead, and has been since the dawn of time. It's the feast day of Samain. The dead are honored, time is abolished, and the gods and heroes from the other world come mingle with the living.

It's also the end of the light season and the beginning of winter, the dark season, during which time warriors must cease their hostilities."

There's a smile on her face. Roman feels exhausted. The woman is not to be underestimated. But the peace she proposes is impossible.

"Show me your ancient idols," Roman asks finally, also breaking into a smile. "I'd like to see what your sins look like."

"I can't," she says pleasantly. "We don't make statues of our gods. They live freely in our hearts, in our imaginations, and in the other world of the Sidhe. But they often come into our earthly world, and not only on Samain's Day! Often they visit humans by taking the form of animals and forest creatures: Fairies might become swans, the mother goddess a crow."

From then on, Roman understands why Moira makes such frequent reference to the Holy Mother. In her mind, Mary has become one with the mother goddess, just as the Day of the Dead has taken the place of Samain's Day. Christians were wise enough not to totally wipe out all Celtic beliefs, but rather to incorporate in their gospel several important Celtic symbols. And that explains why Christianity spread so rapidly in this region. Moira is an exception, because her family secretly persisted in keeping its culture. However, she's only partly an exception. For the absence of pagan idols, the total destruction of the ancient sanctuaries and of the druids, the only people allowed to officiate in ceremonies, all those things give Roman great joy. Yet what's a religion without rites, without priests? Not really a religion at all any more, just thought reduced to baseless bits and pieces, to distant memories, to old wives' tales, foolish though charming.

Roman remembers Moira's sudden interest when he told her about the saints' lives, and he realizes that reason alone will never bring the woman around. The only way to convince Moira is to uproot the nostalgia affecting her like an evil spell and to replace her heathen poetry with poetry from the Holy Book. Lying there in his bed, he tells himself that he must show her the richness, the beauty, the mysticism, and the depth of those verses of faith so that she might bury her blasphemous beliefs away forever. He must win her to God through her heart.

5

LYING ON HER PSYCHOANALYST'S COUCH, JOHANNA BREATHED a sigh.

"It's . . . it's like nausea," she said, putting her hand on her chest, "constant nausea, and I haven't been able to get rid of it since my latest dream. It's not so bad that I need to throw up, but it's unpleasant, a constant feeling of malaise, as if my body is quaking inside, as if my heart is trying to climb into my throat."

"All right, that's enough for today."

Johanna sat up on the edge of the couch, eyes staring.

"And what about sleep? Are you sleeping better?" the therapist wondered.

"I . . . well, I'm still taking sleeping pills to get to sleep," she admitted. "I'm afraid my dreams will return. At least the pills knock me out and keep me from having nightmares."

"Hmm. . . . It'll probably take some time to get your normal sleep patterns back. But you should start reducing the dosage, or you'll become dependent. Keep a notebook by your bed, and if you dream, write down everything right away. Then we can talk about it together. All right?"

"Sure," Johanna answered, thinking about the notebook she had when she was a little girl. "See you Saturday," she added as she stood up.

"You know," the psychoanalyst went on, "I think a second weekly session would allow you to make better progress. Would you be able to come on Tuesday or Wednesday?"

"No, I can't. Because I work all week in Cluny, and I can't come back up to Paris before Friday."

"Okay. Too bad. See you next Saturday. Have a good week."

Noon. Like noon every Saturday when she walked out of her psychiatrist's office. The "archeologist of my unconscious," as she liked to refer to her. Rain was falling. She raised the collar on her beige raincoat. In rue Saint-Louis-en-l'Île, she stopped at a shop window that tempted her with a black waterproof hat.

"Hmm, that's ridiculous," she thought. "I'd be better off buying an umbrella."

So she didn't buy anything and crossed the Seine, her hair soaked by the October downpour. She considered taking the bus, but decided against it when she saw how many people were waiting in the shelter, as if defending it from intruders. No desire, either, to go down into the Metro. She'd just catch a nasty cold, which would give her a good reason to stay in bed all weekend. Rue Henri-Barbusse: At last she was close to shelter, if a little intimidated by the stairs. Come on, I've got to go up. Third floor. Finally. She closed the apartment door with immense relief. She had never appreciated her home so much. It wasn't anything special, a typical one-bedroom Paris apartment with a kitchen for midgets, a squeaky floor, ceramic tiles, and the basic decoration she had never had the time to fix up right. But it was her refuge, and nobody could disturb her there. She collapsed on the sofa and dried her long, dripping hair with a bathrobe that she'd left lying on the cushions. She took a sip of cold verbena tea from the cup she'd put on the lamp table the evening before and noticed that the answering machine was blinking. She pulled herself up from her seat and pressed the button despite her weariness of listening to other people's voices.

Beep. "Hi, this is Philippe! You left the dig in such a hurry yesterday evening that I didn't have time to tell you anything more about Paul's forty-fifth birthday party. Well, anyhow, we've organized everything in secret with his girlfriend. He's not expecting anything at all; it's going to be great fun! And don't worry about a gift. We'll add your names to ours. So don't lock yourself up in your room this evening like a nun. Come join us! We'll all be in the café below Corinne's apartment, at eight o'clock. Don't be late. Here's the address again: metro Blanche, 16, rue . . . "

Johanna moved to the next message.

"Honey, it's me," François whispered. "I left a message on your cell phone, too. So, it's a little complicated, but I won't be free this weekend. But I promise to do the best I can to come to Cluny during the week, maybe Thursday; and if so, we can come back up to Paris together Friday evening. I'm sorry, love. I miss you terribly. Hugs and kisses. Call you later." Beep.

"So, Jo, what are you doing? Isa here. This is the third message I've left on your cell phone, and you never call back! So either you're with François or you're sick. I hope it's not the latter. Anyhow, this time you'll call me, won't you? If not, I'm going to call the fire department! So long." Beep.

Johanna smiled, picked up the telephone, and dialed.

"Yes, Isa, it's me. . . . No, no, I was with my shrink. . . . Oh, yes, I turned off my cell phone last night when I went to bed and didn't turn it back on this morning. . . . Sure, things are fine! . . . No, not this weekend. He's tied up with his wife and kids. . . . In the rain? Sure, if that's what the forecast says. At one o'clock in the Luxembourg Gardens on our favorite bench. See you tomorrow. Me too, Isa. Ciao."

On Sunday morning the rain had stopped, but the sky was the color of the typical winter sky in Paris—a dirty opaque white. Wrapped up in her overcoat in the gardens, Johanna stood near the pond, where she watched the boats kids were guiding with sticks. Isabelle arrived late as usual and, like always, blamed it on her family.

"Morning, girl," she said, giving her a kiss. "Sorry, but there was real drama this morning. Jules had lost his special teddy bear. I searched through his room for an hour, and finally it turned out that Tara had hidden it in the dishwasher to get even with her brother for saying her doll was ugly. Say, you don't look well!"

Johanna forced herself to smile. A journalist with a feminist magazine, Isabelle was an old friend from high school in Fontainebleau and had become a lifelong friend, though they led totally different lives. Not very tall, with short blond hair and brown eyes, always elegant in spite of the weight she had put on with her two pregnancies, Isa was fortunate to be anchored in the realities of daily life, those realities that always annoyed Johanna.

"Come on," said Isabelle. "Let's go eat. A little glass of red wine will do you good, and I need to talk to you."

"Well," Johanna asked once they were seated, "what's up? Any problems?"

"My dear Johanna," Isa answered. "Once again, I think you're a little out of it. Sorry to speak so frankly, but you're the one who isn't well, in case you hadn't noticed. I don't know where you're going, but you look like a ghost in some cheap movie, and you've been like this for weeks. Psycho-analysis isn't helping?"

"Yes, but . . . ," she stammered, eyes filling with tears.

"Oh, my dear," her friend said. "I understand, you're going through a difficult period. It happens to all of us, you know. Remember the condi-tion I was in after Jules was born? You're at a delicate age for a single woman, and François isn't often here to give you any support. Listen," she said after a moment's pause. "I've just had a crazy idea! You know, on Wednesday my paper is sending me to Italy for a week to do an article on the great tourist sites in Puglia. Why don't you come with me? You know, sometimes it's better to run away from your problems and then deal with them later with new perspective—"

"Puglia?"

"Puglia, the heel of the boot! The weather's still great there this time of year, they say you can really eat well there, and it's still kind of wild. And don't forget the handsome Italians! All you need to pay for is your airfare, and I'll work out the rest with my newspaper. Come on, Jo. It's been years since you've taken any vacation. It would be great to try out the hotels and restaurants together. Come on, don't leave me to face those handsome Italians all by myself. Think of my dear husband's honor!"

"Isa, Wednesday's only three days away. I can't. My dig! We're in the middle of the All Saints' Day holidays, and all the others have taken time off. And what about François? He was planning to come see me in Cluny on Thursday."

"Well," Isabelle said kindly but with a touch of anger in her voice as she lit a cigarette. "Did your dear François ask your opinion before he went to Cabourg for a month last summer? And your dig, your dig. Excuse me, but Paul's the director, not you, even if you are indispensable. You, too, have the right to take some days off, damn it! And how about the thirty-five-hour work week? Your skeletons can surely wait a week for you, can't they?"

THE CAPTAIN ANNOUNCED that the plane was beginning its descent into Brindisi and that the ground temperature was 22 degrees Celsius. Isabelle closed the guidebooks and the map she had been studying during the flight, and Johanna stopped thinking about François. She felt guilty for refusing to see him before she left and for what she had put him through during that memorable weekend at Mont-Saint-Michel. But she wasn't really very sorry. It was as if her life force and her will had been wiped out. She was letting herself be carried along by the course of events, without trying in any way to influence them. She still clung to her profession, more out of habit than out of true conviction, as she was certain that she would never find Hugh de Semur's grave. She had finally given in to Isabelle's urging, because she was simply too tired to put up any resistance. Even if François should announce that he was leaving her, she wouldn't fight it. It seemed to her as if she had been swimming upstream in her life's current. . . .

Today, although she was only thirty-three, her spirit seemed dead and her muscles as worn out as an old man's. She had started psychoanalysis as one accepts a crutch, for she knew full well that therapy wouldn't necessarily keep her going but that it might keep her from totally collapsing. It was now just a matter of time, and the numerous medicines she was swallowing morning and evening reinforced the impression she had of floating, of a slow, inevitable slide into nothingness that it was useless to resist, just like it was useless to keep rushing forward.

"We'll rent a car and take the road along the Adriatic to Lecce, Otrante, and Santa Marina di Leuca, at the bottom of the heel," Isabelle decided. "And then we'll come back up the other coast, along the Ionian Sea, toward the north."

"Fine, you're driving," Johanna answered.

. . .

THREE DAYS LATER, thanks to the sun, there were even more freckles on Johanna's nose and cheeks, and her eyes had a sparkle again. Sometimes the sparkle was due to the heady regional wines, sometimes to the enchanting foreignness of baroque cities, the turquoise sea, the red soil, the winter wheat fields dotted with poppies, and the groves of hundred-year-old olive trees with their dry trunks knotted like the arms of old circus contortionists.

Isabelle had certainly not lied about the region's gourmet treasures, and, for next to nothing, the two gastronomes ate their fill of pasta, warm squid salads, fresh shrimp, roast lamb, and creamy ice creams that would have made the toniest Italian restaurants in Paris pale in comparison. The few tourists normally in Puglia had long since disappeared, because it was only a few days before All Saints' Day; as they drove along the tiny roads in the valley, they were the only ones left to marvel at the *trulli*, those strange little huts with their cone-shaped roofs made of stone without mortar, looking for all the world like the houses of sylvan elves whose forest had been surrendered to vineyards.

"How strange!" Johanna exclaimed. "They look like smurf houses. What's that little sign painted on the roof?"

"Nobody knows for sure," answered Isabelle, blowing the horn as they neared a curve. "It's linked to the stars, I believe. Somewhere I read that they were inhabited as early as the thirteenth century. Can you imagine?"

Those jumbled stones, assembled by men according to some impenetrable mystery, intrigued Johanna's soul.

"And just wait, the best is yet to come!" said Isabelle. "We're going to Alberobello, smurf city. There are *trulli* everywhere!"

And indeed, once they passed the town's industrial suburbs, vestiges of regional splendor turned to misery, a whole town of whitewashed houses with cone-shaped stone roofs surged into view.

"Well," said Isa, shutting the car door. "I'm not sorry we came. What a change from Florence and Venice!"

Johanna couldn't help remembering that François had never taken her to Venice, and then she swept aside any feelings of romantic self-pity.

"Jo, could you stand over there beside the *trullo* with ivy climbing up it?" the journalist asked. "I'd like to take your picture."

When she wasn't behind the wheel of the car, Isa was forever taking pictures, both for her job as a reporter and for souvenirs to show her husband and children. She insisted that Johanna or the locals pose, a demand that Johanna found annoying, because she didn't think the old wall's natural beauty had any need whatever of a human being's publicity smile.

"Oh, no, Isa, that's enough!" the archeologist exploded. "The next time, drag along one of your newspaper's top models and then you can make the style section. That's not my thing!"

"Okay, don't get upset. For once I'll do the posing, and you can take the picture. All right?"

"That's fine. Give me the camera."

Isa moved over to the white wall. Her apple-green ensemble from a young designer's boutique matched the color of the ivy climbing up onto the round roof.

"Perfect!" Johanna cried, her face to the eyepiece. "Lovely! Wait, I've got to zoom, there."

Then Johanna lowered the camera, face frozen in an expression of utter surprise.

"Finished?" Isa asked. "What's the matter? You look like you've seen the seven dwarves!"

Without answering, Johanna walked on past Isa toward the building and, passing her on the left, she looked up, her mouth hanging open in surprise. The street name was engraved in golden letters on a marble plaque. Johanna couldn't pull her eyes from the sign. Isabelle came over and read what was written: *via Monte San Michele*.

"How about that!" she said with astonishment. "Whatever is Mont-Saint-Michel doing here?"

They found a shopkeeper who explained. It had nothing to do with the mountain in Normandy, although the Normans had indeed ruled Puglia for a time, but was a reference to an important local site, Mount Gargano, where Saint Michael had once appeared. The holy site could be found about one hundred kilometers away, in the town of Monte Sant'Angelo.

"That's impossible," Johanna murmured. "The damned place has a twin here at the other end of Europe, far off the beaten path, and it's just my luck to happen upon it!"

First, she cursed fate, or fortuitous coincidence. The situation would have made François laugh, but Johanna was soon cursing everything— her unconscious, her conscience, chance, bad luck, Isabelle's newspaper, and even Isabelle herself, who was so sorry to have been instrumental in bringing out Johanna's old demons. They left Alberobello and hurried to Ostuni, a marvelous village built on a hill. Isabelle hoped the oriental charm of Ostuni's stones would ward off the spell that seemed to have taken possession of her friend.

Unlike Alberobello, a small hamlet in the plain built by tiny farming people, Ostuni looked more like a Moroccan city perched on a hilltop, a white Kasbah clinging to the sky like a proud Catholic Essaouira. Isabelle and Johanna left their car in one of the modern city's squares, at the foot of the slope, and walked up into the medieval city. It was a gradual climb, the little streets wide enough and winding peacefully up. They were lined with square block-like white buildings, and the welcome scents of stew and fried vegetables filled the streets as they wafted out through flower-bedecked windows and from little trattorias opening out onto the pavement. Johanna looked at all the street names but could find no trace of the Archangel. A painted plaster Madonna, housed in a niche in the wall, looked out sadly from behind its iron grill. High above the old village there wasn't an abbey but a splendid cathedral with a Venetian fronton and a rose window chiseled like a Gothic sun. At the summit of the mountain, the two friends looked out over the panorama beneath: A sea of olive trees formed a bronze bay with silvery specks, from which baroque breast-like stones emerged. Beneath the wind's teasing music, the vegetation undulated like a belly dancer. Beyond the land and sky lay a somber blue desert: It was the glassy sea, and it seemed lifeless.

"It's magnificent, isn't it, Jo?" Isabelle ventured. "White Ostuni, the city on three hills. Really like a miniature Rome, but not the same style.

It must be terrible in the summer, with tourists and heat waves. But it's worth writing about in my paper. This evening we're going over there," she said, pointing out into thin air, "to an old farmhouse they've turned into a fancy hotel."

Little by little, cooler air enveloped the town, and the sky turned dark blue like the sea. Johanna didn't answer but couldn't keep from shivering.

"You're shivering!" said Isabelle. "Are you cold?"

"A little," she responded, looking off into the distance. "And I'm famished. Shall we go eat? Have you made a reservation anywhere?"

"No, I thought we might happen upon a nice little restaurant for my article. Come on, there are plenty of inns around here, and at this time of year we won't have to fight for a table. Here, put this on," Isabelle added, pulling a leather jacket from her bag.

Johanna slipped on the jacket and followed her friend. The sun had set and, in spite of the streetlights reflecting on the chalky walls, Johanna couldn't see anything except her tennis shoes, which were having trouble navigating the steps.

"Don't worry," Isabelle said reassuringly, taking her arm. "We'll find a lovely restaurant, enjoy our meal, and tomorrow will be another day."

"Isa, I love you, but if existential angst could be cured by forking food into our mouths, we would be in bliss, happy and . . . obese!"

"Maybe," she answered, trying to get serious, "and then newspapers like mine might stop showing girls carved in a grain of rice, and the fat happy ones would get all the attention! My motto is: *fat power!* We'll be the winners, because we're the most optimistic. . . . "

Johanna broke into a smile. Isabelle paused beside an interesting sign.

"Look here, Johanna!" she exclaimed. "*La taverna della gelosia*—'The tavern of jealousy.' What a great name! I'll bet you a plate of squid that the owner is a nice-looking woman who feels good about the way she looks."

"And full of spirit," Johanna added. "We sure make a strange pair. We're both fascinated by Italian signs, but not the same ones."

"What do you expect? You're obsessed with some sacred mountain near the English Channel, and me with the mounds of lard ensconced on my hips. We each have our cross to bear."

This time Johanna burst out laughing and reached out tenderly to Isabelle for support as they walked down the steep stairs leading to the restaurant. Two little enchanting terraces lit with Chinese lanterns opened out on the night. Isabelle was right about the restaurant's owner, and the woman suggested a table inside, in a vaulted cellar with the stones exposed. It looked like a rustic grotto cleaned up and refined, thanks to the careful decorating done by a woman of taste.

"It's lovely, but if you don't mind I'd rather stay outside," whispered Johanna to Isa. "I'm afraid I'll feel claustrophobic in there."

"Don't you like medieval stones any more?" Isabelle asked in surprise.

"If you aren't afraid of getting chilled, just now I feel better outside."

"Fine with me, girl. I understand. No problem, I've got another sweater in my bag."

They sat down under the protective branches of a giant pepper tree with a wrinkled trunk and leaves that exhaled a delicate odor of pink berries. Right away Isabelle struck up a conversation with the restaurant owner, in Italian and English interspersed with French. When the woman left them alone with the menu, Isa scratched some words in her notebook, then lit a cigarette from the candle on the table.

"She won't tell me why her inn is called the tavern of jealousy," she explained to Johanna. "Personal life. In any case, the house specialty is medieval cooking centered upon meat. She found some old recipes and has adapted them to suit modern tastes. What a great idea!"

"Hmmm," Johanna mumbled, scowling at the menu. "I hope the meat isn't medieval! And there's no squid, either. Too bad. In that case, I'll just order a pizza. Not much risk."

Isa didn't try to answer. She knew that Johanna's bad mood wouldn't last any longer than it took to drink two glasses of fourteen-percent wine. So she ordered the best regional red immediately. Johanna couldn't really have said whether her sour mood came from the feeling that Mont-Saint-Michel was following her everywhere, even to the medieval contents of her plate, or if it came from the anger she was beginning to feel about François. In that romantic spot, more propitious for a couple's harmonious relationship than for jealousy, she realized that he had never spent even a week's vacation with her. He would have loved this medieval village, these poetic old lamps, this picturesque character who was bringing back to life the cuisine of another time, her time, their favorite time period. By candlelight they would have talked passionately about her discovery of Mount Gargano, like the specialists they were. But instead of being here with her, touching her, he was more than a thousand kilometers away, and she was letting herself get upset in conversation with her best friend who was doing everything to improve her mood. She felt like borrowing Isabelle's cell phone and giving François a call.

"Are you sure you don't mind sharing the antipasti with me?" asked Isa. "It's for two."

"That'd be great."

"And then I would like to try this medieval rabbit stew. And for you, my dear, shall I order a pizza? What would you like on it?"

"No, no," Johanna answered, finishing her second glass of wine. "I've changed my mind, after all. It'd be stupid to order a pizza. Rabbit like you."

A bit later, the two women were cleaning up the last drops of the spicy, vinegary gravy.

"Pass me a cigarette," Johanna asked. "I'd like to ask you something."

She coughed a bit, for she didn't normally smoke, and began to explain what she wanted.

"Isa, I'd like to go see Mount Gargano. I know it's crazy, but it's almost like the more I try to run away, the more it all tries to catch me by surprise, to hit me in the back. And I hate being attacked from behind, just like I hate all these coincidences. I'm not afraid, I'm with you, and after all, I'd like to understand what's happening, to see what's there. I wonder if it's different from Mont-Saint-Michel, what the abbey's like, its style, its history."

"We wouldn't have to go in person. We could buy a book!"

"No, it's not far away, and I'd never forgive myself to be so close, knowing it's there and not having the courage to go see it. Please, we can do it in less than a day, and there may be some interesting things for your paper."

Two DAYS LATER, on a Sunday morning, the little car was negotiating the hairpin turns toward Mount Gargano. A vast, forested massif plunging down into the Adriatic, Gargano was a nature reserve, a large green mountain lined with resorts and dotted with sloping villages, including Monte Sant'Angelo, the town that sheltered the sanctuary devoted to Saint Michael.

"As you can see, the countryside is nothing like Normandy," said Isabelle joyously. "No plains, no island standing alone in the sea, no tides, no sheep in the salt flats, not even any cows!"

"Yes. Apparently it's just a little village hidden on the mountain. It's strange how little the two regions have in common."

"All the better."

The contrast was even clearer as they entered the town. The sign said it was Monte Sant'Angelo, but rather than old medieval stones, lines of sordid modern buildings greeted Isabelle and Johanna. Johanna was dubious. They must have found the wrong Monte Sant'Angelo. And then, in the distance, they saw the old village, built on the top of the mountain like a white medina, similar to Ostuni. That was reassuring, and they continued. Johanna was gripped with intense excitement. A square bell tower emerged above the sea of houses, but it didn't look anything like the thin Gothic spire of the French mountain. Was it a part of a monumental abbey, with an underground crypt and its twin choirs? They needed to get closer to find out. Her legs tingled, and she was sweating even though the air at that altitude was cool. Finally they made it to the summit, and Isa stopped the car along the sidewalk. Johanna leaped out of the car and started looking for the monastery. There was the tower, standing alone, without any cathedral, just a tower, a campanile. Tiny cobblestone streets, shops with religious souvenirs, trattorias for tourists, but no abbey.

"*Scusi,*" she said to a shopkeeper dressed in black and bent over a pile of transparent plastic virgins. "*San Michele santuario, per favore?*"

Her accent must not have been very convincing, because the shopkeeper didn't say a word, just pointed toward an ordinary building near where Isa had found a parking place. Dubious, Johanna walked over to it. Facing the campanile, a large square led to a building made with limestone, its façade obviously recent, maybe nineteenth century.

It was pierced with two ogival arcades, twins, with two doors, and the white wall was capped with a triangular fronton decorated with friezes. Above the two identical arcades, between two little rose windows, a niche sheltered a plaster statue—the statue of Saint Michael decapitating the dragon, an exact replica of the golden sculpture crowning the spire on the Norman bell tower.

"Oh, here it is!" said Isabelle from behind her. "You must admit that it's not very spectacular!"

"Read this," Johanna urged her, her eyes caught by the epigraph above the right door. "*Terribilis est locus iste hic domus dei est et porta coeli*: 'This place is terrifying, for it is God's dwelling place and the gate to heaven.'"

"So? That's not surprising for a church! Come on, now that we're here and since it looks like there aren't any monks around, let's go see this terrifying place."

The walked through the door. There was a religious relic shop on their right, and a large flight of stairs led down somewhere. No place to buy tickets.

"You've been too tied up with your work, Johanna," said Isa. "Don't forget that we're in Italy now. Here the government and the Office of National Monuments don't have total control over the churches. The Vatican manages its own historical patrimony. So you're not going into a museum but into a place of worship, where shorts and bare arms are forbidden."

Johanna put on her leather jacket and started down the stairs. Immediately, her soul was caught up in the characteristic smell of old limestone, the half-erased medieval frescos, a huge cross, the large Gothic arcades, and the rib arches above her head. A feeling of mystery, of time standing still, kept her from speaking. They went down five flights of stairs separated by four landings. They might have been descending into the depths of the earth and of the human spirit; the staircase seemed endless. What could there be at the end of this dimly lit world? Johanna recognized the traces of old tombs on the walls. Finally the staircase ended. They could see light coming through a doorway framed by twisted columns and crowned with a fresco that was almost completely obliterated, but they could still make out the shape of a bull. Under the fresco a marble plaque with an opulent border was held up by two angels. Johanna translated the Latin:

"'This is the crypt of the Archangel Saint Michael,'" she murmured, "'known throughout the world, where he deigned appear to men. O pilgrim, as you prostrate yourself, venerate these stones, because the place where you are standing is holy ground.'"

They went through the doorway and blinked in surprise at the sunlight pouring directly into the atrium. Marble sarcophagi and statues of saints lined the patio. Across from them, a remarkable Romanesque doorway framed a heavy bronze door that opened onto a dark area—the Angel's dwelling place. Spurred by curiosity, Johanna hurried ahead of Isabelle. Her heart was pounding as she entered. Never could a stone-lover like her have imagined what she saw. She took a few steps and then, captivated by the atmosphere, stopped. She was standing in the middle of a grotto, a natural cave, formed with huge blocks of ageless limestone. The shadows played over the rock's crevices, and she raised her eyes to a Gothic ceiling with ribbed vaults. Across from Johanna, in the back of the cathedral, an apse was hollowed out, yellow like the sun, a man-made baroque temple attached to the rock like something from Jordan or Petra. Yes, just like subterranean Petra. A covenant between earth and men, this strange church was only a prelude to something else.

As soon as her eyes had grown accustomed to the dark nave, her attention was drawn to the right, toward the choir. Under a vault made of uneven rocks, surrounded by pulpits and behind an altar, a point of light was shining. In a large urn made of silver and Bohemian crystal and supported by the rock mass, it was a statue of Saint Michael, sculpted from amazingly pure white marble, that was shining so brightly.

Enchanted, Johanna walked over to the statue and looked carefully at the head of the heavenly hosts—golden-winged, dressed in the short armor worn by Roman legionnaries and a military mantle, armed with a long horizontal sword—in the posture of a warrior cutting off the head of a demon with the face of a monkey, the thighs of a goat, the claws of a lion, and the tail of a serpent. This Saint Michael wore an expression she had never seen anywhere else. It was the face of a smiling adolescent with thick, curly hair, and his eyes had the crystalline innocence of a child.

"How truly extraordinary," Isabelle commented when she caught up with Johanna.

"Yes, Isa," whispered Johanna emotionally. "I hadn't expected any-thing like this. It's overwhelming."

They slowly took in all the details of the place: altars, sculptures, the little chapel housing the relics of popes martyred during the third and fourth centuries. The dark bones displayed in such opulent fashion im-pressed Isabelle. Johanna was more taken by the lovely sculptures and medieval bas-reliefs. There was a Virgin of Constantinople from the twelfth century; a Saint Michael, which must have been from the eighth or ninth century, with his scales weighing the souls of dead sinners; and in the center of a little hollow in the rock, protected by a pane of glass, a charming sculpture of a Renaissance Saint Michael. Visitors were tossing coins to the saint through an opening in the glass.

"A wishing well!" Johanna exclaimed joyously. "For once I'm going to make a wish."

So she did, as her friend watched in amusement. Won over by the place's mystical beauty, Isabelle was delighted and only too happy to see that Johanna was again relaxed and enjoying herself. Loud voices brought them back to the middle of the grotto.

A crowd had gathered on the benches surrounding the choir, and even in the nave where men and women were standing, waiting for Sunday mass. A priest stood before the urn with the statue of Saint Michael. When the mass began, the two women remained a moment in a corner of the church, where, their backs to the rock, they were touched by the obvious fervor of the exclusively Italian audience. Then, out of decency and respect for such real piety, they slipped out of the cavern and climbed back up the steps in silence. At the top, Johanna found a guidebook in French, and they didn't speak to each other until they found themselves once again out in the open square.

"Are you all right?" Isabelle asked Johanna.

"Great, imagine that!" she answered. "I'm not sorry I pushed us to come here. I feel liberated . . . but I can't understand why more people in France don't know about this place. For me, it's every bit as important as the Sistine Chapel. Let's find a place to sit down. I'm eager to see what this book can tell us about it."

"Sure. How about lunch? It's about time," she said, licking her lips.

. . .

THE VILLAGE ITSELF was worth a visit. It included a medieval fortress that had once belonged to the Normans and would have been worthy of the Knights of the Round Table, a baptistery named Saint John of the Tomb that dated from the eleventh century, churches from the High Middle Ages, and poppy gardens. Clearly, there was no monastery, nor had there ever been one. Johanna and Isabelle particularly enjoyed Junno, the oldest section of town, where tiny, twisting streets lined by whitewashed houses with wrought-iron balconies offered splendid views of the sea.

"It's crazy. The sanctuary dates from the fifth century!" said Johanna, her mouth full of mountain lamb, a local specialty. "That's earlier than Mont-Saint-Michel! So it's just the opposite of what I thought. Mount Gargano is the model for Mont-Saint-Michel, and the chapel is the historical twin of Saint Aubert's grotto."

"Twins? Sorry, but I don't think they have much at all in common for brothers," Isa responded, chewing on the lamb chop bone. "Those two brothers are surely not identical twins!"

"Yes, they are," said Johanna, her face growing pale. "There are major differences, but they both have the same legendary matrix, the triple apparition. In the year 490, the Angel appeared a second time to the Bishop Laurent, prelate of the city of Soponto, where he had been summoned when the city was besieged by the enemy. The chief of the heavenly hosts guaranteed the town's victory. In 493, to thank the Archangel, the bishop decided finally to obey him and establish a grotto in his name. Saint Michael appeared a third time, saying that it was too late because he had already done it himself. The bishop went to the cavern, escorted by the clergy and the people. There he found that a stone altar had already been set up, and engraved in the rock was Saint Michael's footprint. The bishop officiated for the first time in the sanctuary. It was the twenty-ninth of September, and that day became Michaelmas all over the world."

"That's interesting. This lamb is really good."

"You're right," said Johanna, her eyes bright. "Like the lamb from Mont-Saint-Michel, and it fits all the symbols! Saint Michael loves wine-producing regions, for they venerate Christ's blood; regions where lamb is produced, for the Lamb of God; mountains near the sea, for the New Jerusalem; the number three, for the Holy Trinity; and bishops!"

"So? Why is he a bishop-lover, in your opinion?" asked Isa with a smile.

"I don't know," Johanna answered, amused at her crazy demonstration. It would have made all her old professors scream. "Perhaps because he has to have some vice, saint though he may be!"

"Talk about vices, bishop-loving has to be one! And what's more, they sure don't reciprocate. They never even listen to him."

"That's right, Isa. Whereas Joan of Arc, when he appeared to her as a shepherd girl, she listened to him right away. In the French legend of Mont-Saint-Michel, the Angel stuck his finger through Aubert's skull so he would finally build the grotto on the mountain and stop thinking he was crazy. And so it's true that, in spite of angels' passions, men remain men."

The rest of their lunch was pleasant, filled with bizarre accounts and finally with scabrous details about their respective partners. They continued their conversation as they strolled along through the old village past outdoor cafés. Isabelle took lots of pictures, noted her impressions, wrote down addresses of cafés, as she hoped to correct the injustice done to Monte Sant'Angelo by those of the French guidebooks that didn't say one word about it. As the afternoon came to an end, they passed old people dressed in their Sunday best on their way to have a drink and play cards. Isa checked her watch and Johanna looked at her cajolingly.

"Isa? What's on for this evening?"

"Trani, a lovely fishing village on the way to Bari. We ought to be on our way. I told the hotel we'd be there around eight."

"Isa, I'm not trying to be difficult, but I'm getting tired of always being on the road. I'd like to stay in one place for a while. Wouldn't you like to stay here tonight? And then we could leave tomorrow morning. I noticed a little hotel across from the sanctuary. A hotel address here could be useful for your article. Come on, and to thank you for bringing me here, I'm paying for the meal."

Isabelle exhaled her cigarette smoke and frowned.

"Tell me, Jo. I may be blonde, but I'm not a natural blonde, you know. Why can't you just come right out and say that you don't want to leave your Saint Michael now that you know there have never been any monks here and so no Benedictine ghost can come pull your hair while you sleep?"

THE HOTEL MICHAEL was nothing fancy. Smoking wasn't allowed, especially in the rooms, and that annoyed Isabelle. She was also a little upset by the unfriendly girl at the desk, but she calmed down when she learned that they were the only guests and so they could have the nicest room. It was the "matrimonial" room, and it had a great view out over the roofs and the sea. Standing on the balcony, the two women admired the panorama. Opposite and to the right, there were white houses with red tile roofs, and a multitude of singing swallows swooped here and there as if to defend them. On the left, the Romanesque arches of the closest building, the old baptistery, stood out against the sky like a friendly star. Further away, the impassable deep blue sea sucked at the mountain's green base. Below, several children at play added life to a small square surrounded by churches with baroque entrances. Seeing the local children, Isabelle stayed on the balcony and tried to take some pictures while she smoked, whereas Johanna went back to explore the holy grotto before it closed. That evening, her passion for old stones came alive again. But it wasn't Johanna the archeologist who felt renewed. It was a little girl freed from a primitive fear—fear of dying in her sleep. Later, after the typical feast and a short walk in the tiny streets for digestion's sake, she lay down beside her friend and fell asleep without taking a sleeping pill.

The next morning, Isabelle woke up when the travel alarm went off. She threw off the covers and drew open the pink velvet curtains. The sun painted the sky and the distant sea pale blue, with no clouds and no waves. Facing the water, rocks and vineyards glistened. The light turned the mountain houses white, and it looked as if they were raising their old tiles up as an offering to the new morning. Delighted to see such a beautiful day, Isa opened the window, and when she turned around to awaken Johanna, she realized she was alone.

"Jo? Are you in the bathroom?" she asked. Then, when she got no response: "Where has she gotten to? Gone to mass, maybe?" she said with a chuckle.

Johanna's suitcase lay open in a corner. Isa deduced that Johanna wasn't far away, and she took over the bathroom. A few moments later, dressed in red suit pants and a little sailor's sweater, her makeup on and her hair carefully combed, she walked up the stairs toward the hotel's breakfast room; her perfume scented the stairway as she climbed. In the corner of the veranda built under the roof, a large man was grumbling as he worked the espresso machine. Johanna was sitting alone in front of the bay window, having her breakfast. On the table lay a pen and a little blue school notebook.

"Morning, my dear!" said Isabelle, giving her a kiss. "Have you been here long? I didn't hear you get up."

"Good morning, Isa," she answered, discreetly turning over the notebook. "I woke up a little before dawn and slipped out so as not to disturb you."

"Did you see the sunrise from here?" she asked, waving at the window. "It must have been marvelous!"

"Yes it was, absolutely magnificent," Johanna responded, raising her cup to her lips.

Isabelle sat down, ordered a black coffee, and looked over at her friend. She seemed a little strange—not very talkative, her face drawn, her eyes staring out over the bay. She was rubbing her forehead. She must have gotten dressed in the dark without bothering to wash up. She was wearing her usual dark canvas pants, the flat shoes she always wore, and an ordinary gray wool V-necked sweater pulled over a white T-shirt. She was thin, but not skinny, and you could see her pleasing shape beneath her unisex clothes. Isabelle would have given anything to have her body, still unmarked by motherhood and the trials of ordinary living. If only she had the opportunity to look like that, she would try to keep her shape; she'd eat natural foods, she'd go to the pool or gym. Not like Johanna, who ate everything she felt like eating and declared she was against all sports. If she were her friend's size, she would wear long, tight, low-cut dresses, snug jackets, short skirts, and high heels, and she would never hide her beauty under such shapeless, nondescript rags.

For once, Johanna had not tied her hair up, and the lovely, dark mass rippled down over her shoulders. Without her glasses she looked less scholarly, and Isabelle could see her lovely, almond-shaped eyes, light blue with gray circles. If only she would try to use a little makeup, she would stop every man in his tracks! Her mouth was naturally pleasant and her curves didn't need any silicone, but with a little lipstick she wouldn't be quite so pale. Her work wasn't stressful, and she didn't smoke or drink too much tea and coffee, so her teeth were white without a dentist's ruinous help. As for her skin—it was smooth and fair, with irregularly spaced freckles—it stood in stark contrast to her black hair and thick eyebrows. The contrast was charming, it gave her a mischievous air. She needed to watch out for wrinkles, though, and there were already a few star-shaped lines near her eyes—the first ravages of time. Johanna couldn't have cared less, but just because she was an archeologist, that didn't mean she had to look like an old wall! Isabelle promised herself that she would tell her about the new generation of creams and bring some samples back from the newspaper room if her colleagues hadn't already taken them all. But it didn't seem like the best time to start talking about cosmetics. Johanna hardly seemed to know Isabelle was there. She was engrossed in watching the sky being torn apart by the ballet of whistling swallows.

"Did you have trouble sleeping?" Isabelle asked.

"I didn't get much sleep," Johanna answered after a short silence, "but enough."

"Good. Do you want to go back to the grotto before we leave for Trani?"

"No, that's not necessary. I've seen what I needed to see. But I do want to go wash up before we give up the room. Isa, could I borrow your blue sleeveless sweater? You know, the one that's so soft?"

"The cashmere one . . . of course," Isa answered in surprise. "It might be a little large for you, but sure, take it. It's on the chair."

Johanna thanked her, picked up her notebook and pen, and left her friend sitting there puzzled.

. . .

TRANI'S LITTLE PORT smelled of salt and fish. A few meters away from the fishing boats, on a flowered terrace, Johanna was concentrating on a seafood platter and her table mate on a grilled sea bream. The sleeveless sky-blue sweater brought out the color of Johanna's eyes and the natural elegance of her arms.

"Are you sure you don't want some?" asked Isa, lifting the pitcher of white wine.

"No, thanks. Today I feel like drinking water."

"You're not sick, are you?" Isabelle wondered. "You've seemed a little strange all day. What are you thinking about? Is there something wrong?"

Looking right at her friend, Johanna raised her head and swallowed an oyster. Then she stopped eating, hesitated, gazed out over the sea, and finally launched into speech.

"I'll tell you, Isa. Last night I had a dream."

"A dream? What kind of dream?" Isabelle sounded worried. "An ordinary dream, or your famous nightmare in Latin with the monk in robes?"

"At first everything is dark," Johanna began. "Then a shadow leaps into a brightly lit room. In fact, the human form was hiding in the ceiling and then jumped down to the earthen floor. Everything is made of wood, the ceiling, where I can see the hole the form jumped through, as well as the walls. There's a fireplace, a table with parchments on it, burning candles, a small jug of wine, a pewter goblet. In one corner there's a stranger sleeping on a mat, a blond man with long hair, a beard and mustache, and he's covered almost entirely with a rough wool blanket. Above him hangs a magnificent tapestry showing Saint Michael with his scales, weighing souls . . . "

"Say, that reminds me of something," Isabelle interrupted.

"Right. The eighth- or ninth-century sculpture we saw in the grotto yesterday," Johanna answered excitedly. "The same theme, but woven into tapestry. So then the shadow walks over to the sleeping man, I can hear him breathing, and it reaches out one hand. And I can see very clearly that it's a man's hand."

"But," Isabelle stammered, "how about the rest of the body? Who is it?"

"I have no idea. I can't make it out. All I can see are the hands. In short, with his strong right hand, he grabs the blond man's arm, lifts it up and lets it fall back. The arm falls motionless on the mat, and the man doesn't wake up. The shadowy form picks up the wine jug and throws it to the floor. It makes a red stain and smells like cheap wine. The other man still doesn't move."

She pauseed and took a deep breath before continuing:

"And then he picks up a candle and sets fire to the blanket. It smokes and burns, but the man under it, with his eyes still closed, doesn't make a sound and doesn't make any attempt to get away. The fire grows stronger, reaches his beard, his skin, and it starts to smell like roast pig. It's horrible. Soon the flames reach the tapestry; the scale burns up, and soon Saint Michael does, too. Beneath it the straw mat is flaming like a torch. A human torch. . . . Suddenly I'm in the crypt Notre-Dame-sous-Terre. Everything is dark, but I can see the stones and the twin altars with their candles. On one of the altars I even see a Black Virgin. Up on the steps, to the right, the headless monk in the same Benedictine frock is waiting for me as a priest waits for his flock before the sermon. He's standing opposite me, his arms hanging down beside his headless body, and he says in his cavernous voice: '*Ad accedendum ad caelum, terram fodere opportet.*' 'You must dig into the earth to reach heaven.' There I am, opposite the altar; I reach my arms out toward him, my hands; he raises his hands toward the heavens and repeats louder still, '*Ad accedendum ad caelum, terram fodere opportet.*' I'm petrified. He looks at me with his nonexistent eyes, and I realize I'm completely naked. Suddenly he flies with his wingless body, he dives toward me like a blackbird. He reaches out his hand and points at me! There he is, only a few inches away from me, hovering in the air, and suddenly he touches my forehead, repeating his sentence, syllable by syllable: '*Ad accedendum ad caelum, terram fodere opportet!*' His index finger is about to drill into my head. It burns, it hurts . . . and then I woke up."

Isabelle didn't say anything for few moments. Johanna, rubbing her forehead, sipped her carbonated water.

"Well," Isa finally said, "I'm not a specialist in interpreting dreams, but there's plenty of material. You should call your Madame Freud, she'd be delighted. There's enough stuff there for a whole year of sessions."

"On the contrary, Isa, she won't be at all pleased, because as soon as I get back I'm going to tell her that I'm stopping our sessions."

"What?" Isabelle exclaimed.

"Oh, I know what you're going to say," said Johanna. "I've heard it before, I can hear François saying it, and my shrink insinuates it too. Yesterday I told you about Saint Michael's third appearance, when he pierced the bishop's cranium, and then, as if by chance, last night my headless monk comes back the third time and touches my forehead. Yesterday, in the grotto, we saw a medieval sculpture of the psychostasis Archangel and—"

"Psycho what?" Isabelle asks.

"Psychostasis: 'he who weighs minds,' the sins, the souls of the dead, and in my dream, I find myself facing a tapestry showing the angel and his scales, in the very same position, with the very same design. I agree, it doesn't seem at all like a casual coincidence. During the night I witnessed a tragic death I can do nothing about, but I still feel guilty when the headless monk points at me. I wasn't at all involved in my brother's death, but I've always unconsciously felt that I'm responsible. When it comes right down to it, I guess it's hard for me to accept being alive when he's gone. That's why I don't want to be a mother, to give life. Okay, I know all that, I got all that out during analysis, you're right. But that's not the important thing."

Isabelle made the decision not to speak, to let the wind blow over her friend's anguished words. Johanna's blue eyes stared painfully into Isabelle's dark ones. Her hands were twisting up her napkin as if she was trying to tie her fingers together. Her lips were tight and razor-thin. Isabelle knew that her friend was at the edge of a personal abyss. She needed to use all her skill and prudence.

"I'm not sure you can say I'm right," Isabelle finally said firmly. "Because I'm not an interpreter, I didn't say anything or even think anything except that 'psycho-thing.'"

Johanna's eyes grew wide. Her fingers froze on the white cloth.

"So? What is so important?"

Johanna leaned her face closer and took Isabelle's hands.

"But . . . heaven is important! I've been focusing on the earth and I've forgotten heaven, and that's where the answer is! Heaven! That's why he came back again last night. I didn't understand why, but suddenly, this morning, it came to me there on the terrace when the sun came up."

"Jo, I don't follow, I—"

"I'm not crazy, Isa, relax. On the contrary, for the first time I can see clearly. This dream is a parable for my neurosis. It's true, the shrink helped me figure things out, and I needed to know so that I wouldn't confuse everything and so I could finally understand that I'm not the cause of everything that's happened. Do you understand? There's something else I vaguely sensed, but I couldn't identify it until this morning. Now I know there's a story that's not my own. It echoes within me because I've lost my brother, but it's not my story. The source for all this is a real story from the past that has nothing to do with me. Someone has surely been committing murders, but it's not me. The headless monk isn't judging me, contrary to what I thought, but he's inviting me to see clearly and start digging somewhere else rather than simply within myself. In some terra incognita that's hiding the key to my dreams, an enigma from the past. In short, Isa, I was mistaken. He's given me the order to search elsewhere, and it's not a condemnation of my own personal ground."

Isabelle wasn't able to follow Johanna's explanations. They seemed sibylline and irrational to her. She hoped that it was just a passing eccentricity and that her friend's mental health wasn't at stake. For the moment she decided to humor her.

"Maybe so," she said with skepticism, pulling her hands away. "If that's how you see it. What do you plan to do? Take off for Patagonia with a pickax?"

"Perhaps," Johanna answered with a smile. "The headless monk keeps reappearing because he knows that I'll keep at it and that sooner or later I'll figure things out. I've got the necessary background, and the right soul, too, if I let it guide me. Anyhow, I'm done digging around in my own navel; I'm finished with all those sleeping pills and I'm going to find the key to all my dreams right where it is, in history's fertile soil, in the past and in the legends about Mont-Saint-Michel. I'm no longer afraid in the least, because I know the monk's not trying to harm me and that he'll help me in my dreams. As soon as I have a little free time, I'm going to dig through libraries, find the real source of the myth, leaf through old books, and plow through that crazy mountain's archives."

ON THE FIRST of November it was raining in Paris as it often does, and as it almost always does on All Saints' Day. She had come back the day before but hadn't seen François, because he had gone along to Cabourg with Marianne to place chrysanthemums on the family graves as is the custom. He had pretended he had a meeting at the ministry the next morning, November 2, Day of the Dead, and intended to rush over to her apartment, but Johanna wouldn't let him. She preferred instead to meet him for dinner in a restaurant of his choosing. He had rightly thought that she would be tired of squid and white wine, so he had invited her to a chic beef restaurant in Saint-Germain-des-Prés known for serving meat from beer-fed animals that were said to be given daily massages by geishas. He took pleasure in admiring her body—poured into a velvet dress the color of blood—as she devoured an enormous steak with pepper sauce and lifted to her red lips a glass of Pomerol.

"The vacation was really good for you. You look fantastic!" he said.

"That's true," she admitted. "It'd be hard for me to say the same thing about you. You look worried."

"Do you think I've gained weight?"

"Not really, no," she answered. "But I don't have a set of scales in my eyes. I'm not kilostasis!"

"The last few days have been stressful," he continued, pretending not to notice her sarcasm. "I've got a problem at the office, and—"

"Oh?" she interrupted. "Tell me."

François was a little embarrassed, but his face stayed pale. He took a sip of Bordeaux.

"Don't be angry, but I prefer not talking about it."

Her eyes, darkened with eye-shadow that accentuated their brightness, were piercing.

"It's not what you think!" he said defensively. "I'm not playing games, and it's not really a secret. But it's something I've been trying to avoid talking about with you since our surprising little weekend back in September," he added, holding her gaze, sure that his words would discourage her from asking anything more.

She calmly laid down her silverware, wiped the corners of her mouth, and began to caress his hand and its gleaming wedding band.

"You misunderstand me, my dear. You're forgetting that I'm seeing a psychiatrist," she lied. "I've changed. I don't understand it all, but at least I can talk about it. It's not a taboo subject any more. On the contrary. Tell me what's worrying you. I promise there won't be any tears, any insults in Latin, any murders," she finished with a wink.

He hesitated. He could still picture himself that Saturday afternoon in September, driving alone through the Paris streets, not daring to go home, both furious at Johanna and worried for her. He could still remember their meaningless conversations, his feelings of guilt, Johanna pulling back, how hard it was to talk and again get close to her. He had thought she would leave him, but no. It was worse, she just hid from him. Since then it was as if he was floundering in dangerous waters, not knowing if it was better to leave the pool or learn a new stroke. But this evening he was pleased to be with the woman who had first attracted him, a woman full of life and good humor. And there was something new, something irresistible: a seductive manner that affected him deeply. He couldn't take his eyes off the black curls escaping from her chignon, the bare neck he would have loved to devour instead of his beef, her breasts rising firmly under the red velvet, not to mention her satiny, tanned legs, which he could touch under the table; he hoped she was wearing stockings and not pantyhose. He could smell her Guerlain perfume, Shalimar, and it, too, was new. Growing heady from the perfume's oriental fragrance, he began:

"In two weeks an important project was supposed to get under way on Mont-Saint-Michel near the treadmill. That's where the abbey's old Romanesque cemetery and ossuary were located, later destroyed during the Revolution. This is only a hypothesis, but we think that before the abbey church was built and the cemetery laid out, there was an older building, Saint Martin's Chapel, Carolingian, built to house tombs. We had come across pre-Romanesque bones during other excavations. So we decided to open a dig and work for one year in the hopes of finding either the chapel's foundations or some tombs. I've been working on the dossier for months, negotiating with the administrator of the Mount, a fellow who isn't easy to work with, the Fund for Historical Monuments, and the minister's cabinet. The National Association for Archeological Digs has promised a budget, the National Archeological Research Council has accepted the project, I've gathered together the best possible team, and we have the official authorization to proceed. I signed off on everything. In short, we were ready to start on November 15, the time of year when we have the fewest tourists.

"And then, last week, Roger Calfon, our project director, announced to me that his wife had been diagnosed with cancer and asked for a six-month leave of absence to take care of her. As you know, in such cases a leave of absence is automatic, but here I am without a good archeologist to direct the project. Catastrophic! Given his reputation and experience, Roger is really irreplaceable. He's the eminent specialist in medieval archeology. Thirty years of experience, including twenty at our Saint-Denis site, are not to be sneezed at. I can't send someone without experience to Mont-Saint-Michel! Roger's assistant is not in the ministry's good graces because of an article he's just written about the Office of Architecture and Patrimony, so I can't simply promote him. For the last week I've been trying to find an assistant from some other site, someone I can name the temporary director while we wait for Roger to come back. But specialists in these kinds of tombs aren't a dime a dozen!"

That evening, Johanna blessed her fate: It wasn't by chance that Isabelle had encouraged her to buy that red dress in Bari, along with a pair of garters.

"François, the expert on hidden medieval carcasses, current dig assistant, and easily available for a job at the Mount—that's me!" she exclaimed, making a mental rendezvous with the dead monk who occupied her heart and mind.

6

SAINT MARTIN'S CHAPEL IS DARK, AS DARK AS THE SUPERSTITION weighing heavily on Moira's soul, as dark as the Benedictine frock behind which Roman is hiding. Walled off behind the choir, the Celtic and Breton dead await the confrontation. Roman is the first to arrive, and he feels he's entering a cave. The cold humidity eats at his bones, and at the same time, his chest is overwhelmed with waves of heat.

He wipes drops of sweat from his forehead with his sleeve. Perhaps fever is stalking him again. He limps over to the altar, crosses himself, and lights three candles. Then slowly he lets his trembling body drop to a stone bench. He closes his eyes for a moment to calm his breathing. But he can hear his breathing get louder. When he opens his eyes, he senses other eyes burning into his back. They burn into his heart and it begins to beat faster. Suddenly, sweat pearls on his forehead, and the rough homespun robe sticks to his skin, scratches and burns like stinging nettles. It's as if bees are swarming in his head; his legs are like those of a dragonfly, weak and wobbly. His fingers throb like insect wings, in uncontrollable frenzy. Awkwardly he stands up, exhales, and lays his hands against his thighs. And then he realizes that he's forgotten the sentences he so carefully prepared in his solitude, and his throat feels pinched, as if by an invisible cord. Laboriously he tries to swallow and breathe deeply. He has to turn around. Instinctively, he holds his breath and whirls around; he feels his face grow red.

She has dared to remove her woolen wimple and veil before coming in. Her hair has been carefully combed, and her flowing braids are embroidered with wildflowers. She's wearing a long coat, which is held closed over her breasts by a piece of chiseled gold jewelry. She spent two nights embroidering the cloth gloves that adorn her hands. She bathed while singing songs known to her alone and then anointed her body with odiferous plants. She has reddened her lips and cheeks with petals, she's brushed her golden eyelashes.

The letter had been brief but clear: a secret meeting, at the same place they had first met, as night fell. She hadn't struggled with her decision; giving free rein to her happiness, understanding how strong their connection was even before it was completely woven, she'd enjoyed the sweetness of her preparation. He had been gone for two months, and she had waited every evening for a sign. Just before Christmas, the abbey's cellarer had brought her some vegetables from the abbey's lands, along with some eggs, some fish, and three amphorae of wine from the abbot to thank her for her hospitality. The monk had told her that Roman was improving, thanks to Hosmund's care, but that he was still bedridden and very weak. That was the only sign she had received from up there at the abbey. Up there! So near and yet so far! He lived in a temple in the sky, she in a hut on the earth, and a sea separated them.

Once, recently, she had tried to ask about him when she was called to the Mount by some villagers whose only child had fallen on the rocks. But when she got inside the house decorated with holly, the boy was already dying, his body mangled, enveloped in pain in spite of the unction the priest administered. She held him as he breathed his last, and didn't have the heart to ask his parents, whose hearts were dying, about Roman. She refused to interpret the child's death as a bad omen and went back to Beauvoir to wait. She wouldn't try to read the runes; she preferred instead to look into the water in her brother's eyes, a peaceful caressing lake that encouraged her to keep up hope. That morning, it was raining, and Brewen, too, had storms in his eyes. Dark black clouds veiled the lake's normal green color. For a long time she had caressed his lovely blond hair, her soul aquiver.

Just after morning mass, Hosmund had arrived on foot. When he saw him coming, Brewen left the house, bags for herbs tied to each side of his body and knives hanging from his belt. The lay brother was smiling through his brown beard dripping with rain. She showed him to a bench near the hearth and gave him a jug of monastery wine. He laughed. He said that Roman was still limping but that he was better. She found it hard to speak, so emotion-filled was she, but she answered that it was thanks to Hosmund who had taken such good care of him. And then he stood up and, as proud as the Archangel Gabriel, pulled a rolled parchment from a pocket in his scapular. Blushing, he announced that it was thanks to God and one of his faithful servants named Moira, whom Roman also wanted to thank with this paper. With his thick hands and dirty nails, he delicately placed the letter on the table, then said good-bye to the young woman and started back toward the abbey. She waited before picking it up. She was afraid. There he was finally, but it could be the end of her hope, a final adieu. Hosmund couldn't read; she could tell by his timid deference when holding the parchment. She took the letter and held it against her breast; shaken with sadness and abandonment, she was sure that she was going to lose Roman. Finally, resigned to the loss, she opened it.

For two days she adorned herself to forget the doubts she had had during all those nights without him.

Tonight she stands still, mute and motionless like the first time when he mistook her for a ghost. But no spirit could have a body like hers, or that look in her eyes, like gentle stars. Her veil glistens with the raindrops from which she protected her pale, freckled face.

He doesn't dare move, for fear of breaking the enchantment. There they stand, each gazing into the other's eyes, both listening to the silence play their love song.

"I . . . I'm so pleased to see you, Moira," he finally blurts out. "Since I came back, you've often been in my thoughts."

"You've never left mine," she admits with a sigh. "I'm happy you're better and that you've braved the Rule to come see me."

She lowers her eyes and looks at Roman's hands, his lovely hands. When will he open them?

"We must see each other," he says. "Often. And in secret. No one must find out."

Moira feels tears welling up, tears of joy. It's all she can do not to throw herself into his arms.

"No one will find out," she answers, controlling her voice and her desire. "Only Brewen. He's always known, but he'll not betray us."

He reaches out his hand. She exults. Feverishly, she gives him her own hand, feels his warmth through her glove. He leads her over to the stone bench. Their robes brush against each other. They sit down.

"I left so suddenly," he continues, keeping her hand in his. "You saved my life . . . but something feels unfinished. It came to me like a revelation. I had to see you . . . "

She stiffens with desire.

" . . . to teach you more about the Christian religion."

The young woman's heart stops. Is he joking? Is he just toying with her? Against the light of the flickering candles she has trouble seeing his face, but there's light enough to know that he wears no smile on his face. The ring of his tonsure looks like a dark wall, like ramparts, built up on his smooth skin. The fortress is in his head. Of course. What had she imagined? That a man cloistered in a strict monastery since adolescence would suddenly renounce his commitments because of a woman, a creature despised and feared by monks, even though she's the woman who has bound his wounds and opened her soul to him? She had been crazy and stupid. She clenches her lips so as not to burst into tears. Idiot! He doesn't even realize that she loves him! How can he not know? All her actions have proven it. Suddenly, she realizes that the only thing they have in common is that they were both born of a mother. Certainly his mother was the only woman the monk had ever been near. Brewen is a deaf-mute, but now Moira is the one who is deaf and dumb. Dizzied by her own flame, she hadn't once considered Roman, though he was always in her thoughts. He does love her, though. Of that she's sure. But he must be terrorized by a feeling he's never known before. She must be patient and tame him little by little, soothe his fear, save him from himself, guide him toward her.

"I'll listen to you joyously, Brother Roman," she answers after a short silence and superhuman effort.

Roman, too, is quiet a few moments, as still as a magician before a disappearing act.

Since returning to the Mount, at the beginning of Advent, Roman has often thought about the young woman. Sometimes, dressed in her sylvan robe, she has even appeared in his dreams and filled his nights with strange fire. He would wake up in the morning feeling shame and guilt, but he'd never told anyone about it. Then he decided that the dream visions weren't coming from some dark, hidden corners of his soul, but rather that they were inspired by God himself. Moira wasn't able to recognize God's light! Roman had sought refuge among his brothers' pure hearts, but still he decided to bring the young Celt to the Lord's divine light. Hiding the real source of his strategy from his own conscience, he decided to meet Moira again somewhere out of his brothers' sight, convert her in secret, and then tell the father abbot, and him only. He was still too weak to get on a horse and ride unseen to the hut in Beauvoir. So Moira needed to come to the Mount. The place for their secret meetings was obvious—Saint Martin's Chapel. And it was also clear when they should meet—in the evening, after Compline. All that was left to do was to summon the young woman, send her a letter by messenger, an involuntary accomplice who couldn't read, someone unbound by the monastery's normal constraints: Brother Hosmund the infirmarer.

The only experience Roman had had with women was with his mother's cold eyes, the interchangeable arms of his nannies, and then his holy love for the Virgin, and so he doesn't understand the origin of the joy that takes possession of his body and mind when he sees Moira again this evening. A diffuse warmth in his abdomen, a tingling on his skin, rapid breathing, a bird singing in his head. . . .

"Moira," he asks, "do you know the story of Adam and Eve, our ancestors?"

Moira doesn't know much about them at all, except that they were a man and a woman, and especially that they were lovers. She thinks that Roman has chosen a most appropriate religious story.

"I've heard about them at mass," she answers.

"The Bible tells us that God created the earth, the sea, the sky, the firmament and the luminaries—the sun and the moon—then plants, sea animals, animals that live on land, and finally the first human couple. Contrary to the plants and animals, he created man and woman in his own image and likeness."

"What image," the young woman interjects, "since God has no face?"

"The internal image, the soul! That's why only Man has a spiritual soul, and not plants and animals," he says with a smile. "The soul has three qualities: intelligence, love, and domination. Intelligence allows Man to read the world around him and, by knowing all creatures, to understand that God created them. The second quality, love, is the will reaching out both toward human goodness and toward supreme goodness, which is God. As for domination, Man alone dominates creatures, and that's why God has enjoined Man to name the plants and animals. Master of the noun, Man is the master of all creation."

"And since Man thinks, loves, dominates, is that why he and not other beings is in the likeness of God?" asks Moira.

"It's because Man thinks, loves, and dominates nature that he is in the image of God. Likeness is something else. It's the hierarchy among those three qualities. In the beginning, domination serves intelligence, and intelligence serves the most important among them: love."

"I didn't know the Bible said so much about love!" she says, her eyes bright.

"The Genesis text says simply that God created Man in his image and in his likeness," he adds sagely. "Doctors of the Church, like Ambrose, Jerome, Gregory, and Augustine, inspired by God's spirit, have managed to understand the deep meaning of the Scriptures and extract their full savor. They are the ones who have taught us the deep meaning of the holy text, especially the three qualities God gave Man and the relationships among those qualities."

Moira's eyes stray over the ground, and she thinks about Conan, Geoffroy, Ethelred, all valiant princes, sanguinary heroes, resting there under the paving stones.

"Brother Roman," she says teasingly, "contrary to what God had planned, I think that the world of men is not governed by love, not even among Christians!"

"Moira, it's their own fault if men aren't governed by love. The first couple lived in an earthly paradise in harmony with the world. But one day Satan, in the form of a serpent, invited them to disobey the only order God had given them—not to eat any fruit from the Tree of the Knowledge of Good and Evil. Thinking that they would become gods, Eve and Adam ate the fruit and were banished from the Garden of Eden. Since the day of that original sin, Adam and Eve's descendants have inversed the hierarchy of the three qualities, putting love and intelligence in the service of domination. Man is motivated now by his desire for power, and no longer by love. Thus, Man remains in the image of God but has lost his likeness with the Creator—"

"Except for monks!" the young woman exclaims.

"No, not even monks." Roman answers, chuckling. "Because monks also descend from Adam and Eve. We, too, are poor sinners, and we don't resemble God. We serve him, and through prayer, in his love and the love of the angels, we intercede so that he might forgive men for being sinners. But even man's purest and most fervent faith will never expiate original sin. Only one man, also the son of God, born in his likeness, suffered and died to atone for our sins. But later I'll tell you about Christ."

"Yes, I'd rather you talk to me about men's sins. That's something I understand more easily, although sin doesn't even exist in my ancestors' religion."

Roman pays no attention to her teasing. He knew that his job wouldn't be easy, but patience and perseverance are among the virtues. He continues his story.

"You see," he says calmly, "every man feels nostalgia in his soul for the Garden of Eden, but that paradise is lost. Yahweh posted angels at the gates to keep people out. That means that every man who seeks happiness only in earthly things goes astray. Man is now in exile on the earth and must journey toward the true kingdom, which is in heaven. God alone can gratify our hearts' desires. That's why all human efforts to become like God through power are but pride and vanity. Only love can bring us close to him, and there's one being we are well acquainted with here, one who is like God—the Archangel Michael, for in Hebrew,

Michael means 'he who is like God.' Yes, Saint Michael is the perfect reflection of the divine image."

Roman pauses, gazing off into the distance. His mind fills with sketches, granite arcades and arches of a grand abbey, so far existing only on the parchments of his imagination.

"You're dreaming, Brother Roman," says Moira. "What are your heart's desires?"

Roman comes back to earth from his tunnel-vaulted clouds. Through the high windows he can hear rain falling in the darkness outside and turns toward Moira. She looks at him intently, with a touch of provocation. Her lovely green eyes glow like the apple of temptation. Roman is convinced that it's really the glimmer of ignorance and that he mustn't try to extinguish it with violence as his predecessors had. All trace of defiance has disappeared from her eyes, and she observes him with infinite tenderness. He dares to lose himself in her eyes, and in them embrace the depth of her intelligence, the clarity of her soul. From that moment, he's sure that although Moira's thoughts might be corrupted by her ungodly beliefs, her soul has remained pure.

Yes, he had always been sure of it, the woman's soul is beautiful, as beautiful as the face there near him—the bright eyes, the pale, smooth skin, a mouth the color of petals. Roman shivers. He represses a sudden desire to hold her in his arms, but his eyes are already embracing her. Moira drinks in his eyes and, gracefully, calmly, she extends a bare hand out to him. He hadn't seen her remove her glove. The hand comes closer, and she lays her pale fingers on Roman's. The contact with her skin hits him like a thunderbolt. Inside, it's as if lightning has taken control of his heart, has overwhelmed it and given it light. Joining their hands is like joining their souls. At that moment, he realizes that their two souls recognize each other like soul sisters, like twin souls. Roman blushes and pulls his hand away.

"To punish men for having so much evil in their hearts," he continues, his voice uncertain, "and sorry for having created them in the first place, Yahweh decided to wipe from the face of the earth all men and the animals that fed them. He sent the flood to destroy all perverted flesh. But one man, just and upright, found favor in his eyes: Noah, who was six hundred years old. Rather than destroying everything that lived under the heavens, God bade Noah to build an ark of rosewood coated with tar—three hundred cubits long, fifty cubits wide, and thirty cubits high—with compartments on three levels, so that Noah, his family, and a pair of every kind of animal could find refuge."

Moira notices that when he talks about the ark, it's as if his soul is speaking.

"When they all were in the ark," he goes on, "the animals below, food on the next floor, and people on the top level, Yahweh sent waters over the earth. Rain fell for forty days and forty nights, flooding everything and lifting the ark. The waters covered the mountains and all flesh perished. At the end of the forty days and nights, the sky's floodgates closed. The ark stopped on Mount Ararat. After the waters had subsided, the people in the ark came out to replenish the earth. Noah built an altar to Yahweh on Mount Ararat. And Yahweh promised never to curse or destroy the earth again. He established a covenant with Noah and his descendants so that as long as the earth should last, sowing and harvest, cold and heat, summer and winter, day and night, would never cease. That was the first covenant between God and men. As a visual reminder of God's promise, the central nave of the future church on our Mount will have the exact same proportions as Noah's ark."

Moira hangs on his words. She looks questioningly at the monk, and Roman can't help but feel a wave of delight to see how much his story piques her interest.

"And just as Noah's ark represented salvation for humankind," he continues, "our abbey will be a place where men can seek redemption."

His heart's desires are those of a builder. His deepest love is love for stones. When he talks about "his" abbey, his eyes, the color of the evening, are flooded with lunar dawn.

"The Bible says that, in spite of the flood and the ark," he adds, "man's desire for power and domination was not extinguished. Afterward, we even tried to build a tower that would reach the sky."

"Others would like to build a church that will reach the sky."

"Moira!" Roman exclaims. "We're building a basilica in praise of God. The Tower of Babel was built so that men might steal some of God's power."

Suddenly, echoing Roman's words, a bell's voice rings out in the distance. Panic seizes the monk.

"It's time for Matins!" he cries. "They're ringing Matins already! You must leave, we'll be caught, I've got to hurry to the church! Hurry, hide somewhere, and as soon as you hear us chanting, you'll be able to get out and leave this place."

"Don't fear, Brother Roman," she tries to reassure him, "no one will see me. Go on, don't worry about me. I've learned so much this evening, and I can't wait to listen to you again."

"Five nights from now, after Compline!" he says, turning around to leave.

She wants to shake his hand, but he slips away and limps pathetically toward the door. This time, he's the one fleeing Saint Martin's Chapel. Calmly, she hides behind a pillar and waits for the psalms that the wind, in spite of the rain, will carry from the Carolingian church that stands a short distance away.

"*Michael archangele . . . gloriam predicamus in terris . . .*"

"*. . . eius precibus adiuvemur in caelis . . .*"

On this night, Moira listens to the monks' prayers. On this night, Roman has trouble sleeping. He has pain in his leg and his abdomen. The beating is only a memory, but his flesh, throbbing regularly like a heart beating, remembers the suffering. Beneath the shadows, his flesh slowly begins to keep rhythm with his heart and its fervor spreads throughout his body.

"ON THIS ROCK I will build my church, its main axis running east and west, the transept running north and south, and on the very tip of the rock, where the two axes meet, the spire, like my prayer to heaven, will rise to dominate the monastery, the island, the sea. There will be many difficulties, but we have eternity before us, and by Montjoie Saint Michael, our reward will be to overcome them all," Hildebert, seated under the tapestry of the Archangel near the fire blazing in the fireplace, writes to Abbot Odilon in Cluny.

A few days before, so that the abbot would not be disturbed by the coming work, they had moved his hut to the north face of the mountain, the steep, dark face where black trees grow and the cold salt wind wears down one's blood and eats at the intestines. Down below gushes the only freshwater spring on the island, Saint-Aubert's spring, reputed to heal fevers. But the small stream of water the Archangel brought forth is insufficient for hydrating the lime needed for making mortar to fix the stones together. Nor can the sacred spring quench the thirst of the army of workers soon to be swarming over the mountain. So, on the walls, Roman had wooden cisterns built to collect rainwater in this country where there's plenty of rain. Indifferent to the blasts of briny wind, leaning on a cane that functions not only as a cane but also as a measuring stick and punishment for the lazy, he commands a detachment of peasants carrying the cisterns. Hildebert's hut is made of wood, fragile and precarious, vulnerable to fire and to invaders. Hildebert and Roman both dream of tearing it down and replacing it with large granite rooms in the abbey church. Only stone can defy human aggressors and that eternal assailant—time. Only stone can stand up to the centuries and maintain an image of eternity. From now on, everything must be built of stone—the convent buildings, the walls, the arches, the pillars, and especially the vaults in the church choir. They have to place tons of granite above their brothers' heads because the sky is immortal.

Of course, that kind of architecture requires rare technical skills, but Pierre de Nevers has thought of everything, even a system of arches and supporting crypts, so Roman will be able to direct the stone blocks' downward forces and their horizontal thrust. In a few weeks, in the middle of the Lenten season, Master Roger's barges will begin to ferry the stones to the island, and there Master Jehan and his stonecutters will shape them one by one into the form appropriate for their place in the edifice. They will inscribe their signature, the workman's mark, a sign of recognition among the different lodges, on the bill enabling them to receive payment from the master builder. After Palm Sunday, Roman will prepare a ground sketch of each part of the building. Using compass, square, measuring rod, and especially the rope with twelve knots, and with the Pythagorean theorem and the golden number in his head, he'll draw the outlines for the foundations directly on the ground, and later they'll be marked by stakes. During Holy Week, craftsmen will be arriving—mortar-mixers, roofers, ironsmiths, fresco-painters, glass-cutters, interpreters mastering the different dialects spoken on the site, and then the army of workers, hod-carriers, those who'll carry stones or water. Finally, at Easter, Hildebert will give the sign to begin. At Easter, after Lent and its accompaniments of deprivation, fasting, and painful purification, when everyone has received the joy of Christ risen from the dead, when spring has come, then the everlasting life of the Angel's palace will begin.

While they wait, the people prepare themselves for Lent's forty days and forty nights by singing, dancing, and gorging on meat. This period of feasting is not the best time for converting souls, and yet, this evening, Roman has a meeting with Moira. Since early this morning, he's been strangely excited by a kind of apprehension tinged with joy that he blames on the upcoming building project. Now he limps resolutely into Saint Martin's Chapel. Immediately, light from his lantern catches a shadow that turns red like the burning bush when it gets close—the thick, free-hanging hair, burning cheeks, the purple coat. Roman blushes red like her wide-brimmed hat. His heart seems about to explode in his chest. He tries not to show any emotion and smiles at her. In the torch's halo, Roman's face appears delicate, his thin face's sharp features are drowned in the warm glow, his eyes grow brighter.

"Good evening, Moira. Are you ready to continue our discussion?" he asks with no further introduction.

"Is the lesson continuing, my dear preacher?" she asks, already sitting down on their usual granite bench. "I prefer hearing you talk about covenants, about stones."

Before extinguishing the lantern and setting it down, he uses it to light a candle and then sits down beside her. For a moment, Roman listens to the silence in the chapel, bells pounding in his heart, and then he continues his tale.

"The first covenant was established with Noah, as you recall," he begins. "That covenant was a promise of peace between God and men. God will conclude the second covenant, the covenant of posterity, with one of Noah's descendants named Abraham. One day Yahweh appeared to Abraham and commanded him to leave his home country and go to a far-off land. The man obeyed, abandoned his idol worship, and left his homeland. His wife Sarah was already old, as he was, and already sterile. But the All-Powerful said to Abraham: 'Lift your eyes to the heavens and count the stars if you can,' and he made him a promise: 'Your children will be like that.' Sarah had a child, Jacob, and from Jacob, twelve sons were born, and they became the twelve tribes of Israel, a people allied with God. The sign of their covenant with God is the circumcision of all eight-day-old males, from generation to generation."

Immediately Roman is sorry to have mentioned circumcision, because he's afraid she might ask what it was. Of course, he could cite the Genesis text, which is very explicit on that point. He knows it by heart, as he does the entire Holy Book. But he would prefer not talking about circumcision with her. He continues on quickly:

"Several centuries later, the people of Israel had multiplied but were being held captive in Egypt. Sorely oppressed, they supplicated their God, the one true God, to deliver them from the yoke of the Egyptians. God heard his people's prayer and sent Moses to lead them out of Egypt. Pharaoh's army was swallowed up by the Red Sea, whereas the Israelites were able to cross on dry land, for Yahweh had parted the waters to make a path for them. . . . "

Moira rolls her big eyes. She seems fascinated by the history of the Hebrew people. She doesn't know much about it, like most lay people of the time, because the Bible is accessible only to clerics. Then Roman picks up his story again, more slowly, with the Exodus, and fortunately there are no references to foreskins.

The descriptions of the plagues brought down on Egypt bring cries of stupor, horror, and admiration from Moira. She can imagine the water in the Norman swamps changed into blood, her peasant neighbors covered with sores, devouring insects, hail, darkness covering the Cotentin, and she bows her head when he tells about all the first-born children dying. These people's history could be her own. She drinks in the words of this marvelous storyteller. For he exalts the primary qualities sought by the Celts—supernatural powers and the art of war. Caught up in the emotion of their escape from Egypt, she grabs Roman's arm. Her mouth drops open when he recites the victory song, the psalm of thanksgiving sung by Moses, his people, and Miriam, the prophetess who dances and plays the tambourine:

> *I sing for Yahweh, for he has shown his glory. He has tossed horse and rider into the sea.*
> *Yahweh is my strength and my song, to him I owe my salvation.*
> *He is my God. I praise him, the God of my father, and I extol him.*
> *Yahweh is my warrior, his name is Yahweh.*

"Yahweh is not the God of my fathers," she exclaims. "But Yahweh is a great magician and a fearsome warrior."

Stirred by the close physical contact with the young woman, Roman stands up. Candle wax drips on his robe.

"However," he goes on, rubbing the wax spot with the back of his sleeve, "as soon as they leave Egypt, the people of Israel begin to murmur against Yahweh and against Moses. They preferred their slavery, the oppression they knew, rather than their wandering through the wilderness toward an unknown land. So God established a third covenant, a covenant particularly for the Jewish people. Yahweh called Moses to Mount Sinai and told him: 'If you, the Israelites, hear my voice and keep my covenant, I will make you my own people among all the people, for the whole earth is mine. I will make you a kingdom of priests, a holy nation.' With this promise, God made the Jewish people his chosen people. But while Moses was on Mount Sinai receiving the Ten Commandments, written by God's own hand, the people were perverting themselves and making a golden calf, bowing down before it. In a rage, Moses broke the stone tablets. However, God did renew his covenant, writing the Law on other stone tablets. But he tested his people's hearts for forty years as they wandered through the wilderness. When Moses was finally leading them into the Promised Land flowing with milk and honey, he died, and God delivered the land to his successor, Joshua."

Roman paused.

"Moira, today I promise you the earth," he says, his tone more intimate. "This story is the history of the Jewish people. It's also the story of all humanity. And the story of each person, your own personal story. Listen."

He sits back down, puts his hands on Moira's shoulders, and his face is close to hers.

"Like Abraham, you must leave your country," he whispers, "for your country is dead. Renounce the past. It's rotting within you like a corpse, infecting your living flesh. Give up your old beliefs that keep you in slavery, and stop feeling nostalgic for that slavery! God knows that old habits, even if they're bad, are more comfortable. But you must dare to accept the adventure of faith. You've got the strength and courage to do it! The Lord has sent you a guide to accompany you in the wilderness. Purify your heart. I'm here, walking with you, walking beside you, and I'll show you the path to his kingdom."

She watches his lips move like a bird. Some of the notes ring true. She is indeed a prisoner of bygone days. A guardian of death. But believing his song, singing it with him, would be renouncing her love for her people for a man who knows nothing of love except for God's and who loves only God. And yet he is clasping her shoulders and she can feel him trembling. He seems so near at this moment, so familiar! She looks into his gray, probing eyes, she gathers in the warmth of his hands on her body, warm waves that pass through her clothing and engulf her chest. Suddenly, she pulls him to her, holds him with all her might, and takes in the scent of his neck. It's like the smell of sea spray and wind. She holds a tempest in her arms.

On that night, when bells for Matins are rung, they separate without a word, as they had met. For a long time their bodies had remained welded together, Moira's head on Roman's shoulder. They breathed in each other's scent without moving, without communicating except through their unified breathing. When the bell begins to toll, she loosens her grip. He walks slowly away; she leans up against a pillar and the stone is cold.

Before joining the black army, the terrestrial angels who live with their eyes on the heavens, he turns back and sets another meeting, the night of the second Sunday of Lent.

Fasting is difficult for ordinary people. It begins on Ash Wednesday. In the church, the priest marks their foreheads with the dusty cross of their human condition. Reminded that they are doomed to die, they will live on herring, peas, dried whale meat, and prayer. As for the monks, penitence began back in mid-September. From then on, they have eaten only one meal a day, the *prandium*, or dinner, after Nones, for they give up supper until Lent. During Lent's forty days and forty nights, however, the only meal is supper, or the *cena*, after vespers. So the brothers fast from midnight, when they rise for Matins, until Vespers at the end of the day, and yet they go on about their daily work as well, do the required reading, and sometimes impose additional mortification upon themselves. The edifying ordeal is tiring, even for a monk. For a convalescent like Roman, who, in addition, has such major construction responsibilities, it's pure torture. Already exhausted after Matins, he drags his body around like a dead weight while fighting to keep the morbid inertia from contaminating his spirit. But not because he's fasting. Moral remorse and carnal desire have taken possession of him and, jousting one against the other, are overwhelming him. His conscience feels guilty for embracing Moira, but his body is tempted, filled with an unfamiliar appetite that leaves him no peace. Why hadn't he pushed her away? He had breathed her soul, like a flower's soul, fragile and fragrant. Her soul? Nonsense! He let himself be touched by her skin, her breath, her inviting flesh! The woman isn't evil, but has just lost her way, and he is her shepherd. He, a shepherd? More like a pig-keeper, wallowing in the pigpen's stinking mud! The woman's breath is like filth. She's an ungodly woman trying to lead him astray! Her arms were so soft, so different from his nannies' arms, and the very thought makes him shiver. Debauched, corrupt, betraying God! Roman gathers all his strength against this new emotion, almost a sickness, that must not infect his reason. He must combat it constantly to rip it out of his vile body, which seems to feed on it at all hours of the day and especially at night. His head has called the diabolical passion lust; and to protect himself from it, he calls on the purifying power of the passion of Christ.

The Lenten season of the year 1023 is marked by this singular combat. For the first time, Roman observes Lent as true contrition and a means

THE ANGEL'S PROMISE | 119

of personal redemption. His abject flesh must be chastised; and often, in spite of Hosmund's gentle disapproval, he refuses the one daily meal so as not to interrupt his prayers.

On this second Sunday of Lent, Roman's cheeks are hollow and his thin body, floating in his frock, needs a cane's constant support. His face is yellowed and lined, dry like Brother Almodius's face. But Roman wears these physical stigmata like the banner of his spiritual victory over impurity. His gray eyes shine like a sword, and his mouth seems to be frozen in a warrior's snarl. He can't wait to confront Moira this evening, for he's sure that this time he can persuade her to accept conversion. But, after Compline, Hildebert summons him to his hut to ask him to renegotiate labor costs. Bored with the recurring problem he thought he'd taken care of, and annoyed because he'd be late to Saint Martin's Chapel, Roman listens to Hildebert and imagines the father abbot in the place of Saint Michael, the weigher of souls, in the tapestry, with his gold pieces in one tray of the scales and workmen on the other. In spite of their size and their muscles, the workers are surprisingly light compared to the heavy coins belonging to an abbot and a Duke of Normandy. Suddenly, Moira, hidden behind Hildebert/Saint Michael, kicks over the contents of the scales in fury, and he catches a glimpse of her naked thigh as her skirt flies up to her waist. She disdains the coins and, her eyes as blue as the sky, runs off laughing, holding by the hand one of the stone carriers.

"Brother Roman?" asks the abbot curtly.

"Excuse me, Father," Roman answers, looking back at the abbot, " I . . . I was distracted. Fatigue, no doubt. But I do understand your concerns and tomorrow I'll talk to—"

"I should have exempted you from Lent this year, my son," the abbot interrupts him with a frown. "Your body is still frail; this construction project is sapping what little strength you have left. These deprivations are damaging to you."

"Not at all, Father," exclaims Roman, his eyes wide.

"In his great wisdom, Saint Benedict saw that sometimes voluntary martyrs were not so very different from proud fanatics, more filled with sin than the most sinful pagan. From now on, I dispense you from Lent. You'll will break your fast both morning and evening; that seems most prudent," he adds in his fatherly voice. "I need a clear-thinking, healthy master builder," he says firmly, "not an old man who looks like a ghost! Now go sleep."

"I . . . I'll do as you bid, Father," Roman answers, bowing his head.

He leaves the abbot's cell and hugs the walls all the way to Saint Martin's Chapel. This evening, the tide is especially high and the wind is gusting more strongly than usual. And what's more, it's cold. Bent slightly over his stick, he stops for a moment. Leaning back against the chapel door, he listens to the dark sea trying demonically to couple with the august mountain. Anger rises along with the waves. He had sinned by touching the woman's body, but why was the abbot depriving him of expiation? He had sinned by not confiding in his brothers during the chapter meeting for repentance, by protecting the creature he's continued to dream about, although he constantly hands his sins over to the Lord. Why does Hildebert prevent him from following the path of redemption? Why give nourishment to this guilty flesh and set him apart from his monastery brothers who must fast? To his feverish mind, treating him this way is like pointing a finger at him without letting him redeem himself. The gusts of wind, like acid, irritate his eyes, as they assail him in their fury. He must convert the young Celtic woman. Now his own salvation depends on it. Forcefully, he pushes open the door with his cane. Apparently nobody there, except the shadows. A fresh fragrance washes over the old incense of the stones in the choir. Roman lights some candles and notices, on the altar, a bouquet of large flowers. He takes the flowers and scatters them over the Breton tombs.

"You seem upset," she says from behind him.

He turns around, eyes and mouth stern and aggressive. She utters a little cry when she sees him.

"Roman," she says. "You're in pain! You're nothing but skin and bones!"

"I'm doing fine," he answers. "And if my impure flesh should disappear, it's only justice."

"I don't understand. Why mistreat your body? What has it done to merit such punishment?"

"You should know, since you're the cause," Roman blurts out with a dark look. "The contact of our flesh. . . . "

She in turn is caught up in anger. Hearing him revert to distant politeness revolts her as much as listening to his fanatical words and seeing his crazed look. She feels like fleeing from his clumsy attack, but the sight of his skinny body and the moribund face is distressing. He's still struggling with the truth of their love, and flagellating himself relentlessly! Her violence turns to sadness. No, she can't abandon him to his error, even if she has to pay with the tribute from her own inner conflict. First of all, she needs to calm his fury. Slowly she looks up at him.

"Brother Roman," she murmurs reassuringly, as she takes in his disarray and sits down on the stone bench where he has already collapsed. "Forgive my audacity the other evening. In spite of all your efforts, you see, I'm still a weak Christian. But I think I can understand what's tormenting you."

Roman sighs, too spent to react.

"In the beginning," he says, forming his words with difficulty, "Christians couldn't avoid being martyrs as they were hunted down by the Romans. Martyrs bearing witness that God was greater than the Roman emperors. But when Constantine converted, Christianity was no longer outlawed, and it became the dominant religion. From then on, martyrs were voluntary. In Egypt, they went off into the desert to bear witness that God was greater than anything else. Those anchorites, totally dedicated to God, vowed poverty and chastity to prove to the world that life depended on God alone. When the hermits began to form communities, monasticism was born. Saint Benedict, organizing our lives through his Rule, tempered the mortifications that the Desert Fathers imposed upon themselves. But contrary to ordinary lay priests, a Benedictine cannot marry, because he has taken the vow of chastity. You see," he says, turning toward Moira, "a monk lives away from the world of men, orienting all his desires and energy toward God. Today we bear witness before men that God is all-important."

Roman is silent for a moment.

"If I allow you to dominate me," he continues, looking directly at her, "if my heart, my body, and my spirit reach out to you, even for just an instant, then I'm no longer worthy of being a monk, for I wouldn't be totally devoted to God."

"But . . . you are really a builder!" she objects. "You're already obsessed by stones!"

"The stones are for a church, Moira. The task is dedicated to God. It's my duty as a monk."

Both bitter and full of pity, she remains quiet. Once again, she is tempted to give up and run away. She can't win against a rival like God! Why has she given her heart to a monk who's like the cold, dry stones of a church? But regrets are powerless to break the unusual link that grows stronger even when they are apart. Her eyes scan the dark, rough frock hanging heavy on his body like a lead shroud. That's her enemy. As he said, lay priests can get married. So how can she get him to trade his frock for a priest's cassock? She turns her head toward the granite vaults. Vain hope. A parish priest doesn't build his own cathedral! She has known for a long time that, for Roman, sacred architecture is not just a monk's duty but a man's vocation, a vital passion that does indeed unite him with God, and more importantly, with himself. And his passion is the absolute sun that now irradiates Moira and shapes her love for him. No, she doesn't want to destroy that angelic light and end up with just a hollow human being, a shadow without mystery. If she leaves now, if she removes herself from reality, she will regret the physical separation but not the remorse of breaking a magical enchantment. It will continue to live within her like eternal grace. She looks again at him, to engrave in her memory the dusky eyes. Then she stands up.

He realizes immediately that she is giving up. He knows that it's not because she respects his monastic state or because she fears struggling with God, but rather because of her love for him. Wordlessly, she leaves him sitting on the bench and turns away. No, she's not the creature he had imagined. He had realized that from the very beginning, right here in the chapel, and he's done everything he could to forget her. Slowly she walks away. What has he done? He looks at his hands, trembling with weakness and emotion, and then at the measuring rod he's using as a cane to prop up his ravaged body. He's only thirty years old, an age when many men of the time die, and he's letting himself waste away. After being spared, he is now braving God's will and allowing himself to be invaded by despair, by scorned fury: Hildebert was right. She's already walking through the nave. The chapel door is only a few feet away. Bewitched by the hidden demons he thought he had vanquished, he has gone back on his engagements. He's even neglected his work on the construction site.

She's leaving, she who gave him new life; she's abandoning him so that he may live in peace with himself, so that he may devote himself totally to the task he was born for, and so that everything may be accomplished according to destiny. She is slipping away, about to open the door onto the darkness and to return to her night.

"Moira!" he calls out. "Wait!"

She turns around. He's standing there in the choir without his cane.

"You know," he says quietly, "when I speak to you about faith and about the Book, I am also being faithful to my duty as a monk. We haven't finished. There's still the end, Solomon's temple, the coming of the Savior who redeems all sins, the final promise and the end, yes, the end of the earthly realm."

Suddenly he totters, grabbing the bench for support. She hurries back and helps him sit down.

"I'll listen to the end of your story on one condition, Brother Roman," she whispers, just inches from his face, her voice trembling like the monk's body. "This is the last time we'll see each other," she avers, her throat tight, "we both know it. And I want you to swear that you'll never give in to despair's selfish mortification and that you'll keep fighting for what makes you live, for those sacred stones. And that you'll never feel contempt for the love living people feel," she says with a sob, "simply because they aren't God or God's granite stones! They know that," she adds with a forced smile, "but they don't deserve contempt. Don't love them if you are unable to, but ask for their help when you need it. They are there for you, in secret, and they want the best for you."

He's also struggling against his tears. Eyes fixed on the candles burning on the altar, he takes her hand.

"I promise, Moira."

"Good. Then I agree to listen to you," she concludes, sitting back down and squeezing his hand. "Speak to me. Tell me about the final covenant between God and men; tell me about the end of the world, since it must be told."

"The end is on earth, but eternal life is in heaven."

"And where is hope?"

"Between the two, Moira. Hope lies between earth and heaven, in the human heart, embodied in the magnificent stone palace that soon will take shape, a castle of perfect love, a bridge between men, a passage between the living and the dead."

She turns and looks him in the eyes.

"Take me to your palace, and tell me about perfect love."

Roman clears his throat to get control of his emotions, and he begins to speak:

"This palace will be called the New Jerusalem, Jerusalem, the 'mountain of God.'

"There are two Jerusalems in history. First, there was the earthly Jerusalem, the city of David, the temple built by his son King Solomon, the house of Yahweh built in the land of Israel and destroyed by Nebuchadnezzar, king of Babylon. At the end of time, when all those now living are dead, the dead will live on in the heavenly Jerusalem. The abbey church we are building will be set between the two. It will be like the earthly Jerusalem and the heavenly Jerusalem, like a symbol linking them in the natural order of the world. It will be a reminder of the beginning and will also announce the end. It will stand between the earth and the heavens. It will stand for hope, for it will embody the promise of eternal life."

"I know that you and your brothers love God above all, and that you want to build in his honor a most beautiful dwelling," she says. "But why dedicate it to an angel, who is like God but is not God?"

"Because Saint Michael is the path between men and God! This basilica will be the new city of the Most High. He will descend among men, but men must also be able to ascend toward him. You know, men love God, but God loves men even more. He loves them above all, Moira. Their relationship with God is like the union between husband and wife, in perfect love. When Yahweh created man, he announced to the angels around him, the first of which was Lucifer, 'the light bearer,' that mankind, though imperfect, was God's favorite creation. Filled with jealousy and pride, Lucifer rebelled. He turned away from God, taking with him the other fallen angels. Ever since that day, he has kept trying to prove that God made a mistake when he created mankind. He penetrates the dark side of God's imperfect creatures, trying to push them to self-destruction," Roman says, thinking of himself. "The greatest victory for Satan will be to prove to God that mankind is so perverse that he exterminates himself. So, to protect mankind, God did two things: first, he gave each human being a guardian angel to fight the devil inside," he continues, thinking of Moira.

"Then he called upon Saint Michael, who had become the first among angels in place of Lucifer. He gave him the mission of defending mankind against the angel of darkness whenever mankind was besieged by the master of the fallen angels or his army of demons. And that's how the Archangel faced the dragon, one of Lucifer's many incarnations. He brought him down but didn't kill him, because Lucifer is immortal and because the goal of a Christian's life, and Saint Michael's as well, is to combat without ceasing. The indestructible head of the heavenly host, Saint Michael helps men against the forces of evil throughout their lives, and even after death, by leading them to Paradise and working to keep their purified souls from being stolen on the way by demons."

"Yes," Moira states coldly. "His constant efforts ever since the dawn of time are worth a church."

"His devotion and his noble love for sinners," Roman corrects her, "must be answered by the love of men, who can pray to him, thank him, and ask for his intercession with the Omnipotent in a palace worthy of him. You must understand that, as for a man and a woman who are in love," he says, hesitating, "love between the divine and the human is not unilateral but reciprocal."

"However, with a couple, we are never sure that the other one loves us," Moira objects gravely.

"Perhaps because the signs of love he gives are not the ones we expect," Roman answers after a moment's silence. "God gave men irrefutable proof of his love, the best possible proof. He freely gave his own son. Jesus, which means 'the savior,' came to tell men that God loved them deeply. Jesus' first apostolic act, when he was thirty years old, was to go to a wedding feast. It happened that there wasn't enough wine. Jesus took water, changed it into wine, and gave it to the wedding guests. With that act, the first of his miracles, he shows that God, through his love, wants to give joy to the heart of men. As wine warms the body, so does a husband his wife."

"And Jesus dies for mankind."

"'There is no greater love than to lay down one's life for a friend,' he said himself. He dies, but his love saves the world. Like a new Moses, he has delivered his people, all of humanity. As God promised to Noah, Jesus, son of God, has sealed the final covenant. He is the new Adam, the perfect man who brings together in one body both divinity and humanity, who atones for Adam and Eve's original sin and reconciles God and men forever. He'll come back at the end of time to judge the living and the dead."

"The end of time," she repeats with a somber tone. "I don't know if we should hope for the end of the world, even to find Love."

"You mustn't be afraid, Moira," he says with a smile, "for it'll be joyous, a deliverance, and all suffering will end. It won't be an end but a beginning. Listen to Saint John's Revelation: 'And then I saw a new heaven and a new earth, for the first heaven and the first earth disappeared, and the sea was no more. And I saw the Holy City, the New Jerusalem descending from heaven, from God's dwelling place. It had adorned itself like a young bride decorated for her bridegroom. And then I heard a voice shout from the throne: "Here is the dwelling of God with men. He'll take his dwelling with them; they will be his people, and he, God with them shall be their God. He will wipe the tears from their eyes. There will be no more death; there will be no more tears, lamentations, or suffering, for the old world has disappeared."'"

"That's beautiful, Roman . . . your Jerusalem will be lovely—the city of God and the city of men. Your life on earth to construct heaven, what a beautiful life!"

Roman is deeply touched. His eyes burn with sacred fire.

"I . . . I'll show you," he murmurs, pulling a parchment from his cowl and unfolding it in the young woman's lap. "You must see this! Look at God's mountain! This is our Jerusalem!"

The dark lines sketched by Pierre de Nevers are spread out there on Moira's thighs. She contemplates Roman's mystery as if she were surveying a fabulous, inaccessible sun, a luminary made of juxtaposed squares and triangles.

"Roman, I can't read this," she stammers. "There aren't any words. . . . "

Roman stands up, and the air, set in motion by his newly alive body, blows the sketches to the chapel floor.

"I'll explain it to you, yes, that's better. Listen, Moira! Come here!"

He picks up the parchment, grabs his cane, walks to the choir, and spreads the drawings on the altar, there where the bouquet of flowers lies.

"Look here," he says, pointing to a mark with his stick, "here is the rock. That was the major problem, given that its peak is not flat, and also the primary goal, given that the peak is high and that the Archangel's dwelling needs to be as near to the heavens as possible. My master and Abbot Hildebert had the great idea to place the church's center of equilibrium on the tip of the rock and to surround it with crypts. These crypts built up around it can support the choir and the transept arms. The ensemble will form a colossal extension toward the heavens, a series of ascending spaces, including the monastery buildings built on different levels. Seen as a unit, it will look like a pyramid, a gigantic triangle, for the number three is sacred. Three is the number of the Holy Trinity, the three theological virtues, the divine spirit. But now let's look at the abbey church. There, you see the entrance, preceded by the narthex in front of the terrace. A first staircase leads to the nave, composed of seven elevated bays—seven, four plus three, being the cipher of the body augmented by the soul, as well as the seven musical tones, the seven planets in the heavens, the seven days of creation. And then there's the central space, constructed with vaults on both sides, and the transept, also elevated, and finally the choir, and its apse is surrounded by a raised ambulatory. An ascent for pilgrims up toward the Most High, toward Christ's light, from the west to the east."

Standing on Roman's left, Moira is stupefied. A question seems to be burning her lips.

"Roman," she finally says. "Tell me. These crypts, are they beneath the ground?"

"Of course," Roman answers. "There will be four of them, like the four elements, the four rivers of Paradise, the four seasons, the four cardinal virtues, and the four Evangelists. They will support the church and will themselves be small churches. There will be one under the nave, one under each transept arm, and one under the choir, the most beautiful of all—right there." He points with his stick. "That's where the work will begin, in fact, right there in the choir crypt, so that we can put Aubert's relics there. It will house our founder's sacred remains and hold up the choir, the holy of holies with its altar of Saint Michael. There will be three bays ending with an apse with five walls, for the pentagon is the symbol of creation augmented with divine unity. It's the cipher of man, his five senses, and of God become man—Christ's five wounds—"

"But the relics already lie in the current church!" she interrupts again, worry in her eyes.

"I know, Moira," he answers with a smile. "But you see, our church is going to be destroyed. It's tiny and ugly, a symbol of bygone times."

"Yes, of the days when the Breton canons were here!" she adds bitterly. "So it's true," she says, her face suddenly pale.

"Yes," he answers gently. "The symbol of sinners who ill served God and the first of the angels will be erased. But the place where we stand, also built by the canons, will be preserved and transformed into a crypt supporting the nave. Your people's tombs, cherished in your heart and memory, will be spared. Don't be sad."

But it isn't sadness—or relief—that Moira feels at what the master builder has said. She seems to be terror-stricken. In a voice as colorless as her face, she dares to raise an objection:

"But the canons' church was built over Aubert's grotto!"

"Aubert's grotto embodies the birth of the holy mountain, but also it was built on the model of the Italian grotto on Mount Gargano. And our city must be unique, created to impress upon men force and beauty never

seen before. When we finish the choir and the transept, the church holding the wall of the primitive sanctuary will be razed," Roman admits, "so
that we can build a brand-new structure and support the future nave by
setting pillars directly on the rock itself—"

"No!"

Moira's shout rings out as from the dawn of time. Roman is astounded
and looks at her livid features and her horror-filled eyes.

"What's the matter?" he asks worriedly. "It's as if you've seen Lucifer
himself," he tries to joke.

"You must never dig under the church," she screams. "You must not,
for any reason at all!"

"Moira, relax. They'll hear us. Why not dig under the church? What's
got into you? Tell me!"

She puts her hand to her mouth. Her eyes are like a crazy woman's.
Her brow is wrinkled in pain. Roman moves toward her and gently forces
her to sit down.

"It's the end of time! The end of time is already here," the woman says,
her voice flat.

"Please, Moira, please! I don't know what you mean. Speak to me!"

"I can't, I mustn't. If you love me, don't dig in the earth under the
church, don't dig! Promise!"

"Why? What does the church have to do with you?"

She looks at him and bursts into tears.

"The church isn't important. It's . . . it's . . . "

"What?" he asks, sitting down beside her.

"Roman," she answers, pulling herself together, "I'm going to tell you
a great secret; I have to reveal it to you. May you never betray it, never betray me!"

Roman sits mute with stupor. Moira's attitude is a dizzying enigma.
He looks into her eyes, where he hopes to find part of the answer but sees
only dark anguish. What can this secret be that makes her so different
from the woman he thinks he knows? He is troubled by her disarray. He
gazes into her eyes, which are staring back at him with intense despair.
Then, determined to accept the upsetting mystery because it comes from

her, he leans toward Moira like a confessor. His reassuring face promises that he'll never divulge what she reveals. Calmed by his silence, she regains confidence and begins to speak.

SHOCKED, WEIGHTED DOWN by what she has just told him, Roman sits in silence beside her. Then, pale, his eyes wild, he stands up with the help of his cane.

"Roman, don't tell anyone," Moira murmurs, touching his arm timidly. "I know that you'll not say anything, I know that what I'm asking is serious and that if you agree, you'll need to make big changes to the plans for your abbey. But I beg you to give serious thought to it. Think about the peace we enjoy today on the rock. And let me know your answer. I'll wait for you here, the night of—"

"No!" he interrupts vehemently. "No, Moira," he repeats more gently, a little surprised by his violence. "You mustn't come back to the Mount. I'll come see you when I've made my decision."

Fear. A new, brutal fear now. In light of what Moira has divulged to him, everything at this moment has taken on a new meaning.

"Fine," she says, trembling. "As you wish."

She stands up. He stares at the cross on the altar, and the smoke from the candles burns his eyes. He has trouble breathing; he begins to suffocate. She takes his arm, and he offers no objection. Supporting him like a second cane, she leads him to the exit. She looks unblinkingly at her fate, she peers into the future that her story, now entrusted to one other person, the man brushing against her side, will bring. Moira pulls open the chapel door. A gust of wind rushes through her hair. Everything is dark; all surrenders to the gusting wind and the waves pounding once again against the mountain in their war-like passion. Above her, she can sense the church's silhouette, and she feels the warmth of Roman's body. Desperately, she turns and holds him to her.

"Roman, Roman! Roman, I need to say . . . whatever you decide, my love for you will not grow weaker."

Roman squeezes her to him, first timidly, as if a little frightened, then with greater assurance. The cane falls to the ground when he puts both arms around her. He can feel his soul filling up with sweet warmth, with an unknown tenderness, that chases away his anxiety and the sense of oppression arising from his dilemma. If only this instant could last forever. A gust lifts strands of her red hair, and he plunges his face into the salty perfume of her thick mane. May this moment become eternity . . . let their words break like the waves against the mountain, let the battering wind camouflage their differences, let the wind drown memory and carry it away in a muddy torrent!

"Roman, our love makes us immortal," she says.

He pulls away and, intrigued by her remark, looks at her, but the darkness prevents him from seeing the expression on her face. She turns away, and, without saying good-bye, she flees. He remains alone with the wind, with the furious elements' crushing noise. And then he limps toward the dormitory.

As ROMAN IS limping through the darkness, a tall figure moves away from an angle in the chapel's outside walls.

Lantern in hand, it moves along the sanctuary toward the scriptorium. The big lock is easy to see in the bluish moonlight. With difficulty, a key turns. The figure enters and double-locks the door behind it. Inside, it lights a candle. The flame reveals a man's downcast face, his skin pale like old parchment, his black eyes, from which tears roll down, making his emaciated face seem even more hollow. He crosses the big room with wide windows, and an immense fireplace, a room empty of human presence but filled by Greek and Latin thoughts in manuscripts lining the walls or standing proudly on the tables near pens and brightly colored inks. In the back of the room, the monk opens a door and enters a tiny office, where the copyists' latest work is waiting to be checked. He places the candle on the desk. Almodius falls to his knees and sobs silent tears. His monk's frock is shaken by spasms. His long, elegant hands spotted with ink clasp his head in tears. Finally, a sound escapes from his pitiful body, a sound like an animal whose throat is being slit. The monk collapses face-down to the office floor. Moaning, he pronounces unintelligible words. Then he rises to his knees, reaches out his hand into a hidden cavity, and pulls out a whip made of leather straps with bits of lead embedded in them. He pulls his robe down to his waist. His skinny, white back stands out like a starving light.

"Almighty Lord, please help me!" he begs, his voice breaking.

Keeping his eyes closed, Almodius begins to brandish the whip. Smiting his back, he murmurs a prayer. The metal balls tear into the naked skin and make little red furrows where tiny streaks of blood appear from his waist to his shoulders. He pauses regularly to breathe, then flagellates himself once more. Shivers of pain rise through his shoulder blades, his lips are clenched, red droplets form on the folds of his frock. Soon his back is nothing but a raw wound, a lovely carmine red. Bent over, he moans to repress his suffering. Then one word manages to escape from his mouth in whispered rage. As his blood oozes when the metal strikes, the whisper becomes a cry:

"Moira . . . Moira . . . Moira, Moiraaaaaaaa!"

7

"HERE, JO. SAUSAGE, BUTTER, AND PICKLES!" SOMEONE WAS HAND-
ing a sandwich down to her.

"It's really chilly today," Paul added, kneeling at the edge of the deep
trench. "You're going to catch your death of cold."

Johanna smiled at her boss, the director of the archeological dig. Her
down jacket was covered with mud, as was her long hair. Using a soft
brush, she was cleaning off a stone in the square of earth, clearly marked
by strings and numbered stakes, that she had been assigned to explore on
the trench's uneven floor.

Paul smiled back. An eminent professor at the University of Lyon, he
was quite attached to his assistant, the only woman on the dig for the past
two years, even if sometimes he found her behavior hard to understand.
He didn't approve of her relationship with François, who, for him, was just
a self-satisfied, high-level technocrat. Everybody was talking about their
liaison, even though they tried to be discreet. In her presence, Paul and
the others pretended not to know anything about it, since she never
talked with them about her private life.

Often, Johanna would dream that she was not working with a group,
but by herself, when and where she felt like it. She preferred communicating in total intimacy with stones instead of with so many people.
However, she respected Paul a great deal. Cluny was his life, and he had
been a member of the jury for her doctoral thesis: *1928–1950: Excavations Led
by the American Architect Kenneth John Conant on the Site of Cluny III: Architectural
Breakthrough and Archeological Outline,* eight hundred pages in which she had

demonstrated that, in spite of his inestimable contributions to knowledge about Cluny, the largest medieval abbey, now destroyed, the famous
scholar had neglected certain archeological leads that still needed to be
explored. Three years later, when Paul was named to lead a large dig at
several places on the Cluny site, he was delighted to be able to hire the
study's author as his assistant, and she was beginning to get restless in her
CNRS laboratory. At the time, the forty-year-old Paul was in the throes
of divorce proceedings, and he would have liked to see Johanna's professional gratitude turn into more personal feelings. But the attractive
young woman seemed to be interested only in her work, and Paul was too
timid to let her know how he felt. Together they had surveyed hundreds
of stones, one by one, as they checked out the eighteenth-century cloister where the medieval cloister and the remains of Cluny II had stood.
Cluny II was how they referred to the second abbey church, Saint-
Pierre-le-Vieil, three times larger than the first. The first had been built
in the eleventh century and razed in the twelfth, so that Abbot Hugh de
Semur could undertake building the third abbey, Cluny III, the *maior ecclesia,* the largest church of medieval Christendom, a church that it took
twenty-five years to dismantle after the Revolution.

For the last six months, instead of forming a reciprocal personal relationship, Paul and Johanna had directed their love toward the same goal:
finding the mythical tomb of Hugh de Semur, sixth Abbot of Cluny, master builder of the great Cluny III church. He had led the abbey for sixty
years, from 1049 to 1109, and had died at the ripe old age of ninety-five.
In her thesis, Johanna had pointed out that the Cluny monks had been
specialists in commemorating the dead during the Middle Ages. They
were the ones who had invented the Day of the Dead, November 2, and
they had created rich liturgies for the dead that brought material wealth
for them as well. There were many people, both lay and religious, a few
poor but many more wealthy people, who, for a nice donation to guarantee their salvation, were buried at Cluny. Now the abbey was gone, and
although some graves had been uncovered, the earth still protected most
of the tombs, including the abbot's. It had been placed in the choir of
Cluny III and was described by ancient texts as being the jewel of Clu-

niac funerary art. In 1928, the American Conant dug up some fragments but didn't pursue the excavation. And just a few years ago, Paul's predecessor had unearthed by chance a piece of frieze from the mausoleum's cornice in a wall dating from the nineteenth century and standing at some distance from where the church had been. Some experts had concluded that the mausoleum had been destroyed along with the abbey, and that its stones had been used for another structure. Others, like Johanna and Paul, believed they could still find the tomb and wanted to continue Conant's unfinished work.

As soon as Johanna had arrived in Cluny, she and Paul worked up a proposal for an excavation where the choir of Cluny III had been. However, the place where the holy of holies of the *maior ecclesia* had stood no longer belonged to the abbey grounds managed by Historical Monuments. There now stood stables belonging to the government-subsidized Haras Nationaux, the National Stud Farms, with purebred stallions, mares, and colts. The farm reported to the Ministry of Agriculture, a ministry whose primary mission was not studying medieval archeology.

"And what are you thinking about, my dear assistant?" asked Paul.

Paul was short and chubby, he wore thick glasses, and his blond hair grew sparsely like a crown around his bald head.

"I'm beginning to doubt we can find it," she said, looking away, ashamed to admit it. "We've been at it six months, and still nothing. What if we've been wrong? What if it was destroyed in the nineteenth century?"

The negotiations between the Ministry of Agriculture and the Ministry of Culture, represented by François, had dragged on for more than a year, not long when compared to Cluny time, but still exhausting for the people doing the negotiating.

Finally, one Thursday in November, François had been able to wrest a decision from Agriculture. They could have eight months to dig in the stud farm's garden, from June to January of the following year. There, they had what they wanted, and euphoria had swept away the married man's final scruples. That evening, they finally acted on the strong attraction they had felt for each other during the previous year.

"How can you doubt?" asked Paul. "You know he's real and that he's still right here! You spent years on your thesis to prove just that. We've got to be patient and keep on working. We'll find him, I'm sure."

"Paul, we have only two months left! Think for a minute! We calculated that the tomb would have to be at least two and a half meters long even without the base. A monument of that size can't just disappear! Soon we'll be down to the water table. No, I . . . I think we haven't picked the right place to excavate. . . . "

"What do you mean?" shouted Paul. "This is where the apse was, in this garden, right under this grass. We can tell because of the transept arm. Everybody knows that, even complete idiots. You're out of your mind, Johanna!"

"Don't talk to me like that, Paul," she scolded. "What I mean is that they might have put it in the axial chapel, or in one of the chapels radiating behind the ambulatory, right over there!" she said, pointing to an imaginary spot in front of her. "And that's not where we're digging."

Paul sighed and sat down on the ground.

"You're right. That's not where we're digging. We must be fools, for all we'd have to do is rent a bulldozer and raze the farm's office building. Of course, if we stole some dynamite from the quarry, we could work even faster. And then, while we're at it, we could also blow up the stables!"

"Barbarian! Not the horses!"

She smiled and, sitting down beside Paul, placed her hand on his big shoulder.

"I'm sorry," she said. "I'm exaggerating, as usual."

He put his hand on hers.

"That's all right," he reassured her. "It's nothing, Jo. Your love is stronger than mine, that's all . . . for Saint Hugh, I mean. Don't worry! I know it's not very scientific, but I've always had the knack for such things, if not for most things, and can sense something big right here, not under the stud farm director's office. Trust me, Hugh is right here somewhere. We'll find his tomb together, and we can talk about it all the way to . . . to Luxor!"

Finally Paul left her alone with her moodiness and her sandwich. As usual, he'd come back an hour later with a hot cup of coffee and the rest of the team. She had dragged herself out of the trench to eat and stretch her legs, stiff from working down there on her knees so long. At times, she would go over and give a bit of her lunch to Firmament, the nervous stallion with a shiny black coat, soft as silk. She was attracted by horses, and they were calming to her. They seemed so fragile with their thin legs, and yet they had so much power! True athletes.

As she left the stables, she almost bumped into François.

"There you are! I'm so pleased you've come!"

They slipped off into Cluny III's meager ruins, away from the dig. François always enjoyed trying to imagine what the great abbey church had been like, but that was impossible. Near the entrance to all that was left of the nave, he looked around and then pulled Johanna against his long cashmere coat.

"I can't believe it extended all the way to those trees over there," he said. "Amazing."

"Yes, one hundred eighty-seven meters long, with a nave thirty meters high. Only Saint Peter's in Rome could match it, but that was five hundred years later," Johanna said. "François, I'll be more comfortable in our little chapel. Here we're out in the open and I'm afraid everyone will see us when they leave the restaurant."

She didn't know why she was reacting like that. She didn't have anything to hide, and she certainly wasn't ashamed of François. To be sure, since their dinner in Saint-Germain-des-Prés when she got back from Italy, she had constantly been harassing him to name her as project director at Mont-Saint-Michel by using all the arguments she had in her arsenal, some of which were irresistible. She hadn't seen him for a week, and now here she was giving him a lecture about the size of the abbey rather than showing how pleased she was to see him.

"After all, it is freezing here in this wind," François admitted. "Yes, let's go to our little sanctuary!"

Secret lovers also have their habits, especially if they find them romantic. Johanna and François liked to meet in a fifteenth-century Gothic chapel hidden in the only vestiges of Cluny III's second level, the south arm of the transept. Winters in Burgundy were harsh, and Jean de Bourbon, a fifteenth-century abbot, was tired of suffering from the cold like his sons. So, beside the frozen chapel where the freezing monks held their services, the abbot had a small private antechamber built, where a big fireplace kept his back warm during mass.

One evening, Johanna had built a fire in the fireplace and opened a bottle of Meursault, then they had made love. François had found their little sacrilege exciting. Later, Johanna had told him that what they had done was not nearly as outrageous as what the monks themselves used to do. She told him that by the thirteenth century, the Cluny monks often went to taverns, dives, and prostitutes, and that in the eighteenth century they used drugs. Although an atheist herself, she wondered if the destruction carried out after the Revolution could be considered divine punishment, with God's instruments being the local population disgusted with the monks' long-standing decadence.

"The wine might be a little warm, but we'll drink it anyway," said François, leaning up against the stone fireplace and taking a bottle and two glasses out of his briefcase.

"Are we celebrating something?" wondered Johanna with surprise.

"Yes," he answered, taking her in his arms. "Our anniversary! We've been together for a year! Most men forget these things, but not me!"

"Oh, François, I'm very touched," she said, looking down at her muddy jacket. "How adorable!"

They kissed. His delicate attention was unexpected, and she melted like sugar in his arms. He was such a loving man; she needed to remind herself more often. Sometimes she thought she must be crazy to let her head fill up with dead people from the past, with dry stones and dusty bones, when the present was proposing a living, loving human being. Couldn't she stop looking for the impossible, aspiring to a nonexistent heaven, when life was giving her such a present? Wasn't she being blind and ungrateful? Shouldn't she break away from her dreams and live free and happy?

"And then there's something else we need to celebrate, too. Something I didn't want to tell you before," François added, pulling away and popping the champagne cork. "Do you remember two years ago? Our story began thanks to Hugh de Semur and the authorization to begin the dig here. And two years later, almost to the day, look what I have here, my love!"

Full of emotion, he pulled a paper from an inside pocket. Johanna almost stopped breathing.

"Look!" he repeated. "Today, our story continues under the auspices of Saint Michael the Archangel. Here's your assignment to the Mount!"

GRAY PYRAMID WITH golden summit, bursting forth out of a liquid desert. Fortified castle with entrails of stone. Constantly kissing the heavens, fleetingly caressing the earth. A monster assailing the infinite, a monster of beauty and of the impossible, embracing the gods and lowering its gaze on men, baring its flanks to the white-capped sea. The myths of its mysteries, its eternal desire, its very flesh . . . like the Angel's erection.

Johanna stood contemplating it, unable to turn away. Cluny was made of white limestone, like the off-white of a straying virgin. Mont-Saint-Michel was gray, gray like a knight's armor. Different shades of anthracite, cut in brilliant facets, echoed the clouds and the waves without losing itself in them. Granite's victory over nature and time. Arrogantly facing the elements, part man, part god, the Mount radiated captivating virility. What could the powerful, armored colossus be hiding?

"If it existed at all, Saint Martin's Chapel must have been right here," explained Christian Brard, administrator for Historical Monuments, standing near the treadmill. "An old manuscript tells us that in 992, the Count of Armorique, Conan I, who died at the battle of Conquereuil, was buried here in a 'chapelle Saint-Martin.' We've deduced that it was this chapel and that it must have been used as an ossuary. Several skeletons have been uncovered, but not Conan's. We think that one of them might be Geoffroy, Duke of Brittany and son of Conan. The others are monks, more recent, from the Romanesque period, when the chapel was destroyed and replaced with a cemetery or perhaps when Abbot Robert de Thorigny constructed another ossuary. During the Revolution, both the ossuary and cemetery were destroyed, but there are surely still bones to find. In fact, we'd love to put our fingers on the tomb of Judith of Brittany, spouse of Richard II, Duke of Normandy. He's the one who chased

out the canons, gave the abbey to the Benedictines, and financed building the great Romanesque abbey church. If two months ago somebody
had told me that instead of Roger Calfon there'd be a woman in charge
of looking for Judith, I'd have never believed it."

He was a big man pushing sixty, dry as a bone, with sloping shoulders,
thin lips, tortoiseshell glasses, and piercing eyes the color of hazelnuts.
He had solved the baldness problem by shaving his skull, and in these
walls, that made him look like a scholarly convict. Johanna had expected
more hostility on his part. So far, he had been in a hurry but polite. This
was the first such comment he had made since she had introduced herself
to him a half hour earlier.

"Don't interpret that as a sign from heaven, for sure," Johanna answered with a smile. "And relax, I'll be here only six months, just so Monsieur Calfon can take care of his wife before coming back to devote
himself to Judith."

Her irony, unusual for her, came from strong emotions that had taken
hold of her as soon as she arrived at the Mount: fear, a young girl's fear of
a dream that was becoming real, as well as an adult's fear in facing a task
for which she felt inadequate. Everything had come together: her phobia
about the decapitated monk and her anxiety at never being able to find
him; her fear of directing an empty dig and her eagerness to discover exciting tombs.

"Tell me, Monsieur Brard. Why was Saint Martin's Chapel destroyed
during the Romanesque abbey's construction?" she asked, changing the
subject.

"We don't know," he admitted, looking at her through his spectacles.
"What we do know, although the plans for the Romanesque abbey have
been lost, is that initially the Carolingian church was to have been razed
and this chapel preserved. In the end, the inverse happened. They destroyed Saint Martin and kept the church, using it as a crypt supporting
the Romanesque nave and baptizing it Notre-Dame-sous-Terre. There
is indeed a crypt under one of the transepts called Saint Martin's Crypt,
but it has nothing to do with the chapel. The name may have been chosen in homage to the place they demolished. In any case, whether due to

the whimsies of the master builder or the abbot, such changes were frequent in the Middle Ages."

"Yes, I know," she said, touching the masonry work on the walls, thinking about Notre-Dame-sous-Terre.

"The best thing you could do would be to dig into the abbey's history. You'll find what you need in the library in my office. You're free to use it as you like," he offered pleasantly. "Listen," he added, looking at his watch, "this evening I've got a lecture to give in Rennes and I still have some work to do on it. Could I ask you to come with me to my office so I can sign your contract? And I still need to give you the keys to the abbey. My assistant will show you to your housing. With everything that's happened, we're slow in starting the excavation. The team and all the equipment won't be here for another week. When do you plan to start?"

It was clear that he accepted Johanna but would be watching her every step.

"Immediately!" she answered.

IT WAS A large house beneath the abbey walls, behind the historical museum where Geoffroy, son of Conan, was resting, and it had an unbeatable view of the village cemetery. So Johanna would be surrounded by tombs day and night. The white-shuttered medieval building had a small courtyard and a round tower, from which sentinels could watch the bay during the Hundred Years' War. At the top, in the sentry box, she knelt down and looked out through the loophole. It was great. She felt like she was in control and safe in the watchtower. As evening fell, she went back to her room to prepare her headquarters. She pulled the iron cot to the middle of the room so she could see in all directions. She pulled the velvet armchair and the little desk over to the window overlooking the cemetery.

She'd have to go back to Paris to get the things she needed, but she could already spend her first night on Mont-Saint-Michel. Yes, her first night as project director, her first night so close to Notre-Dame-sous-Terre and whoever was haunting it. She shivered. The humidity was worse than the cold. At Cluny, winters were freezing but direct; here, the cold was tricky. The air seemed mild, but then it slipped under your clothes like a damp snake and slowly bit your skin with insidious little acidic nibbles, gnawed at your muscles, froze your bones, sapped your energy. Johanna crumpled up a few pages of a newspaper lying in a box, tossed them in the fireplace, struck a match, and placed some logs on the paper. Acrid gray smoke filled the room.

A few moments later, the night wind blew in through the open windows. It dissipated the smoke and nearly snuffed out the candles that Johanna had lit instead of turning on the fancy halogen lamp that would have clashed with the medieval setting. Sitting in the middle of her bed, wrapped in her dirty black down jacket, taking a swallow of Calvados now and then along with some cookies she found in the kitchen, she was deep in a big book lying open beside a dozen other books and a notebook spread out over the blanket. How they had organized the construction of the Romanesque abbey church was still a mystery, and the name of the builder hadn't survived through the ages.

"What a magnificent architectural and mystical achievement," she thought as she looked at the drawings. "Everything has meaning, nothing left to chance. What purity and harmony! Decades of construction, and no trace of its history. Why hadn't they razed the old church, Notre-Dame-sous-Terre? Perhaps because of the decapitated monk? Everything here is legend, the tale of the struggle against death and the forces of evil: the birth of the mountain, the Benedictines' arrival, the huge building projects, the constant battle between Normans and Bretons, the Hundred Years' War. Unbelievable, the Hundred Years' War at the Mount," she thought, looking around her at the walls dating from that period. "All of Normandy was in English hands, including Tombelaine nearby. All but Mont-Saint-Michel, for it resisted and never was taken. It was under siege for thirty years. At the beginning of the siege, in the middle of a service, the abbey's Romanesque choir collapsed on the monks," she read.

"The choir was rebuilt in Gothic style thirty years later. The mountain was defended by knights serving the king of France and by the monks, who never gave in to the invaders in spite of their abbot's treachery. The father abbot went over to the English, and he later voted to put Joan of Arc to death. All that is incredible," she sighed, looking up at the sky. "Like its Archangel, the Mount is more than a church. It's the symbol of collective and individual wars, of patriotic, even nationalistic fervor," the book added as she adjusted her glasses. "After the defeat of 1870, it was the secular, even anti-clerical Third Republic that saved the Mount, closing the prisons and restoring the abbey church. The Republic saw it as a national symbol, an emblem of resisting the occupier, and not a cathedral. . . . "

The holy fortress served as an allegory for resistance in the battle against both outside forces and inside enemies. Johanna didn't know what demons were awaiting her, both outside and within her, but she sensed that the place was transmitting some of its power to her. She had to use her time wisely, before the others arrived and the dig began. She needed to take advantage of the freedom the administrator was giving her to go looking for the mysterious man who had led her here in the first place. The next morning, she would go to Avranches to consult old manuscripts from the abbey. She might possibly find some reference to the headless monk or to the murders that took place in the monastery. But before that, she would go alone to Notre-Dame-sous-Terre. Maybe she would go that very night. It wouldn't be dangerous, she was sure. She no longer was afraid. The headless monk was like the Mount: He stood straight and dark beyond time, indestructible, full of secrets. He spoke to her like a valiant paladin struggling against invisible forces. Johanna rose and closed the windows but not the white shutters. She wanted to wake with first light, the dawn of a new day. She undressed and laid the books on the red floor tiles, all but one. She kept that book near her, open to the page where in 1469, after the Hundred Years' War, the Knights of the Order of Saint Michael swore the following oath:

To the honor and reverence of Monsignor Saint Michael, the first knight, who, for God's quarrel, struggled victoriously against humankind's arch-enemy and threw him out of heaven, and has always with good fortune guarded, preserved, and defended his place and oratory, called the Mont-Saint-Michel, without ever being subjugated nor given over to the former enemies of our kingdom.

The underground crypt was surprisingly light. The sun, if one could call the pale disk that awakened her the sun, had brought her peace after a restless night. Dressed in a coat of mail, sword in hand, she had fought against winged Englishmen with horns, beards, and long tails. They looked a little like Paul, François, Isabelle, her lab director at the CNRS, Hugh de Semur, a former lover, Judith of Brittany, her mother, or even a baby—her dead brother, Pierrot. In a corner, without moving, a statue of the Commander was watching her, looking like Christian Brard. And behind him rose the flaming silhouette of Mont-Saint-Michel smashing Cluny's last tower. She had finally opened her eyes after she found herself in a dungeon, shackles on her feet, waiting to be burned at the stake in the middle of the village cemetery under the gaze of skeletons dressed in worn homespun frocks and chanting Latin phrases from her thesis. All the people she knew had come, all except the one she was hoping most to see. She woke up sweaty and left a message on François's cell phone to say that she'd be back in Paris by late afternoon. For a long time she stared at the ring of keys to the abbey lying on the mantel, a rusty iron ring holding lots of heavy keys. The people employed by Historical Monuments walked around with them hanging from their belts; they looked like prison guards. Strangely, she was tired of wearing old tennis shoes, jeans, turtlenecks, and the padded jacket that hid her femininity. That morning, to visit Notre-Dame-sous-Terre, she felt like dressing up. Fortunately, thinking the administrator might invite her to dinner, she had packed a black wool dress, some pumps, a short tweed coat, and a gray Bakelite bead necklace. Her rudimentary bathroom was cold, but at least she wouldn't need to share it with the rest of the team. They would have three other bathrooms on the floor below; she was pleased about that.

Five people would be arriving six days later. Roger Calfon's usual assistant, three other men, and a woman. Johanna was relieved to know that she wasn't going to be the only female on the dig. At least if the woman didn't see her as a rival. She still had six days to organize an important dig and to plan how to lead a group of complicated human beings, she thought as put her lipstick on. There was no sign of coffee in the kitchen. She'd have to get some groceries. After all, she was in charge. And she'd need to set up a schedule to rotate household chores so the woman didn't get stuck with doing everything, as had happened in Cluny when Johanna first got there two years ago. Cluny! Poor Paul! When she had gone to his room to tell him she'd been named temporary director at the Mount, the day after François had visited her, he had been dumbfounded. Pale and mute like a corpse, he sat there on his bed, and then exploded in anger—raged like she would never have guessed. He called her an ungrateful, unscrupulous, careerist hussy, and, slamming the door, he walked out on her. That evening she had begged him to come to a smoky café with her. After a few vodkas, he was willing to forgive her for deserting him if she'd agree to come back to Cluny once her assignment in Normandy was completed. Later that night, alone in her room with the walls spinning, she realized that there was room in her life for only one man. The man had no name, no head, and no longer really existed, but he was more clearly present with her than anyone else. He had been always been with her, in her mind, body, and soul. He had formed her like a father, he appeared in her most private moments like a lover, and he showed her the way like a brother, all the while leaving her free. And he needed her, she was convinced.

IT WAS AS if she was seeing it for the first time. Her anxiety and uncertainly gone, Johanna looked up at the double stone staircase with a smile. She would have liked to have thrown her arms around the twin altars, caressed the granite pillars, and soaked up the scent of the place that now was hers. He wasn't there, but she could sense his presence up above; so near!

"Well, here I am," she whispered. "I don't know who you are, except that you're surely right here, in Notre-Dame-sous-Terre. I don't know what you expect from me, or perhaps I'm expecting something from you. We are linked beyond time, I know that. We are connected by our expectations, our hopes, our quest. These stones have given me your strength, courage, and passion. As I've been digging in search of soulless bones, it's really you I've been seeking, an incomplete body like me."

Suddenly a stranger burst into the crypt.

"Oh, here you are! You are an early riser like me. My name is Kelenn, Guillaume Kelenn, a local guide at your service. Delighted to meet you, madame!" he said, holding out his hand.

Johanna was startled by his sudden appearance, but finally pulled herself together and shook his hand.

"Pleased to meet you, too," she answered. "Jo—"

"Johanna. Yes, I know. What a lovely name! The feminine form of John, author of the Book of Revelations. He provided the inspiration for Romanesque abbeys."

"Perhaps," she said curtly, not at all pleased to be bothered during this private time in the crypt. She hoped that he hadn't heard what she had been saying.

He must have been about the same age as she was. He looked quite charming with his finely tailored jacket, his long reddish-blond curls tied back in a ponytail, his thin mustache, and his big green eyes with brown specks. Unfortunately, he had a big, hooked nose and an unusually long neck that reminded Johanna of a vulture.

"Forgive my intrusion. I didn't mean to disturb you, just meet our new archeologist. People say that you're an expert in Romanesque art, and I wonder if my expertise could be helpful to you. I was hoping to take you around my castle before it's open to the public and share some of my little secrets with you," he added with a wink.

"Your 'castle'?" Johanna wondered, already finding the fellow annoying.

"Manner of speaking, to be sure. You see, I was born here in the village, and, believe it or not, my whole family has been born here ever since the ninth century. I've been guiding people through the abbey for more than ten years, so I tend to think of it as my own home. That's not surprising, is it?"

"Perhaps not. Thank you for your offer, but it'll have to be some other time. I've got to go to the library in Avranches and then drive back to Paris. Sorry."

"Oh, that's really too bad! I could have told you things you can't find in books or archives, could have shown you the abbey's soul. For example, are you aware that its soul is right here? Can you sense it?"

He was indeed annoying, but his words piqued her interest.

"Yes," she whispered. "I . . . I mean . . . I'm not sure. The atmosphere is so strange here in Notre-Dame-sous-Terre."

"Because it's the source of everything!" he responded excitedly. "This crypt was a church built by Bretons right where Aubert's sanctuary had been. You can still see a piece of the old sanctuary wall right there. And before that, it had been a Celtic temple!"

"Yes, that's what I've read," she said with disappointment. "Aubert built his sanctuary on a megalithic mound, razed by the first missionaries."

"That's the important thing," he concluded eagerly, raising his arms. "Do you think that our Celtic ancestors chose their temples by chance?"

"I thought you lived here and that your family has been here for centuries," Johanna said skeptically.

"Yes, right here on the Mount, so we're Breton!" he answered forcefully. "The Norman bastards stole it from us in 933. We were here before that, and we were Celtic!"

Johanna sighed. Age-old quarrels bored her to death.

"I thought this place was Christian from the sixth century on," she reminded him.

"Christian, yes, but they were Celtic Christians! I'm talking about a people, not a religion. A separate people, with their own history, their own roots, their own physical characteristics and customs! Furthermore, Bishop Aubert was from around Avranches, and Avranches belonged to Brittany until 933. His canons served the Archangel, but they were Celts. The Norman Benedictines chased them out in 966."

"All the same, after all that time, now you're Norman."

"That's an insult," he answered sorrowfully, raising his chin like a shamed knight. "My family calls itself Norman, but not me. I refuse to be considered like one of those hypocritical savages pretending to be scholars. They took our land and tried to wipe out our culture."

Johanna felt like laughing. She restrained herself, thinking that this unusual man might be able to tell her something about the headless monk.

"The Normans have also done some amazing things," she said gently. "All we have to do is look around us."

"That's true," he admitted quietly, a little calmer. "That's what I explain to tourists every day. They did indeed develop a magical site, but it doesn't belong to them."

"Magical? Like Notre-Dame-sous-Terre?" she asked, hoping that he would say a little more about the crypt's history.

"This crypt is more than a simple chapel," he said finally. "They completely razed the Celtic sanctuary that was here before, but we can still sense its soul. Furthermore, every Celtic temple had two identical parts and twin taurobolic altars. Just as Aubert, in 708, copied the circular model of the Mount Gargano grotto when he built his round cave, his canons, in the tenth century, followed the same Celtic architectural principle by building this church with a double nave and a double choir. Do you see? It was a way of paying homage to their ancestors, even though they were Christians. They didn't forget their people, even though their religion was different."

Guillaume's knowledge began to captivate Johanna. She motioned to him to continue. He didn't need to be asked twice.

"The druids celebrated the dead and took care of the living here. We are exactly at the point of convergence of major telluric currents, it's scientifically proven. That's right, the earth's supernatural force can be found right here. The druids honored the god Ogmius, or Ogma, the opposite of the god Dagda, worshipped on Mont Dol nearby. Dagda is the god of light, Ogma the god of the shadows—chief among the dead, the god of war, of magic, guiding the souls of the dead to the other world. Doesn't he remind you of somebody else?"

"A psychopomp, the guide and protector of dead souls on the path to heaven. Saint Michael, of course," Johanna responded in amazement.

"Yes, indeed. Saint Michael. And it's not a coincidence!" Guillaume said, flushing with satisfaction. "All that means something. All the Christians did was take our traditions and expand on them with their own myths. So effectively, and with so much force, that we've forgotten the source—our own culture! I could give you other examples: Saint Michael combating the dragon is just a variant of our legend 'The Shepherd and the Monster,' and the Day of the Dead is like the Celtic feast day Samain. And how about Saint Aubert's skull, venerated by the faithful in Notre-Dame-sous-Terre? When you go to Avranches, you should see it in its golden reliquary in Saint Gervais rather than holing up in a Norman library!"

"A skull? In Notre-Dame-sous-Terre? Aubert?" Johanna stammered, paling.

Guillaume walked over toward her, leaned against her shoulder, and, facing the stairway the headless monk had climbed, whispered into her ear: "Do you see those steps up there, above the altar dedicated to the Trinity, leading to the wooden door under the vaulted ceiling?" he asked.

Hardly daring to move, Johanna held her breath. The staircase and the door were identical to the ones above the second parallel altar, dedicated to the Virgin.

"Well," he said without waiting for a response, "these steps continue beyond the door and go all the way up to the nave in the big church. Same thing over there. Today the two passages are closed off, but in the Middle Ages they were used to carry down to the prostrate pilgrims in the crypt the coffer containing the relics of the founder Aubert, buried in the abbey church's choir. The reliquary held one arm and a head, supposedly belonging to Aubert, that the canons had hidden when the Benedictines arrived. And then the Benedictines discovered them by chance when they were running out of money to finance the construction of the Romanesque abbey church. The skull has something very unusual about it. According to the legend, in the middle of the forehead, it was pierced by the Archangel's finger when he appeared the third time. An angelic perforation. But, you see, it can't be Aubert's skull, because the perforation is not in the forehead but off to the right side, near the top of the cranium. You can go to Avranches to see for yourself in the Saint Gervais church. They continue to display it as one of Aubert's true relics! And do you know why the hole is on one side and not in the forehead? Because it's a Celtic skull. Surely Neolithic or dating from the early Christian era, because it carries the mark not of some strange apparition, but of trepanation, a sacred ritual that the druids performed on those who died!"

8

ROMAN RAISES HIS EYES ANXIOUSLY TOWARD THE CEILING IN THE form of a double stone stairway. He prays. He feels like smashing the twin altars with his own hands, breaking the granite pillars, burning the sacred place and obliterating the fragrance he can still sense, so near.

"Divine Archangel," he prays. "Guide me. Which path must I follow? Must I keep this terrible secret? Perhaps I can modify my master's drawings so as not to destroy this church in which I'm lifting up my prayers to you. I was supposed to turn the church into a forest of pillars, standing directly on the rock, designed to support the nave of the great abbey church that will rise above me. Saint Martin's Chapel, on the mountain's flank, was to be the support for the nave's outside walls. The best way to make the change would be to raze the chapel and keep this church intact, so as to use it as a supporting crypt for the nave—a dark, subterranean crypt. Of course, we would need to reinforce the stonework," Roman says, looking around him, "double the south wall, make the central pillar thicker, add an extension to the western end of the church so that it could support the bays in the nave. None of that would require digging in the earth. But how can I convince Hildebert? I might be able to persuade him if I invoke Aubert's grotto, for this is exactly where it was, saying that we'd be destroying its sacred spirit if we destroyed these walls. Should I try? Must I preserve this church? My master, Pierre de Nevers, didn't want to. My master, dear father, how I miss you. . . ."

Roman closes his eyes. He can feel the parchments hanging against his chest inside his cowl. It seems as if the sketches are burning his skin, penetrating his blood, being engraved on his heart. He stands up suddenly, crimson red.

Standing there in the church, he scrutinizes the statue of the Black Virgin as if she were a human being or a monster rising out of the shadows—one that he needed to confront alone, with his measuring rod instead of a sword. He drops his rod. He hasn't needed to use it as a cane for several days. And then he falls to his knees before the altar.

"Dear master!" he exclaims, holding his head in his hands. "I can't betray you. Rest assured there at the Lord's side; all will be done according to your will. I do love that woman; yes, I do, but with chaste love, with no dishonor to the flesh. This love torments me, but I can no longer struggle and risk destruction. So I accept it as a gift from God sent to test me. I love God and his angels no less. I love her like a lost sister who I need to bring back to God and the angels. She's included in my adoration of the Most High! My goal is to bring her peace. Today, led by the chains that keep her in bondage, she has asked me to commit a false act of love that would make me, too, fall into bondage by being unfaithful to my master's memory. No, that I cannot do. Holy Mother," he murmurs to the statue, "as a woman, you can help me tell Moira that her cause is lost. This evening I'll go to Beauvoir. Give me the strength not to give in when I see her, for I know I'll be taking away her reason for living, tearing away both her past and her future. She was orphaned by both her parents; this evening she'll be orphaned by all her people!"

THE WATER IS the color of the ink the monks use in the scriptorium. The little pond, bordered in springtime by green illuminations, is for Moira a book of sacred history. Every morning she comes to read the legends her people have constructed over the centuries. The swamp is sacred, for, like a book, it's a door, the passage to a world where time has stopped, where in gold and crystal palaces immortal beings live. And sometimes they enlist living people to transport them in their glass boats to eternal peace. For hours Moira watches the surface of the dark waters as she waits for a god to show her the entrance to the joyous, delightful world where she knows her father is living. But the heroes remain hidden at the bottom of the pond. They'll never take a woman to the world of the Sidhe.

Like her mother, Moira will come back to life in another body, and the best she can hope for is that one day her soul will be reincarnated as a man and that his exploits will open the gate to the gods. She can't see them, but she can feel their presence there under the water; she knows they're looking at her. Sometimes they send her signs. When her father died, a dog, their messenger, came into the hut in Beauvoir and led her and her brother here to the pond. A crow was circling over the pond; it was Morrigan, the mother goddess, the fairy of death and fertility, who flies over the battlefields to choose the future dead and couple with the heroes. Brewen and Moira had realized that Morrigan this time had chosen their father, that she had accompanied him to the Sidhe, and that his progeny were expected to make an offering of thanks to the swamp spirits. Moira had wondered then if the prophetess of doom hadn't also come to warn them about an impending danger. Now, since she last met Roman, she is almost convinced of it, as the crow has come back and is cawing at the edge of the pond. Using gestures, Brewen has told her that if the Reaper is lurking about, it means that Moira is in grave danger, but today the young woman can think only about the secret she has divulged to Roman. This morning she darkened her eyebrows, put rouge on her cheeks, plaited her hair in long braids that hung over her shoulders. She is wrapped in a large wool coat, madder red, the color of knowledge but also the color of war. The coat had been her father's. Ordinarily she would not have dared to wear it, but today is different. She must be the incarnate symbol of the two greatest qualities her people possess in order to speak to the gods and ask for their help. She must represent the powers of both knowledge and war.

Standing on the banks and gazing out over the dark pond, she puts her hands behind her neck and removes her baptismal cross, a little wooden crucifix hanging from a cord. She holds the crucifix out in front of her and quickly throws it into the water. In the old days, her ancestors would offer to the gods the bent swords of their vanquished enemies or the bound bodies of their rivals; after battle, too, the victors would decapitate their dead adversaries and tie the heads to their horses' collars as trophies. She, however, would prefer her enemy's head and body, for he might be her savior if he gives up his weapon, the Christian symbol, the crucifix, that the gods in the world of the Sidhe might obliterate. Moira pulls from her pocket a tiny object that her father had given her. She'd taken it from its hiding place this evening.

A cross made of gold and bone, it sums up the druids' knowledge of cosmogony and metaphysics. Its four gold arms of equal length are engraved with tiny geometrical signs, oghams, which in part constitute the writing system used by the druids and the god Ogma. The four arms represent the four elements, water beneath, fire above, air to the right, and earth to the left. They extend outward from four concentric circles: The smallest is the Gwenwed circle, symbolizing the soul's ascension to be with the gods; the second is Annouim, the circle of the abyss; the third, the Abred circle, represents fate, which is equally divided between good and evil; and finally, the largest, Keugant, is the one from which souls leave, like sparks, to begin their migration toward other bodies. These four circles are engraved on a circular piece of bone set in the cross. The bone is an amulet that dates back to the origins of her people, to the time when druids would practice trepanation on the skulls of dead warriors by taking a small disk of bone, an operculum, which they often wore as combatants to gain strength and courage. After trepanation, they would joyfully bury the dead with their perforated skulls. Moira kisses the druidic cross and places it around her neck.

"Ogma!" she calls out, lifting her arms above her head and keeping her eyes on the water. "God of war, master of eloquence, writing, and magic, chief in the realm of the dead, conductor of dead souls, your kingdom is in danger. Ogma, old man in a lion skin, our enemy doesn't carry a sword. He's a language warrior, he fights for love, and his battlefield is a stone castle that will reach into the heavens as it digs into the earth at the Mount! The offering I gave to you, that cross, is his weapon. Ogma, don't destroy him, for I love his love, but inspire him, give him the magic words that will keep him from digging in sacred earth. May he cease struggling. May he be conquered without becoming our enemy!"

A breeze rustles over the tree trunk a few feet behind her. A honeybee, noisily celebrating the rebirth of its favorite flowers, is brushed away with the back of a hand. A round black eye stares avidly at the young woman. On hearing her prayer to Ogma, he leans his frock-clothed body against the tree and stifles a cry.

He was attracted to her when she took care of Roman, but this morning he realizes who she truly is. He is overcome by what he has learned, but not as much as he was when he found out the other evening in Saint Martin's Chapel about the love she and Roman share. Almodius has always been ignorant of women.

Given to the abbey by his parents when he was three, along with a large donation, he naturally couldn't remember his mother; and for him, the word "family" had meant only one thing—the monastery. The only woman admitted to the monastery—and during the eleventh century not very often—was the Virgin, and so Almodius had grown in perfection, his heart turned resolutely toward his imposed vocation, and all the while he was surrounded only by men. When he became an adult, the abbot had asked him, as he asked all the oblates, if he wanted to go back into the world. But Almodius was passionate about books and his faith, so he had chosen to remain in the abbey as a novice. Later, he pronounced his vows and became a monk. The books he read and then copied so carefully did indeed reveal to him the stories of Mary Magdalene and the women martyrs of early Christianity who perished in the arena, where they were devoured by lions because they would not renounce their faith in Jesus. But their mystical power was beyond him. Some women did come to mass, but the master of the scriptorium saw them only as vessels for bearing children, and sometimes he wondered, as others did in those days, if God had even given them souls.

But when Almodius had seen Moira for the first time in her hut in Beauvoir, he'd suffered a huge shock. Although his mind still attached no value to women, his body had been dazzled in a brand-new way. In the grips of violent physical attraction, he fell prey to some wild instinct, and his desire for possession became an obsession. The subprior's body seemed to be possessed by the devil, and that woman was the cause, that woman he hated by nature and by circumstance. Each time he appeared at the builder's bedside was pure torture. Torn between his sensual attraction to the young woman and his moral duties toward the patient, he had to mobilize all his strength to hide his unhealthy bent. He would have liked to have borne his poor brother out of the claws of the demon, just as he would also have liked to have been in his place—lying on that bed at death's door but within reach of Moira's lips. Yes, in spite of Roman's wounds, he envied him.

As soon as it became clear that the patient wouldn't die, Almodius had hastened to have him moved back to the monastery, to get him away from that female. He'd thought that he himself would thus be saved as well. But the demoness had not left him in peace. Day and night she haunted him: she instilled in him a poison that paralyzed his will, excited his imagination, took hold of his flesh like a carnivorous animal. Unable to free himself from the jailer imprisoning his heart, he had begun to spy on her in secret. Given his rank as subprior, he had the right to leave the cloister, and when his duties allowed, he would gallop out toward Beau-voir, where, hidden in the brush like a vulgar thief, he could watch the vil-lainous woman's comings and goings. That's how he learned about Moira's daily visits to the pond. He hoped he would see her bathing, naked, but she never even touched the water. She simply stared at it, like Narcissus looking into his mirror, and passed hours contemplating her devilish beauty. Only her brother, the deaf-mute, had once dipped his hands into the water and then made hideous sounds like a crow cawing.

It was purely by chance that Almodius had learned about Roman and Moira. That evening, assailed by infernal visions, as he often was, he had woken up before Matins and left the dormitory to get away from his sleeping brothers. The tempest outside matched the state of his soul, and he had taken refuge in nature's elements as he imperviously met the night chill and the rain beating down in harmony with the sea's furor and the wind's exaltation. And then, hoping to put an end to his nightmares, he was planning to entrust his sins to God and with a whip to purify his flesh of desire for that woman, as he often did when he suffered too much from temptation.

Hildebert, however, forbade his sons to mortify themselves, because for him, as for most men of the time, the Passion was above all an act of love, not of torture. Monks who voluntarily inflicted torture on them-selves were viewed as proud fanatics, who gloried in useless selfish suffering rather than serving God through love of men, whose suffering was never voluntary. So Almodius had fixed up a secret niche in the office he used as the head of the scriptorium, and that's where he hid his whip. To reach his office, he had to walk past Saint Martin's Chapel. That stormy night, he had at first thought he was seeing a ghost and had barely had enough time to hide behind a supporting wall in the chapel. In fact, he would have preferred meeting a phantom from the abyss, the king of fallen angels himself, rather than powerlessly watching that horrible scene with two people he immediately assumed were lovers.

He was as naïve as a novice. The creature had held his brother close to her breast, in her den, with no witnesses. A man on his deathbed, such easy prey! The demon has no scruples, he carries off his victim. How had she been able to seduce Roman? Roman was an aristocrat like him, but Roman wasn't a Norman oblate who'd been locked up in a monastery since he was three years old. He had been born far away, he had seen the world with his master Pierre de Nevers, had walked through valleys, had sailed the seas. Perhaps he'd even met some women! He must have spoken to Moira about other lands, and she had proposed her own land, a land smelling of sin and corruption. And at night, she spread her sulphurous charms even into the heart of the holy mountain, into the dwelling of the Most High!

Several times he'd come close to denouncing Roman in the chapter meeting for confession, before the entire community. But each time an inner voice had held him back. A monk's sins against the flesh are a grievous sin, and Roman would pay dearly. But he would pay it alone. The creature who had led him astray wouldn't pay at all. And yet she was the one who should be punished. She was the truly guilty one—Eve, the source of all the earth's evils, holding out the apple to Adam—fornicating with Roman and bewitching Almodius. She was the one who must be removed from their world. Guided by a mysterious instinct, the subprior had increased his surveillance around Moira and started watching Roman. He noticed that she had never come back to the Mount after that fateful evening during Lent and that, unless she had slipped past his vigilance by some magic spell, she hadn't seen her lover again for weeks. Furthermore, in proof of the woman's dangerous influence, now that she was not around, Roman seemed to be regaining his strength. He had lost most of his old man's limp, he was not as pale, and he was able to give himself completely to his holy mission—building the great abbey church. He spent days and nights bent over his master's drawings, stylus in hand, obviously calculating and recalculating the tensions and thrusts of the stones. Indeed, with her gone, his brother is once more on the path of light. Almodius is satisfied, and his jealousy is as well.

She, on the other hand, is in torment, assailed by indwelling shadows. Her courtesan's complexion has taken on death's pallor; her green eyes have grown darker and seem to be looking for unlikely answers in the leaves of the trees and the clay from the path she follows to the pond.

On this morning, once his initial surprise has dissipated, a fertile joy washes over the subprior as if he'd been plunged into a sea of happiness. His combat is something greater than the struggle between lust and purity. The battle he wages, inspired by the Angel, is the battle between Christians and absolute evil, paganism, false religion! The woman is more than temptation for the flesh. She is the incarnation of the old religion; she's like the devil himself. Leaning there against his tree, Almodius watches Moira walk away. He smiles. He gives thanks to Saint Michael for having shown him the woman's true nature and the real stakes of the battle the subprior must wage. A providential battle for which he is now armed, a battle that will free him once and for all from his dangerous passion for Moira. Suddenly he thinks about his brother Roman. Does he know who his mistress really is? Vengeful flames rise in his eyes. No, impossible, inconceivable for a Benedictine, the best servant of God, elite among men! His brother has surely been bewitched, and Almodius must save him. And yet Roman deserves to be punished because he was unable to fight against the spirit of evil. He gave up; in his weakness he betrayed the habit he wore. The vile, cowardly, miserable man was trying to build a cathedral, yet he'd groveled in filth—he must be severely punished. For sure, he doesn't deserve any pity. Almodius himself had been blinded by the devil's charms, but now, now, he's been delivered, and he feels within himself the Archangel's invincible bellicose power, not a soft heart for renegades! As for her, her . . . the subprior runs to his horse, leaps on it, and gallops toward Mont-Saint-Michel.

. . .

ROMAN IS RELIEVED to have come to a decision and leaves the church. Seeing the mountain and what he has so longed for takes his breath away. From top to bottom, men are swarming over the Mount like bees in a hive. On the sea at high tide, dozens of boats loaded with granite blocks are moving.

On the slopes, big oxcarts with small wheels carry the stones through the village. There are people carrying wood for the scaffoldings. Near the cisterns filled with rainwater, kilns are baking limestone, and vats bubble where the mortar-mixers, sweating in the heat, are stirring the quicklime with iron rods. Further on, workmen are mixing the cooled, slaked lime with sand and cow hair into the mortar that others will carry on their backs to the top of the mountain. There, at the tip of the rock, opposite the Carolingian church, on the east side, construction of the choir crypt is under way. For the work on the steep slope, Master Roger's team has built wooden terraces, held in place by stakes driven into the earth. Above these levels, on one-legged stools or on an assemblage of beams forming a table, the master stonecutters are at their work. Other craftsmen are carving capitals to decorate the columns. Opposite them, one part of the wall is already standing, along with scaffolding held in place by beams placed in temporary holes. The masons, working on small platforms, check the wall's verticality with their plumb lines or mason's levels. Imposing lifting devices with names like "goats," "gallows," and "she-wolves" grasp stones in their iron jaws and raise them to the needed height. Laborers are setting up the "colt," a huge wooden treadmill powered by men for lifting blocks that might weigh up to ten quintals. Cries ring out in every language; the interpreter runs back and forth to translate. Songs are raised. They aren't in Latin, but Roman knows that heaven can hear them all the same. Joyously, he contemplates his work. Yes, his work, and the work of Pierre de Nevers.

The day before, Easter Monday, Father Hildebert had officially launched the construction site, and his blue eyes were shining with tears of joy. Never had Easter festivities been as joyous as they were that year. It was as if all the angels had gathered, with their leader at their head. Three days before Easter, the monks, alone on the mountain, celebrated the night service, the "tenebrae," by slowly extinguishing one after the other all the candles in the church. Then, for the next three nights, they chanted Jeremiah's lamentation.

On Maundy Thursday, the bishop of Avranches came to consecrate the holy oils and administer public penitence. The villagers and pilgrims were joined by some workmen from the future construction site. In the evening, the monks removed all cloth and decorations from the altars, and before celebrating mass, as at the Last Supper, Hildebert washed the feet of all men present. By that time, the stone-carriers had arrived, exhausted after their long journeys from the far corners of France. The abbot knelt before them and washed their dusty feet. The next day, while the monks were raising the huge cross they'd carry on their backs to the top of the mountain, thus replicating the stations of the cross, they were joined by a large crowd of workers who would soon be carrying their own loads up the same path. The brothers knew, by the way the fervent crowds were watching the Benedictines climbing the slopes of the holy rock, that the Omnipotent One was blessing their construction site. The most exciting moment occurred on Saturday as they waited for Easter, when Hildebert came out of the church, which was filled with monks and villagers, to light and bless the Easter flame. For that's when he saw the huge crowd of people waiting on their knees outside the church. Everyone was there—those who would toil with their hands, their legs; those who would die building the Angel's dwelling place—and the church couldn't hold them all. Hildebert lit the brazier in front of the sanctuary door, and immediately the chant of the risen Jesus burst forth from the multitude. "*Exultet,* let the angel host exult," they sang. And the abbot saw the angels that had appeared to him. Then, leaving the church, he mixed with the crowd and blessed them one by one until late in the night.

"Oh, Master Roger, can you supervise placing the stones for the vaults?" says Roman to the carpenter who, hand on his hips, is directing a cart loaded with wooden arches that would be instrumental in building the barrel vaults and groined vaults.

The carpenter turns toward Roman, and Roman can see as usual in Roger's eyes the mischievous flame of his own brother Henry's eyes.

"Oh, Brother Roman," Roger answers with a smile, "I've been so eager to show the Archangel what good work my men can do!"

In Master Roger's mind, at this moment the Archangel has taken on the features of the man who authorized the construction, Hildebert, and his messenger has taken on the features of Roman, the master builder. And heaven's grace must be round like pieces of silver. As Roman begins to answer, his assistant, Brother Bernard, interrupts, saying that the abbot requires his presence immediately in his cell.

"Well, that gives me the opportunity to vaunt the merits of your men," he says to the carpenter.

Roger winks, and Roman walks away, hoping that the abbot will approve the agreed-upon costs and not ask him to negotiate further with the different guilds. That's something he hates. He's more concerned about the walls' height than with their cost. Roman walks past the old monastery buildings and the chapter room. He knocks on the door of the cell inherited from the canons. It will be destroyed once the stone buildings are finished.

"Come in!"

The abbot speaks sharply. Roman enters the room. Hildebert is seated behind his desk, beneath the tapestry of the Angel, weigher of souls. His eyes are ordinarily warm and friendly, but now they are hard and reproachful.

"Father, you asked for me?"

Hildebert stares at him but doesn't answer. Standing in front of him, the monk waits, eyes lowered. Hildebert's lips are pinched together, and the blue in his eyes looks like ice. In the fireplace, flames are consuming a log. Roman can't feel their heat but can hear the voracious crackling that fills the heavy silence.

"Have you seen the healer from Beauvoir since you came back to the monastery, Brother Roman?" the abbot finally asks, his tone suggesting that he already knows the answer.

So that's why he's been summoned. It had been foolish to have her come to the Mount. One of the brothers must have seen them. I have to be straightforward and tell him the truth.

"Yes, my Father," Roman admits, looking up. "Three times she's answered my call and we've met in Saint Martin's Chapel between Compline and Matins."

"Infamy!" Hildebert interrupts him, pounding his fist on the table. "You, a man of God, a servant of the first among angels, a companion of Pierre de Nevers, designated for the highest mission. You, the must erudite of my sons, in whom I had total confidence, whom the Lord cherished. I couldn't believe it, but you confess your lust like a primitive ignoramus who doesn't know anything about sin. You!"

"My Father," says Roman. "I have committed a grievous sin, but not the sin you're accusing me of! My flesh has not been not defiled."

Hildebert stands and walks over to Roman. He scrutinizes his son as if the monk has become a stranger to him.

"In that case, your sin is even greater!" says the abbot, his face just a few inches from Roman's. "For you have given away your soul! And do you know to whom? Do you know what's hidden behind that woman's inoffensive appearance?"

The abbot's garlicky breath envelops Roman in damp fright. The monk looks up at the Archangel with his scales. Moira is kneeling on one of the pans, and she's falling into darkness. Hildebert knows everything. She's lost. Who? Who saw that heresy was attacking her? Refusing to speak, Roman is the victim of a white veil that passes before his eyes and blinds him. His legs seem to belong to someone else, and they collapse beneath him. Overwhelmed by unmanageable emotion, he falls at the abbot's feet.

"Father!" he exclaims, face toward the ground, like a penitent at the chapter meeting for confession. "Father, Moira is not who you think she is. It's my fault," he says between sobs. "I wanted to help her by myself, out of pride or out of love . . . for I do love her, Father, it's true, I'm torn with my love for her. Torn between heaven and earth, but I've always chosen heaven! You must understand. She's not a dangerous demon but a slave, and I've tried to free her! Her skin smells like the forest, her hair is like trees, her eyes . . . she . . . I need to . . . I have to save her," he stammers.

The old man is taken aback by these words; he lets the monk's pain pour out in silence. He kneels before Roman and lays a paternal hand on his sobbing son's shoulders.

"Now, tell me everything, my son," he gently orders. "I'm listening. Unburden yourself."

Roman lifts his head a little. With his eyes on the cross hanging on the abbot's chest, he begins to speak. He tells about his conversations with Moira in her house in Beauvoir; he recounts how she saved his life, why he resolved to see her again, his distraction over her, his attraction to her, the night meetings in Saint Martin's Chapel, Moira's beliefs, his efforts to bring her back to the light, the temptations of the flesh, his own internal struggle.

"But never has she turned me away from my vocation nor from my tasks, Father! Never!" he concludes, thinking about the secret she entrusted to him and that he hasn't mentioned. "Her only sin is that she can't see the truth. Mine is to have tried to show her what the truth is."

"Explaining Christ's words so secretly, in the night, as if they were ungodly! What a beautiful mission!" says Hildebert, struggling to get back to his feet.

"But I've succeeded, my Father!" Roman objects. "I believe I've opened her soul to the divine word. I've touched her heart, even if she doesn't yet admit it."

Hildebert walks over to the fire. The red flames dance on his tired face. He turns back toward Roman, a sarcastic smile on his face.

"It's true that her heart can't admit it, my son. And her acts, witnessed by our subprior, communicate in fact an entirely different message."

And then the abbot begins to describe the scene by the pond and Moira's prayer to the pagan god Ogma, just as the master of the scriptorium had told him. On his knees beside the wooden table, Roman is overwhelmed. So, she hadn't truly heard Christ's message, she hadn't understood Moses' anger when he saw the Golden Calf, she hadn't seen the New Jerusalem. Once she was away from Roman's eyes and mouth, she had gone back to the scoria of the past! The monk feels great bitterness invading his heart. When he glances at the Archangel's scales, he sees that now he's the one falling from his lofty illusions. Disappointment and resentment eat at his heart like a poisonous scorpion, and he drinks the poison to the dregs.

"You have failed, my son," the abbot continues, seeming to read his thoughts, "for you mistakenly brought together two desires: one, reprehensible, of the flesh, and the other, legitimate, to save the poor sinner's soul. You confused grain and chaff, mixed good and evil. You appeased your conscience by placing the Bible between that woman and yourself, when in fact your only desire was to possess her body. The intangible proof is that you acted in the dark, in the utmost secret, and not in the light divine! Plans carried out in the darkness belong to the darkness."

The old man stands with his back to the fire that crackled in the fireplace, like a man vanquishing the flames of hell. Roman knows that his words are accurate. If his intentions had been as praiseworthy as he had thought, he would have told the abbot about Moira. The old man's temperance and experience would have kept him out of danger. What Roman had been fearing unconsciously wasn't telling the abbot about Moira, but rather unveiling his own motivations, because although he hadn't understood them himself, Hildebert would definitely have been able to read his thoughts. He does carnally desire the woman, in spite of everything, and he has always desired her. Yes, it's true, and yet Roman feels confusedly that that's not the whole story. He has managed to get beyond the sensual temptation and control his body, yet his desire isn't dead. That means his nature is different and not limited to concupiscence. Now that Hildebert knows about Moira's deepest beliefs and the link between her and Roman, Roman should be able to confide in the abbot, to tell him Moira's secret, the secret of the Mount.

"Father," he begins, hoping to lift his burden.

And then his lips freeze. Something holds him back; something infinitely powerful is constricting his throat and pressing against his mouth like a gag.

"Are there other sins you haven't yet confessed?" Hildebert asks, his white eyebrows frowning.

He must speak, get it out, purify his soul. He looks down at the earthen floor, as if he could find there the liberating words. But the earth is as a silent as a tomb. It has recently been turned over, when they moved the abbot's hut to the present location. The earth yields nothing; it's mute. Roman picks up a few tiny dark particles that stick together in the dampness. He's holding Moira's land in his hand, and with one gesture, with one forbidden word, it will slip through his fingers and return to its secrets. She had fooled him by letting him think she was eager to hear his fervent message, but she wasn't lying when she declared her love. He was mistaken about his love for her. He had let himself believe that his love was like a shepherd's devotion to his lost sheep, but it was really a man's love for a woman. Moira always knew he was lying, and she accepted that. To what truth should he be faithful now?

"I'm waiting, Roman."

The abbot's words startle him. He drops the dirt, and it falls on his frock. He needs time to think, time to pray. Right now he's incapable of betraying Moira, any more than he can betray Pierre de Nevers.

"Father, forgive my confusion," he says, looking at Hildebert from the corner of his eyes. "I've entrusted all my sins to you, and I know they are weighty. I deserve punishment, and I'm ready to accept it. But I'm still concerned about her. My love for that woman, however guilty it may be, is driven by compassion and—"

"In penitence there is also compassion, my son," Hildebert answers more gently. "You will appear before the chapter and we will decide your fate together. Your special position as master builder requires of you exemplary spiritual qualities that you have not displayed. And paradoxically, your position also makes you indispensable, so we'll need to be unusually careful. But the truth is, we need you to build the Archangel's dwelling place. On the other hand, one thing the holy mountain does not need is a resurgence of pagan cults! I will see Moira immediately, and then I'll decide. I formally forbid you to leave the monastery or to try to contact this woman in any way. Go to your place on the construction site, and I'll call you when she comes."

Roman leaves Hildebert's hut in shock and wanders around over the construction site. The bustle of men and materials, which a few minutes earlier had seemed to him to sing like a religious ode, now assaults him with a cacophony like chaos.

At the sixth hour, while the workers are seated on the slopes and the monks in the refectory are having lunch, he notices a cart being pulled up the hill by two horses. It is carrying a strange load. In front, Almodius sits enthroned beside the abbey's lay groom; in back two hefty village men who work in the abbey kitchen sit on both sides of Moira, whom they guard like a prisoner. Roman's nerves can't bear the sight. He turns away and hurries toward Hildebert's cell.

Once again the abbot is seated at his desk under the tapestry in which the Archangel is weighing souls, and his eyes are the eyes of a judge—strict, not closed-minded but filled with goodness and compassion, yet at the same time implacable in the face of sin. Standing behind the abbot is Brother Robert, the prior. Facing Hildebert, Moira is staring at the tapestry, and on either side of her stand Almodius and Roman. On Almodius's left, near the fireplace, a brother from the scriptorium sits at a little desk holding wax tablets and a stylus. Roman still hasn't met Moira's eyes; he's avoided the moment. Seeing criticism, fright, suffering, or a call for help would devastate him. His feelings of powerlessness and guilt are so strong that it's as if his spirit has been separated from his body, his sinful body, and is watching from above like a ghost visiting the living. The crackling fire in the hearth seems to come from far away, like an echo. He concentrates on keeping his eyes on the abbot's hands—his knotted, wrinkled hands wearing a ring decorated with his coat of arms. The hands lie there motionless, waiting, on the table. Suddenly the fingers stir. The scribe picks up his stylus.

"My daughter, please tell us your Christian name, your parents' names, and your means of subsistence," Hildebert asks.

Moira looks straight at the abbot. In spite of his years, she discerns in his eyes perspicacity, intelligence, and such unusual humanity, inherited no doubt from the time he's spent with the angels, that she loses some of her fear. When Almodius, accompanied by an escort with menacing muscles, had pounded on her door, she saw such hate in his eyes that she found herself fearing for Roman. Back when the master of the scriptorium would come to his brother's sickbed, she always felt uncomfortable with his ambiguous coldness. Whenever he talked to her, his eyes seemed to be throwing darts at her, yet they would fondle her obscenely whenever he thought she wasn't looking.

As for his relationship with Roman, she always found it enigmatic. He seemed to be Roman's protector, devoted and full of compassion, but one day when the injured man lay unconscious she had caught Almodius with his hand at Roman's throat, as if he were about to strangle him. But it had all happened so fast, she wasn't sure what she really saw.

That morning, Almodius had simply told her that the father abbot wanted to speak with her, but he'd said it as if he were inviting her to a torture session. In spite of her questions, he would give no explanation. Living on land belonging to the monastery, she had no choice but to obey Hildebert, as a vassal would a lord who has power over all his subjects. Brewen had tried to intervene, but as one, Almodius's guards had bared their ugly teeth. Useless. She'd signaled to her brother that all would be fine and climbed into the cart. Still, her head was filled with unanswered questions. She worried about Roman, who might have had another accident, or perhaps he was sick, or worse. She of course considered the possibility that she herself might be in danger, but since she couldn't imagine for a moment that Roman had divulged her secret to the abbot, she kept thinking about Roman and tried to forget about Almodius and his henchmen. The sight of the new construction amazed and frightened her. Had they destroyed the church? No, it was still there. But why, then? Her heart leaped when she saw Roman's back in the abbot's cell. Total relief, for he was alive. She made a tremendous effort not to touch him, speak to him, or look at him, but he himself also seemed to be ignoring her. And while other questions, more pernicious questions, filed through her troubled mind, she had to answer the handsome old man with blue eyes.

"My name is Moira," she says. "It's my Christian name, meaning Marie. I'm the daughter of Nolwen and Killian, both deceased. I live in the woods near Beauvoir with my younger brother Brewen, and I still practice the same profession that my father and my father's fathers practiced. As you know, I try to take care of sick bodies," she answers proudly, glancing over at Roman standing still at her side like a statue. "I live off the few animals I raise as well as vegetables from my garden and fruits from the forest."

"How do you heal the sick? What kind of medicines do you use?" Hildebert continues.

"Brother Hosmund can verify that my medicine is like the medicine practiced by the monks, my Father," she says with respectful assurance. "I use simples, trees, animal material. . . . "

She again turns toward her former patient, and this time he begins to blush.

"Do you also pray when you heal?" the abbot wonders, pretending not to notice that his master builder has changed color.

Immediately Moira pales. She grows suspicious.

"I do pray, and not only when I care for the sick," she answers. "I pray to the Holy Mother, the Most High, and especially the first among the angels—"

"The first among the angels . . . hmmm . . . the first during which period of angelic time, Moira?"

At first she doesn't understand his question. Hildebert came to Beauvoir soon after she had taken in Roman, so he knows how she cares for people and he can see right before his very eyes the proof that she's a good healer! A little annoyed, she feels like interrupting this grotesque interrogatory to ask what she's doing here and what exactly the abbot wants. But then she remembers Roman, standing motionless there beside her, and she tries to think: Let's see . . . angelic time, different from human time . . . which period of angelic time? So there must be several periods. The time of the angels, the first angel nearest to God, that's always been Saint Michael! Then she remembers the strange, impressive story of Lucifer that Roman had told her in Saint Martin's Chapel. Might the tricky abbot be asking her if she prays to the devil? How stupid! Why would she invoke someone damned in Hell that her father and mother had always presented as an enemy of God and men?

"The first among them since the angelic time when Lucifer, who disdained God's love for men, these imperfect creatures, was thrown out of heaven with the fallen angels," Moira answers, proud of her Christian teaching. "The Archangel who lives right here, my Father, and who guides all of us: Saint Michael!"

Hildebert permits himself a kindly smile before continuing. This woman is interesting and knows how to speak.

"Good, my daughter. And where do you pray to our Archangel?"

"Well . . . in the village church in Beauvoir, during mass on saints' days, and sometimes in my house."

"Do you not come sometimes to pray here in his dwelling since you are fortunate to live so close by, on monastery lands, and since you are part of his flock?"

Moira begins to sense the abbot's malice and to understand why she's been summoned. Some brother must have seen her inside the monastery when she came to one of her meetings with Roman and told the abbot. With luck, the tattletale hadn't seen Roman, and the only reason Roman is here now is because he knows her. It must have taken the monks some time to identify her, that's why they waited several weeks before sending for her. Three weeks exactly, three weeks during which she hadn't seen Roman. According to her calculations, Saint Martin's Chapel lies outside the monastery, so she doesn't risk much for having gone there at night, even if such visits are prohibited. She lowers her eyes strategically.

"My Father, I must admit . . . I have come, yes, but. . . . " she speaks with hesitation, twisting her hands.

"Speak, my girl. Come on, don't be afraid," he prods gently. "When did you come?"

"Several weeks ago, during Lent. I had the sudden urge to be close to him, to Saint Michael, to pray to him here. I went up to Saint Martin's Chapel . . . but it was after Compline."

"How strong and pressing your faith must be to push you like that at night into our Archangel's arms; don't you think so, Roman?" the abbot asks, looking at the poor petrified monk, once again as white as alabaster.

The business is more serious than she had imagined. Someone had seen her with Roman, perhaps even in a compromising position, when they embraced at the chapel entrance, for example. They must all believe the two are lovers. Now what should she do? Deny everything? She doesn't fear anything, but how about him? How has he disobeyed the Benedictine Rule? What should she do to keep him from being too severely punished?

"There is nothing reprehensible between Brother Roman and me," she blurts out finally.

"Ah, so you do admit that you came to see him secretly?"

Moira doesn't know how to answer without harming Roman. She remains quiet and helplessly lowers her gaze.

"I'm waiting for your answer!"

"My Father, we've done nothing wrong." she says imploringly. "By Saint Michael and all the angels of creation, he's only done his duty as a monk!"

"Lies!" Almodius suddenly blurts out, his eyes blood-red.

Moira and Almodius watch each other like two wild dogs eager to rip each other to bits.

"Quiet!" the abbot intervenes, rising to his feet. "Brother Almodius, you'll speak when I give you permission. Moira, you say that Brother Roman came to your meetings at night out of his 'duty as a monk.' What did he owe to you? What was his debt, and how was he to pay it?"

Almodius frowns. Roman's eyes grow wide, but he doesn't dare intervene. Moira is taken by surprise once again. Hildebert stands there leaning on the table and staring impatiently at the young woman.

"But, but . . . that's not what I meant!" she answers. "Brother Roman didn't owe me anything. I've never made anyone pay for my medicine; we shouldn't make money off human suffering. Sometimes people give me a chicken, and you, my Father, you were kind enough to give me some produce from your gardens—"

"I'm not talking about material things," the abbot interjects, "but rather spiritual debts, just as you've already admitted. What did you want this monk to give you, if not his body? Perhaps the pure soul of a servant of God, perhaps his soul?"

Moira shakes her head, not knowing where to look. Sobs rise up in her throat; she attempts to swallow them, but because she can't understand what's happening, she can't keep tears from veiling her water-green eyes. She looks at the prior standing beneath the tapestry, she can see accusation in his face. By all means, don't look at Roman, and surely not at Almodius.

"Roman's soul belongs to God and means nothing to me!" she finally shouts back to the abbot. "You're mistaken about me, Father." she adds more calmly, but anger still in her voice. "I do not adore Lucifer, and I don't eat either the flesh or the souls of your monks. I prefer my geese! Would you like to know what kind of sustenance he offered, though I never asked for anything?" she asks, turning toward Roman, who lowers his gaze. "He gave me, a Christian, but a poor, ignorant Christian, the nourishing food of God's word. He explained the meaning of Christ's message to me, a poor woman who could only repeat it without knowing what it meant! That's what we talked about, nothing demoniac like you think."

Hildebert slowly sits back down.

"Woman, I haven't come to any judgment yet," he answers coolly. "So you claim that Brother Roman, in the middle of the night and in secret, was teaching you about Christian faith. Is that right?"

"Call it what you want—"

"Yes, words are important!" he says, smiling teasingly. "They can change everything, you know. In this case, we have to determine whether it was supplementary Christian teaching or rather evangelization!"

She had seen the attack coming. So that was the weapon he had been sharpening for a long time and that he now plunges into her heart with a smile. The old man knows everything. Moira must not panic.

"Evangelization? Father, I've already told you that I'm a Christian!" she objects, playing her last card.

"I believe that I, too, may need private lessons from Brother Roman," he continues. "For I wasn't aware that our hagiography included a certain Ogma!"

She freezes. Roman closes his eyes. Almodius jubilates in silence, his eyes bright. The scribe sits waiting, his stylus raised. Hildebert decides not to pursue his advantage. He stands up and walks over to Moira.

"Come, my daughter, let's stop this verbal jousting. I'm going to ask you one final question, and your answer will be capital. Think carefully; it's useless to lie. Our subprior saw you beside the pond. Do you admit that you were praying to pagan gods?"

Almodius! So it was him, the spy, the tattletale, the traitor! It wasn't Roman! That thought welled up within her, it occupied her for a moment. What should she say? He must have seen her near the pond. Had he also heard her invoke Ogma and ask him to protect the mountain's secret? Roman hadn't said anything, she's sure of that, but might Almodius have seen them in Saint Martin's Chapel? Had he heard her tell the story to Roman? How could she find out?

She realizes that the only way out is to admit her beliefs. Hildebert knows about them in any case, and she would never be able to convince the wise old man otherwise. If she doesn't deny everything, and if that's the end of the interrogation, then he can't find out what she told Roman. But if he keeps asking questions, then. . . .

"Father, I pray to Saint Michael, and sometimes I pray to Ogma, his ancestor. It's true," she says, deciding how much she can admit, "I am a Christian, but I also remain faithful to my people's ancient gods. Brother Roman was the first to learn it, and he tried to get me to give up my old beliefs by showing me the beauty and strength of the Bible, which apparently doesn't tolerate any competition. He made every effort, using reason and his monk's pure heart, to convert mine," she adds in tears. "He recounted marvelous stories, told me about heroic combats, pronounced words of such intelligence and love. He showed me my errors without ever accusing me. I opened my soul to Christ's message, but I have not been able to erase the memory of the celestial messengers of my forebears, and I've continued to honor their memory. There's the truth, Father; I've told you all my sins. Now do with me what you want."

Silence hangs heavy. Moira is trembling. Now the truth will come out, in the abbot's words. Now he'll speak about the secret or remain quiet forever. She realizes that beside her Roman is also trembling. Hildebert has crossed his arms and stands there calmly. The prior, Almodius, and the scribe disappear completely from Moira's mind. There's just the abbot, Roman, and her. Just those three.

"There is only one God, Moira," the abbot finally says, his voice amazingly gentle. "You cannot unite in the same prayer both darkness and light, both the revelation of Christ and the adoration of the Golden Calf. Of the past, you must of course revere the memory of human beings—your parents' love, your mother's breast, your father's arms—but not those spirits thirsty for sacrificial blood as they drag you down the path toward the shadows."

Moira raises her eyes. She looks gratefully at Hildebert. She holds her right hand tight against her coat so as not to enlace her fingers in Roman's, so as not to grasp his robe, for she realizes that she now has proof of his love, his loyalty, and his trust. Roman had not said anything; Almodius had not heard anything. Roman had kept their secret, had preserved a link between them that was more powerful than his deference to his father and brothers.

He does indeed love her, with a love like hers for him, the love of one human being for another. And there's where Moira's strength lies; it makes her invincible, whatever the abbot may decide. Past and present are united in her heart, the future is no longer important.

"I believe you understand me, Moira," the abbot continues. "You must renounce Ogma and the gods of your ancestors. Forever."

Moira awakens from her moment of sweet torpor. Renounce them? Abandon the past now that it's taken on its full meaning?

"I cannot, Father," she answers.

"How dare you say that?" he asks. "You clearly have admitted a sin of the utmost gravity, and then you say in the same voice that you would like to continue persevering in your sins! Are you aware of what you are saying? You confide in monks that you venerate the devil and that your desire is to continue venerating the devil! Do you think that I can accept that? You're living on my lands, my daughter, on sacred ground, chosen by the Archangel. Do you think that I can tolerate giving a parcel of that land over to Satan? Abjure your religion, Moira, abjure. You have no other choice!"

"I know that in your clemency, Father, you are offering me forgiveness on that condition," she says in a strained voice, "and I thank you for your magnanimity. Unfortunately I can't accept that forgiveness, for I cannot renounce the blood that flows within me, whatever its nature may be. I am yours. Do with me what you think necessary. I'm in your hands and submit completely to your will."

At these words, the abbot leaps from his chair, steps toward her, and points an accusing finger.

"My will? My will? My will is indeed all-powerful, equal to your crime! Do you know that I could give you over to the secular authorities? They hate even more than I do what you represent. Richard will put you to torture, and that will be quite different from the polite conversation we are having. Have you never heard of the Manicheans, who insisted on praying both to a god of light and a god of darkness, on worshiping both good and evil? They were burned, yes, burned, at the stake! That's what you risk if you refuse to renounce the devil within you."

Moira drops her head. Her empty gaze takes in the cell's dirt floor, earth from the Mount. The chains tying her to this earth are stronger than the ones the abbot evokes. The pure power of the tie between Roman and her is more important than her own life. Their love was never made real by the union of their bodies, and she suddenly realizes that that's why it's so strong, that's what will make it eternal—the union of their minds, their souls. The body is nothing. It will return to nothingness, but the soul will come back in another body, again and again. Different human forms will follow each other, just as they have done since the world began. Her soul will not die but continue, migrant yet eternal, in harmony with its universe, and richer for having experienced this man's love. Moira thinks about the suffering that can be imposed on a body, the suffering that Hildebert seems to be threatening. She must not give in, not dirty her soul with physical torment. A wave of fear engulfs her, but she gets control of herself again. Her decision is irrevocable. Her only wish is to commune once more with Roman's spirit. She looks intently at him. He's looking straight ahead, and then a breath of life seems to startle him. He is about to turn toward her, he must look at her one last time. . . .

"Don't count on help from Brother Roman," the abbot says, a metallic gleam in his eyes, and Roman goes back to his former posture. "He can't do anything for you. Your fate depends on me, but mostly on you, yourself," he adds less harshly. "I'm asking you one last time, Moira. Do you renounce your ungodly beliefs?"

If only it were over! Moira can't stand it any longer, and Roman seems about to collapse. Sweat is dripping down his temples, and it looks like he might faint. With a final gesture, Moira shakes her head again and awaits the abbot's lightning bolts to strike her. His response is totally unexpected.

"Moira, on this Tuesday after Easter, in front of these witnesses," he announces as if reading her sentence, "you've admitted your sin. I, Hildebert, the third Benedictine abbot of Mont-Saint-Michel, I remember that Jesus died for the sins of mankind and that he rose again. I'll grant you four days and four nights to pray and reflect on the mystery of faith. Sunday, the first Sunday after Easter, I myself will come at daybreak to hear you recant. If you refuse to abjure your religion, then your possessions will be confiscated, and you'll be excommunicated and banished forever from my lands, you and your brother, and neither you nor any of your descendants will ever be allowed to come back. I've spoken. Now, get out of my sight. Return to your dark forests and your cursed dwelling. I'll be praying, asking God to help you. Go now!"

Moira stands for a moment in shock, she's so surprised by the verdict. She looks around like a caged animal who suddenly sees that the door is open. Almodius is fuming as he strives with all his strength to keep from protesting, to keep from leaping on her and grabbing her by the throat. Roman weeps in silence. Hildebert turns and walks slowly to his desk and, helped by the prior, collapses in his chair. He looks exhausted. His heavenly gaze meets hers, a little shocked that she's still there. Then, after a furtive glance at Roman, she turns away, opens the door, and runs out toward the Beauvoir forest as if pursued by a terrible monster.

Moira,

    Master Roger agreed to bring you this letter, but he is totally unaware of the agitation in the monastery that's spreading like an epidemic and might contaminate all our lands. I'm afraid for you, Moira; I fear the petty anger of ordinary folks without education, and I fear the villagers' vengeful flame directed against those who are different from them. I'm afraid they've forgotten the pain and suffering you've relieved them of and that they may try to avert their fright by making you suffer. Roger doesn't know anything about all that yet, and he still remembers that you healed his daughter Brigitte. But tomorrow he may see you as the devil's servant. And yet, Moira, you could see for yourself our dear abbot's sharp intelligence and the goodness of his heart, so quick to forgive our trespasses, no matter how serious they are.

Do you understand that I entrusted my trespasses to him without hesitation, as you did? Divine light possesses that man, and he
is indeed merciful. He's waiting for you. He gave up an important
trip in order to stay here close to you. He knows that you won't
run away, and he is praying day and night for you, for your salvation and for your soul. He loves you as God loves you, and he
wants to keep you in his heart. Don't reject his generosity and
kindness. They are unusual for such an important lord. Welcome
him on Sunday like Christ who lives within him! Open your home
to him, let him cleanse you of your sins! One word from you is
enough, and please, Moira, say that word!

I'm writing in the secret of candlelight, seen only by Brother
Hosmund, in the makeshift infirmary where I found refuge yesterday. My body has once again betrayed me, and I can do nothing
for it. Nor can anyone else. I'm writing to you about Hildebert's
love, about the love of the Most High, but all the while my whole
being is shouting out another love, relegated to suspicion and concupiscence. And yet it came to me like a violent dagger thrust that
I loved you without shadows, without sin, with the simple desire
of knowing that you exist, that you are close to me. We are already
beyond the corporeal world, we've gone beyond what our flesh requires of us, and the recent events have made us strangers to the
ephemeral satisfactions and tortures of the flesh. You loved me
when I lay dying, feverish, and losing my life's blood. I'll love you
whether you're a Christian or a secret pagan, as long as you are
here!

We can always find ways to see each other and to communicate.
But how can we, if you are banished? Our first meeting was a gift
from heaven. Yes, Moira, today I bless the brigand and his hunting
knife! Tomorrow I would bare my chest to him again if his knife
could lead me to you! I'm always thinking about those days in your
house in Beauvoir. How sweet they were; it seems that they existed outside of time, removed from this world's contingencies
that are assailing us now! I've forgotten everything my body suffered. What I remember is your voice, the first time I heard it,

your loving expression, your pale hands, your evanescent presence by my side, like an angel. Yesterday, Moira, yesterday heaven's generosity was even greater. After granting me life, heaven granted you the same favor, and I have no doubt that heaven approves of our love. So now do you have the heart to destroy everything, now that life is opening up before us? Why? For this land you'll be banished from if you remain faithful to it? To save old beliefs that will disappear along with you? Our love is alive, and its enemy is a dead religion, a defunct era, an empty shell that lost its soul centuries ago! Relax, I've not breathed a word about your secret, but I haven't yet had the strength to change my master's drawings, for they are his testament. What keeps you from living will disappear in a few years.

I beg you, Moira, don't exile yourself from an existence heaven is promising to us. Protect our love, the most important thing in the world, and we'll construct a new land, not a land filled with corpses, but with the roots of trees!

Don't leave me alone with my stones, Moira. Without you, they are cold and mute, like my soul. Without you, I'm a prisoner in a dark fortress, and my heart is a dungeon. From here on my knees I implore you! Give me peace, my beloved, give us peace!

I'll see you soon, my earthly angel, I'll see you soon. Promise me.

Roman

Destroy this letter as soon as you've read it, to be on the safe side.

Brewen is standing still beside the smoking fireplace. It's dark outside. Moira breathes in the smell of the manuscript, her eyes closed. Her russet curls caress the parchment. She's racked by quiet sobs. She lifts up her head. Her face is sad, tearless but sad. And then a ray of hope brightens her countenance, a weak, pale ray that grows brighter until it becomes incandescent like the sun. Finally—the enchantment of love shared, unveiled, declared! A shadow passes over her face and her features stiffen, then she breaks into a smile. She listens to her desire. She dares to believe in Roman, in herself, in them together; she dares to renounce the past. Everything is different now that he has declared his love! They'll be able to see each other, hidden from others but in their hearts' true light. Moira hesitates, her soul torn. Her fingers retrace Roman's words, his lovely upright script on the vellum tanned by monks. Suddenly, someone's pounding on the door of their hut. Moira looks at her brother and hurriedly burns the letter in the candle's flame. Fire had given life to the letter; now fire destroys it. The pounding grows louder. The unhoped-for letter is now nothing but ashes. Moira walks over and opens the door.

"HOW AMAZING!" EXCLAIMS Roland d'Aubigny, bishop of Avranches, standing at the building site of the choir crypt. "My dear Hildebert, what a change in just one week! Last Thursday the mountain was bare when I came to consecrate the holy oils. Today it's beautiful, it's swarming with activity, the abbey church is being built, it's rising toward the heavens!"

"Yes, Monsignor," the abbot answers. "On Maundy Thursday, the mountain was still wearing its rough homespun monk's frock, just like me and my sons. Now, and for decades to come, it'll be putting on the simple courage and pure strength of all these people who, far from being simple ornaments, will be devoting their lives to building the basilica."

The two men look coldly at each other. Although the April weather is mild, Roland d'Aubigny is wrapped in bearskins as, escorted by his four vicars and the father abbot, he walks through the sweating, half-naked workmen. His impromptu arrival in the church just after the conventual mass surprised the entire community. The tide was high and he had to take an uncomfortable boat. But Mont-Saint-Michel is not Cluny, and only the abbey in Burgundy has the privilege of exemption, freeing it from the yoke of the secular clergy and from reporting to the pope. On the Mount, in spite of the abbot's residence, the bishop is in his home territory and has the right to show up at any moment, day or night. The bishop, younger than Hildebert, is Aubert's successor in charge of the diocese, and he's passionate about the holy mountain. Sometimes the fifty-year-old bishop seems omnipresent on the island, and sometimes he seems to disdain it, concentrating instead on the bishopric's lands. He's close to Richard II, and shares his noble attributes: fine clothing, palace, banquets, hunting parties, women. A handsome man, blond and lithe, Roland d'Aubigny looks haughtily at the abbot.

"Our walk has made me thirsty, my dear Abbot," he says, wiping the sweat from his face with his sleeve, "and all this dust is scorching my throat. Might you agree to proposing a little of that good Beaune wine your cellarer gets from Cluny?"

"Our home is your home, my dear Roland, and my cellar is yours," Hildebert answers sharply, a little annoyed at having to share a pitcher of his favorite wine with this worldly drunk. "Let's go to my cell where we can be more comfortable, and you can warm up by my fireplace."

"By the way, I don't see your master builder anywhere, that gifted student of Pierre de Nevers, for whom I shed tears daily during prayers."

"Brother Roman is not well; he's resting in the infirmary. This damp climate exacerbates the wounds he received when he stood up against an evil bandit preying on pilgrims."

"Oh, yes. I remember something about that heroic act!" the bishop answers, raising his arms. "But that happened back around the time of the dedication festival. I thought that since he had such good care, he'd be back on his feet."

Hildebert pretends not to understand the allusion. He continues on toward his cell without pausing. Off in the distance he can see Brother Bernard, Roman's assistant, helping Master Jehan supervise raising the huge blocks of stone.

"Brother Roman's mind and soul are made from the hardest granite there is, and he's proven to be a remarkable master builder. But his body was weakened by his struggle against death. The wound is near his heart. Every now and then he loses his strength, but a few days of rest put him back on his feet and he is able to work with more energy than ever."

"It's true that some people's hearts are weaker than others," Roland d'Aubigny notes. "Please, my dear Hildebert, after you!"

The abbot enters his cell ahead of the bishop. He asks the lay brother stoking the fire to bring them a pitcher of his Burgundy red and two goblets. The prelate doesn't know that Hildebert's good friend, Abbot

Odilon, has just sent him several casks of a delicious white wine made from grapes grown by the Cluny monks around Auxerre, where vineyards had first been planted by the Romans. Clearly, Roland hasn't come just to enjoy his wine cellar, and the abbot is pleased about that. But the bishop's words notwithstanding, he doubts that he appeared just to admire the construction site. The bishop's ambiguous words suggest something else entirely, and don't bode well at all. So the abbot decides to make the first move.

"Have a seat, monsignor!" says Hildebert, offering him a chair across from the desk where he himself sits down. "Now that we're seated comfortably in this ancient cell, by the warm fire, tell me, have you been pleased with your visit?"

"I've been overjoyed by what I've seen, absolutely overjoyed. But to be completely satisfied, I need to complete my mission. I've got a curious story to tell you—oh, nothing very formal, but there's information I couldn't pass along while others were within hearing."

"I'm all ears, Monsignor, and I can assure you that the only ears here are mine, and the only spirit the Archangel's," he answers, gesturing toward the tapestry.

Just then the lay brother knocks on the door. He serves the two dignitaries and retires. The bishop tastes the elixir, congratulates the abbot for having such a valuable friend as Odilon, and clears his throat.

"It's about something that happened yesterday, at night," he begins. "It's really my responsibility, but I thought I should also alert you."

Roland pauses to glance at the abbot, who, beginning to worry, is filled with foreboding. The bishop seems pleased with the effect his announcement is having and takes another sip of wine.

"Can you imagine," he continues, his manner falsely lighthearted, "that I've discovered a heretic in my diocese, and, what's more, on your lands!"

Hildebert grows as still as a corpse.

"Richard II's soldiers arrested her yesterday evening," the bishop continues with obvious pleasure. "She's locked up under guard in one of his prisons, in Avranches, not far from my palace. I haven't yet interrogated her; I thought you and I should talk before I did. The prisoner is a healer named Moira."

The abbot seems to come back to life. Standing up suddenly, he knocks over his pewter goblet with the back of his hand. The red liquid spreads out over the table.

"You didn't have the right!" he shouts. "Moira lives in Beauvoir, and that's my domain. She's one of my people!"

"Ah, so you know the creature?"

"Someone came to speak to you; I demand to know who did! I judged that woman two days ago, and she has until Sunday to abjure her ungodly faith. If she doesn't, she'll be excommunicated and exiled from my lands!"

"Only to come find refuge on mine? A lovely sentence, Father Abbot!" Roland answers, his eyes as full of fire as the abbot's. "You shouldn't blame any of your sons for demonstrating the lofty views appropriate in such a serious affair, for it extends far beyond the borders of your domain."

"Who?" the abbot repeats, standing erect behind the table. "Are you going to tell me who committed such an odious act?"

"Brother Almodius, your subprior, came to ask my opinion about this business. He wisely thought that I should be aware of the woman's heresy, for heresy is a crime of lese-majesté, a crime against all Christians, and not simply against your monastery. You know that. And so you should have told me about it. I'm not holding it against you, since your subprior did it for you."

"Almodius did not have the authority to act in my name! The traitor will be severely punished."

"Come now, my dear abbot," the bishop answers, pouring more wine in the goblets. "Don't get so upset. True, Almodius failed in his duty of obedience, but his failure was motivated by a higher, more imperious authority. The crime is not your son's; it resides only in the damned soul of that pagan woman. She's the one who needs to be chastised publicly."

"What are you going to do with her?" Hildebert asks resignedly.

"What you yourself failed to do! Sound the depths of her heart and determine how rotten it is!"

"By force!" the abbot says, getting angry again. "Quite right, I refused to use force, because torture is unworthy of the man of God I claim to be and of the Church I serve! Might you have forgotten Pope Gregory's edict, in which he said that the Church must not shed blood?"

"Shed blood, no. But as bishop, I'm the successor of the apostles, and it's my job to determine the danger this woman brings by using any means I think appropriate, and to pronounce a decision in the name of the Church! I won't punish her myself, of course. I'll leave that to Duke Richard, as I should. It's his job to enforce peace on earth and to help the Church in its battle against the devil, using force if necessary."

"Richard is not an executioner!" the abbot objects.

"Of course not. He's a good prince, a lover of justice, and a fervent Christian. As soon as he received my messenger, he sent an armed detachment to apprehend the so-called healer and make sure she was secured. Fortunately, princes who underestimate heresy's perils are rare. That reminds me that six years ago, the same year that Richard married Judith, the same year she died, the year we found Aubert's relics in this very ceiling," he says, looking up, "the year the duke made the decision to build the great abbey church and the year you brought in the honorable Pierre de Nevers, that very year, the king of France, Robert II, appropriately called the Pious, had the Manichean canons burned. Normandy is not France, but I imagine that our good Duke Richard certainly remembered that precedent when he learned that the Mount's blessed earth, which he cherishes so much and where he's funding the future abbey, was harboring such evil in its bosom!"

It's a perfidious attack, but it's skillfully done. Hildebert tries to evaluate the situation pragmatically. Moira is already in the hands of the bishop and prince. For the moment there's nothing he can do for her. Because the woman foolishly refused to abjure her faith here in his cell, and now because of the subprior's horrible act, the affair has moved to a different level. Now it's become political, a struggle among three men: Richard, Roland, and Hildebert. The abbot's authority has been seriously questioned, and Hildebert thinks that perhaps even the building project might be threatened. No! Richard cannot jeopardize this grand project that will be his glory! All the same, the abbot must soon arrange a meeting with his lord and try to reestablish his influence, in the hope of preventing the worst for Moira. For the moment, he must fight the skillful prelate, who so far has parried all his arguments. But the abbot still has a weapon left, a sword he uses with the greatest dexterity: the sacred word.

"Be it far from me to try to preach to a man like you, so versed in celestial things," he begins, pouring a little more wine, "but as I share this holy drink with you, I'm reminded of Christ's Last Supper and the words he used when he was arrested. Peter pulled out his sword to defend him, and Jesus said: 'Put up your sword!' If the life of the Lord himself doesn't justify spilling blood, then no life does. Our swords, for those of us who serve God, are words, the Lord's words. We must convert by using words, not weapons."

"Christ also said: 'I came not to bring peace but the sword,' indicating that the sword of truth is preferable to peace built on error and lies."

The two men survey each other.

"I realize that our visions do not agree, even when we talk about Holy Scripture. So let's appeal to the pope, letting him decide!" says Hildebert sharply.

"I'm the pope's representative!" the bishop answers, sitting up straighter. "It seems to me that you might be confusing the Mount with Cluny," he adds in his honeyed voice. "Is that an unexpected effect of Odilon's good wine?"

"Odilon is a saintly man," the abbot responds shortly. "Like Benedict and all of our order's members, he refutes violence in the struggle against heresy. We can vanquish evil only through the witness of prayer, faith, and love. Of course, we must have the courage to break with this world's illusory enchantments," he adds, glancing at the bishop's fur coat, "in order to feel the full power of heavenly love and faith."

"I understand that you find the company of angels edifying. That's an ideal that brings honor to you and to those in your order. But I didn't realize that your dear Archangel Saint Michael slew the dragon using only fervent words!"

"Saint Michael used his sword against other angels," Hildebert says, furious at the bishop's condescending tone. "Lucifer knew his mistake. He knew full well he was sinning, and it was a combat between equals. This woman, on the contrary, sinned from ignorance and not from pride."

"From ignorance? And yet I believe I heard that she had been taught by one of your intensely dedicated sons, cutting into the precious little time he had for sleep."

"My monk's lives, sleep, and other activities are my business and no one else's."

"As you wish. I have no desire to infringe on your duties, my dear Abbot. I have my own, and they are heavy enough. And now I must be on my way to interrogate that demon. I bid you good-bye."

Without another word, the bishop rises and leaves the cell to join his vicars waiting outside. Shocked by the turn of events, Hildebert remains alone in his cell. Then he is hit by a cataclysm like those that strike the mountain: a fury that he has never experienced before, a boiling rage, frightening to him because it's so foreign to his nature and vocation. The old man, overwhelmed, is unable to calm his raging anger. Like a young man, he leaps up and rushes out of his hut, just as the bell is ringing the sixth hour. He bursts into the refectory, where the hungry monks stand waiting. Brother Robert, the prior, is not at his place. The day before, Hildebert had sent the prior in place of himself to a high-level Benedictine meeting in Anjou, so that he could hear Moira's abjuration on Sunday. From behind his empty plate, Roman raises his head to watch the abbot come in. Roman's face is ashen, the same color as his eyes, but this morning, when Master Roger came to the infirmary to reassure him that he had delivered the letter, Roman got up and went back to work; he would no longer try to hide from his brothers and the workmen what he had quit trying to hide from Moira and from himself. The abbot stares furiously at him. Roman feels punishment's pain burning into him, but Hildebert keeps walking and heads toward the subprior.

"Almodius!" the abbot sputters. "Follow me at once to my cell! The rest of you, eat!" he shouts at the astonished monks.

He whirls around and, followed by the head of the scriptorium, storms out of the refectory. He leads Almodius into his cell and slams the door.

The sound of the door slamming startles the subprior, and his ears begin to redden. The abbot sits down at his desk, petrifying his unworthy son with a burning look.

"My Father, I—" Almodius begins.

"Quiet!" Hildebert interrupts him, his voice crackling with anger. "Your words shall not corrupt the holiness of this place! You, taken in by Abbot Maynard when you were only a child! You, whose body and mind we've nourished, whose soul we've forged, whom I raised to the rank of subprior, to whom I entrusted the scriptorium key and with it the memory of all Christendom and our community's knowledge. You have betrayed us all, you miserable worm!"

"My Father," Almodius answers tentatively, frightened by the abbot's uncustomary anger, "I admit I disregarded your orders. I was led by the faith you and your predecessor instilled in me as a boy. My faith is stronger than anything else, and it serves the sanctity of this place whose integrity I thought was being threatened."

"It's my job to preserve this mountain's integrity!" the abbot thunders. "Your deed puts it at risk from the bishop and the prince! 'Obeying one's superiors is obeying God,' Benedict wrote. By your disobedience, you have demeaned the Lord himself! You have repudiated everything: your blood family that entrusted you to God, your brother monks, your spiritual father, and the family of angels!"

"My sin is nothing compared to the sin of my Brother Roman, who let himself be tempted by the devil's sensual pleasures," retorts the subprior, raising his head defiantly. "Yes, it's true that I disobeyed you, but it was to save our abbey's soul, for it has been infected by that infernal female and by your soft, old heart!"

Hearing these words, Hildebert nearly suffocates with rage. Red as a beet, he begins to cough violently and is forced to try to catch his breath before he can continue speaking.

"For some time," says the abbot, pausing to spit into his handkerchief, "I've been worried about you. You've been looking less and less humble. At night you've often been out of the dormitory, and during the day you've been leaving the monastery for no obvious reason and suddenly straying from your daily tasks. I didn't think you had broken completely with our deepest convictions. Today I see, and I understand. This old heart you criticize can hear the arrogance and ungratefulness of your mouth and can see the mortal passion that's eating away at your heart. Yes, I understand your hate for your brother Roman, for the woman, for our clemency toward those whose sins are due to naïveté and powerlessness rather than to vanity. That's what faith has done to you," he concludes, breathing heavily. "Almodius, I relieve you immediately of all your duties. I'll call the chapter council together right away to begin the official exclusion process. When Robert gets back from Anjou, I'll designate a new subprior and choose another brother for the scriptorium. You have already abandoned us. I'm just making your choice official. I only hope that you are not irretrievably lost and that you will be able to make your way back to us."

Hildebert holds his head in his hands, like a father broken by a favorite son who has come to kill him.

"You don't understand at all!" Almodius suddenly exclaims, walking toward the abbot. "You prefer forgiving the weak and unfaithful and blaming me because I didn't give in! Your justice is arbitrary and good only for the feeble. I'm not sorry for denouncing your justice to the bishop. He will be able to eradicate the evil!" he shouts, fingers balled into fists, inches away from Hildebert, whose breathing grows more and more labored. "Your so-called clemency is nothing but cowardice, and your faith has become your alibi! I. . . . "

The monk pauses when he sees the abbot's face turn pale. The patriarch's eyes grow wide and his mouth opens, but no sound emerges. A little foam appears at the corners of his mouth. Hildebert brings his hands up to his chest and collapses onto the table with a groan. Almodius is stupefied. Not knowing what to do, he waits motionless for a moment, then moves closer and timidly helps the abbot to sit up. Hildebert is white and stiff as a corpse. Almodius bends down. He's still breathing. The young monk moves the abbot's hand and checks for a heartbeat. It's still beating, but feebly and unevenly. Hildebert isn't dead yet. Almodius runs out of the hut.

A FEW MINUTES later, Hildebert is lying on his bed, mute, motionless, his eyes haggard. The fire in the fireplace casts reddish shadows in the room.

Brother Hosmund is bent over the sick man as he tries to get him to swallow some medicine.

Beside the bed, Almodius is praying on his knees. Outside, all the monks, priests, and lay brothers, who gathered at the rattle's first sound, are quietly chanting the *Credo in unum Deum*. Hosmund straightens up and meets Almodius's somber stare. He can see in his eyes what Almodius is wondering.

"I don't know, my brother," answers the infirmarer. "He is closed up within himself, dead to the world. His muscles and tongue are stiff. It must be his heart, too worn out to keep beating. No fever, but intense internal exhaustion. His age, the stress related to construction, the recent events," he says, bowing his head. "Anger is always dangerous for the soul. We must pray for him. I'll take care of the rest, with the help of our Lord."

"And mine, Brother Hosmund," says Almodius firmly. "Since Brother Robert is not here, I'll take charge of the abbey . . . and of our father's care, too, until he's back on his feet."

"Fine, Brother Almodius. I'm going to the infirmary to stir up some ointments and boil some simples. Letting a little blood might help relieve some of his bad humors. Oh, my father," he says, his big, bearded face suddenly bathed in tears, "our dear father. Don't you think we should send for the prior and ask the bishop to come for the last sacraments?"

Almodius puts a comforting hand on the infirmarer's shoulders.

"Come now, my brother. Our affliction is infinite, but it cannot help our father. We must pray, we must all ask the Archangel to bring succor to his soul! Brother Robert will soon be back to add his prayers to ours, but there's no reason to rush things. On the other hand, it does seem wise to ask the bishop to come to anoint the abbot. I'll send Brother Guillaume to Avranches. Our father needs calm and serenity, so I'll see that our brothers don't disturb him. You and I will take turns at his bedside, while the brothers raise their fervent prayers to the Lord. I'm counting on you, Brother Hosmund."

Almodius turns around. Through the hut's only window he can see the worried monks gathered outside. He goes to report on the sick man's condition and give them orders. As he is speaking, already in mourning, his eyes catch Roman's hard gaze, which seems to defy him in wordless indictment. But the master builder says nothing and joins his brothers walking toward the church where they will implore Saint Michael with their pure tears and their fervent prayers.

In the evening, calm settles back over the mountain, a calm that's not of true peace but simply of submissive waiting for the divine decision. The heavens themselves seem to be withholding their evening breezes. The gray clouds dissipate, the weak sun fades slowly away, and the dark night slips furtively in, lightly and delicately, like the petals of a lunar calyx. The sea has risen, is singing its sweet songs, flattering the earth, stammering its ephemeral murmurs against the rock. Up above, everything is waiting. The construction site seems abandoned, and the cranes erected for lifting stones stand there like gallows, imaginary corpses swinging beneath them. No stars in the dark sky. No light in the church, which night has emptied of humans and filled with spirits. Only the arched windows of Saint Martin's Chapel are glowing with their yellow haloes.

THE NEXT DAY, Friday, Roland d'Aubigny gallops up at low tide. The abbot is still hanging between life and death; mute and rigid, he's suspended between two worlds. Almodius has not left him for one moment; he has pronounced the three prayers that normally the prior must recite over desperately sick people, recited the *Confiteor* for Hildebert who is unable to speak, administered when Hosmund joined his brothers praying all night in the chapel.

Soon after dawn, as he came out of the sanctuary whose stones reminded him of Moira, Roman had tried to see Hildebert, but the subprior would not allow him in and closed the door in his face. Not eager to start another quarrel, Roman didn't persist. Instead, he went off to the building site to greet those workmen who hadn't slept right there on the site as they began. Now Roman's soul oscillates between Hildebert and Moira, the two people he loves, for their fate is uncertain and all he can do for them is pray. He supplicates the Most High fervently and hopefully, without bitterness, in the certainty that heaven will help them. Last evening, standing in Saint Martin's Chapel, he'd turned with his whole being, with a love unfelt before, toward the Archangel. That new love came without worry, without pain, without regret, and looked resolutely toward the future. He'd confidently entrusted his love to the mouth of the first among the angels, and he could feel the angel's spirit comforting him. Yes, in the deep night's shadows, the invisible had enveloped him in its blue-gray breath.

When Roman sees the bishop and his entourage, hope washes over him, and he recalls in all his senses the mystical moment the night had held for him. He places himself in the bishop's path and waits.

But Roland d'Aubigny passes without pausing, without even a glance at him, and goes directly into Hildebert's cell. Brother Hosmund is sent away immediately. Almodius and the bishop are alone with the abbot to anoint his eyes, ears, nose, lips, hands, feet, and loins, all those places where sin can enter. To redeem his sins that found life through his five senses, they wash a crucifix in water mixed with wine, symbolizing the blood from Christ's five wounds, to wash away the sins of the world. Roman meanwhile questions Hosmund, who can impart no new knowledge as to the patient's condition. Roman can only keep waiting, and praying.

FRIDAY, THE SECOND night of prayers. This time, the bluish mist has a strange scent, strong and sickening, like burning feathers. Roman would have loved to have talked about it with Hildebert. "But the abbot is still unconscious," Hosmund had told him, "carefully guarded by Almodius." During the day, nothing had filtered down of the conversation between the bishop and the subprior after the prelate had given the abbot the last sacraments. Nothing about Moira. But a voice as sweet as celestial breath orders Roman to keep faith in her, in himself, in the winged protector watching over them. In the secret of his silent prayer to Saint Michael, he even forgives Almodius his infamy concerning the young woman. Isn't the subprior's total abnegation regarding the old abbot's care proof of his remorse and of his desire for redemption?

During the day, the abbot's face had twisted into a rictus resembling a smile, and he'd opened his eyes before dropping back once more into the space between two worlds. A messenger was sent to alert Duke Richard, while Hosmund and Almodius spread a hair shirt out on the floor and traced out a cross on it with ashes before placing Hildebert's motionless body on the cloth.

THE THIRD NIGHT in Saint Martin's Chapel, between Saturday and Sunday, between light and darkness, between angels and demons. The celestial vapor fails to bring comfort to Roman. He feels a chilly dampness beneath his ribs, near his heart, and struggles for breath. With the first glimmers of light in the Sunday sky, Hildebert wakes up from his long torpor. Almodius raises his head.

Under the Saint Michael tapestry, the two men look at each other. The subprior, alone with the dying man, doesn't say a word. The abbot struggles to move, to pronounce words, to throw off his serge blanket, as if he wants to get up and complete an important mission. His veins swell with thick blood that seems to be coagulating in the cold air. His face and neck turn blue, he begins to pant, eyes fixed on the wood ceiling. Suddenly his body gives up. He tries to rise one more time, makes one last effort, and then his breathing simply stops. Hildebert falls back. One last gasp escapes from his throat. Then the silence returns.

9

I T WAS AS NOISY AS A SCHOOL LUNCHROOM WHEN DIMITRI brought to the table the two sea bass he, burning his fingers, had just taken off the grill in the fireplace.

"Fish again!" Sebastian exclaimed. "This is getting a little tiresome. Couldn't we buy some nice, juicy steaks for a change?"

"Poor little boy," Florence retorted. She herself was getting tired of eating bass, though it had been caught that very morning. "You can always go console yourself with a hamburger and ketchup if you don't like it. And do the grocery shopping for the next time."

"Okay, okay, Flo," Sebastian answered. "Relax, in two days it'll be my turn. I'll go to the supermarket and buy some nice rib-eye steaks and some fat sausages, that's for sure!"

Dimitri went back to get the potatoes cooking in the coals. He had gone to a lot of trouble to get one of the few commercial fisherman living on the Mount to sell him at a reasonable price these two fish, which normally would have gone to market in Paris and ended up in a Parisian restaurant. Dimitri was about thirty years old, thin, a little timid, but endearing. He was coquettish and delicate, with feminine movements, and he usually kept his distance, because his male colleagues often made fun of him.

"So, Seb," began Patrick Fenoy, Johanna's assistant, "you're like the medieval construction workers at Mont-Saint-Michel. Before they would agree to come work, they always demanded assurance that they would not have to eat barracuda, sea salmon, or sturgeon every day."

"Meat sticks to your bones better in a climate like this!" added Sebastian. "I'll never get used to this humidity. It's freezing. Have you noticed that our sheets are always damp when we climb into bed? And our clothing always stinks, even when it's clean and we manage to get it dry. It smells like seaweed. Ugh!"

"Try to imagine what people lived like during the Middle Ages. There weren't any glass windows, just some little openings covered with poor-quality paper blackened by candle and fireplace soot. I recall that they did use to heat the scriptorium here, contrary to the normal Benedictine practice of heating only the kitchen and the infirmary—they heated the scriptorium, but not because they were concerned about the copyists' comfort. Rather, they worried that otherwise the room would have been so humid their precious books would have rotted!" Patrick answered.

That's what things were like in the archeologists' group house. And how they had been for the three weeks since their project had gotten under way. Patrick Fenoy was giving them a lecture on the medieval history of Mont-Saint-Michel. That would have been enjoyable if the man had shown a little more humility in his words, and especially in the looks he threw at Johanna. His face wore the expression of a superior being not pleased to be obeying orders given by a younger woman with less experience. As he saw it, she didn't know anything about the Mount's past and had been parachuted in by unspeakable means that were no secret to anyone. He didn't know exactly how it all had happened, but it was hard for him to swallow being passed over for his rightful position by this little goose who had never even worked with the grand master, Roger Calfon.

Johanna stared at Patrick Fenoy's thin, sharp features. She looked at his dark eyes hidden by little glasses, the beginning of a beard. She examined his straight brown hair, already thinning, his ashen hue, his fingertips yellowed by the cigarettes he rolled himself, and his holey gray sweater. She herself wasn't much more elegant in her rough wool jacket, but she was getting tired of the arrogant, disdainful man and all his bragging. All in all, things weren't going too badly. Dimitri was an asexual angel, Sebastian an eternal adolescent of thirty, like some she had already known at Cluny. Jacques was a heavyset, self-effacing man, a little self-conscious about his weight but very effective on the job; Florence was a small, lively woman whom Johanna enjoyed, even though they hadn't become close friends. Patrick was the only one who presented a problem. She couldn't trust the one person who to her was the most indispensable, her assistant. Of course, she could understand why he was hostile, but she thought his bitterness would disappear with a little time. But not only was his rancor tenacious, it seemed to Johanna that it was getting stronger daily. One evening she had surprised him as he was calling his former project director and ideal, Roger Calfon. It was perfectly normal to make such a call. After all, Johanna called Paul from time to time to ask his advice. But, hiding in the kitchen, she had witnessed a no-holds-barred personal attack. Her assistant was revealing everything about the team, both professional and personal, not only by amplifying Johanna's little mistakes, and exposing any hesitations as if they were signs of her incompetence, but even by engaging in direct attacks. And finally he had asked Calfon to find out more about her. If ever he learned the truth! She had paled, then shrugged her shoulders. After all, she hadn't killed anyone, damn it! In the presence of the others, and especially in Patrick's presence, she had always repressed her anger, but this evening she was losing patience.

"So," said Patrick. "What do you think of our discovery today?"

"I think it's fascinating," Johanna answered, swallowing a piece of fish, "even though it belongs to a much later period than the one we're interested in. And it has no connection to what we're looking for, Judith's tomb."

That afternoon they had dug up a small piece of stone, the remnant of a pointed arch, probably dating from the construction of the Gothic abbey.

"I share your fascination for the Gothic arch," he continued in honeyed tones, "but I'd be less categorical than you about the period and about its lack of connection with what we're looking for. Although it wasn't systematically used until the Gothic period, let's not forget that it was already widespread in the twelfth century. In fact it was invented near the end of the eleventh century, at the height of Romanesque art, of which it's the summit, the perfect outcome, before Romanesque art began its decline. Let's imagine for a moment that it was here on the Mount before then. Saint Martin's Chapel was destroyed to build the nave and the monastery buildings between 1060 and 1084, and we all agree that we can date the end of Romanesque construction in 1084. So, what if by some extraordinary means the Romanesque architect had already discovered the pointed arch? That would make us rethink everything, and so we'd have found something immensely important, an archeological and architectural revolution. For that would mean the Gothic pointed arch was created right here on the Mount!"

Johanna lowered her gaze. Did he really believe what he was saying? Or was he just trying to put her to the test? In any case, he had piqued her curiosity. The table was unusually quiet, and the charged atmosphere was heavy. She laid her silverware down on both sides of her plate. He'd catch it now.

"There are two parts to my answer, my dear Patrick," she began with a mocking smile. "A carry-over from my graduate-school days. First of all, the historical theory and its practical example. We all know that in the tenth century the pointed arch was invented in the Orient, in Syria and Armenia more precisely, and that it was brought to Europe by the first crusaders around 1099 or 1100. The first known use of the pointed arch was in Cluny, an abbey I'm not totally unfamiliar with, during the construction of Cluny III, which started at the end of the eleventh century. Secondly, the application of the theory to the abbey here at Mont-Saint-Michel. Certainly, with its strictly round Romanesque arches, the abbey was finished in 1084, but you've forgotten that in 1103 the nave's north wall collapsed on the monastery buildings, and their arches, round arches, were destroyed. They had to be rebuilt. And so the damaged building was redone around 1106—after Cluny, and after the Crusaders' return—and that's when the pointed arch was used for the first time at the Mount, particularly in the rebuilding of the Salle de l'Aquilon. In conclusion, I also have two points to make, if you allow me. One: about our discovery. I lean more toward a vestige of the work undertaken by Abbot Robert de Thorigny, perhaps the arcades of the ossuary, of Saint-Étienne chapel, or the south buildings, all in the second half of the twelfth century, for which he used pointed arches and vaults. And two, that's not to say that the architects in charge of building the Mount were not geniuses. First, there was the architect in 1023 who came up with a very sophisticated system of redirecting forces and counterbalancing weights. And others, too, for example the architect at the beginning of the twelfth century who reconstructed the monastery buildings that had collapsed in 1103 by using a true Norman invention, the cross-rib vault. It is said, poetically, that the cross-rib vault pays homage to the drakkars of their Viking ancestors. And it's true that when we see it, like in the Salle du Promenoir, we do think of the strange boats of those men from the North."

Pensive, she stopped speaking. She noticed Jacques's admiring glance and Florence's pleased look. But Patrick hadn't finished.

"Whatever date we might accept," he continued, "it's clear that the pointed arch is a major symbol and a technological advance when compared to the round arch. It allows us to open bays in our churches so light can finally enter! In addition, it reduces the horizontal forces and allows us to redirect them onto their supports more efficiently. In short, the pointed arch is the culmination of Romanesque art, its absolute perfection."

Johanna had to contradict him one more time, because he'd touched on an important point, her unconditional love for pure Romanesque, the round arch.

"Sorry, Patrick, but I don't share your opinion on its symbolic value. I agree with you about the progress in technology, but for the rest, I believe on the contrary that the pointed arch represents the decline of Romanesque art and of the Romanesque understanding of the world, not its apogee. Let me explain. By its shape, the round arch, a perfect curve in the image of the heavens, doesn't allow much light to enter, and so asks men to look inward, become humble, turn back upon themselves, as does the Romanesque church, in order to understand their deepest nature. Only then can they rise above the terrestrial world, imperfect by nature, toward the heavenly kingdom that's the only goal for the living on earth. By breaking the round arch in the middle, the pointed arch breaks the celestial vault in two and, raising the arch in space, above the pure Romanesque arch, lets in the light, as you say. It's a major philosophical break, the advent of duality. Heaven's arches are broken, and the profane, secular, earthly world penetrates both church and man. That's a radical change of viewpoint! One historical example: That period is also when the Benedictines were in decline, and their monastic order had led the Western world. By the end of the eleventh century, nobody observes the letter of Saint Benedict's Rule. Secular customs and earthly life have become more important than the text, and that what causes the scission in 1098. Some of the monks living in Molesmes, at the Benedictine abbey, want to return to the purity of the original Rule, to poverty, to manual labor, and so they leave to found Cîteaux."

That's how she had won over François. Her words had quite an effect on the group that evening, too, and they all seemed to hang on her words. But Patrick couldn't resist breaking the charm.

"That's all very interesting," he admitted, "but it sounds like you are nostalgic for pure Romanesque art. And what's more, it's an oversimplification, you'll agree, to explain history through architecture, even if your explanation is poetic!"

"It would be schematic and an oversimplification," she responded, "to forget religion's symbolic influence. In the eleventh century, everything is symbol, everything carries meaning, for it's a century of faith. If we admit that the best criterion for judging the art of this period is faith, then we need to consider the theologians of the High Middle Ages, for whom God's primary attribute is simplicity. For the monks of that time, men who were attempting to get closer to God, simplicity is the goal of their spiritual life—by purifying themselves, they leave behind passions, human contradictions, the constraints of the flesh. And what is Romanesque art if not asceticism and simplicity? On the other hand, Gothic art brings in practical aesthetic concerns, implying that the spiritual life is no longer life's only goal. Yes," she added, dreamily, "the Gothic rises toward the sun. It's erectile, aggressive, and masculine, whereas the Romanesque, with its curves, seems feminine by nature. Romanesque architecture descends toward the earth in order to reach heaven."

"As I said, you sound nostalgic," Patrick said, "and mystical as well! That's strange for a twenty-first-century archeologist. Given what we know about the Cluny monks, I don't think it's been their ghosts that have made you nostalgic for eleventh-century Benedictines and their round arches!"

Hearing his words, Johanna blanched. Her own last words echoed in her mind—"Romanesque architecture descends toward the earth in order to reach heaven"—as did Patrick's words about ghosts. "You must dig in the earth in order to reach heaven," she thought. Suddenly she stood up and left the room, so Patrick could joyfully assume that she was angry while Sebastian attempted to lighten things up by changing the subject.

"Christmas is coming soon. What's everyone doing for vacation?"

"STUPID GIRL," SHE thought aloud, climbing up the steps toward the abbey with the huge key-ring in her hand. "I had all the information I needed, but I didn't realize it until that pedant put me on the right path! It's clear now that the decapitated monk did really live. He gave me all the details: Notre-Dame-sous-Terre, Carolingian church built in the tenth century, and 'you must dig in the earth in order to reach heaven.' The tenth or eleventh century, perhaps the beginning of the twelfth. In any case, my favorite period, as if by chance! He did it on purpose, or perhaps I have. I've got to dig through the manuscripts from that period, from the Romanesque period, and he's got to help me. Why hasn't he appeared again since I've been here?"

As she went on like that, looking down at her feet, she didn't notice the man, also lost in his thoughts but looking up at the stars, who was coming from the opposite direction. They bumped right into each other.

"Oh, sorry, I didn't see you. I was lost in thought."

"Me, too. Did I hurt you?"

"No, I'm fine. Excuse me, but I'm in a hurry."

"If you're hoping to visit the abbey, it's too late. They close it early in winter."

"Oh, that doesn't matter. I've got the keys!" she said, holding up the key ring like a kid holding up a rattle.

"Are you a new guide? I don't think we've met."

She paused to look at the man. He was tall, on the thin side, about forty years old, with black hair that formed thick curls like a halo around his head. It looked like he had green eyes, but she couldn't be sure in the dark. His eyebrows were dark, and he had olive-colored skin, pale lips that were breaking into a timid smile, and a magnificent tweed coat. He was handsome and carried himself well. She glanced down at her muddy vest, then taking on the voice of a femme fatale, she looked him straight in the eyes and said: "I don't believe I know you either."

"Oh, sorry! Simon Le Meur," he said, removing his leather glove and reaching out his hand. "I'm an antique dealer in Saint-Malo, and this is where I come during the off-season. I got here this morning."

"I got here a month ago," she answered, shaking hands, "and I'm in charge of an archeological dig in the abbey."

"Are you the person replacing Calfon?"

Surprised, she looked at him suspiciously.

"Well, say, there's nothing you don't know!"

"You're forgetting, perhaps because of all the tourists, that the Mount is really just a village," he explained. "Actually, I own a house here, and that changes everything. I'm a true resident. I vote here; I know the mayor, the people, the dignitaries, and I like to keep up with everything that's happening on the rock. Although I realize I don't know everything important, since I don't even know what your first name is."

"Johanna."

"Pleased to meet you. Johanna is a lovely name. Say, how about continuing our conversation somewhere out of this wind?"

"That would be nice, but I have to check on something at our dig," she lied. "Perhaps some other time."

"Madame, you've noticed that in the wintertime, and especially on winter evenings, there's nobody around. That's why I'm here, of course, but on the other hand, the chance to chat with a lovely young woman who bumps right into you with a heavy ring of keys is quite rare. Personally, it's the first time that's happened to me, and I'd like to celebrate with a drink. Don't worry, I won't have the bad taste to try to lure you into my house. We'll go to some public, well-lit place—somewhere I can see your eyes more clearly, here it's pretty hard—and we'll have a beer or some chamomile tea, if you prefer. Then I'll let you go, and you can return to your private nighttime visit of the abbey."

She smiled. She was already too tied up with a man to get caught up in flirting, so she told herself there was no danger in accepting his invitation. What's more, who knows? A local who has so much information about the Mount, even if he's only there in the off-season, might be able to teach her something that would put her on the trail of the headless monk.

"I'd prefer a glass of Calvados, and though I think you've got a skilled sales pitch, I find you interesting. Let's go."

Buffeted by the wind, they walked down the main street and found one of the few bar-restaurants not closed during the off-season. As she sat down in the café bathed in yellow light, she put the heavy key ring into her pocket. It had yet to open any doors for her.

"You seem mighty quiet," Simon Le Meur said. "Is that the effect I have on you?"

"Not at all."

"You must be preoccupied by your work. Tell me about it. Archeological digs are my passion. Not surprising for an antique dealer, you'll agree, when we know that history's first archeologists, during the Renaissance, were antique dealers."

Johanna studied him carefully. He did indeed have green eyes, an astonishing pale green surrounded by emerald. On each side of his face, his well-trimmed sideburns were beginning to gray, and there were a few gray streaks in his thick, curly hair. He was a handsome man, if a little too sure of himself, and altogether too curious.

"What sort of antiques do you deal with?" she asked. "What time period?"

"I dabble in boats, my dear. Sextants, telescopes, and other navigational instruments, boat furniture, logbooks, figureheads, and even some clothing and flags. From all eras, although I have things mostly from the nineteenth century and the beginning of the twentieth. But some rare priceless pieces from the seventeenth or the eighteenth. I do most of my business in the summer and fall, and then I close up shop and come back here. There. And how about you? What period?"

"The Middle Ages, especially the Romanesque period."

"I understand completely. What a fascinating time! The golden age of Benedictine monasticism, the construction of the great abbey here on Mont-Saint-Michel, the round arch, the kingdom of the angels, the quest for perfection of the soul so that it might find the path to heaven."

She remained silent but watched him with interest. The waiter brought their Calvados.

"So," he said, raising his glass, "to your future discovery of Judith of Brittany's grave and three cheers for the piece of pointed arch!"

"Cheers. You know about that, too? You surprise me."

"So you won't think I'm a magician reading your thoughts," he added, lowering his voice, "when you bumped into me on the steps, I had just finished having dinner with Christian Brard. He dropped the information in passing as we were having dessert. He was skeptical about the origins of the piece of stone. He thinks maybe it dates from construction begun during the time of Abbot Robert de Thorigny."

Johanna couldn't help but smile inside at her little victory over her assistant. So the administrator of Historical Monuments shared her opinion!

"Brard is a friend of yours?" she asked, a little more warmth in her voice.

"A friend—well, not exactly. More like a client. This evening I sold him a magnificent logbook from an eighteenth-century English frigate, a real museum piece. He loves old manuscripts."

"Oh, I didn't know. Our relationship is purely professional."

"I'm sure it's not sensual, since Brard is gay."

Johanna almost choked at how indiscreet Simon was. The man was like a town crier! She'd have to be careful not to reveal anything about herself, but this meeting could be providential if he knew as much about the mountain's past as about what was happening now. She needed to get him to keep speaking without divulging anything herself. She ordered two more glasses of Calvados.

"Don't misunderstand me," he said, turning pink. "I mentioned that only because Brard never tries to hide it. I'm neither a doorman nor a cad."

"No," she admitted reassuringly. "You're just aware of everything that happens around here, and I find that interesting. Because everything remotely connected to the Mount is fascinating. Like so many others, I think I've fallen in love with this mountain."

"And I'm sure it's reciprocal," he answered with a dark glint in his eyes.

And that's when she blushed. The fellow intrigued her. He seemed superficial, invasive of others' privacy, and nothing seemed sacred to him. And then at the next moment he was secretive, deep, and ready to flee.

"What do you know about Brard?" she asked somewhat abruptly.

"Is this an interrogation?" he asked.

After a third glass of the Calvados, he did end up telling her that the administrator was a Freemason, but Simon didn't know which lodge he belonged to. Like all Masons, Brard revered mystical, spiritual places, especially the Mount. He hated the dozen or so monks and nuns belonging to the Community of Jerusalem who came to the abbey in 2001 after long negotiations with the State, which owned the abbey. If they could have at least been Benedictines! But there weren't enough of the black monks who came back to the Mount in 1966 for the monastery's millennium to keep up such a large abbey with so many tourists. Their contemplative vocation, which exacted withdrawal from the secular world, didn't fit well with the swarms of tourists in shorts invading the crypts during offices. The Benedictines had relinquished all claims on their mountain. Founded at the end of the twentieth century, the Community of Jerusalem, made up of men and women who wished to live a monastic life in the world, now celebrated the liturgy in the abbey church and resided in a part of the abbey that people couldn't visit. One of the exploits the administrator was proudest of was keeping the church doors open to tourists during high mass at noon, although that exasperated both the officiating priests and their followers. In short, Brard was doing everything in his power to chase off these "modern" monks and nuns from the sacred ground he considered his own domain. Simon even called him the abbot. In private, the administrator said that since the black monks—the only ones who had any historical claims on Mont-Saint-Michel—had voluntarily left their sanctuary, now there should be lay rituals, Freemasonry, for example, that could reestablish the connection to the Mount's symbolic purity and mystical beauty. It had been saved from destruction by lay people back during the Third Republic, when the Republic took it over and began reconstruction efforts. The government spent huge sums to understand and explain its past, and for that the Mount needed to become a lay temple.

As Johanna listened to the antique dealer's stories, she was careful not to take sides, like a policeman when listening to an informant. But she could understand Christian Brard's nostalgia for the Benedictines, and she was pleased to learn so much that might help her. She was trying to figure out how to take her leave when she saw Guillaume Kelenn coming down from the restaurant one floor above with a young woman. He smiled warmly at Johanna, started toward her, caught sight of Simon and turned away rapidly, his smile disappearing.

"Oh, it looks like Guillaume isn't one of your clients!" she said to Simon.

"That little kiss-ass calls himself Breton, but he couldn't tell a compass from a thermometer!"

"Perhaps not," she laughed. "But he, too, knows a lot about this place. Less current things maybe, but what he knows is magical, and they're things I could never have found in the library in Avranches."

"What has he told you?"

"He told me about Notre-Dame-sous-Terre," she answered with a provocative glance, "about healing underground forces, about the Celtic sanctuary that was destroyed, about Aubert's skull that probably isn't Aubert's at all but maybe belonged to a Celt who underwent trepanation."

"More fanciful tales!" he cut in. "That choir boy must be confusing Celtism with some rock group."

"You sound pretty vehement."

Immediately he calmed down and took her hands in his. She didn't pull away.

"You see, Johanna, as you can tell by my name, I myself am Breton. My father is from Saint-Malo, and my mother is Spanish, another race of navigators with a rich past. And I must say that this modern esoteric re-constitution of our ancestral myths is terribly annoying. We reinvent the past, present, and future to fit our fancies, creating new superstitions. We think we must see our ancestors' lives as legendary, when really they were probably just struggles for survival, with nothing poetic about them. And so our own little lives become a marvelous tale and we think we're demigods. That's all just usurping the past to meet our own needs! Tales can be found in books, and only in books. Kelenn, that romantic soul, is trying to defend so-called Celtic identity, but I defy him to tell me what that really is. Tomorrow he'll no doubt announce that he's a descendant of Merlin the Magician and expect us to believe him."

"No, we'll just think he's ridiculous. And he's surely used to that. He's just a dreamer, reinventing his past because he finds the present so colorless and uninteresting."

"You're right," he concluded, pulling his hand away. "Say, you, on the other hand, you must have your head on your shoulders."

The remark made Johanna uneasy. She glanced at her watch—twelve thirty. Not too late for a headless monk. He saw her glance at the dial.

"You intend to go up to the abbey now?" he wondered. "Aren't you afraid?"

"Afraid of what?"

"I don't know. The ancient stones, the place's soul, the old tales, maybe the ghosts."

"I thought we could find legends and tales only in books," she answered sarcastically.

He paid for their drinks and they stepped out onto the pavement in the Grande-Rue. A fine, cold, penetrating mist filled the air, and they could hear the waves crashing at high tide. Johanna could feel the alcohol's effect on her head and legs. She offered to walk him back home because she needed to walk to clear her head. He lived beside the ramparts dating from the Hundred Years' War, along a wall connecting the North Tower to the Boucle Tower. So, following the rock looking out over the sea, they took the watchman's walk and then a steep staircase. All Johanna would have to do would be to continue on through the North Tower to reach the Grand Staircase leading up to the abbey.

"The Benedictines would have let themselves be hanged rather than dare to enter the church between Compline and Matins," he said in a sepulchral voice. "They say that the monks could hear angels singing in the church at night and that everyone who tried to see them died when daylight came. Of course, what killed them was their guilt at having broken a taboo, not the vengeful hand of some celestial force, but I find that leaving the invisible alone is not a bad idea. I think that even our brothers and sisters who belong to the Jerusalem Community respect the rule that daytime is for people, nighttime for the angels."

"Come now, Simon," she said, taking his arm. "Don't worry, I'll respect the tradition. My dig is not in the church, and I'm not the kind to go pray in the middle of the night; not during the day, either. Tell me," she added, trying to sound flippant, "does that taboo involve just the big church built after 1023, or does it also affect the old Carolingian church that later became Notre-Dame-sous-Terre?"

She could sense him hesitating.

"I'm not sure," he admitted. "But I believe the custom was followed already in the old church built by the canons. And it was even worse in that sanctuary. There you could hear demons screaming at night!"

"That's not surprising. Even logical when you consider the mentality of medieval man," Johanna retorted. "But what you're telling me still makes my blood freeze. Or maybe it's this rain!"

"We're in a place that is still caught up in medieval logic," he said gently. "Even the weather reminds us of the medieval world, and that's what we all come here looking for—a little bit of eternity. I'm a twenty-first-century Cartesian, and I don't believe in angels or demons. But here on the Mount, I . . . it's hard to explain, but here it's all still so alive, so palpable. So I have a great deal of respect for this place's weather and customs, so different from our own. I try not to break the charm, letting magic do its work. In short, Johanna, here the night belongs to the powers of the night. At night, human beings have other things to do, like sleep, dance, and so on."

She smiled at him. His words about Mont-Saint-Michel had touched her. Yes, even though he'd never admit it, this man was sensitive to tales about life. He could hear legends that weren't printed in books, legends the stones were telling. Hell was singing in Notre-Dame-sous-Terre. He would remember other things about these walls, but not tonight. If she asked him anything more about the old church, she risked divulging too much. She decided it was best to change the subject. She thought about Sebastian.

"Speaking of celebrations," she asked, "will you be staying on the Mount for the Christmas holidays?"

"Absolutely! Like an old bachelor, I'll pull a soft easy chair up to the fireplace, listen to a Mahler symphony as I savor my oysters, drown my-self in a bottle of white wine, and then I'll stumble down to look at the sea."

"What a plan!" she laughed.

"Like to join me?"

"I love Mahler and white wine, but I don't think I'll be here for the holidays. I've got other plans. But if I change my mind. . . . "

"For sure, don't hesitate. It'd be a pleasure. Well, here we are!"

The façade of his house was typical of the old local buildings. Built of granite, it had windows with tiny panes, a dark red door and shutters, and an old, rusty lamppost. Below it lay a tiny garden crossed by a stairway whose wrought-iron rails were woven with hibernating rose bushes and wisteria vines. He timidly invited her in, but she refused. Then he awk-wardly scribbled his telephone number on a piece of paper and handed it to her. He shook her hand vigorously, waved good-bye, and went inside. Alone in the drizzle, lost in thought, she started up toward the abbey. What a fellow! Hard to figure out. Certainly more inclined to divulge other people's secrets than his own. And why had she brought up the subject of the holidays with him? She didn't even know him and certainly wasn't going to sacrifice François for him. Except maybe François would be the one abandoning her. After all, he wasn't even sure he'd be free. Last year, he didn't tell her he could spend New Year's Eve with her until seven P.M. that same day! Until he finally showed up, she had assumed he had cancelled out and that she'd have to spend New Year's Eve alone. It wasn't so much being alone that frightened her, but rather New Year's Eve. Every year she grew anxious during the holidays, with the feeling that she was in mourning while everyone else was celebrating.

This year, how far away François seemed! And he was far away, farther away than when she was living in Cluny. They did often call each other, but she hadn't gone back to Paris for three weeks, and he hadn't been able to come to Normandy. And yet she didn't really miss him. On weekends, the rest of the team left Mont-Saint-Michel, and she stayed there alone with the mountain. There were of course more tourists on Saturday and Sunday, but they didn't bother her because she was so caught up in her dreams. She had tried to see the room she had slept in as a child, where she had seen the headless monk for the first time. But that house remained closed; it was open only in the high season when the prices for rooms skyrocketed. She had ignored the other room, where the second apparition happened, as she was sure she'd find nothing there. She spent long hours in Notre-Dame-sous-Terre, where she sat motionless on a stone bench and stared at the steps until her exhausted eyes ached because of his absence. But the rest of her body seemed to be filled with the monk. Her body was tormented with the hope he would appear, and it was becoming an obsession. Suffering was an indication of his diffuse presence within her, everywhere except in her eyes, which obstinately refused to see him.

She had looked everywhere in the abbey for him, in the many books written about the history of Mont-Saint-Michel, in the monastery's manuscripts, but she had found no trace of him anywhere. All she had was her memory alone to connect his image to the reality of his existence. Johanna knew that if some day, or some night, he reappeared a fourth time with his procession of dead people and his Latin sentence, he'd perhaps push her over the edge into madness. And yet, that didn't seem to worry her.

Panting, she kept climbing the Grand Staircase and reached the round towers of the Châtelet, the entrance to the abbey. She climbed the steep stairway called the abyss, took out her keys and opened the huge wooden door. She was having trouble catching her breath. She realized that the drizzle had soaked her windbreaker and her hair hanging down behind her. She remembered the curse, the ancient beliefs Simon had told her about, and she felt a chill, not knowing whether it was due to the rain or to fear. Up above, beyond the steps in the grand vestibule, everything was black. Like all archeologists, she always carried a flashlight in her pocket. She reached down for reassurance, and yes, there it was. Christian Brard hadn't thought it necessary to give her the keys to the transformer, where she could have turned on the lights in the abbey. In any case, this was supposed to be a secret visit. She didn't want to have to explain to anyone what she was going to do in Notre-Dame-sous-Terre in the middle of the night! She climbed two more steps and shone her flashlight around on the dark stones. Her glasses were fogged up, and all she could see was a bluish haze. As she was looking for a handkerchief to clean her glasses, she felt a warm breeze on her forehead, a damp silent sigh like an invisible kiss, some breathing. She put her glasses back on and looked around in fright. Nothing, nobody; just the wind. The wind? Suddenly she paled, closed the door, put the keys and the flashlight back in her pocket, ran down the stairs, and fled along the watchman's walk skirting the high Gothic walls. When she got to the historical museum, she turned and hurried down to her house. She made it into the dining room, where Florence was reading beside the fireplace.

"Evening," said Flo quietly. "What a face!"

"Is there still some Calvados in the cupboard, or some cognac? No, I've already had enough to drink," she said, rubbing her forehead. "I'm going to bed. Good night, Florence."

"Wait. Your friend Isabelle called. She can't reach you on your cell phone. And Paul called, too, from the dig in Cluny. He sounded strange and wouldn't tell me anything. But he wants you to call him as soon as you can. Even tonight."

Florence was looking at Johanna, who seemed as strange as her former director had been a little while before on the phone. It was clear that too much responsibility could drive you crazy!

"Thanks, Flo. I'll take care of it tomorrow. Now I'm heading upstairs. Good night."

It was one twenty. She had left her cell phone on the nightstand, and when she walked into her room, it was vibrating, the signal that she had a message. She took off her wet clothes and laid them over a radiator, then tried to get back in touch with reality. There was a message from Isa, who was worried about her and proposed that they join some friends from her newspaper for New Year's Eve. Out of the question. And then one from François. As usual, he wouldn't know until the last minute if he'd be free for New Year's Eve, but he loved her, he missed her, et cetera. He wasn't going to come through on the thirty-first, she just knew. And finally, a message from Paul. It was unusual for him to call like this. They were still on good terms, but not nearly as close as when she had been at Cluny. His message was laconic. He repeated what he had told Florence, but Johanna could sense strong emotion, an urgency in his voice suggesting that something important had happened. She was so worried that she called him right back.

"Finally!" he shouted. "Listen. It's unthinkable, extraordinary, fabulous! A sensational discovery! Good God, I can finally admit it. I had given up believing. A tomb, Jo, a tomb! Don't panic, it's not Hugh de Semur. It's better yet, and so totally unexpected! The man I found was buried in 1022, can you imagine? In 1022! He was an important local figure, a Benedictine monk and master builder of Cluny II, or at least one of the builders, and I think he's the one who finished the church. He must have been buried along with Abbot Odilon in the choir of Cluny II, then transferred later to the choir in Cluny III. His name is Pierre de Nevers. Amazing how well he's preserved! And that's not all. In the tomb we found a manuscript from 1063, a letter addressed to our own Hugh de Semur in Latin, and I've started deciphering it. And it's amazing, Johanna, you won't believe your eyes. You've got to get back here right away. I want to keep it a surprise, and I swear you won't be disappointed. Get a couple hours sleep, then jump in your car and hurry back!"

10

W HEN HE HEARS THE NEWS, ROMAN IS DEVASTATED. BROTHER Robert, the former prior, shares the master builder's consternation.

"She was tried in Rouen," Robert adds, "by an ecclesiastical court presided over by Roland d'Aubigny, under Duke Richard's authority. Our brothers Romuald, Martin, Anthelme, and Drocus were among the judges. You must keep your hopes up, my brother. She's a bright woman, and she knows it's useless to persist. She will surely recant before she's tortured, so she'll be saved!"

"What kind of torture have they condemned her to?" Roman asks without expression.

"Well," Robert answers, paling and looking down. "They removed her clothes to see if she bore the devil's mark on her skin, and hanging around her neck they found a piece of a human skull set in a gold cross, a druidic cross with the four cosmic elements."

The news fills the master builder with foreboding. He tries to look Brother Robert in the eyes, but the former prior keeps his gaze averted, first down toward the ground he's sweeping, then up at the blue sky.

"And?" Roman asks, pulling at his shoulder. "Tell me, Robert, I beg you!"

"I don't know who had the vile idea, Roman," Robert says finally. "But this is the judgment: Because Moira extolled the four elements, she'll be tortured by each of those four elements until she abjures the Celtic cross and the faith of her ancestors. The sentence will be executed right here on the holy mountain. By air the first day, water the second, earth the third, and, if she still hasn't recanted, by fire the fourth day, until death. And the fourth day will be Ascension Day."

Ascension Day, forty days after Easter, celebrating Christ's ascension into heaven.

Alone in Saint Martin's Chapel, overcome by what he has just heard and by the weight of time flowing by, Roman kneels beside the tombs. He feels that he has powerlessly witnessed the end of the world. He had been so elated when the construction of the new abbey church got under way. But now his joy has been swallowed up by the anguish he suffered over Moira's arrest, by the revulsion he felt on discovering that the traitor Almodius had turned the Celtic woman over to the bishop and prince, and then by the shock of Abbot Hildebert's death. Since only a monk holding the same rank as a dead brother could prepare the body, the Abbot of Redon had come to the infirmary to wash Hildebert's body where it lay on the stone of the dead. Once his hands had been joined under the stitched-up cowl, and the hood pulled down over his face, incense and holy water sprinkled over the dark robe that had become his shroud, the abbot of Redon and Brother Hosmund carried him to the sanctuary, Saint Martin's Chapel. They laid out his corpse and lit two candelabras, one at his head, near the cross, the other at his feet.

His thirty sons then formed a circle around Hildebert and began their wake. Not for a moment did they leave him alone, as they implored Saint Michael in their prayers to accompany and protect him on the perilous path to the Omnipotent One. Prior Robert, back from Anjou, wrote the date of the abbot's death in the local obituary, and Brother Guillaume went off to carry the news of the death to all the order's monasteries, where he'd gather their condolences and praise for the abbot on a long parchment scroll. He wouldn't be back for months with his scroll of the dead. Accompanied by litanies, psalms, and the gusting wind, the brothers buried their father near the church, near where Abbot Maynard I and his nephew, Abbot Maynard II, lay in their tombs. They marked the spot with a stone cross so his remains could later be moved to the choir crypt in the great abbey church, when the reliquary chapel was completed. Thus had Duke Richard ordered. It seemed appropriate to him that the brothers and the other faithful, when they went to the crypt to venerate the relics of Saint Aubert, founder of the mountain, could also honor Hildebert, for he was the founder of the new abbey church. So it is that Roman must hurry to finish the crypt under the choir, and then the choir itself.

That's his mission as well as his salvation. Like Hildebert, Roland d'Aubigny and Richard II had spared him only because he was the master builder. If equity and probity had been respected, he, too, should have been accused and found guilty at Moira's trial for complicity in heresy, but his name wasn't even mentioned. The monastery court, the chapter of faults, even exempted him from corporal punishment, due to the state of his health, and imposed only a lenient spiritual punishment comprising supplementary prayers. Now, as every time Roman prays, his thoughts turn to inevitable and surely horrible divine punishment. He has lost his real father and Pierre de Nevers; once again he is spiritually an orphan. And no longer can weeping relieve his suffering. In fact, nobody on the Mount has been able to help Roman work through his pain, because as soon as Hildebert was buried, the struggle for power began.

According to the charter Richard I granted the Benedictines in 966, the monks had the right to choose their own abbots; often they choose the prior as well. But their choice, Brother Robert, came from Saint-Brieuc and was a relative of Duke Alain III of Brittany, an adversary of the Duke of Normandy. So it mattered little that Robert had been shaped by Hildebert and remained faithful to the man who was his abbot for fourteen years, for Richard's son was not so attached to the principles laid out by his father. Richard II and his bishops' council chose instead Thierry de Jumièges, one of the duke's nephews and cantor at the Jumièges abbey, to be the new abbot. Richard's nepotism infuriated the community of monks on the Mount, and they elected Robert. When the duke threatened to cut off all funds for the building project, however, Robert himself asked the monks to vote in Richard's protégé, because the construction of the Angel's dwelling place was their divine duty, ordered both by Saint Michael and by Hildebert, and that task was greater than any secular arguments over governance. They would have to accept a Norman abbot, said Robert, and at least pretend to be pleased that he was related to their overlord in order to guarantee continued financing for the construction of their great abbey church. The brothers gave in, and Richard passed the pastoral staff to Thierry de Jumièges. Robert resigned from his position as prior before the new abbot could dismiss him, and Thierry named Almodius as Robert's successor. The monks ratified the choice, for they believed that the scriptorium master would be able to protect the abbey's integrity against the new abbot Thierry. Now that the quarrel over the succession was over, construction had resumed and they would be able at last to get back to their normal life of prayer. So all the brothers were thinking, all except Roman. He could think of nothing but Moira, and he had no idea what fate held in store for her.

But today, Brother Robert has told him just what it holds in store, and his words have destroyed everything Roman believes about earthly things. His gaze wanders over Princess Judith's tomb. True justice is not of this world, but can the world of men really be so vile and so full of ignominy? Will Moira now be lost to him forever, just when he's begun to realize how much he loves her and needs her presence? He can't stand not being able to see her. He looks around the chapel at the walls and altar. He can make out the yellow Scotch broom she had given him, and he can imagine her sitting there on the stone bench and listening to him tell her Bible stories. There she is, in her long autumn-colored dress, her hair in flaming red braids, lips parted, leaning toward him and laughing. He bends forward to inhale her presence, blue like the clouds. Her face twists in pain and she disappears. Roman is left with only his memory, his body and soul empty. The chapel's gray stones mirror his helplessness. Soon Moira will return to Roman's mountain, and her body and too-lively memory will suffer martyrdom. He won't be able to do anything. Except watch from a distance when she's given over to her ermine-robed executioners, except pray to God who hasn't answered their other prayers, except try to communicate with her spirit so she will finally listen to her body's pain and suffering and recant. If she'd only recant! Then she could be with him again.

SHE TAKES THE same path the monks follow on Good Friday with the cross, the same one the stone carriers use every day along the rock's north face. Three days before Ascension, when the tide is low, a cart is moving slowly up the mountain, which echoes with the shouts of all the people who have gathered to witness the sight promised by criers in lands even as far away as the enemy Brittany.

She is standing in the cart, her hands and feet tied, her dress a dirty, granite-gray shift. Through a veil of long, tangled hair her green eyes stare off into the distance. They seem to be searching for the sea, now hidden from view. Behind her is Tombelaine Island. On each side of the earthen path lined with gardens and orchards, people have poured out of the inns and houses and, walking alongside her, they shout out hateful epithets and spit on her. Some among the crowd remain quiet like her brother Brewen—Master Roger and his family, the abbey monks, young Andelme, old Herold, some of the patients she has healed. Others of them, tormented perhaps by the fear that they've been healed by the devil, shout more loudly than the rest. In vain she tries to pick Roman out of the noisy crowd. The horses stop in the square between the village cemetery and the little parish church dedicated to Saint Peter.

Protected by armed soldiers, four men stand waiting: Enguérand d'Eglantier, representing Duke Richard; Roland d'Aubigny, bishop of Avranches; Father Abbot Thierry; and Brother Almodius, the prior. When she sees Almodius, her features harden. She raises her eyes toward the abbey far above. The first thing she sees is the abbot's wooden cell, the monastery buildings, and the walls of Saint Martin's Chapel, almost hidden in a heavy fog that is surprising for the end of May. The sky, chalk-colored like a winter sky, makes the stones in the buildings seem darker in comparison, especially at their base. She can picture the chapel's interior and the Breton tombs, and, near Judith's tomb, she can imagine him sitting on a bench: her beloved, in silhouette.

"MOIRA, DAUGHTER OF Nolwen and Killian, residing in the forest near the village of Beauvoir, fief of the Mont-Saint-Michel abbey," the bishop calls out after raising his hand to quiet the crowd. "You were seen practicing pagan rituals, and you've admitted it. Yet you've refused to renounce your ungodly beliefs. At your trial in Rouen on Saint-Pacôme's Day in the year of our Lord 1023, you were found guilty of the mortal sin of heresy and sentenced to undergo torture in this holy place until you recant your demonic faith. Before we begin the first torture, I ask you this question: Will you renounce your ancestors' false religion and publicly espouse the one true faith?"

Moira's face is as pale as the fog now engulfing Saint Martin's Chapel. Her freckles fade into her transparent skin. In the threatening silence, she stares at the silver cross hanging on Abbot Thierry's chest. The public is savoring this reprieve while at the same time awaiting the promised spectacle.

"Well then!" the bishop says. "Since you persist in the error of your ways, I'm handing you over to Count Enguérand d'Eglantier, in the service of our suzerain Richard the Good, so that he might carry out God's sentence! At any moment you may stop the torture and come back to the fold of the Most High."

Shouts from the crowd drown out the prelate's last words. A soldier grabs the reins of the horse pulling the cart, others fall into place on either side, and they escort her along the path to the top, the four dignitaries leading the way and the crowd following. The overcast sky seems to hang lower as the cart rumbles slowly and crookedly toward the east. Everyone stops to take in a strange scene: At the far end of the rock, at the base of the slope, they see, rising from flat ground, walls with arches that seem to be clinging to the Mount, thanks to the magic of wooden lifting machines that look like huge insects. Since the construction site is deserted, it's almost as if the mountain itself, with this strange protrusion, has given birth to a granite temple. Under a threatening vault of mist, wooden forms are already partially covered by stones that have been carried up long ladders and put into place to shape the arches. Suddenly filled with hope, Moira looks out over the dark base of the unfinished choir crypt. She can see its pillars, but there's no man there, no monk's frock. A soldier unties her and motions to her to get down. The crowd shouts deafeningly. Now it's her brother she's looking for. Soon Brewen's eyes meet hers. The thirteen-year-old stands head and shoulders above the crowd. He's not weeping, he's standing as tall and erect as a stone pillar. They push her along toward the construction site.

And that's when she spots the iron cage on the ground. It's not like a bird cage at all, but rather like one of those cages that show off bears or other ferocious animals at the fair or in village festivals, only smaller. She understands immediately and creeps into her new prison. Although Moira is not as tall as her brother Brewen, she can't even sit up straight in her iron jail, so she must bend her back and bow her head. Enguérand d'Eglantier locks the door and turns toward the soldiers.

One of the them ties the cage to a long beam taken from Roman's construction site, and the others slide the cage along toward the abyss. Out at one end of the beam, the iron prison swings in the air. Then the soldiers, helped by some construction workers, weight down the other end with enormous granite blocks. Hanging out in thin air, bent in two, Moira feels a wave of nausea. The people scream. Some of them rush out onto the sand to look at her from below, hanging there at the mercy of the angry wind soon to be rising along with the incoming tide. Moira tries to move, but every movement makes the cage swing madly, right and left, and it squeaks harshly on its rusty hinge. Her vertigo grows; she can see nothing but the sand forty rods below. Now and again, hoping to block out the emptiness, she closes her eyes, but then another wave of nausea hits her and she has to open them so as not to throw up. She clings tightly to the bars. She must hold on, not give an inch, for her people's memory and for the future of her love for Roman. She thinks about the letter she burned, Roman's beautiful letter. Is he really serious about what he promised if she would recant? Their love is not of this world; peace is not of this world. They are condemned to secrecy on this earth, to flight, to denying themselves, to betrayal. Yes, the decision she's come to is the right one: Faced with the choice between heaven and earth, she has chosen heaven. But she is being punished for her choice by being suspended in air between earth and heaven. Tomorrow her deliverance will come; she'll be free to love, free for eternity. With a supreme effort Moira flattens her body down against her legs and twists her torso around. As her prison swings, she manages to look away from the sand, out into the pale ether, spider-like and as milky-white as an angel's kiss. The crowd's shouts are echoed by the calls of gulls, ducks, and terns. As the day draws on, the air becomes more turbulent, and Moira's flesh, racked by cramps, confinement, hunger, and especially thirst, is transformed into a body that knows only pain. Her spirit alone remains indomitable; it clings fast to Roman's memory just as her reddened hands cling tightly to the iron bars of her rabbit cage. The sea begins to rise, surreptitiously at first, with silver tongues sliding over living swamps, and then unfolding its brutality. Rising up from nowhere, or perhaps from the heart of Hell, the waves swallow up the earth in their heaving disarray before gathering their strength for one last impressive rush.

Seen from above, the picture would be magnificent if the water weren't joined by the terrifying, freezing north wind pounding the poor cage. In its arms, Moira is buffeted like a tiny feather, a speck of dust subjected to the raging master of the winds. Fear digs into her mind and her body. Her eyes begin to bulge out. Panting, freezing with cold, she mutters a prayer in the teeth of the raging wind.

"Ogma! Saint Michael!" she murmurs, seized by a spasm of pain, her voice cracking. "Soul of this mountain, you who vanquished the abyss of Evil, I beseech you, carry me away from these skies. Cast off the chains that hold me to this rock! I beg you, spare Roman the tortures I'm suffering and the torture of vain hope. O powerful spirit! You have always watched over my life, now watch over my death. From now on, my existence can offer me nothing more than a defiled dungeon, even if I recant. You know that, you who know everything. I refuse to renounce the things of this earth, and all that's left for me is heaven. Call on the wind to smash this cage on the rocks. Crush my body; I willingly leave it. Take my soul and lead it out of time into another body, another world, a world in which I can love Roman!"

Moira can't repress her sobs, but she's not weeping for her own fate or because of the pain that is afflicting her bones. Her tears are tears of hope. The north wind gains strength as evening draws near, and it brings rain. Moira is pleased, because the rocking cage now seems to be announcing her death on the stones below. The wind speaks to her through its violence, but it refuses to kill her. Perhaps night will grant her wish.

Fog descends from the church, it envelops her in its damp shroud. A crow brushes the cage with its wing, and then the shadows fall.

. . .

"MOIRA, I'LL ASK you the same question again. Will you renounce your ancestors' false religion and publicly espouse the one true faith?"

Two days before Ascension. At dawn the soldiers had lowered the cage back to the ground. Moira was soaked with rain and unconscious, but she was alive. Richard's envoy ordered that she be taken out of the cage and tied to the beam on the ground while they waited for her to come to her senses. Her body was bruised; her hands, purple like her face, clung to the bars. Her joints cracked as they dragged her out and tied her up once more.

The people wait. Hung over though many of them are after the festivities of the evening before, they are delighted that the witch is still alive and excited by the prospect of further torture and another holiday. At the time when the construction workers normally sit down by their tools and break their fast, the villagers and visitors, seating themselves on the ground near the unconscious heretic, do the same. Abbot Thierry has set up a table outside for his important guests, the bishop and the prince's emissary. While the abbot is celebrating the office of Prime, Moira opens her eyes. Roland d'Aubigny and Enguérand d'Eglantier are seated before roasted Cancale oysters, sturgeon pâté, swans cooked in verjuice, monastery cheeses, and some jugs of the wine Odilon had sent to Hildebert. Moira, not realizing that she's still chained, tries to stand up and reach for some food but falls back with a moan.

"It's about time!" says the bishop when he sees her fall back. "We were beginning to get impatient, Moira! You must be starving . . . and thirsty. You may join us if you like. With one word, you'll be able to eat all you want."

When she remains silent, he straightens up, and so does the crowd. Two soldiers remove her chains and help her stand. Then the prelate raises his hand to silence the crowd, walks over to her, and asks the solemn question. She feels like spitting in his face, but the bishop isn't close enough and her mouth is as dry as old parchment. Water . . . what wouldn't she give to have some water! But she will not trade the memory of her people for a few swallows. How her legs and side ache! Why had the north wind refused to smash her on the rocks? Why hadn't the night carried her off, and why had it allowed her such a deep sleep that she would forget her wish to die? Now that she's lucid once more, she can once again struggle against her torturers. She looks with loathing at the prelate. He's standing, on ground that belongs to her and gives her strength. The wind brings her echoes of the psalms the monks are now chanting in the church. The monks, including Roman. And their chant brings her courage. She looks at the banquet table, then turns away arrogantly. Her attitude provokes Roland d'Aubigny to anger.

"As you wish," he shouts. "Since our wine doesn't appeal to you, I'll give you a drink that can quench your thirst for a long time!"

The count gestures to the soldiers, who then drag Moira down the path through the village. The sun has been up for barely two hours, and it, too, seems to be eager to watch the spectacle. Under the vaulted heavens, transparent like water, it casts its rays on the Mount, dries the sticky mud on the path, turns the bay blue, and warms Moira's aching bones. The guards support her by her shoulders because she can hardly walk. Head down, she hopes the torture will be quick, horrible, and final so that everything will soon be over. She knows she'll never see Roman again, at least not in this world. So why resist? The only fear she had was for Roman, and that evaporated during the trial because the master builder's name was never mentioned once. Thus Roman is still free, alive, and he'll keep their secret. He'll build his New Jerusalem and die an old man, at peace with himself and with God. Then, perhaps, if Moira's soul is still living in the other world, he will recognize her and they will love each other forever, either in the kingdom of the dead or on earth in different bodies.

The procession arrives at the base of the mountain, which is still lapped by the retreating tide. Empty granite barges and fishing boats bob on the waves. Tombelaine Island watches the sea leave just as rapidly as it came in. Moira realizes that her life is like a wave. They've erected a post in the bay, not far from Aubert's spring, and they tie her to it like a figurehead on a ship. Moira remembers that her last image of Roman is his dark, sobbing body that day in Hildebert's cell. The old man's eyes were like the sea. And then he died the very morning he was supposed to hear her recant in Beauvoir. A nostalgic smile spreads over her face, and she looks off into limbo. Lost in her thoughts, her mind clouded by hunger, ignoring the clamoring crowd, Moira seems not to realize that now she has become the water's prisoner and that this evening the tide will rise up around her. And then she thinks she sees a large, dark, bearded angel hurrying toward her, flask in hand, the robes of his companions floating in the wind. Brother Hosmund is immediately intercepted by the duke's soldiers.

"Monsignor, Prince!" he says to the bishop and the count as if in prayer, while holding forth the leather flask. "A little wine diluted with water. Please allow the Lord to lighten her thirst if not the burden of her sins."

"The Lord has judged her!" the prelate answers curtly. "And the sentence must be carried out as he wishes, with no relief of any kind, Brother! Besides," he adds, pointing to Aubert's spring, "a source of pure water is available to her, and she can watch it all she wants until the tide comes in!"

Hosmund, Drocus, Robert, and Bernard are shocked by the bishop's callousness. Seeing their reaction, Roland d'Aubigny tries to justify himself.

"Please understand, my brothers," he explains. "She does continue to deny our Lord, and her insolence adds to her crime against the Most High and against the community of Christians everywhere. She throws her contempt in the face of the Archangel himself, in his own dwelling, and you, his devoted servants, you come here to quench her thirst! I doubt that your abbot ordered you to do it."

"Our father did not require it, that is correct," retorts Robert, the former prior, with a sardonic glance at the bishop. "As you say, we are the Lord's servants. We are motivated by Christ and by the Gospels to do what we do."

"But Jesus cannot accept heretics!" the bishop shouts, pink with rage. "The wicked woman doesn't dwell with Christ, and thus she's unworthy of his mercy until she crosses the threshold of his dwelling."

"Fine," Robert answers with a slight bow. "Then we'll go pray for her, asking that Christ might welcome her into his dwelling."

"Pray for her soul's salvation. That's what she needs," the bishop concludes.

The monks turn away quietly and walk off through the crowd. It opens up to let them pass.

"Roman!"

Brother Bernard, the builder's assistant, pauses a moment and then continues on. Moira had seen the dark backs and couldn't stifle a cry from the heart. Strapped tight against the pole by the cord wrapped around her shoulders, she twists her neck to watch them walk off toward the rock, away from the waves.

For the first time since she was arrested, tears of sadness fill her eyes. The bishop walks over and whispers in a voice too low for the others to hear:

"Roman couldn't care less about you! You need to know that even if you recant, you will never see him again. Never! The only love he's ever experienced is his love for God and for the stones he's erecting to God's glory on this mountain. He's wiped you from his memory. He's free to move about as he wishes, you know. He could have come to see you long ago, even during the trial, and he apparently didn't wish to. Yes, the only thing that matters to him is the construction site. So don't think you can renounce your crimes in hopes of being free to reach him. He has already renounced you in public, and your whore venom can never touch him again. Do you understand? Never again!"

Tears course down Moira's cheeks. She closes her eyes in concentration and spits in the bishop's face.

"Let divine justice be done!" the bishop shouts to the people, wiping his face. "Let the ocean that God created do its work!"

The crowd responds in noisy acclamation. Enguérand d'Eglantier orders his men to keep the crowd away from the victim, and the two dignitaries withdraw to observe mass in the Carolingian church.

Moira misses her cage, for at least it separated her from this mass of people screaming insults at her between swallows of wine or mead. The crowd is joined by pilgrims, boatmen, merchants, and acrobats coming on foot from behind Tombelaine. The day is as long as the sinuous liquid serpents evaporating in the sun. The sun dries Moira's rain-soaked shift and makes her thirst grow unbearable. The tide is out, but the salt carried by the land breeze irritates her skin even more than the hemp rope did.

She's like a slowly eroding rock. She hasn't the strength to keep her head up. Her salt-caked hair hangs in shapeless clumps over her breast and hides her stone-gray face. Her mind begins to wander. She imagines Roman in the church, pictures him climbing the steps above the twin altars with granite blocks in his arms, then turning so that the faithful might venerate them. Then he's near her. She's turned to stone, and he begins to sculpt her, to transform her into a pillar to bear the weight of the vault in the crypt beneath the choir.

Suddenly a sound awakens her. The crowd comes joyously awake as well, for off in the distance, beneath the setting sun, weakened already by the promise of the coming moon, the tide is beginning to turn. Moira is happy. Finally, the waves. The sea she had contemplated from high above, the day before, will swallow her up today. She's facing north, and the north wind, too, begins to rise once more and, joining the waves, prepares to run her through. The wind gathers strength and, like a sword, it's stabbing at her ears, flattening her head and body against the post, crushing her flesh, prodding her body with its sharp point. The onlookers exhort the timid tide, applaud the swelling serpents that turn into dragons pouring watery flames from their mouths with sepulchral moaning. The crowd and the soldiers, growing fearful, begin to back up when the foaming monsters draw near. But Moira longs for the water's embrace. The water is her friend. They have spoken so often, by the pond, during storms, out on the sea. Water washes away all our stains, the sea's abyss protects the dwelling place of the gods, it carries the crystal boats on their journey to the other world. The water will gather her up and take her back to the mysterious world of human origins. Moira begs for the water, mother of life, to caress her cheeks, bathe her hair, soothe her eyes, kiss her mouth, and drown her heart.

LOW TIDE. RAOUL, captain of the regiment, struggles to cut through the rope that the salt water has swollen tight against her skin. Cut by the wet rope, her legs and arms are bleeding, and her distended face has been discolored by the cold water that is now retreating with the coming day. Her whole being is quivering from head to foot, and Raoul can't tell if that means she will live or die. She mutters several incomprehensible syllables and begins to cough. Some liquid dribbles out from between her bluish lips. It sounds as if she's reproaching her mother. She must have lost her mind. Raoul and another soldier lay her on the cart; the rabble watches. The cart begins rattling its way up toward the village through the drizzle sent down by the heavens. There are tents everywhere, set up to house the curious crowds whose commerce brings prosperity to the island's businesses. Near the square and the parish church, in the lay cemetery, Raoul's men have finished digging a hole. Moira has completely lost touch with reality. Her body is bruised, her spirit broken, and she isn't able even to recoil when she sees the gaping hole.

It's plain that she isn't able to think clearly, for even with Raoul holding her, she is rocking back and forth like a crazy woman, and pays no attention to the radiant faces of the masters of ceremonies. Only Almodius, standing next to the abbot, has a frown on his face, and for a moment his dark eyes seem to be filled with pain. Roland d'Aubigny abandons his irony. For the third time, he asks the customary question:

"Moira, on this day, eve of Ascension, I ask the same question: Will you renounce your ancestors' false religion and publicly espouse the one true faith?"

Moira turns her vacant eyes toward the bishop and bursts into crazed laughter.

"That's the mark of the devil!" the bishop concludes. "You can see, Count, Father Abbot, you can hear. He appears in broad daylight; these divine tortures have ripped off his mask! There he is, Lucifer, come to defy Saint Michael on his own territory, and to tease us! Demon from the depths of Hell," he says, speaking to Moira, "go back to Hell!"

With these words, Raoul and his assistant drag Moira by her arms over to the hole and push her in. The trench isn't very deep, but it is dark and narrow. Her body lands in a motionless heap. The four dignitaries lean down to see what they have done. There Moira lies like a corpse, unmoving, in the fetal position, eyes closed, her hair, sticky with salt water, spread out over the ground. The steady drizzle is turning the ground into thick mud, and it sticks to her body like a lover. A slight blow to her leg brings her out of her lethargy. Disappointed that there's nothing to watch, the crowd has begun to throw stones and horse dung into the hole to rouse her. Trapped in her earthen prison, Moira cringes like a buried wild animal; her eyes roll with fright. The duke's guards have trouble holding back the crowd. Moira decides never again to utter human speech, and she hopes that "never" won't be very long. She presses herself back against one wall in her tomb. Feverish and hallucinating, sweating, she stares at the walls; her hands are kneading the wet clay as if it were living flesh. She closes her eyes and tries not to breathe, as if to withdraw from the world's filth. She offers a silent supplication to the earth of her ancestors:

"O earth of this mountain, you who brought to life the gods, the Celtic people, and the angels. Wind and sea have always struggled to possess you; today men are trying to steal your power for themselves. Both wind and the sea have refused to separate me from you, you to whom I've belonged since the dawn of the stars. I've entrusted your secret to a man who belongs to you but who doesn't yet know that he does. But I'm sure you've chosen him to celebrate your union with the heavens. He'll not betray you. He's one of heaven's creatures, but his love for you is stronger than he can imagine. He makes you fertile by using stones blessed by the azure heavens, and those stones will make you invincible! O rocks, I've now accomplished my task. You became incarnate in me, I loved him and felt his love. A heavenly love, in his image, with passion and vigor like yours. Today, air and water have left me life so that I might come back to you. You alone, blessed earth, can tear me from this body. I entreat you, don't let fire devour my soul! Don't deprive my soul of eternal life. . . . "

Music. Villagers and pilgrims, with garlands of flowers on their heads, dance and sing around the trench to the sound of pipes and fiddle. The songs spread throughout the cemetery and out onto the square, and the rain stops. Soon, it will be time to gather the fruits of the earth, blessed by long processions. Moira smiles at the fertile ground, for she is sure that her own body, this night, will turn to humus.

"MOIRA! MOIRA, WAKE up, I beg you! Hosmund, do you think . . . ?"

The infirmarer shakes his head. He moves his torch closer, but no, she's still alive. He can hear her irregular breathing. Night has come, a night with no moon. All is completely dark, and that suits Roman's purpose. He's come in secret along with Hosmund. Almodius asked Hosmund to bring some wine and food to the woman who will surely die the following day. It's like a condemned man's last meal, and for Moira, it's her first meal in three days and two nights. Raoul has taken advantage of the monks' visit to go for a beer with his soldiers in the nearby inn. A few hours before she's going to die, perhaps the heretic might wish to confess to those fellows, you never know. Down in the hole, everything is dark. In the torch's halo they can see, at the bottom of the trench, a shape stirring feebly like a squashed earthworm.

"Moira!" Roman says again, his voice hollow.

She tries to stand up by supporting herself against the muddy wall, she starts to fall, she straightens up once more, and Hosmund's torch shows them the horror: Her hair has so lost its color and curl, it might be the fur on a dead rat. Her face is gray, mud-splattered, swollen, and her eyes burn with fever. Kneeling there at the edge of the hole, Roman has to slap his hand over his mouth to keep from screaming.

"Is . . . is that you?" she hardly dares ask.

"Yes, my love, it's me, Roman!" He can barely speak.

"Turn the torch away from me and shine it on your own face!" she orders.

Roman pulls down his hood and, swallowing his sobs, anger, remorse, and despair, shows her the loving face she's hoped to see again. She says nothing, but reaches up her hands, which almost touch Roman's when he leans down.

"Moira," Roman begins again. "I beg you on my knees, recant right now, recant. Do it for me, even if you won't do it for yourself!"

She remains silent for a long time and then her disembodied voice answers:

"I'm further gone than you think, Roman. I've already left that dilemma behind. I'm still imprisoned here beneath the earth, but I've already left our earthly world. My body is dying, but I'm no longer suffering. So that our love might live, I must die. And I want to die, out of love for this mountain and for you. If you want to help me now, pray that I might depart this very night and that my soul might reach heaven."

"Moira, what are you saying?" Roman bursts into tears. "These barbarians have stolen your reason! You can't just give in to them and leave me.

I can't let you go! Recant, my love, recant right now, and we'll be able to love each other freely. Moira, I've given a great deal of thought to it, and if you renounce your faith, I'll give up my robe, the monastery, the Mount, and we'll go off together to Bamberg. We won't have any trouble making a living there. I own a little land, and we can live from its fruit. Call the guards, Moira! We must wake up the bishop. Recant, and let's flee far from here!"

"My dear Roman, the fruit of your land is the New Jerusalem, and right here is where it must rise. Do you think physical pain has corrupted my heart so much that I am willing to sacrifice you for our ephemeral, uncertain happiness? Roman, your people created you with heaven, mine created me with the earth. We have been chosen by the spirit that governs this rock, me to protect the past, you to father its future. My ancestors were the flesh of this rock and I the mortar for your stones. I've passed this mountain's secret on to you, a link between past and future. My mission is completed, and now I must rejoin my people. I leave you all, you and your brothers, with the soul of Mont-Saint-Michel, so that you may construct eternal glory in its honor."

"What are you saying? You must be crazy. You can't leave me alone; you can't prefer torture and death to life with me!"

"Some day we will cherish one other, my love, but not in this world. Here it's been our destiny to love this holy mountain's Angel and to devote ourselves to him. Listen to me, Roman. This evening, the last evening of my life on this earth, I'm making you a promise," she said, reaching out her hands toward him. "My soul is sealed by your love and will never forget it. My soul takes this oath: Wherever, whoever you are, I'll always be able to recognize you! I'll cross any rivers and every sea in the universe of the dead and the living to find you, I'll raid your tomb and carry you off with me to the heavens where we can love one another until the end of time."

Roman remains mute. Stunned by her surprising words, he can't fully comprehend what she's saying. And then the noise of weapons clattering on leather belts caps Moira's oath.

"The soldiers!" Hosmund whispers.

"Moira! Recant! Recant!" Roman's hoarse voice entreats her.

She doesn't speak. The lay brother grabs a basket and lets it down into the hole on a rope. Roman pulls his hood back up over his haggard features.

"So, my brothers!" Raoul greets them, clearly a little drunk. "Still with the heretic? Having a meal with her? They don't feed you enough in the monastery? Maybe you ought to go over to the inn. Things are more lively there!"

Hosmund has trouble getting to his feet because he's so heavy. He looks disapprovingly at the blasphemer and signals that Compline has rung and so he can't speak. He pushes Roman along in front of him, and they hurry back to the abbey.

"Okay now!" Raoul says to one of his men. "Down there it's as quiet as a tomb already! No kidding, here the wine is pretty cheap. And that's good, 'cause the weather's nasty and the conversation isn't much better. Sure need the wine to warm us up a little! Brrrr," he shivers, hearing the waves crash against the rocks, "I won't be sorry to get back to Rouen when all this is over. My blood's starting to freeze in this god-awful place!"

"That's for sure, Captain!"

Raoul walks over to the trench and holds out his lantern. The condemned woman is on her knees, her head hidden in her hands. The basket of food lies there beside her untouched.

"Hey, sweetie! Still down there? D'you know you'll be roasted on a skewer tomorrow?"

Moira looks up and stares right at him. There's no worry or sadness in her eyes. They stare straight ahead, burning like the eyes of a ghost, but at the same time they are astonishingly gentle and kind. The look of a saint, of a woman touched by the grace of immortal love. Raoul's mouth drops open in surprise, and he crosses himself.

"I . . . do you want me to call the bishop or the duke? Do you have something to say?"

Without looking away, she shakes her head.

"I'll be praying for you," he promises. "And you really should eat something, or at least drink. Believe me, if your body is full of wine, it won't fight the fire so much and you'll pass out sooner. Drink your wine, get some sleep, and I'll come back when the night's over and bring you some more wine. Then during your last moments you'll be too drunk to suffer much."

Raoul walks away a few steps. There's a long, thin shadow watching every move he makes from behind one of the trees in the cemetery, a dark human shape. The man can't hear any of the captain's words, and his lips, pressed tightly together, are marked by the same silence as Roman's and his sister's.

The master builder has been totally devastated by Moira's words. His prayers and tears spent, he's lying prostrate in Saint Martin's Chapel. Like Brewen, he can no longer speak. All words have been able to do is demonstrate how powerless his love is. However, both Brewen and Roman can hear doleful kisses. The embracing darkness whispers that with night's end their own shadows will begin.

SINCE DAWN A large fire has been imitating the brightly shining sun on the village square, between the parish church and the cemetery. The blaze roars like a bonfire and people are dancing joyfully around it to celebrate Ascension Thursday. Nothing suggests trial by fire. There's no post, and the base of the flames is protected by a large square platform of built-up stones. One might expect to see an ox carcass nearby waiting to be grilled and distributed to the hungry crowd. But there's no meat or skewer anywhere nearby, just a crane borrowed from the building site, a wooden gallows with a winch attached along with a rope and a hook normally used to lift wooden beams. The machine seems out of place, but Raoul doesn't appear to pay any attention to it. He stirs the embers like a true roasting master. He's traded his sword and coat of mail for a large apron and an iron poker. He rubs his hand over his sweaty, emotionless face. As soon as morning mass is finished in the Carolingian church, a solemn procession comes down from the summit of the mountain. At its head is Duke Richard in person, escorted by his court—the bishop of Avranches, Thierry, and Almodius—who are followed by all the brothers from the monastery and then a huge crowd of lay people dressed in their holiday best. Bringing up the rear, soldiers are carrying a steel frame. Soon the square and village cemetery are swarming with a mass of humanity. The captain is still calmly stirring the fire, now mostly burned down. A sea of scarlet embers lies glowing before him. Facing the crowd, Richard the Good, Enguérand d'Eglantier, Roland d'Aubigny, Thierry de Jumièges, and Almodius stand behind the trench where their victim is kneeling. The judges' faces portray the grave majesty people expect from men of their rank on such occasions. Around the abbot's neck hangs a chiseled cross, and he wears a ring with the coat of arms of the Duke of Normandy's family. The prior's eyes glow incandescently, like precious stones. The bishop wears his brilliant miter and carries his golden staff embedded with rubies and emeralds. In his best ceremonial dress, the mountain's uncontested master, Richard II, sweeps his eyes over the crowd like a god from Mount Olympus and looks down regally at his warriors. A ladder is put down into the pit and a soldier starts to descend. In the silence everyone waits with bated breath. Raoul turns toward the pit to see the man climbing back out with the victim on his shoulder. Once they're out, two guards seize Moira by the shoulders and display her to the prince. A third guard grabs her hair and pulls it back so that she has no choice but to raise her head toward her sovereign. The crowd can see her only from behind. Her matted hair is dark like the earth, and as for her shift, it's hard to tell if it's the color of mud or of blood.

"Moira, on this holy day of Ascension, a day that unites all mankind in fervent joy," says Roland d'Aubigny in his strong voice, "I'm going to ask you one last time the same question I've asked you three times in the course of the past three days and which you've refused three times to answer. Moira, daughter of Nolwen and Killian, residing in the forest near the village of Beauvoir, fief of the Mont-Saint-Michel abbey, you've practiced the suspicious role of a healer, and in spite of being baptized, you've maintained commerce with the Evil One using pagan rituals. You've undergone three purifying ordeals so that your soul might return to the Lord. Today, on this holy day when Christ ascended into heaven, tell me if your heart is ready to rejoin God's family!"

Once more, Moira's silence is her answer.

"Since air, water, and earth have not gotten the better of your unclean soul, I sentence you, in the name of our Lord, to perish by fire! May your damned soul never reach heaven! May it return to Hell from whence it came!"

The crowd explodes in joyful catharsis. The soldiers bring the gallows crane closer to the carpet of glowing embers.

They spread Moira's arms and legs and attach her to the steel frame by her wrists, ankles, and waist. Then, with the crowd clapping and screaming, four soldiers carry her over to Raoul who attaches the hook hanging down from the crane to the rope around her waist. He goes around behind the machine and starts turning the crank. Now the improvised grill is in place. Moira is hanging horizontally over the coals. The cruel rotisserie swings for a while and finally comes to a halt. Richard nods to Raoul, and he begins to slowly lower the poor woman. The people grow excited beyond measure. This is far better than the tortures they've witnessed the last three days. The monks, though, are as motionless and as quiet as Moira herself. They cross themselves and pray. In one corner, Brewen stares dry-eyed at this final torture, the present moment's last pain. From now on, his life will be nothing but memory. For him, too, it's the final moment, his last rites. When the grill stops about waist-high above the embers, frying sounds and the smell of roasted flesh begin to waft out through the scorching air. Roman loses control and starts elbowing aside the gawkers, so pleased at the spectacle, to get through to the front row.

Moira's hair begins to melt like a tallow candle, pieces of cloth burn off from the back of her shift and exposes her blistering skin, the rope around her waist begins to loosen. She puts up no struggle; her eyes and features express no emotion. Roman lets out a scream that's camouflaged by the shouting crowd. He leaps toward the machine taken from his own construction site in hopes of maneuvering the pulley and cranking the frame back up, but strong arms grab him and pull him back.

"Please, Roman, don't do that!" Hosmund says, holding him tightly.

"Let go of me, Hosmund!" he shouts. "Let me go!"

"By all-powerful God, listen to me!" the infirmarer begs. "Listen," he whispers, keeping his grip on Roman's arm so he can't budge. "Roman, Moira is already dead, do you understand me? She can't feel anything because she's dead. She was already dead when they lit the fire."

Roman looks at Hosmund, his eyes frozen like stone.

"Just after Lauds," the lay brother explains, "as I was going back to sleep, Almodius came and ordered me to follow him. Outside, Father Thierry was conversing with the bishop, who had just gotten out of bed, and with the captain of the guards, the fellow we saw last night. The abbot was visibly upset, and he told me she had died during the night and that the captain had finally realized it. He asked me to go to the pit to verify that she was dead and not to say one word to anyone. I obeyed. Almodius went with me. The captain told us that he had seen her just after we had been there, and that she was still alive then. Strange, according to him, as if some spirit was living within her, but alive all the same. She wouldn't say a word, but he promised to come back when the night was over to check on her again. Just before dawn, when he held his torch down into the hole, she wasn't moving. He thought she must be sleeping, and he spoke to her, trying to rouse her, but she didn't move. Finally he went down into the pit himself and found that she was no longer breathing. Her eyes were closed, her body was still warm, and her skin had a bluish tint. But she was indeed dead. I checked myself, and there was no doubt. The earth granted her wish, Roman. The earth carried her off to be with her own people. The ghoulish spectacle we see now is designed simply to satisfy the duke and entertain the people."

Roman is both relieved that death saved Moira from the fire and devastated that she's left this world. He looks up again to watch the farce. His beloved's flesh is no more than a few inches from the coals. The heavy smell constricts his throat. Off to his right, some peasant is claiming that it smells like roast pig when you singe its hair after slitting its throat. Hosmund releases his brother's arm. Tears stream down Roman's face. Suddenly, flames shoot up from the coals and, engulfing Moira, devour her savagely. The dead woman's body turns into a torch. The crowd howls with glee. Roman turns and catches Brewen's eye. And then he collapses to the ground.

THE DAY CHURNS on with masses and rogations presided over by the abbot. Out under the sun, Raoul keeps stirring the fire, guarded by armed sentinels, so that nobody can steal a piece of the corpse and use it in some pagan cult or for black magic. There must be nothing left of the cursed body, and incineration is the surest way to destroy it completely, now and forever. Moira's life on the fringes, her crimes against faith, and her terrible painful death all make it likely that she will try to return to haunt the living and exact vengeance on the villagers by causing epidemics, bad harvests, and other catastrophes. There are many witches and healers who have been condemned to death and then buried without the proper precautions. And then they devour their shrouds, eat up their bodies in the coffins, and bring death to the people who condemned them. But on this night, the people of the Mount can sleep peacefully. The flames have exorcised everything. They have deprived Moira of proper burial and of any life in the future. They have prevented her possible return as a ghost.

ON THIS THURSDAY evening after Ascension in the year 1023, Hosmund is on his knees on the infirmary floor praying when Abbot Thierry comes in. Unlike Hildebert, Thierry de Jumièges is young and heavyset.

"How is he?" he asks, starting over toward the bed where Roman is lying.

"Stay away, Father!" answers the infirmarer, getting up and blocking his path. "It's serious. A violent, mysterious fever, and I'm afraid it might be contagious! Stay over by the door; don't put yourself in danger."

The abbot steps back in astonishment and places a handkerchief over his nose and mouth. He watches the sick man's delirium. Roman is extremely pale and is shivering from head to foot. Dripping with sweat and racked with spasms, he rocks his head back and forth, his eyes are open wide, his hands are raised in the air, and alternately he's making little raucous sounds like a carnivore and high-pitched squeaks like a caged bird.

"By all-powerful God!" the abbot exclaims. "I've never seen anything like this!"

He stands quietly a moment behind his handkerchief, looks at Roman again, and then turns back to his infirmarer's poor, defenseless face.

"It must be that woman!" he proclaims in terror. "She has possessed him. She's come to take him along with her to Hell! The heretic must have made a pact with the devil before she died. She's in possession of her lover's body and soul! That's horrible, for she won't be satisfied with her partner in lust. Her soul, faithful to Lucifer, will then begin to harvest even pure souls. By Saint Michael, she's bringing down a contagion on us that will carry off even the souls of the Archangel's servants. We shall all perish!"

"Unfortunately, my Father," the lay brother answers, his voice trembling with fright, "this strange fever did indeed appear this morning at exactly the same time the condemned woman's flesh was being consumed. He was watching her burn when suddenly he collapsed. After we brought him here, he woke up in this condition. My medicines and prayers are powerless against such evil. It's beyond me. I've never seen anything like it. Maybe if we sent for the bishop, he could free Roman from this evil spirit!"

"The bishop left with Richard after Nones," the prince's nephew says, and his face is almost as white as the sick man's. "My uncle invited him to join a hunting party near the borders of the duchy."

"Brother Bernard used be called for exorcisms before he became Roman's assistant," Hosmund suggests, looking at the man in the bed.

"Then he should come immediately," the abbot orders in his rich baritone voice. "Stay with him, my son, and I myself will get Bernard. He must come without delay!"

AFTER NIGHTFALL, BROTHER Bernard, exhausted, leaves the infirmary. His eyes are bright.

"I've done my duty, Father," he reports to the abbot, who's waiting nervously outside with the monks. "He seems to be resting now, but I don't know if he'll live. When he came to, I heard his confession. An exemplary confession, brightened by the breath of angels! He gave me the parchments drawn by Pierre de Nevers, his master builder's rod, and some instructions that I am to give to you if he should seem to be dying. But tonight the appropriate thing to do is pray so that he not be swallowed up by the shadows surrounding us and coveting him. If he lives through the night, he'll be saved."

While Hosmund keeps watch over Roman, the abbot and brothers go back to Saint Martin's Chapel to watch and pray. They chant to make the devil relinquish his claim on Roman as well as his claim on them. Yes,

232 | *Frédéric Lenoir and Violette Cabesos*

now they are also praying for themselves, imploring the Archangel to protect them from the devouring dragon. Just before Matins, Abbot Thierry returns to the infirmary. Almodius, accompaning him, carries a lantern, though a lantern is not really necessary since the night is so clear and so filled with stars. There's no rain, no wind. The elements are calm. Tonight, men alone are tormented. A few feet from the infirmary, they hear screaming from inside. The abbot pounds on the door. Soon Hosmund appears. Thierry and Almodius step back.

"Ah, my Father, Brother Almodius!" says the infirmarer in fright, raising his arms. "It's horrible, worse than before the exorcism! He woke up a few minutes ago, and he's worse off than ever. The fever is higher, he's foaming at the mouth and roaring like an animal! I . . . I had to tie him down! I don't dare let you in. Just look in through the door, and listen. Just listen!"

The two superiors do as he suggests and witness a horrible scene. Roman is tied down to his mat, and he's screaming like an animal. His chin and neck are covered with spittle, his eyes are haggard, his features taut, and his mind appears to be a prisoner to infernal visions.

"We've lost him," Almodius notes coldly. "I'm not at all surprised, but he does endanger the monastery."

"You're right, Almodius." the abbot responds. "We must act swiftly, or we'll all succumb to this calamity. Hosmund, you must take this incubus far away from the Angel's dwelling immediately. You're strong. You won't have any trouble carrying him to a boat and rowing him over to shore."

"But," the lay brother tries to protest, twisting his chapped hands in anguish. "Can't we wait until the sun's up? Where can we go in the middle of the night?"

"The situation is so serious that we can't brook any delay. The hospice in Avranches seems like a suitable refuge," Almodius suggests unfeelingly. "If you'd stop arguing and leave right away, you could be there by daybreak! What do you think, Father?" he asks obsequiously.

"I agree with you, my dear prior. The hospice in Avranches, yes, that's where you need to take him," the abbot decrees. "That's where you can take care of him, and Our Lord will decide his fate. My son, explain things to the good people at the hospice and don't bring him back here until all danger has passed. Besides, you've been in close contact with him during these demonic hours. You've been very kind, but you must also look after yourself. Whatever happens, my dear son, be sure to stay in solitary confinement as long as you need to."

"All will be done according to your will, Father," Hosmund replies with a bow. He has no choice but to obey the abbot, even if the order does seem to be a death sentence. "Have no fear, I'll let the hospice know, and if I catch it, too, they'll keep me away from the monastery whatever transpires. Father, we'll leave right away!"

"Almodius," says the abbot, turning toward the prior, "have some food brought to him for the trip. My son," he says solemnly, looking at the infirmarer but staying a safe distance away, "I give you my blessing. May the Archangel guide and protect you. My son, don't forget. Tonight you hold the future of our abbey in your hands."

Later, beneath the bright full moon, the abbot, prior, and brothers watch the stocky infirmarer walk away with Roman's thin body, bound and gagged, thrown over his shoulder. The monks are greatly relieved to see the dangerous madman being carried off. Their courageous lay brother is surely removing the devil himself from the community. May the Lord judge Hosmund according to his sacrifice, for he might have to pay with his own life.

The brothers are infinitely grateful to Hosmund for what he's doing. Only Brother Bernard, Roman's assistant, remains filled with anxiety, for he failed to help his master regain his reason and now he's the one carrying in his cowl the drawings for the great abbey. He thinks about the people who have carried them before—Pierre de Nevers, Hildebert, Roman, now all either dead or on the path to Hell, and the sketches hang heavy around his neck like a block of stone.

LATE IN THE day on this Thursday of Ascension in the year 1023, at a time when angels and devils desert the Carolingian church, in the tiny office belonging to the master of the scriptorium, a dark, kneeling form pulls his robe down to his waist. A whip punishes the prior's pale back. Soon, blood begins to ooze, and with the blood comes a plaintive cry.

"Moira . . . why did you come to torment this weak soul?"

Almodius continues to strike his back. Old scars from earlier whip-pings open; the pain is immense. His back is shredded, torn, broken like his heart.

"Moira! Everything I've done, I did it for you. Moira . . . Moira . . . Moiraaaaaaaa!"

"MY SONS," SAYS the abbot to the monks, whom he has called together for a special chapter meeting. "As you know, two nights have passed since our brother Hosmund left this rock to carry out a sacred mission for us and for the Angel. This morning, a messenger arrived from the hospice in Avranches. My sons, I must announce to you the passing of our master builder. He was consumed by the demonic fever that had taken hold of him, and he died out on the open waters of the bay before he even got to Avranches. His brave guardian anointed his corpse with holy oil and burned it, so that the purifying flames could destroy the disease, cleanse his tarnished soul, and prevent him from coming back from the nether world to seek us out in his anger. My sons, the Archangel and Hosmund have saved us! Your brother, sorely tried, will stay in the hospice until his quar-antine is finished. I ask you to pray that the contagion from which he saved us might spare him, too. You can see, my sons, how prompt and fearsome is heaven's justice. We, poor mortals that we are, thought we should spare Brother Roman because he was in charge of building the Archangel's dwelling. But Saint Michael could not tolerate an impure soul acting in his name. He condemned his unworthy servant as our Lord had condemned the ungodly woman. And both perished, both were consumed by the weight of their sins. Fear divine justice! Yes, fear it above anything else! You see what horrible punishment was inflicted on an apostate for keeping an illicit relationship with the heretic! Keep in mind how he suffered! My sons, now we will pray for our benefactor Hosmund's safety and for our master builder's soul so that it might be freed from its sinister companion. Let us redeem his sins, my brothers, let us redeem his mortal sins with the purity of our own souls and actions. Let us work for his forgiveness."

"Father," the former prior, Brother Robert, interrupts him. "Hos-mund is a saintly soul, but he's not a priest. He wasn't able to preside over the burial ceremony."

"In his great foresight, the All-Powerful put in his path a group of pilgrims leaving our mountain, my son," Thierry continues affably. "They were among the faithful who had come to celebrate the Feast of Ascension with us, and they were on their way home with their parish priest. On that morning, after the possessed man's body had been consumed in the flames, the priest assisted Hosmund. Inspired by the Archangel and edified by watching the pagan woman's torture, he buried Roman's remains in a swamp. Before burying him, he carried the remains around in circles so that Roman would never be able to find his way back to the Mount, and he pronounced the customary formulas of absolution so his soul might find peace. You have nothing more to fear, neither his return nor his eternal banishment."

Everything falls silent. The relief is palpable.

"And now, my sons," the abbot goes on, "now that the peril has passed and Saint Michael's will has been accomplished, we can continue our secular mission—building the grand basilica. Our master builder is no more, but he has left us his assistant. Brother Bernard learned from both Pierre de Nevers and Roman, during the time Roman was uncorrupted. Bernard's experience and fervor are allied with our prince's support and our devotion to this place's spiritual master. Beginning tomorrow, my sons, the work will start again in the choir crypt, under Bernard's direction. In his great prudence, your brother communicated to me Roman's confession. He was able to get it when the demons deserted our master builder's soul momentarily, and I shall reveal to you all his astonishing confession, for it concerns the entire community."

Thierry pauses, whetting the monks' curiosity and attention. Hildebert could sometimes achieve such effects, but the new abbot is a true master of the theatrical arts. Robert thinks bitterly that Thierry must get his inspiration more from the buffoons and jesters at Richard's court than from mystery plays presented in the cathedrals.

"Yes," the abbot continues. "The demons had temporarily fled from Roman, frightened away by your brother Bernard's prayers and holy water. And then the angels possessed him. With his mind and heart illuminated by Saint Michael, Roman took on the voice of our founder Aubert! Bernard certified it, and he can certify it for you as well. He saw

236 | *Frédéric Lenoir and Violette Cabesos*

his master in full ecstasy, guided by the Divine Spirit! Finding refuge near the Lord, the saintly bishop ordered that some of the sketches for the future abbey be modified. The sky opened for a moment above the poor man who was about to end up in the shadows, and the heavens, through Aubert himself, ordered him not to destroy the church now sheltering his sanctuary. The mountain's first builder forbade us to touch his oratory, the one he built with his own hands in accord with the Archangel's orders when he appeared for the third time!"

Stupefaction could be seen in everyone's face; it was followed by intense religious fervor.

"My sons," says the abbot, himself almost in transport, "we know the price of disobeying divine injunctions. We've heeded the warning the Angel has sent us. The Angel spoke to Roman, but unfortunately, our brother allowed himself to be caught up in evil and it killed him. May God's infinite grace have saved him from Lucifer's claws at the last instant! We who serve the forces of Good, we shall respect Saint Michael's wishes and the wishes of our founder. We will preserve the Carolingian church, for it holds within its walls vestiges of Aubert's grotto. The saintly man's relics will be displayed for the faithful to venerate in his chosen place, the current church, and we will transform it into a crypt to support the new church's nave. Through the hand and mouth of Brother Roman, Aubert modified the drawings and gave precise instructions so that we might accomplish his sacred will. Hildebert will rest with his predecessors, as Richard has planned, in the choir's crypt. As Aubert wished, he'll be in the old church, built where his original sanctuary lay. Bernard, you've told me that these changes would mean that we can no longer use Saint Martin's Chapel. I should be able to convince our good prince that the change is necessary. When work on the nave begins in a few decades, the church will become a dark underground crypt, suitable for reflection and humility as Aubert would have liked. And the underground crypt will support the nave of the abbey church, which shall be bathed in angelic brightness. The crypt beneath the earth will carry the heavens! My sons, if the Lord grant us life, we shall see that crypt. But already this day I will baptize the edifice in honor of the statue of the Black

Virgin it houses. The Black Virgin has come to us from time immemorial when the pagan gods were destroyed and the mountain converted to Christ. For today the old religion's dragon has been definitively vanquished! So that we always remember the sacred order the Archangel and Aubert have given us, I name this crypt Notre-Dame-sous-Terre!"

II

H E HAD TRAVELED ACROSS TIME, NEARLY TEN CENTURIES, THANKS
to a copper tube that looked like a telescope. The tube had been
hermetically sealed and placed in the stone vault that had protected it
and its contents from rats, worms, mold, and damage from the ground.
Paul had taken the time to put on gloves before he very carefully unrolled
the parchment sheets so they wouldn't break, then checked their moisture content, took detailed photographs, inserted them in plastic sleeves,
and placed them in an album. He had set the album on the desk in his
bedroom, beside the copper cylinder, a Gaffiot dictionary, and a notepad.
Johanna would come first to the dig. He had calculated that it would take
her about eight hours to drive from Mont-Saint-Michel. Paul hoped that
she had slept a little before starting out. He himself hadn't been able to
sleep, even after the party the team had organized, because he was so excited about the discovery.

After lunch, representatives from Historical Monuments showed up.
They were never in much of a hurry, as was the case yesterday morning
when they were supposed to send a crane to lift the sarcophagus. But the
good news was that François hadn't come down from his office in Paris.
In fact, Paul hadn't let him know, for if François knew Johanna was coming, he'd be in their hair within two hours, and Paul wanted to be alone
with her when she read the manuscript.

Local journalists showed up at three o'clock. Paul had his picture taken
with the vault, the way Howard Carter had done with King Tut. He refused to make any announcements, however, and said only that the work

was just beginning. Nor did he say one word about the parchment. Finally, at four, Johanna rushed into the dig, her clothing wrinkled and her hair in disorder. There were rings under her eyes, but Paul could see that they were glowing with anticipation.

"He's waited nine and a half centuries, so he can surely wait five more minutes," Paul exclaimed, standing in the middle of his room with a champagne glass in his hand. "First we'll drink, and then I'll tell you all the details!"

Johanna agreed, though impatience and fatigue were gnawing at her. She had had to wait, too. She had waited until morning to tell her team and to leave her assistant instructions for the work to be done before the beginning of Christmas vacation a few days later. She would have preferred to leave as soon as she had spoken with Paul, but didn't want to risk giving Patrick Fenoy more ammunition to use against her. So she had slept fitfully until seven and then announced the tomb's discovery over breakfast. She had left her cell phone number, given Florence a letter for Christian Brard, wished everyone a good vacation, and said that they would start work again on January 2. As she drove away from Mont-Saint-Michel, she had a strange feeling. On the causeway, when she looked at the rock in her rearview mirror, she felt that it was speaking to her, that it was saying it had prepared a little surprise for her—one that was going to significantly change her life; that, when she came back to the Mount, she would view it in a totally new way. Her love for the rock would be stronger still. Immortal. And she would belong to it, body and soul. A woman by the rock possessed. For eight hours, Johanna's imagination roved from the Mount to Cluny and back as she drove. Cluny . . . Paul hadn't given her any clues, purposefully.

"This is the best Christmas present that chance or fate has ever given me!" Paul was saying, choked with emotion. "I was about ready to say good-bye forever to Hugh de Semur and Cluny, you know. After you left, things just weren't the same. I had begun to have doubts. In short, yesterday morning, as usual, I headed to the dig, knowing that my days here are numbered. But I couldn't bring myself to jump down into the pit. How can I explain? My lassitude, the cold, exhaustion, the others . . . the earth seemed to be harassing me, and I was about fed up with digging through it as if I were digging my own grave. And then I thought of you," he admitted, blushing. "And I went to see Firmament, like you used to do when you were discouraged. He was snorting nervously in his stall, and whinnying, and that didn't reassure me at all. The stable boy told me that horses are very sensitive to weather and to things people can't see. That made me smile, but all the same I was a little intrigued. What might the horse be sensing that I couldn't? I walked closer to him, and suddenly he calmed down. Firmament let me rub his nose and neck. Feeling the horse's warm, soft skin did me good. Just that simple, magical contact calmed me down, too, and I was able to go back to work. For some reason, I left the square I had been working on and started digging in one of the few sections left. A section that, when we first laid things out, was going to be one of yours. I was digging rapidly but without much conviction, thinking that you must be doing the same thing there on your mountain.

"And then around noon," he continued, looking out the window, "I heard it: the characteristic sound of a hard object. I was immensely hopeful, but also afraid that once again it'd be something ordinary. At the same time I had a feeling I can't explain, but from instinct or experience perhaps I had the premonition that finally I was discovering something important. Only it was something you yourself should have discovered. I slowly brushed away a few centimeters of soil, and I saw the letter 'R' appear on some local stone, quarry limestone. My heart stopped, and so did I.

"But I already knew it couldn't be Hugh's tomb. I tried to calm down, and then I brushed some more. Finally a whole name appeared: PETRUS. Yes, Pierre. I was paralyzed, captivated, unable to continue. I thought it might be the abbot Pierre le Vénérable. And then I called the others over. Things weren't easy, because over the years the tomb had slipped sideways and was now turned diagonally, but it was still sealed and hadn't been opened. The Latin inscription on the stone was Romanesque in its simplicity: Pierre de Nevers, Cluny monk, master builder of the church, deceased in the year of grace 1022—and there were the customary formulas wishing peace to his soul. It was the date that startled me! The year 1022, when Odilon was abbot! I knew that Nevers was the architect who had finished Cluny II, and I knew that he had died in a building accident during its construction, but I wasn't expecting to find his tomb. As I said on the telephone, we can thank Hugh for helping us find Pierre de Nevers, who should be resting in the choir of Cluny II with Odilon. Hugh must have moved both of them to the holy of holies in Cluny III. Or perhaps it was Hugh V or Bertrand I in the thirteenth century, when they reorganized the tombs in the choir. Whatever the case may be, it means that we were right about where the choir of Cluny III was located, and this discovery opens up the possibility of many others. Now everything is possible, do you see? Of course we can start looking for Hugh, but also for Odilon, Bernon, and Pierre le Vénérable!"

"That's right. But first of all, you don't yet have permission to do that. And secondly, we have to start with what you've found and learn all we can about it by dating it with archeometry," said Johanna, interrupting him.

"Yes, of course!" he answered, pouring and drinking another glass. "So, we waited all day long for the crane and the conservator. And then finally we were able to extricate the tomb and open it. I was so afraid I'd be disappointed! But it was beyond my wildest dreams. There he was, wrapped in his moth-eaten monk's robe. At his side lay this copper cylinder. Oh, dear corpse, lovely skeleton, flower of my dreams, you've become my best friend!"

Johanna could hardly wait. She put down her champagne glass, glanced over at the copper tube and then at the album containing the manuscript.

"Just a second, my dear angel," he said, already a little drunk. "I'm getting there, to the main show! I'm the one who read it first. In fact, I'm the only one who has read it. I forbade anyone else even to touch it! I've kept it for you, so you can be the second person in the last thousand years to read it. I've prepared it for you, watched over it all night long, and now it's yours. There it is, go ahead!"

"Paul," she said, taking his hands. "I already know that I can never thank you enough for this, and for many other things. I love you deeply, Paul, and I'm moved by all that you've said. But you're the one who discovered it! You're the one who should now reap the benefits. You must authenticate it, learn all that it can reveal to us about the period, and publish everything in your name! Pierre de Nevers waited more than nine centuries for you, and he shouldn't have to wait five more minutes. Go talk to him. He has thousands of things to share with you. But now what I'd like to do is to be alone with it," she said, gesturing toward the manuscript, "before giving it back to you. Please, let me study it alone for just a few moments."

Paul looked like a whipped puppy, but he raised his chin proudly and walked out without a word toward the dig where his new study partner lay. Johanna hurriedly locked the door. Slowly, she sat down at the table. She began by examining the copper cylinder that had protected the manuscript from air, light, and water. Then she laid it back down. Her fingers moved slowly toward the album. She closed her eyes and breathed deeply before opening it. She felt like she was excavating a sepulcher from the long-silent, mysterious earth, and that a tomb was opening up before her. The writing was a promise. The dark ink letters, tight and oval-shaped, in the tiny Carolina hand inherited from Charlemagne, displayed the skill of an educated man if not the artistry of the complex forms used by scriptorium monks. For the author, the contents of the manuscript were more important than its form. It was clearly a hand used for drawing up charters and basic documents rather than sacred texts. And yet what beauty emanated from these thousand-year-old characters scratched onto on the yellow parchment, some of them rubbed out and written over! She couldn't resist touching them, and with a lover's gestures she removed them from their transparent plastic prison.

Contrary to what was normal for ordinary medieval manuscripts, the parchment was of excellent quality, the quality usually reserved for copying Bibles—a lovely sheepskin, without defect, tanned according to the rules of the art by a first-quality monastic workshop. Which workshop? Cluny, or somewhere else? Each one had its own particular method of fabrication, but Johanna wasn't an expert in such matters. They'd have to call in a specialist. Whatever the case, the author had done his best to try to preserve what he was writing. Johanna couldn't help running her fingers over the smooth skin, as smooth as a man's back. She lifted it to her nostrils. To the Russian novelist Bulgakov, old parchments smelled like chocolate. This one smelled more like autumn at the seashore, a scent of dry leaves and salt, no—not a sea breeze but rather the scent of dried tears. Johanna spread the nine sheets of sheepskin out before her. She kept putting off her actual reading of the manuscript, for her heart was already troubled enough by the presence of the parchments themselves. Their significance confused her, overwhelmed her. They held a power that had crossed centuries, a sensation of eternity mixed with tragic urgency. She polished her glasses on the sleeve of her sweater, put them back on, looked over at the Latin dictionary, and dived into her search for the manuscript's meaning and for the unknown man who had composed its words.

CLUNY ABBEY, EASTER, THE YEAR OF OUR LORD 1063
TO ABBOT HUGH DE SEMUR

My Father in Christ. For forty years I've been living in this place dedicated to Saint Peter, prince of the apostles and keeper of the keys of heaven. Forty years like the Israelites in the desert, and my soul and body have performed acts of contrition and repentance. On this very holy day when our Savior rose from the dead, I cannot share my brothers' joy because I'll be leaving you. The urgent trip I must undertake, here in the evening of my life, is not the trip we all hope for. That precious moment is indeed near, but before leaving this earth I have one final mission to accomplish, and my duty demands that I fly far from you. I am not running away from anything, Father, even if you may so believe. I'm ashamed to cast dishonor on our house by this perceived affront, and that's why I'm composing this confession for you. I'm not asking for your forgiveness, for I know I'm not worthy of that. But if you read what I am confessing, you will know that my soul has already been judged.

I'm entrusting this manuscript to Brother Grégoire, and he has promised to give it to you if I'm not back by the New Year. And only death can keep me from coming back and prostrating myself at your feet to ask your mercy for the sin I'm about to commit. Knowing the purity and the legitimate expectations of your heart,

I have never confided in you the trouble I'm embroiled in, for I know that your venerable authority and your keen intelligence would have changed my decision. So I'm leaving Cluny in sorrow, painfully aware of my villainy, but at least I shall have told you the true causes of my outrage. In order to do that, I, who am now an old man, need to remember my youth and faithfully narrate my story, whose wounds are still painful after forty years of praying. Father, this is my story.

You know of course that your predecessor, Abbot Odilon, allowed me to enter these walls in the year of our Lord 1023. I did not hide from the saintly man the things I am now ready to tell you, and in his immense kindness, he opened the monastery doors to me all the same. I've always wondered if Odilon, before he set out on the path to heaven, might have told you the secret surrounding my arrival in Cluny. If my memory serves me correctly, you came to Cluny around 1040 when you were about fifteen years old, and Odilon, noticing your merits and virtues, quickly named you grand prior. Perhaps he did tell you about me. I never had the misplaced audacity to ask you, given that you always treated me like the other brothers. You were strict, just, and magnanimous. Today the question is no longer important. Back in that long-ago year of 1023 I was a young man of thirty, and I wore the Benedictine habit I still wear today. When I entered this cloister, my brothers surely believed that I had come from one of the many establishments that had adopted Cluniac customs. I admit that I was deathly afraid that one of them would ask me about my past during the times when we were allowed to speak! The first days, I tried to avoid them whenever speaking was authorized. However, with Odilon's agreement, I had retaken my baptismal name and resolved never to tell my brothers the whole truth. Thanks to God, I soon adapted to the community's way of life, although I didn't know anything about it when I first arrived. I rapidly took my place among the eighty monks as harmoniously as if I had been an oblate living here for decades. Whenever a priest or a lay brother asked about my past, I said only that I was an aristocrat

born in Bavaria and that I came from a Benedictine monastery in
Cologne. I hid that I found refuge in Cluny when fleeing Normandy and an abbey that is not a Cluniac abbey, where I had
spent more than six years. For years, whenever a brother from
Normandy happened to stop in Cluny, Odilon kindly authorized
me not to appear in the choir or refectory so there'd be no risk
that the brother would recognize me.

Odilon was well acquainted with that abbey in Normandy. It's a
monastery perched on a mountain, between earth, sky, and sea. The
ancients called it Mont Tombe, and we call it Mont-Saint-Michel.

Johanna uttered a cry. She rose and went over to the window to calm
her nerves, as Paul had done a few moments before. Paul, dear Paul! Mechanically, she looked out over the vestiges of Cluny III off in the distance framed in the evening light. Her eyes rested on the top of the
tower, the Tour de l'Eau Bénite, and she could imagine seeing the black
tip of the Mount appear above it in the threatening sky. She went back to
the table and turned on the lamp.

I lived almost seven years at Mont-Saint-Michel, from 1017 to
1023, as the assistant to Pierre de Nevers, my master, whom I had
followed to Normandy, and then I myself became the master
builder of the new abbey.

Incredible! Phenomenal! The man who wrote this letter was the architect of the Romanesque abbey at Mont-Saint-Michel! Johanna had
the sudden urge to turn immediately to the name on the parchment's last
line, a name that had been lost for centuries. And then she realized that
to do so would be a profanation. Patience! A little patience! He had
waited forty years to confess, and it had taken the words almost ten centuries to reach her. She needed to allow the narrator to proceed at his
own pace. Relax.

Stones were my life. God, and then stones. My master had
taught me their languages from construction site to construction

site, all over Europe. I venerated Pierre de Nevers for what he was teaching me and for himself. He was a pious, generous monk humbly serving the Lord in prayers, but especially by building churches with such mystical force that their stones helped build men's souls. I no longer fear confessing that he was the man who instilled fervor in my heart by transmitting his art to me. With him, I learned that the master builder is above all a missionary, an evangelist with a visionary spirit, a man who builds in order to reveal faith to men, faith and the glory of God, now and for all eternity, guided by the Most High.

At that time Hildebert, whom you never met, though I'm sure you heard his infinite wisdom praised, was the abbot at Mont-Saint-Michel. He asked my master to come to the Mount to build a new abbey, and we both set out proudly for Normandy, overjoyed as we were to serve our Lord through that grand project. If only I had guessed that my entire existence and everything I believed in would be turned upside down by that trip! Nevertheless, such was my destiny.

We arrived at that strange mountain, battered as it is by the elements, isolated from mortals and so near the heavens that it was chosen by the first among the angels as his dwelling place. From the year 1017 until the disastrous year 1022, my master and I lived among the angels, totally committed to the sacred task ordered by the Most High and Hildebert his servant. I'll not describe the marvelous creations Pierre de Nevers drew on his parchments to give form to that fabulous undertaking that no man had ever dared imagine before. The heavenly Jerusalem now standing on that rock in Normandy, although it's not completely finished, we owe to my master, and he was inspired by All-Powerful God.

That's the year Abbot Odilon called Pierre de Nevers back here to Cluny to finish the building planned by the Abbot Maïeul, the abbey church Saint-Pierre-le-Vieil, in which I'm now writing to you. During the forty years I've spent among you, not one day has passed that I didn't affectionately touch these stones that were my dear master's life and are now his tomb. They are his final prayer,

his soul, his blood, and they are as much his gravestones as the
stones in the choir. Every day they bring me comfort and warmth.
May the Lord grant me the favor of finishing my life here in their
shadows! Their protective, familiar shadows, that's what I asked
for when I came to see Odilon and speak to my master's soul so
long ago. But if you are reading this letter, then I now am already
under other skies. May God's will be done.

When Pierre de Nevers left Mont-Saint-Michel in the late
spring of 1022, when, without knowing it, my eyes looked into his
for the last time, he entrusted to me his sketches and his master
builder's rod, bequeathing to me the heavy responsibility of supervising the construction until he got back, which he never did. Although worried about the responsibility, I did confidently accept,
supported by Brother Bernard, a monk from the Mount whom my
master had also taught the stones' secrets. Construction was set to
begin at Easter, 1023. Summer went by like a flash. Life on the
mountain was tough, filled with nature's demonic rages and with
apparitions, but everything remained under the protection of a
powerful patron saint. However, our fervent souls were often put
to the test, and I myself was not spared. The trial sent to me by
heaven was as big as the task it had entrusted to me and that occupied all my thoughts.

All thought suspended, Johanna listened to the night silence and recognized the calm that often precedes great storms.

Her name was Moira, Marie in her people's language. Her hair
reminded me of fire because of its color and life. Her eyes looked
like leaves in the springtime, her skin was pale and transparent like
clouds, speckled with sun-like freckles, and her mouth was a
changing sea, lively, animated and dangerous at one moment, then
calm and serene the next. She could communicate with trees,
rocks, and ponds, and her whole being carried the perfume of a
forest beneath salty rain. She was the trial heaven had chosen for
me, a joy engendered from centuries of human misfortune, the

earth angel I felt I had to save from ultimate disaster. Excuse me, Father, I hope you don't take this wrong. I'm finally bringing myself to speak after forty years of silence, prayer, and supplication, so don't fall victim to the confusion that caused our loss. I was a monk, I'm still a monk, in full possession of all my faculties in spite of my advanced age, and never has this habit of virtue been sullied by breaking my vow of chastity. You must believe me. Never did I commit that sin, even if many others have stained my soul, and I've expiated those mistakes during the past forty years. But I see I'm still trying to defend myself, me the guilty one, when really she alone is the one I should have helped. Alone, for alone she was, with a younger deaf-mute brother only thirteen years old, named Brewen, a strange, strapping fellow who communicated with his eyes and whose infirmity she was unable to heal. However, never had I seen such skill in easing the body's suffering. She was well versed in the herbal arts, and she was my devoted doctor for days and nights after I had been grievously wounded by the knife belonging to a man who robbed pilgrims.

She cared for me when Brother Almodius, subprior and master of the scriptorium, had already heard my confession and administered the last rites, and when Brother Hosmund, the monastery's infirmarer, would never have managed with his remedies. She healed me, and then I was taken back to the Mount to be with my brothers, to my great misfortune and theirs. She was already in love with me then, and I loved her already. My heart, in its hidden corners, knew that I did, but my mind didn't.

Johanna raised her head, removed her glasses, and rubbed her eyes. The master builder of the great abbey. She had expected some long lists relating to its construction, a profusion of technical details, some abstract ideas, or perhaps some religious symbols, but not a love story with a real person! And yet she was far from disappointed. The author, whose name was still unknown to her, had caught her up in the meanders of his tale. The description of Moira and the monk's passion had shaken her, and little by little Johanna was overwhelmed with the strange feeling that she was being attracted by something very personal, something she seemed already to know about but was unable to identify.

However, Moira had confided something in me, and that was our tragedy. Moira was Celtic, descending from a long line of druids, the latest person to have received a portion of their ancestral knowledge. Although she had been baptized and did venerate Christ, the Virgin, and Saint Michael, she continued to observe pagan rites and to remain faithful to her ancestors' false religion. Certain that such was our Lord's will, I took it upon myself to meet Moira, alone and in secret, in order to convert her to the true God. That was my unspeakable sin—not trying to convert her, but believing I was doing it to serve God. For God had already assigned me my sacred earthly mission, to build the New Jerusalem for him! I should have been contented with that mission, of course, but it was already too late. If only I could have known myself then as I do now! Too late. It had been too late for a long time, for I didn't suspect that my love for stones was moribund and that it had changed into something stronger, something more perilous, into love for a woman.

She had transformed my heart, the heart of a master builder, had turned it into a man's heart, and I couldn't see the difference, for I was fighting to save a part of me that no longer existed, a part that had disappeared with my master. I should have confessed my plans to Hildebert, but, blinded by the vanity of youth, I said nothing to him. I was able to send a letter to Moira, asking her to come to Saint Martin's Chapel by night.

Three different times she came, and three different times she watched me struggle with my feelings for her as if I were fighting against dragons. She knew she had won and was just waiting for the moment when I would lay my weapons down at her feet, and at the feet of our undeniable love. I had nearly given in but was still resisting. She could see me suffering, and during our third meeting, on the second Sunday of Lent in the year 1023, she's the one who tried to break it off, out of love for me. She tried to slip away and leave me to my stones. As I was about to lose her, my eyes finally opened and I listened to my heart. Not fully knowing what I was doing, I revealed the passion that had been driving me until then. I showed her the drawings of the great abbey, Pierre de Nevers's sketches. And then, knowing full well what she was doing, she entrusted to me the mountain's secret, the enigma of her own sacred earthly mission. I've always hid the mystery in my heart. Father, do allow me to continue keeping it secret, in memory of her, because that's all I have left.

That evening, I listened to Moira's soul, though I couldn't fully understand it. She was already far away and I needed time to reach her. And yet I had already waited too long! The delay proved fatal. On Easter Day in the year of our Lord 1023, exactly forty years ago, construction began on the great abbey church. On the following Tuesday, Hildebert sent for me. He accused me of sinful relations with a woman, and, what's more, with a heretic. Brother Almodius had seen us together, and, even worse, he had heard Moira invoking Ogma, a pagan divinity, near a pond. That very same day Hildebert summoned her, accused her, and demanded that she abjure her religion. I witnessed the meeting, dumb with confusion, and it's still engraved in my flesh like a scar. Almodius had divulged her grave sin to Hildebert, but I was the one who was really the infidel! She had saved my life, and she was preserving my life's meaning right before my eyes, and in return I was disowning her by my silence. She kept her faith until the end, refusing to recant. The abbot threatened to exile her forever from the abbey's lands, but for the moment he sent her back to her forest, free, telling her to think about it, and saying that he himself would come to hear her abjuration at dawn the following Sunday. Alas, if I had been a little wiser, I wouldn't have been so pleased with his benevolent verdict, nor would I have wasted any further thought on my sacrosanct construction site. I was so relieved, for I believed our story was now bound to turn out right! If I hadn't been so weak, I would have fled the monastery immediately. I would have rushed to her and taken her away far from that sinister

mountain, using force if necessary, yes, even force! Instead, sick of
body, I collapsed on a mat in the infirmary.

The next day I managed to get a letter to Moira, and in that
letter I finally confessed my love. I begged her to do what the
abbot was asking. It was important to act quickly, and I wrote to
her, supplicating her to renounce her ungodly faith, promising to
love her in secret however uncertain our chances to meet, giving
her assurances about some indefinite future. Valetudinarian clum-
siness! Even though I was tragically devoid of the courage to act,
there were others who were not. As soon as the abbot released
Moira, my brother Almodius, exasperated by Hildebert's magnanimity, went straightaway to see the bishop of Avranches, Roland
d'Aubigny, an insignificant, presumptuous man, to denounce
Moira. The bishop seized the opportunity to reduce the abbot's
power and immediately alerted our suzerain, Richard the Good.
Moira was arrested by the prince's soldiers and taken to prison in
Avranches.

Johanna suddenly realized she was trembling. She stood up and
poured herself a glass of tepid champagne to regain her courage. The
poor man was so torn by remorse, forty years after the events, that she
herself ached for him. She was convinced that most men in his situation
would not have shown any more courage, instinct, or lucidity about their
real feelings. The bitter, cruel wound he described remained an open
wound, and not many other men would have imposed such suffering on
themselves. All those years of silence in a monastery had failed to weaken
his love for the woman or to moderate his suffering. On the contrary!
Those years had exacerbated his understanding of the difference between Moira and himself. Yes, everything had happened as if the young
Celtic woman had always been one step ahead of the monk by anticipat-
ing their misfortune and then resigning herself to it. Indeed, she had
acted as if everything had been planned long before, as if she was aware
of their destiny and had no choice but to follow her dark star from the
day she was born. This realization made Johanna ill at ease. In any case,
she was enthralled by the tale and felt its effects deep down inside her.

The monk's passion, alternating between an abbey's cold stones and a woman's heart, captivated her. And so did Moira's reaction. Everything conspired against her, but her head high, motivated by a personal secret that the monk refused to divulge, she continued down her chosen path. That secret made her stronger, able to resist everything, even the worst. And the worst did arrive. Moira expected it and was waiting for it. Johanna, too, was waiting for it.

> And then Hildebert burst into the refectory, looking for Almodius. I had never seen my father with such an expression on his face. Yes, I can see him now, a man so wise and thoughtful, in an indescribably furious rage, burning from within. I've never forgotten his face, for that was the last time I saw Hildebert alive.
>
> According to Almodius, our father suffered a malaise during their conversation in his cell. Afterward, Almodius himself was the one who organized and dispensed care for the sick man, often refusing Hosmund's help. We never heard anything about the nature of the conversation that had triggered the abbot's collapse, and Almodius was careful to keep us away from the cell where he was lying. It would have been easy for him to leave Hosmund with the abbot, go to the infirmary, and pour some poison into the lay brother's medicines! Naturally, I have no proof of what I'm suggesting, but when I tell you, Father, about all of the turpitudes Almodius committed in the years that followed, you will surely understand my grave doubts.

No book stated categorically that the famous Abbot Hildebert had been murdered. But Johanna remembered reading one book in which the author proposed such a hypothesis, though he couldn't prove it or even give details about the circumstances surrounding Hildebert's death. She knew she had come across the name Almodius but couldn't remember in what context. She would need to check on it, only she was almost sure it had nothing to do with Hildebert. She realized that she could learn more about Hildebert's death from this totally unknown manuscript than by poring over any history book.

For two days and two nights, my brothers and I prayed fervently in Saint Martin's Chapel. At dawn on Sunday, at the very time Hildebert had set for hearing Moira's abjuration and for welcoming her into God's dwelling, at that same fateful hour, he expired.

That's when the world I thought I knew escaped my reason, so much did it change. I felt totally lost during those events, for they provoked violent, confused thoughts within me. Along with Hildebert, all clemency and thoughtfulness disappeared. The rock was prey to greed, intrigues, and plots. Duke Richard imposed a new abbot on us, Thierry de Jumièges, none other than his own nephew. Almodius was named prior and also kept his appointment as head of the scriptorium. Thus did evil men take power on the mountain. As for Moira, they judged her in Rouen. The church tribunal, manipulated by Richard and presided over by Roland d'Aubigny, pronounced a sentence that even today fills me with terror and wrath!

"Well, now," Johanna thought. "What a curious coincidence. Joan of Arc, a saint to whom Saint Michael had appeared and whom he'd asked to take up arms, was also judged in Rouen, by Robert Jolivet, a former abbot at the Mount who had betrayed his sons, his king, and the sacred rock when he joined the English invaders. And she was burned as a heretic in that very city on a day near Ascension Day, May 31, 1431, near Saint Michel, a church belonging to the abbey at Mont-Saint-Michel.

I was kept away from the trial. I didn't find out what happened until the judgment was pronounced. My Father, I'm not confessing that to lessen my guilt. On the contrary. She's the one they judged, but I was really the guilty one. Guilty of blindness, guilty of allowing Almodius to give her over to the prince and bishop and of doing nothing to save her. And she protected me once again like an experienced guardian angel. As they interrogated her, never did she pronounce my name! For another reason, her judges, four of whom were my monastery brothers, didn't bring my name up, either. They were keeping in mind the abbey's stones, in their belief that the stones were surely more powerful than my love for Moira! I was needed to direct the construction project. Since my brothers, mere mortal men, failed to judge me, Father, God and the stones will do so. When Almodius was heard as a witness, he, too, respected their decision and didn't mention my name. He poured out his bile on Moira. And with his cruel, diabolical imagination, perhaps he's the one who came up with the horrible sentence. In reference to the Celtic cross she wore around her neck, Moira was sentenced to be tortured by the four natural elements until she either recanted or died. The judgment would be carried out on the Mount, in public, on Ascension Day.

Dear Father, suddenly my quill freezes like my blood, and I'm powerless to describe calmly for you the spectacle I witnessed from afar. The wretched images will forever be engraved in my memory. They are my everlasting wound, and I can never remember Moira's torture without bursting into tears. That's the cross I've borne for forty years. The air. A day and a night. She wouldn't recant and was still alive. Water. A day and a night. She wouldn't recant and remained alive, calling my name. Earth. A day and a night. She wouldn't recant and died. The earth had killed her. On the day we celebrate Christ's ascension into heaven, they built a huge fire on the village square. They had hid her death from the duke and from the people, and they moved her corpse around like a puppet. Then they tied it to an iron frame that was lifted by one of the construction cranes out over the carpet of embers. Fire. A day and a night. The flames consumed her.

Johanna moved away so that her tears wouldn't spoil the manuscript.

You will understand, Father, that continuing my job as master builder was inconceivable. The sacred duty inspiring me now was not to abandon to a second death the person I had abandoned in life and sacrificed to the abbey stones. Now I needed to fight to save the soul of a woman who had never stopped trying to save my life. Naturally, this house came to mind, Father, this sacred haven

THE ANGEL'S PROMISE | 255

totally devoted to respecting the dead. I thought about Abbot
Odilon, Hildebert's friend, who was said to be as magnanimous in
mind and spirit as my deceased master. I could see Pierre de Nevers's face once more and imagined what his tomb must look like
here in this church. I confess, too, that I thought about Cluny's
privilege exempting it from the authorities, both bishops and
princes. I realized that I had to leave the Mount and seek asylum
in Cluny, where, if my deceased master and Odilon granted me
protection, I would be able to live in silence, expiate my sins, and
above all set my beloved's soul free so that she might welcome me
to heaven the day I died, for we were promised to each other for
eternity.

Immediately I revealed my project to Hosmund and he raised a
sound objection. Thierry and Almodius—Almodius had a great
deal of power over the new abbot—both mistrusted me and would
never allow me to leave the abbey, because of the construction.
Suddenly I saw the solution. I would fool my peers into believing
I was possessed by Moira's diabolical soul and had fallen victim to
a deadly contagious fever that might kill them all if they kept me
in their midst. I had to persuade Hosmund to be my accomplice
in this subterfuge, and that wasn't easy.

I confess the deception, Father, and I've often asked God to
forgive me for it, me and Hosmund, but in those circumstances I
didn't see any other way out. So after Vespers I swallowed an
herbal potion my friend had stirred up to induce a fever, a physical
fever that wouldn't reduce my lucidity but would make people
think that I was gripped by some powerful mysterious malady.
Hosmund was in terror, and that helped my plans. Once, during
my travels in Saxony with my master, I had seen a man truly possessed by the devil, and I used that memory as inspiration. The
brew induced sweating, paleness, spasms, and chills. I added piercing screams, incoherent mumblings, and flailing limbs.

As I thought he would, the abbot came to inquire about my
health near the end of the long day of ceremonies. He convinced
himself that the sinful woman's soul was pursuing me and that it

would soon begin tormenting all the brothers in the same way. All Hosmund had to do was to suggest that only Brother Bernard's exorcism could save us. And my assistant played his part well. I confess, Father, that I took advantage of the esteem and deference he felt for me. As soon as he sprinkled me with holy water and pronounced the appropriate words, I stopped thrashing about. And then I played a sacrilegious scene I'm ashamed of and for which I still feel the need to repent. But it was absolutely necessary. You should know that I had Pierre de Nevers's drawings in my scapular, and I absolutely had to make one important change. His sketches called for our church—inherited from the canons and from the time when the Mount belonged to Brittany, built right at the place where Aubert's sanctuary stood—to be totally razed when work on the new abbey church started. But now the church had to be spared. It was the church where we prayed during the day and which was off limits at night, the holy place where Richard the Good had married Judith of Brittany. The double sanctuary had indeed become too small, and that's why it had become necessary to build a new abbey. But now it could never be destroyed! It would be easy to change the church into an underground crypt to carry the weight of the new church's nave. It would be easy to change the sketches, but it would be much more difficult to get the abbot to accept the changes without explaining the real reasons.

That's why I came up with the ignominious idea of becoming the mouthpiece for Saint Aubert, founder of the mountain, approving the construction of the grand abbey church but now forbidding us to touch his sanctuary that had since been transformed into a church and ordering us to use the church for his relics. A person can be possessed by a demon or an angel, and I made Bernard believe he had delivered me from Moira and that now the forces of Good were speaking through me.

Unbelievable! So that's why that unexplainable change had happened during construction. This was the man who had signed the birth certificate for Notre-Dame-sous-Terre! But why did he go to all that trouble? Perhaps he would explain later on.

I'm not at all proud of my trickery, Father, but I confess that it worked better than I ever expected. Not without experiencing great emotion and nostalgia, I handed over to Bernard Pierre de Nevers's sketches, which I had just modified before his eyes. From then on, my mission at Mont-Saint-Michel was over. My spirit was freed from the abbey's stones. But my body and my soul were not yet free. For that, I needed to put on one more performance, the final act. As soon as Bernard left the infirmary with my master's drawings and the weight of Aubert's sacred order, Hosmund began to reproach me, and justifiably so. My faithful friend could hardly stand it that I had betrayed not only Aubert's memory but also the memory of Pierre de Nevers. So I had to lie to him as well, to the man without whom I'd have been dead for a long time already. To the most loyal person I had ever met, I had to pretend that my master himself had planned the change and left it to me to carry it out or not as I saw fit. I continued my lie by saying that I had come to the conclusion the changes were necessary after the work had begun, but that I hadn't yet had the courage to undertake the mod-ifications because I didn't know I'd be leaving so soon. Hosmund believed me, or at least pretended to do so. At any rate, I knew that he wouldn't betray me, and in fact, he never did.

No real technical justification! Nothing architectural! But what, then?

However, since I was forbidden to explain to Hosmund the reasons that led me to such blasphemy, I can't explain them to you, either, Father. Indeed, the real causes behind changing the sketches must remain hidden forever from everyone.

Night had fallen, but luckily the moon and stars were bright. Hosmund had me drink a potion whose effects I'll never forget. People say that the mandrake, with its human form, grows under the gallows, and that it's used by magicians and evil spirits. He had mixed it with other magical herbs, belladonna and black henbane, and the result was powerful. My whole being slipped into unconsciousness, and I was the victim, this time for real, of unbearable demonic apparitions. I was being devoured alive by fantastic creatures ripping at my hands and entrails. I felt as if my skin was bleeding everywhere, that my whole being was oozing out in slow painful agony. The monsters were gnawing at my eyes, my cheeks, my tongue. My head was nothing but a putrid stub, my body a black liquid swamp.

I could feel myself disappearing but was unable to die. When I regained my senses, early in the morning at the edge of a field of rye, it was reality. I had disappeared but wasn't dead. Hosmund was looking at me, he himself now haggard and worn. He smiled. I was saved. He described my terrified screams, my horrible rolling eyes, and the speed with which the abbot and Almodius wanted to see me leave the monastery and go to the hospice in Avranches. I had counted on the prior's unlimited devotion to the abbey along with, and excuse me, Father, for saying this, the abbot's cowardice, to produce the result I wanted. I hated Almodius because he had condemned Moira to a horrible death by handing her over to the secular authorities and because he had probably also caused Hildebert's death. But I knew that he had done all that in the name of his faith. You see, for him, faith was a mad passion, a violent, jealous love, stubborn and almost bloodthirsty. It was so different from the gentle moderation practiced by Benedict and Hildebert, and his faith was incarnate in his abbey. That I finally understood much later, within these walls. At the time, I only sensed it. For him, the abbey was like a woman. It was his mother and his exclusive mistress. Moira represented everything he held in contempt, and I, possessed with the devil, I was putting the monastery in grave danger. He couldn't tolerate that, for it was as if I were threatening him in his own flesh. That night, if he could have strangled me with his own hands to save the abbey, I have no doubt that he would have done so. But he was content to require my immediate departure for the hospice.

I drank a little wine to help me gather my wits, and I nibbled at a piece of bread while Hosmund recited the epilogue to the drama that he had been forced to play alone. When he got to Avranches, he announced that I had died a horrible death in the boat while we were crossing the bay during the night as the tide rushed in. He had carried my clothes to dry land and burned them to wipe out any trace of contagion. In the morning some pilgrims and a priest returning home from the Mount had helped him conduct a Christian burial in the swamp, thus warding off demons. Fearing that he, too, was contaminated, the lay brother said that he would stay away from the hospice. Since he couldn't write, he also asked that a messenger be sent to the abbey. After a short quarantine, he would then go back home to the monastery. I hugged my brother and his stubbly beard for a long time. We were both in tears, ashamed of our lies, happy to have succeeded, overwhelmed because we had to part after all those difficult moments we had spent together. I suggested that he come along with me to Cluny, but with a wink, he answered that he hadn't mixed the mandrake potion right and that I was still talking out of my head! My heart was aching, but I knew I needed to leave him. I've often prayed for him, prayed that the Most High forgive him for taking pity on me.

And then I started my long journey toward Odilon, Pierre de Nevers, and the soul of my beloved.

After two weeks of walking I made it here to this abbey. I was exhausted, hesitant, suddenly uncertain that I would be granted mercy I didn't deserve, but I could immediately see Hildebert in Odilon and I made confession to him as today I'm confessing to you. He told me that this house was for the dead and the needy, and that I was acceptable on both counts. He added that the long road I had covered on foot was nothing in comparison to the path now in store for me and that I'd need to cover it on my knees. He forbade me from ever asking for a position of authority in the monastery. I promised, for the only charge I was seeking was silence and contrition. The only task Odilon ever asked me to per-

260 | Frédéric Lenoir and Violette Cabesos

form was to write a part of the manuscript *Liber tramitis* devoted to describing the abbey buildings.

The *Liber tramitis,* the Book of the Way, a Cluniac daybook written between 1020 and 1060, described in astonishing precision the monks' liturgy and especially their daily life and surroundings! The book had been preserved, and Johanna had spent a lot of time with it when she was writing her thesis, especially the part about architecture, the part written by this very monk.

That was, in forty years, my only contact with stones.

It was difficult work, in fact, because stones no longer communicated with me. They tolerated me in their midst like a distant memory, as you might agree to shake the hand of a good friend who once betrayed you. They did sometimes bring life back to my soul, but it was primarily because I remembered my deceased master, their own master. As for me, I was just a cold, inert heart for them, for I had betrayed them for a woman's heart.

As for that poor woman without a grave, without refuge, I prayed for her day and night for forty years at every mass, at every office, and even between the offices. At the Mount, it took us a week to chant the complete Psalter. At Cluny, I would chant the whole thing every day. The numerous masses for the dead made my arid heart rejoice like water in a desert. Requiem. I begged, I supplicated, praying that Moira's soul would find peace. I called on Mary. I invoked Peter. Requiem. I still implore heaven, hoping that her soul has come into God's presence. I've grown old in silence, but the silence has not been serene. I've lived in the midst of fervent faces, and for me they have all been ghosts. A human specter, a shadow in the light, mirage of a snuffed-out existence, I no longer aspire to anything else but dying so that I might see life gush forth, that I might embrace her breath and hug her voice. She's waiting for me, and I'll recognize her amidst all the souls of the firmament. At the moment you are reading this, perhaps I've already joined her! No doubt I've already completed my final earthly task, done it in her memory, faithful to the secret she entrusted to me and to our immortal love.

My heart is heavy, for I must leave. I cannot shirk my duty. Pray for me, Father, you who are wisdom and the supreme intercessor. Pray that my soul may again find peace . . .

Adieu.

Brother Jean de Marburg, formerly Brother Roman

12

THE ARCADES, WITH THEIR ROUND ARCHES AND STAINED-GLASS windows, share the color of the sky, a deep blue with yellow tinges, that increasingly gives way to the reddish-blue bands announcing sunrise. The sun itself is not yet visible, but the sky is getting lighter and the gusty wind is not so penetrating. Down below, the crashing waves are beginning to retreat and surrender their nocturnal grip, and the rock will soon be free from their whip-like kisses.

"*De Angelis... Michael archangele veni in adjutorium...*"

From a column of monks, black like the night, a glow as gentle as the modest, bluish, celestial light caressing the Archangel's altar begins to emanate.

"*In excelsis angeli laudant te. In conspectu.*"

Beneath the glass panels depicting the Saint Aubert legend, a second column of Benedictines, parallel to the first, answers in harmony. Standing in the round choir that ends in the five alcoves of the apse, and framed by the pillars marking the ambulatory, the Angel's servants are singing, chanting from both sides of the primary altar, in communion with the invisible universe. Their master, the prince of the heavenly hosts, has watched over them during the dark moments that have now come to an end, and the monks have protected men through their prayers. The intercessors between the two worlds fall silent. The priest of the week, praying aloud, marks the end of the office of Lauds. Two by two, the monks bow before a tall, withered old man with dark eyes as he blesses each of his sons before they slowly file out of the holy of holies in careful order. Outside, the now voiceless monkly columns pull their hoods back over their heads; their silhouettes stand out against the dawn sky. The monks at the front of the column blow out their lanterns and, heading toward the dormitory, walk past the entrance to the transept and past the tall, square bell tower rising up from its center. The tower was finished three years before, in 1060, and houses a huge bell named Rollon in honor of the Viking navigator, the first Norman nobleman.

The bell's deep voice can be heard for miles around, and when there's fog, it rings incessantly to guide sailors lost in the perilous mists. On this spring morning, the air is so crisp that the bell is silent. A novice raises his eyes toward the thin clouds. Such a peaceful sky is unusual here, and the novice takes it all in as a precious gift. Suddenly, he stops dead. The monk following him, head bowed, bumps into him and grumbles. Looking up, the novice claps one hand over his mouth while he grabs his neighbor's robe with the other. Finally the other monk looks up in the same direction. He, too, freezes, then lets out a cry and poins up toward the sky. Soon both columns break into disarray. The monks are pointing and shouting in horror. They call the abbot. He's the last to leave the church, and he comes running as fast as his seventy-year-old legs allow. All of his sons are looking up at the church tower. He raises his eyes and stands there in astonishment. Under the tower's arcades a man is hanging! With one end of a rope around his neck and the other attached to the frame holding up the bell, a monk hangs, his head drooping to one side, his lifeless body swaying in the wind, brushing against the stones as it rocks back and forth like a censer on a chain.

"Who is it? Who is it?" the monks keep repeating, crossing themselves. "That's impossible, how horrible. By all-powerful God. . . . "

The abbot is just as appalled as his sons. He stares up at the corpse, but it's too far away to identify. Finally he tries to get control of the situation.

"Calm down, now!" Almodius says. "Someone untie him and get him down right away!" he orders. "You three there, go on! Hurry now!"

A few moments later the three monks deposit at the abbot's feet the mortal remains of Brother Anthelme, one of the oldest monks at the Mount. His blue eyes are rolled back into his head as if he had seen the devil. His skin is purplish, his mouth hangs open, and the rope loops around his neck like a necklace. The monks pour out their despair, for everything leads them to believe that the old man took his own life. And that's almost unheard of, for a man who has chosen religion and who stands among God's chosen.

"We can't keep someone who's committed suicide within the monastery walls," Almodius says immediately, his voice breaking with surprise and emotion. "We must lay him under the construction workers' shelter. Don't allow the workers to go in. And, you infirmarers, examine him carefully, for if he has killed himself, we can't give him a Christian burial. My sons, finish your office of prayer for poor Brother Anthelme! I'll call you together for chapter meeting later, after our brother infirmarers have finished their work, so that we can decide the fate of our brother's mortal remains."

Almodius takes one last look at the dead man and turns away. Brother Anthelme! An old man! And yet he still had his wits, and he was still governed by his faith and his love for the monastery. What could have pushed him to commit such a serious deed, a mortal sin that condemned him to repudiation by the Lord and by the community of the faithful? No, surely suicide wasn't possible. Anthelme had already been part of the abbey when Almodius entered as a child. The abbot remembers those days very well. Anthelme had been a young novice then, and he's the one who explained to Almodius how things worked in the monastery. Deep in thought and unsure what to do, Almodius retires to his wooden cell, the abbot's cell where Aubert's relics had been discovered. As he goes over to the fire, he's gripped by a preposterous thought—in two days and two nights the great feast of Ascension will be taking place in this year 1063, and Almodius, as he does each year, will celebrate in the secret of his flesh a more fateful anniversary, the anniversary of Moira's death. Four decades. Exactly forty years ago, at this very hour, she was swinging in the air in her iron cage. And it suddenly comes to him—she was swinging in the air just like Brother Anthelme was today! A striking coincidence. The abbot pales and sits down behind his desk to keep his old legs from quaking. No, that would be impossible; his aged mind must be playing tricks on him, these forty years having been so stressful. Stressful, even chaotic, and Almodius still has a bitter taste in his mouth when he thinks about all that's happened on the rock after Moira's death. Three decades of intrigues and struggles had inflamed the mountain and all of Normandy like an insatiable bed of coals. Yes, for thirty years the duchy and Mont-Saint-Michel fell victim to a murky, unstable fate. Both Duke Richard the Good and Abbot Thierry had died in the year 1026. One of Richard II's two sons took the throne but perished a year later, poisoned. His brother Robert, called Robert the Magnificent, followed him. In the Angel's dwelling place, when Thierry died, Prior Almodius was certain he would be named the abbot's successor.

Almodius's assumption didn't take into account Brother Robert's rancor. Robert had been prior under Hildebert, but Almodius had supplanted him three years earlier. A rumor circulating in the abbey suggested that Thierry's sudden, mysterious death was very much like Hildebert's and that in both cases Almodius had personally watched over the sick man. Because they were nervous about any scandal that might arise, the monks were careful not to choose Almodius as their abbot. Instead, they named Aumode, a monk from Le Mans who had close ties with the Bretons. Almodius was devastated; he resigned his position as prior and took refuge in his scriptorium. But he also plotted with Robert the Magnificent, who was at war with Brittany, and denounced Abbot Aumode for his dangerous sympathies with the enemy. When Duke Robert pushed the Bretons out of the Cotentin and the Avranches region, and ended the hostilities, he also brought to pass Aumode's disgrace as a collaborator with the enemy. Thus had Almodius managed to get rid of Aumode, but the former prior was still not rewarded with the position he coveted. The prince himself named the new abbot—and chose a foreigner over Almodius! Suppo was from Rome and had been an abbot in Lombardy, so he knew nothing about the regional conflicts in France. Duke Robert, believing peace had been restored, entrusted Normandy to Alain, prince of Brittany, the duke's former enemy and now his ally, and then left on a pilgrimage to the Holy Land. He died on the way home, but he had time to choose as his successor one of his illegitimate sons, the seven-year-old William, whom he'd he had by his concubine Arlette, a woman of the people, a harness-maker's daughter. War again broke out, and Alain, respecting the oath he had taken in Robert's presence to keep

Normandy from chaos, intervened with his army, not to take the duchy for himself, but rather to protect young William's rights, for he was under attack by rebel noblemen. Eventually William the Bastard, later known as William the Conqueror, assumed the reign over Normandy. Though very young, he managed to quell the rebellion, and little by little he restored a lasting peace that protected peasants, pilgrims, religious, women, children, and merchants from the noblemen's bloody hostility. The new duke proclaimed it God's peace, and in God's name he outlawed fighting during Advent, Lent, the Easter season, and on Sundays throughout all this territory. But the armistice naturally didn't apply to him, for the truce was in fact not God's but the prince's. He married a queen, Mathilda of Flanders, and he made Normandy Europe's most dynamic province. As a sovereign prince, he would cross the Channel to conquer England in 1066, on Saint Michael's Day.

Though calm had returned to the prince's household, the same could not be said of life in the Angel's dwelling. Abbot Suppo did expand the abbey's lands, its treasure, and its library, but he also increased the wealth of his family on the other side of the Alps. Like his brothers, Almodius soon discovered Suppo's avarice, but he made no effort to stop him. He decided simply to wait and feigned to have no interest in the monastery's secular affairs. On the other hand, Robert, who had been prior under Hildebert, soon fell into conflict with his abbot and was forced to leave the Mount. He lived as a hermit on the neighboring island of Tombelaine, where he began to work on a commentary on the Song of Solomon and became known as Robert de Tombelaine. With one enemy gone, Almodius decided that he, too, would profit from the greedy Suppo's prodigality. He arranged to have valuable books added to the library and expanded the scriptorium's activities so greatly that it became famous. The social and military peace the duke had restored made it easier for manuscripts to circulate and for expert copyists and brilliant intellectuals to establish a school in Avranches. During those years, Almodius's world was made up of sheepskin parchments or of fine vellum made from newborn calves. His universe contained bird feathers, ox horns, rabbit feet, gold leaf, and colored pigments whose secret alchemy produced the red and green illuminations typical of the work done at the Mount. His dreams were filled with circular tracings, with palmettes, with big letters that looked like dog heads, masks of dragons, eagles, and lions. The master builder had built the legend of the Mount with stones, and Almodius was erecting it on animals' skins as well as his own skin, now wrinkled and yellowed by time, desiccated by unfulfilled desires, and whipped by penitence. His flesh was striated with stigmata as dense as flowing ink. His black eyes, worn out from the close examination of manuscripts, could sometimes imagine that the strange creatures in the animal-shaped letters at the beginnings of texts were truly dancing.

His team copied Plato, the Bible, the Venerable Bede, various saints—Augustine, Jerome, Ambrose, Gregory the Great. He also had many profane scientific treatises copied, but the work he was proudest of was *De introductio monachorum,* the sacred history of the Mount, the legend of Aubert and the mountain, written like the story of Moses and Sinai, with the Benedictine abbey taking its form as the New Jerusalem. Construction of the abbey church wasn't yet finished, but the glorious epic of the Benedictines on "Mont-Saint-Michel in peril of the sea" was already alive for all eternity. For the purpose of edifying the souls of pilgrims, Almodius also arranged to have a book written called the *Miracula,* a collection of anecdotes about the apparitions and miracles that had occurred thanks to the Archangel, such as that of the pregnant woman who was saved from the rising tide by Saint Michael—he kept the sea at bay at a place marked with a large cross that appeared and disappeared with the tide's ebb and flow.

While Almodius devoted himself solely to his books, the conflict between Abbot Suppo and his indignant sons became so great that the monks began to threaten the abbot. William had to intervene, and he sent Suppo back to Italy. One more time Almodius thought his day had come, but once again his hopes were dashed. Even though the monks were relieved to see Suppo removed, they were still angry, for an abbot had tried to steal their abbey! Suppo had betrayed God himself! They needed to stop recruiting abbots from the world outside the mountain, and the dukes of Normandy had to stop intervening in their elections and let the monks choose their own abbot according to the Rule. Although Almodius was indeed one of them, the Benedictines distrusted him because he had benefited so grandly from Suppo's greed. They seemed to be forgetting that Almodius had indeed enriched the scriptorium and the abbey but had never become rich himself. Embittered by their stupidity and ungratefulness, Almodius let himself get carried away by a fit of emotion that lost him the position of abbot. He accused his brothers of reveling in the disorder that reigned on the rock and of personally enjoying those years of negligence. In the refectory, they were served pure wine in ever-increasing proportions, and they stuffed themselves with roasted meats, fat pork, and other foods the Rule forbade. They neglected the manual labor prized so much by Saint Benedict and preferred saying private masses, for which they kept the money rather than giving it back to the community. In a word, they had benefited from Suppo's largess, and like their former abbot, they, too, were corrupt.

Almodius's attack angered the monks, for they were not eager to be reduced to poverty, diluted wine, and mashed fava beans. So they relegated Almodius to his holy scriptorium by refusing to make him abbot. They were to regret it sorely. Duke William took advantage of the situation once again to impose a stranger as abbot, a monk from Fécamp, Raoul de Beaumont. That was in 1048. Almodius was fifty-five years old; by then he had been hoping to become abbot for the last twenty-five years. Raoul turned out to be rather a sorry abbot, and circumstances became only more untenable on the rock. In 1050, Raoul left Mont-Saint-Michel on a pilgrimage to Jerusalem. Exhausted by the trip, he died on the way home, just like Robert the Magnificent. Trying at all costs to keep the duke from imposing one of his men as abbot, the monks continued without an abbot for three months, and meanwhile total anarchy overtook the rock. During those three months, Almodius doggedly tried to persuade his brothers one by one that he was the only person who could restore order and glory to the monastery. Careful not to repeat what he had said after Suppo died, he worked more diplomatically. Mainly he argued that he had become a vital, integral part of the abbey, as he had been devoted to it for fifty-seven years. Few of the brothers could claim to have been faithful to the monastery longer than that! He promised that if he were elected, he wouldn't try to alter their practice of charging for masses or change the way things were being done in the refectory.

Once he managed to convince the monks, he still faced a major obstacle, the Duke of Normandy. Playing on William's military difficulties in fighting the king of France and on his constant need of money, the monks obtained permission to choose their abbot themselves if they made a monetary gift to the duchy. It was really simony, something they had criticized Suppo for, but the end seemed to justify the means, for it was the only way to guarantee that the Mount would remain in the hands of its own people. The monastery brothers—called Bocains because they were mostly locals from the Norman *bocages,* or groves—were deep believers in their island's autonomy and independence and thus managed to wrest some power from their Norman lords.

A few years later, when outside control of the abbey had begun to run so counter to their unique ways of doing things and their desire for sovereignty, Almodius and his monks went so far as to compose a false papal bull granting the monastery the freedom of elections. William was taken in. So finally, in the year 1053, after thirty years of waiting, Almodius could begin reigning over his fifty brothers and over the holy rock. At the age of sixty, he attained his lifelong dream—the staff, the chiseled cross, and the ring with its coat of arms. He now owned the abbey, he owned Mont-Saint-Michel.

Peace had come at last to the Angel's mountain, and there had been no further troubling incidents until now, a few days before Ascension in the year 1063.

"THERE ARE NO signs of wounds on Brother Anthelme's body," says Brother Godefroi, one of the infirmarer monks, speaking in the chapter meeting. "No wounds at all, except the one caused by the rope. So I believe it must have been an accident. It was very dark, and we know that he could no longer see very well. In the darkness, he could have got caught up in the ropes, hit his head on something hard, like maybe the bell Rollon, and then unfortunately fallen when he lost consciousness. He must have been strangled by the tangled ropes that kept him prisoner."

"Fallen on the outside of the bell tower? And besides, what could he have been doing in the bell tower?" Almodius objects. "Brother Anthelme was more than eighty years old. He was indeed almost blind, and what's more, he could hardly walk. He moved no more than necessary to devote himself to a life of prayer. He had no reason to end his days, I agree, but also no reason to impose such a difficult climb on himself!"

"I don't know why he climbed the tower," says Brother Mark, a young priest, "but what I can say before you all, Father, my brothers, is that I saw him climb the steps and then come back down."

The monks are stupefied.

"What?" asks the abbot in the midst of the tumult. "Explain yourself."

"It's like this, Father. God has willed that in the dormitory I be Anthelme's neighbor; and, as you said, he had trouble moving about. So I had gotten into the habit of helping him get to bed and get up, with all the respect due his rank and age. Last night, after Matins, I was surprised not to see him come back into the dormitory. I was afraid he had had a malaise, so I picked up a lantern and started back toward the church to look for him. That's when I saw him at the foot of the tower. Leaning on his cane, he went inside the tower and started climbing the stairs, with a great deal of difficulty. Disregarding our Rule, I called out to him, but, as you know, he was a little deaf. He didn't hear me, or maybe he didn't want to answer. I was worried, so I moved some distance from the belfry and waited. A few minutes later, he appeared at the bottom of the stairs. His hood was up, and he was still leaning on his cane. But instead of coming toward me, he began to hobble toward the outside walls. I almost called out to him again, but then decided that I shouldn't dare to interfere with our patriarch. I was afraid he would scold me roundly, as he sometimes did," he adds with a blush, "accusing me of acting like an old woman. I went back into the dormitory and slept until Lauds."

"Did you not look up? Didn't you notice the body hanging in the air?" Almodius wonders.

"Unfortunately not, my father. I was concentrating on the door because it was so dark, wondering if I, too, should go in. And from where I was hiding, I couldn't even see the other side of the tower, and that's where they found our brother."

The abbot reflects a moment as he rubs his long, thin, ink-stained hand over his head, no longer tonsured but bald, with just a few strands of gray hair. The terror-stricken monks meanwhile whisper that Mark must have seen Anthelme's soul leaving the tower. His soul, or maybe his ghost!

"That's enough," says Almodius sharply, his ill-humor growing. "Stop that nonsense. There's a very simple explanation. Anthelme may have waited outside the walls until Brother Mark disappeared and then later went back to the tower, where he committed some sin that the Church condemns and would excommunicate him for. Or perhaps it's just an accident, as Brother Godefroi has explained, though I doubt that. Another possibility is that someone waiting at the top of the tower lured our brother up, hanged him, then came back down, and that he was the person Brother Mark saw leaving, mistaking him for Brother Anthelme."

The abbot's final words bring a chill to the chapter. A murder! A murder in their abbey! But who could wish harm to one of the Angel's oldest and most devoted servants? Unless perhaps it was . . . the devil?

"My sons, I beseech you," the abbot says firmly but gently, "don't let panic overwhelm you! We can't be sure of anything yet, and the Archangel will help us clear up this unfortunate business. Let us go pray to Saint Michael, my brothers, asking him to enlighten us as he has always done. Let us pray, asking him to care for Anthelme's soul; let us go celebrate mass. I request that our prior Brother Jean de Balbec question the many pilgrims and the villagers as discreetly as possible. Come, my sons, let us seek the light!"

On this morning, the day's first mass takes place in the crypt of Our Lady of the Thirty Candles, as it does every morning. But today's ceremony is cloaked with sadness, with fear, and also with an ecstatic hope that reinforces the underground sanctuary's atmosphere. The crypt is crowned with two groin vaults and a half-domed vault in the apse, and its walls are painted to resemble building blocks, so that it has the effect of a dark cave, yet it's intimate and reassuring like a womb. It has a low ceiling, and its single narrow nave is dedicated to the Mother, the Virgin, a white Virgin of mercy. It takes its name from the thirty candles burning there, and because it's within the monastery walls, it's accessible only to the monks. That's where the first morning mass is celebrated, as well as

Compline, the last office of the day, whereas the other offices now take place in the new church's choir. The crypt of Our Lady of the Thirty Candles bears the weight of the great abbey church's north transept.

To the south, Saint Martin's Crypt lies beneath the other transept. It's majestic and monumental with its mammoth continuous barrel vault. The crypt forms a perfect square that's surmounted by a pure semicircular vault. Considered to be outside the enclosure, it's open to all. Richly decorated, it represents death and the soul's lyrical ascension to heaven. Destined to be the resting place of the monastery's great benefactors, the crypt offers new space for the dead, its cemetery filling up the space between its walls and the old Saint Martin's Chapel, which, no longer in use, has been turned into an ossuary.

When morning mass is over, Almodius leaves the monk-priests to their lucrative private masses. With Ascension just two days away, there's a huge crowd of pilgrims. Lost in his thoughts, Almodius walks through the abbey church, of the domain of which he is the uncontested master. Ten years ago, when finally he was elected abbot, his first concern was the construction site. For thirty years, master builders had come and gone about as fast as abbots, and the resulting confusion had slowed down construction.

From 1023 to 1026, Brother Bernard had slaved away at building the choir crypt, but it seemed as if the master builder's rod was burning his hands. Little by little, he came to believe a curse fell on everyone who touched the drawings for the new abbey. Pierre de Nevers, Hildebert, and his own master, Roman, had all died, and he began to fear that he might be next. Abbot Thierry had tried to explain that if the rod ever really bore a curse, it had been removed the night Saint Aubert inspired Bernard to modify the sketches. As they were now carrying out the will of the mountain's founder, even though some of the abbot's predecessors had not shown proper respect to Aubert's wishes, death no longer had any reason to stalk those in charge of the drawings. For a while, Bernard had believed him. But then Jehan, the master stonecutter who often handled the drawings, died in an accident, and Bernard fell first into depression, then into outright panic. Yet it had been an ordinary accident, the kind of accident that often occurs on a construction site. A crane lifting a huge block of stone that weighed several quintals had broken, and Master Jehan, standing nearby, had been crushed by the enormous stone. He hadn't died immediately; he screamed for several days in the infirmary where he was taken, his members maimed, his spirit haunted by infernal visions, until he finally succumbed.

Seeing Jehan's suffering brought back to Brother Bernard the painful memory of his demon-possessed master and rekindled his fears. After that, he interpreted every accident on the construction site as a direct threat to him. He often neglected his work so he could pray. More and more, he preferred the silence in Saint Martin's Chapel to the noisy construction site. When first Abbot Thierry and then Richard the Good died suddenly in mysterious circumstances, Bernard lost his mind. He proclaimed that there was a curse upon him, and threw the drawings along with his builder's rod onto one of the altars in the Carolingian church that people were beginning to call Notre-Dame-sous-Terre, although it was bathed in light. Then he fled. No one ever found out what became of him.

Aumode is the abbot who built the choir with the help of a new master builder from Brittany, a man who had constructed the choir at the Abbaye de la Couture, in Le Mans, the abbot's native city. The holy of holies, strictly limited to Saint Michael and the priest-monks, was built according to the plans drawn by Pierre de Nevers, its top extending beyond the rock and choir crypt's walls holding up the extension. Even before the choir was finished, the Angel's servants knew that their master had come to take possession of the place when supernatural events began occurring. They were recorded immediately by Almodius's scribes. Brother Drogon saw three angels disguised as pilgrims holding candles near the major altar during the night. He failed to bow, and suddenly he was slapped by an invisible hand. The next morning he was dead. On another occasion, two monks carelessly saying their breviary were burned up by a flame from the altar. The Archangel himself, always at night, passed through the choir as a pillar of fire. And apparitions often accompanied magnetic storms. For these reasons, access to the sanctuary during the night was carefully controlled, as was already the case for the Carolingian church. In that consecrated space, night was reserved for spiritual beings alone, and no mortal could enter the new church between Compline and Matins.

Suppo built the transept on the rock's flat peak. As for Raoul de Beaumont, he barely had the time to construct the pillars for the transept crossing and to start the tower that would rise above the pillars. Finishing the tower that would later prove fatal to Althelme was the first project undertaken by Almodius and the new master builder—one Eudes de Fezensac, a layman from Gascony, unusual though it is to give a lay person responsibility for construction.

The conventual buildings around the Carolingian church have been demolished and replaced temporarily with wooden buildings on one of the slopes, so that the construction of new multistoried stone buildings can continue against the nave of the abbey church, also still under construction. Because Almodius hopes to write his name in history as the man who completed the grand abbey church, he tries to speed things up. The Carolingian church is finally worthy of its new name, Notre-Dame-sous-Terre. It's been surrounded by stone walls, while its own walls have been reinforced, its central pillar thickened, and a vestibule added so that it can support the weight of the nave being built above it. A high gallery now envelops the chapel, and it's flanked by the monastery building rising beside it. They've closed up its windows, so no light can enter; the absence drastically changes the atmosphere. Now, instead of the exalted chants of former times, it houses dark silence and obscure introspection, only barely lit by the flame of the candles burning on the Holy Trinity altar and on its twin where the Black Virgin, the queen of angels, is displayed. Aubert's skull, marked by the hole the Angel made, and his sanctified arm have been placed in a closed opaque urn decorated with brocade and precious stones. No one can ever cast impure eyes on the relics without going blind immediately, but, as Aubert wished, all can come to venerate from a distance the abbey's treasure, the illustrious heart of its glory beating in the mysterious setting, before they continue on to reach the upper church's illumination.

ESCORTED BY HIS master builder, Almodius is examining the nave under construction. Above Notre-Dame-sous-Terre, a stone floor lying open to the elements has been invaded by machines and swarming workers. A few pillars stand here and there so that, for the time being, it looks like the ruins of a Roman temple, but the abbot can already envision its magnificence to come in a decade or two. The long nave, part of a Latin cross, will be composed of seven identical bays separated by columns three stories high. Up above, wide windows will be surmounted by round relieving arches that will close each of the bays in on themselves. The stained-glass windows will represent the Passion, and a lovely paneled ceiling will cover the nave. It will be magnificent, original, powerful, and eternal. It will be his, and he dreams about it every night. Unfortunately, on this particular morning, Eudes de Fezensac interrupts the abbot's grandiose dreams.

"Father, excuse my asking, but the porters are surprised to see that they can't use their shelter. They've seen the corpse surrounded by your infirmarers and can't talk about anything else. They're afraid there's an epidemic. Can you explain what's happened so I can relieve their worries?"

The abbot is displeased to be brought back to reality.

"Do you really think that to save my monks I would endanger the lives of the men building our immortality? That's slanderous, totally slanderous!" he shouts, looking coldly at his master builder.

The Gascon is a big, blond-haired fellow with a beard and mustache that would make him look like a Viking if they weren't so neatly trimmed. He's devoted to the abbot, but always slightly apprehensive, because it's hard to predict how Almodius will react. The skinny old abbot looks feeble, but he's as strong as vine stock, and his mind is as sharp and as tough as a weed. Above all, he's very secretive and never tolerates anyone trying to delve into his thoughts or into what's happening within the community. He tries to carry everything on his own shoulders. Eudes de Fezensac bites his lip and looks down. Damn the old man! He's so suspicious and easily angered. It's not a crime, after all, to ask about a dead man that's been deposited in his workmen's shelter. His own men, yes, to each his own. The abbot protects his monks, but Eudes de Fezensac is responsible for the construction workers, and there are a lot more of them. He can't keep them from talking, and what'll he do if they leave the Mount because they're afraid of some contagion? The monks surely won't carry stones and make mortar. The master builder looks back up to answer Almodius, but the abbot is gone.

Back in his cell, Almodius is fuming. Whatever the cause of Anthelme's death, there's the risk that it'll cause problems on the mountain just when he needs everyone's support to finish the buildings, and especially the duke's. He tosses the sketches for the church on the table. As he looks at the drawings made by Pierre de Nevers and modified by Roman's hand and Aubert's words, he can't repress a wave of emotion. The old man stands there alone in his cell—the same cell in which Moira was interrogated forty years before, where both Hildebert and Thierry had died, where several disgraceful abbots had lived; the cell that he had so long coveted and that now belonged to him. Today, long-gone shadows seem to be reappearing through the walls, painful ghosts he thought he had tamed once and for all. He stands with his hands on the parchments that Bernard avouched were fatal, and he thinks that maybe the old master builder was right after all. All that commotion, those deaths and intrigues, and now the mystery of this new death! Taking a little cool water from a basin and dripping it on his head, he wonders if he's losing his mind. No, Saint Michael is watching over him, over them all. As proof, not one of those unworthy abbots, not Aumode, Suppo, or Raoul, experienced the grace and honor of dying in this blessed cell. Almodius hopes that he, at least, will be able to die on the holy rock. All this time he has spent loving the Mount, sighing, working so that one day his spirit would join the Archangel in the clouds and his body would unite with the earth right there on the mountain! Yes, everything he's done his entire life has been dedicated to that purpose. May the Lord grant him the joy of that long-awaited hour, may he bring peace to his soul and permit him to serve, allow him to complete the New Jerusalem. Almodius, all-powerful, feels his eyes misting up. His eyes sting, and he blinks; he stands up energetically. The heavens will surely help him come to grips with his past and shape the future.

THE DAY BEFORE Ascension. Prior Jean de Balbec's investigation among the pilgrims and villagers has not explained Anthelme's death. Brother Mark is still the last person to have seen him alive. The body of the man who died in such suspicious circumstances is still lying in the shelter, without benefit of the sacraments. Eudes de Fezensac has tried to counteract the gossip circulating among his men, but the prior's questioning and comments by the monks have stirred things up. The rumor on the mountain is growing that it was either suicide or homicide. Both are equally serious for Christian consciences; but for Anthelme's soul, they are very different. In the first case, he's likely to end up rotting in Hell, whereas in the other the heavens will welcome him. The abbot knows that in either case a heavy cloud will hang over the monastery. This morning he must come to a decision about Anthelme's fate, and it's not clear to him what he should do. Absent clear proof, which solution would be worse for the abbey's reputation? The least damaging for all of them, including Anthelme, would be to decide it was an accident.

Almodius doesn't believe that for a moment, and he knows that few others will, either. But above everything else, he must think first about the glory of the Angel's dwelling. He must allow no stain ever to come upon it. At the end of high mass in the church, with the crowds of villagers, workers, and pilgrims looking on curiously from the transept, the abbot officially announces that the old man got caught in the ropes in the bell tower and that he'll be given a Christian burial. The faithful and the monks leave the church. Almodius remains in the choir to reflect and pray by the main altar. On his knees, head bowed, eyes closed, he is asking forgiveness for the lie he's committing in the Archangel's name when he feels a hand on his shoulder.

"Father, please excuse me for disturbing your prayers, but you need to come right away."

Almodius turns around, his eyes as rigid and dry as his body.

"Well, Jean, what's the problem?"

"Please, Father, follow me. It's very important."

Almodius starts after him, his heart filled with foreboding. Outside, two fishermen are waiting, a father and son, wringing their big, red, calloused hands. The abbot walks up to them quietly.

"Father," the older man begins, "we are to be pitied! The Lord has sent another misfortune!"

"You can lament later. What's the matter?" the abbot asks impatiently.

"It was this morning, not long ago," the son answers. He's a redhead with stained teeth. "At low tide, my father and I are checking our boat. Some shouts we hear over on the shore near Tombelaine. 'Must be another pilgrim caught in quicksand,' my father says. We start off to help the poor, imprudent fellow. It happens a lot. Sometimes they give us a little money, and we're happy to oblige."

"Yes, yes, and then?"

"We get nearer, and there are a lot of people screaming, weeping, and raising their sticks up in the air. But, but it wasn't quicksand. Someone had drowned in the sea, Father, and it wasn't one of the pilgrims, it was one of your own!"

ALMODIUS HAS THE body carried to the infirmary.

The drowning victim is Romuald, a sixty-year-old brother who's been in the monastery for more than fifty years. One of the older members, but younger than Almodius. The abbot knew him very well, because he had worked in the scriptorium as a copyist until his sight had failed. He, too, lived off by himself and passed his days praying and waiting for death. Death had come this morning, but some other man had hurried death along. This time there could be no possible doubt. Anthelme and Romuald did not kill themselves, and they didn't die accidentally. No, there's an assassin on the mountain.

The brothers wash the victims' bodies; their robes are sewn shut and their hoods lowered. Then Almodius has them carried solemnly to Saint Martin's Crypt. They lie there side by side, their bodies incensed and sprinkled with holy water, while ritual candles flicker at their heads and feet. The monks keep watch over them all day long, until just before Compline on this day before Ascension. Then the two victims lie alone in the dark, powerful air of the burial crypt, while the living meet in a makeshift chapter room. There the atmosphere is explosive.

"It's the Archangel's work!" Etienne, one of the community's patriarchs, proclaims in his loud bass voice. "It's not a man who has committed these crimes. It's the hand of the Archangel, punishing us for breaking the vow we made to him forty years ago!"

"Come now, Brother Etienne," Almodius intervenes. "You know full well that we've been careful to honor the vow we made to the Archangel to complete his dwelling."

"Nonsense!" shouts the old man, pointing accusingly at the abbot. "You've been serving Saint Michael through outrageous behavior, and you insult his good servant, Saint Aubert! Yes, Saint Aubert! Forty years ago he spoke, asking us never to touch the old church that holds his holy oratory! And you, what have you done but sully that sacred space! The forces of heaven are taking vengeance on us because of that profanation. The murders are surely a warning from the angels, my brothers. I'm sure!"

All the monks begin speaking at once as they deliver their arguments one way or the other. They divide into two camps, some supporting Etienne and some Almodius.

The point of the argument is crucial, for it has to do with Saint Aubert, the angels, and Notre-Dame-sous-Terre. The underground crypt has in fact been closed to everyone for several days, by the abbot's order. Some new construction has just been started there, or rather some studies have been launched to determine how they might dig around the sanctuary's foundations to see if they might discover additional relics. It was unusual to undertake such work, but the abbot, in the year 1063, thinks he has no choice. Construction costs are running higher than expected and far exceed revenues from monastery lands. Unfortunately, the abbey's primary financier, the Duke of Normandy, has not been so generous since his cousin Edward the Confessor, king of England, has promised the duke that he would inherit the throne. Duke William knows that the English noblemen, and particularly Count Harold, are opposed to that prospect. And so, while he waits for Edward to die, he's beginning to prepare an expedition to England. The expedition will make history, but for the moment those preparations monopolize all of William's funds. Keeping the abbey uppermost in his mind, Almodius remembers the discovery of Aubert's relics that had been hidden in the ceiling of the abbot's cell. It had been after that legendary discovery forty years earlier that Richard II, the Duchess Gonor, and many other prominent and less prominent people made substantial contributions to the monastery, which allowed Hildebert to begin work on the abbey church. So to complete the construction, Almodius needs some new relics. Where better to find new relics than in the old church built on the site of Aubert's sanctuary? If necessary, Almodius is not averse to inventing some, as many people have suspected Hildebert himself to have done.

However, and this the abbot would never admit, the dig has also been prompted by a less obvious reason, something Almodius has been wondering about for forty years. Why did Roman modify his master's drawings before he died? Why did he insist on protecting the old canons' church, which everyone had hated? Almodius had doubted from the very beginning that Saint Aubert really had spoken through Roman, and he'd forbidden his scribes to note the event in their miracle books. Maybe the master builder was possessed by that ungodly woman's soul, but how could the mountain's venerable founder indeed have asked Roman to change the plans? Yet everyone seemed to believe it, and even Almodius had pretended to accept the claim in order to protect the abbey and get rid of Roman. But in fact he had always been skeptical. Abbot Thierry and Brother Bernard both had been persuaded that there was a miracle, but neither was around any longer to convince Almodius.

The abbot hoped that people would forget about what had happened in the absence of a written record. But the old monks remembered, and they passed the tale along to the younger ones—a tale embellished, decorated, illuminated like a manuscript, but one that would exist only in the brothers' minds. Forty years later, several different versions of the story are floating around, but nobody in the monastery is unfamiliar with it. And today Brother Etienne is trying once more to convince the abbot that it was a real miracle, as are some other monks, both young and old, who tremble at the thought of disobeying Aubert's injunction against digging under the church. But Almodius is the master of the mountain, and he doesn't need to obey credulous, stupid old men. Soon he will have an answer to the question that's been tormenting him for decades. As far as the murders are concerned, an idea has come to him, an explanation that appeals to him more than the punishing hand of an angry angel.

"My sons! Listen to what I have to tell you," he orders the noisy chapter. "The angels are watching and protecting us, and the greatest among them governs this house. Numerous times Saint Michael has displayed his will and his wrath. Many of us have been witnesses, and some of us victims. But remember that on each occasion heavenly powers appeared, there was never any ambiguity, never any doubt, about what they wanted, and remember that they always proved their determination by providing obvious stigmata! Remember when Brother Drogon insulted the angels by entering the new church's choir between Compline and Matins. When he died the next morning, there was a clear outline on his cheek where he had been slapped! Aubert himself still wears the imprint of Saint Michael's finger on his skull. But you've all seen the bodies of Anthelme and Romuald, and they display no trace of any supernatural signature!"

Almodius has managed to get the monks' attention. Now abandoning his defensive strategy, he continues by going on the attack.

"Do you think I'm the kind of man who would dare to defy our supreme master's plans? I've always worked to protect the abbey, to protect you all, to safeguard our collective salvation. Today Brother Etienne wakes up from his torpor to accuse someone, but what did he ever do during our house's darker days, when it was imperiled by decadent abbots and controlling Norman lords?"

Etienne's anger is obvious, but the brothers bow their heads in the heavy silence.

"I can assure you that if such were the will of the Archangel, I'd put an end to our excavation immediately. Its only purpose is to allow us to finish building the abbey church!" he affirms. "You see, I'm sure these deaths were not caused by an angel's hand, but rather by a very human one. Besides, I have an idea who committed the murders, but it's still too early to talk about it."

The monks begin to stir nervously again.

"Whom are you accusing?" Etienne asks in surprise.

"As things stand now, I'm not accusing anyone, but if there is an assassin hiding in this abbey, you can be sure I'll find him! And now, my sons, let's all go finish our last office on this fateful day. As we chant together during Compline, let us proclaim our eternal devotion to the Archangel."

All the monks look at each other with terror in their eyes before starting off toward Our Lady of the Thirty Candles. When the office is finished and the night's silence has fallen, they walk toward their dormitory to try to sleep until Matins in spite of their fear. Some of the brothers leave to watch over Anthelme and Romuald in the crypt. As for the abbot, he returns calmly to his cell. He stirs up the fire in the fireplace, sits down with a glass of red wine, and plans how to unmask the killer. He seems to be waiting for someone, and indeed, someone knocks three times at the wooden door.

"Come in!"

A dark form, short and stocky, dressed in a dirty frayed frock, enters the abbot's cell and brings with him the smell of manure. The man's hair is white, and bits of straw are caught in the tufts. His thick beard hasn't been trimmed in a long while, and his ravaged face is covered with red splotches. His eyes are dark, and he looks as secretive as a condemned crypt.

"A goblet of wine, Hosmund?" the abbot asks.

The former infirmarer looks grimly at the pewter pitcher and shakes his head.

"Where were you last night and the night before?" demands Almodius, not even asking him to sit down.

The lay brother's brown eyes are as empty as an abyss. He looks around like a trapped animal.

"Where I was? Where I was?" he repeats as if he doesn't quite understand the words. "With my horses, damm-get-thou-behind-me-Satan!"

Time has altered Almodius less than has his constant self-flagellation, but it has gotten the better of the lay brother. The old monk has slowly sunk into senility. His face, once so full, now has grown thin, and is covered with scabs. Hosmund spends his days scratching them and then eating the clumps of clotted blood. He's lost his Latin, and he now speaks a mixture of some Viking dialect, French, and words of his own invention. Whereas he used to live in terror of horses, he now spends all his time with them. In fact, his passion for horses is what has saved him from going to the hospice in Avranches, where some of the brothers wanted to send him to finish out his days, as his dementia placed him outside the community. Of his own accord, he had deserted the dormitory, refectory, and church, and taken up residence with the horses in the stable. Although he had worked with medicinal herbs a good part of his life, he has forgotten all his knowledge and eats nothing but hay. The oblates and novices make fun of him constantly because he smells like manure, yet he's never violent with them, and he still makes himself useful by helping the blacksmith and lay brothers who take care of the stable.

"Do you know what happened last night and the night before?"

Hosmund stares wide-eyed and shakes his head.

"You must certainly remember Brother Anthelme and Brother Romuald, although they don't come to the stables."

Nodding, the monk mouths a weak "yes."

"Well, yesterday morning we found Anthelme's body hanging in the wind, and this morning, Romuald's drowned in the bay."

Hosmund crosses himself, but says nothing; he seems unsurprised.

"It's a tragedy for all of us, and an inexplicable mystery. For there's a troubling coincidence. These two deaths seem to be an echo of events that happened here a long time ago. A perfect echo, because tomorrow we'll be celebrating Ascension."

Almodius looks into the brother's impassive face.

"Do you know what I'm alluding to?" he asks.

Hosmund remains silent. He's content to stare down at the earthen floor.

"I know you understand. And chance has willed it that Anthelme and Romuald were the last survivors among the judges who officiated forty years ago at the trial of that woman. Brothers Martin and Drocus have not been with us for many years, nor has the bishop, Roland d'Aubigny, nor Duke Richard, nor Abbot Thierry. The only ones still alive were Anthelme and Romuald. That's very striking, don't you think? Except for me, and I was simply a witness, not one person from that trial now survives. What do you have to say about that?"

"About what, Father?"

Almodius frowns, and his salt-and-pepper eyebrows furrow. He can feel himself getting angry. It seems useless to interrogate the senile old man, but the abbot is sure that Hosmund is hiding something and that he's not as crazy as he looks.

"That it all looks like odious vengeance, you old idiot!" he spits out, pounding on the table. "One crime by air, on the anniversary of Moira's

284 | *Frédéric Lenoir and Violette Cabesos*

first ordeal. A second by water, and both victims were among the heretic's judges! Don't you think that's a little strange? You were Roman's friend, and aside from me, today you're the only person left who was part of that event that occurred so long ago."

"Horses! I was with my horses," the poor monk shouts.

"You're lying. I know that you're lying and that you're not as senile as you would like to have me think. Your strategy might work with the naïve people in this monastery whom you can fool like you fooled them forty years ago when you said that Aubert was speaking through Roman. But with me, understand me well, your perfidious trickery won't work!"

For the first time, Hosmund's eyes grow bright, but a moment later they are filled with helplessness.

His helplessness doesn't escape Almodius. The abbot calms down and begins to speak again, this time in a surprisingly gentle voice, the voice of a warrior who has thrown down his weapons now that victory is assured.

"I've learned a great deal about my fellow men and about myself over the years," he says. "I've searched the depths of the human soul, and no mortal can fool me. I'm finally in my rightful place, this position that should have been mine for thirty years, and I'll not let anyone threaten it. In three decades of battles I've vanquished fear, treachery, ingratitude, negligence, and chaos. And I've beaten Duke William himself. So today I'm not going to be frightened off by the violent memory of a dead woman. You're denying it, but I'm sure that you must be trying to avenge Moira and cast anathema on the abbey. I don't doubt, in fact, that I, too, am on your list of reprisals. And logically, there must still be two more murders, one by earth and one by fire. I even believe that you've reserved fire for me, a final conflagration, a true apotheosis! The only thing I can't explain for the moment, though I'm sure I'll soon be able to, is why you've waited forty years. . . . "

Almodius lets out a little condescending laugh, then stands up energetically and opens the door. Two large lay brothers are standing on the threshold. Hosmund looks at them in terror. At the abbot's signal, they come in and tie Hosmund to a chair. The former infirmarer doesn't put up any resistance. The two fellows drag the chair with poor Hosmund in it over to the fireplace and remove his sandals.

"Brother Hosmund," Almodius continues. "The fire that you're planning to bring down on me, I present to you!"

The torturers each grab one of Hosmund's ankles and push them toward the glowing embers. Twisting like a poor worm, the old monk tries to struggle

"I'll ask you the question once more: Brother Hosmund, are you the one who hanged Brother Anthelme and who drowned Brother Romuald to avenge Moira the pagan woman?"

"I'm innocent!" cries Hosmund. "It wasn't me!"

"Lies!"

His two filthy feet now rest on the bed of firebrands. Around his flesh smoke is beginning to rise, and Hosmund lets out a horrible scream. The lay brothers relax their grip.

Roaring like an ox, Hosmund twists around, and the chair tips over backwards. The old man's pain is so intense that he loses consciousness. What Almodius and his henchmen couldn't hear before because of Hosmund's screaming, they hear now. Someone is beating at the door. Almodius looks over at one of the torturers, then hurries over to open it. It's the prior standing there in the night. Brother Jean scarcely looks at the body down on the floor where Hosmund is beginning to regain his senses. The prior is in a great panic.

"Father, there's indeed a curse!" he says to Almodius. "A fire, a horrible fire, started in the master builder's hut! Eudes de Fezensac is dead!"

13

W HAT A SHOCKING CONFESSION!" SAID JOHANNA, LOOKING UP
from the notebook in which she had Roman's letter. "I can't
think about anything else. I've almost memorized his words, and you're
the first person I've talked to about it—except Paul, of course. You're the
first person on the Mount, for sure. Soon everyone will know about it,
because the original manuscript is being evaluated. But I still have a little
time before other people hear about this fabulous story," she said, holding the pages against her chest. "It's still my story, and mine alone. I've got
to be the one to find the secret, Roman and Moira's secret, the mountain's enigma, you know. Why in the hell did he change the plans for the
abbey? Why did he leave Cluny? Where did he go? What did he do?
When did he die? The key was at Cluny, but I know that the door is here.
I'm sure he came back to Mont-Saint-Michel. I can just feel it, and the
stones know it, too. I've got to get them to speak!"

"So that's what you went looking for at Cluny. It's a horrible, marvelous story, that's true, but what stones are you talking about, Johanna?"
asked Simon Le Meur, getting up to throw another log on the fire. "Because there's not much left of the Romanesque abbey. You surely don't
expect your dig in what used to be Saint Martin's Chapel to produce another copper cylinder with a parchment telling the rest of the monk's
story? And why not look for your own name on the manuscript: 'From
Brother Roman in the eleventh century; to Johanna, twenty-first century'! Come on, you've got to be realistic, and grateful for the gift life has
just given you. It's already amazing enough to have a text that made it

through so many centuries and so many places. You can't expect too much."

She was sorry she had even shown Roman's testament to Simon. She had trusted him, and now he was acting like an ungrateful wretch.

"You don't understand," she answered quietly. "I'm not expecting anything particular, but I'm hoping for everything! I absolutely have to know what happened to him. So I'm constructing all kinds of theories. I have no choice but to be inventive and to trust the stones' memory, because everything has been erased from human memory. There's nothing left of the abbey's daybooks. They all burned in 1944 in Saint-Lô. And as for the Avranches library, it houses nothing but religious texts. I've been spending all my free time there, but I haven't even come across the story about Roman becoming the spokesperson for Aubert. Yet the monks ought surely to have included it in their collections of miracles. I have found some information about the infamous Almodius, but nothing about Brother Roman, nothing anywhere, and so I'm reduced to touching the stones that perhaps he himself touched, stones that he loved at least, hoping that they might whisper some of his story to me."

"Of course you realize that Roman is a great name for a Romanesque builder, but it also suggests a romancer, a creator of fanciful fiction."

"Very funny," she said as she stood up. "I point out to you that before the nineteenth century, all medieval construction, without exception, was called Gothic. Romanesque art wasn't called Romanesque until 1818, when a Norman architect, Charles Dehérissier de Gerville, linked it to the version of popular Latin spoken in the Middle Ages by ordinary people, the *rustica romana lingua*. In Normandy, as in all of Northern Gaul, it was simply French! And anyway, Brother Roman was educated like all the monks, and he communicated not in French but in Latin when writing and speaking. As for the fanciful fiction that we call novels today, it didn't even exist when the man was alive. It wasn't invented until the twelfth century to awaken dreams and to celebrate courtly love and chivalry, the mystical ideal of love for a woman, totally different from the religious ideal of love for God."

He walked over to her, his eyes bright.

"Oh no, professor," Simon said. "I would say that this monk invented the novel without realizing it. What is his tale if it's not the singing of a woman's praises, a hymn in the cult of lost, absolute love marked with tragedy and dreams of a better world? All the elements are there, and that's what makes the text so beautiful," he added, putting his hands on Johanna's waist. "I'm sorry to have hurt you. That's because I'm such a romantic. For me, this story is not a historical document but rather a magical tale, like those my mother told me when I was a child. The truth of Roman's story is not even important. I don't care whether the monk really existed or not or what really happened to him. I don't give a damn whether the story is authentic or not. The only thing that matters to me is its fabulous beauty, for it carries me off on imagination's paths! And the fact that I don't know what happened next doesn't frustrate me at all, because that means that all sorts of things may have happened. The sky's the limit, don't you see?"

She smiled. He was irresistible.

"I know that you are a gentle dreamer and that you enjoy fiction, but my job is to decipher history. We don't have the same vocation, that's all."

"And you know," he said like an excited kid, "in my shop I often invent fantastic adventures for the objects I'm selling. I don't really lie about their past, but I do embroider a little, and people love it. They're not so much buying the object as its history. I make up storms, shipwrecks, trips around the world, treasures. My clients know that what I'm telling them may not always be true, but they enjoy listening to me, and it helps them travel themselves."

"Simon, you're in the wrong profession. You should be a novelist!"

"Well, in fact I have started a novel. Maybe some day I'll read you a few pages."

"A love story?"

"Of course," he said, lightly touching her ear, "but it'll never have the mythical power of Brother Roman's fable, alas. . . . "

"Simon," she said, taking his hand, "I understand the way you see things, and I find it tempting to see things the same way. But I can't share your views completely. I, too, can feel the emotion you're talking about, but I don't think you should call the story a fable. Sorry to insist, but for me it's not a fable. It's a true story, and I have to try to prove it is!"

Looking a trifle vexed, he nodded his brown curls.

"There's something I just don't understand, Johanna, and it fascinates me. Why must you insist on confusing dreams and reality? You are becoming obsessive, and I like that. Whatever you might say, when you talk about that manuscript, you're not acting like a historian but rather as if the story concerned you personally and had some link with your own life. And it's not because you once studied the fragment written by Roman at Cluny, the *Liber tramitis*. There's something more, something deeper. I can sense it. Is the monk among your ancestors, or what?"

She forced herself to laugh so she wouldn't have to answer. She had not mentioned one word to him about the three dreams that had led her that far, but he had guessed something similar nonetheless. They hadn't known each other for very long and they weren't lovers, yet he was able to read her as if they had been friends forever. That had never happened to her before, and she found it troubling. They didn't know each other sexually, and yet they seemed to be able to sense each other's intimate secrets. It was clear they would become lovers, but for the moment they hadn't given in. It was obvious that they were taking their time and enjoying the wait. She would be the one to let him know when she was ready; she could sense that, even though they had never talked about it. She was in no hurry. In fact, Johanna was frightened by the unexpected, new feeling. How could she explain that suddenly François seemed to be a stranger and that she was spending New Year's Eve with Simon? She felt a little guilty. Isabelle had reassured her; she'd teased her a little for not realizing how powerful love could be and for treating it much like an unfortunate accident. Then Isabelle had congratulated her and had said horrible things about François, even though up to then she had seemed to like him! Johanna was flabbergasted. Nothing had prepared her for such a radical change in her life. She had spent Christmas with Paul at Cluny, with Paul and his companion Corinne. As François had planned it, he was celebrating with his family at home in Cabourg, just a few dozen miles from Mont-Saint-Michel—but completely out of reach from Cluny.

The Christmas holiday was unusual, and their spirits were high. Paul couldn't talk about anything else but Pierre de Nevers, and Johanna couldn't talk about anything but Jean de Marburg, alias Brother Roman. Corinne looked at them askance; she found herself jealous of two dead people who managed to bring two archeologists to life and make accomplices of them. She would have preferred having François there as well, to balance things a bit. Corinne relaxed when Johanna announced that she'd be going back to the Mount on December 26. She had finished transcribing the manuscript and was eager to find some trace of her builder monk back among the stones of the abbey. She thanked Hugh de Semur aloud for not having destroyed the document, for not having revealed its existence, and for having placed it in the tomb of Pierre de Nevers, Roman's master. She went to say good-bye to Firmament, the horse who had been, she said, Paul's muse. She caressed the manuscript lovingly and then kissed Paul, who began to frown. He tried to talk her into staying, but to Corinne's great relief she left.

She arrived at Mont-Saint-Michel the night of the twenty-sixth, without even stopping to see her parents in Fontainebleau or Isabelle in Paris, and with no detour to Cabourg, where François was waiting for her in a little out-of-the-way hotel. She lied to them all; she said that Christian Brard had called her back for an emergency, even though she knew that François could easily find out that the administrator was also away on vacation. She also told them all about Paul's discovery, but she didn't mention to any of them that a manuscript had been found in the grave. François would learn of it soon enough when he got back to his office in early January. When she saw the Mount's enchanting silhouette lit up against the shadows of sea and sky, she realized that the gift she had just been given came from the mountain. The Archangel had chosen Roman to build the New Jerusalem, and the rock's soul had chosen her, Johanna, for a mission as yet unknown, but one that was beginning to take shape in her mind even as the abbey was taking shape before her eyes as she drew near. As she drove over the causeway, her eyes transfixed by the stone castle, by the golden spire crowned with a statue of the Archangel, her fears evaporated. She accepted her fate. She sensed that she would have to face intense upheavals, but she would face them with confidence. The spirit reigning on the Mount would continue to help her, to enlighten her during her moments of doubt, to instill in her its combative spirit. Yes, she would fight for it, she would discover the key to her dreams, and she would solve the enigma trapped in the sacred rock.

She left her car in the parking lot reserved for residents and walked through the three fortified gates leading to the village. Ten P.M. The weather was worthy of medieval tales. The canons and paving stones were glistening from a misty, almost invisible rain. The crashing waves were responding to the *aquilon*, the north wind, and spreading humidity like the sweaty fear one feels upon seeing a sudden apparition. The cold was so violent that it penetrated the flesh, paralyzed the muscles as cruelly as dungeon chains. She thought about the Benedictines during the Middle Ages, how they were able to survive without any source of heat. Yellow tavern lamps swung in the darkness, and you could almost expect at any moment to meet a furious knight or a cantor drunk with wine and armed with lyre. Johanna did meet a couple of lovebirds gushing over each other. They seemed out of place here, where time had been suspended, in their modern clothing. She smiled at them and struggled up the slippery steps. When she reached the parish church dedicated to Saint Peter, she turned left and walked into the village cemetery. Closing her eyes, she could see in her mind's eye a pit hollowed in the earth and Moira, dressed like a Celtic goddess, rising from it, leaving behind her a monk robed in black and weeping as her wings brushed against him. Johanna looked up. She saw her empty house, and for the first time she considered it her only true home, with the wrought-iron balcony of her shuttered room facing an incongruous palm tree that had been planted in the street below. The streetlight on the way cast a pale gauze over the tombs lined up in the grass along the wall. She discovered that the tomb just under her window, where another improbable palm tree was planted, was the grave of a poor soldier from World War I who had died on the field of honor when he was thirty-three years old, exactly her own age, just before the 1918 armistice.

Her heart ached; she shivered from the cold. She could feel in her pocket the weight of the abbey keys, and they seemed to be burning hot. She picked up her travel bag and continued up the stairs toward the monastery. As she unlocked the heavy wooden châtelet door, she thought back to the night she hadn't dared to enter, when she had felt a strange, frightening breath, the night Paul had called with his discovery. It was just the week before, yet it seemed like an eternity. Between last week and today almost one thousand years had passed. She smiled. She hadn't been able to go any further that night because she wasn't ready then. Today, he knew that she was ready. He had done what he needed to so that she would be ready. The beam of her flashlight cut a sharp furrow over the stones. Johanna was led forward by what seemed to be a bride's veil. Milky white night lights crowned the granite walls like garlands of orange blossoms. The happiness that had washed over Johanna's soul at Cluny now completely engulfed her. She walked through the frightening rooms with a calm and serenity she had never felt before. It was only when she reached the closed door leading to Notre-Dame-sous-Terre that she began to shudder. For the first time, she was going to enter the old church at night, and she recalled Simon's words about the angels and demons that haunted it. Slowly, she opened the door. Immediately, she was reassured by something she hadn't noticed before. It felt surprisingly warm in the crypt, when everywhere else it was freezing. The abbey's ancestral entrails were as warm as a human womb. Mother Earth gave life to this feminine place. Yes, the place seemed to be gendered. The rock and most of the monastery were masculine, but this sanctuary was clearly feminine, and it sheltered a man she half expected to see on the steps above the twin altars. There wasn't anyone there, but the crypt wasn't empty. She could feel a confused presence of life, mute and almost imperceptible, but surely there was life. Guillaume Kelenn had told her that although they knew nothing at all about the place, and even if they didn't believe in God or the devil, some tourists went into a trance when they visited Notre-Dame-sous-Terre. Telluric energy! Johanna knew that such forces would not be dangerous for her. She had nothing to fear because one of those forces was protecting her. She took off her down vest and leaned up against one of the pillars. Might her headless monk be linked to Brother Roman? Certainly, or why would he have sent her the manuscript across the ages?

For she no longer had any doubts that the manuscript had been sent to her just as personally as her three dreams had been. The mysterious spirit who had communicated with her through her dreams had also played with destiny so that she would find the manuscript, so that she would learn about the marvelous love that had united two beings whom everything conspired to keep apart and whom tragedy finally had separated. In the comforting warmth of the crypt, she realized, though, that she was missing an important link in her full understanding of what had really happened, the link between Brother Roman and the headless monk. She now possessed the beginning and the end, but she couldn't resolve the whole mysterious story without untying the central knot, without finding the unknown piece: what had happened to Roman after he left Cluny in 1063.

"I know that the answer lies here at Mont-Saint-Michel," she murmured to the invisible presence. "I know that you'll help me. Guide me. Which path must I take? Show me, I pray."

When she left the underground crypt around midnight, she had the strange feeling that she wasn't alone. A protective soul seemed to be accompanying her, filling the night's silence with a gentle murmur. It was like an old prayer in Latin, like plainsong. Perhaps it was the wind, or the abbey stones remembering the Benedictines' office of Matins. Perhaps it was nothing.

During the days that followed, Johanna took advantage of her team's absence to explore every nook and cranny in the monastery and village. The rock could no longer hold any secrets from her. During the day there was tourist bus after tourist bus, but once the winter dusk came, the mountain was given back to the natural elements that made it so impressively unique. She often met Simon Le Meur, who invited her to go sailing with him. But she was prey to seasickness and preferred going with him to gather shellfish when the tide was out. Wearing plastic boots and carrying a rake, he explained bay life to her and showed her magnificent birds, which reminded her that the Mount was also a nature preserve. They dug up little white shellfish called Saint Michael's cockleshells, like the emblems medieval pilgrims pinned on their coats. They took a long walk, and that evening he invited her to come eat the shellfish they had collected. Everything had begun during that long walk and the following evening. Johanna discovered a man who wasn't like the insatiable chatterbox she had met in the café the first time. He was subtle, sensitive, and discreet. She attributed his gossiping that first evening to the awkward impropriety that timid people sometimes display.

Simon's house was as charming as he was. It had a splendid view over Tombelaine Island and was guarded by a stone gargoyle fixed to the top of the granite wall. Above the entrance an old lantern welcomed visitors. Inside, the antique dealer had designed the rooms for comfort and elegance, but unpretentiously, in harmony with the mountain's ambiance. There was a large kitchen with a colorful ceramic-tile stove, decorated floor tiles, and copper cooking pans; the warm living room was decorated with old paintings, ship's instruments, a huge, carefully restored fireplace, soft sofas, and a celestial globe from the eighteenth century. The desk was an authentic medieval chest surrounded with rows of books stacked from the floor to the rafters. The bedrooms contained all sorts of huge, finely decorated Norman armoires, and the sheets they held smelled like lavender. That first evening was light and cheerful. They didn't talk about the Mount. Simon entertained her with stories about how his Spanish mother tried to make Breton cookies for his father, and how she couldn't keep from using olive oil when she made them. And Johanna told him about her memorable culinary catastrophes. He asked her about her love life, and she heard herself say that she used to be with a married man, but that now things were over. What had gotten into her suddenly to make her like that? She changed the subject, and they discovered they enjoyed the same kinds of music and literature. After dinner was over, Simon repeated his invitation for New Year's Eve, and Johanna accepted. As she walked back home, she wondered why she had accepted. Had she lost her mind? She had told this man yes, but she had already promised François she would spend New Year's Day with him in Paris. All evening long it seemed like there was someone pushing her into Simon's arms. It was as if someone had cast a spell on her! Johanna was upset enough to call Isabelle in spite of the hour.

Her friend was concerned about one thing only. Was Simon unmarried, free, alone, without a wife and children hidden off somewhere? As soon as Johanna answered in the affirmative, she heard a joyous shout at the other end of the line, followed by such encouragement that she was a little perplexed. On the twenty-eighth she was in such a panic that she got sick. Her gastroenteritis came at a good time, as she could cancel her trip to Paris. She begged François not to come; she said that she didn't want him to see her in such a condition. She vomited her guts out, started a purifying diet, stayed in bed, and by the thirty-first she was better. She felt like she had a new body. That evening at Simon's, she realized with surprise that she had been delivered from the macabre despair she often felt at year's end. She was changing, and she could swear that the friendly spirit possessing her was no stranger to the change. But she couldn't speak about that to anyone.

Simon had prepared a table fit for a princess. The evening was a fairy tale. They were living in a book of legends, out of time, away from the present. At midnight he led Johanna to the open window, sat down close behind her, and gave her a copper telescope so she could admire Tombe-laine and the moon. Johanna's resistance had melted away, and when she saw the cylinder, she had a strong desire to tell him about Roman and Moira. Conspiratorially, she reached into her bag and took out the note-book that never left her person. Then she sat back in an armchair beside the fireplace, and, as the air filled with the honeyed scent of the Dutch tobacco with which Simon packed his sailor's pipe, she read him the monk's words she had translated into French.

It was easy to forgive Simon his bent for literature rather than for rational history, especially since it was just that fanciful spark that attracted her to him.

She realized that she was moving further and further away from the Cartesian she thought she was. History didn't really belong to the "hard" sciences, to be sure, but it did demand rigor and verification. An archeologist was, above all, a scientist. Yet she had immediately assumed that the manuscript was authentic without waiting for the experts to give their opinion. Worse, she considered herself an atheist, only now she believed she was possessed by some kind of guardian angel dressed in a monk's frock and without a head! And finally, on top of all that, she found herself under the charm of a forty-year-old man who enjoyed looking at the moon! She told herself that just a few months earlier, she would never even have noticed Simon. Occasionally she had met these kinds of supersensitive people and had always carefully avoided them.

Life was too serious to go in for romanticism, which for her was an obvious sign that a person hadn't grown up, and wouldn't. Her love of stones came before love of men, and certainly before any men who might jeopardize the passion she had for her profession. Johanna still unquestionably venerated stones, but she couldn't deny that she was also wildly in love with Simon and that there was no contradiction in this turn of emotional events. She desired Simon like she had never desired François or anyone else. Her body did enjoy intimacy with François, but now her whole being was burning, body and spirit, in perfect harmony. She had a crazy idea: Might it be a heavenly force driving her, pushing her toward love? Did that force want to test her or confront her with a love as passionate as the love that united Roman and Moira so that she might understand it better? Or had the monk's tale made such an impression on her subconscious that she herself needed to experience such a consuming relationship, one that was clearly impossible with François? In any case, she had no desire to go back home and leave Simon. But she didn't want to give in completely, either. Thinking about the powerful but chaste link uniting Roman and Moira, she explained to Simon that she wanted to sleep with him but didn't want him to touch her. She felt like a child, but he agreed. Simon was deeply moved.

He loaned her a pair of pajamas that smelled like linden blossoms, and she spent the first hours of the New Year cuddled in his arms and curled up against his chest, while he delicately kissed her hair as if they inhabited a chivalric novel by Chrétien de Troyes.

ON THE MORNING of January 1, not knowing exactly why, she took leave of Simon and hurried back home. The house was empty, for the team wasn't due back until the next day. But an hour later, as she was leaving the bathroom, someone unexpectedly rang the doorbell, and she saw that François was waiting down by the door. He said he was worried because her cell phone wasn't on and nobody answered the house phone. He had spent the evening in Cabourg with Marianne and the children after all, and he had come over to the Mount to see how she was doing. Johanna didn't have the courage to tell him the truth. She said she still wasn't feeling well and because she hated New Year's Eve parties, as he was well aware, she had taken some sleeping pills and gone to bed early. He agreed that she still didn't look well and said that maybe she needed to get out a little. He suggested a walk on the ramparts. Johanna felt a little guilty and searched for a way to keep him from running into Simon. It would happen inevitably, because it shouldn't happen, and the two rivals would probably guess the truth at first glance. And in fact, perhaps François already suspected something. Never before had he shown up without warning, even when she couldn't be reached by telephone. She answered that she'd like to go somewhere off the island, and since the weather was nice, she proposed a day in Brittany. So as not to make him suspicious, she hurriedly added that Cancale, during the Middle Ages, was part of the abbey's lands and that she be delighted to go see it. François smiled. He first wanted to see the new dig, and they went down to what used to be Saint Martin's Chapel. Absentmindedly, she described the archeological work that was going on, the bones that were being studied. She was thinking all the while about the meetings between Roman and Moira, for they had taken place right there, and she wondered if she and Simon would also be condemned to secrecy. "Love is always secret for someone," she thought, remembering Marianne. "The important thing is not to keep it hidden from one's own heart." Roman himself had denied his feelings for Moira for such a long time! It wasn't the same situation, of course. Johanna wasn't a nun, although she, too, was directing a project. The more she reflected, the more she was convinced that her soul was like the soul of the master builder, Jean de Marburg, Brother Roman. And might he be her headless monk?

They had an enjoyable day. They ordered a gigantic platter of shellfish down at the port in Cancale, the turquoise point of the Grouin, from where they could see the Mount off in the distance and then the ramparts of Saint-Malo. She claimed she didn't want to go inside the walls of the city because there weren't any old stones—the city had been totally destroyed during World War II. In fact, she wouldn't be able to hide her emotion if they happened upon a certain shop featuring marine antiques. She was afraid to go back to the island, and not simply because she didn't want to run into Simon. No, there was another reason, less clear but more powerful, as if the holy mountain, which welcomed three million tourists every year, was rejecting François. How grotesque! Except that François wasn't just any old tourist. He had been into her house, her bed, and her body. Was that fact painful for the spirit of the rock to accept, or was it painful to her? Everything seemed so unclear that she was confusing the rock's spirit and her own. She did belong to the Mount, and its mystery was becoming part of her because she had laid bare her soul. She could no longer distinguish her own breath from the mountain's. And yet, after all, it had been François who had arranged for her to live and work there! She couldn't deny that, but still she couldn't bring herself to go back with him. She took him to the commune of Courtils, to an old manor house transformed into a hotel-restaurant that had a magnificent view of the Archangel's dwelling. All through dinner, she kept reminding herself that she owed her present happiness to François, and she began to relax. She even enjoyed being with him. She laughed, told him about Paul and his discovery, about Christmas and Corinne, but didn't mention the parchment. While they seemed to be admiring Mont-Saint-Michel through the hotel window, in reality, she felt, the Mount was looking at them, watching them. When the meal was over, she didn't want to return home. Her house was cold, impersonal, and she was sure that Patrick Fenoy had come back. He was exasperating and, if he saw them together, everyone in the profession would know about it, maybe even Marianne, and he'd make life unbearable for her. Naturally François agreed, and they took a room in the hotel. To top it off, she came to a climax immediately.

GETTING BACK TO work on the archeological dig was dismal. Johanna's colleagues had come back from vacation exhausted. They had clearly drunk a lot. Her assistant hadn't lost any of his bile, and he poured it out on everyone, but primarily on Johanna. He accused her indirectly of losing interest in their work at the abbey, of thinking more about the discovery at Cluny and about Pierre de Nevers's grave. And that was partly true. She did have her mind somewhere else, but not in Burgundy. She was in fact thinking about the Mount, for she'd become obsessed with Brother Roman as well as with Simon. She kept looking for Roman in the Avranches library and in Notre-Dame-sous-Terre. In the crypt she could sense his presence there, but in the library she would lose herself in magnificent volumes, in their red and green allegories, in angel and demon faces that fatigued her eyes and gave her nightmares. She was beginning to get a better feel for Almodius's work than for Roman's. Roman kept avoiding her.

As for Simon, on the other hand, she met him every evening but kept it secret from the group so as not to give Patrick's mean spirit and the others' curiosity something to feed on. Her assistant had mentioned that her missing dinner with the team was contemptible, and so she made an effort to share their unchanging ritual and to put up with Fenoy's lessons about history and life in general. But as soon as dinner was over, she would flee and try to stay out of sight, while back in the team's house they all gossiped about her. Florence and Dimitri, the sharpest ones, had probably already deciphered her vaporous looks, her flushed cheeks, her greater attention to how she dressed, and especially her impatience to leave once dinner was over. But they were discreet enough not to show it. Johanna knew that sooner or later they'd find out about her liaison with Simon. It wouldn't be a scandal, and it certainly wouldn't harm anyone. Still, she took fanciful pleasure in covering her face with a wool or silk stole, running along the ramparts at nightfall, her heart pounding at the thought of meeting someone she knew, and then tapping in Morse code on the door of the tower where her Prince Charming was waiting. Her joy, like that of a little girl, was followed by a woman's exhilaration. She had overcome her fear, and for the past two nights sensuality had erupted between Simon and her. They they'd experienced a symphony of emotions in a major key and attained the essence of love, greater each time in their union, the surprise and the sharing more sublime. For Johanna, it was a revelation, this miracle called love.

François had flown into a rage when he learned that Johanna hadn't told him about the Cluny parchment. The document was now undergoing chemical analysis in the Bibliothèque Nationale. At first glance, the expert thought that the parchment and the ink could indeed date from the eleventh century and that they came from the Burgundian abbey's workshops. At the other end of the line, Johanna smiled. Of course the manuscript was authentic! She cut short her conversation with François, who fortunately knew only the document's major points. His Latin wasn't very strong and the text hadn't yet been officially translated. She hurried down to Notre-Dame-sous-Terre to thank the forces that had enlightened her soul. She bumped into Guillaume Kelenn, who was strutting about like a peacock while numerous Saturday-morning tourists flocked around him.

"Oh, how fortunate!" he exclaimed when he saw Johanna. "Ladies and gentlemen, I would like to introduce the director of the archeological dig that's keeping us from admiring the treadmill and its fabulous ramp leading down to the base of the rock. Could you speak to us about your work and about Judith of Brittany? This is a group from Brest!"

It certainly wasn't an opportune time to see Kelenn, as was often the case. But this time she was especially annoyed because he was getting between her and the stones in the crypt. She looked at him, lips tight. Her eyes were like cannons, ready to send a salvo of bullets filled with lethal poison. Then she turned around and, slamming the sanctuary door, walked out. Good heavens! Rarely was she in such a bad mood. And Simon had gone away for the weekend. He'd needed to visit his parents, not far from Brest, as a matter of fact. Did she ever need to visit her parents? For her, telephoning was enough. Why did he need to spend three days with his parents at his age? Or maybe it wasn't his parents. That was what he said, but there was nothing to prove it. Jealousy ate away at her like bad alcohol. That desire to possess the other person, to share his every gesture, every second, every breath—jealousy, too, was new to her.

And now that fellow Kelenn was preventing her from seeing Roman, or her headless monk, or both of them, since there was probably a link between them. She could try to get along without Simon for a few nights, but nothing could make her forget Roman. She was eager to find him. She hurried determinedly down through the village, got in her car, and sped toward Avranches.

"But I'm telling you he does not exist, at least as far as I know," said the library's chief conservator, trying to be patient.

"Just because you can't find him in your dusty old volumes doesn't mean he doesn't exist," answered Johanna. "There's bound to be some reference to him in one of these books!"

The conservator looked angrily around at the documents. With its books in their worn leather bindings piled up to the ceiling, its wooden bookcases, and the little staircase leading up to the top of the book-covered walls, the room looked like a museum or even the Bibliothèque Nationale.

"Madame," he said, spitting out his words, "these 'dusty old volumes' that we have the honor of owning have miraculously escaped numerous fires in the abbey, collapsing buildings, the covetousness of princes and greedy prelates, the Revolution, the expropriation of the monasteries, pillaging, war, the American bombing of 1944, the weather, the humidity, artificial light, saltpeter, mold, insects, and readers' carelessness. We're the ones who've saved these books, disinfected them, inventoried them, microfilmed them, and then classified them and brought them together here. From the abbey of Mont-Saint-Michel alone we've counted four thousand volumes, including two hundred and three medieval manuscripts. They are survivors, treasures, and I can't let you insult them like that! Good-bye. It's noon and we're closing."

Not sure what to say, blushing, Johanna dropped her head. He was right. It was as if someone had called her own Hugh de Semur or Judith of Brittany old carcasses and her Romanesque stones piles of pebbles! Sheepishly she smiled at him. His passion for old books really was very endearing. It was the first time she had spoken to the head conservator. Usually she managed alone by digging through the files, or sometimes she got help from an employee. But today, believing that her quest was near its end, she was in such a hurry that she had decided to consult God instead of his saints, and she had offended him.

"Please accept my sincere apology, sir," she said. "I . . . I'm not sure what got into me. For the last two months I've been searching unsuccessfully, and I'm getting testy."

"You have exhumed a piece of a pointed arch and a few skeletons. That's not bad, even if it's not what you were hoping for. And surely you're not telling me that you're despairing after only two months. You spent two years on your dig at Cluny."

"You know who I am?"

"I've seen you here several times a week for the last two months. I've had time to find out who you are," he answered with a wink. "This isn't

Paris. Here it's difficult to remain incognito. But just between you and me, I don't understand the connection between Saint Martin's Chapel, Judith of Brittany, and this obscure 'Brother Roman' you're looking so hard for! In 1063, Judith had been dead for more than fifty years."

Johanna was transfixed. Should she show him a copy of Roman's manuscript? He was a man who was used to working with such things. If he read it, something might click in his head so that he'd remember something he had seen in his books. She hesitated. Would he keep it to himself? If he was like her archeologist colleagues, it would be better not to tell him. The librarian took pity on her.

"Listen," he said finally, adjusting his glasses, "I've got an idea. I haven't been here very long, and I haven't been able to study four thousand volumes. But I know someone who has spent thirty-five years of his life doing just that."

Johanna's eyes lit up like a lighthouse on the coast.

"In fact, it was thanks to him that we were able to save the books," he added, looking down at his cigarette. "They were being eaten by death-watch beetles and by microscopic fungi, and he made a real fuss. He kept nagging the city, the department, the region, and finally he came close to attacking the Ministry of Culture! In 1986 they finally listened to him. They took all the books to the Bibliothèque Nationale to be treated. In the meantime, we renovated our space so that they could be kept properly here. As you've noticed, we maintain a constant temperature of eighteen degrees Celsius and even have ultraviolet filters on the windows."

"Who is this man? The former conservator?" Johanna asked.

"Oh, no, not at all. Although he did play that role for the works we inherited from the abbey, he really didn't have the title or the clothes," he answered with a chuckle. "He's a monk, a Breton Benedictine who came to the Mount in 1966 when they reestablished a religious community—the first Benedictines to live in the abbey since 1791, exactly one thousand years after the first black monks conquered the mountain, can you imagine?"

The lighthouse beam grew brighter.

"To make a long story short, the abbot had given him the job of making an inventory of the abbey's library, of determining the extent of the damage, if you will. So he would spend all day long here, never going back to the monastery until Vespers, riding his moped whatever the weather. He was so caught up in his work that in 2001 when the Benedictines left, giving the abbey over to the Community of Jerusalem, he preferred retiring and going back home. And he was plenty old enough!"

"What's his name?"

"Placide, Father Placide. He still lives in Brittany, in a retirement home for religious, in Plénée-Jugon, between Dinan and Saint-Brieuc. Apparently it was really hard on him to give up the manuscripts that were so dear to him, and he's lapsed into silence, just waiting to die."

Johanna was already on the way out. In the doorway, she turned back to thank the conservator and ran to her car. She hadn't expected to meet a modern Benedictine. A black monk, of course!

SHE GOT LOST twice, asked her way, and finally found an old, decrepit-looking nineteenth-century building in thorn-infested grounds where monks of various orders were walking about in robes of various colors. They had spent their lives praying among brothers belonging to the same order, but here they were getting old together—Franciscans, Dominicans, Benedictines, Cistercians, and Carmelites. The only things they had in common were their age and that curious spark in the eyes that comes from living apart from the world. A nun tried to keep Johanna from seeing Father Placide. She couldn't understand what a young woman who wasn't even a relative could possibly get from an old man who would no longer speak, who perhaps couldn't understand anything, and who simply was waiting to die in the Lord.

But Johanna was too determined to be frightened off by an old monk's voluntary silence. She finally got his room number and hurried up the stairs. The steps were easy to climb compared to those at the Mount. The eggshell paint on the wall was starting to peel and showed the somber gray behind it. The doors, painted piglet pink, struck a happier note that might make you think for a moment you were in a maternity ward. Johanna knocked several times but got no answer. She decided to go in nonetheless. An artificial heat wave and the smell of urine caught in her throat. On the greenish wall across from the bed hung an engraving of

Mont-Saint-Michel. On the bed, surrounded by all sorts of medical equipment, lay a corpse-like man dressed in an old, wrinkled-up, black robe. His bald head was yellow, with a few white hairs standing up. He seemed to be sleeping, or maybe dying. The robe fell over him in creases like waves, his cheeks were sagging, and his thick beard made his neck look as if it were floating. His liver-spotted skin seemed to bear no connection to his muscles and bones. He must have been at least eighty years old, maybe ninety. Ill at ease, Johanna sat down on a squeaky metal chair. His eyelids opened; his eyes looked like a faded sky.

"Sir," she began, standing up. "Oh, I'm sorry. Father, I mean. You don't know who I am. My name is Johanna, and the conservator at the Avranches library gave me your address."

He kept looking at the engraving of Mont-Saint-Michel on the wall.

"I . . . I'm an archeologist," she continued, reciting her lesson like a school girl, "a medieval historian, and I'm conducting a dig in the abbey at Mont-Saint-Michel."

When he heard her mention the Mount, he deigned to look at her. He had magnificent eyes, but they were covered with a translucent film. A moment later the spark went out, as if it had been drowned in a dark abyss. Without waiting to find out what Johanna wanted, he turned away. Although the conservator in Avranches and the sister had warned her, she hadn't expected that. The spirit of the monastery manuscripts was dead! She couldn't say a word. He communicated nothing but eternal silence.

She tried once more. "Father, I don't want to disturb your well-deserved rest, but you are the only person who might be able to help me."

Not a word. Desperately, she looked over at the engraving on the wall for inspiration. Protected by glass, in an elegant gilded frame, the etching was signed by Georges Gobo and issued by the Louvre museum. It must certainly have been a retirement gift from Historical Monuments. It was a view from the south, and the mountain at low tide stood out against a sky filled with undulating mists. At its base, the new causeway was an earthen path lined by pleasure craft and fishing boats. The Mount as it must have been at the beginning of the twentieth century, after the prison was closed and the restoration completed under the Third Republic. That was when they had chanced upon the walled-in and disfigured Notre-Dame-sous-Terre, which had been lost since the end of the eighteenth century. One hundred and thirty years wiped out for the Mount's ancestral soul. How long would it take for Johanna to open it back up? Slowly she turned around and looked back at the man stretched out on the bed; she listened to his rasping breath. How long? Suddenly she reached for her bag and pulled out the cahier where she had copied Roman's confession. She had nothing to lose. She had to make one last effort before it was too late. After all, Father Placide would surely not be telling anybody else about the contents of the master builder's testament.

"I have here what a colleague just discovered at Cluny, in the tomb of a man named Pierre de Nevers," she started out, sitting down at the foot of the bed. "*The Cluny abbey, Easter in the year of our Lord 1063. To the abbot Hugh de Semur. My Father in Christ . . .*"

As she read, she could sense that Father Placide was beginning to move and then realized he was staring at her. But she made herself keep reading. Only her voice betrayed her emotion.

When she had finished, she sighed, and, like a person on trial, she fearfully looked up at her judge. He was sitting up in bed, pillows behind his back, and his position made him seem different, as if he had rejoined the world of the living. The light in his eyes was bright but serious. Only his brown-spotted hands and his lower lip kept up their trembling. Johanna had to bite her tongue to keep from spoiling everything with inappropriate words. She waited.

"That's quite an impressive discovery," he finally said weakly. "And what exactly are you looking for?"

"Officially, I'm looking for medieval bones, particularly the remains of Judith of Brittany; but in fact I'm really searching for Brother Roman, Father. Secretly, of course. I absolutely must find out how his story ends."

"Why?" he asked curtly, almost threateningly, and it appeared to her that he might indeed know a great deal. She hadn't told him anything about herself, but like Simon, he had been able to guess. He knew that her search was affecting her very existence. This man, too, had been filled with the rock's supernatural quintessence, Johanna was sure. She didn't hesitate to tell him more.

"The first sign was sent to me the first time I went to the Mount, when I was only a child," she began. "That was twenty-six years ago. One night, I dreamed about a Benedictine monk tangled in ropes, hanging from the top of a tall tower. And then, in a place I identified later as the crypt Notre-Dame-sous-Terre, the body of a headless monk appeared to me saying, in Latin: 'You must dig in the earth to reach heaven.' The second time happened in September of last year when I went back to the Mount for my first visit since I was a child. Once more in a dream I saw a hand push a black monk off a rock, and the victim fell into the night sea and then drowned as his brothers were chanting Matins in the Romanesque abbey. And then the headless monk reappeared, once again in Notre-Dame-sous-Terre, and he repeated the same sentence in a supplicating voice. The third and final time I saw him was around All Saints' Day, at Mount Gargano in Italy. It was at night, while I was sleeping. But that time I clearly saw an assassin's hands burn a straw mat where a lay person seemed to be sleeping, and I didn't recognize him any more than the others. The blond-haired man lying there was burned up, along with a tapestry representing Saint Michael weighing souls, and then the flames reached the walls of the wooden hut. Afterward, I found myself again in Notre-Dame-sous-Terre, where the same headless monk was waiting on the stairs above one of the twin altars. And he repeated a third time: 'You must dig in the earth to reach heaven.' And the third time, he flew over and pressed his finger against my forehead. Just like the Archangel did to Aubert, according to the legend, when Saint Michael repeated the third time that Aubert was to build a sanctuary.

"That's my story, Father. And at the same time, you understand, it's not my story. I'm not sure what to do!" she concluded, bursting into tears. "I've been living at the Mount for the last two months, and I've been searching vainly for the headless monk in Notre-Dame-sous-Terre and in the Avranches library. I never see him anywhere, but I sense that he's taken possession of me, that he expects something from me. Yes, he's waiting like an angel or a devil, and I know that he's the one who made sure I got Roman's manuscript. Now I need to find out why. I need to find out who the monk is, if it's Brother Roman or someone else. If I'm right or if I need to be locked up somewhere!"

She was weeping hot tears. Father Placide closed his eyes. It looked like he was praying. Slowly, he leaned forward and took Johanna's hands in his. The old monk's hands were warm and rough.

"Being locked up somewhere is not what you think, my daughter," he said, his voice gathering assurance. "When you're in prayer, it's not a prison but a gate, a gate between earth and heaven. In your case, I believe that communication between the two worlds has already been established, deep within your soul. Don't be afraid that you're going crazy, and listen to what your heart is telling you, for your heart is on the path of light!"

Johanna didn't understand everything he was saying, but wisely, leaving her hands in his, she kept quiet.

"Your heart is pure," he continued. His eyes were still closed, and it was as if he were reading deep into her soul. "No, your heart is not mistaken, for others have seen what you have seen, have heard what you have heard."

"What? What are you saying?" she asked in astonishment. "Excuse me, Father, but that makes me so happy! For the first time in twenty-six years, there's confirmation that he exists. The headless monk exists! What is his name? Have you seen him?"

"He comes from the holy mountain's dark past. I've never seen him myself, but other people have, a long time ago, and they've left descriptions."

"The manuscripts in Avranches! You found him in the Avranches manuscripts? Where are they, Father? Please! Which shelves, which volume? Where are those archives, my dear Father?"

As peacefully as he had closed his eyelids, Father Placide reopened them. His eyes were feverishly bright. It seemed as if there were an immense fire burning within him, in stark contrast to his words and gestures. He released Johanna's hands, raised his fingers to his old head, and, placing his forefinger on his forehead, he answered:

"The archives are right here!"

14

WHEN ALMODIUS ARRIVES AT THE SCENE, THE BURNING HUT has just collapsed and the monks and lay people are watching in consternation, with words of despair running through their minds. Eudes de Fezensac's assistant, a lively little Gascon, is digging into the smoking debris to reach his master's body. Blackened timbers crash down. The abbot notices a pewter pitcher lying on its side, a pewter goblet as well, and charred strips of something troubling. It's the tapestry showing Saint Michael weighing souls. It has been badly burned and all that's left is the Archangel's menacing head and the handle of the sword he had been brandishing in his right hand. Ten years before, when Almodius became abbot, he had taken the ancient tapestry down from where it had always hung in the abbot's cell and had it placed in his master builder's lodging. He associated too many unfortunate memories with that piece of cloth, even if it was sacred: Hildebert interrogating Moira, the confrontation between Hildebert and Almodius, Hildebert dying, then Abbot Thierry as well. And finally the succession of corrupt abbots. Almodius had feared that the tapestry would daily awaken too many of the ghosts he was trying to dispel. He had reasoned, too, that living with the Angel could be useful in opening up Eudes de Fezensac's soul, up the mountain he didn't know very well.

This evening, as the master builder's assistant and two water-carriers pull out what's left of the builder's charred remains, Almodius is filled with compassion.

"Take him to Saint Martin's Crypt," he orders. "That's where we hold wakes for souls that are pure and for the benefactors of our monastery. My sons," he says to the monks, "Matins will soon be ringing. I ask you to intercede with the Lord for the man whom he has just summoned to be with him. Invoke the Archangel's clemency, ask him to come help and to protect his soul on the way to heaven. Go on, my sons, Eudes never shirked his earthly duty. Let us help him reach heaven!"

The monks look despondently at the abbot and then pull their hoods back up and start toward the church choir.

"Bertrand!" Almodius calls out to the master builder's assistant and pulls him off to one side. "Tell me, Bertrand, do you know anything about how the fire got started?"

The young man watches them carry the corpse away in a blanket, his eyes red from the smoke and sadness.

"We were both in Notre-Dame-sous-Terre," he begins. "It was after Vespers. The sun hadn't set yet, but down there it was dark, like eternal night. We were considering the day's progress, but it was disappointing. After removing some loose soil, the men had bumped up against solid, impenetrable granite. Eudes de Fezensac was looking over the measly mole tunnels with disgust when suddenly his eyes lit up."

Almodius can scarcely breathe, and his weasel eyes stare at Bertrand.

"He was looking at the twin altars," the assistant continues, "where candles were burning. More precisely, he was staring at the base of the pedestal. He glanced over at me and I realized what he was thinking. That was the only place his men hadn't yet thought of digging! We moved over to the altar with the Black Virgin, and with a few tools and a great deal of effort, we managed to loosen it from its base. Eudes was praying aloud to the mother of our Lord and the Queen of Angels to forgive him for that offense. But beneath the altar there was just some dirt, and under the dirt, rock and more rock. He crossed himself and hurried over to the altar of the Holy Trinity. Although it was even more difficult, we did manage to loosen it, too. Under the altar there was dirt, but under the dirt we saw chiselled stones!"

Almodius's eyes open wide, gleaming like black suns.

"My master and I pulled the stones up. We were sweating; we were afraid, but euphoric in a way that often accompanies fear. Suddenly he gave a shout. Under the granite debris there was a circular opening. It was large enough for an ordinary-sized man to slip through, and it extended down through the rock toward the darkness. The walls of the hole were vertical like a well, and it had certainly been dug out by human hands. My master held his lantern down in the hole's black mouth and dropped a pebble down its stone throat. We couldn't see where it landed, but we did hear it come to rest on a flat surface. There's something down there, probably a grotto, and we immediately deduced that it must be another temple that Aubert dug out under his sanctuary. Perhaps it's the secret hiding place for the holy relics you were hoping to uncover!"

The announcement takes the abbot's breath away. Joy overwhelms him. Finally he will get the answer to the questions he's been asking for forty years!

"Given the legitimate attachment you monks have for Aubert's work," Bertrand continues, "and given its sacred character and the time it was getting to be—Compline was about to end and demons would soon be invading the crypt—my master didn't want to climb down. He was afraid he'd be desecrating a holy place with his unclean hands, he was fearful of outraging heavenly powers, and he was especially in terror of disturbing Aubert's soul and going against the Archangel's will, for they had forbidden touching the former church and had just taken revenge on poor Anthelme and Romuald."

"Eudes de Fezensac, too, can believe such stupidities!" Almodius thinks. "This man is just as superstitious as a mindless serf!"

"Consequently," Bernard goes on, "stricken with apprehension because he had touched the sacred altars and by his fear of committing even worse sacrileges, my master decided not to try anything and to tell you about it immediately. We put the altar of the Virgin back in place, lit some candles, and then left the crypt, relieved to get out into the fresh air. We were going to awaken you since Compline was over, but we were surprised to see your door barred by two lay brothers who, with a vehemence unsuitable for their position, wouldn't let us in. My master was forced to admit that his discovery would have to wait until the next morning. He bade me to go to bed and went to his own lodgings. He was pale, and his eyes were filled with terror. I'm sure he had sensed what was going to happen to him. Heaven's fire would strike the person who had offended Aubert and Saint Michael's sacred will. And their lightning struck him indeed!"

Bertrand sobs uncontrollably.

"Father, I beg you, we must stop the work in Notre-Dame-sous-Terre! Otherwise, worse things will happen! Heaven is conspiring against us poor mortals, and we are powerless against it. Father, I . . . I must warn you that as soon as my master is buried, I'm leaving for the south, going back to Gascony. I won't deprive my soul of God's salvation by obeying your orders. You'll have to find another master builder, someone who fears Hell less than I do."

Without taking proper leave of the abbot, he turns away, sniffling, and flees toward Saint Martin's Crypt to pray over his master's remains. Almodius tries to take in the news. He looks up toward the dark clouds. The firmament appears dry and lifeless, seemingly impassible. Only the faithful north wind still continues its nightly struggle.

The next morning will be a holiday marking Christ's Ascension into heaven, with crowds, parades, and the three funerals the abbot will have to celebrate under the monks' quiet, recriminating stares. Anthelme, Romuald, and now Eudes de Fezensac. At midday, for high mass, the bishop of Avranches and Duke William will arrive, and they won't fail to criticize him severely. Yes, both of them will be there, the bishop and the duke, like every year, just like their predecessors forty years ago. But this time, Almodius will be the one under attack, the one held responsible for all the chaos. The prelate and the prince have no idea who Moira was, the woman Almodius has tried for decades to forget and who now has returned from the dead, more demonic than ever. Almodius will have to confess that the legend of stone, the legacy that was to have crowned his earthly mission and given him immortality, must be suspended for the moment, because there is now no master builder. At the next office, he'll need to put down the revolt by his gullible sons, for they all believe in the Archangel's wrath. Although he hasn't told his suzerain about their digging in the crypt, he'll soon need to do so, and he'll need to tell him about discovering the underground passage and grotto. He'll need to convince him, too, that the three murders must not keep them from exploring the grotto, for it almost certainly holds a treasure. And then he'll probably have to combat William's greed. He forces a grin on his wrinkled face, clenches his fists, and walks back to his cell like an old soldier ready to fight. He opens the door. Hosmund's chair is still lying overturned by the dying fire, but the lay brother has disappeared. That doesn't concern the abbot, for now he knows that Hosmund is innocent. Almodius wraps his heavy serge cape around him, grabs a lantern, and, while his sons are chanting Matins, makes his way furtively to the crypt under the new church's choir. And then he reaches Notre-Dame-sous-Terre.

The candles Eudes and Bertrand left are still burning, and the abbot can see the holes and piles of dirt. Beside the Black Virgin on the left altar a lantern is flickering. The altar on the right, dedicated to the Holy Trinity, has been moved over against the wall so that it now stands perpendicular to the other altar instead of parallel with it. Near its usual place is a pile of stones. In spite of the candles and lantern, the crypt is still very dark.

Although the temperature has dropped outside, inside the air is warm. Wrapped up in his black cloak, Almodius moves toward the mysterious opening. He looks around to be sure no one is there. The vertical passage Eudes de Fezensac discovered is exactly as Bertrand described it, and it had clearly been dug through the rock's entrails by human hands. The abbot extends his torch, but the light isn't strong enough to reach the bottom. But the hidden grotto must be there. It holds out a promise for the future and especially a way to clear up the past.

"That must certainly be the reason those three poor men were killed," Almodius murmurs, rising to his feet.

"Perfectly well reasoned!" cries another man.

The abbot turns around to look for the voice that seems to have come from beyond the grave. Over near a pillar he can pick out a frail, dark form bent over like the arches in the crypt. Avoiding the mounds of dirt, Almodius walks toward the shadow. The form is wearing a frock just like the abbot's and carrying a pilgrim's stick. A thick ring of white hair crowns its head. The man is as old as Almodius, but there is life in his eyes. They are gray like dusk or like a delicate dawn, with dark sad rings under them. The stick reminds him of another stick, and the eyes. . . .

"Roman!" Almodius cries out, just a few feet away. "Is that you, Roman?"

"Unless I'm his ghost, coming back to avenge the death of the poor innocent woman whom you delivered up in cold blood and watched perish!"

"Keep your stories of ghosts and possessions for Brother Etienne and the other monks," the abbot replies, once the first moment of stupor has passed. "They still like them as much as they did forty years ago. So, four decades ago my instinct and reason were right to doubt you had really died! I now have proof that the whole business of your fever, of your being possessed by the devil and then by Aubert, was nothing more than a setup organized with Hosmund's help. I knew the rascal was covering up sinister misdeeds!"

"I had no other choice but to act as I did," Roman confesses, bowing his head, "no choice but to drag Hosmund into that infamous comedy. I had no other choice but to flee the abbey, Abbot Thierry, you yourself. I had to abandon my mission as master builder and be sure that you'd leave me in peace."

"I always thought that, unfortunately for all of us, you loved that woman more than the sacred stones of this abbey church," says Almodius, his voice suddenly gentle, looking up at the barrel vaults in the sanctuary. "You were the best master builder the Archangel ever chose, and you betrayed him for a woman, a mortal woman, and what's more, an ungodly woman whose cursed soul must still be suffering in the abyss."

"Her soul is not in Hell!" Roman roars. "How do you know she is not in heaven? For four decades I've been in the abbey at Cluny praying for her."

"Oh, that's where you've been! I'm not surprised to hear that Odilon took in a black sheep. But I find it curious that you didn't defrock."

"Why would I defrock? I did lie, of course, and I faked my death, but I've always remained faithful to God and to the Benedictine Rule."

"Brother Roman, whom do you expect to believe that an assassin is still worthy of wearing the Benedictine habit? This time you couldn't fool even the stupidest among us!"

Roman doesn't deign to answer. Almodius tries to take advantage of the opportunity.

"Moira certainly told you about this grotto," he says, pointing to the opening, "and you've come back forty years later to keep me from finding out about it. I don't know what fabulous treasure it holds, but it must be considerable. For, to protect it, first you changed your master's drawings and today you are spreading terror in our community with odious crimes! You haven't struck randomly, and your devilishly clever actions serve a double purpose. By these murders, you're trying to stop my excavation campaign in the crypt and at the same time eliminate enemies from your past! What an ingenious maneuver. Anthelme and Romuald were the last survivors of the court that condemned the heretic, and so you chose them to undergo your vengeance. As for poor Eudes de Fezensac, let's say that he was imprudent enough to discover the grotto, that his position as master builder made you bitter, and that by killing him you were also attacking me."

"You're mistaken," Roman answers, shaking his head. "You're talking about the work of a cold-hearted, satanic mind, and that description fits you more than me!"

The abbey feels hot, and anger rises in Roman's chest. He wags an accusing finger.

"How dare you claim that you haven't premeditated all of this? Nonsense! In a few hours it will be Ascension Day. You have calculated everything to the day, reproducing the symbols of the four elements. And unfortunately, everything has gone according to your evil plans. You prepared your barbarous misdeeds so carefully that you had no need to hurry or show impatience. So, the dark figure Brother Mark thought was Anthelme coming down from the bell tower after Matins the day before yesterday, that was really you. You were leaving the scene of your crime so calmly that Mark didn't for one moment suspect the horrible truth."

The cold, stark reality hits Roman. Trembling, he leans on his pilgrim staff and sighs before continuing:

"At Cluny, for four decades, I have lived a life of compunction and prayer, a life filled with silence, remorse, and memories," he says, looking down at the candles. "I've never forgotten the events that took place here, never, and I wasn't trying to hang onto them. Remembering was my condemnation. It was an open wound that kept growing with the passing of time, and even my supplications for the salvation of Moira's soul couldn't lessen the pain. And yet my heart always rejected any desire for revenge. Vengeance belongs to those who are revolted by life, who believe they are masters of a life that in fact is designed by God. I don't share such vehemence and pride. At Cluny I thanked the Lord for having given me so much, for having given me both heavenly and earthly love. My greatest crime was to have refused earthly love so long, to have remained blind in the face of the splendor of such a gift. My remorse comes from that self-imposed, voluntary infirmity. And then I imposed the same infirmity on Moira and caused her downfall. The only revenge I can conceive of is vengeance directed upon myself!"

Almodius crosses his arms under his cloak and looks mockingly at Roman. Roman pretends not to notice and goes on speaking.

"I left the mountain, now you know why and how, and I took refuge at Cluny under my baptismal name, Jean de Marburg. And there I hoped to finish out my days. But it's true that I had sworn forty years ago, in memory of Moira, to modify the drawings for the abbey. I did it to prevent any digging under the canons' old church, so that it would not be destroyed and so that nobody could find the passage to the grotto. In my exile at Cluny, I tried to keep myself informed about progress here on the abbey church, and I was reassured to learn that you had ordered the old church to be transformed into a crypt supporting the nave and named it Notre-Dame-sous-Terre. I thought the grotto was now out of reach, but I underestimated you. This year during Lent, my friend Hosmund had a letter sent to me secretly, the first in forty years, written for him by a pilgrim. Hosmund doesn't know about this cave, but he knew how strongly I felt that no one should ever dig here. So he told me about your plans to look for relics in Notre-Dame-sous-Terre. I confess that without his help I would never have known, or would have found out too late, since you placed the excavation under the seal of secrecy."

"So, as I thought, old Hosmund isn't crazy after all. Deceitful fellow. As for keeping the excavation secret, that wasn't to hide it from you but from Duke William, the bishop, and any relic thieves that are so common around here."

"Of course. And the secrecy let you act freely, as the region's grand lord."

316 | *Frédéric Lenoir and Violette Cabesos*

The two old men watch each other, each wondering which knows the other better, which hates the other more.

"I thought a long time before coming back to the Mount," Roman continues, "for the very idea filled me with terror. Seeing the mountain where Moira was tortured again, without being able to go back to where we met because Saint Martin's Chapel is gone; discovering the great abbey church that I had dreamed of so much when I was young and that I should have built myself; running the risk of meeting you and the other brothers—all that seemed well beyond my limited strength. But I couldn't fail to honor the oath I had given to Moira in my heart. So I put on a pilgrim's mantle to hide my monk's frock, picked up my stick, and set out, my soul filled with dread."

"Your fear soon left you!" says the abbot mockingly.

"My fear of myself did leave me. It became clear to me that I needed to awaken fear in other people, in the abbey monks, such intense fear that they would force you to stop digging in the crypt. The way to do that was obvious, since everyone thought me dead. Everyone, or at least those who were in the monastery back in those days and were still alive. After my long trip back, I went dressed like a pilgrim, to see Hosmund in his stable. He had been waiting for weeks. It was as if I had just left, although we were both changed men. He told me everything that had happened here during those forty years. He told me all about you, about my brothers. I unveiled my plan to him, and because Anthelme had condemned Moira and still enjoyed a reputation for wisdom, he's the one I chose."

Almodius sniggers, expecting Roman to confess his crimes.

"The day before yesterday Hosmund took it on himself to tell Anthelme that he had seen my ghost—that, like a phantom wandering for forty years, I had appeared to my friend Hosmund because I could sense that my enemy Anthelme would soon be leaving this place to join the Lord. Hosmund led him to believe that I was seeking revenge because I couldn't free myself from earthly contingencies and from my rancor. My greatest wish, Hosmund told him, was to block the road to heaven for those who had sentenced Moira. If Anthelme wanted to reach heaven immediately, without me keeping him here on earth and making him suffer the same tortures that Moira had suffered, he needed to make peace with me."

"Oh, I must say, this time you really surpassed yourself," Almodius interrupts with a sneer. "What diabolical imagination! Better than back in the old days!"

"Anthelme was convinced," Roman continues, unruffled by the abbot's sarcasm. "The poor fellow was in terror. During Matins, at darkest night, I took off my pilgrim cloak and climbed to the top of the tower in my monk's habit to wait for him. He showed up right on time, pale and trembling with fear, sure that he was talking to a ghost. I told him that I was furious about the sentence he had pronounced on Moira, and that her damned soul had been pursuing me for forty years demanding vengeance. When he asked what he needed to do to free me from her, and for him to be free from me, I answered: 'Serve the Archangel, obey Aubert's sacred injunction as he told it to me just before I died. You have until Ascension Day to be sure that all desecration ceases in Aubert's sanctuary and the old church. Until then I will leave you in peace. But if by the evening of Ascension Day the defilement has not been purified, I shall come back to find you. I shall carry off your soul and punishment will begin.'"

"But," Almodius asks, "then why kill him that same night?"

"Exactly!" says Roman, pacing back and forth in the crypt. "I'm telling you all this because I did not kill him, and the angels were my witnesses. I simply wanted to frighten him, make him persuade his brothers to stop the digging. He would have told everyone about our meeting, and that would have served my purposes much better than killing him."

The abbey is flabbergasted. He narrows his eyes.

"You're lying, Roman," he concludes. "You have always lied, back then and now. I believe you're trying to fool me because you haven't the courage to admit your human emotions, just like back then. You drew Anthelme up into the tower, as you said. But then, rather than give him your edifying speech, you threw yourself on him and hanged him from the tower. The symbol was too obvious for you to resist, and you worked in the same way to get rid of Romuald and Eudes de Fezensac."

"False!" Roman answers firmly. "When I came down from the tower, Anthelme was still alive. He was still living, I swear! No, I did not touch him. But the next day, when I learned he had died, I understood what had happened. Sometimes you are quite shrewd, Almodius, and as far as Anthelme is concerned, your first impression was correct. He killed himself, that's the only possible explanation. He was frightened beyond what I could have imagined, he was afraid that he wouldn't be able to get you to stop the dig and that he would see my 'ghost' again. He preferred risking Hell and hoping for Paradise all alone rather than facing inevitable torments in limbo with some ghost."

"You are probably going to tell me now that Romuald wanted to go swimming and so threw himself into the sea, and that my master builder was so cold he deliberately torched his own hut?"

Roman's back is turned. Slowly, he turns back around.

"I was as surprised as you to find out they were dead. I had not seen Romuald for forty years. And as for poor Eudes de Fezensac, I did catch glimpses of him here, but I've never had the honor of meeting him."

"What are trying to tell me?" the abbot asks impatiently. "The victims, the motive, the timing of the murders, and the way the men were killed— by using air, water, and fire—all that carries far too much meaning for me to think that you're innocent. Your very presence here on the mountain is an admission of guilt."

"I understand your reasoning, and I even agree up to a point. Although I still think Brother Anthelme killed himself, I believe, like you, that Romuald and Eudes de Fezensac were killed in keeping with the symbolic system surrounding Moira's tortures. They were surely killed to stop any digging in this crypt so that the grotto wouldn't be discovered. The last crime, the master builder's murder, unfortunately proves that the goal was to stop the excavation. For Eudes de Fezensac had nothing to do with those tragic events that happened so long ago. He had nothing to do with any vengeance related to Moira's tortures, but he was guilty of finding the entrance to the underground grotto. And that's why he was killed, just moments after his discovery. So, in fact, someone is killing to protect this grotto. Only, you must admit, I'm not that someone."

"But then who is? And why?"

"The why you've guessed. Both to protect the grotto and to get revenge for Moira's death. But, in my opinion, neither the way to get revenge, using the four elements, nor the choice of victims was premeditated. The unexpected way Anthelme died, hanging up in the air like Moira did four decades ago, must be what gave someone the macabre idea to carry out the project the way he did. As for the name of the assassin, I have my ideas, but it's too early to tell you. In any case, I can assure you that it wasn't Hosmund, whom you unjustly tortured."

Almodius for a moment remains silent. Standing at opposite sides of the crypt, the two religious contemplate one another, each tormented by his own memories. The two old men are like those memories; sometimes they meet, but never are they alike. On this night, nothing has changed between them. Like back then, time has reunited them, and their understanding of people and events brings them together, but between them a dissonance burns as hot as the air in the crypt. Almodius and Roman are like the two altars in Notre-Dame-sous-Terre. They look like twins, carved out of the same granite, but in reality they are polar opposites. One stands on the north, attached to the earth and the rock of which he is abbot, the solid rock that he venerates completely—his sacred woman, a Black Virgin. The other, on the south, is dedicated to the Father, Son, and Holy Ghost. The altar has been moved from its former place to open up a steep clandestine path that was dug in some other, older time with immense effort. It descends through the stone down to a womb-like grotto. Roman knows it holds secret treasure, but he has never been inside.

"I'm willing to admit that Hosmund did not commit the crimes," says Almodius, sitting down on a granite bench, "but he is your accomplice, as he was your accomplice in the past. And I cannot believe that you are innocent. No, your demonstration has not convinced me. For me, you are the only assassin, and I believe that this time you must truly be possessed by the Evil One. If not, how could you dare commit such infamy in a holy place, dressed as you are in a Benedictine frock?"

Roman sits down on a stone bench across from the abbot, his hands on his pilgrim's staff. Finding it useless to keep trying to defend himself, since his old enemy has decided he's guilty, Roman goes on the attack, though his voice remains calm.

"You, Almodius, do you think that our habit preserves those wearing it from the most sacrilegious crimes? You, who were wearing the habit when you tortured an innocent woman and poisoned an abbot?"

Almodius sneers. Now he's the one who has to defend himself in this strange courtroom where ghosts become judges.

"So you, too, believed that I poisoned Hildebert. Many people thought so and used their suspicion and false opinion to keep me from becoming abbot. However, I assure you that my only crime involving Hildebert was to make him angry, and his anger got the best of him. His was a cold nature, and his body couldn't stand the sudden heat. My words, without meaning to, did light the fire that consumed him, but the angry flames emanated from his own heart, and I did not stir them up with any poison. On the contrary, I tried everything I could to cool his body back down, but in vain. He died because he was in conflict with his own nature. Though I was in no way responsible, I ended up paying for a crime I did not commit. Unlike you, who live in regret, I took responsibility for my acts and finally became abbot. Better to accept what everyone thinks about you, even if they're wrong, than to insist on a truth that others refuse to believe."

"Interesting metaphysics. And you dare reproach me for lying!"

"I'm not reproaching you for anything, Roman, except for refusing to accept your actions, serious as they are, and so refusing to accept yourself. As for me, I don't have any experience with repentance. I think, and I act."

"You seem sincere," Roman admits, "and yet I have trouble believing you did not poison Hildebert. His dying served your ambition all too well."

"You'll believe me, perhaps, if I confess that I did administer poison, but not to our abbot."

Roman looks at him with satisfaction. Almodius looks back in the same way.

"Abbot Thierry, I suppose, so you could have his crosier?" Roman asked. "He died so suddenly in such suspicious circumstances, and then it didn't even help you."

"You disappoint me, Roman," the abbot responds condescendingly.

"Forty years of remorse haven't taught you anything about people! You see, in order to kill, you must either hate with your whole body or love passionately, and my feelings toward Hildebert and Thierry didn't reach that level of attachment."

Roman stares at the abbot, annoyed that he had misunderstood.

"The only substance I ever poisoned," Almodius finishes, "was the food you carried to Moira when she was at the bottom of the pit."

Stupefied, Roman blanches. Almodius savors his victory as he would a tasty wine from Burgundy.

"*Atropa bella donna, solanum dulcamara, hyoscyamus niger . . .* " he says, as if he were reciting a list of good wines. "A dozen fresh belladonna berries, an equivalent amount of red fruit from the bitter nightshade, some black henbane roots. I stole it all from Hosmund's infirmary, ground it up, and mixed it with wine and food to be sent to Moira."

Roman stands up, flushing with anger.

"You . . . you're a monster!" he shouts.

"You really don't understand me," the abbot responds calmly, staring off into the depths of the crypt. "Are you still as blind as you used to be? Can't you see that what I did was to spare Moira the cruel pain in store for her the next day, ordeal by fire? Yes, I did kill her, but I gave her what she was hoping for, death. For I knew that she would never recant. What good would it do to watch her suffer? I freed her from the earth by answering her prayers and delivering her back to earth, and I did so out of love."

"How could you have done that?" Roman shouts angrily, his eyes filling with tears and his fists clenched. "How dare you speak of love? Oh, yes, I was mistaken about you, and today I see how greatly. Good God! You killed her, and I'm the one who gave her the poison food. I was trying to save her, and I killed her. I killed her!"

"I would say rather that finally you gave her what she was longing for. That was the only time, it seems to me, that you did what she wanted. And you did so out of ignorance. For you never really understood her, naïve child that you were. You would never have had the courage to do something like that deliberately. I was the only one who understood the depths of her soul, because our souls were identical. While you were still entertaining futile hope, I heard her heart calling out for death. I was listening to her supplications, I answered, and she understood me! She was too experienced in herbal medicine not to recognize the taste of those poisons. If she had wanted to follow you, she would not have eaten. But she swallowed it all, thanking, I'm sure, the kindly hand that was saving her, knowing that it could not have been yours. Perhaps she guessed that I was the person giving her the only proof of love she wanted, proof that you were incapable of providing. I've always hoped that she knew. Yes, at the hour of her death she found out who was strong enough to love her and who had abandoned her like a coward."

"Abandoned? But you're the one who condemned her! And not content to give her over to the authorities, you're the one who sentenced her to torture and then condemned her to death, to irreparable death!" Roman shouts angrily, raising his arms. "How I deceived myself, how you deceived all of us. Look down, Lord, witness your son's confession, observe this man's self-delusion. Far from being guided by the faith he proclaims, he's governed by deleterious passion! Finally you let me see your true face, your vanity, and your rebellion against God. For a believer would have expected that divine grace could have descended on Moira even at the last minute to illuminate her heart and motivate her to change, and thus save her life. But you, you wanted to take the Creator's place, take for yourself the power of life and death over her. I thought your faith was so strong, so imperious, so vehement, that it had killed your capacity to love. But it was just the opposite. You were trying to stifle love and human passion because they had killed your faith. You denounced Moira, but it wasn't to save the abbey. It was out of spite, spite and vengeance, because she couldn't love you. Your faith has been nothing but an alibi for your own passions!"

Almodius rises from his bench.

"Are we really so different, my dear Roman?" he asks in honeyed tones. "Are you really as pious and pure as you claim? Didn't you use converting Moira to the true faith as an argument to attract her to your secret rendezvous and to cover up your sensual desires? Wasn't faith also an alibi for your own fondness for her? You see, what separates us is that you've always been hypocritical and cowardly about your feelings, whereas I welcomed that powerful, dark desire that was ravaging my soul and my body. You speak of passion, but you don't even know what passion is, a mortal epidemic that wipes out everything in its path. I refused to flee from those burning fires. I let them take possession of my whole being, and then I faced them. Valiantly I fought against the flesh as long as was necessary, and I won!"

"You fought by giving up Moira, and when that wasn't enough to put out the fires you're talking about, you killed her. That was the only way for you to be free, but you didn't care a whit about her, about her feelings, her thoughts, or her plans."

"Her plans? Her feelings? Do you think they had anything to do with you? You couldn't understand her love until she was tortured, and she needed to die before you'd admit your love for her! While Moira was still alive, you disdained the flame she was giving to you, waiting until her death before you began to venerate her nonexistent ashes. That's what the power of your 'love' was like; it was more a disregard for the living and veneration of the dead! She an icon, you worshipping the dead! What a great idea, to flee to Cluny! Of course, what could you have ever promised to Moira when she was still living? A miserable existence with a defrocked monk?"

The abbot lets out a loud laugh. On the other side of the crypt Roman can feel his blood boiling. His lips are clenched, and his gnarled hands grasp his rod with all his strength.

"When Moira was alive, she was a puzzle you would never have been able to solve," Almodius continues. "For you, Roman, have the same kind of blood as Hildebert did, cold blood, lukewarm in the best of cases. Fire can destroy you because it's so different from your putrid soul, putrid like a swamp. On the other hand, Moira was fire incarnate, and fire is also part of my own constitution. That's how I knew she would never renounce her beliefs. That would have meant renouncing her very essence, and like me, she was the kind of person with the conscience, tenacity, and warlike energy to prefer death to a pale existence torn from her Creator's matrix. To pay her homage, I spared her that final conflagration; I connived with a kindred spirit, perhaps out of my mad love for her. But I did not do it out of jealousy or spite. I gave her the poison that gripped her entrails in order to defend your corrupt soul, and to protect my own, 'tis true. But I did it especially so that our mother earth, our sacred mountain, would not be besmirched, for my greatest passion lies at the summit of this rock, and it could not be altered! It rises up above our heads, a stone castle reaching up toward the sky, and never could I let anyone bring peril to it, especially not Moira. I did indeed love her, but she threatened to bring horrible contamination to our community. What she did to you was proof enough. You, whom I so admired. . . . "

Moving toward Roman, Almodius continues to speak.

"You, chosen by the Archangel, you allowed yourself to stray from him and from his ardent stones. You, to whom he spoke so that you would build on the Mount heaven and immortality for him and eternity for all people. You, whom Moira dragged through filth, where you continue to wallow alone, without even struggling. Just as he did for me, the Archangel dubbed you with his sword, he showed you the path and you were too weak to follow it. She was certainly not an ordinary human being, and you didn't have what it took to resist. I alone was able to beat her. If only you could have understood that I was trying to help you when I delivered her over to the secular authorities, that I was trying to remove your chains! Then, instead of fleeing and hating me, you would have stayed here on the mountain, on our holy mountain, and together, we could have spared the Mount all those years of chaos."

Roman in turn walks toward Almodius. The abbot has tears in his eyes.

"Instead, you remained a prisoner in that woman's chains, even after her death. You were a holy alchemist, changing granite into divine gold, and she brought a stop to your art. You were a master, and she turned you into a slave. She's the one who killed you forty years ago, and I hope that in the depths of Hell she's paid for it!"

"Quiet!" screams Roman, barely a few steps from the abbot.

Roman drops his pilgrim's staff, reaches into his cowl and pulls out a dagger, which he brandishes before Almodius. The abbot recoils in surprise and backs toward the opening in the floor.

"That's enough!" Roman cries. "You've lost your mind, and your words are the words of a madman. You blame me for my weakness, only I was never weak enough to hate you, until tonight. But you've just opened yourself up as you have never done before, and the degree of your ignominy helps me understand much. Never did you really love Moira. All that your shady character could imagine was vile concupiscence and desire for possession. She managed to slip away from you as I, too, slipped out of your grasp, and you've never forgiven us. Moira gave her life for this grotto, and you are planning to sully it with your abject breath; you expect to violate its entrails as you burned to violate Moira's, but I shall prevent you. Yes, she may have died, but this cave is her beating heart, to which I've sworn fealty."

Almodius is standing right beside the gaping hole. He stops, pulls the folds of his cloak around him, and arrogantly confronts his opponent.

"Kill me if you wish. Assassinate me as you've already killed three others! This will be the fourth and final murder, the murder by earth, the earth in whose arms Moira died. End my days if you have the courage, for I'm not just some poor fellow you happen upon by chance, pretending you're a ghost. Go on, but before you continue, you must surely realize that if you don't, my men will enter this underground womb and find everything it contains. What could be so important that it's caused so much bloodshed?"

"You yourself will go down through this passage and will be able to satisfy your own curiosity," Roman answers. "When you've disappeared, I'll block the passage back up, stone by stone. Then I'll return the Holy Trinity altar to its rightful place, and you, with no air, you'll suffocate. Just like Moira did with your poison at the bottom of her pit. And I'll walk away, certain that no one will ever dig here again!"

"Do you really think that I'll be accommodating enough to leap into this hole simply because you're threatening me with that little dagger? No, Roman, once more you underestimate me. If you want me to die, you'll need to cut my throat yourself and then answer to the Lord for all eternity for what you've done."

Almodius stands motionless beside the opening. Unable to wait any longer, Roman raises his weapon and leaps forward to stab Almodius. The abbot does not move. Just as Roman is about to thrust downward, something stops him, and his body collapses. The dagger drops to the

326 | *Frédéric Lenoir and Violette Cabesos*

ground. Roman opens his mouth in astonishment, but no sound comes out, only a little dark blood. Roman is impaled on a long sword, a knight's sword that Almodius was hiding under his cloak. With one movement, the abbot pulls the sword back out of Roman's abdomen. Roman drops to the crypt floor, moaning gently.

"You betrayed the Archangel," says the abbot, "and you thought you could trick Almodius, the first among his servants. You who sowed death in our community, you die at my hand by Saint Michael's sword, the same sword with which the prince of the celestial hosts decapitated the dragon!"

Gathering all the strength he's bottled up for forty years, the vigorous old man raises the blade. He brings it down on Roman's neck and chops off his head. The tonsured cranium ends up at the edge of the hole. Almodius is breathing hard. He drops the sword, bends down, and picks up Roman's head.

"So, you'll not be back to haunt me!" he says. "Since you've remained faithful to her, even beyond death, well, then go to Hell to find that demon woman who gnawed at your heart until you died."

He tosses Roman's head down into the opening leading to the grotto. He can hear the skull striking the bottom down in the darkness. The old man wipes his forehead with his sleeve in exhaustion.

"This is the last impure blood ever to stain the Archangel's rock!" he says finally. "Now I can go down and discover the secret. At long last I'll know why Moira sacrificed her life and died to save this place."

Almodius looks around him and tries to catch his breath. His anger fades away. There's a rope ladder rolled up in one corner of the crypt. With his yellow gnarled hands he ties one end to the Holy Trinity altar.

Slowly, he unrolls the ladder out on the floor, walks around Roman's headless body, and drops the rope down the opening. He's a little too old for such physical activity, but on this particular night time has been abolished. The abbot seems four decades younger, still vigorous, his soul fortified by the blood he's shed and his spirit appeased after executing the revenge that for him is justice. With a lamp in his hand, leaning out over the opening in the stones, he takes delight in waiting. Long though his curiosity has been frustrated, he now knows that soon the mystery surrounding Moira will be cleared up. Delicately, as if entering a flower, he climbs down the ladder and disappears into the abyss.

A long time passes before his lamp's halo again emerges from the opening. The abbot's physiognomy is totally altered. Rivulets of sweat course over his wrinkles, and his eyes are filled with horror. Almodius is finally standing again on the floor of Notre-Dame-sous-Terre. Pale, he looks at Roman's headless body lying facedown beside Saint Michael's sword. He stands a long time staring. Then, looking up, the old man lets out a long, painful sigh. Pulling his cloak around him, he crosses himself and begins hobbling toward the crypt door when he is startled by a muffled sound behind him. The abbot turns back toward the twin choirs. A form comes out of the darkness and walks slowly toward Almodius, like a wild animal stalking its prey. His eyes bulging with terror, the abbot backs toward one wall of the nave. The huge shadow keeps coming closer.

"No, impossible," mutters Almodius, frozen in horror against the wall. And then an avenging hand rises above his head.

15

Sitting up in his bed, Father Placide keeps his eyes on the opposite wall, where the engraving representing Mont-Saint-Michel hangs.

"The three pillars of my life have always been silence, the liturgy, and books," he explains. "Sometimes books' voices are too loud, but I've always enjoyed the notes they fill my head with, for they're the laments of people who've been freed from time's constraints."

Johanna is burning with impatience, but she doesn't say anything. She must allow the old man to rediscover at his own rhythm the path of words so long unused.

"Before I went there," he says, pointing to the Mount, "I was in the Abbey of Solesmes, working in the new library built after the last war. There was nothing left of their medieval manuscripts and almost nothing from before the Revolution, for unlike Mont-Saint-Michel, a valiant warrior, my abbey couldn't defend itself and fell victim to the vagaries of history. Back during the Hundred Years' War, the Mount resisted and never did fall into enemy hands, but Solesmes was taken by the English, occupied, and destroyed. When the precious books at Mont-Saint-Michel were carried across the sands and the bay to Avranches during the Revolution, the library at Solesmes was sacked. Note that during the Revolution and after, England redeemed itself for the outrages it committed during the Hundred Years' War by becoming a land of refuge for monks from all the French abbeys persecuted by the Revolution. I believe that the irrepressible monks from the Mount, the Bocains, as they were called, and the English were basically similar. They both had the unique temperament of islanders, eager to preserve their freedom at all costs. In my opinion, the English had never forgiven William the Conqueror's victory, although the Normans brought them much."

He pauses for a moment and then seems to wake up from a dream.

"Oh, William the Conqueror has nothing to do with our subject. My words are drifting and getting lost in my head," he admits. "I locked them up in there so long ago that now they're getting even, all trying to escape at the same time."

"Let them out!" Johanna says with a gentle smile. "We'll pick them out of the air and put them in their places."

"No, no, mademoiselle. Order and rigor are the children of virtue. In chaos, there's no salvation. Would you please give me a drink of water?"

Johanna does as he asks. Her being here surely is tiring the octogenarian. Speaking is a normal faculty for most people, but for him it's a luxury he's deprived himself of, like a good monk. However, as soon as he has finished drinking, Father Placide seems to want to revel in the opulence of language. Johanna sits back down at his feet.

"So, I was at Solesmes," he continues, "where I was in charge of the many books the abbey edited or purchased. In 1966, in honor of one thousand years of monastic life, André Malraux agreed to have some monks go back to Mont-Saint-Michel temporarily. For nine months, one hundred brothers from various Benedictine, Cistercian, and Trappist monasteries took turns living in the abbey. Finally, in 1969, a small community moved in to stay. My abbot asked me to go there to take care of the abbey's manuscripts. I was already fifty, but that's why my superior wanted to send me. He wanted people with experience, people who could stand the climate's rigors and the Mount's constraints, especially the constant presence of so many pilgrims and tourists, although back then there were fewer tourists than there are now."

He stops for a moment to breathe deeply. There's a bottle of oxygen near the bed, but he doesn't seem to need it. He's filled with new energy.

"As soon as I got there, I was gripped by the grand mystery of the place and worried about the pitiful state in which I found the Avranches manuscripts. They were in serious danger!"

"Yes, I know," Johanna interrupts. "The conservator told me how you fought to save them."

"Alas! What was left was quite limited, compared to the treasures the medieval abbey held. I don't know how, but both the Mount and the Archangel, as soon as you get close, give you an irresistible desire to fight for them. They give you incredible strength, courage, and will!"

Du Guesclin and the French knights from the Hundred Years' War who fought to defend Mont-Saint-Michel, especially during the siege, would probably agree with Father Placide. Johanna keeps expecting the old man to tell her about some document hidden away on the shelves in the Avranches library that she wasn't able to find. She's a little surprised by the turn the monk's story is taking.

"About twenty-five years ago, when I was in the throes of my fight to save the manuscripts, I had a visitor, a Benedictine colleague, an expert in manuscripts, and an Englishman."

She frowns.

"He was the prior of the Benedictine abbey in Ampleforth, in the north of England, near York. He was on his way to Solesmes for a gathering of the superiors from our order's various congregations. Fortunately, he spoke French better than I can speak English. He came with a gift for our abbey at Mont-Saint-Michel. By order of his abbot, he solemnly gave me a hard little notebook with a worn, dark cover that he had discovered in his abbey's library a few years before during inventory. It dated from 1823. He told me that its contents were related to the Mont-Saint-Michel monastery, and that's why he was giving it to me, since there were once again Benedictine brothers on the mountain. He added that now I would be responsible for the strange little volume. He didn't seem to want to talk about it much, and he went on to his conference. I was intrigued, and when I opened the notebook, I found a lovely script with flourishes, but it was written in English! I had learned a few words of English during the war when I was in the Resistance, but I didn't know enough to decipher the text. The brothers brought in from Boquen or Bec-Hellouin couldn't read it either. The only 'foreign' language we used was Latin! My prior recommended a lay person with a reputation for piety and humility, someone born on the Mount, an older man who had worked and lived in London until he retired from the world of business. He was discreet and very religious, and he invited me to his house several evenings in a row to read me the text, promising he would tell no one else. The contents of the manuscript were one of the greatest shocks I've ever had in my life."

The mystery surrounding the English notebook piques Johanna's curiosity.

"It had been written in 1823 by an English Benedictine in the Ample-forth Abbey, and his name was Aelred Croward. Though it was written in the nineteenth century, the events it recounts happened much earlier."

"That's it! Now he's going to talk about the Middle Ages, about Notre-Dame-sous-Terre and the headless monk!" Johanna thinks.

"In fact, Aelred had put down on paper a tale told by another Ample-forth brother on his deathbed. His name was Joseph Larose, Brother Joseph, and according to Maurist tradition, he was called Dom Larose. He came originally from the Mont-Saint-Michel abbey."

"But what was a monk from the Mount doing in England?" Johanna asks.

"You know that there were many large old Benedictine monasteries in England: Westminster, Canterbury, Gloucester, Saint Albans," Father Placide answers. "But they were all dissolved in the sixteenth century by Henry VIII and then Elizabeth I, and Catholics were persecuted by the Anglicans. Our order can count numerous English martyrs! In short, in 1607, only one Westminster monk was still alive. He was Brother Sige-bert Buckley, and he sought refuge in France. Where he ended up in exile, at Dieulouard near Nancy, he founded a Benedictine priory that thrived until the French Revolution. In 1791, it was France's turn to sup-press monastic orders, persecuting, imprisoning, or executing religious, and Great Britain became in its turn a place to seek refuge. Brother Anselme Bolton and his Dieulouard monks went back to their home country and founded a new monastery in the north, at Ampleforth. They welcomed many French monks who had fled their own country, espe-cially Breton and Norman brothers, for whom the journey to Albion was not long. They had met Dom Larose and other monks from the Mount on the boat taking them to England. And that's how Dom Larose happened to follow them to Ampleforth, where he helped found the new abbey."

"The origin of the notebook is a great deal clearer," says Johanna. She can certainly appreciate Father Placide's historical knowledge, but she'd prefer he stick to the story that really interests her.

"The connection between France and Great Britain is much stronger than we normally think, and I've always found it interesting," Placide goes on. "Since the conquest of England by William the Conqueror and the Plantagenet empire, our destinies have been intermingled in an unusual manner. Collectively, we've always fought each other bitterly, but individually, we've always known that the other country was a clear refuge in times of danger in one's own country."

"And Dom Larose was aware of that, too!" Johanna adds a little impatiently.

"Oh, yes, Dom Larose. In short, he never came back to France and died in Ampleforth in 1823. The notebook contains the strange story he told Brother Aelred before going to sleep in the Lord."

"Do you think you are strong enough to tell me that story, Father?"

"I'm old, but stronger than I look," says Father Placide impishly. "And if I should begin to fail, Saint Michael will give me strength," he adds, looking up at the engraving.

"Well then. Fifteen or so years before the monks were expelled from Mont-Saint-Michel during the Revolution, around 1775, strange things began to happen on the mountain, and Dom Larose, about twenty at the time, was a witness. In those days the Mount, like many monasteries, was in the hands of black monks belonging to the congregation of Saint-Maur, a Benedictine reform movement. There was a lot to be done on the rock. Buildings were falling down and there wasn't money to pay for repairs. The Hundred Years' War and then the Wars of Religion had ruined the monastery financially, and the birth of printing had long since sealed the end of the scriptorium. Mentalities had evolved over the years with the development of cities and the advent of the mendicant orders and then the Jesuits. Religious vocation began to turn away from contemplative monasticism, already in decline. Yes, the medieval 'golden age' was slowly dying; it had become a thing of the past. Nonetheless, the brothers were still living as best they could in the abbey and kept doing what Maurists were known for, research and historical preservation. Unfortunately they didn't have the means to restore the abbey buildings and used them for different purposes. But thanks to those Maurists, many medieval manuscripts copied in the abbey's scriptorium were saved and passed down to us. Dom Larose, like most of his brothers, worked in the library, which had been moved to the kitchen in the thirteenth century. His job was removing medieval bindings damaged by humidity, collating the different volumes into groups of three or four, and rebinding them in black calf leather."

"And one day, he discovered a strange manuscript!" Johanna breaks in.

"Not at all. One day the prior told the chapter that he had seen a supernatural apparition in the crypt Notre-Dame-sous-Terre. On the stairs above the Holy Trinity altar, he had seen a Benedictine monk, without a head, and he had heard the headless ghost say to him, in Latin: 'You must dig in the earth to reach heaven.'"

Johanna is too excited to speak.

"The news had a huge effect on the community. As I was saying, the times were difficult, and they all feared for their own salvation. The brothers were convinced that the apparition was a sign to the prior from God, a message sent by the Archangel. For like the headless monk, the brothers had lost their reason. If they wanted to be saved and stay on the path leading to heaven, they needed to delve into the shadows of Notre-Dame-sous-Terre and seek the light of an immaterial treasure: their deliverance from sins into purity, the goal of any religious man's eternal quest. To help him, the prior selected three of the wisest brothers, and they began to dig under Notre-Dame-sous-Terre, looking for a mystical ideal, the redemption of mankind from sin. With the feeble light from their lanterns, they dug on their knees with their bare hands in the semi-darkness, punctuating their digging with incantations and sacred chants for forgiveness. They dug all the way down to the rock, twenty or thirty centimeters beneath."

"What did they discover? Did they meet the headless monk again?"

"Never. I hope they did reach heaven, for all four of them soon met death."

"Death?" she repeats. "What happened?"

"Dom Larose doesn't exactly explain. The circumstances were not very clear, but apparently the four monks were killed."

Johanna's mouth drops open. Four Benedictine monks killed! Might they have been the murders she saw in her dream? She hardly thinks so, because she saw three corpses, not four. Furthermore, the last victim, the one who burned up in the hut, was a lay person, not a monk, and was dressed in medieval-style clothes. Finally, the architectural details she recalls were Romanesque, with no trace of the Gothic construction undertaken later.

"Father, do you think they are the victims I saw in my dream? Did Dom Larose describe a hanging, a drowning, and a fire?"

"Dom Larose didn't describe anything, my daughter. He simply mentioned the four murders without giving any details, as he was more interested in the brothers' reactions to them. They were terrorized, sure that the headless ghost must be an evil spirit or a demon who had cast a fatal curse on them. They stopped digging in the crypt, and the abbot, repentant for having asked his prior to follow those diabolical injunctions, asked his sons not to tell anyone about the incident. He himself didn't say a word about it to Louis XVI, king of France. Dom Larose didn't speak, but his memory did. He remembered one of the abbey's old daybooks on which he had replaced the binding and whose pages he had cleaned some years before. He was certain that he had run across a story about suspicious deaths that had taken place in Notre-Dame-sous-Terre, but he had not paid much attention to it."

Johanna begins to shiver.

"Dom Larose dug up the medieval manuscript in the library and was able to find, to his stupefaction, the amazing story of a thirteenth-century monk, starting on a page added two hundred years later, in the fifteenth century, by another monk."

Father Placide pauses to catch his breath. He must surely be a victim of Parkinson's disease, for his legs and arms are trembling.

"The fifteenth-century addition had been written in the middle of the Hundred Years' War during the siege of the Mount. Captain Louis d'Estouville and his one hundred nineteen French knights were holding out against the English who occupied the rest of Normandy. The English blockade of Mont-Saint-Michel was total on both land and sea, the Breton sailors from Saint-Malo, who smuggled things over to the rock, notwithstanding. In short, the Mount became a stronghold circled with ramparts and cannons, housing indomitable monks and knights who kept resisting the invader against all odds."

Johanna can hardly repress a smile as she recalls the famous comic books recounting the adventures of indomitable Gauls who, against all odds, kept up their resistance against Roman invaders.

"Since Charlemagne, Mont-Saint-Michel had always been, and still is, the emblem of the nation's defense, of the struggle against adversity on the historical, geographical, and spiritual levels!" the old monk exclaims, as if in answer to the young woman's thoughts. "And during the Hundred Years' War it never fell! For the courageous men defending it trusted God and their hero the warrior Archangel."

"Yes, I've read some amazing documents about the defenders' valor, about how they routed the better-equipped English artillery. What the defenders lacked in numbers they made up for in fervor."

"Yes, like the battle of Valmy in 1434. But we're talking about 1425, my daughter, 1425, the same year that Saint Michael appeared to the maiden of Orleans, four years after the abbey's Romanesque choir collapsed on the monks during an office. That was the year a brother librarian reported in the introduction to the thirteenth-century manuscript the adventure of a French knight who had seen a ghost one morning in Notre-Dame-sous-Terre."

Johanna stares intently at the old man.

"The noble knight had been disturbed in his sleep by a headless black monk, who had appeared to him on the steps above the Holy Trinity altar, saying: 'You must dig in the earth to reach heaven.' I forget the name of that worthy knight. What I do remember is that the knight decided to go back to the crypt alone after nightfall and start digging. He was sure that he'd find some treasure monks had hidden a long time before, real booty, perhaps gold, silver, and precious stones."

"What became of the brave knight?" Johanna wonders, dreading the story's conclusion.

"Early the next morning they found him lying dead on the floor of the crypt. His mouth was stuffed with dirt. He apparently had eaten dirt and been suffocated by it."

"Why had he eaten dirt from the crypt?" Johanna asks.

"Nobody knows, and nobody can ever know," says Father Placide. "The librarian monk's text ends with a warning about the monk without a head, with exhortations about not digging in the crypt floor and respecting the ancestral tradition of never entering the sanctuary between Compline and Matins. He says that whoever sees the ghost and obeys his injunction to dig will be sure to die. According to him, the black monk is the demon of death, a grim reaper gathering souls to carry off to Hell."

Johanna tries to swallow but can't, because there's a huge lump in her throat. Father Placide sees how frightened she is and changes the subject.

"He also refers to a daybook from the thirteenth century, in which he inserted the page with his story. He says it's important to read the next anecdote in the daybook that explains why the Benedictine monk haunts the crypt. He also says finally that he doesn't know what happened to the thirteenth-century monk who narrated the strange story, but that it can't have been good because the crypt is cursed!"

Johanna turns pale.

"The monk's name was Brother Ambroise. The incidents he relates happened in 1204, and that's an important point, because in 1204 there was a huge fire that destroyed the Romanesque buildings on the north side of the abbey. Besides, if I may add a personal note, it seems that every appearance of the headless monk has happened in a particular historical and architectural context. It's always been when some of the past was being destroyed. In 1425, when the Mount was squeezed between English armies, the abbey choir collapsed and the jewel of the Romanesque church was destroyed forever. The choir would be rebuilt as we know it today, in flamboyant Gothic style. In 1775 the abbey is moribund, the buildings and monks are in ruins, and the final agony of monasticism at Mont-Saint-Michel will take place during the Revolution when the monks are driven off. The sacred stones seem to be dying, too, announcing the end of the religious who built their legend. The decapitated monk appeared three different times in the distant past and then three times in the context of an earlier world dying. I find that interesting, don't you?"

"Yes, it's fascinating," Johanna says.

Father Placide must have done a lot of thinking during his years of silence. Johanna thinks that the phantom is linked to the abbey's political history, but perhaps it's linked more closely still to its architectural history. He lives with the stones, the Romanesque stones, and he shows up whenever those stones disappear! That means the ghost might indeed be Brother Roman, one of the former master builders of the abbey church. However, there's one thing that doesn't fit with that theory, the headless monk's fourth appearance, her own vision when she was a child. That was a different context altogether. It wasn't a time of death to some part of the past, but rather of rebirth! Because in fact that was the time when the Benedictines had come back to the rock, including Father Placide, and Historical Monuments had in fact undertaken considerable restoration projects, particularly in Notre-Dame-sous-Terre! No, twenty-six years ago the stones of the abbey were not dying, but rather they were being brought back to life. Twenty-six years ago, like today, death existed only in her dreams, in the three corpses, and the other witnesses didn't mention them. As she thinks about the phantom's various appearances over the years, Johanna realizes that she's the only person to have seen the monk in a dream and not in reality, the only one to have seen the three suspicious deaths, the only one to have seen the monk several times and not only at Mont-Saint-Michel. She was also the only one to be involved in an architectural context, of restoration rather than destruction, of life rather than death, and she was the only woman to have seen him.

"It's strange," she admits to the old monk. "It's as if with me he changed his tactics. We see that the spiritual and historical surroundings are different. For now our struggles are individual struggles, more internal than external, and thanks to Freud, we now believe dreams more easily than ghosts."

"You're right," he says with a smile. "We're a long way from the Middle Ages and parades of revenants, as real then as leprosy. For in those days it was simply assumed that the dead could appear to the living; it was feared but accepted. Perhaps we can understand it all better if I tell you what Brother Ambroise saw back in 1204. You probably know that during the Middle Ages people believed in the concept of good deaths or bad deaths. The irony of the story is that it was in fact someone named Ambroise, Saint Ambroise, living in the fourth century, who formulated the idea of good death. To go to sleep in the Lord and reach heaven immediately, one must, before dying, follow the path of redemption—contrition, confession, and expiation. Victims of sudden death don't have time to go through these three steps, so their death may be problematic. They are victims of bad death, and there are primarily two categories of those predisposed not to reach the other world immediately, whatever their fate may turn out to be: people who die prematurely, like suicide or homicide victims, and thus who still need the help and prayers of their friends; and people who have lived badly—brigands, assassins, sorcerers, healers. The dead in these two categories wander between two worlds. Revenants are such vagabond souls, trapped between earth and heaven, victims of bad death."

"I understand, Father. Tell me what happened to Brother Ambroise."

"During that month of May in 1204, around Ascension Day, I believe, Brother Ambroise, a copyist in the scriptorium, is inspecting the disaster after the huge fire. He's walking alone in the midst of that somber misfortune. Under the nave of the church, on the west side, Notre-Dame-sous-Terre is still intact, except for a pillar that was added at the end of the twelfth century. The pillar takes up a lot of space but hasn't dramatically changed the crypt's atmosphere. When he goes into the crypt's darkness, he feels a breath wash over his face and hears a strange sound like a broom sweeping. Brother Ambroise's lantern picks up a shadow at the usual place, up on the stairs above the Holy Trinity altar. And it's the shadow of a headless Benedictine monk, his arms crossed as if he's waiting. After his initial fright, Ambroise realizes that he's seeing a revenant and that the revenant needs him! He tries to relax. The ghost keeps standing there at the bottom of the steps. Ambroise knows that it must be a familiar spirit, because ghosts appear to people they know to ask for their help, and they haunt places they're familiar with. Looking for reassurance, he tells himself that demons normally pursue the living during the winter months. But, he reasons, now spring is here, so this revenant must not wish him any harm. It must be a good spirit, trapped between earth and heaven. Ambroise tries to speak to him, asking what his name is. The monk doesn't answer, but he does make a horrifying sound! Ambroise concludes that since he doesn't have a mouth, he can't speak. Trembling, he makes the sign of the cross. The ghost raises his arms toward heaven, joins his hands as if in prayer, and begins to speak, in Latin!"

Johanna, instinctively imitating the monk, joins her own hands. Father Placide solemnly continues his story.

"The headless monk says that his name has been outlawed. Ambroise works up the courage to ask how he can speak since he has neither mouth nor tongue. The revenant answers that it's not his body speaking but his soul, that the body is only an instrument of the soul. And that his soul's spiritual voice can freely speak to human ears, for such is the will of God. Ambroise asks him how the living might help him, and the revenant tells his story."

A deathly silence hangs over the room. Johanna can scarcely breathe.

"The headless monk says that he's trapped between the two worlds and that he needs the help of the living to reach heaven. He needs their support in the form of prayers, masses for the dead, and odes to angelic choirs. Mortals need to help him, especially the brothers at Mont-Saint-Michel, with whom he used to live, for the Archangel himself condemned him to the prison he's in long before. He explains that he experienced a bad death, sudden and premature, that he hadn't had enough time to do his acts of contrition, confession, and expiation. He explains that he was killed, by decapitation, in Notre-Dame-sous-Terre."

Johanna's blue eyes are bulging from their sockets.

"At his death, a winged Saint Michael appeared to him on foot. He was dressed in his armor as prince of the heavenly host and as divine herald. His eyes were clear and hard. He held his sword in his right hand and his scale in his left."

Johanna remembers her third dream, and she can still see the fire eating away at the tapestry representing the Archangel in that very posture.

"Saint Michael weighed his soul. It was heavy with sin, but also with love and pious acts. Beside him, demons were waiting, ready to carry his soul off toward the abyss. But the scale was in equilibrium; it signaled neither Paradise nor Hell. The Archangel looked at him with his whirl-wind eyes and delivered unto him God's judgment. He said that the monk had faithfully served the Most High but that he had also commit-ted grievous sins, so he was not worthy of joining the Lord immediately. Therefore, the Angel would not take him directly to the Lord's side. His soul would have to wait for time to amend it. This was the sentence: The decapitated monk is condemned to wander for centuries between the world of the living and the world of the dead, between earth and heaven, in this very place, in the crypt Notre-Dame-sous-Terre, until his head has been reunited with his body. That terrible judgment is linked to a promise. The Angel promises the monk that the curse will be removed at the very instant some living person places his head once again on his body. Only then will be he delivered from this uncertain world; only then will the Archangel come to take him to the other world, to eternal Paradise."

"So, whatever the monk's name might be, he's a poor wandering soul, not an evil spirit," Johanna thinks, remembering Brother Roman, her heart aching. "If Roman is the headless monk, the heavenly angel con-demned his soul to stay here on earth and thus blocked the road to peace and to any reunion with Moira. Saint Michael promised him heaven, but heaven has been waiting for centuries. And so has Moira, because nobody has been able to set the ghost free. Roman and Moira are still separated!"

"Ambroise was greatly affected by the wandering monk's story, and he promised his unfortunate brother to pray for him and to try to reunite his body and head and lift the Archangel's curse. He asked the ghost how he should proceed. The ghost answered: 'You must dig in the earth to reach heaven.' Ambroise asked where the body and the separated head might be. The soul in pain repeated: 'You must dig in the earth to reach heaven.' Ambroise asked one more time, and the specter responded in the same way."

"The crypt's earthen floor," Johanna thinks. "That's where the others thought they needed to dig in the past, and it's logical because that's where the monk's head was cut off."

"What happened to Brother Ambroise afterwards?" she asks. "Did he dig in Notre-Dame-sous-Terre? Did something horrible happen to him like to the others?"

"I can't answer you," Father Placide sighs. "Ambroise's story ends with the words *ad accedendum ad caelum, terram fodere opportet*, 'you must dig in the earth to reach heaven.' I don't know if Ambroise lived or died in strange circumstances. But we can assume that he wasn't able to keep his promise since the ghost has returned to beg others for help."

"Father," Johanna asks, "what happened to the medieval daybook Dom Larose found, the one that included Ambroise's story as well as the story about the knight? I assume it was burned in 1944 in Saint-Lô when American bombs fell, as were all the other daybooks from the abbey?"

Father Placide's anger is decidedly unexpected for a monk.

"No, my daughter! Alas, in 1944 it had already turned to dust! In 1775, when Dom Larose found the document in the library, he showed it to his abbot. Fearing that other monks might read it, then try to dig at the cursed spot and consequently be killed, the abbot destroyed it right before Dom Larose's eyes. The monk was shocked," the former codicologist explains, "and he was furious that someone would dare treat an old manuscript in that way. Of course it wasn't the first sacrilegious act committed by the Maurist abbot. He had already transformed the old Romanesque dormitory into a recreation room, the kitchen into a library, Notre-Dame-sous-Terre into a wine cellar, the room beside it into a beer cellar, the Aquilon Room into a cider cellar, the Saint Étienne chapel into storage for firewood, and Saint Martin's crypt into the site for a horse-powered mill! How unfortunate! Young Dom Larose, in spite of his love for manuscripts, was powerless and had to watch the daybook burn. His memory alone preserved the story for fifty years, and he passed it on to Brother Aelred Croward in Ampleforth the evening of his death in 1823. The strange thing is that a few months after the abbot burned the book, a huge fire broke out in the church, causing a great deal of damage. The façade and the lower part of the Romanesque nave, just above Notre-Dame-sous-Terre, threatened to collapse, and they would take with them the supporting structures below. Not having the financial means to rebuild it, Dom Larose's abbot decided to pull down the ruins. That's when the nave was cut in half; the current façade was built, and, down below, Notre-Dame-sous-Terre's twin choirs were hidden by the foundation for the façade. Now that it was walled up, the accursed crypt was hidden away from everyone, and the construction prevented any new appearances by the headless monk. Notre-Dame-sous-Terre was rediscovered at the beginning of the twentieth century, but we had to wait until 1960 for the architect Yves-Marie Froidevaux to remove the walls that were hiding it and return it to its original state. By giving back its original appearance and its soul, Froidevaux may be the one who liberated the soul linked to Notre-Dame-sous-Terre and allowed the ghost to return."

"Do you think Froidevaux saw it?" Johanna asks.

"I have no idea. In any case, although the architect did superbly restore Notre-Dame-sous-Terre, I'm sure that neither he nor anyone else in the twentieth century undertook excavation. And I'm sure there were no suspicious deaths!"

"Are you sure that the decapitated monk never appeared to one of his Benedictine brothers when the community of black monks returned to the rock?" she asks.

"I can assure you that between 1969 and 2001, the year we left, he didn't talk to any of us. The first time I heard about him was in Brother Aelred Croward's copybook, and I admit that I was very dubious. Since then, nobody has mentioned him until today, until you showed up to tell me your story, and your story does have troubling similarities with the contents of that little English copybook."

"What's become of it?" she asks nervously, hoping to gather some information that would support her own story. "I'd love to see it. Don't worry, I can read English, and I won't show it to anyone."

Father Placide lowers his feeble eyes and breathes deeply.

"Alas! Just like the old daybook from the abbey, the notebook no longer exists."

Johanna is stunned.

"Just as Dom Larose in his day was the only one to know about the daybook," says the old man, "I'm the only witness to know that the copybook existed, and this afternoon my memory faithfully passed along its contents to you."

His hands and mouth are shaking convulsively.

"I didn't want the text to fall into just anybody's hands," the old monk goes on to explain. "After it was translated for me, and with my prior's agreement, I chose not to place it in the Avranches archives but rather to preserve it inside the abbey walls, in the monks' small private library. And then, two years before we left the Mount, one morning we found that the lock had been broken on one of the entrances to the monastery buildings. Everything seemed to be in order, and it looked as if nothing had been taken. However, I realized later that Aelred Croward's notebook had disappeared. That was the only document stolen. The only one. But what a disaster, and I was responsible. If I had known, I would have kept it with me, here under my habit."

Johanna is filled with consternation. Stolen! But by whom?

"Someone else besides you must have known about it!" she exclaims. "Who, Father? Who else could it have been but your translator?"

"You're on the wrong trail. That man would never have committed such a sacrilegious act. I've never suspected Fernand Bréhal. And besides, when the notebook was stolen, he had already been dead for several years, God rest his soul."

"He might have mentioned it to someone before he died, maybe on his deathbed."

"No, no! I've turned this over and over in my head. No. Fernand Bréhal never told anyone about it. He had sworn he wouldn't, and he was a man of his word. So much so that after he finished the translation, he wouldn't talk about it even with me."

"So, you can vouch for him," Johanna admits. "But someone else must have known about it, you can't deny the evidence. Forgive me, but how about one of your brothers on the Mount? Or perhaps one of the monks from Ampleforth Abbey?"

"Impossible," he replies vehemently. "None of the brothers in either place would have had to break the lock to get into the building. All he would have had to do is go inside and take what he wanted."

"Exactly. Doing so would have been like leaving proof that a monk had been the thief, because only monks could enter the monastery. By smashing the lock, one of the brothers could make people believe that some lay person was guilty."

"You're wrong!" he answers. "In fact, not one of my brothers even knew about it. At Ampleforth the booklet had been forgotten, and here I had told only my prior about it. You're surely not going to accuse my superior of stealing from his own monastery?"

Johanna smiles sadly. Father Placide seems to be about done in. She decides to give up.

"Unfortunately, I think that such things have happened over the years here in this abbey and others," she says. "But you're right. That was a long time ago, and I wouldn't think of incriminating your former prior. So the theft will have to remain a mystery."

Father Placide is totally exhausted from all that talking, and he closes his eyes and falls back. Johanna rushes over. He's still breathing. He's just drifted off to sleep. Gently, she fluffs up his pillows, pulls the white sheet up over his frock, and sits down on a chair beside him like a guardian watching over his sleep. For years, as they slept, ordinary men were protected from demons by monks who stayed awake at night, chanting and praying. Today, it's Johanna's turn to protect this old monk in his weak condition. He has just given her an invaluable gift—historical verification about the headless monk, proof of his existence, the reasons why he appears, and the attestation that she is not crazy. She is indeed possessed, but by a defenseless being who is counting on her for salvation. Yes, now she finally has the answer to the questions she has been asking herself for twenty-six years: Why has she been the one to see him and what does he expect from her? She's still unsure who he really is, of course, but now that question doesn't seem so important.

What a lucky break it was for her to hear what Father Placide had to say before he went to sleep forever! She looks at the old man with enormous gratitude colored with admiration. What a sharp mind he has for his age! What an amazing memory, twenty-five years after Fernand Bréhal had translated the notebook that Father Placide himself had been unable to read. Just like Dom Larose, who had kept his story secret for almost fifty years, until his death. Johanna frowns, and a horrible idea crosses her mind: Nothing is more fallible or partial than human memory, especially when the memory was conveyed orally and indirectly. Only the written word can preserve facts with any semblance of objectivity. The notebook's author, Aelred Croward, didn't experience any of the events he wrote about. All he did was repeat as best he could what an old dying monk, Dom Larose, had told him about things that had taken place a half century earlier, things the Benedictine brother from the Mount had himself read about only once in an old manuscript! As for Father Placide, also an old man, he's passing along not a visual memory but one he had heard, a translation of a tale taken from a notebook that itself was a collection of secondhand memories! How could reality not have been affected? Some facts must certainly have been altered. The only indisputable fact is that not one single material piece of proof about any of the story exists.

As she has no possibility of finding the book that Dom Larose's abbot burned, Johanna decides she must do her best to find Brother Aelred Croward's little English notebook. But first she must find the person who stole it! The theft was recent. There's a good chance the thief is still alive and that he's kept the object he coveted so much that he risked stealing it. At the moment, though, she has no idea who the thief might be. Her thoughts are interrupted by somebody knocking at the door. The nun who gave her such a cold greeting comes in with a tray, on it a bowl of hot chocolate and some bread and butter.

"His snack," she says, looking over at the sleeping old monk. "Oh, I see he's as talkative as usual," she adds, frowning. "I told you so!"

"Yes, you were right," replies Johanna. "But that's no problem. Let me have it," she offers, taking the tray. "I'll take care of it."

"As you wish," the nun says, and leaves the room.

"Damn!" says Father Placide when she has closed the door. "With her, it's much better to be deaf and dumb."

"Oh, you're awake," Johanna notes with a laugh. "I'm exhausting you, Father. I'm sorry. I'll leave right away."

"Absolutely not," he answers. "I was afraid you'd be gone. For once I can talk about that place with someone who loves it as much as I do," he continues, pointing to the engraving of the Mount. "It's the first time since I retired. That's why I had decided never to tell anyone. The conversations of old men here hold no interest for me. Give me that," he orders, looking over at the tray she's holding; "today that looks good."

She hands over the tray and helps him drink the cocoa. But he doesn't touch the bread. Johanna herself devours it and realizes that she hasn't had any lunch. When they're finished, they look at each other like old friends, two accomplices, connected by a powerful, invisible link.

"My daughter," he murmurs, taking her hands, "by confiding in me, you have cleared up Aelred Croward's story. I admit I was dubious. You've lit up a portion of the rock's history; and the rock, though I came late to it, was at the center of my life. As for me, by telling you about the notebook's contents, I've shed light on your dreams and the meaning of your quest, at the center of which is our holy mountain, where it's been since your childhood. However, I must warn you. Today I'm seeing you for the first and perhaps the last time, but I can read you, and what I'm reading fills me with fear! I'm afraid that now your plan will be to dig in Notre-Dame-sous-Terre, and that, my daughter, I beg you not to do. Because if the story about the headless monk that Dom Larose and Brother Croward are telling is true, then the murders of those who dare dig in the crypt are also real. You do realize that over the centuries someone has been systematically killing anyone who tries to see what lies under the crypt floor! And don't tell me that those things could happen only back in the old days and that the modern world is different. The fact that the English notebook was stolen just recently, inside the monastery walls, is proof enough that even today there's still danger."

That's exactly what Johanna needs to hear to decide that she can't lose one more moment and that she must spend every night digging in the crypt, alone and in secret. It's natural that Father Placide's warning causes fear to rise within her, but along with fear comes a feeling of urgency and the certainty that she's on the right path. She'll get some tear gas for protection. And if needed, maybe the breath of the headless monk or the Archangel will protect her! Nonetheless, she doesn't want to make the old monk worry unnecessarily. She chooses to change the subject, for she doesn't want to lie to him, either.

"Father, I've always wondered about the meaning of that famous sentence: 'You must dig in the earth to reach heaven.' What do you think?"

Father Placide isn't easily fooled, and he closes his eyes as if in defiance, but then he answers:

"I do remember a section from the story in Aelred's notebook saying that Brother Ambroise asked the ghost about it in 1204. The ghost answered: 'You must combine the three meanings of these words so that all may be accomplished.'"

"The three meanings? You didn't say anything about that a moment ago!" Johanna says in surprise, skeptically wondering if Father Placide has forgotten other details or if perhaps he has just invented the monk's answer to please her. "That answer is more enigmatic than the question," she adds.

"For an atheist, certainly, but not for a religious," he says, a little annoyed. "I don't need to say anything about Christian symbolism related to the number three. In your profession, you surely know all about that."

Johanna remains silent.

"Three like the Holy Trinity," the old man continues learnedly, "the three divine beings: Father, Son, and Holy Spirit. Three like the three theological virtues: faith, hope, and charity, the paths by which men can reach God. Three like the three archangels: Michael the warrior, Gabriel the messenger, and Raphael the healer."

"I always forget about Raphael," she confesses.

"As I was saying, medieval theologians taught, in their exegesis of the Holy Scriptures, the three meanings that every sacred text possesses: a literal meaning, a symbolic meaning, and a spiritual meaning. These are the three meanings we must no doubt seek in the words of the headless monk and then bring together."

"On the spiritual level, 'you must dig in the earth to reach heaven' surely means that by digging into your personal earth you can free your spirit," Johanna proposes. "That's a very Romanesque way of looking at things. And not only that, for it's also a way of saying 'know thyself,' the philosophical maxim inscribed on the temple of Pythia at Delphi, and it's similar to ideas in modern psychoanalysis."

"And it's also the essence of the spiritual life and of monastic life in particular. Throughout the ages, introspection and prayer have served to purify the soul and make it as perfect as possible, ready for heaven. You've grasped the spiritual dimension: The ghost encourages us to undertake that internal work and asks us to pray for him. How about the symbolic and literal dimensions?"

"The headless monk's soul is imprisoned between the two worlds because he's a phantom. By digging literally into the crypt's floor we might be able to find his skull and his body, place them back together, and remove the Archangel's curse. That will set his soul free and allow it to reach symbolic heaven, Paradise. That's how the three meanings are combined, the spiritual, the literal, and the symbolic."

"That's right. Whatever the case may be, Johanna," he says, squeezing her hands, "I'll repeat what I said earlier. Cling to the spiritual meaning of the sentence and don't follow any path strewn with corpses. You're risking your life, I'm convinced!"

Johanna remains seated, but she's no longer paying attention. Deep within, she's already calculating that she'll never be able to undertake any secret dig in Notre-Dame-sous-Terre as she had first thought. She needs help, equipment, computers, electric light, and she could never undertake such a task without people finding out. In that case, there's only one solution—she has to open an official dig in the crypt. Historical Monuments has never undertaken a similar dig, its policy being always to opt for restoring what's there rather than to look for something from the past. So it won't be simple. The project in Saint Martin's Chapel required years to negotiate and get underway. How will she be able to manage, one against many, to get a second dig authorized? She thinks about Patrick Fenoy, Christian Brard, François. Yes, François is her last chance! How wise she had been to hide her affair with Simon and not to break up with François. What could her arguments be? She can't tell him or anyone else about her conversation with Father Placide. And even if she did, they wouldn't believe her since there were no solid proofs. It might take months, even years. Suddenly her eyes light up, just as the old monk's eyes begin to close from fatigue and age. She looks at him through the veil of tears that begin to well up in her eyes. She feels for the poor man. He has given her so much, in just a few hours. She whispers that now she's going to let him rest, but he doesn't answer.

Gently, she removes her hands from his. His hands, thin and lifeless, fall back on the sheet. She'll come back to see him, bring him chocolate and keep him company before he joins the company of angels. Slowly she gets up, looks back one last time at the old man and the engraving on the wall, and tiptoes out. In the corridor with pink doors she begins to consider her options. Yes, Roman's manuscript, that's what she can use as an argument. It speaks about the crypt; it suggests that the crypt hides a secret, a secret linked to Moira, a secret so powerful that Roman had to change the plans for the abbey church. The document has been scientifically authenticated, and its contents cannot be put in doubt. And it'll soon be made public anyhow. So she may as well use it as the basis for her request for authorization to dig in Notre-Dame-sous-Terre. If only she can begin to dig, to keep the promise she has just made to the headless monk: the promise to set him free!

16

CHRISTIAN BRARD'S SHAVED HEAD GLISTENS LIKE A PUDDLE OF water in the sun after a spring shower. Behind his tortoiseshell glasses, his eyes stay focused on a document as he motions to Johanna to sit down.

"*But it was absolutely necessary.*" he reads. "*You should know that I had Pierre de Nevers's drawings in my scapular, and I absolutely had to make one important change . . . the church had to be spared . . . the real causes behind changing the sketches must remain hidden forever from everyone . . .*"

"*At the moment you are reading this, perhaps I've already joined her. No doubt I've already completed my final earthly task, done it in her memory, faithful to the secret she entrusted to me and to our immortal love,*" Johanna continues from memory, for she has practically memorized Roman's confession.

"And do you know this quotation?" he adds. "'The stones were like sugar lumps soaked in water.'"

"No, I . . . "

"Prosper Mérimée, the writer," the administrator answers. "He was also an inspector general for Historical Monuments, and wrote those words in the report he sent to the Ministry in 1841 after visiting the Mount. He had found the abbey in such a horrible state of affairs that he alerted the government. But he said that they should not undertake major repairs, because if they did, the penitentiary authorities would take advantage of the opportunity to house still more prisoners. Fortunately, in 1863, the government realized that the only way to save this historic jewel was to close the damn prison."

He stands up and takes off his glasses.

"That's what things were like when they entrusted it to us," he concludes. "Since 1872, the French government has poured billions into restoring it. And since the restoration is never finished, billions are still being spent to keep it up. You can imagine what talent, imagination, and energy have been required to save it, to restore its glory and soul, to allow as many people as possible to visit it, according to the principles of a democratic republic. Each year I have a million visitors in the abbey, nine thousand a day during the summer, and I'm delighted! But if we listened to you archeologists, the abbey would be closed to the public and reserved for you alone. It would fall into ruins, and you'd transform it into Swiss cheese by digging everywhere, simply because you have some intuition or because some eleventh-century manuscript makes reference to some hypothetical mystery. If we had given you people free rein, there'd be nothing left of the abbey, nothing at all. Just holes here and there where your curiosity and momentary inspiration led you to dig. Not one stone would be left on top of another. As administrators, we spend years trying to save a site, encouraging people to visit and love it. As for you people, you'd like to close it so you can destroy it."

"And yet," the young woman interrupts him, "you did authorize our dig in Saint Martin's Chapel on the basis of an old manuscript. We both report to the same people, you know, the government and the Ministry of Culture. And we have the same goal—to exhume a past that history has wiped out, to give it new life and share it so that it might enlighten our contemporaries."

"You claim to be preserving history by officially destroying a different version," he cuts in sharply. "The campaign to dig in Saint Martin, the former chapel, didn't endanger any vestiges or any other site. But digging in the crypt is something else entirely! Froidevaux spent more than two years of his life restoring Notre-Dame-sous-Terre, the oldest site on the Mount. He removed the scoria and tried to interpret everything; he replaced the walls that had disappeared, the 'epidermis,' as he called them. He had such a keen sense of the place, restored it with such sensitivity and skill that I would defy anyone to see any difference between the contemporary masonry and the original walls. He even discovered a piece of the wall from Aubert's sanctuary. He managed to restore the crypt so skillfully that his restoration is still considered a model, surprising and enchanting every visitor. And you, on the pretext of uncovering history that's older still and that probably has left no vestiges, you'd be happy to destroy everything!"

"I understand your point of view and why you're worried, sir," she responds, rising to her feet too. "You love your profession; you love this abbey. But you see, I do too. Nobody can deny what Historical Monuments have done, and are still doing—amazing things—and I would never want to detract from that. As far as Notre-Dame-sous-Terre is concerned, I promise not to touch Froidevaux's restoration."

"I doubt that very much. In any case, you'll find nothing but rock!"

"Perhaps. We'll see."

"You say you understand me," he says, sitting back down behind his desk and cleaning his glasses, "but I can't say that I understand you. You're a respected and well-recognized expert on Cluny, and excuse me for saying so, but then you go out of your way to get yourself appointed as Roger Calfon's replacement in an abbey you know very little about. Maybe I could explain it all by ordinary professional ambition and your interest in the excavation in Saint Martin's Chapel. That, after all, is the biggest archeological project we've opened up. Of course, it's based on an old parchment, but it is a parchment that gives precise, verifiable details. But where I can't follow you is why you don't take advantage of this wonderful opportunity, why you try to rub everyone the wrong way, me most of all, and why you've used your influence in the ministry, at the risk of your career, to have the project moved from the old chapel to Notre-Dame-sous-Terre on the basis of an old Cluniac manuscript. Its obscure, sibylline arguments, you know as well as I do, are not enough to justify opening a new dig. And on top of everything, and this I can't forgive because your attitude is unworthy of a civil servant, instead of coming to talk to me directly about the manuscript and the project, which after all is directly linked to the Mount and thus to me, you secretly go over my head. And then the Ministry imposes the decision on me from above."

She sits back down before answering.

"I admit I didn't show appropriate loyalty toward you. But frankly, do you think that if I'd come to see you after discovering Brother Roman's testament, you'd have agreed to my request? Come on, now. I would then have had no choice but to attack you directly."

"At least you'd have satisfied my passion for old manuscripts. For it is truly an exceptional manuscript, and I would have loved to be able to study it earlier. But you're right; I would have refused your request, that's for sure. Yesterday, just like today, I would have found it baseless, aberrant, and dangerous, for what you would like to do works against preserving the abbey's stones."

"And what if I told you the crypt hid a treasure?" she asks, seeing that the administrator is in a better frame of mind than he was when their meeting began.

He stares at her like a psychiatrist examining an incurable madwoman.

"You're kidding, I hope," he says in a neutral voice. "You've deduced from Brother's Roman's words that he changed the plans in order to hide a treasure? Is that what you hope to find? A Viking or Celtic treasure? Or maybe one hidden by the Crusaders or Norman monks? Or who knows what kind of treasure, to justify this plot, this ministerial masquerade? But that's impossible! You've read too much Stevenson or Dumas, and it's all gone to your head."

She's sorry she mentioned the word "treasure," but it's too late now. Might as well expand on the idea to show how serious she is, but she needs to keep her real reasons hidden.

"When I use the word 'treasure,' sir, I don't mean necessarily gold or precious stones. Listen, you can't deny that the crypt holds a secret. Brother Roman, master builder, is keeping a secret he wouldn't reveal even to his abbot. In protecting it, he was even guilty of blasphemy, an act unheard of for a monk at that time. No one has ever been able to penetrate the secret. Perhaps there are relics of ancient saints, dating back to the first days of Christianity or back to Aubert himself. Perhaps there are manuscripts, Bibles, or pottery dating back to Celtic days or to when the canons lived here. Perhaps there's something linked to Moira, yes, to Moira, the love of his life. Something that she herself hid there, something that might have been discovered if Roman had not prevented them from destroying the old church. In any case, there's a mystery, something real, something modern archeology could find out without ravaging the crypt. It would be a crime not to try."

The administrator hopelessly puts his head in his hands.

"Moira? How about that! And I thought you were a professional," he says sadly. "You're doing all this just to satisfy your romantic nature. My crypt, Notre-Dame-sous-Terre, is going to be turned upside down, transformed into trenches, dug up, and sullied because some ambitious young archeologist has decided that nearly a thousand years ago, a tortured woman with whom a monk had fallen in love must have buried a 'secret' that's never been discovered? That's crazy! Listen, get out of here! I don't want to hear another word about this, because in any case there's nothing I can do to prevent the desecration. Wait!"

He throws her the ministerial decree authorizing the dig. He had received it earlier that day.

"I'll leave it to you to explain everything to your team, and especially to Patrick Fenoy. Tomorrow you'll clean up and secure the project in the old Saint Martin church. I don't want some tourist stepping in a hole and breaking his leg. You can start in Notre-Dame-sous-Terre the day after tomorrow. But I warn you, the Ministry gives you no more than two months in the crypt, from April 15 to June 15. Though I'm opposed, I have no choice but to accept the decision, because I, at least, do respect hierarchy. But you won't have one day, one hour, more. The crypt will reopen on June 16 for guided tours and soon after that for night visits. Count on me to insist that you return it in the same condition you found it in; that means in perfect condition, with no traces of your wild fancies."

Sheepish and furious, she walks out with her authorization in hand. But what else could she have done? She couldn't have told him about the headless monk, about Father Placide, about the burned daybook and the stolen English notebook. If she had done that, Brard would have had her locked up with the old monk! But at least the Cluny manuscript, Roman's testament, really does exist, and it has been officially authenticated. And that's part of what saved her. The parchment dates from the eleventh century and had indeed been prepared in the workshops of the Cluny abbey. The ink was made according to the techniques of the Cluny scriptorium and with ingredients they used there. It could indeed have been written in 1063, the date on the letter. The hand, the language, and the style also correspond to that period. The only uncertainty is related to the time when the document was put in the copper tube and placed in Pierre de Nevers's tomb. The tomb has also been authenticated, by Paul himself. Paul is of the opinion that Hugh de Semur, when he knew that Roman, or rather Jean de Marburg, had died, opened the master's tomb so that his disciple's testament could be placed in it. Later, Hugh or some other abbot moved the tomb to the choir of Cluny III. For the past four months, Paul has been carefully examining the tomb and its occupant, and what he's found seems to corroborate that theory. He's found slight traces, very old, indicating that the tomb had been opened and then closed back up. So the manuscript was not invented by some counterfeiter. The date on it was accurate. But its contents, under examination by Latinists and medievalists specializing in the history of Cluny and the Mount, are raising controversy. Some experts would like to believe the historical accuracy of the story and are vainly looking for traces of Brother Roman and Moira. The Norman dukes and the various abbots are not a problem. Whether or not Hildebert was poisoned has been an open question in historical circles, and the name of the person who might have poisoned him, Almodius, has been passed down through the ages by virtue of his being head of the scriptorium.

The name Jean de Marburg can't be found in the Cluniac daybooks, and there's no way of finding it in the daybooks from the Mount because they were all destroyed in the 1944 fire. However, everyone agrees that the writer Roman is well acquainted with monastic life and that he could easily have been a monk at the Mount and then at Cluny. He could also have known Pierre de Nevers, but it still hasn't been demonstrated that he had in fact been the master builder of the abbey church at Mont-Saint-Michel. And there's no way of proving it, because the archives have disappeared. In short, Brother Roman is a phantom monk, invisible, untraceable, unverifiable. But his spirit has traveled through time, thanks to the manuscript. As for Moira, historically she's nothing. There is no trace of her trial in Rouen or her ordeal at the Mount. She lives only through the words of the manuscript's author. That's why some experts no longer consider the manuscript a historical document, but simply some monk's gripping fantasy: an original, even revolutionary, work of fiction; a fable invented by some lively, tormented intelligence with a great deal of imagination. For them, this tale addressed to Hugh de Semur stands as a short novel, the first novel written in the West, a century before the appearance of books in verse transposing Latin writings, and more than a century before the work of French writers Chrétien de Troyes, Béroul, and Thomas, often considered the inventors of the novel in Europe. When Johanna learned about the controversy opposing "the partisans of historical revelation" to "the partisans of the novel," Simon came to mind. He had chosen his camp as soon as she read him Jean de Marburg's testament on New Year's Eve by immediately assuming it was a great literary creation with no connection to reality. She decided to use the controversy to her own ends.

It had been back in early February, that gloomy, dark, abortive month. Obsessed and deeply affected by Father Placide's revelations, she was no more than pretending to concentrate on Saint Martin's Chapel, for she had already moved on to Phase Two of her plan. Phase Two meant starting an official dig in Notre-Dame-sous-Terre on the basis of Roman's confession, the only tangible evidence anyone knew about. She told Simon she was going to visit her parents, but the following weekend she met François in a deserted old luxury hotel in Etretat. When he brought up the in-house quarrel dividing historians over the Cluny manuscript, she leaped at the providential opportunity. If library research proved unfruitful, the only way to choose between the two sides lay in her art—in archeology. The author of the manuscript clearly said that Notre-Dame-sous-Terre hid a secret and that he had changed the plans for the abbey church because of it. There was no architectural reason for making that change. So, a simple way of finding out would be to dig in the crypt. If the story was a historical document, the archeologists would uncover the secret. If they couldn't find anything, then those who thought the story was a romantic fiction would be right. In both cases, the document was incredibly valuable and it was worth shaking up Historical Monuments a little. But François was far from being naïve, and it saddened him to realize what Johanna's idea really was and why she had come to spend three days with him.

"And if by chance you were the person chosen to direct the dig in the crypt?" he asked, hiding his pain.

"Listen, François. It so happens that a complete team of archeologists is already operational at Mont-Saint-Michel. It'd be great to take advantage of that, much simpler and less expensive than bringing in another team. All we'd need to do is move the dig from Saint Martin's Chapel to the crypt. The project wouldn't take long because the crypt is very small. And then we'd go back to our earlier work. Of course I can't deny that I'd love to direct the project in Notre-Dame-sous-Terre myself. Remember what I confided to you, and to you alone, back in September when you took me to the Mount," she said, lying. "Symbolically, for me, I think digging in the crypt could be like digging into my unconscious, liberating me from those little-girl dreams I had. However, there's one problem: We need to work quickly! Because my authorization to work at Mont-Saint-Michel is temporary, good for only six months."

She had the good sense to drop the subject for the rest of the weekend. François held all the cards, and it would be useless to harass him. For the time being. Johanna knew that Roger Calfon's wife was failing rapidly, for Patrick Fenoy had recently been going to the hospital to see her. The chief archeologist wouldn't be coming back to work any time soon. There was no way François could not be aware of that, but it would have been tasteless for her to bring it up. She concentrated on letting him realize how far she had moved away from him over the past few months. She didn't say anything about Simon, of course, or even suggest that she might dump him if he didn't help her. It was bribery, she knew, but that didn't bother her. Her highest priority now was to lift the curse hanging over the headless monk. She had to free him in order to set herself free, and that was all that mattered. She would complete her mission and keep her promise, and she was committed to using every means at her disposal. Every means, and help from François wasn't the worst. Sure, she was using him, but hadn't she given him a lot during the time they were together? And what about him? As a married man, what had he given her other than secret meetings with no future? That was what Isabelle liked to tell her, but Johanna knew deep down that it wasn't quite like that. For she had chosen François, knowing full well that their relationship would inevitably be frustrating. At the time, his lack of commitment had been reassuring, but now she pretended to forget all that. Isabelle was right, she thought. The best thing François could give her was professional support, and she would have been crazy not to ask for it. She knew men well enough to see that if François thought she was at his mercy, weak, and imploring, then he wouldn't help her. But if he was afraid he might lose her, then he'd help so she would realize how much she needed him.

The strategy worked. François was so worried she might leave him that he had moved heaven and hell at the Ministry to get her the authorization to dig in the crypt and to extend her time at the Mount. Immediately, Christian Brard opposed the idea, by rightly arguing that neither the objective elements in the Cluny manuscript nor the battle raging among the specialists warranted changing the policy of preservation that Historical Monuments had been following for a hundred and fifty years. All the same, François had won, with the support of historians from both camps, but he knew that the administrator was right. Brard had at least managed to get the project limited to two months.

AS SHE LEAVES Christian Brard's office, she knows that another test awaits her. She must still announce the change to her team. Rumors have been circulating, none of them very precise. François had purposely kept things quiet so that the groups protecting the Mount—and any bitter archeologists like Patrick Fenoy—couldn't intervene. Respecting the rules of the game imposed by their hierarchy, the administrator hadn't tried to elicit help from others in his effort to prevent the new dig. François respected him for that, though he himself didn't demonstrate much professional loyalty in this battle. Brard is an intelligent man, and he may have guessed the truth, but for the moment he has only made a few allusions. Johanna and he need to be careful.

"IT'S A REAL surprise, but I'm excited!" says Florence, leaning up against the treadmill near the dig in Saint Martin's Chapel. "Too bad we won't be able to enjoy the sun any more."

"Yes, really surprising," Jacques adds. "I love the idea of digging to look for the real value of words from the past, whether they are real or imagined."

"Yes, but personally," Dimitri says, delicately pulling off his gloves, "I hope we won't find anything in this crypt, so the manuscript can be considered the first novel ever written."

"What a romantic soul!" Sebastian teases. "I'll go along, too, Johanna, but I hope we'll find a huge treasure hidden away by Aubert and his canons—gold censers with rubies, silver chalices, a diamond tabernacle, the sword of Saint Michael himself! Say, madame, as our director you've been pretty secretive about all this. We could sense that something was brewing, but we didn't expect this. How did you manage to get the authorization so quickly from those bigwigs in the Ministry without anyone knowing anything about it? That's not how they usually work."

Johanna blushes.

"Well, after the parchment was discovered at Cluny," she begins clumsily, "we couldn't let anyone know because of pressure groups."

"Pressure groups, come on!" Patrick cuts in. "Miss Johanna has the ear of people in the Ministry, that's all. Cluny wasn't enough for her. She managed to work things out to get sent here, and she's used the parchment to get her latest whim approved—digging in the crypt. And of course we'd better not interfere." He looked around condescendingly. "The rest of you seem to be happy helping her carry out her foolish little ideas, but I have too much respect for our profession. Never will I support such a grotesque, half-baked project, and I refuse to be treated like a peon presented with a fait accompli."

And with that, he turns to walk out.

"Hey, Patrick, where are you going?" Florence asks.

"Tell Brard I'm resigning!" he spits out.

Johanna isn't sure how to react.

"Drop it, it's no big deal," Florence tells her. "It's just an egotistical reaction, the macho reflex of a man whose power is threatened. He's upset because you didn't ask his opinion before you acted, that's all. It's his way of saving face. In a couple of hours, tomorrow at the latest, he'll be back

360 | *Frédéric Lenoir and Violette Cabesos*

on the job. No one has ever dug in the crypt, and he wouldn't miss that for the world."

"I don't like him very much," Johanna answers, "but I must admit he's a good archeologist. And it's never good for a team when one of its members leaves like this."

"Don't worry," Jacques says. "Let him go. I bet you a bottle of Calvados that he'll never resign."

"You're on! If you're right, Jacques," Johanna answers, "I'll give you a twenty-year-old bottle."

Later that evening, while Sebastian is taking his turn fixing dinner, heating up Caen-style tripe to build up their energy, Johanna's assistant still hasn't rejoined them. Simon is waiting for her in Saint-Malo, but she has put off leaving in case Patrick should come back. They need to come to an understanding, and she's eager to have it out with him. Johanna looks at her watch, sighs, smells the tripe beginning to cook in the pressure cooker, and then decides to leave. As she walks down the cobblestone street, carefully because of her high heels, she looks up at the red evening sky. Two days later, the dig will begin in Notre-Dame-sous-Terre. She should be elated, but in fact she feels stifled. Yes, it's as if she is being suffocated by some invisible hand, and it's not the hand of her revenant. On the way to Saint-Malo, she tries unsuccessfully to figure out what's causing the feeling of suffocation. She's delighted to see Simon again. She hasn't seen him for several days because of Easter vacation and the first influx of tourists. He's gone back every weekend to Saint-Malo to open his shop and is only living on the Mount part of the time. Far from disappointing Johanna, his obligations have been a relief, because she doesn't want everyone to know about their relationship. She's been trying to keep it as secret as possible, to Simon's dismay. And yet she does love him, more than she has ever loved François or any other man. But it's beyond her, she can't stand the thought that others might learn of their special love, might be aware of those moments they've stolen away from the insignificance of their daily routines. For Johanna, for those moments to retain their beauty and reality, they need to stay hidden away from the devouring public eye. Once the romantic ecstasy of the first weeks passed, their trysts in Simon's house on the Mount had made her fearful and nervous. Although it's a long way between the Mount and Saint-Malo, Johanna finds the distance reassuring. It allows her to protect François, Simon, and herself from village gossip, but she realizes that's not the primary reason she feels reassured. Meeting Simon elsewhere than on the Mount allows her to keep control of the relationship and not yield completely to him, for she suspects that if she does, she'll lose him.

Before ringing the bell at his luxurious apartment above the shop, she stops to buy a bottle of chilled champagne. She feels like celebrating the start of her excavation in Notre-Dame-sous-Terre. He gives her a big hug as if she has just come back from a ten-year expedition to the North Pole.

"I can't wait until Sunday evening," he whispers in her ear, after a passionate kiss, "when I can close my shop and come back to the island. And then it's only a week until the end of Easter vacation. I'll be able to come back home, and we can see each other every day like before."

"But I love to come here," she answers. "The change does me good."

"Sure, and then, too, there's no danger of meeting someone you know. I don't understand that. Are you ashamed of me, or what?"

"Simon! How can you say such a thing? No, I've told you a thousand times. My private life is my own business, and I don't want to give my team and people living on the Mount something to gossip about."

"Let them gossip!" he answers with irritation in his voice. "What do we care about that? We're consenting adults, and we're free. Your concern about what people might think is ridiculous and so old-fashioned. Or maybe the year you've been with that married man has made you especially secretive?"

"Please, Simon, don't start that again. Let's not fight this evening, I've had a tough day. Listen, I've got some great news to tell you."

She pulls the bottle of champagne out of the plastic bag.

"Bubbles?" he says with surprise, putting his hands on her waist. "Have I forgotten your birthday? I thought it was in the summer."

Setting the bottle down, she looks at his black curls with silver streaks, his gray sideburns, his lovely eyes, his skin tanned like a Mediterranean sailor from hours out on his boat. She breathes in his perfume; it smells like madly galloping horses in a dark, magical forest. Staring deeply into his anise-colored eyes, she pulls his face toward her.

"It's much more important than my birthday," she answers. "It's like a second birth. Yes, coming back to life from the dead, back to the land of the living. Me and someone else."

"I feel the same way, Johanna," he whispers. "I was dead, and you've brought me back to life."

She doesn't understand what he means. And then she realizes the danger.

"That's true," she stammers. "But I wasn't speaking about us. It's something else. In fact, I'm going to supervise a dig in Notre-Dame-sous-Terre, and we're starting in two days!"

Simon is flabbergasted, and then grows pale. Johanna would never have thought that his dark olive skin could turn so white. He thought she was going to tell him how much she loved him, but all she was really talking about was her passion for a crypt and the headless man who haunted it. She feels like an idiot. He pulls away, and she thinks she sees disgust in his eyes.

"I'm blown away," he admits. "Blown away and shocked; yes, shocked. Like everyone who loves the Mount," he says, pronouncing each syllable distinctly, "I'm especially attached to the crypt, the oldest part of the abbey. It bears witness to the mountain's origins and its unusual atmosphere, and it keeps a perceptible medieval charm. I find it truly unfortunate that it'll be turned topsy-turvy. It's sacrilegious, a desecration!"

"You can be sure you're not the only person who feels that way," she answers quietly.

"What do you think you'll find there? And why didn't you say anything about it before?" he asks angrily. "As it turns out, when I was talking about your love for secrecy, I was still far from the truth. What you really love is intrigue, plots, and deceit! How I pity you! If you show so little confidence in the people who love you, you must truly hate yourself!"

"Not as much as you do right now," she answers weakly, tears in her eyes.

"Good heavens! You must be blind! Now you think I hate you? Blind, and paranoid on top of it! What's happened to you, to make you reject human love like this? At least with your stones, your old tombs, and your married men you're not taking any risks! No danger, no domestic fights, no promises to keep, no commitment, no possible betrayal or abandonment! Well, are you going to answer instead of standing there looking like a victim? I don't believe for a moment that you're a victim!"

Never would she have thought he could be so vicious. Taken aback, she stands there with her coat still on and faces this strange, angry Simon boiling with disappointed passion as he paces around in the vestibule like a hungry lion near feeding time. Then, as on that memorable evening in September with François when she saw and recognized Notre-Dame-sous-Terre for the first time since her childhood, a wave of sadness engulfs her. She runs and locks herself in the bathroom, where a child's screams and tears rack the grown woman's body. Simon is left speechless by her reaction, and he begins to deploy all the remorse, excuses, and tender words he knows—and he knows a lot—to get her to open the door. When she reappears, he hugs her like a mother hugging her child, speaks to her like a brother consoling his sister, and finally, he gives himself totally to her like a man pouring out his pain to a woman.

Exhausted and broken by her tears, she collapses in a chair in the living room, near the fireplace. Here, too, one can hear the tide's violence, and Johanna compares herself to the stone ramparts that the foaming waves unremittingly crash against. When Simon takes the risk of handing her a glass of champagne, some of the same champagne that started the whole scene, she looks at the glass first with hostility, then as if she doesn't even see it.

"Let's raise our glasses in spite of it all," he whispers anxiously. "At least, even if I hadn't yet had a drop, the champagne helped me tell you things that had been weighing on me for a long time, though I know I said things poorly."

With red, swollen eyes surrounded by streaks in her mascara, she breaks into a sad little smile.

"Yes, and maybe I need to set my own heart free from all the things that have been weighing on it for longer still."

She raises her glass to him, empties it, and begins her story. She tells him about her three dreams, Aelred Croward's notebook, Father Placide, the ghost, and the Archangel's curse. When she's done, her glass, which Simon has refilled but she hasn't touched, stands beside the bottle that

Simon finished while she was talking. Without a word, he rises, fills his curved pipe and lights it as he walks to the other side of the room.

"Do you think I'm crazy?" Johanna asks. The silence makes her uncomfortable.

"Johanna," he answers quietly, "you know what I feel about you. So I won't lie to you. I'm glad you've finally confided in me, and I understand how difficult it must have been. But I must say that your story makes me very uneasy."

Her lips tighten as she waits for him to explain.

"From a purely rational point of view," he continues, puffing on his pipe like Sherlock Holmes, "you have no material proof that the ghost really existed and appeared in the past. As for it being the same 'person' as the author of the Cluny manuscript, about which we know nothing at all and which may have been a total invention, however good it may be, then that's going too far. And worst of all is that you're willing to destroy the oldest crypt on the Mount to check out his allegations. That's the official reason, of course, because your own personal reasons seem to be pure fantasy. How can you believe anything that senile old man told you? He was all too happy to tell you what you wanted to hear, all too happy to have someone visit him. In short, the whole story is surely the creation of supersensitive, neurotic minds whose imagination has gone wild."

She's already up and heading for the door.

"Wait," he says gently, grabbing her arm, "I'm not finished. I've not forgotten that I'm dealing with a brilliant scholar, and so my remarks are divided into two parts. That's the first part, the Cartesian model."

"Excuse me, but I've been out of school for a long time," she answers curtly, "and I'm not in the mood for games."

"Sorry, I was trying to cut the tension," he confesses like a schoolboy. "Won't you sit down and hear me out?"

She looks at him with steely eyes, but she does go back to her armchair, sits down, and crosses her legs.

"As I was saying," he continues, picking up Johanna's glass. "That was the logical, reasonable, contemporary, 'normal' view. Bu—and there's always a 'but'—you know that I'm Spanish through my mother and Breton through my father. So I'm a passionate, romantic, literary soul, and sometimes I toss sacrosanct scientific reason out the window."

He's standing right behind Johanna with his hands on the back of her chair, and she feels a sudden wave of warmth.

"So, let's consider—and this is just a hypothesis, not a certainty—that this headless monk does indeed exist, that he's trapped in Notre-Dame-sous-Terre because of some powerful archangelic punishment, and that from time to time he calls on living beings to ask them for help out of his predicament. Let's imagine, and I emphasize the word 'imagine,' that he did appear in the past to Brother Ambroise, to the fearless knight, and to Dom Larose's prior, and that in the present, or recent past, he has indeed appeared to you in your dreams. That would be crazy, inexplicable, paranormal, irrational, but why not? Why not? Although I'm not a fervent Catholic, I don't believe that the world is limited to its material dimension, at least I hope not, because that would be too depressing. I believe there are some things the human mind cannot understand, and that's why your story, even if it seems absurd and crazy, might be plausible on some points."

She turns around and accepts the half-full glass from him.

"Conceivable," he continues, as if he were thinking aloud. "But I doubt that we should hope it's true, because that would be horrible, maybe even like something out of Dante. For the ghost can't be Roman, that poor brother lost in the meanders of his own imagination, that poor, frustrated monk. No, that's impossible. If there's any truth to the story, the ghost you want to set free, the ghost others have also tried to set free, must be a maleficent spirit!"

Standing by the fireplace, pipe in hand, Simon faces her.

"Listen," he continues. "If what Father Placide told you really did happen, you're confusing this ghost with Brother Roman, the manuscript's author. First of all, there's no link, direct or indirect, between the two stories. Furthermore, you're forgetting about the murders! The ones you saw in your dream aren't at all like the ones described in the English copybook. In fact, the murders you dreamed about seem totally disconnected, and that leads me to say that your headless monk is teasing you, just as he teased the other 'witnesses.' What's more, I can't believe Saint Michael's so-called curse. If there is a curse, it should come from the devil rather than from an angel! This phantom, if it does exist, can only be an evil spirit, marked by maleficent forces that first attract, then kill, the people who see it, surely so it can take their souls. Yes, that's probably who the murderer is, and if the ghost didn't kill those men with his own hands, he may have done so indirectly by taking possession of some people's poor, sick minds. And then those people, once empowered, they themselves destroyed or killed their brothers. In conclusion, even if this fable has any semblance of reality, you should in no case start digging in Notre-Dame-sous-Terre."

She watches him with interest and feeling, but doesn't speak.

"Basically," Simon goes on, "I'm very skeptical. It's either one of two things. Perhaps it's all just a made-up fabric of lies and superstitions, more at home in a novel than in your lovely head. In that case I'm sorry you believe it, for you and for that crypt you're getting ready to violate. Or perhaps the story does haves some basis, in which case it would be suicidal to start digging in Notre-Dame-sous-Terre, and I won't let that happen because I don't want anything to happen to you!"

"It's kind of you to think of me, but if I follow you correctly, that means that I'm either a gullible idiot or a mindless kamikaze, and neither is very flattering."

He kneels down at her feet and caresses her ankles.

"I'm sorry, but that's what I think," he admits quietly. "Don't hold it against me. I'm not trying to pick a fight. Let me help you."

"And if you had to choose, which would it be?" she asks more calmly. "Am I naïve or suicidal?"

"If we think about it, things aren't so clear-cut," he says, backing off a little. "I admit that in your place, I wouldn't know what to do. It's all very disconcerting. Personally, I've always made it a point of honor to separate dreams from reality, fiction from concrete fact, but I recognize that for a personality like yours that wouldn't be easy, nourished as you have been by books and immersed in your long study of history."

"You've already made that compliment," she answers bitterly, pulling her ankles free and standing up. "On New Year's Eve, when I read you

Roman's confession, you accused me of not knowing the difference between the real and the imaginary. Whether you like it or not, it's not something I believe, but something I know is true! Do you hear me? I know that the headless monk exists and not only in my head, I know that it's not an evil spirit, I know that it won't hurt me. On the contrary, the ghost needs me, and it must be Brother Roman."

She's almost shouting. He stands up, disconcerted by Johanna's rage, but getting angry himself.

"Since you lap up any legend you hear, at least do me the honor of listening to the legend I'm going to tell you now," he says angrily.

Simon walks away a few feet and relights his pipe. The gray smoke smelling like vanilla and molasses fills the room. As still as a statue, Johanna stares acrimoniously at him.

"In fact," he begins, drawing on his pipe, "I suspect the old man in the retirement home—you said he's Breton—of drawing inspiration from the tale I'm going to tell you when he invented, in whole or in part, his story about the phantom. Because it's a well-known legend in Brittany. It's called 'The Revenant's Mass,' and it takes place in the Plougasnou presbytery, in the Finistère, a long time ago around All Saints' Day. One evening near the end of October, one of the young curates was praying so fervently in the church that he didn't hear the sacristan lock the sanctuary. When the curate realized he was locked in and that nobody could hear him calling, he decided to spend the night in the choir. He made himself comfortable in his stall and fell asleep. Suddenly he was awakened by a strange noise and saw an unknown priest, dressed in black and holding a candle, come from the sacristy. He walked to the altar to light the altar candles. Once he had finished, he spoke with a deep, dark, cavernous voice. Three times the priest dressed in black asked: 'Is there anyone who will respond to my mass?' The curate was terrified and couldn't say a word. Then the mysterious priest blew out the candles and disappeared. The curate looked all over the church and in the sacristy but could find no trace of the priest. The next morning, when the sacristan let him out, he told his story. But nobody would believe him, and they accused him of dreaming or, worse, of having drunk too much. That upset the curate, and to put his mind at ease, he vowed to go back to wait in the church the following night. So he did, and once it was dark, he went back alone to his stall in the choir. At midnight, the same priest dressed in black appeared once more, again lit the altar candles, then asked the same question three times. The curate didn't move. Then the religious extinguished the candles and disappeared. The next morning the curate repeated what he had seen and persuaded the dean of the presbytery, still incredulous, to spend the next night in the church with him. On the third night, at midnight, the priest dressed in black did appear again, and as the dean and curate watched in astonishment, he prepared the altar as usual. But when he asked his habitual question: 'Is there anyone who will respond to my mass?' the curate stood up and presented himself. Then the enigmatic priest began to say a mass for the dead, and the curate assisted. When the mass was over, the priest turned to the curate and told him his story. Three hundred years before, he himself had been the curate in that parish, and he had died suddenly, before he could say a mass that a poor woman had requested. And she had already paid him for the mass. Since that time he had been appearing every year during the week of All Saints' Day, hoping that someone might respond to the mass he still owed to God and the woman. But before this particular night he had never found anyone and always had to return to purgatory. He thanked the curate for setting his captive soul free. Before going to heaven, he said his name aloud—he hadn't been able to say it for three hundred years— and he warned the curate that he would die before Christmas. For anyone who answers a dead person or helps a revenant is sure to die soon thereafter. But the help he gave to a soul in pain guarantees that he'll go to Paradise. The priest said they would meet again, in heaven. And two months later, the young curate did die."

Simon stops speaking. He looks at Johanna. She's white as marble, and the streaks in her makeup look like black veins.

"How incredible," she whispers, her mind off somewhere else. "Whoever makes contact with the other world must die, for he has crossed the border between the earthly and celestial worlds. He's seen the underside of things and so now belongs to the other side of the mirror. That's amazing, still another meaning for 'you must dig in the earth to reach heaven' that I hadn't understood. If I set him free by digging in the earth, he'll reach heaven. But so will I, immediately thereafter!"

Simon strides over to her in exasperation; he's ready to explode.

"You're crazy!" he shouts, shaking her by the shoulders. "Do you know what you're saying? Your imagination has clearly won out over reason. Where's your common sense? Do you want to die? Are you trying to die just to prove that some old legend might be true? Go ahead and lock yourself up in that crypt! That's where you want to be. And strangle yourself by swallowing dirt, like that crazy knight! When they find your body, I'll explain that you were out of your head but that at least you found the head of the man of your life and went off to heaven with him. And how about me?" he asks, his hands on her collar, breathing in her face. "Would you rather be in love with a nonexistent phantom, or maybe a killer revenant if he really does exist, than with me? What have I done to you to deserve this? Or what haven't I done? Can you tell me? Must I keep telling you macabre stories to keep your attention, give you nightmares to get you to look at me, become a killer to get you to love me?"

"You're getting close; you're strangling me," she says, choking, her voice without expression.

Frightened by what he has done, he drops his hands immediately. He looks down at his large brown hands and then at Johanna, who's breathing fast. She stares sadly at him and then starts toward the door.

He's unable to move. When he does regain his wits, weeping, stammering out excuses, he hurries to the apartment door, but she's already gone. He runs down the stairs and into the street just in time to see Johanna's little car speeding off under the streetlights.

Several kilometers away she stops along the road back to the Mount. She leaves her cell phone turned off so she won't have to answer if Simon calls and arranges her hair in the rearview mirror. She looks like someone who's escaped from an insane asylum with her hair flying and mascara streaking down her cheeks. She closes her eyes, puts her head down on the steering wheel, but she's unable to weep over Simon's behavior. She's shocked, for the harsh words, his doubts and his indictment of her motives, are more upsetting than any action motivated by passion. Of course, he did try to humor her by admitting—even if he doesn't believe it—that there might be some truth to her story, but he's far from the truth if he thinks the decapitated monk is an evil spirit. And Johanna knows she was mistaken if she thought that Simon's love was strong enough for him to support her. No, nobody can help her, not even Simon, who loves her. She'll remain forever alone on her chosen path. Not Paul, François, Isabelle, or Simon—none of them has the guts to accompany her. She's the only one to have been touched by the revenant's breath, and that's what distances her from the world of the living. She thinks back on the legend Simon has just told her, and she realizes how vain and useless it is to tell her own story to anyone else.

The path she has chosen leads to the edges of the earth, to the borders of heaven. It's her own path and she doesn't have the right to make anyone else walk it with her. Yes, that's all become clear to her. She's far away, too far away for the living. If she expects to reach her goal, she must give up the norms and realities of the world she has been living in. Contrary to the legend Simon told her, she doesn't believe that her journey will end in death, in her own death. No, the phantom will not carry her off to heaven. But rather he will make her whole. In spite of all the strange things that have happened since she's come to the Mount, she realizes that never has she felt so close to her true self, so close to what she had been unaware of before. Her quest has allowed her to become a woman who's intuitive, lovable, aware of what she wants, sensitive, committed, and complete.

Complete, yes, that's the right word, no longer jerked back and forth between the appetites of her mind and the divergent, misunderstood appetites of her body. She has become a complete, harmonious being embarking on a quest that sometimes is beyond her but that gives her life new meaning by removing all doubt. It doesn't matter whether or not other people believe her or think she's crazy, whether or not Roman and Moira actually lived, whether or not the headless monk is just a fantasy in her own mind or in the minds of monks many years ago. The true reality of the whole story, perhaps the only reality, is that it has placed Johanna at the heart of her own story. It's put her at the center of the only truly important adventure, the quest of self-understanding. No one else can understand that, of course. She looks up through the windshield at the stars, points of light scattered over the dark sky like angelic sugar. She sighs, realizing she has to leave Simon. She'll use his violence as the pretext. Later perhaps, once she's completed her mission, she'll be ready to meet him halfway and walk by his side, once she knows herself fully. If they still love each other. But for now, it's too early. She turns her cell phone back on. She checks her messages and listens to Simon's remorseful music. Then, her mind made up, she starts back toward the mountain.

As she climbs the steps toward her house, she realizes that she no longer has the oppressed feeling she had had a few hours before when she was on the way to see Simon. In its place, hunger is gnawing at her stomach. She hasn't eaten anything at all since noon, and she sees that it's already twelve thirty. With a little luck, there'll still be some tripe left. If she's out of luck, Patrick will be back, waiting in the living room to engage her in a battle she's no longer interested in. She'd be happier if he went ahead and carried out his threat and resigned. That'd be one less person in her way. She's thinking about that possibility when she hears panting and hurried footsteps behind her. She turns around and realizes that it's Guillaume Kelenn.

"Johanna!" he calls out. "I saw you go by. I was in a café. Do you have a minute?"

His long, flowing blond hair, the grayish-green gleam in his eyes—surely alcohol-induced—and his thin mustache make him look like a Viking. That'd be too much for someone so proud of his Celtic origins! She nods suspiciously. She never says very much to the young man because his excitability is a little irritating.

"How about a drink?" he asks.

"Well, I haven't eaten yet," she admits. "And I'm exhausted. I'd rather go on home."

"Fine, no problem," he says, although his expression says just the opposite. "I just wanted to congratulate you."

"Congratulate me? What for?"

"For the dig you'll be starting in Notre-Dame-sous-Terre, of course. That's great!" he exclaims confidently.

Johanna can't hide her surprise.

"Thank you, Guillaume. You must be one of the few people who aren't opposed to the project. That's a nice surprise," she says, with a warm smile.

"Yes, I know," Kelenn answers, "and especially Fenoy. Nobody's heard anything from him, by the way. Brard hasn't seen him, in any case. It looks like your assistant has deserted you."

Indeed, that's good news for Johanna, and she's feeling better all the time.

"That shouldn't be a problem. You can get along without him," he continues, the expression on his face showing how little affinity he has with her assistant. "How marvelous to start digging in the abbey's most secret sanctuary. I envy you, you know. I'd love to be part of the team. Perhaps I could replace Fenoy?"

Johanna is surprised and reassured. At least there's somebody who isn't vilifying her project.

"I'm afraid that's impossible," she answers sweetly, "but there wouldn't be any problem if you'd like to visit the site regularly, and I'd be pleased to talk to you about the work."

"Thank you," he says, coming over to shake her hand. "That's nice of you. Say, Johanna, couldn't we start being less formal with each other?"

17

MAY HAS ARRIVED WITH ITS LONG HOLIDAY WEEKENDS, BUT Johanna doesn't leave Mont-Saint-Michel. She prefers to stay on the island, down in the crypt where springtime never comes. On the abbey's outside walls, the yellow lichens make it look as if sunshine has melted over the stones. The sun's rays are not yet incandescent, and the nights are still cold when the north wind blows. Along with buds on the trees come more tourist buses, and as regular as the tides they pour into the shops to buy T-shirts and fluorescent Saint Michaels. Old stones attract plastic. Only about a third of the visitors are interested enough to climb all the way up to the abbey. It's not yet the human flood that summer brings, but the village and abbey church already seem different, at least during the day, and Johanna isn't pleased to see the change. Fortunately, at night the mountain seems purified by the elements, and, hidden behind its windswept black armor, it and its deepest mysteries are protected from the crowds. Closed to visitors, shrouded by shadows for more than nine centuries, Notre-Dame-sous-Terre still remains hidden from the archeologists, who have already been digging for three weeks by the light of huge projectors. It still hasn't yielded the secret that Brother Roman was guarding, and in spite of Johanna's passionate prayers, the headless monk has not reappeared. On the other hand, Patrick Fenoy has been back for a week. This evening, in the team's house, just a few days before the long weekend of May 8, Johanna gives a case of Bourgueil wine to everyone, and to Jacques she gives an old bottle of Calvados because she lost her bet with him. They have all gathered in the common room for dinner.

"Oh, thanks so much!" Jacques exclaims when he sees the label, winking at her. "Say, anyone else for an aperitif?"

They all hesitate. Patrick doesn't even do that. He sits there the way he's been ever since he came back—angry and taciturn. Sebastian, Jacques, Florence, and Dimitri think that his efforts to stop the dig while he was gone have worn him out; Johanna thinks he's up to something. During his absence, Patrick had indeed tried to get the authorization for the project revoked. He went to see Roger Calfon in Paris, and then to the Ministry, where he made a scene in the department François directs as well as in his office. In vain. François called Johanna to tell her that even though she'd need to work with an enemy, at least she could keep working. Her assistant didn't get back for a few more days, because Roger Calfon's wife died. François represented the government at the funeral. Brard hesitated, but finally he went to the funeral, too, though he had never met Calfon's wife. It was more like a diplomatic maneuver. It allowed him to show his support for Calfon and Fenoy, say a few words to François to help calm things down, and bring Johanna's assistant back to the Mount.

In the team's house Patrick was not warmly welcomed. The team was angry that he had tried to sabotage the new project. Johanna had prepared herself for a confrontation, but Fenoy's attitude has surprised everyone. Usually he is an aggressive, know-it-all braggart, but since his return he's been reserved and sullen and kept his thoughts to himself. He's avoided all confrontation, especially with Johanna, and hasn't spoken out of turn down in the crypt. Johanna hasn't lowered her guard and still mistrusts him, but the others have let themselves get caught up in good springtime feelings, not to mention enjoying a few bottles of some of the good Bourgueil wine as an aperitif.

"Maybe we're not drilling in the right places," Sebastian suggests as he pours the wine. "What if there is indeed a cavity behind the wall but we're just missing it with our probes?"

"I doubt it," Johanna replies. "It's true that sometimes more widespread drilling is necessary. But we don't want to damage the masonry too much. We can't turn the wall into Swiss cheese. Don't forget that we must move each stone we touch very carefully so that we can restore its original appearance afterwards. And also, it would take too long to probe the walls more systematically. We don't have much time."

"There aren't thousands of places in the crypt where a chest, a reliquary, or a box could be hidden," says Florence.

"Or a corpse hidden in some secret tomb," Johanna adds, thinking of the revenant's head separated from its body.

"A corpse?" Jacques says in surprise, putting down his glass of Calvados. "What does a corpse have to do with it? We're not digging in Saint Martin's Chapel any more, Jo; nor in Cluny! Paul already found the tomb that was awaiting discovery, and Roman wouldn't have gone to so much trouble to protect the effects of a dead monk. Unless perhaps it's a sacred skeleton, or at least sacred for you, or shameful. Maybe the bones of a fetus or a newborn baby, the fruit of his secret love for Moira, or maybe the charred remains of Moira herself, who knows?"

"Or do you think it might be the bones of Saint Michael in person, with armor, cloak, sword, shield, along with dragon fossils and a set of scales?" Sebastian says, jokingly.

"Idiots!" Dimitri shouts out, already a little drunk. "I say we won't find anything, anything at all. Because we're talking about a novel, and we can't expect a novel to be real."

"No, but all fiction has some basis in reality, even if it's just to reinvent it," Johanna objects.

"Well," says Jacques, "for me the banal reality is that Moira was some peasant girl Roman knocked up—that must have happened more often than people think—and she died in childbirth. Or maybe she killed herself in shame or out of spite, and the unworthy monk, who was alive while the abbey church was being built but wasn't the master builder, was banished from the Mount as his punishment. Hidden away at Cluny, he came up with this farfetched story to salve his sinful conscience."

"Why must you always make pure things sound so dirty?" Dimitri cuts in. "And why do you have to trivialize beautiful things and make them sound disgusting?"

"What do you think about Guillaume's suggestion to probe the floor to see if there might be an underground cave?" Florence asks Johanna, trying to forestall an argument.

At the mention of Kelenn's name, Patrick's mournful expression changes. The guide is his bête noire. When he returned to work, he found the man in the crypt watching them all and commenting on their work, sometimes lending a hand. Guillaume now routinely spends all his free time on the dig, and he seems delighted to be there.

At first, Johanna didn't pay much attention to him, but he knew so much about the abbey and Notre-Dame-sous-Terre that she began to tolerate his presence in the hope of picking up some information that might be meaningless to him but essential for her. He's not without a sense of humor, and the team has been glad to accept him for that reason. Little by little Johanna has come to appreciate the fellow, for he has proven himself to be brilliant and generous, and she enjoys having him around. But she does wonder why Guillaume never showed any interest at all in the work on the earlier project. She attributes his interest in the Carolingian structure to his obsession with his Celtic ancestors, who had placed a dolmen here during the Neolithic period. Patrick is too caught up in himself to think the guide is trying to supplant him. But as a professional, he's offended by having a stranger present, a vulgar amateur who knows nothing about archeology sharing in the work of carefully chosen, highly trained specialists.

"I do think we should check to see if there's an underground cave, even if the rock makes that hypothesis not very probable," Johanna says.

"Not very probable? Ridiculous is more like it!" Patrick roars suddenly. In spite of his best intentions, he has to say something. "Why and how could they have dug a grotto out of this rock back in the eleventh century or before? Can you imagine how much work that would have required with the tools they had and without dynamite? This dilettante is filling your minds with childish ideas that make you forget the meaning of your profession. If there is anything to discover, it's just some mad adolescent fantasies. The Cluny manuscript, even supposing it is authentic, has no archeological import. But let's suppose it does, since that's why they're paying us, and so we have no choice. But in fact, if there is anything at all, it would be evident to any professional worthy of the name that it must be behind one of the crypt's outside walls. They could be hiding a secret cavity, a room, or a corridor, for example, built when they first constructed the church or when they turned it into a crypt to support the nave. Or perhaps even when they built the monastery buildings around Notre-Dame-sous-Terre. Their plan could have been to hide some treasure or to provide a way for the monks to escape from the fortress in case of danger. That kind of parallel construction was quite common in the Middle Ages, I remind you, just as I must also remind you that we've already seen some of the abbey's secret passages."

The group falls silent. Everyone knows that Patrick is partially correct, but they're all waiting for the "adolescent" to react. Strangely, she doesn't seem upset.

"That was indeed quite common," Johanna begins, looking at her wine, "and that's why we started by probing the south, north, and east walls. It's useless to drill into the west wall, since, except for the Romanesque stairway, it is open on the other side. The most likely hypothesis is that there could be a secret chamber hidden behind a wall, we all agree on that. But there's a problem: Our probes have come up empty. On the one hand, as I was saying, it's because we can't drill as much as we might like, for fear of damaging the structure, and on the other, it's because behind the first Carolingian wall there's another, older wall, dating from the eighth century when the mountain was founded. That's the wall of Aubert's oratory, and it probably surrounds the crypt. Everyone knows that, and has for a long time. And when Froidevaux restored Notre-Dame-sous-Terre, he found a section of that wall right behind the Holy Trinity altar. So, it's evident that if there's a chamber or passageway, it must be either behind the second wall or between the Carolingian stones and Aubert's own stones, and it could date from well before the time the Romanesque abbey was built. Our dilemma is how to reach any such cavity without demolishing the sanctuary. If Brother Roman insisted that the builders of the great abbey church not destroy this chapel, perhaps it was because in order to discover the secret, one has to completely demolish the sanctuary!"

"Now that you mention it, that does seem reasonable," Florence chimes in, relieved to see that Johanna didn't react to her assistant's personal attacks. "But how are we going to go about it? We can't ruin this place! Brard will never let us proceed, nor will the associations protecting the site. We'd risk having serious problems."

"I've been thinking," Johanna responds. "I spend my days thinking about it, and my nights, too," she adds with a sigh. "And here's one idea: If what we're looking for does exist, it must be in the choir, or very near. Any treasure has to be placed near the holy of holies, not out in the nave with pilgrims. Consequently, that's where we need to concentrate our work. Starting tomorrow, we'll remove the stones one by one from Aubert's wall, which Froidevaux exposed behind the Trinity altar. Then we can see what's behind it. With a little luck, we'll find a passageway that leads around the crypt and we won't need to touch the other walls. If we don't find anything, well, I'm sorry, but then we'll need to consider moving a wall, the wall behind the Virgin's altar, for example. Or maybe decide that Guillaume Kelenn's idea wasn't so stupid after all."

"Johanna," Dimitri cuts in, "Froidevaux laid stones over the entire floor. We'll need to break them all up, and that'll be a massacre!"

"We're not there yet, Mitya," she answers, emptying her glass. "First, Aubert's Cyclopean wall, and then we'll see."

Patrick frowns. They go to the dinner table and begin talking about other things. Jacques deglazes the pork roast with apples and a little of his Calvados and takes advantage of the opportunity to drink a third glass in the kitchen. It's a joyful dinner, with a little more wine that usual. When they get to the cheese course, Dimitri announces that it's his thirty-first birthday, and they all wish him well, all the while complaining that he should have told them sooner. Florence improvises and comes up with a banana gratin, and the big white candle Johanna sets in it looks like a lighthouse rising out of burned rocks. Dimitri tries to hold back his tears when he sees his birthday dessert. He thanks everyone vociferously, but he's too drunk and too emotional to realize that he's mixing Russian words into the conversation. Then he runs off to his room to weep. As they're all, including Jacques, drinking up the Calvados, Florence explains that Dimitri's boyfriend has just left him. Sebastian rolls his eyes when he learns that his friend is gay.

"What difference is there?" Jacques complains in his slurred voice. "A man or a woman, hetero or homo, love is simply solitude's banal façade."

"Of course, and as for you," Florence answers, "you've pulled down the façade. What you see is what you get."

"Right," he says. "I've broken the distorting window. One hundred kilos of solitary meat, with the label 'confirmed bachelor,' and I'm glad to be who I am!"

"You're kidding," Sebastian responds. "We all know that song. You're glad because you have no choice. Nobody wants to buy."

"That's what you think!" he shouts, standing up. "You think I can't attract anyone? If I told you the story of my life, you might be surprised."

"Not fooling me with your Casanova adventures," Sebastian laughs. "But if you say so."

"You little jerk," Jacques shouts at him, trying to pull him up by his shirt, "I'll teach you a thing or two."

"Relax!" says Johanna. "Sounds like a kindergarten playground!"

Jacques looks darkly at Sebastian, empties his glass, and says he's going to take a walk. The door slams noisily. Patrick sits watching the scene, then he smiles and gets up to go to bed. Sebastian, still muttering, helps the women clean up.

"We didn't treat Jacques very kindly," Florence points out, looking over at Sebastian. "He's a good man. The poor fellow, I'm almost sure he's never touched a woman. But he always sees sex in everything, and that explains his interpretation of Brother Roman's story a few minutes ago. He's sex-deprived. You can tell by the way he looks at women's legs, right, Jo?"

"As you said, he's a good man," Johanna says, changing the subject. "As for stones, he knows how to look at them, and that's all that matters to me."

"Oh, come on. For once stop acting like the boss. There's more than work to life," Sebastian says teasingly.

"You don't understand," Florence objects. "Johanna doesn't like to gossip, because she doesn't want other people to gossip about her own love life, that's all. You know, Jo, in spite of all your efforts, everyone knows about it. And we almost envy you. Your Simon Le Meur is as handsome as a prince. So distinguished! And what lovely flowers! Nobody's ever brought me flowers like that."

Johanna almost decides to drop the pile of plates she's carrying and to slap Florence. Florence can tell that she's gone too far. Johanna calmly puts the dishes down on the dishwasher.

"There's no longer any Simon Le Meur," she answers in a mournful voice, as if he were dead. "You see, you didn't have up-to-date information, Florence. Now you do. Good night."

She leaves them standing there and goes to her room.

She didn't explode back in the kitchen, but now she does, inside. Roman and Moira sleeping together? What nonsense! To try to relax, she thinks about her impossible dream of digging alone. She's beginning to consider the possibility more and more seriously. Ever since the work in the crypt began, she's had trouble putting up with the presence of all her colleagues. If only they would all just disappear! Only Guillaume Kelenn finds grace in her eyes. There seems to be a mysterious understanding between them. It's not so much an attraction, and certainly not a physical attraction, or even friendship, but something else outside themselves. It must be the passion they share for the crypt and their receptivity to its telluric waves, which seem not to affect anyone else. Or perhaps it's their burning interest in archeological digs, though they may have different goals. Johanna has never revealed anything about her secret goals to Guillaume; neither he nor anyone else knows anything about them. Roman's manuscript made an impression on him, especially the story about Moira, a Celtic woman who might have been one of his ancestors. Johanna imagines that Guillaume is hoping to find the vestiges of an old dolmen in the crypt, or maybe Moira's soul, a soul from his own real or imagined past, something haunting him so much that he has trouble living in the present. Like Johanna, there must be something within himself that he's seeking so fervently. As it is for Johanna, the true meaning of his quest must be personal, mystical, and spiritual. As she is doing, he's trying to solve a personal enigma, and he, too, needs to dig back into personal ground. Yes, it must be their symbolic quests' similarity that's brought them together instinctively, a deep understanding that their unconscious has sensed. Johanna suddenly sees him as a brother, and suddenly, encouraged by alcohol, she feels like picking up the telephone and telling him so. But she thinks better of it. She remembers the decision she made: She must follow her path alone. She thinks back to that fateful evening three weeks ago with Simon when she told him the whole story. And how it put an end to the story they shared. She refuses to feel any regret. For a week Simon had tried everything to win her forgiveness, but for her, the flowers he's sent, even though Florence envies her, are as cloying as the mistake she made by telling him the story in the first place. She's not sorry she met Simon, for she thoroughly enjoyed their time together. But she's sorry to have confided in him, to have opened herself up as she did. And yet she should have known that he would swallow her up! "Abandoning oneself to others always leads to the others abandoning us," she thinks.

Of course, she's the one who left him, but all she was doing was making his rejection official. She had exposed her soul, and he had insulted her. Not only had he refused to believe her, but then he even tried to strangle her! Disowned her, he had completely disowned her.

When she finally saw things that way, she tossed the roses Simon had sent into the sea as night fell. She'd kept her cell phone turned off until he tired of trying to call her, and she'd asked her ally Dimitri to screen her phone calls at the house. At the Mount she hasn't gone anywhere, so as to not meet him in the streets, and she's counting on her colleagues—as well as on Simon's distaste for publicity—to protect her if he should decide to show up at the abbey. Last weekend she'd gone to Paris to see Isabelle and François. She'd tossed the letter Simon sent into the trash, unopened. Silence and flight are her armor, and Simon's masculine pride is what she touches with her sword. And her intuition has proven to be right—after trying unsuccessfully for a week to make contact with Johanna, Simon became vexed. To keep his self-respect, he stopped calling, and she has received no more letters or flowers. She still has to stay clear of Simon's house for another week. Soon, as May progresses with the beginning of tourist season, Simon will be forced to return to his little shop behind the ramparts of Saint-Malo, and Johanna will be cut off completely from him.

· · ·

THE NEXT MORNING, trying to recover from their hangovers, the team is sitting at the breakfast table. Dimitri's face is as swollen as if he has been in a fight; Russian benders are as strong as fists. Sitting quietly across from Johanna, Florence and Sebastian stare into their bowls as if they might find the crypt's treasure there. True to his nature, Patrick remains impassive as he eats silently. At eight thirty, Johanna begins to worry because Jacques still hasn't shown up, and nobody heard him come in the night before.

"He was probably barhopping," Sebastian suggests feebly, "and too drunk to come home. He didn't dare come back, given the racket he made last time when he came in at three o'clock and the tongue-lashing you gave him afterwards! He must be lying somewhere in a medieval gutter."

Suddenly they hear a knock at the door.

"Here he comes!" Sebastian says.

Filled with foreboding, Johanna goes to open the door.

No Jacques, but standing at the door is Christian Brard, outlined against the beautiful sky and accompanied by two policemen. Everybody sits up. Brard looks ashen.

"Good morning. I . . . I'm sorry, but I've got some bad news," he says. "This morning early, a street cleaner found our friend Jacques, uh, lying at the base of the ramp below the treadmill. Unfortunately, he . . . he's dead."

Sebastian turns blue-green; Patrick drops his spoon. Dimitri claps his hands over his mouth, and Florence lets out a cry.

"That's horrible; I can't believe it!" Johanna says. "What happened?"

"Well, we hope you can help us figure that out," one of the officers answers. Like many important members of the police force, he has a strange accent and an impressive moustache. "All we can say for the moment is that he fell through the opening near the treadmill. A thirty-five-foot drop through the air, and the poor man was crushed on the rocks beneath. He's not a pretty sight."

"When did you see him last?" Brard asks, sounding like a policeman.

Johanna briefly goes over the events of the evening before.

"Hmm," says the policeman, rubbing his moustache. "He was intoxicated, and at first sight that makes it seem like an accident. We'll know better when the inspector and the coroner have seen him, and still better once the autopsy is completed. You," he says, looking at everyone. "Don't leave. The inspector would like to ask you some questions."

"Autopsy? A police inspector?" Florence murmurs, horror-stricken.

"Yes, my dear," the policeman confirms. "He did fall, perhaps accidentally, perhaps on purpose, or maybe someone pushed him!"

"Johanna," Brard says quietly. "I'm counting on you to notify his family."

She knows that the poor fellow has no wife or children. When she goes through his belongings, she finds a little red address book with only a few names. She finds an entry for Jacques's parents, who live in Paris, but can't bear to call them. Instead, she calls a sister living in Strasbourg.

His sister promises to come that very evening and to tell her parents. Johanna hangs up the phone and goes back to join the others. They are devastated, but still they manage to make conjectures about his death. Since the treadmill was near their earlier dig, Jacques may have gone back there for some reason, perhaps to sleep it off. Perhaps he leaned out past the protective barrier and through the opening so he could see the stars. Yes, that must be it. There were lots of stars last night, and because he was so drunk, he slipped and fell to his death. Poor Jacques, he was so kind, so friendly, so competent, so admirable; they all were so attached to him! Johanna can't stand their morbid sentimental outpouring and leaves the house. She thinks back to the wish she made the evening before, that her colleagues would all disappear so she could dig in the crypt by herself. She feels very ill at ease. She feels the need to breathe, to think, to get some air, like Jacques last night. Air! The word strikes her like a whip, and more than the word, the idea itself terrifies her! Jacques died falling through the air, just like the monk she had seen hanging in her childhood dream. And like Moira, who nearly a thousand years ago swung in the air above the Mount during her first ordeal.

"Could it possibly be more than a coincidence?" she wonders. "If so, that'd be horrible, because that would mean that Jacques was killed and that someone, some crazy, demented person, killed him by imitating the medieval murder. But Jacques had never seen the headless monk. No, but he was digging in the crypt. That's it. Someone is imitating the original murders as they are described in Dom Larose's notebook; someone is striking down people who are digging in Notre-Dame-sous-Terre. In that case, the whole team is in danger!"

Johanna shivers as she climbs the steps toward the abbey church. She stares out over the sea and the ebbing tide.

"The sea, water, the second ordeal," she remembers. "What if the warning Dom Larose read in that daybook was warranted? What if the crypt was indeed cursed and the revenant an evil spirit as many monks— and Simon, too—believed. No, no! They can't be right. Think, Johanna! Think! The killer has to be the person who stole that notebook. Or the person who has it now. That's the person who is evil and dangerous. He has used what he found in the notebook to kill Jacques, but surely that can't have anything to do with the four elements that inspired Moira's tortures. Nor could there be any link with Brother Roman's manuscript, nor for that matter with any diabolical monk without a head. It's all surely the work of a psychopath, but it has to be a contemporary, a real flesh-and-blood man or woman."

As she thinks, she continues on toward the abbey. Without really realizing where she is, she ends up a few feet away from the base of the ramp below the treadmill. What she sees seems surreal. A police van, a fire truck, and an ambulance block the narrow street. The different uniforms moving around in every direction partially hide a gray shape covered with a blanket at the bottom of the steep slope. With rocks and shrubs on both sides, the man-made stone ramp looks like the launching pad for a missile. High above, it ends at the abbey's south façade, at an opening between two arcades dating from the nineteenth century, when the abbey was a prison. Johanna looks at the launching pad and suddenly feels she's in a different world, a world unfamiliar to her. She walks closer. Nobody pays any attention to her. The EMTs prepare to lay the gray shape on a stretcher. As they lift it up, the load shifts and the shape slides back down to the ground, so that it's lying on its back, the blanket askew. Johanna would never have imagined what she sees for the few seconds it takes for the EMTs to correct their mistake. She sees the corpse of a man she would never have recognized. Except perhaps for the clothing draped over his body. But not by the face. In fact, there is no face. Just a dark mass of blood, bone, raw flesh, like some horror-show makeup that has totally obliterated his nose, eyes, mouth. Makeup reproducing an insupportable reality, a reality that no dreams could protect against. Johanna turns away suddenly and throws up on the pavement.

As in a fog, she seems to see Christian Brard's smooth features, and then she drops into a black hole.

When she comes to an hour later, she's in bed, and Florence is sitting beside her. She has a bitter taste in her mouth.

"Hi," says Flo. "Glad to see you're back, Jo. You passed out. The EMTs brought you up here."

"Oh, I remember. How horrible! Indescribable!"

"Yes, I know. Don't try to talk about it."

"Florence, could you please bring me a pot of coffee?"

"You need to eat something, too."

"No, nothing!"

"All right. I'll bring some. By the way, an inspector is asking Patrick some questions."

Johanna sits up, and the whole horrible scene comes back to her. And no, it wasn't a play or a film. It was real. It's still real. Poor Jacques! Finally Johanna is able to weep. Sobbing, she realizes that it's absurd to think her team member was killed by the person who stole Dom Larose's notebook. That idea is just the irrational invention of her own fantasies, which can't even begin to explain the corpse she saw. Seeing the body has brought her rudely back down to earth—but, for her, the fall wasn't fatal. She has to stop seeing everything through the prism of Roman's legend and her own story of headless monks. Other people's reality is not the same! It's not her reality that killed Jacques, but rather his own—his despair at being alone, the bitterness and weight of his own life, everything he tried to find relief from by drinking. Yes, surely his inebriation caused the suicide or the accident, and maybe for Jacques suicide and accident were one and the same.

All day long the police continue questioning the team members and the people in the Mont-Saint-Michel office of Historical Monuments. The body has been taken to Saint-Lô for the autopsy. That evening in the team house, it's like a wake with no body. A few of the villagers come by, out of curiosity or compassion, to present their condolences to Jacques's professional family. Guillaume Kelenn's presence comforts Johanna and sends Patrick, as morose as usual, off to his room.

The next morning they go back to their dig in Notre-Dame-sous-Terre, but nobody can work. Dimitri is off weeping in a corner; Patrick just sits there; Sebastian and Florence are talking together and drinking coffee from a thermos. Johanna stares at the Holy Trinity altar and, behind it, at the little section of wall Froidevaux had discovered. She wonders if it could be hiding a secret chamber where her monk's skeleton and skull could both be found. She's burning to remove the rough-joined stones from the wall one by one, but she doesn't dare, given the way her team is feeling.

Finally, at noon, a shape shrouded in white, a sister from the Community of Jerusalem, comes down to ask if they would like to join the Community in prayer for their friend's soul and to attend high mass in the church. Except for Dimitri, they are all atheists or, at best, agnostics, but they accept with some relief. They take their places on benches in the Gothic choir, alongside tourists and pilgrims with their sticks and cockleshells, just like their counterparts in the Middle Ages. Johanna looks up at the evanescent blue color suffusing the stained glass windows with its heavenly light to create an almost supernatural atmosphere. She thinks about the Romanesque choir that collapsed on the Benedictine monks in 1421 during the Hundred Years' War, about the knight who shortly afterward saw the headless monk in the crypt, and about the knight's corpse lying there, mouth filled with dirt. She forces herself to get rid of such thoughts and to concentrate instead on the service and on the Community's brothers and sisters dressed in white. She is surprised to find herself offering up a silent prayer to Saint Michael, asking him to accompany Jacques's soul to heaven. Heaven is there above her, in flights of graceful stone, in fine majestic lines that communicate an irresistible sensation of elevation, of pious verticality. A dull roar pulls her out of her architectural prayer. Tourists in Bermuda shorts and headphones, cameras around their necks, are walking around behind the faithful like fat, curious honeybees. From their headphones, the voice describing the church drowns out the priest's voice. The monks and nuns are used to this daily outrage and continue singing as if it were nothing.

Johanna makes an effort to concentrate on the priest's sermon. She stares at his cross hanging like a pendulum over his immaculate robe. Little by little, to her eyes, a homespun robe and scapular replace the priest's white robe, and his cassock seems to grow darker, until it's black like a Benedictine's frock. Suddenly, the priest has no head. And then she sees Father Placide's head, wrinkled and emaciated, and it repeats three times: "Is there anyone who will respond to my mass?" and Johanna answers quietly: "*Ad accedendum ad caelum, terram fodere opportet.*" Florence elbows her, and she opens her eyes. When she looks up, the priest dressed in white, arms raised, is singing "Our Father." She looks around. The archeologists are all standing and surprisingly, they're all joining in the prayer. Johanna stands up and tries as best she can to remain upright. Fortunately, except for Florence, nobody seems to have noticed that she had dozed off.

The mass ends. Johanna hurries outside to the terrace. The sky can't seem to decide between blue and gray-black, and its low, dark streaks seem to weigh down on her like a granite tomb cover. Johanna gives her team the afternoon off. She needs to be alone to gather her thoughts. She closes herself in Notre-Dame-sous-Terre and removes from the Holy Trinity altar the drills someone has put there. She lights the candles and turns off all the electric lights. There's a strange feeling in the air, and across the crypt's white stones move shadows that seem centuries older than the candle flame that brings them to life today. Johanna rubs her hand across the stones' contours, as if she might find there traces of another hand under hers, its fingers dark and pointed like the legs of a spider crawling across her skin. She leans her forehead against the magical stones, then places her mouth against them. She can feel the wall's heart beating. She can sense the stone's painful memories coursing down her cheeks.

"Roman," she murmurs. "If I am able to set you free, you'll fly away. You'll join Moira, and you, too, will abandon me. You've been with me for so long! The closer I get to you, the more, I fear, you move away. You see, I need you. We both are like this crypt, each the other's double, and twins. You've given so much of yourself—the love of your art, unceasing dialogue with a past that's more alive than the present, solitude, and the comfort of dead souls. But you've condemned me to silence! I can't speak to anyone about you, except to your old accomplice, Father Placide. Simon did in reality exist, and you took him from me. But I know you had nothing to do with Jacques's death. He died because he was alone, by himself, whereas you and I are alone, but bound to each other. We sustain each other. Two parallel lives. We're dead to the world, Roman. You can't reach heaven, yet you are my heaven. I know, Roman. I must hold you close, I have to embrace your body for you to join the star that's been waiting nearly a thousand years for you. But who will then be my star?"

For a long time she stands leaning against the wall. Then she looks over at the rough, irregular blocks from Aubert's oratory, and she thinks of Aubert, whose perforated skull lies in state in the Saint Gervais church in Avranches. She's sure that the head and body she needs to exhume can be found behind those stones. But she can't possibly remove them without the others' help. The huge, heavy blocks stand one on top of the other. Halfway up the wall there's a large stone that would require a crane. She lets out a sigh. Johanna would love to be the only person to discover him, to see him, to touch him! Paul found the manuscript that was supposed to be hers; Father Placide was given a precious notebook he couldn't keep. But she's the one who has managed to put together all the pieces, and so the final liberation should belong to her! Fenoy, Dimitri, Florence, Sebastian, and even Guillaume have no interest in a skeleton and head lost in time and stone. The tribulations of that poor soul have nothing to do with them. Unfortunately, she needs their arms so that her own hand can write the conclusion of her own personal story.

Sighing once more, she places her hand on Aubert's wall. The mountain's founder tried to imitate natural rock and grottoes, like the grotto on Mount Gargano. None of the stones are shaped, and there's little mortar. There in that circular sanctuary, Saint Aubert and his canons must have felt that they were in the center of a cavern, in God's dwelling, in a secret chamber like a womb. Johanna blows out the candles, locks the door, and returns home. She finds no one there but Dimitri, moping in the living room, trying to read.

"Simon Le Meur called," he says indifferently. "He heard about . . .

Jacques and wondered how you were. Anything new about Jacques?"

"I don't know. Oh, yes, I should call Brard right away."

The administrator tells her that he expects to get the autopsy report later that evening and that he'll keep her posted. The funeral will be held the day after tomorrow in Paris. He thinks it would be appropriate to close the dig for a week and give everyone the week off. Johanna doesn't let him get away with reducing the time for her project. She tells him she's given her team the afternoon off. Since the funeral is the seventh, they'll take a long weekend but no more than that. She doesn't call Simon back, but manages to persuade François to spend the weekend with her. Given the circumstances, he's not hard to persuade. She has dinner alone with Dimitri, and the tragedy has clearly made his depression worse.

At nine that evening, Brard comes to tell her that it was clearly an accident, and that it happened around two A.M. There's no sign of a struggle on the body or near the treadmill, no strange substances in his body except for the high level of alcohol. Unfortunately, he was drunk, and he must have simply fallen. That's what she expected, but she's relieved to hear it nonetheless. She opens the cabinet to offer her boss something to drink and pulls out the Calvados she had given to Jacques. The bottle is three quarters empty. She pales as if she has seen a revolver, as if she herself shot her colleague.

THE NEXT DAY, Guillame joins the team and they begin to attack Aubert's wall. Slowly, with careful movements, they remove the stones from where they've lain undisturbed since the year 708. The granite doesn't come from the Chausey Islands, but from the Mount itself. According to the legend written down by the canons and then later by the Benedictines, after the Archangel's third appearance Aubert finally went to Mont Tombe. And there he discovered that the spot where the future sanctuary would stand had been marked by Saint Michael, just as the Angel had announced in a dream. In his dream, a bull stolen by a thief and hidden so the thief could sell it later was awaiting the bishop at the center of a large circle drawn by the morning dew. At that center, near two big stones, was where he was to build the oratory dedicated to the first among the angels. And that's where Saint Aubert indeed did build it.

Historians and archeologists believe that the two stones, removed so the floor would be smooth, were in fact the two upright rocks from a former dolmen that had fallen into ruin, while the circular area was a mound from the megalithic monument. The Celts always built their temples at special places, particularly at places where they could feel the earth's power. So it was generally assumed that Aubert's cave, an artificial cave, had taken the place of an old dolmen no longer in use, as Christianity had supplanted Celtic religion. Though many of the old beliefs were retained and Christianized, the pagan temples were destroyed. Nothing is left of the dolmen at Mont-Saint-Michel, but Aubert's walls, taking the exact shape of the pre-Christian sanctuary, still keep its memory alive. As soon as Patrick, Sebastian, and the little crane remove the first stones from Aubert's wall, Guillaume Kelenn rushes over with a lantern. Quickly, Johanna cuts him off.

"May I?" she says aggressively. "You can look later!"

He backs off sheepishly. With a jubilant smile, Patrick leans a ladder up against the wall. Her heart is about to explode as she climbs up and pushes the lantern into the opening they've just made. All she can see is rock, a natural, impenetrable wall similar to the one Aubert had built. No secret passage or chamber. But she wonders if perhaps at the base of the wall the rock might have been hollowed out to make a large enough space to hide a skull and a body. She looks down; she strains to see what lies between the rock and Aubert's stones. She sees nothing but a small, empty space. She clings to the granite so as not to burst into tears. Where can Roman be if he's not here? She begins to feel sick to her stomach.

"Well, Johanna. Can you see anything?" the others ask excitedly.

Slowly she comes back down the ladder. She takes off her glasses and rubs her eyes. They assume that dust has caused her tears.

"Nothing," she says dully. "There doesn't seem to be anything. Just the vertical rock wall. But let's remove the rest of Aubert's wall. We need to make sure. Come on."

"Do you really think it's necessary?" Dimitri wonders. "The wall is the oldest part of the whole abbey. It's almost thirteen hundred years old. If you didn't see anything, why destroy it?"

She stares icily at him.

"Because we're scientists," she answers curtly, "and a quick glance is not enough to make a true scientist give up his thesis. He needs proof. So we're going to tear down the wall to be sure nothing is hidden there. And if we need to, we'll tear down all the others as well, one by one."

Mitya looks away sadly. So Johanna is prepared to wipe out Notre-Dame-sous-Terre. He's surprised. He's always admired Johanna, but now she's changed. She used to talk passionately about the stones in the crypt, and now she's willing to destroy them! Maybe Jacques's death has affected her more than she's letting on. Or maybe it's the end of her affair with that antique dealer in Saint-Malo. She must be feeling really bad, just as he, Dimitri, is. He feels as if he's breathing the stench of death.

JACQUES'S PRIVATE FUNERAL doesn't take long. The only religious service held for him was the mass said by the Community of Jerusalem that the team had also attended. Incineration takes place in Père Lachaise, and his father carries off Jacques's ashes in a black urn. This time Brard takes Dimitri back to the Mount with him.

"There's nothing I want to do in Paris," Dimitri says. "I want to go back to the village where I feel at home."

He plans to spend the weekend by himself, wallowing in melancholy.

"Come to Marseille with me," Florence says. "I'll be with some friends. We could go swimming."

But Dimitri refuses and walks away toward Brard's big car parked along Ménilmontant Boulevard. The face Sebastian is making shows what he thinks as he watches the two men leave, but he doesn't say anything. Johanna is afraid Dimitri will tell the administrator that she intends to take the crypt apart stone by stone, but she puts that worry aside. Patrick is unusually friendly as he says good-bye to go home to Montmartre, where his wife and two children expect him. Sebastian takes the train to Cergy, where his parents live. And Johanna takes a taxi to the Left Bank.

Sitting outside in the sun in a café on Saint Sulpice Square, she tells Isabelle about the funeral. Her friend shows compassion and asks if she's seen Simon again. Johanna says that she's forgotten him completely and that she's planning to spend three days with François. An hour later,

392 | Frédéric Lenoir and Violette Cabesos

when they part, they know that things are different. For the first time since junior high days, even though they have gone their own individual ways, there's now something separating them, something they can't quite put their fingers on. Johanna thinks that Isabelle is materialistic and superficial, too unimaginative. She was bored sitting with her. Not knowing anything about Johanna's recent discoveries, Isabelle thinks that Johanna is wild, and at the same time cold and distant, especially when it comes to normal human love relationships.

Johanna goes back to her apartment on Henri-Barbusse to wait for François. The apartment doesn't seem welcoming. She suddenly recalls that she's living in an apartment on a street named after a famous World War I soldier, a man trapped in the trenches, a man who survived the ordeal of living in the ground while waiting for death to free him from his suffering and let him reach heaven. Two hours later, she's still thinking about Barbusse when François rings the doorbell.

He's able to get her mind off these morbid thoughts by taking her to a magnificent castle in Puisaye, the northern part of Burgundy, in the town of Prunoy, far from Cluny. It's not a medieval structure. The room is decorated in art deco style, in the evening an orchestra plays baroque music, the owner is delightful, and there's not a single Romanesque church for miles around. In short, a complete change of scenery, and Johanna is grateful to François for coming up with the idea. As she begins to relax, she closes the door on her personal crypt. They take long walks in the gardens along the lake, they eat well, they drink some excellent wine, they avoid any references to Mont-Saint-Michel, and they make love. Johanna takes comfort in the familiar smells—his skin, his sweat. But a strange phenomenon begins to take place. She finds herself imagining Simon in the place of François, and the memory of her lovemaking with the antique dealer almost supersedes her interest in François's embraces. The first night she gets angry with herself and tries to force herself to enjoy the reality of the moment. But her body stiffens in rebellion. Finally she gives in and lets her mind revel in her memories. Only then can her mind and body accept her lover's kisses in total harmony.

At noon on Sunday she has to leave the chateau with its dreamy calm and go back to her underground battles. On the drive back to Paris, she sighs as she thinks about the section of Aubert's wall they've completely dismantled and behind which they've found nothing. Now she'll have to choose between drilling into some other wall or into the stone floor.

François wants to take her back to the Mount. At first she's upset.

"It's just so I can spend a little more time with you," he says gently, "and help make things easier. Don't worry, I'll drop you off in the parking lot by the causeway. I'm not keen on meeting Brard in the streets."

She smiles and accepts. He's a considerate man and communicates a sense of security. Since the weather has been so nice, François is nicely tanned, and some more freckles have appeared on Johanna's nose. The traffic is bad on the way to Paris, but once they're on the road to Normandy, driving is easier. When they get to the mountain, she gives François a long hug. He says he's glad to have found her again. She's touched, but knows she has to let him go. She feels sad, as if she's said good-bye for the last time. Every separation leaves her feeling morose, sometimes for just a few minutes, sometimes for her entire life. She looks at her watch. Barely five P.M. She breathes a sigh of relief, because the others surely haven't come back yet and she'll still be able to enjoy a few moments of peace before having to wage war once more against the stones in the crypt. Dimitri will probably be there, wandering around in sadness, but she won't let that bother her. On the contrary, his melancholic soul is touching. She decides to have a talk with him, to help him talk through his sadness. Yes, she needs to give him some support. He's a good man, and so far she hasn't tried to support him at all.

The weather is still lovely. Johanna fights her way against the waves of humanity walking back down to the cafés and parking lot. There are kids bawling, and a big man bumps into her, his huge stomach protruding as if he were pregnant. Her travel bag catches on someone else. Finally she reaches the cemetery, and, just above it, the gray-granite house with white shutters welcomes her.

She unlocks the door and calls out for Dimitri. There's no answer. If he's gone out, he must be feeling better. She walks into her room, throws her bag on her bed, opens the window, stretches, and decides to have a bath and drink some tea while she waits for Dimitri. She puts some Argentinian tangos on the CD player on her desk and goes back down to heat some water in the kitchen. She carries a tray back up with a teapot, a cup, and some butter cookies; she sets it on her table. She opens the door to her private bathroom, and then she freezes.

The bathtub is already full. There are some bubbles floating around a thin, naked body. In spite of the music by Astor Piazzola, Dimitri lies motionless, his beautiful, lifeless eyes staring. His skin has a bluish tint, and his thin arms hang down like dead branches. Beneath his arms, two dark puddles spread out in dark circles: blood from the slit veins in his wrists.

18

DIMITRI'S FUNERAL IS EVEN SADDER THAN JACQUES'S, AS HIS young death is clearly a case of suicide. Dimitri was a believer, and the Orthodox church in Lille is filled with people and with his mother's sobs. He was an only child. In spite of the autopsy, the examining doctor has restored his body well, except for a few additional scars and the telltale marks on his wrists. The whole team is in deep sorrow over Mitya's decision to kill himself. Johanna is stricken with remorse for having left him alone that weekend. Christian Brard, who had gone back to the Mount with Johanna after the other funeral, is also guilt-ridden. He was perhaps the last person to have seen Dimitri alive; he had talked with the young man about unimportant things and then stopped speaking—when another word might have changed everything. Dimitri had been taciturn, and the administrator had wanted to respect his mourning with silence. François tries to comfort Johanna. There's really nothing to be done in such cases, he says; Dimitri had made the decision to end things, and he would have done so no matter what.

Johanna knows that if fate has appointed her to save anyone, it's surely not Jacques or Dimitri, but still she is burdened by the brutal deaths that ended the lives of those two young men. Yes, death surrounds her, but she hopes it has struck at random. Aside from the police and Christian Brard, Johanna is the only person to have seen both corpses. In her nightmares they blend into one, with the expressionless face of Jacques on Dimitri's skinny body. She goes off to bed right after dinner, takes a sleeping pill from her nightstand, and swallows it as she closes her eyes, though her eyes are pulled toward the bathroom door. Before the police even put up their tape, in her mind she has already closed off the bathroom. Never could she go back in there, for how would she be able to take a bath in that tub without being prey to hellish visions?

On that fateful Sunday, paralyzed by the reality she couldn't handle but that she had to deal with, she had stayed a long time at the door. There was no way to hide from it; the reality was inescapable, white, cold, and still, just like Mitya himself, with that expression of surprise on his face. She didn't scream; she didn't cry. She felt fragile, like an ephemeral sand castle facing down a frightening, invincible rock fortress; like a delicate house built by a child on a dune waiting to be destroyed by guardians of reality, throwing stones.

Yet she didn't faint. Calmly, walking like a clock pendulum, she went downstairs to call the police. The rescue squad would be useless. She even remembered to alert Christian Brard. It was only when Patrick Fenoy got there two and a half hours later, with the house already invaded by policemen both in uniform and in civilian clothes, that she started to tremble, was unable to speak. She spent two days in bed in a state of shock; she was taken care of by a doctor and what was left of the team—Patrick, Sebastian, Florence, and Guillaume. Through her drug-induced dreams, Simon kept talking to her, begging her to wake up. When she did wake up, she would be in the middle of a cemetery with open tombs, the dead people obscenely stripping off their skins and displaying their worm-eaten bones.

"Don't you think we should get her to a psychiatrist?" Florence asks Patrick, who's sipping a cup of coffee in the living room. "That's what Inspector Marchand suggested."

"I know what she's made of," Patrick answers, "and it's medieval stones. Tomorrow morning we'll go back to work, and I'm certain that once she's in the crypt she'll be fine. No, it's not her I'm worried about."

"Who, then?" wonders Sebastian.

"Us!" Johanna's assistant exclaims.

"That's right. It doesn't seem important enough to talk about," Sebastian answers, "but with fewer people the work's going to be more difficult. And they won't send us any replacements. I know you're not fond of Kelenn, but it's good he's here to help a little. He's just told Johanna that he can come every afternoon."

"I don't give a damn about Guillame Kelenn," Patrick retorts sharply. "Let him come all day long if he wants, and even at night up there in her bed," he says, looking up toward Johanna's room. "I wasn't worried about him, either, or about the dig, when I said 'us' a second ago."

"So then what do you mean?" Florence cuts in.

"Don't you people think it's strange, an accidental death *and* a suicide in less than ten days?" Fenoy asks, getting to his feet.

"What are you trying to say?" Sebastian asks, paling.

"That we need to ask some questions," Patrick says, rolling a cigarette. "One: What was Jacques doing in the middle of the night by the tread-mill? And two: Why did Dimitri absolutely insist on staying here by himself?"

"Are you joking?" Florence stammers. "Do you mean that Jacques may not have fallen by accident and that Dimitri may not have committed suicide?"

"I don't know," he continues, lighting his cigarette. "I don't know what I think. But it seems to me that there are too many coincidences. This dig in Notre-Dame-sous-Terre is perturbing. Too many people were against it. I wonder if someone isn't trying to stop us."

"By killing us off one by one, like in *Ten Little Indians*?" Florence wonders. "What are you trying to do, Patrick, scare us off? Is that the new weapon you're using to fight the project? Because I have to point out that you yourself have been among those strongly opposed to digging in the crypt!"

"I know," he admits, blushing. "Fear makes me imagine all sorts of things. In any case, after the autopsy tomorrow, we'll know more."

The next morning, on May 19, Patrick and Johanna silently climb up to the abbey rooms where Brard has his office. Johanna's eyes are puffy and her features are drawn. She thinks of Simon. She nearly called him in Saint-Malo so he could comfort her. Her pride alone made her call François instead.

"I'd like to introduce you to Commissioner Henri Bontemps," the administrator says. "You already know Inspector Marchand. The commissioner is in charge of the department's criminal branch."

"Criminal?"

"Unfortunately, madame," says the pleasant-looking fifty-year-old policeman in a friendly voice, "the autopsy performed on Dimitri Portnoï showed that the veins were cut post mortem. He had been dead approximately fifteen minutes when his wrists were slit in that fashion. He drowned in bath water; his lungs were full. Someone held him under and then cut his wrists to make it look like a suicide."

"That's impossible!" Johanna exclaims, growing ashen. "A murder!"

"I'm afraid so; there is absolutely no doubt," the commissioner goes on. "I'm going to look again at the file on Jacques Lucas, for, like they say around here, 'if there's one, there might be two.' But don't be upset. The investigation is just beginning, and with your help, there's no reason to suppose we won't soon find the guilty person. I'll be questioning the entire team of archeologists, one at a time, at the station. I'll be expecting you tomorrow morning in Saint-Lô."

"I wonder, sir, if we couldn't come in the late afternoon? It takes an hour to drive to Saint-Lô, and we're already far behind schedule on the dig."

Astounded, Commissioner Bontemps looks strangely at Johanna, as he fails to realize that for her, after hearing such news, getting back to work on the dig is essential for her psychological survival.

"Six P.M. tomorrow, you," he says, pointing at Johanna, "you," he adds, looking at Patrick, "and the two others."

The two others are beside themselves when they hear the horrible message. They stare at Patrick, but he doesn't break the awkward silence. So he was right! But was the motive to stop their dig? Why? And, more importantly, who?

THE NEXT MORNING, on May 20, the four survivors—Johanna, Patrick, Sebastian, and Florence—are once again in the crypt. Johanna acts as if nothing has happened. Standing behind the Trinity altar, she rubs her hand over the natural rock behind Aubert's wall, now totally dismantled, its stones lying at her feet. Sighing, she comes back to the center of Notre-Dame-sous-Terre, beneath the arcades of the wall separating the twin naves and choirs.

She can't decide what the next step should be. Should she knock down the wall on the left, behind the altar of the Virgin; dismantle the walls lining the choirs on the south and north sides; or remove the square stones from the crypt floor and do some drilling there? She appears to be trying to find the answer in the sanctuary's warm, dark air. When she looks up at the two tribunes above the choirs' barrel vaults, it's almost as if she's praying.

"Right there," Johanna says, speaking like a water witch standing before an invisible spring and pointing to the wall behind the altar of the Virgin. "The passageway may stop between the two altars before continuing on toward the north. We've got to hurry. We've only three weeks left."

"You're wasting your time, and ours too!" Patrick answers. He has become the assertive Patrick of before. "Do you understand the situation, Johanna? We've just found out that one of our colleagues, maybe two, have been killed right here on the Mount, and all you can think about is which wall to knock down? Don't you think that's inappropriate?"

Calmly, Johanna takes off her glasses. As she walks over to her assistant, she's careful to be keep Sebastian and Florence in sight. She has expected this mutiny. It's a critical moment, and the fate of Brother Roman, the headless monk, is at stake. She mustn't think about her secret wish to get rid of her colleagues and work alone, she mustn't think about Moira, a torture by air, a torture by water, Jacques falling through the air, Dimitri drowning. She must forget Dom Larose, the notebook, all the corpses of the past. She must cling to a reality the archeologists can accept. She's the only one to suspect the truth. But is it really the truth? In any case, she can't admit her suspicions; she's got to be strong and fight to keep the project going.

"Listen," she says to her three team members. "Like you, I'm sad, and like you, I'm afraid. Don't forget that I'm the one who discovered Mitya and I saw Jacques. I can't get that out of my mind, and frankly, I'm frightened. But I'm trying to control my emotions. I'm sure that Jacques's death was an accident—the investigation came to that conclusion—and that poor Dimitri was killed. I don't know who did it or why, but we all know that Dimitri was having serious personal problems. We've paid our last respects to Dimitri and Jacques, we've even prayed for them, we can't stop thinking about them, and we'll do everything we can to help the police find out who did what to them. But I don't think we should give up the dig. That wouldn't make any sense. On the contrary, I tell myself that Jacques and Dimitri are still right here in this crypt with us. They were archeologists, and that's not an easy profession. They had won difficult battles. You and I know that you don't become an archeologist by chance! They loved stones, these stones, and they loved to dig. They would have been eager to find out what treasure is hidden here. Each had his theory. I'd like to keep working for them, to keep them in my mind. You can do whatever you think best."

Sebastian and Florence drop their heads after the sermon. For the moment, Patrick has failed to get the project stopped. He grabs a pickax and rushes angrily over to the wall behind the altar of the Virgin. Pounding soon echoes again through the closed crypt.

"AND YOU DON'T have any idea who might have had it in for Dimitri Portnoï?" Commissioner Bontemps asks again from behind his desk at the police office.

"I've already told you, not the slightest idea," Johanna responds with assurance. "He never talked about his private life; I've told you how we learned that his boyfriend had left him."

"Was he opposed to excavating in Notre-Dame-sous-Terre?"

"No. I . . . no. He wasn't against it, just worried about damaging the crypt. But that's a normal reaction. Many people feel the same way, including me. It's the abbey's oldest structure, the oldest on the Mount."

"Who was against allowing the archeological work in the crypt?"

"Against? Christian Brard, the administrator," she answers, taken off guard by the question.

"You're forgetting Patrick Fenoy, your own assistant," the commissioner says sharply. "He did everything he could to stop the dig."

"You surely don't suspect that he killed Dimitri?"

"I don't suspect him any more than Brard, who hasn't hidden his hostility to the project. He also volunteered information about your assistant's opposition, as well as about the unusual circumstances under which you received the authorization," he says, and he can see her flushing. "May I simply remind you to omit nothing from your deposition."

"Mitya's murder has nothing to do the with dig," she exclaims, irritation in her voice, "and I'm sure that Jacques's death was an accident."

"Perhaps, but perhaps not. It's my job to make a decision about that, and for the moment, absent proof in one direction or the other, I must follow every lead. But I, too, think Portnoï's death is a crime of passion. And, in fact, the Paris police have arrested his ex-boyfriend, for it's not clear he's unrelated to the case. Portnoï apparently was taking their separation badly and kept harassing him. His friend threatened him, according to witnesses, and the man has no alibi for the night your associate was killed. Tomorrow I'll be in Paris to interrogate the suspect myself."

Johanna can't help breathing a sigh of relief. So there's no link between his death and Notre-Dame-sous-Terre. Once again her doubts were based on her imagination. Simon was right. Simon. How she missed him! In spite of everything that was in the newspapers—although Simon would have needed no newspaper to know what was going on at Mont-Saint-Michel—he hadn't called her. If he had, she would have answered, because she would have loved to talk to him, to feel his skin next to hers, to cuddle up again in his arms! He hadn't tried in any way to make contact, and Johanna's self-respect kept her from trying to contact him. Yesterday, however, she had dialed the number of his shop, but when he answered, she hung up. François, on the other hand, has been calling her a couple of times a day. The Paris police had even interrogated him, in his office. Brard is pushing hard to have the dig stopped, and François is afraid for Johanna's safety. He almost accepted the administrator's arguments, but Johanna was able to counter them, on the grounds that the odious crime had nothing at all to do with their work. Fortunately, François doesn't know anything about Dom Larose's notebook! After all he did to get the dig under way, after all the risks involved, was he simply going to give up on her?

. . .

MAY 24. BEHIND the altar of the Virgin stands the Carolingian wall. Behind it, Aubert's wall. And behind Aubert's wall, no passageway, no head, no human bones.

Two days before, the police had methodically searched the team's house. What were they looking for? Nobody knows, but Mitya's suspected murderer, his lover, is still in prison on the Quai des Orfèvres. The natural granite is cold and damp, like a dungeon. This morning, Florence was convoked to the police office in Saint-Lô; she hasn't yet returned. Just Florence. Why? This afternoon, Guillaume is not around to help. The walls remain mute. Deaf to their entreaties! Should they start ripping up the floor? Roman, where art thou?

"You won't believe what's happened," shouts Florence, rushing excitedly into the crypt. "They've just arrested Mitya's killer!"

"Oh, there you are finally!" Johanna answers. "Thanks for the news, but it's not all that new."

"It's not what you think. Dimitri's lover was released yesterday, all charges against him dropped."

Johanna, Patrick, and Sebastian turn to look at Florence.

"It wasn't him," says Florence, feeling important. "You won't believe your ears; it's crazy! We've been lucky, let me tell you."

Johanna feels dizzy.

"Do you know what the cops were looking for in our house yesterday?" Florence asks.

All they can do is shake their heads. Florence shakes her head too, before answering. A strand of her blond hair hangs over her forehead.

"Hair, my friends! Our hair. Or at least mine."

"Tell us what you're talking about," Patrick orders impatiently.

"As always in these kinds of investigations, the police keep some details away from press and suspects alike, so they can use it against the criminal. They kept two things secret about Dimitri's death. The first is that one of the bathroom windows looked as it was closed from the inside, but in fact it had been pulled closed but not locked, so someone could have come in and left through the window. The second is that when they combed the bathroom, they found some hair that didn't belong to either Dimitri or Johanna. And in fact, after verification, it doesn't belong to any of us, even though it's much like mine."

"Blond?" Patrick concludes.

"Natural blond, almost red, slightly curly, and long. Not from a wig. Unfortunately, or perhaps fortunately, I've dyed mine. I'm not a true Viking!"

Johanna can feel her ears ringing.

"With evidence like that, the police lab can reconstitute someone's DNA," Patrick adds.

"Exactly!" Florence confirms. "And it's irrefutable proof that the person was at the scene of the crime, but it doesn't necessarily mean that person killed him. In short, since they were focused on Dimitri's brown-haired former companion, the police didn't go looking for this mysterious blonde woman until they knew Dimitri's boyfriend was innocent. And then they descended on all our hairbrushes."

"And did they find the woman?" Sebastian asks naïvely. "Who is she? There's no lack of blondes around here!"

Johanna leans up against the Altar of the Black Virgin. Her head is spinning. Florence puts her hands on her hips like a fishmonger gabbing to the crowd.

"They found the person with hair like that, and that person's DNA as well. Someone we all know, someone who has lovely reddish-blond hair, worn long and curly, and a mustache: Guillaume, Guillaume Kelenn!"

It's as if a bomb has exploded in the crypt.

"Has he admitted he killed him?" Johanna asks, bewildered.

"I don't know. The cops didn't say," Florence answers. "In any case, the bathroom was cleaned Saturday morning; the crime was committed Saturday night, and you found the body at five P.M. Sunday. Guillaume must have gotten in during that time. But why, if it wasn't to kill Mitya? Not to take a bath!"

"But why would he do that?" wonders Sebastian, who's gotten along well with Guillaume. "I can't believe it. He's a good man. He doesn't look like a killer, and he would have had no reason to kill Dimitri!"

"One more person who thinks killers have the word 'assassin' engraved on their foreheads," remarks Patrick. "Well, it doesn't surprise me that they could pin it on him. He was dying to take our place."

"And wait, that's not all," Florence adds. "The name Kelenn is not his real name! It's his mother's maiden name, and it sounds like a real Celtic name. His father's name is a typical Norman name, Bréhal. His name really should be Guillaume Bréhal."

Johanna rushes out of the crypt. She can hardly breathe. She runs down the Grand Degré staircase and takes the rampart walk to Simon's house. The shutters are closed. Everything is locked up tight, and there's no sign of life. Off in the distance she can see Tombelaine Island in the sun and wind.

"Bréhal . . . Bréhal," she repeats. "Fernand Bréhal, the man who translated Dom Larose's notebook for Father Placide! Surely Guillaume's father! By Saint Michael! Guillaume must be the one who stole the notebook from the Benedictines' library several years ago. He read the notebook. And he knows. He knows the headless monk's story! Maybe he, too, has seen the link with Brother Roman's manuscript. Guillaume knows the past, knows about the murders in the crypt, and today he's a copycat murderer! No, that's impossible. I've got to see him, I've absolutely got to see him."

MAY 27. SINCE Guillaume's arrest forty-eight hours ago, Johanna hasn't been able to see him. She hasn't been able to see Simon either. She tried to call him twice, but hung up both times as soon as he answered. And now journalists have picked up the story. She stays away from them and lets Brard handle the press. This morning, Guillaume was formally accused of killing Dimitri. Nothing about Jacques. The investigation has just gotten under way. The stones of Notre-Dame-sous-Terre have closed over a man who loved them as much as she did. Guillaume watched the archeologists dig during the day and killed them by night. Why? To bring back the notebook's past? To keep alive the curse that affects anyone desecrating Notre-Dame-sous-Terre? For what purpose? The crypt can defend itself! It slips between your fingers, for even when you've taken down some walls, there's nothing except stone that the hand of man has never worked, barbarous rock that history's magic has never touched. Just natural, sterile granite. Commissioner Bontemps has told her that she could see Guillaume today. But first he wants to talk with her.

SAINT-LÔ, IN the commissioner's office, 2:00 P.M. "He denies he killed your associate," Henri Bontemps explains, "and the story he tells is incredible. Sounds more like a novel! Sure you don't want some coffee?"

Bontemps is of average height and thin. He has light brown eyes, and his skin is tanned. He must be a sailor, like Simon. Bontemps never wears a hat and doesn't smoke a pipe. No ham sandwich, no mug of beer or glass of cognac with water on his table. Only a cup of coffee. A double dose. With artificial sweetener. Johanna looks out the window. The weather is beautiful. Too beautiful for a detective novel.

"No, thanks. What exactly does he say?"

"On the evening of the murder—the time of death was between twelve thirty and one A.M.—he was walking down below the abbey. As he walked on the ramparts behind your house, he says, he saw a dark shape—but he can't give any details—climb out a window, leap down to the parapet, and run off. He says he went over near the window and saw it was wide open. The light was on in the room, and he recognized your bathroom. From where he was standing, he couldn't see the bathtub, off to the side. He was worried, wondering if you had come back and if something might have happened to you. He says he rang the doorbell, but nobody came to the door. Since he didn't have a key, he says, he went back to the bathroom window, climbed over the little wall and into the room. And that's when he says he found Dimitri Portnoï's body, lying there dead in the bathtub. He says there were signs of a struggle—water all over the floor, bottles knocked over. A crime, and he had just spotted the killer. He says he was too shocked to do anything for a few minutes. But then, instead of calling us, he apparently tried to make the crime look like a suicide. He wiped up the water, put things back in their places, and sliced the poor man's veins with a razor he found on the stand. And then, after wiping away his own fingerprints, he claims, he climbed out the window, pulling down the curtain and then closing the window and running away like the killer fifteen minutes earlier."

"His version of the facts is plausible, except why would anyone try to disguise a murder as a suicide unless he wanted to protect the killer? Maybe Guillaume knows who the killer is?"

"That's exactly what I think. Either Guillaume Kelenn, or Bréhal—that's another problem—is himself the killer, or he knows who the killer is. And in either case, he's lying to us."

"How does he explain what he did?"

The commissioner, a little embarrassed, scratches his head.

"Well, that's where things get a little sticky. If you can shed any light on the subject, I'd appreciate it."

She watches as he clears his throat.

"The words he uses are all Greek to me, though I don't speak Greek," he begins. "From the outset he's been acting strangely. Usually, when suspects deny what they've done, they deny everything, facts and motives. But when they brought him in and we started interrogating him, Kelenn-Bréhal admitted right away the details I've just shared with you. But he has refused to say anything about why he did what he did."

"Of course, but he's been caught in the act. You've got proof, DNA from his hair!"

"We never told him that, so he had no idea. Right away, he told us his version of the facts, so we never needed to tell him about the DNA. He spoke as if he were telling a beautiful story, a fictional tale, and, for the twenty-four hours his interrogation lasted, he refused to offer any explanation for his actions. And then his attitude changed. When the net started closing around him, suddenly he realized that he was going to be charged with murder. He became nervous, agitated, worried, and it almost looked like he was hallucinating. We were afraid that something had happened to him, and the doctor gave him some tranquilizers. And then he finally cracked."

As it had back in the crypt, Johanna's head begins to spin. She tries not to show it.

"He wasn't making any sense, but he never changed his tune," Bontemps continues. "They're words of a crazy man, but I'll tell you what he said anyhow. There's a headless phantom, a Benedictine monk no less, who was supposedly punished by Michael the Archangel and has been haunting Notre-Dame-sous-Terre for years because he's looking for his head! So our friend Guillaume apparently got it into his own head to set the revenant free by reassembling his bones, which are hidden somewhere in the crypt. But—and this is even more interesting—some mysterious person who hates ghosts is apparently opposed to anyone giving the monk's head back to him, and that's the person he thinks snuffed out your two colleagues to bring the work in the crypt to an official halt. Guillaume apparently disguised the murder as a suicide so nobody could stop the dig in Notre-Dame-sous-Terre. Because if the project were closed down, there'd be no way of discovering the monk's bones. It all sounds like the ravings of a madman, as you can tell."

"Did he say where he got this information?" Johanna asks. Her throat tight, she hardly dares to breathe.

"He mentioned an old notebook he says he stole from the monastery from some monk named La Tulipe. But you can well imagine that we've already searched his house and found nothing. He must have told us that to confuse us and gain time. So, it's one of two things: Either he really believes what he's telling us and he needs to be in an asylum, or it's just a tricky maneuver to get himself declared unfit for trial and avoid going to prison. In either case, I know that I've got Dimitri Portnoï's killer, and maybe the person who killed Jacques Lucas, too, although he denies that and I can't yet prove that it was really a murder. There's still the problem of premeditation."

"Where is Guillaume now?" Johanna cuts in.

"Where he wanted to be, and the reason he made up such a crazy story: in the madhouse! No matter what I tried, I couldn't get him to change his story, so I sent him to be evaluated by the hospital psychiatrist. I know the psychiatrist. When he runs across someone who tries to tell him a story like that, he's never easily taken in. You've got to admit that Guillaume came up with a good one. A headless monk. He must be seriously ill. In short, he's temporarily being held in the psychiatric wing of the hospital in Saint-Lô, not far from here."

Bontemps pauses.

"I know you want to see him alone, but I'm not happy with that idea," he adds, throwing his empty coffee cup into the trashcan. "It's not normal practice and perhaps dangerous. But this business defies all stereotypes, and I think this fellow is not really crazy. Perhaps, like a lot of people, he just went into a panic in the police station. I figure that with you, he won't play games. I need a confession, understand? So let's give it a try, and I'm counting on you to get something coherent out of him. But be careful. Crazy or not, he's a killer, I'm sure of that, and he's violent and unpredictable. I'll go along with you and stay close by."

Saint-Lô, psychiatric hospital, 3:00 P.M., in the section where they keep dangerous inmates. It's a modern building in the middle of well-groomed grounds. Nobody is out walking. People dressed in white coats hurry by. Inside, patients dressed in royal blue pajamas are moving around, without a sound, past loud lemon-yellow doors. The blue shapes walk among their brothers belonging to the same order, and their order puts a strange gleam in their eyes that shows they've pulled back into their own nightmares. Led by a nurse's aide, Commissioner Bontemps and Johanna get into a steel elevator. Restrained by his chemical strait-jacket, Guillaume can't get out of bed. "Delirious psychotic." That's the diagnosis given by the psychiatrist the commissioner sent him to see. But Johanna isn't afraid. She knows that she could easily be in his place, and she doesn't let society's definition of madness frighten her. When they reach his door, the aide first looks in through the little window, then un-locks the door, moves to one side, and crosses his arms. Bontemps mo-tions to Johanna to go in, and he, too, waits just outside the door, where he can look in through the window. He won't be able to hear anything, but he can see everything. At the slightest sign, he'll come in. Johanna goes into the room.

It's a round room, padded from floor to ceiling. No window. An over-whelming medicinal smell. Slowly her eyes adjust to the semidarkness. She can see Guillaume on the bed, straps around his arms and ankles to keep him in a horizontal position. There's no pillow, so he can't smother. Like sunflower petals, his long blond hair frames his face. The hair that gave him away. He'd have been better off shaving himself bald, although with a shaved head and without a mustache he would no longer have looked like a Celtic warrior. His eyes are closed. He seems to be sleeping, or maybe just giving up on reality. There's no chair, and the bedside table is screwed to the floor like ship's furniture. Everything is battened down as if for a storm. Johanna sits down on the bed; she tries not to think about Bontemps looking in. Delicately, she touches one of Guillaume's manacled hands. His fingers move feebly.

"Guillaume! It's me, Johanna," she whispers.

He tries to emerge from his artificial fog.

"Dear Guillaume," she murmurs, leaning down. "What have they done to you? Guillaume, please wake up!"

He's smiling, and she begins to shed tears, not sure whether she's crying because Guillaume is strapped onto this hospital bed or because she herself could as easily be in the same place.

"Jo, Johanna, how nice," he mutters. "I, I didn't kill him. Nobody. I haven't killed anybody. He was already dead."

"I know, Guillaume. I know. I'm going to try to get you out of here, but you've got to tell me," she whispers. "How did you come up with that story you told the police about the headless monk?"

His mouth moves, and wrinkles appear on his forehead. He looks like an old man.

"I knew I shouldn't say anything," he confesses. "I had never told anyone about it, and I knew I shouldn't, but I couldn't help myself. I was so tired, and they wouldn't stop asking questions. I couldn't. . . ."

"Don't worry about that. They didn't understand; there's no way they could understand. But I can, because my soul belongs to the Mount and to Notre-Dame-sous-Terre, just as yours does. Don't forget who I am. I'm the one digging in Notre-Dame-sous-Terre. And Guillaume, I promise I'll keep digging for you, thanks to you, but I need your help."

He seems to relax. Injection chemistry, or spiritual alchemy.

"When I was little," he begins, "there were still Benedictines on the mountain. One of them, the only one who dressed the way they used to, like the black monks of days gone by, used to come every evening with an old notebook to see my father, and my father would translate the story in the notebook; it was written in English. My mother would always send me to my room. I would pretend to go to sleep, but as soon as she was gone, I'd slip back to listen at the living-room door. My mother would go to bed, but sometimes she would get up for a bowl of milk to drink.

Whenever I heard her steps in the hall, I would hide inside an old grand-father clock that no longer worked. As soon as Mother went back to her room, I'd go back to the door. My father would be reading out a story about Notre-Dame-sous-Terre, about an anonymous Benedictine monk without a head, a revenant that had gotten lost in time and was con-demned to wander between earth and heaven. It was extraordinary. The notebook explained what needed to be done to set the crypt's prisoner free, but it all seemed fabulously dangerous.

"A few years later, my father and mother divorced. My mother and I went to Montpellier. I'll spare you the details, but that was a difficult, painful time (the more so because my parents were already old), and I never did see Papa again. I was lost, rootless. That's when I took my mother's name, Kelenn, and started studying history. Although I was liv-ing far from the rock, I became passionately interested in its Celtic ori-gins, and mine, too, since my mother was from Brittany. When my father died, we finally came back to the Mount. I had never forgotten that headless monk, and he became an obsession. Just before the last Benedic-tine monks left the rock, I stole Aelred Croward's notebook, because I was its only rightful owner, the only living witness of those past events. I became a guide so I could go down into Notre-Dame-sous-Terre as often as I wanted. For years, I hoped the phantom would appear, speak to me, designate me as his savior, because I had been walking along with him for so many years that I knew him better than I did myself. But I never saw him. And alone, I could never set him free. Two years ago, my mother also died. I no longer had a mother or father, but I did still have Notre-Dame-sous-Terre and the headless monk who haunts my life and gives it purpose, even though I never see him! And then you came. When I first met you, it was in Notre-Dame-sous-Terre."

"Yes, I remember."

"Something intrigued me right away. I'm used to people wandering through the abbey with half-crazed eyes, or sensitive people who collapse in the crypt because of telluric forces, but with you, I sensed that there was something else, something linked specifically to that place. But what? When the dig was moved to Notre-Dame-sous-Terre, I became fright-ened. What if you knew something about the revenant? What if you had seen it and wanted to set it free instead of me? Back then, you weren't very friendly. I knew that you couldn't possibly know anything about the revenant, because I knew it belonged to me! I realized that the dig was an unexpected opportunity for me, just what I had been waiting for so that I could do what I owed the medieval ghost. When you let me join the dig, I knew that we were allies and not in competition, and that by combining our forces we could both reach our goals, our primordial goals, even though they were not identical."

Johanna forces herself to smile and puts her hand in his. How wrong she had been about Guillaume! He's like a brother, a symbolic brother who knows everything but to whom she can reveal nothing. Because Guillaume thinks he's the only one, the only one who knows those words, the only one who knows that childhood magic, that clock with frozen time, that sense now of absence. He has no room there, in that secret world, for Johanna. So she must remain out of sight; she must stay hidden from his green eyes with hazel specks, those eyes that are watching her and seem able to read her thoughts.

"The dig had to stay open, don't you see?" he continues nervously. "We must find him! At all costs! Like back in the old days, spilled blood could stop the dig. So I cut his motionless wrists. He did bleed, and this time spilled blood will help the monk."

"Guillaume, you saw the killer running away. Can you describe the person?"

"Like the notebook says, the shadows get their revenge on the living," he mutters, "because they covet the revenant's soul, a soul that's so rich from wandering a thousand years between two worlds! Darkness wants his soul, and darkness also comes to take the souls of those who want to steal the monk's soul by digging in the bowels of Notre-Dame-sous-Terre. Criminal darkness. But I was able to recognize the old monster of the abyss, the monster from the past. The crypt has become a dark force, and the crypt wants to keep its own. The crypt's dark shadow, condemned to the shadows, protecting the earth's womb, so that the monk may return to the sacred darkness and so that the living can no longer reach him. . . . "

"Guillaume, relax. The notebook you mentioned. That's proof, the only proof that what you're telling us is true. The police couldn't find it when they searched your house. Tell me where you've hidden it. I'll go get it, and the notebook will prove that you're innocent and you'll get out of here."

His face grows still. Then he wrinkles his brow. Things are getting dangerous, and he's not sure he trusts her.

"What do you think?" he mutters. "I'm not stupid enough to leave it at my house! And nobody will ever find it, not even you."

A heavy silence hangs over the room. Johanna doesn't know what to say to get him to see reason. But he has to understand that his notebook is the irrefutable link between imagination and reality, between the past and the present.

"Anyhow," he says calmly, "I think I must have been mistaken. You're just like all the others, and you haven't believed one word that I've said about the revenant. You managed to get me to speak, but all you really want is Dom Larose's notebook. It's true, just like with Brother Roman's manuscript, if you read the notebook, you'll believe me. You believe in paper. But it's not true that you want to get me out of here. Because then you'll know what's needed to liberate the headless monk and you'll try to set him free yourself. You're trying to steal him from me! I've finally understood why you came to the Mount! To steal my ghost!" he screams, trying to sit up even though his arms and ankles are strapped down. "You're trying to steal my childhood and all its secrets! Help! Help! She's trying to kill me!"

When he starts shouting, Bontemps and the aide rush into the room. Johanna is standing a few steps away from the bed, defenseless. Quickly, the commissioner grabs her arm and leads her out. A nurse and a doctor go in and give Guillaume a shot to calm him down. He's turned bright red, his eyes are bulging, and he's pulling at the straps with all his strength, all the while spitting insults. Johanna stands motionless in the hall as the white coats work in his room.

"Guillaume," she mutters to herself, "you share my dreams, you're my brother in imagination, and I'll never abandon you. I'll never abandon you."

Distraught, she lets Bontemps lead her out of the building. She thinks about Father Placide. She must go see him again, tell him about Guillaume and about the murder, ask his advice. The commissioner sits her down like a child's doll on a bench in the garden. Bending over her, he tells her to breathe deeply.

"How are you feeling?" he asks kindly. "Would you like me to get you something to drink?"

She shakes her head, and her color starts to come back.

"I'm sorry," he says. "I was right to be worried. With those kinds of people, you never know how they'll react. But it looked like things were going well at the beginning. He was telling you a great deal, it seemed to me. Anything new? Or just the same fable he fed us?"

"The same things he told you, but I don't think it's a fable," Johanna answers excitedly. "What I mean is that I don't think he's lying. He hasn't killed anyone, and he sincerely believes in that legend about the headless monk in the crypt he needs to set free. I know, at first the whole idea seems totally crazy, in our day, but not when you live on the Mount and are saturated, like me, with the rock's history and spend your days in the Middle Ages. Medieval man truly believed in revenants. The people who didn't believe in them were considered crazy!"

"I'm not calling into question your authority in medieval history, either of you," he answers, looking sharply at her. "But haven't you noticed that we no longer live in the Middle Ages?"

Johanna blushes.

"Listen," he says, in a kinder tone. "You tried, and you failed. Don't feel bad; that's proof that the fellow is really crazy, that's all. Thanks to you, now I'm sure of it. It's not his famous phantom that's trapped in time; he's the one trapped in the Middle Ages. But don't worry, the psychiatrists will bring him back to the twenty-first century. And finally he'll confess that he killed Dimitri Portnoï. While we wait, he'll stay locked up. And you can be thankful for that. Given his state, if he hadn't been arrested you can be sure that he'd still be killing, maybe people on your team, maybe you yourself. Yes, you're lucky we've caught the killer, mademoiselle, for if we hadn't, I'd have halted the dig, just as Brard requested."

·　·　·

ON THE ROAD back to Mont-Saint-Michel, Johanna can feel the weight of the centuries on her shoulders. The thousand years separating the eleventh and the twenty-first centuries are as heavy as time gone before it's even been lived.

"Guillaume," Johanna thinks. "What a disaster, what a mess! He has spoken, and his words have sentenced him to that prison with no sharp corners, with no opening to the sky, his body screwed down to a bed. Now his dungeon is in his head." How could she save him from himself? Without Aelred Croward's notebook there was not a chance. Unless they found the real killer. Air, and then water. Like Moira. "Like my first two dreams: a man hanging from the tower, another drowned in the bay. No. I can't keep thinking about that. That would be impossible. Just coincidental. It can't be more than a coincidence. I've got to look clearly at reality. Analyze. Keep things separate. Otherwise I'll succumb to my dreams, like Guillaume. But who? Why? A complete mystery. Hang on to reality and to the present moment. For the time being, Guillaume's sacrifice is working, for the dig is still open.

MAY 30, THE day after Ascension. Just seventeen days left on the dig, minus weekends. The earth lies beneath our feet. Guillaume had sensed that something lay hidden under the ground. So Johanna has not hesitated. She has had some of the paving stones removed from the twin naves. Beneath them, a few centimeters of earth, and then rock. More rock. Their drilling finds only rock, impenetrable stone. Nothing's moving forward. Neither on the dig nor in the criminal investigation. The investigation hasn't come up with anything new, except the description of Guillaume's condition: paranoid schizophrenia tending toward hallucination. He's still strapped down and heavily medicated. Through Guillaume, Johanna herself feels condemned. If she were to speak, if she were to tell them what she knows, she, too, would be diagnosed as crazy. So she doesn't say one word and keeps on fighting.

The four archeologists come back to the crypt after lunch. They normally have lunch outside on the western terrace when it's not filled with tourists and it's not too windy. Or sometimes, taking advantage of their having access to places that the public doesn't, they may sit on the benches outside the church choir, where they can look out over the fairy-tale-like view of the gargoyles, the flying buttresses, and the lace staircase a hundred meters above the shore. After they've eaten out under the sky, returning to the earth and the crypt always seems a little strange, as if they were descending into the very origins of humanity. Immediately, something incongruous catches Johanna's eye. Lying on the Trinity altar, against one of the drills, there's an ordinary white business-size rectangular envelope marked with a single letter—a stylized "J" written with red ink, like a manuscript illumination. Instinctively, she puts the letter in her pocket and hopes the others haven't noticed. While they're busy removing more stones from the floor, she slips off to the choir of the Virgin and opens the envelope in a corner. A sheet of paper, just as ordinary as the envelope. But the contents are not ordinary at all. She recognizes the tiny Carolingian hand, the same hand that Brother Roman had used to write the Cluny manuscript. The missive uses alternating colors, red and green, the two colors used in the scriptorium at Mont-Saint-Michel. The initial letter is illuminated like that of a medieval manuscript. However, the text is in modern French, unsigned, and you didn't need to be a specialist to decipher it:

> *Stop your sacrilegious work*
> *In Notre-Dame-sous-Terre*
> *Or death will claim you . . . all!*

Johanna hides the letter in her pants pocket. She hopes that nobody has seen it and that nobody else has also received a letter! They would be afraid and stop working.

"Dimitri's killer must have written the letter," she deduces. "The hand that formed these Romanesque letters so carefully is the same one that held Mitya's head underwater. How horrible! But how could the killer have gotten into Notre-Dame-sous-Terre to leave the letter? When we went to lunch, there was nothing on the altar, for I would have seen it. I remember clearly double-locking the crypt door on the way out and unlocking it myself when we got back. Unless he came through the walls or through a secret passage we haven't discovered, the killer has a key! But every guide and everyone who works for Historical Monuments has a key. Plus everyone on my team."

She turns toward Sebastian, Florence, and Patrick. "Fenoy! He was gone for about fifteen minutes; he said he wanted to buy some orange juice! Fenoy . . . is that sneaky traitor also a criminal? I need to ask the administration for a padlock for which I alone would have a key. Yes, that's what I need to do first. And after that, we'll see."

She hurries through the big wooden door and bumps into Christian Brard coming in.

"Oh, I was just looking for you," he says. "Come to my office. This is serious."

The administrator had received the same letter that morning. An original, not a photocopy. But he had no reason to try to hide it! So he showed it to Commissioner Bontemps. Like Roman's manuscript, it is now being analyzed. By graphologists and police experts. Not by codicologists. It may be a fake medieval manuscript, but it's a real, threatening letter. Roman's testament allowed the work to start; this scrap of paper could put a halt to everything! Johanna is crushed. Talking to Brard, she tries to minimize what's happened, but he's taking it very seriously. Of course, he's always been against the dig. So he must be delighted! But he seems more worried than satisfied.

"You understand, I can't risk another tragedy," he says. "I could do without the publicity the press has already given us. They all want to see the opening near the treadmill, so we had to close it off. As you can imagine, a murder in this abbey, or maybe even two, stirs up all their fantasies. And it wouldn't take much for people to get really worked up. If the journalists hear about this anonymous letter . . . Kelenn is under guard, so maybe it's just a joke, but maybe not! I'm responsible for all of you, and I can't take any risks. All your lives are in danger."

"For you, the only thing at risk is your job," says Johanna bitterly. "As for Guillaume Kelenn, this letter proves that he's innocent."

"First of all, you can't be sure of that. He might have written it before he was arrested and had an accomplice send it to us. Secondly, whether you believe me or not, I like my job," he answers, offended by her words.

"I don't need to tell you this, but I've alerted Historical Monuments and the Ministry, and I've officially requested that your project in the crypt be halted."

SAINT-LÔ, POLICE headquarters, the commissioner's office. June 2, 11 o'clock.

"Our lab has determined one thing," the policeman tells Johanna. "The letter was written by a left-hander. Guillaume Kelenn is right-handed. But that doesn't mean he didn't have some help. Someone near him, physically and psychologically, who loves the Middle Ages and hates to see him locked up. Someone who thought the letter could prove him innocent, someone who knew about Roman's manuscript and the abbey, someone with a key who could easily have put the letters in the administrator's office and the crypt."

"You suspect me, but you're forgetting that that someone must also be opposed to the dig!" she answers angrily.

"Relax, mademoiselle. I admit that you did come to mind at first, but the graphology test you took shows that you're right-handed, and not the slightest bit ambidextrous."

"That's ridiculous!" she shouts. "I would have had to be not only ambidextrous, but also ubiquitous. I was not at the Mount the night Dimitri was killed; you've already ascertained that. And the only thing I'm interested in is our excavation in the crypt. I would have been sabotaging my own work!"

"We have to follow every possible lead. Humans are complex beings, even when they're perfectly sane. You might have wanted to get rid of your colleagues, frighten them off. And the person who wrote the letter is not necessarily Portnoï's killer. We've already got him, at least I believe we do. But since we haven't identified this mysterious left-hander, my job is to protect your team and you while 'we clear up this business,' as they say in detective novels."

"You don't plan on giving us bodyguards, do you?" she asks with great concern.

"Oh, no, relax. We don't have enough men for that. No, there's a better solution, not so expensive, a solution that depends upon your administrator. As soon as you walk out of here, I'm going to call the person who went to Burgundy that weekend with you and got permission for you to dig in the crypt. I'm going to ask him to stop the dig. If I explain that your life is in danger, I'm sure he'll do everything necessary to grant my wish!"

June 2. Noon. "It's all over," she thinks. "I don't feel like crying. But I'd sure like to hit someone. That dirty cop. Brard. Fenoy. François. I've got to call François. Right away. Here in the parking lot. Oh, what's the use? It's all over. Useless to prostitute myself once more. The battle is over. They'll close down Notre-Dame-sous-Terre. And close me down, too. How incompetent. I've failed, Guillaume has failed, and Father Placide failed long ago. And all because some lefty wrote a letter! I could die laughing. I could die. . . . "

She looks up at the people walking past her in the street.

"These poor innocent people. They naïvely go on living their mournful existence, walking around without ever wondering what their purpose is."

A woman about her own age is pushing a baby in a stroller; Johanna couldn't say whether the baby is cute or ugly. A bent-over old lady hobbles by with her cane and a shopping bag.

"Osteoporosis," Johanna thinks, "a dead skeleton in a living body. The poor thing, she could break at any moment."

A bald man, about sixty, comes rushing by in the other direction. He's holding his cell phone to his ear, and he's clearly not paying any attention to what he's doing. He almost knocks over the old woman in his hurry. Johanna watches the lout run by. Suddenly she stops, and her mouth opens in surprise. She stands there for a moment, then jumps into her car and speeds off. A bald man, a bald man who has all the keys to the abbey! A man who knows about medieval hands, a lefty who has always loved restored stones as much as he's hated excavations: Brard, Christian Brard!

19

Brard never did get over opening the dig in Notre-Dame-sous-Terre," Johanna thinks. "He did all he could on the legal front in vain. It was a bitter defeat. Brard doesn't like women, except Notre-Dame-sous-Terre; in his mind, we archeologists have been eviscerating, sullying, and corrupting Our Lady. Now all the stones are lying there on the ground, and Froidevaux's work is being damaged, all for a dream that means nothing to Brard. What matters to him is that he wasn't able to protect and preserve the crypt. He failed. Brard certainly didn't kill Jacques, but that accidental death gave him the diabolical idea of combating those who were desecrating the crypt by frightening them so much that they'd stop the dig. Something must have happened in the car with Dimitri on the way back from the funeral. Dimitri must have told him that we had started taking apart what was left of Aubert's wall, behind the Trinity altar. Dimitri and I had quarreled over the idea. He didn't agree with my idea to remove the crypt walls. If he told that to Brard, that must be what sparked his hatred, and the fact that Mitya was staying by himself all weekend gave him the opportunity to put his dark plan into action. Or maybe there was some other reason. Maybe Brard was attracted to Mitya's delicate beauty and Mitya rejected his advances. The administrator is proud, and he must have realized that he could get revenge and at the same time stop the work in the crypt.

"Whatever the case, what happened next is clear. Brard spied on Dimitri. Brard lives alone, not far away, so it was easy. Mitya was very depressed and probably couldn't sleep. He knew I wouldn't mind if he used my bathtub while I was gone. Nothing like a bath to help you relax and fall asleep. He opened the bathroom window so the warm night air could come in. But what came in was the killer. Poor Mitya wasn't strong enough to defend himself against such a big man, athletic and powerful in spite of his age. A sixty-year-old man with a shaved head, so he left no strands of hair. The next day, Brard must have been surprised by Dimitri's 'suicide.' He hadn't foreseen Guillaume intervening! If people believed it was a suicide, his plan had failed and the dig would continue. He would have killed an innocent young man for nothing. So then he must have been in a rage, as well as feeling considerable remorse. When they arrested Guillaume and then locked him up, his remorse increased; Brard has always liked Guillaume.

"Brard loves and collects old manuscripts. And he read the Cluny manuscript. Nothing easier than to imitate the Romanesque hand and the medieval illuminations. Using red and green, the colors of Mont-Saint-Michel, of course. He meant to attack me, the person truly responsible for the carnage. He's left-handed and has a key to Notre-Dame-sous-Terre. He knows when we take our breaks, and he can go anywhere in the abbey. He's sure that I won't show anyone the threatening letter, so he also puts one in his own office, one that he can show to the police. He knows that terror will reign on the rock. And the police might doubt that Guillaume is guilty, but they'll never suspect a high official like him. He won't need to kill again, because the commissioner will do the job for him. He'll stop the dig, and thus he believes that this time François or I won't be able to do anything about it. Well done. Well done, Brard.

"But you're not fooling me. I know it won't help to go to the police just now, because Bontemps would laugh in my face. I won't come to the Mount to confront you, because it's still just a theory. But now I've learned my lesson. To bring you down from your abbot-like position, I need some proof, something concrete and real. The most important thing now is to protect ourselves from you and to gain a little time so that I can give Roman one last chance."

The two doors of Notre-Dame-sous-Terre stand along the Romanesque staircase, the gallery that leads upward. The ritual medieval trajectory required that seven doors be opened, one after the other, before the faithful entered the church, the Archangel's dwelling place, the seventh heaven. So pilgrims came into the crypt through one of the monumental doors, prayed in the penumbra, and left through the second door before reaching the building's summit, the abbey church. One of those doors, which were used during the initiatory ascension, has been blocked off, closed forever with a locked gate. The other, however, still allows access to the crypt, and that's the door that Johanna must protect. She stops in a hardware store to buy a heavy chain and an enormous padlock. She'll put the chain and padlock on the only practicable door to the crypt, and she herself will keep the key with her so nobody except her and her team will be able to get in. With the first part of the plan in place, she turns her attention to another point, a major one: convincing François not to give up on her. As soon as she's out of the hardware store, she picks up her cell phone. She clears her throat, breathes deeply, and finds his number on the screen.

"Hello, Johanna. I was just going to call you," he says before she can say a word. "I've just talked to Commissioner Bontemps, and I also had a long conversation with Brard."

"Yes, I know. I can explain everything."

"You won't explain anything at all," he says sharply, interrupting her. "I know all that I need to know and I've come to a decision. This time the situation is too serious. I'm sorry for you, Johanna, but it's over. I'm officially stopping the dig."

"Wait, François. Don't do that!"

"I'm assistant director in the archeology branch, Johanna. That means I'm responsible," he says, raising his voice. "If I don't do anything, that is, if I let you continue after Brard and Bontemps have warned me about the danger you're facing, your blood will be on my hands if something happens to you. You can't, nobody can, ask me to take that risk with full knowledge of what might happen. So I'm closing down the dig, out of regard for you and my archeologists, but also for my own career."

He has used the fateful word "career." Johanna knows what that means: "No more sympathy, no more intimacies. Just work; you are my subordinate and have to obey me." It's one P.M. on June 2. François announces that tomorrow afternoon, on June 3, he'll be sending to the

Mount a team of specialists that he's quickly gathered together to restore the crypt as it was, according to the specifications provided by the chief architect at Historical Monuments and by the administrator. Johanna realizes that it's useless to tell François about her suspicions concerning Brard. She simply absorbs the blow. First they destroy, then they rebuild. Bontemps has even promised that the team will have police protection for the entire job, something he never suggested for her and her archeologists. François orders her to stop the dig immediately. She answers that first she has to let the others know, that they have to gather their equipment and clean up the area, so she asks for a little time. If only the new team could show up no earlier than tomorrow evening, or even the next day, to leave her a little time. . . . He won't hear of it. He says curtly: "This evening." So this very evening the archeologists have to leave Notre-Dame-sous-Terre and wait for the new team to appear, along with François himself. He's categorical, peremptory, incisive. She'd like to stick a knife into him. But she has to accept. All right, she'll quit.

2:30 P.M. JOHANNA is driving around aimlessly. She can't force herself to go back to the Mount. So she takes one of the country roads through the polders along the shore. They lie like a huge flat desert, a vast expanse of mournful lands stolen away from the sea in the nineteenth century, a flat colorless immensity that contributes to the silting up around the Mount. For those farmers who reclaimed the bay's fertile sea-sand, these productive fields are evidence of man's victory over hostile nature. For Johanna and people like her, the land bespeaks a desolation that deprives the holy mountain of its true nature, an isolated island in the sea. The road runs straight. Here and there she can see dark, square farm buildings planted in the gray countryside. Johanna keeps driving, without meeting a single human being. It's easy to get lost in the polders, but she can see the Mount, her reference point, on her right, though most of it's hidden behind a dark panorama of forest. She has to go all the way to the end of the road to see it fully, so she accelerates. The road ends at an embankment covered with salt grasses. Beyond lies the kingdom of untamed water—sand, the bay, the tides. A grassy path runs parallel to the embankment. Mont-Saint-Michel stands about a kilometer away. From here you can see its western flank, where the sun dies and the shadows rise, where Notre-Dame-sous-Terre lies hidden by the stones of the abbey church. Johanna parks her car beside the embankment and starts walking along the path. For two hours she walks toward the mountain, comes back, sits down, stares at it, seeks answers, falls into despair. It's all over, she has lost, and she's as morose as the countryside around her, but she can't release her pain. She's bitter, overcome with fatigue, angry, but not yet ready to accept the verdict. She's not yet ready to say good-bye. They've stopped the dig, and she still hasn't achieved perfect harmony with the Mount. Suddenly it seems as if the rock is calling out to her. By four thirty, she's recovered her peace of mind. She climbs back into her car, leaves the polders, and speeds back toward the holy rock.

On the causeway she doesn't even see the tourist buses gathering at the foot of the mountain in a mechanical procession. Up above, on the bell tower, the narrow steeple reaches upward with the statue of the Archangel at its tip. The sculpture is known the world over. It stands one hundred sixty meters above the bay, and its five hundred kilograms of copper gleam like a sun. With its protective wings, it stands bellicose over mankind and crowns the mountain in the heavens. Johanna has eyes for it alone. It stands so high, so proud; it whispers to her that they must enjoy their final moments of love and mystery. The golden prince cuts through the air like a celestial metronome.

"Tick, tock, the moment of truth has come, my daughter. I'll see what kind of guts you have, I who shared my own entrails with you. Tick, tock. A woman's womb is fertile, but how tough is her heart? The Angel always keeps his promises. Will you do the same? Notre-Dame-sous-Terre is blessed among women, and the fruit of her womb remains hidden. Forget your head. Listen to the memory in your entrails. That's where your strength lies! The memory of your entrails. . . . "

5:00 P.M. Johanna can't go to Notre-Dame-sous-Terre. Not yet. The others must still be there gathering up the tools, and she wants to be alone. So she seeks the memory of Brother Roman at the place where the original choir of the abbey church stood. She probes the atmosphere for invisible traces of Roman and also for traces of herself, traces of the little girl who had been there twenty-six years earlier, when they first met. The church is closed and deserted. She wanders through the ambulatory. She sits down on the bench her mother had chosen on that August 15 when she was only seven. For the first time in her adult life, she offers up a prayer to Mary, just as her mother had, and just as her mother had made her do when she was a child.

"Hail, Mary, full of grace. . . . "

Chapel of the Holy Sacrament. 6:00 P.M. The sound of cloth rustling on the floor and a phantom's screeching jerk Johanna awake. Her back is aching from sleeping against the bench back. She turns toward the nave without her glasses on, and, magically, it looks as if a parade of dead people dressed in white is slipping through a blood-red haze. She puts her glasses back on and sighs when she sees the less-enchanted reality. A nun from the Community of Jerusalem is walking toward her. Dressed in a white robe, escorted by pigeons and gulls, the veiled figure approaches. The birds love the basilica when there aren't many people around. Red is the color of the stones near the door of the abbey church, the color the granite assumed when it was kissed by fire during one of the twelve times the church burned. Johanna smiles timidly. A gray dove lands at her feet.

"I recognized you," says Sister Adèle gently, seemingly unsurprised to see the archeologist sleeping in the church, "and I didn't want to wake you up. I was going to get people for the next service."

"Oh, I needed to wake up," she answers, looking at her watch. "I've got to go home."

"In a few minutes we'll be celebrating Vespers. Would you like to pray with us?"

"Yes, indeed, Sister. I believe I need your prayers. Mine are . . . " Johanna pauses. "Thanks for praying for me."

"I will always pray for you."

Beneath the transept's north arm lies Our Lady of the Thirty Candles, a small, low, warm crypt with a vaulted ceiling. Behind the altar, the oven vault calls attention to a window in the wall. The one small stained-glass window with its simple round arch emits a soft blue light, just as the architect carefully planned. The eye is immediately drawn to the window, which seems to place the final period on the series of repeating vaults. Johanna sits down on a bench. The crypt exalts a Romanesque atmosphere;

it fosters in one a humble piety as it leads one to that calm, simple light above the altar. The light doesn't force itself upon you like a discovery, but rather it reflects the clarity of a path that guides us through earthly life. Salvation is not visted upon us from the outside, it comes from within. Salvation becomes the purpose of one's entire life. There are perhaps ten monks and nuns in white robes, on their knees, the men on the one side, the women on the other, and they are beginning to chant their desire for purity. A few outside visitors are attending the service along with Johanna. She is reminded of the black monks who used to celebrate the first morning mass here when they'd lit the thirty candles, and then the final office in the evening, Compline, before night enveloped the rock. She thinks that perhaps Brother Roman himself must have prayed here, and she breathes deeply, trying to capture some scent of him. Incense wafts on the air and cradles her soothingly. Her eyes are drawn to the statue of the Virgin standing against the opposite wall. Mary has traces of pink and blue paint in the folds of her robe. She's wearing a crown, her right hand is broken off, and with her left hand she's protecting a child, a child whose head has been cut off.

Johanna knows that the statue was sculpted later than the Romanesque period and that the headless Jesus is the work of revolutionaries who decapitated Christ the King in every church. She's fully aware of all that, but she is still troubled by the little headless body and the mother who's holding it up like a trophy. She offers up a prayer to the headless monk as she stares at the mutilated Jesus. Brother Roman has the strength that comes from decades of human suffering, and the revenant has the humility that comes from centuries of divine punishment. May he give her some of his strength so that she might see a way out, a final window with bluish tints. May he guide her to the final light. Serenity. A feeling of quietude sweeps over her, as if she were enveloped in a cloud. The voices of the brothers and sisters soar through the heavens.

7:00 P.M. After the service, Johanna thanks Sister Adèle and starts back resolutely toward the team's house. The few moments of peace she's just experienced have helped her come to a decision. She's going to keep fighting. She must be pragmatic. Realistic and efficient. Like a warrior, she must set aside her conscience so it won't get in the way of action.

From now on, action is all that matters. She still has one last night to dig, though illegally, before François arrives. She has decided to lock herself inside the crypt alone; she'll ensure her safety by putting the chain and padlock on the inside so nobody can break them. No one will be able to dislodge her: Notre-Dame-sous-Terre is in a state of siege. The Mount held for a hundred and fifteen years during the Hundred Years' War. It held out for thirty years during the siege and never did fall into the hands of the English. Johanna can surely hold out for a few hours. She's doing it for herself, and especially for Roman.

"We've looked everywhere for you," says Sebastian. "Of course we know what's going on. At two thirty, Brard came to the crypt to announce that the dig was being closed, and he came with drums, flutes, and pipes! And you weren't even there. We sure looked like idiots."

"We've been worried about you," Florence adds more kindly. "Brard was jubilant. He chased us away from the dig as if we were lepers and told us never to go back. It was like he was trying to humiliate us, or at least get revenge. Is all the uproar due to that anonymous letter?" she asks, though she already knows the answer.

"Yes," Johanna says. "The intimidation plan has worked. They're afraid, not for us but for their power; it's clear. A natural human tendency. I'll be frank with you. Before the others get here, I'm planning to spend the few hours we have left back in the crypt. Tonight. By myself. I think I know who killed Mitya and wrote the letter, but I can't prove anything. So I won't reveal any names for now. But it wasn't Guillaume, I'm sure of that. I don't think the killer will try anything tonight, because he's already achieved his goal of stopping the dig. And if you don't tell, nobody will ever know. The only protection I have is right here," she says, holding up the chain and padlock, "but that'll be enough. As for the rest of you, since what I'm doing is illegal, you stay out of it. All I ask is that you not report me."

"Johanna, don't you realize the danger?" Florence asks. "You calmly announce that a killer is wandering around in the abbey but that you're going to slip back to the crypt tonight all by yourself and might run into him? You're crazy."

"I'll admit that I don't understand you at all, Johanna," Sebastian says calmly.

"Exactly!" Johanna shouts. "I'm not asking you to understand, just to keep quiet for a couple of hours! Listen," she continues more reasonably, "I'm trying to be honest with you and loyal, and what I'm saying is that you won't be going back to the crypt. I am going back, not to work, but to truly say good-bye to Notre-Dame-sous-Terre. With everyone here tomorrow I won't be able to, so it's either now or never. And if it's never, I'll always feel like I didn't finish what I set out to do. Something very personal links me closely to the place, something I can't fully explain. For me, the crypt is like a real person, and I have to say good-bye. It's as if I'm in mourning for someone I've loved passionately for many years. Someone I've always loved, always, and who suddenly is disappearing. It brings a terrible sadness, like that of a second death. I've got to go, and nothing will happen to me. You at least can understand me and let me do that, even if what I'm doing doesn't seem perfectly rational, because you too are in love with stones."

Her words seem to convince Sebastian and Florence, but Patrick has been listening disinterestedly, without saying a word. Suddenly he leaps from his chair.

"Nice sentimental speech," he says mockingly, pretending to clap. "It almost brought tears to my eyes! I'm surprised, because I'm not used to your being honest with us or loyal. This is the first time you've shared your real feelings. Usually you keep us away from your projects. Thanks for the confidence you've shown by letting us be your accomplices and asking us to condone your absurd illegal actions, which might cause us some real problems. Brard has a lot of influence and is quite worked up. If he finds out that we didn't obey his orders, he won't hesitate to make it impossible for us to find work. Thanks, it's very good of you to ask us ahead of time not to say a word about your inept conduct. It doesn't seem to be related to anything professional."

"I'm the one who started the dig, and I'll be the one to close it down," Johanna answers bitterly. "Alone. It's symbolic, that's all. Now, do what you want, since from the very beginning you've done nothing but try to cause problems for me. Go ahead, now you've got a great opportunity to hurt me, to do me in. Go tell Brard everything. He'll be able to reward you and I'll be out of the loop, even more than you think. Go on. But I'm going to bring closure to my relationship with the crypt."

Johanna walks toward the living-room door. "Fenoy will stop at nothing," she thinks. "As soon as I'm out the door, he'll hurry over to see Brard. Too bad. I'll take my chances."

"Sorry that everything has to end like this, and we haven't even found the treasure," says Sebastian to break the tension. "In the end, Dimitri was right. Brother Roman's manuscript was invented so that we could dream. The treasure isn't in the crypt, but in our heads."

"Yes," adds Patrick. "In our heads. And yet it's the face of Notre-Dame-sous-Terre that's been disfigured, and it's our fault! Tomorrow, those restoring the crypt will pull their hair out when they see what condition it's in."

Johanna is near the door. At those words, she turns back toward her assistant.

"It's nice of you to think about the stones, but you're forgetting that Jacques's face was crushed and Dimitri's was frozen!"

Patrick stalks toward her, threateningly.

"Not only am I not forgetting them, but I think you're the one who killed them!" he shouts at Johanna. "You, with your selfish, myopic insistence on digging in Notre-Dame-sous-Terre. You're the one who destroyed them!"

Furious, angry enough to kill, Johanna steps toward him. Sebastian steps between them before she reaches Patrick.

"You're both completely crazy!" he screams. "What's got into you? Go on, Johanna, go on back to the crypt. I promise we won't say anything, nor will he," he adds, looking over at Patrick. "But don't stay long. It could be dangerous."

"All right, Seb, thanks. You," she says, looking at her assistant, "I'll deal with you later. We will settle scores when I get back!"

"I'll be waiting," he says calmly.

8:35 P.M. JOHANNA slips through the late evening shadows and reaches the door of Notre-Dame-sous-Terre. Her travel bag is slung over her shoulder. She unlocks the crypt door, turns on the light, and steps inside. It looks like the sanctuary has undergone an earthquake. Some of the paving stones have been removed and are stacked up against the central arcade. The stones that are left and the contrasting spaces of bare ground make up a strange checkerboard. The walls around the two altars have been taken apart. The walls' stones have been numbered and stacked up, and the rock that has been covered by the walls gives the crypt the look and feel of a grotto: dark and stifling. Johanna takes the chain and lock out of her bag, slips the chain through a hasp on the inside of the door, and snaps the padlock shut. Brard won't be able to get in. Nor will Fenoy or anyone else. She walks over to the altar of the Virgin and dumps out the things in her bag: a wool sweater, a bottle of water, hot tea in a thermos, a knife, her cell phone (though the thick walls render it useless), sandwiches, cookies, her copy of Roman's manuscript, and a canister of tear gas. She looks apprehensively at the door. Will she really be safe? She's still afraid, so with the help of the crane she moves some of the rocks from Aubert's wall over to the door and builds a little rock wall.

9:30 P.M. Dusk fills the abbey church. At night, you can almost hear the stones whispering their horrible legends, and the shadows gather into the black robes of all the Benedictine monks who have tried to survive here—the rough, black homespun robes of the dead, whose tombs have been lost in time. At night, the abbey is filled with the memory of wars: mystical, political, and fratricidal combats, battles with both visible and invisible forces, with internal and external dragons both, our human dragons and nature's alike. Johanna is too caught up in her personal struggle to be afraid. On the contrary, now she feels in complete harmony with the basilica's soul, with the supernatural forces that haunt Notre-Dame-sous-Terre between Compline and Matins. They've given her the energy to build her bastion. The crypt is now finally ready for a siege, and Johanna is in her fortress. She is dripping with sweat when she finally stops to look at what she's accomplished—the entrance is almost completely hidden by the granite wall she's built. It's only roughly constructed, but it's certainly symbolic. The stones are no longer Aubert's stones, but Johanna's. She has founded her own sanctuary to protect her from outside enemies and isolate her in the entrails of Notre-Dame-

sous-Terre. Its entrails. It will take her some time to take the wall back
down with the crane when she's ready to leave, but that doesn't matter.
She's not even thinking now about going back out. All she wants to do is
go in. Go into the secret chambers of her dreams. Johanna nibbles at a
sandwich. It tastes like dust. Granite dust. What should she do now? Call
to Roman, ask him for a clue? Invoke the revenant? As always, the phantom stays hidden in the walls surrounding Notre-Dame-sous-Terre.

"You refuse to show yourself in reality!" Johanna says aloud. "Since I
believe you're real, why do you do that? You are real, so stop keeping out
of my sight! I won't be frightened. I know you're here somewhere. Why
don't you finally show yourself? I can't wait forever. I'm getting sick of all
your cabalistic riddles. Enough games. There's no more time; it's now or
never, and you know it. Help me now, or you'll never be set free! I'm your
only chance, your only chance. You have nobody but me."

Exhausted, Johanna falls to her knees and sobs in desperation.

"Why?" she repeats. "Why do you only appear in my mind? While I'm
sleeping, always while I'm sleeping. This is our last opportunity, Roman.
Tomorrow I'll have to leave; tonight is the last time I can see you. Help
me, I beg you. Saint Michael, please let him give me a sign, just one sign!
Put me to sleep if you want to, Roman. Help me fall into my dream world
so you can appear to me!"

Her eyes close, but her anguish doesn't give her any peace. Dreams are
like the sun: No more than we can order the sun to rise can we summon
up a dream; the sun is in control. Dreams. Johanna had a dream a short
time ago, when she fell asleep in the chapel of the abbey church. A strange
dream, curious like all dreams, with its own logic, as it transformed elements from unconscious memory into something surreal. In the dream,
Johanna was dressed in black like the revenant in Simon's legend. She
was assisting in a mass for the dead officiated by Father Placide in Notre-
Dame-sous-Terre on the altar of the Trinity, which was covered with
burning candles. The old man was raising up a square host, blue like the
light in an open window.

Johanna opens her eyes and stares at the pedestal. Like its twin, the
altar of the Virgin, it's the work of Froidevaux and dates from the 1960s.
The marble table looks very modern, and on the side a Latin phrase is en-

graved in gold letters. The supporting column is unbelievably ugly. It's built with rough-hewn stones, just like some house in the suburbs, and rests on a wider base of granite stones that look like cinder blocks. Froidevaux, though he had managed to restore the crypt's medieval soul, had built altars typical of twentieth-century architecture, and they clashed with their surroundings. It was not an uncommon practice. Since the former altars had been destroyed in the eighteenth century, when the Maurists closed off the crypt, no models remained. The original altars being lost, Froidevaux had to design new ones. Yes, but why had he built pedestals that clashed so with the spirit of Notre-Dame-sous-Terre? So that people would be repulsed by their contemporary style? Johanna doubts it. So that the pedestals could be easily identified as recent additions, and people would therefore know that they had nothing to do with the crypt's ancestral history, with its soul, its secrets?

Indeed, Johanna has never really paid attention to Froidevaux's horrors, she's simply used them as a place to lay her instruments. And yet she remembers Father Placide saying that in the past, the revenant had appeared on the steps above the altar of the Trinity. In her own dreams, too, the headless monk always appeared above the altar of the Trinity, and that's the very altar she looks condescendingly at today. Yes, the altar was in each of the dreams, including her dream a few hours before, in which it figured prominently! By the prince of the heavenly hosts, might it be possible? Might it be the sign she was hoping for? That would be crazy. Almost the entire crypt has been plowed like a field, and only the pedestals haven't been touched. She has no time to waste; she must check it out immediately!

She stands up, grabs a pickax, and begins swinging with all her strength at the altar's base in her attempt to break it free from the floor. It's hard work, but her strength grows as her dream images and the old monk's words about the altar march through her mind. It's hiding a secret, yes; she's sure it's hiding an important secret. Otherwise, it wouldn't always appear as it did in every dream! Froidevaux certainly saw something. He was a firm believer, but did he believe in ghosts? He spent almost three years of his life here in Notre-Dame-sous-Terre. He certainly found something. Or perhaps he refused to find anything. He may have been frightened and didn't want to understand the enigma. After a half hour, the base finally yields. Down on hands and knees, Johanna pulls away the broken pieces. She tries to move the altar with her bare hands, but of course she can't. She'll need Patrick, Sebastian, and Florence to help. No! She must manage alone! She must dig alone. That's what she wants to do, and her bleeding hands attest to it. The foundations of the pedestal are solid and extend deep into the ground. Johanna changes tactics. Back in medieval times, workers used pulleys and lifting machines that could hold stones in their steel jaws. And she does have a small crane. With the altar grabbed in the machine's teeth, she begins to crank. It's tricky work. Come on, little machine, come on! The crane lifts the altar three centimeters off the ground. The weight is enormous. The machine was designed for lifting granite blocks, not an altar with a marble top. Everything might collapse. But gently, carefully, Johanna manages to move the altar slowly and sets it down a few feet away.

She stops the crane and rushes over to where the altar had been. If she finds nothing but rock, she'll know that everything is over. But, instead, she finds a hole, a vertical shaft that seems to extend a long way down. It's plugged with big stones and rubble of all kinds, but there's no doubt that something is down there. Victory! She's found the secret chamber. The room wasn't hidden in the walls, but rather in the bowels of the earth. The entrails, just as the Angel had pointed out! Guillaume's intuition about a grotto was right.

"Thanks, Guillaume," she whispers to herself. "Thanks, Roman. Thanks, my warrior Archangel. Thanks, Froidevaux. Quick, let's get started. I've got to open the shaft. Give me a hand, my little crane!"

10:45 P.M. Johanna has nearly finished removing the stones that block the opening, and the stones tell interesting stories. Most of the granite blocks are from the Middle Ages; some are rough-hewn blocks, others chiseled and bearing the distinctive marks of the individual stonecutters. Johanna recognizes some of the marks, as those are also on the stones in the west terrace: the signatures of those who built the Romanesque nave are identical to the signatures on the stones Johanna has just pulled out of the opening in the earth. Work on the nave was begun by Almodius, and then, after his death in 1063, Ranulphe de Bayeux became abbot and finished the Romanesque abbey church. These stones date, then, from the time the abbey church's nave was built.

"So something must have happened then. Something happened to make them block the passageway. 1063, the year Almodius died. 1063, the year Roman wrote the manuscript, and maybe the same year that Roman died—perhaps he was decapitated right here and then, condemned by Saint Michael to wander between earth and heaven. 1063, the year the passage was closed off? Those three events are surely related! Roman's head and body must surely be at the other end of the shaft. Somebody, or probably several people, given the size and weight of the stones, either monks or construction workers, blocked the shaft after Roman was killed. They must surely have thrown him down the tunnel! But who? And why? Johanna," she says, "stop asking all those questions. Observe the stones and listen to them. They can tell you something. This one, for example, is from earlier than the eleventh century, but I can't date it accurately. No matter, soon I'll go down into the cavity, where I'll be able to find Roman's bones. When Froidevaux built the foundation for the altar, he must surely have seen the shaft, but then I'm sure he left it as it was, plugged up by all those stones. Why didn't he go any further? If he had, the headless monk would never have appeared in my dreams. Now it's my mission, my life's crowning achievement, my childhood dream coming true!"

She hasn't been able to remove the last stones. They lie too deep in the shaft and the crane can't reach them. About five meters down. The only solution is to push the stones down, and hope that they'll keep moving without blocking the other end. One final push before she can discover the treasure. Lying flat on her stomach by the gaping hole, Johanna uses a long metal rod to try to loosen the blocks caught in the rock's uterus.

"Keep pushing, Johanna, courage!" she repeats. "It's the hour of your birth, Johanna. The metronome has stopped. You must leave the warm womb of the earth you know and move toward the unknown! That's the law of life, Johanna. Push, even though you're frightened!

"Aaah!"

A cry of deliverance. The last stones finally gave way. Johanna pulls out the metal tool and looks anxiously down the shaft. Black. Everything is pitch black. She shines her flashlight down. The vertical shaft was clearly man-made. With her bright light she can see traces of steps, and it looks as if someone has tried to destroy them. Originally the passageway hadn't been so steep; it had a staircase. For some strange reason, someone had made the steps impracticable; Johanna's expert eye can see the marks left by whoever had destroyed them. She stands back up. The sudden movement makes her dizzy. She's going to have to go down into the hole. Tears well up in the mix of the joy she feels and the trouble she's borne to get this far. It's a fateful moment, but does she really want it all to come to an end? She can feel the embrace of a world that she's promised to make disappear, the final breath of her long expectations, the anguish that lies in the future, the approach of a nostalgic kiss announcing inevitable death. Roman . . . just then, on the other side of the protective wall she built, she hears someone pounding on the crypt door. Johanna hesitates, then walks over toward the door.

"Johanna! Are you there? Open up!" She recognizes Sebastian's voice.

"Jo! Answer me! Is everything okay?" Florence adds.

"I'm in here!" she says reassuringly. "Everything's fine."

"Come on, let us in."

"No. I'm not finished yet."

"Finished with what, Jo?" Florence calls out. "You've been in there for almost three hours without authorization. That's plenty of time to say good-bye to the crypt! Come on back to the house, or we'll have serious problems."

"Sorry, but I can't do that. Not right away. I need a little more time."

"You don't have any more time," Florence says. "Believe me, even if you're lying about what you're doing in the crypt, we don't give a damn. But now it's over, you've got to get out of there right away or you'll never dig anywhere else again!"

"What happened?" Johanna asks, sensing complications.

"It's my fault," Sebastian begins. "We all three had dinner with Fenoy, and I was keeping my eye on him so he wouldn't call Brard. And then the telephone rang. I turned to answer it, and he slipped out. I'm sorry, Johanna. But that was just five minutes ago, so we came up right away to warn you. If you come out right away, he won't find anyone when he gets here to the crypt with Brard."

"Don't worry," says Johanna. "It's no problem. I'm staying here, and they can't get in."

"No problem?" Sebastian says. "And they can't get in? Are you planning to keep the administrator out of the crypt, out of 'his' crypt? Aren't you considering the consequences for your career?"

The word "career" makes her burst out laughing.

"If only you knew how unimportant my career is now! I couldn't care less about it. Thanks for coming to warn me, but now please go away. Just leave. There's nothing to worry about."

Silence.

"Jo," Florence says suddenly. "What if you were right when you said the killer might still be here within these walls? Maybe you don't care about your professional future, but how about your future life?"

"Oh, that's enough," Johanna answers angrily. "Get out of here! I'm safe enough in Notre-Dame-sous-Terre. The danger is outside. In here there's nothing to fear, so get the hell out, I'm telling you. Get the hell out!"

"I don't know what you're up to in there," Sebastian says curtly, "but I can't let you get by with what you're doing. It's eleven o'clock," he adds, obviously looking at his watch. "If you're not back by one, we're going to knock the door down. Bye, Jo. See you soon."

Johanna makes a face.

"Just let them try to break the door down!" she thinks. "With the chain and the wall I built, good luck!"

She turns back to the dark hole. One o'clock. That gives her another two hours to explore the cavity and put Roman's head back on his body. Plenty of time. She drops a rope ladder down into the granite shaft and is surprised to discover that the floor is seven meters below her. She ties the ladder to the end of the crane, puts her jacket on, and picks up a flashlight. Now the moment of truth has come. Slowly, her heart pounding, she drops down into the secret shared by Moira and Roman.

20

THE SHAFT IS NARROW. JOHANNA'S JACKET SCRAPES AGAINST THE rock walls. She feels as if she's communing with granite while descending into an abyss. It's as if she were entering her own womb. Her fear has dissipated; it's been replaced by a feeling that she is going back in time with each step down, that she is returning to the back rows of history, back beyond the mirror distorted by her imagination. Her feet touch the pebble-strewn ground. She lets go of the ladder and grabs the flashlight glowing in her front pocket. She turns to face mystery. She shines her light inside its heart.

A grotto opens before her. A circular cave, like the one she saw on Mount Gargano. A round cavity about twenty meters in diameter, with a ceiling ranging from one to four meters above the floor. Johanna breathes tentatively, trying not to disturb the shadowy silence. She begins to examine the floor and the walls. There are traces of erosion, so the rock was probably hollowed out by an underground river that later disappeared. All man did was make the opening she'd just come through; the cave itself had been formed by nature. Johanna penetrates deeper into the dark den. She stops abruptly in astonishment when her light picks up two primitive altars in the middle of the room. Twin altars, made of rough-cut granite, similar to dolmens. The top of each altar is concave, presumably to gather the blood of sacrifices. In a niche cut into the wall she sees a small sculpture, the statue of a woman, robed and and with long hair, sitting on a horse.

"Epona!" Johanna guesses. "One of many Gallic representations of the mother goddess, priestess of fertility. Epona, protector of horses, precious symbols of the hunt, war, and death. Epona, the patron saint of warriors, of travelers, and of those souls traversing to the other world, the world of the dead. Incredible! A Celtic sanctuary, yes; it's surely an authentic Celtic sanctuary. But not one single document mentions this place. No one has ever talked about it. Nobody knows about it. I've just made an immensely important archeological discovery! By all the gods, I wonder when this pagan temple could possibly date from?"

Very delicately, in spite of her trembling hands, Johanna picks up the little statue of Epona.

Her familiarity with Celtic art is too limited for her to date the object with any precision, but it seems to predate the Middle Ages. Her knowledge of history does furnish some clues.

"Traditionally, the Celts didn't make images of their gods," she remembers. "The Romans are the ones who introduced anthropomorphic representations of gods. So this little statue must have been carved after the Roman invasion of wooded Gaul in the first century and before Christianization in the sixth century. Not very precise, a span of five centuries! The grotto is surely prehistoric and this sanctuary might well date from the grand Celtic era, the La Tène culture, about four hundred and fifty years before Christ. There's no way I can be sure. But what an amazing discovery! And important on a human level, too. I wonder how long it's been since a human being has been here."

Johanna is overwhelmed by what she's discovered. Guillaume suddenly enters her thoughts. She remembers what he told her when they first met in Notre-Dame-sous-Terre. He had spoken about the Celts and the god Ogma, whom they'd worshipped on the mountain.

"Ogma, god of war, eloquence, writing, and magic; and god of the dead. A psychopomp god leading souls of the dead to the other world, like Epona and Saint Michael. Guillaume didn't know that Ogma was worshipped *under* the mountain as well. I'm in the dwelling place of the pagan ancestor of the Christian Archangel. Ogma's dwelling is like a primitive version of Notre-Dame-sous-Terre. It's round like Aubert's oratory, and there are twin altars dedicated to a mother goddess, Epona, the pagan forebear of the Black Virgin enthroned above, this one consecrated by Ogma, the other by Saint Michael.

"The crypt above took the name Notre-Dame-sous-Terre. But it's really this grotto that deserves that name, because it's truly the oldest part of Mont-Saint-Michel, and in it lies the mountain's origin, its roots, the source, the mother who engendered everything, the womb."

Johanna places the little sculpture on one of the two altars. She steps back in surprise. She has just brushed against something. She shines the flashlight down and sees a skeleton by her feet. She lets out a cry at once of terror and joy. Roman! She shines the light around and sees there are three skeletons lying near the altars. She looks at them each in turn: they all still have their heads. None of them can be Roman. All three, however, have a golden cross around their necks and seem to have been wearing a white fabric. When she examines the crosses more closely, she sees that they are druidic crosses with four equal arms. The corpses must have been laid out over flowers, because pollen is still visible. Around them the ground is littered with pieces of pottery, jewelry, and curved weapons—offerings to the gods.

"Heavens! This must have been a place of worship that was turned into a funerary monument for these three dignitaries. They must have been important people—members of a warrior caste. That would explain why there's a statue of Epona. I wonder when they could have been put here."

Johanna leans down to look at one of the skeletons.

"We'd need to do a chemical analysis of these remains and use archeometry to date them," she thinks. "Paul would be astounded to see this! At first glance, the bones' color and the way they are lying suggest that they're centuries old. How many? It's so frustrating not to be able to tell. Oh, here near the third body is a granite stele with an inscription. I don't know what language it is, nor do I even recognize the alphabet. What can it mean? There are some ideograms, a series of vertical slashes, though some of the lines fall horizontal or at a slant. They look like runes. No, Johanna, they are ogams! Yes, they must be ogamic writing, invented by the god Ogma to be used exclusively by the druids! The sacred lan-

THE ANGEL'S PROMISE | 439

guage they used for divination and for funerary inscriptions. Yes, given the way they are drawn, it must be the language of the god of the dead. But I can't decipher Celtic hieroglyphs. Guillaume would have been able to. These three warriors must have been placed here after some tragic event. Something linked to Brother Roman? These bodies are surely older than that, and in the eleventh century nobody understood ogamic writing any more. Nobody but Moira.

"Yes, that was Moira's secret, the secret Roman was trying to protect at all cost! Of course, how brilliant. The young Celtic woman knew the grotto was here, she knew what lay inside this hidden womb, which was then still completely unknown to any Christian. In 1023, the initial plans for the abbey church called for razing the Carolingian chapel. But if they had razed the chapel, they would have discovered this secret place! Faithful to her people, Moira must have begged the master builder not to touch the old church built by the canons so as to protect the underground sanctuary. That's why Roman changed the plans drawn up by Pierre de Nevers before he left Mont-Saint-Michel and why he hid the real reasons for his proposed changes. If he had revealed the truth, the Benedictines would have destroyed this pagan temple. Roman was also a monk, and he disapproved of his beloved's ungodly beliefs, but Moira had just died and he was beside himself with pain. He organized the elaborate subterfuge he writes about in his manuscript in order to safeguard this Celtic cemetery and to honor Moira's memory. The church above became the crypt Notre-Dame-sous-Terre, as dark as the grotto it hid from sight. In 1063 ,something happened that made Roman come back, so this ossuary must have been in danger. Someone must have been about to discover it. Roman kept his promise to Moira, and the Celtic necropolis remained hidden from Christian eyes. But Roman died in the process. Who cut off his head? Where is his body?"

Johanna turns away from the skeletons and continues looking around the grotto. "You must dig in the earth to reach heaven." The earth, at Mont-Saint-Michel, is solid rock. Roman has to be here, in the heart of the mountain. Trapped in the center of the stone pyramid like an Egyptian mummy. A mummy in two pieces.

At some distance from the altars and the skeletons, her flashlight picks up other human remains, unlike those of the three honorees. This skeleton is seated, leaning back against the wall. There's no offering beside it. No funerary rites. Strips of black cloth hang on the bones like poor decorations. Johanna touches them. They break up into dust, but they were clearly part of a monk's black homespun robe. From a leather belt hang a nearly intact rosary, a small knife, and a wax tablet. A monk. A Benedictine monk. A few inches away lies a skull. His head.

Johanna is petrified. It must be him. She would love to speak to him, tell him everything he has meant to her all these years that he's been trapped within her and speaking to her soul. Soul . . . now Johanna must feed his soul, must accept and then complete their separation. She needs to open the blue window so he can escape and be reunited with Moira. Their souls then will be together forever. And Johanna will then be alone with Roman's body, the black-draped skeleton she has been looking for all her life. Will she be able to keep digging, and keep her heart alive with the thought of discovering other bones? No more quest, no more meaning, no more flesh! Will she be able to resign herself to an existence without mystery, a mission completely detached from enigmatic dreams? Johanna drops to her knees, lays the flashlight down, and touches the skull. Raising her hand to Roman's chest, she notices that some of his bones are broken—some ribs, his elbow, his wrist and legs. She looks at his neck but sees no sign of decapitation. It's clear that the neck has not been severed. As the body decomposed, the skull simply separated from the vertebrae leaning up against the wall and fell to the ground. It's not Roman after all. She's immensely disappointed, and then wonders: "If it's not him, who is it?"

She notices a stylus near the right hand. The man had written on the wax tablet. His last words. In Latin. It's a dead language, but Johanna knows Latin backward and forward. She puts the skull back down and shines her light on the script. The letters look awkward and uneven, as if they had been written by a child. Of course, they were written in total darkness by someone with broken bones. They are the last words of a dying man. Hardly able to contain her excitement, Johanna begins to read. To translate.

Brewen, brother of Moira, hanged Brother Anthelme from the bell tower, drowned Brother Romuald in the bay, burned Eudes de Fezensac, the master builder. Air, water, fire, Moira's torture forty years ago. Earth, where his sister died, he reserved it for me. He broke my legs and threw me into this pagan sanctuary and then closed up the only exit, under the Holy Trinity altar, along with some henchmen. I'll die as she did, under the earth. I'm not afraid of dying, but I do fear God's punishment. May the Archangel intercede for me, because I'm a murderer. Out of love, I killed the two people I loved most. I killed Moira, and I killed Brother Roman. Angel of the firmament, may their souls reign with you in heavenly peace. Prince of War, take pity on my soul that's lost in the midst of demons.

Father Abbot Almodius—
the evening of Ascension, in the year 1063

Johanna has forgotten all about Epona, Ogma, and the three Celtic skeletons. Even the grotto has faded away, as it's been replaced by images from another time, images from her three dreams that are now finally taking comprehensible shape through Almodius and his testament.

"Almodius! What kind of man was he?" she wonders. "A well-known, respected master of the scriptorium, an abbot who died in mysterious circumstances that aren't explained anywhere in the archives but are finally cleared up today. His passion for Moira must have been overwhelming if he led her to her death. But how about Roman? He says he loved him, but then why kill him? Jealous of Moira, surely. But she had been dead for forty years! Jealousy repressed for forty years, and surely some other feelings as well."

Johanna will probably never learn the truth, but she can't bring herself to hate this man who died in the grotto, either from lack of oxygen or from his wounds, more than nine centuries before. Although he delivered up Moira, effected the separation between Roman and the young Celtic woman, and killed Roman with his own hand, she can't hate him. On the contrary, she feels great compassion as she looks at the abbot's bones. How she would love to find out what had taken place between Roman and him. But after revealing so much, now, unfortunately, the skeleton is quiet. No, it still has something else to communicate. It is wearing neither the gold cross nor the typical abbot's ring. What has happened to them? And the big question, where is Roman?

"Roman," she thinks, "you are innocent of the murders I saw in my dreams. They happened in 1063; the testament engraved in the wax tablet proves it. You sent me a vision of those crimes, committed by Moira's brother, to explain why you disappeared. They weren't an admission of guilt as I have always thought. The headless monk is not an evil spirit. But where is he? Why did you want me to dig here?"

She explores the rest of the grotto without finding any more bones.

"What if I'm mistaken?" she wonders. "No, that's impossible. His body has to be here with the man who killed him. Almodius, what did you do with your victim?"

As if he were answering her, she spots a mound of pebbles several feet away from the abbot's bones. Scarcely able to breathe, she scrapes away the stones and finds a skull and a golden Christian cross on a chain.

BENEATH NOTRE-DAME-SOUS-TERRE. June 3, four minutes after midnight. Tears flow silently from Johanna's eyes. She's sure she's found him and reached the end of her journey. She's weeping over the mourning that lies in store for her. She doesn't dare reach out her hand to her beloved Roman. Almodius gave proper burial to his victim's skull, as best he could, under a pile of small stones. And he put his own baptismal cross with him.

"Almodius cut off his head, but he did love him," she concludes. "After preparing this unusual grave, he prayed for him. Almodius didn't try to escape, for that would have been in vain. Given his broken legs, he probably couldn't even stand up. He crawled over here so he could prop himself up against the wall. He wrote his testament and awaited death while imploring the angels."

Johanna rubs her hand over Roman's skull. Where can his body be? She doesn't see any sign of it. She begins looking once more, is examining each corner of the grotto, when suddenly she hears a strange sound behind her. It's coming from the open shaft. It sounds like wood striking rock. She grabs her flashlight and goes over to the shaft. The beam from her flashlight fills her with panic. The rope ladder is gone.

"Who's there?" she screams.

She breaks out into a cold sweat. Silence. Nobody answers, and yet there has to be someone there; someone had to pull the ladder up! Deep in the pit of her, she can sense that someone's above her in Notre-Dame-sous-Terre. The revenant? No, surely not. Some human being? Impossible: the door, the chain, and the lock! Impossible, and yet . . . she tries to get a grip on the rock. Too steep, there's nothing to get hold of, she can't possibly climb with her bare hands. She shines her light up. She can see a section of the crypt's vaulted ceiling.

"Hey, there's someone down here!" she shouts in terror. "I know you're there, whoever you are. Put the ladder back, I've got to come up."

A horrible, prolonged silence. Johanna yells more loudly still. She knows her life depends on it. She's got to get out of there! She feels the walls closing in on her. She begins to pant; she'll suffocate in the depths of the rock. A primal scream. Her hands clinging to the rock, her eyes staring up through the open shaft. A voice: She hears a voice, but it's not loud enough to cut through her screams. She doesn't hear the words, but she recognizes the sound, the timbre, the intonation. She stops screaming. Silence. A head appears in the opening above her, seven meters above her. A head with a halo of curly black hair, green eyes, and olive-colored skin.

"I'm sorry, Johanna," Simon says quietly. "But you'll never come back up. Never."

"You! It's you! What are you doing here? How did you get into the crypt?"

"Through the nave in the abbey church. Hidden by the benches, there are two trapdoors leading down to the crypt, down to the two doors on the stairs just above the twin altars. These two passages have always been there. Everyone thinks they've been sealed off, but I have the key to the gate beneath one of the trapdoors, the one that leads down to the Trinity altar. I've always had the key, and nobody has ever known. You could have built ten walls to block off the crypt door and still not kept me from getting into Notre-Dame-sous-Terre from above."

"Simon . . . but what do you mean by all this? I don't understand. Why did you need the key? And what are you doing up there?"

"Johanna, dear Johanna. I've got all the keys to the abbey, even those that men and time have forgotten, because I'm a sentinel! I'm the secret guardian of the grotto, and unfortunately you found it. I'm Celtic through my father, from a long, prestigious lineage. I'm the descendant of one of Brewen and Moira's cousins. Long before their time, when the Christians took the mountain, my ancestors sealed off this sanctuary to protect it from them. Moira's family belonged to those chosen by the spirit of this place, those born to protect it. Moira fulfilled her mission and paid for it with her life. Her brother avenged her, and he, too, kept infidels from discovering and destroying our past. Over the years, many others have picked up the torch, and many others will continue to pick it up."

Simon's voice echoes off the walls of the open shaft and Johanna can hear clearly its grave, solemn timbre. A church voice. A Biblical voice. Its speech sounds like a sermon. Simon. Her Simon, devoted to the ancient beliefs of a bygone race. He, the agnostic obsessed with reality; he, the destroyer of romanticism, of Johanna's fertile imagination, of Guillaume's neo-Celticism! Johanna is mute with stupor and fright. Never would she have guessed.

"I know what you're thinking," he says. "But I accepted the sacred charge from my father, and I'm not at odds with my realistic self. I'm preserving a real temple, real history, real tombs. The sanctuary exists, and so do I. There isn't any morbid nostalgia in all this. I'm living proof that Celts survive—I, the incarnation of a living past and consequently of the present and the future."

Johanna is in consternation, but at the same time she's enthralled by Simon's words.

"Roman knew that Moira was the sanctuary's guardian," she thinks. "Nearly a thousand years ago, she entrusted Roman with the same information Simon is giving me today. And then she died, a prisoner in a pit, while Roman, like Simon, now remained free in the open air but unable to free her. Tonight I'm the underground prisoner, completely at Simon's mercy. Simon was the link to Moira, and I didn't see it. I've got to make him speak, yes, he's got to speak. I need to understand everything, and only he can clear up all the mysteries."

"Simon, who are the three corpses who have caused so much blood to be shed?" she asks. "Were they warriors?"

"No, Johanna. Those three bodies are the flesh of history. Druids, the three olams, proof that the Celtic world was not a fable. I'm the repository of that history, and I'm willing to share it with you."

Silence, and she doesn't dare break it. Silence, and he savors it like victory.

"In the sixth century," he begins, "when the Christians, led by the Welsh monk Samson, evangelized the region by force, the Mount, then called Mont Tombe, was a place where we worshipped our gods and where lay our entrance to the world of the Sidhe, the other world of immortals. There was a large dolmen on the summit; but, beneath it, this underground grotto had been here for millennia. It was used by druids as a secret meeting place when they performed rites of passage to the other world under the authority of Ogma and Epona. In the year 550, the temple above was sacked and destroyed, and the three olams who were officiating, druids of the highest level, were taken prisoner. Like Moira, they refused to recant. All three were hanged in public, and their bodies were left exposed as an example to all eyes and the elements. But on the third night, as if by magic, their bodies were removed from the gallows. The next morning the ropes were still hanging there intact, showing no trace of being cut. The Christians looked everywhere for the bodies but couldn't find them. People said that the bodies of the three olams had been stolen by our gods and that the gods had taken them to Mont Tombe so they could reach the world of the Sidhe and become immortal heroes. We call the story 'The Legend of the Stolen Olams.'"

"So says the legend," Johanna answers, her eyes fixed on Simon.

"Today the legend of the stolen olams is forgotten because it was never written down, but it's true, or almost true. It wasn't the gods who made off with the bodies of the three olams, but rather their families, including Brewen and Moira's as well as mine. The bodies were carried off by the olams' sons, themselves druids like their fathers and their fathers' fathers had been since the beginning of the world, and like their own sons would not be after Christian evangelization.

"That event was the last in our history to occur in plain daylight; after that our history was written underground. To save their fathers' souls and to give birth to an eternal legend that could keep them alive, they took down the bodies without cutting the rope. They secretly carried the bodies to Mont Tombe, where they laid them in the secret grotto. After performing the funerary rites to give their souls peace and to allow them to reach the world of the Sidhe, they blocked the opening used to reach the cavern—the shaft where you are standing now—and camouflaged the entrance, for they'd promised never to reveal the existence of the underground tombs. No more fathers, no more trunks for the trees, only clandestine roots. A short time later, Christians wiped out those druids too, along with everyone belonging to the Celtic priestly caste. But the three families of the stolen olams kept the secret of the sanctuary and the mysterious funeral. And they passed it on, along with other druidic secrets, from one generation to the next.

"On Mont Tombe an oratory devoted to Saint Stephen was built, and another to Saint Symphorien, and some completely inoffensive hermits were living there. When Aubert arrived in 708 to build his sanctuary to Saint Michael, at the very spot where the dolmen had been, my ancestors were worried at first, but then were relieved when they saw that the canons were themselves descendants of the Celts. The canons were good Christians, but they never forgot their origins. They respected the old customs and lived among the rest of us. They knew the legend of the three olams, and they knew that Mont Tombe was the passageway for Celtic souls, and they accepted that the earth here was sacred for Celts as well as for Christians. They realized that it hid obscure powers and that they needed to be wary. With them appeared the legend about apparitions at night in the holy places, as well as the interdiction against visiting or worshiping here between Compline and Matins, the same interdiction still in force today. In the tenth century they built the Carolingian church to replace Saint Aubert's oratory, with the double choir and twin altars that had been commonly found in Celtic temples. With another wink to history, right above the hidden entrance to the shaft leading down to the grotto they erected the altar dedicated to the Holy Trinity—Father, Son, and Holy Spirit. The name was appropriate, and the altar protected the mouth of the secret passageway.

"When the Benedictines arrived in 966, everything was different. The Benedictine monks lived in heaven, among themselves, bodiless, animated only by the spirit, the Holy Spirit. They mistrusted the local people. They were like 'black druids,' and they were as learned as the olams, but they refused to accept Celtic legends. On the contrary, they aspired to destroy our history, for they were building their own legends. When they announced their plans to build the abbey church and when Moira learned that they were going to destroy the canons' church, she persuaded the master builder, your Brother Roman, not to dig in the earth, not to raze the building. Without violence, with the conviction of love, she accomplished the mission her father had entrusted to her before he died—protecting the three olams' holy sanctuary, by keeping the Christians from finding and destroying it. Later, other guardians kept the same pledge, but they needed to use a different weapon: terror."

"That explains everything. It was your ancestors who over the years killed anyone who dug in Notre-Dame-sous-Terre—the three monks and Dom Larose's prior in the eighteenth century, the knight during the Hundred Years' War in the fifteenth century, Brother Ambroise in the twelfth century, and many others! That means that you, Simon, belong to a family of killers. You are the one who killed Jacques and Dimitri!"

Simon doesn't answer for a moment. He looks down sternly at Johanna. From this distance, she can't see how his eyes are changing, but she can hear the change in his voice.

"I thought you'd understand, but you just don't get it if you think my family is made up of killers," he says harshly. "For fifteen centuries, fifteen hundred years, we've been the guarantors of our roots. We've refused to leave our past in the hands of historians, politicians, and archeologists. We're the agents of our liberty and our memory, without dogmatic ideology, without unrealizable utopias, without bloody revolution. Sometimes we have had to kill, but only to keep from being killed. If ever the Benedictines had discovered the grotto, they would have destroyed it because of their faith. And if people in the modern world had found it, they would have turned it into a museum because of their lack of faith! The sanctuary would have witnessed waves of tourists, just like the rest of the abbey, who would have deprived it of its soul and made it sterile for the people it belongs to. So, yes, I've preserved our soul from corruption by doing what was necessary to put a stop to the dig. And after me, another member of my family, someone I've trained, will continue our work and pass it along from generation to generation!"

He's a madman. And yet Johanna knows that's he's not completely mistaken. The grotto of the three olams would indeed be sullied by both religious people and atheists, for different reasons, if it were no longer secret. However, this man she has loved, whom deep down she probably still loves, this man who has caressed her so voluptuously, is also the man who killed Jacques and Dimitri. Suddenly she feels like throwing up. Such soft hands, his mouth, the smell of his skin . . . Jacques's bruised face, Dimitri's swollen body; Guillaume screaming and locked up in an asylum where Simon should be. Johanna barely has the time to bend over before she does throw up. And then she gathers herself back together. She must think clearly. Simon is dangerous; he's a killer, and he's crazy. She must keep calm. Keep him talking, make him keep on talking. Maybe she can understand what's motivating him. "Crazy people have their own way of looking at things," Bontemps had said. And then perhaps she can talk him into throwing the rope ladder back down to her.

"How did you manage? How did you kill Jacques and Dimitri?" she asks, already disgusted by what she might hear.

"I didn't want things to go that far, but you left me no choice. I tried everything to dissuade you from digging in the crypt, but my words had no effect on you. The only thing I managed to do, you'll remember, the evening you left me, was to lose control and try to strangle you. You were so obsessed with Roman's manuscript, the English notebook, and your stories about revenants. I had to bring you back to reality, by using force since persuasion didn't work. You no longer wanted to see me or listen to me, so I was desperate, backed into a corner. But I knew you'd understand the message if I did things right. Everybody thought I was in Saint-Malo, but I was watching you from the very beginning. I even had copies made of your house keys."

"I see. And you had this key, too. A real jailer. You calculated every-thing from the very beginning, even our affair. That was a nice touch," she says bitterly.

"No! Once again, you just don't get it," he answers sadly. "That's not true. At first I wanted us just to be friends. But when I saw you, then . . . however, that's not the question. In any case, I had lost you and was crazy with pain. Every night I dreamed about you. Every day as well. Sleeping or awake, I saw you everywhere, like a perpetual ghost, in every object, in every room. It was becoming intolerable, and I couldn't stand it any more. My suffering didn't bother you at all. All you could think about was your headless monk. And about digging in the crypt with that half-wit fake, Guillaume Kelenn. If I let you continue, you'd uncover my people's secret. That evening I was wandering through the streets in hopes of running into you and begging you to come back. I would have thrown myself at your feet, told you everything, even about the grotto. But then I saw Jacques Lucas coming out of a bar. He was dead drunk. I realized that the spirit of the Mount was sending me an important signal. Unlike what Moira did with Roman, I needed to stop trying to win you over with love. It was easy, quick, and clean. I greeted Jacques, pulled out my flask of whiskey, and suggested a drink, saying that I'd like him to show me your old dig because I was so interested in old stones, in skeletons, my profession, etc. We went up there. I gave him some more to drink, took back my flask. Then we had a conversation—about you, in fact—and he showed me the old dig in Saint Martin's Chapel. And then I showed him the stars near the treadmill. He leaned out; I barely had to give him a nudge. I'm sure he'd have fallen even if I hadn't pushed him! The others might think it was an accident, but I knew I couldn't fool you. Air. You'd think right away about your first dream, about the man hanging in the air, and about Moira's first ordeal. I thought you'd understand the warning, but you kept on digging."

Nausea again. No, this time don't give in, be strong. Easy, quick, and clean. How horrible! Poor Jacques. . . .

"And how about Dimitri? That must have been more complicated. And not quite so quick," she adds sarcastically.

"I had learned something from Jacques's murder. It was too much like an accident. Since you wouldn't listen, I needed a showy killing to frighten your team so much that they'd stop working. I had mistakenly singled you out, but I realized it was your team I needed to terrorize, just as Brewen had managed to frighten the monks! And I needed to use water, just as you guessed, so that you'd understand the secret meaning of my actions.

"Brard is one of my faithful clients, you know. He happened into my shop on May 8. He had just come back from the funeral, with Dimitri. He's the one who let slip the information that Dimitri was alone in the house. I could well imagine that you were far away and had gotten back together with your slimy family man. I was jealous, but never would I have attacked you. Especially since I saw the opportunity to strike an effective blow. I left the shop in the hands of my employee and came back to the Mount to watch Dimitri. I was waiting for the right moment, and on Saturday evening he provided it. I thought I'd drown him in the bay to remind you of Moira's torture and your second dream, but he wouldn't leave the house. When I saw him open the bathroom window, I saw my chance. What's more, you'd be the one to find him, and so this time you'd finally understand! I came in the front door. I had planned everything— hood, gloves, a jacket without buttons, soft-soled shoes, all of them black, of course. He was splashing around in the bathtub. He was surprised, not just to see me, but doubly so, because he had never seen me before (you had kept me well hidden). I wouldn't have thought such a skinny guy would fight so hard. Afterwards, I went out through the window so the police would think that's how I got in as well.

"I hadn't expected the other idiot to stick his nose in our business. That made me furious! Fortunately, thanks to his fumbling and the scientific expertise of our good national police, suicide was soon ruled out. Soon, too, the effect I had wanted to achieve happened. The survivors were frightened, and they threatened to close the dig."

"And to be sure you'd get what you wanted," Johanna adds, "you wrote a threatening letter, imitating Roman's hand. And you did manage to get the dig halted."

"Oh, no. I didn't write that letter!" he objects. "But I think I know who did."

"Christian Brard?"

"Yes," Simon admits. "The poor man was more frightened than your team was. When I came to show him the logbook from a German warship dating from the First World War, thinking he might want it for his collection, he looked scarcely human. He relaxed a little as I talked to him. He admitted he was totally disoriented by your friend Kelenn's arrest and by your stubborn insistence that the dig should go on at all costs. He feared for himself and for the crypt you were shamelessly ripping apart. He couldn't stop complaining, and he was looking desperately for an effective way to protect Notre-Dame-sous-Terre from your 'destructive folly,' as he said. He didn't trust the authorities at the Ministry, and he didn't think he could get anywhere with them, given the people you knew. Jokingly, I suggested he try the kind of things you see in mystery novels, like killing some member of your team to clear Kelenn's name and get the dig halted. He didn't think that was funny, as you can imagine, but I got what I wanted: He came up with the idea of *threatening* a murder, something intimidating enough to make the team stop the project. And that's what happened. It worked for everyone but you. Because for you an official order to stop wasn't enough. You kept working, alone. You're unbelievable, you know. You give up on men, but never on stones."

Johanna shivers down there beneath the rock. She's trembling with horror and with cold. How can she get Simon to be reasonable? The past, yes, she has to get him to talk about the past, and maybe the past will provide some arguments she can use against him.

"Simon," she says gently. "Tell me why Brewen committed the four murders using the four elements in 1063. Perhaps it wasn't only to avenge his sister's death?"

"Of course not! You're right, I need to explain that to you as well. You need to know it all, absolutely everything. But you see, the truth is that Brewen killed only three times, not four. Forty years before, in 1023, he knew that Brother Almodius had handed Moira over to the bishop and prince, and he had witnessed her torture and death. In 1063, Brewen was the guardian of the sanctuary, the punishing hand of our sacred spirit, the sentinel watching over our dead, our people's glory. And he did act. The first death, however, wasn't a murder. Your first dream, the monk hanging from the tower, looked like suicide. But Brother Anthelme's suicide was like a sign from heaven for Brewen. When he saw the monk hanging in the air, he remembered Moira's first ordeal and realized that Ogma wanted him to proceed by killing Moira's judges. In her honor, he would use the four natural elements not only to avenge her, but to sow panic in the abbey and stop the work in the crypt. So he used water to bring an end to the wicked Brother Romuald. Your second dream. And then he had no choice. The master builder of the abbey church, Eudes de Fezensac, had just discovered the entrance to the sanctuary. Brewen put some sleeping medicine from his plants into Fezensac's wine and then burned down the hut. Fire, your last dream. Brewen, along with others of his clan, was getting ready to seal the opening back up and put the Trinity altar back at its place when the watchman warned him that someone was coming. Everyone fled, but Brewen and my cousins slipped quietly back to watch what was happening in the crypt. They watched an altercation between Abbot Almodius and your man Roman. That's when Almodius admitted he had poisoned Moira. Roman was furious. He wanted to protect the sanctuary, but all he could do was show how weak he was. Almodius ran him through with Saint Michael's sword and cut off his head before throwing him down the shaft. And then the abbot climbed down as well to explore the grotto. But he had signed his own death warrant. When he climbed back up, Brewen and his relatives were waiting."

Johanna is dumbfounded. Simon knew Roman's whole story! He knew who had killed him, he knew he was still lying there!

"Over the following centuries," Simon continues, "in memory of Moira and Brewen, the guardians made it their tradition to use the four elements to wipe out anyone profaning the temple. Once, not too long ago, they didn't need to resort to killing. At the time, the sentinel warrior was my father. He was still young, and he often told me the story. Froidevaux was restoring the crypt, in 1960, and he found the entrance to the grotto while he was cleaning the base of the Trinity altar. But Froidevaux believed in both God and the devil, and he loved Notre-Dame-sous-Terre with a passion. He knew and respected all the mountain's legends. So he immediately realized that the entrance hid a dangerous secret. He was filled with fear, a holy fear sent by the rocks' spirit, and he listened to

THE ANGEL'S PROMISE | 453

it. He didn't touch the stones blocking the passage and made no attempt
to find out what they were protecting. He built those two solid altars and
never told anyone what he had seen. Peace be with his soul. He was a
saintly man; his faith was strong, and the gods spoke to him. Unfortunately, you aren't anything like him. You are too curious, and you forced
me to shed blood!"

"Simon, my dear Simon," Johanna replies, sobbing. "Why didn't you
tell me all that earlier? Why didn't you trust me? I would have stopped if
you had told me. I would have listened to you."

"Do you think I'm crazy?" he shouts. "*You*, listen to *me*? Never did you
heed my warnings, never! You stubbornly kept looking for the only thing
that mattered to you—your old Roman! If I had told you the truth, you
would have worked even harder. I kept telling you I loved you, and that
was the truth, but you could only hear the words of the manuscript and
the old man in the old people's home who told you about the lost notebook. You preferred dead words to the life I was offering you. You're just
like Roman, who scorned Moira for dreams. You refused to understand!"

Johanna puts her hands over her ears. "I'm in real danger," she thinks.
"Save me, save me, Roman, help me, I beg you."

"Yes, you're right, Simon," she stammers. "I was blind. I didn't understand the power of your love because I was obsessed with my mission.
Before giving in to you, I needed to liberate Roman's soul, trapped here
within the crypt's walls. The Archangel entrusted that task to me when I
was a child. Just as you obey Ogma and the spirits of the mountain, I had
to obey the prince of the heavenly host, the one who arranges passage to
the other world. Don't you understand? You're the only one who can
possibly understand, and that's what I saw in you, that's why I loved you
and had to leave you. So that I could fulfill my mission! We're the same
kind of person, both of us born out of a fabulous past and committed to
protecting it. I've almost accomplished my task, Simon. I've found the
skull. Let me find his body and reunite it with his head so the Archangel
might free him. Let him join Moira's soul. They've been promised to one
another for so long and have never been able to live out their love."

"My poor, dear Johanna," Simon sighs. "Since the beginning, your
quest was doomed to failure. If that were not the case, don't you realize

that I would have tried to help you with all my might? But this revenant is an evil spirit, a liar, an envoy from the kingdom of darkness. Remember what I said, you'll never put his head back on his shoulders. It's hopeless. After Brewen smashed Almodius's bones, he had a brilliant idea that would keep the monks from looking for their abbot and from opening up the entrance to the sanctuary that the Celts were trying to keep closed. He pulled the cape, cross, and ring off the abbot before throwing him down into the grotto. While his men were closing up the entrance, Brewen put the abbot's cross around Roman's neck, the ring on his finger and the cape on his back. Beside the mutilated body, he left in plain sight the Archangel's long sword that Almodius had used to cut his enemy's head off and that still carried traces of some of his blood. Both Almodius and Roman were old men, they both wore similar homespun frocks and were about the same size."

Johanna's eyes grow bright.

"That means that when the monks came into Notre-Dame-sous-Terre, they thought the headless body belonged to their abbot and that he had been killed by Saint Michael?"

"Maybe not by Saint Michael himself, but by some supernatural power for sure, for Almodius had flouted two things. First, Aubert's wish that the old church belonging to the canons, once transformed into a crypt, not be sullied by new building projects. And secondly, the interdiction against setting foot in the holy place when it was the prey of angels and demons between Compline and Matins. Some influential monks were already imputing the three earlier deaths to Saint Michael's anger, believing the Archangel was unhappy that they were digging in Notre-Dame-sous-Terre. And the whole monastery lived in terror. In such a context, the affair was easily covered up. The monks buried the four bodies, including one they thought was their abbot's, stopped the dig immediately, and quickly elected a new spiritual leader, Ranulphe de Bayeux, who became an excellent abbot and finished the construction of the Romanesque abbey church."

"But in that case, Roman's head is still here, but his body is . . . in Almodius's grave!"

"His body doesn't exist anywhere, Johanna," Simon continues. "His body is like Dom Larose's notebook, that notebook you're so crazy about. It's gone, turned to dust, destroyed, annihilated!"

"Don Larose's notebook has not been destroyed. It's just hidden somewhere," she answers, biting her tongue.

Shut up, Johanna! He's capable of torturing Guillaume to get the little notebook! she thinks.

"Keep clinging to your illusions if you like, but don't scorn your profession!" he scolds. "You know that here on the Mount all of the abbots' tombs, the cemetery, and the monks' ossuary were emptied, sacked, and pillaged as they were everywhere else during the Revolution! For once try to be reasonable. There's not a single intact tomb remaining on Mont Tombe, aside from the tomb of the three olams. You know that. You yourself excavated the cemetery and old Saint Martin's Chapel, and all you found was some anonymous bones and some pieces of stone! To feed tourists' fantasies, Historical Monuments rebuilt the stele from the tomb of Abbot Robert de Thorigny and Martin de Furmendi back at its original place, but you know that these niches are completely empty, just like your quest—an empty shell! I'm right, admit it. Almodius's tomb no longer exists, and Roman's body has been nothing but dust for more than two centuries. That's why, if Roman's ghost ever did exist, it hasn't appeared since the Revolution. His grave was destroyed back then, Johanna, like all Christian graves. The being you saw in your dreams was an evil spirit, a trickster who fooled you, who slipped into your sleep to try to corrupt your soul! And it worked. You've committed the same error as Roman, who refused Moira's love for too long in the name of his Christian beliefs. At least Roman had an ideal, sincere faith, even if his beliefs are not mine. But you are worse than he was. You pushed me aside to follow your macabre, pathological obsession, your psychotic delirium that's led to two deaths and will now bring about your own destruction."

At the bottom of the shaft, Johanna collapses. The stress of the past few days is weighing down on her, and she feels as if it's crushing her into the stone floor.

"Simon, I beg you," she says feebly. "Help me out of here. You can't leave me here; you love me. Please, take pity on me, help me, I can't go on."

"Alas, Johanna. Alas," he murmurs, his voice filled with sobs. "I do love you, it's true, but now it's too late! You've already spoiled everything. You didn't want to have anything to do with me when things were still possible, and now it's over! You've brought about your own downfall, my love. You should have listened to me. But you insisted on going back to where the past is buried, and you can't travel in time with impunity. Remember the revenant's mass and the parish priest who had to join the world of the dead because he got too close to it. You're already on the other side of the mirror, Johanna. I can't do anything more for you."

"Simon, that's enough of your crazy medieval legends!" she shouts with a last burst of energy. "We're not characters in some medieval fable; we live in the twenty-first century. This is real, and you're not going to kill me symbolically, but in real life! I love you, Simon; save me! I won't tell a soul, I swear. We can leave this place and go live somewhere where we can love each other openly."

Up above her Simon is weeping violently, his face contorted, and he begins to shout wildly.

"No, no!" he screams. "Ogma's sanctuary is holy. It's reserved for druids and olams and must never be sullied by human beings! In the last fifteen hundred years, only Almodius has entered it, and that's why Brewen threw him back down there to die. The graves of the three priests must never be desecrated, and anyone who does so must die! Even I have never gone down there, nor did Moira herself. Nobody, nobody, do you understand? Johanna, if only I could. But it would mean abjuring the faith of my ancestors, putting in doubt fifteen centuries of history, reducing my roots to nothing, forgetting Moira's ordeals and the sacrifices of the warrior guardians, renouncing my father, my family . . . myself!"

"Simon, you're a cowardly fanatic! You find it so much easier to take refuge in the dead past you know than to risk bringing about a living, still-unknown future. Your memory is smothering you, sterilizing you. You're trapped in the branches of a diabolical tree that's grown out of piles of corpses. React! Do something! You're a little kid at the mercy of a cannibalistic father. Stop looking back. Look forward, toward the future! I'll be with you! I'll forgive everything, Simon; everything. We'll make a fresh start, build our own legends, our own chateau unlike any other. We'll be cut off from history, but we'll construct our own history anew, and we'll be together."

This time it's Simon who puts his hands over his ears so he can't hear what she's saying.

"Shut up! Shut up!" he shouts. "You must die in the earth, just like Moira!"

"And how about you?" she roars. "Are you going to close yourself up in a monastery and pray forty years for your soul's salvation? That's enough. Stop it. Find some courage, resist, stop it!"

Simon suddenly seems to calm down. Johanna hardly dares to breathe. As if he's performing some ritual, Simon takes something out of his pocket and throws it down the shaft. Johanna picks up a cross with four equal arms made of gold and bone, a druidic cross.

"That's what I loved the most, except for you," Simon says with a sepulchral voice. "It's Moira's cross. It was passed down to her from her father, and to her father from his father ever since our world began. Brewen removed it from her body before it was burned. It's the insignia of our mission, and we pass it down from guardian to guardian. The engraved symbols represent the four elements that Moira's judges chose as her executioners—water beneath, fire above, air on the right, earth on the left, all emerging from four circles showing the soul's death and rebirth. The inset bone comes from trepanation rites, from the skull of a warrior who died in combat. Now, Johanna, I'm not saying a final goodbye, because I hope to see you soon. Elsewhere, if there is an elsewhere. I'm sorry, but such was our destiny. We can't love each other on the earth, but we will in heaven. I'm leaving you with the earth goddess and the one who guides our souls. May they give you protection until you reach the other world. And may the other world truly exist."

Johanna protests, screams with all her strength, sobs, breaks her fingernails trying to grip the rock wall, but Simon has disappeared. Where is he? She can no longer see him. Then she hears the sound of a motor. The crane! Stones! No! She has barely enough time to move away before rocks start falling. Weeping in silence, deaf to all her entreaties, Simon religiously blocks the passage back up.

21

THE ABBEY, MONT-SAINT-MICHEL. THE WEST TERRACE AT TWO
sixteen on the morning of June 3. Seven shapes darker than night
are waiting on the square in front of the church, where part of the old
nave used to be, near the steles of Robert de Thorigny and Martin de
Furmendi. Sebastian, Florence, Christian Brard, Commissioner Bontemps, Inspector Marchand, and two other uniformed policemen. Very
few words are spoken, and everyone is pretending to watch the stars. Florence bites her nails. Sebastian wonders why Johanna built that wall behind the door in Notre-Dame-sous-Terre. At one A.M. Florence and he
had gone back to get her as they had promised. They'd pounded on the
door, called, begged, but Johanna didn't answer. No sign of life, except
that Florence had thought she could hear for a moment the sound of the
motor on the little crane. What could Johanna be doing down there by
herself? Why wouldn't she answer? Maybe she had had an accident. Or
worse. Worried sick, they'd come back to the house; they were planning
to call the police. They'd found Patrick there splashing water on his face
in the kitchen. He'd said that he wasn't really the jerk everyone thought
he was after all, even though even he himself thought so at times. He
hadn't had the heart to tell the administrator about Johanna because he'd
kept thinking about some comments she had made about the killer. He
guessed that she suspected him, and he wanted to show how unfounded
her suspicions were. He also thought she was hiding something, something serious and maybe even dangerous. He was obsessed by what she'd

said, and, as he sat at one of the bars in town, he tried to figure out what she'd meant, but soon he was too drunk to think clearly. He felt sick and decided to come back home. He was sorry for arguing with Johanna, for the accusations he had made. But most of all, he was afraid for her. He was sure she was in danger and that she knew from whom.

Sebastian and Florence hadn't hesitated. Patrick may have been presumptuous and unlikable, but he was intelligent and had great intuition. So they'd told him about Johanna locking herself in the crypt, about how she refused to come out when they went down there earlier at eleven, and about the complete silence since then. Patrick had grabbed the telephone and awakened Brard so that he could use his authority to get the police to come right away. While they'd waited for the commissioner, Brard and the three others had tried to get into Notre-Dame-sous-Terre. But the chain and the granite wall had kept them out. That's when the administrator had mentioned the word "suicide," and Florence has been thinking about that ever since. To be sure, Johanna was acting strangely that evening, but she didn't seem depressed. Yes, she wanted to be alone in Notre-Dame-sous-Terre so she could say good-bye to the stones, and she had been talking about not being able to mourn appropriately, about a "second death." Oh, it couldn't be that! Bontemps and his team had got there at two A.M.; they were not at all pleased to be called out in the middle of the night for a case they thought was already solved. Brard explained the situation and the commissioner asked a simple question:

"Isn't there another way to get into the crypt without wasting time trying to cut through the other huge wooden door or demolishing the wall you speak of?"

Suddenly the administrator seemed to wake up and slapped his forehead.

"Through the nave in the church," he answered. "There are two trapdoors that used to lead down to Notre-Dame-sous-Terre from above, but back during prison days the passages were blocked off. One is filled with stones and rubble, and there's no way through. The other is blocked by a huge iron gate, and nobody has the key!"

"I'm calling the fire department," Bontemps answered. "They may not have the key, but they do have cutting torches they sometimes use after car accidents to cut bodies out of the wreckage. That should do the job on your gate."

With Patrick dispatched to the abbey's entrance to wait for the firemen, the others went to examine the gate. They moved some benches and exposed the two square trapdoors. As the administrator had said, one of the passages was totally blocked.

"Through this trapdoor to the north," Christian Brard explains, "there used to be access to the platform above the altar of the Holy Virgin. But there's no reason to waste any more time. We can close this trapdoor. Come over here, the gate is on the other side, above the Trinity altar on the south side. These corridors allowed access to the platforms in Notre-Dame-sous-Terre so the monks could show the reliquaries to the faithful waiting below, especially the Aubert relics."

Below the second trapdoor, a dark, steep staircase leads downward. At the base of the steps a wooden door opens into the crypt, just beneath the vaulted ceiling and onto the platform just above the Trinity choir. Between the trapdoor and the door hangs an enormous gate with thick iron bars. Time and salt air have corroded the bars, but the lock and hinges have been carefully oiled. They show no sign of rust. So the gate seems to have been kept up regularly; it stands ready to accept a key, or a human being. Brard is absolutely stupefied. He paces up and down on the west terrace, hands clasped behind him, as surprised as a prison director who's just found out that a detainee has escaped through a tunnel he's dug with a teaspoon.

2:30 A.M. PATRICK, panting, shows up on the terrace, with the silver-helmeted firemen in tow and clanging like knights in armor. The captain examines the gate. Then two thin blue flames as sharp as blades attack it. At two thirty-seven the lock gives, and the steel mass falls to the stairs. The gate opens without squeaking. As if it were his own home, Brard leads the way and opens the door above the Trinity choir. It, too, opens without a sound.

It's the first time he's ever come this way. The yellow light in the crypt makes him blink, accustomed as his eyes are to the dark corridor. He walks down the steps toward the platform. The firemen hand down a ladder, and he leans it up against the stone platform. Soon his feet are on the ground in Notre-Dame-sous-Terre, where the floor is torn up, and where he's joined by the others. As he did the evening before when he announced he was closing the dig, he tries not to think about how badly damaged his dear crypt is. The twin altars are surrounded by piles of stones. The Trinity altar especially. Its base is totally hidden, drowned in a mass of granite stones that have been carefully removed from the walls and clearly labeled. Only the top of the pedestal emerges out of the pile. The top of the crypt door is just slightly higher than the carefully built wall of stones. Stones from Aubert's wall. They look like they've been moved by some crazy mason. They're Johanna's stones, and seeing them reminds everyone that she's not there. At first Florence is relieved not to see Johanna's body lying on the littered earth. So she hasn't committed suicide! But how could she not be in the crypt? There's plenty of proof that she's been there—the contents of her bag, specifically her cell phone, are emptied out on the altar of the Virgin. Sebastian puts his hand on the little crane's motor.

"It's still warm!" he exclaims. "She used it not very long ago. She was here just recently. She was here when we came down a little while ago, even if she didn't answer."

"No doubt at all," Brard says, looking at the wall blocking the door of the crypt. "She had to construct this . . . this thing. And that would explain the crane noise you heard. But where is she now? How could she possibly have gotten out?"

"It's *The Mystery of the Yellow Room!*" Sebastian suggests.

"Very interesting," says Bontemps. "So," he continues, turning around to look at Sebastian, "let's use our brains. Let's recapitulate the facts we know rather than making unhelpful references. One: Johanna is no longer in the crypt. Two: she was here, however, at eleven P.M., since she spoke to you then. Three: at one A.M., she may have been here, but we're not sure. The crane you heard was definitely used. It may be that she was the one using it, or it may have been somebody else—I've got my own opinion about that. Four: Johanna did not get out through this door, because the chain and lock are on the inside and she built this granite wall. She can't have gotten out through the door over there because its lock is unusable. The only other way out, and therefore the way she must have left, is the way we came in, through the passage above the Trinity altar."

"She didn't have the key to the gate, Commissioner," Florence answers. "And like all of us, she didn't even know that passage was practicable, I'm sure of that. In our minds, as was the case for the administrator, just as you saw, this access was blocked off."

"What's in someone's mind is not always as clear as you think, madame," Bontemps answers, and Christian Brard turns red. "If you want my opinion, here it is. This is only a hypothesis, but it seems plausible. Your boss could not accept the decision to close the dig; her attitude in my office when the decision was announced and later with you proves that. She came down to the crypt alone, surely to end her life. But she didn't have the courage. So she decided just to disappear, to get a new life. Perhaps she built this wall to gain time and protect her escape. She didn't know that people would think so soon about the corridor up there. I think she slipped out through the Trinity corridor, and by now she's long gone!"

"Commissioner," Patrick cuts in, "if you please, I'd like to propose another theory. Running away is not like Johanna. On the contrary, she's a passionate fighter, if a little explosive, and that's why we rub each other the wrong way. True, she was greatly affected by the news that the dig would be halted, but she didn't give up. She came back down here to keep on digging, I'm sure. She must have had some idea she wanted to check out here, tonight, all by herself. We are scientists, it's true, but sometimes we make discoveries based on feelings. That's why I'm sure Johanna must still be here on the rock. She wouldn't have run away, leaving all her things here, and certainly she wouldn't have left Brother Roman's manuscript. Check the parking lot; her car must still be there. Although I don't have any real proof, I believe that someone, and it can't be Guillaume Kelenn, was trying to have the dig halted. That person was ready to kill to accomplish his ends, and he—or she—had a key to the Trinity gate. Perhaps Johanna had guessed who it was, and unfortunately, if she's still alive, she must know the killer's identity."

Florence lets out a little cry. Sebastian rolls his eyes. Brard scratches his head. Bontemps frowns.

"That is another lead we have to explore," his big voice booms out. "But let's not let ourselves get carried away by the troubling atmosphere here at night in this old abbey! Listen, whatever your boss's intentions may have been, or the intentions of your Mr. X, let's not waste any more time. The only thing we're sure of is that the woman isn't here any more," he says, picking up the walkie-talkie hanging at his belt. "Do you know what make of car she has, its color and the license number?"

The policeman who stayed out with their vehicles in the parking lot is able to confirm that Johanna's car is still at its usual place. Bontemps clears his throat uncomfortably.

"Well, that proves nothing," he says. "It may be one way to keep us off the scent. She might have called someone to come pick her up or even rented a car to get away without anyone knowing it. However, she might still be on the rock, and since there are plenty of us here, we might as well look for her. Then at least we'll know one way or the other, although I doubt we'll be able to find her. Captain," he says to the fire chief, shaking his hand, "thanks so much for your help. You may as well go on home to bed. I envy you. As for the rest of us, we get to search this charming place! Lopez, and you two," he says, pointing to a uniformed policeman along with Sebastian and Florence, "you take the abbey's bottom floor. Inspector Marchand, Mr. Fenoy, and this patrolman will search the middle one. The administrator and I will take the top floor. Lopez, this time I hope you didn't leave your revolver on your nightstand?"

Lopez shakes his head, showing them his gun. Seeing the gun frightens Florence, but at the same time it reassures her. Bontemps seems pleased with his division of their forces in accordance with official hierarchy and motions everyone away. It's 2:55 A.M.

SAME TIME. SEVEN meters beneath Commissioner Bontemps's feet. Johanna is sitting motionless against the stone wall beside Abbot Almodius, her head leaning toward her fleshless companion. Her flashlight, casting its beam like the sun on the little statue of Epona, turns it into a lunar masterpiece. Overwhelmed by her tragic situation, and totally exhausted, Johanna has escaped into sleep without turning off the light to save the batteries. Total darkness would have too painfully reminded her how blind she had been in relation to Simon. And in any case, the batteries would last longer than she would. It's still warm in Notre-Dame-sous-Terre, deceptively warm, but the air will become thinner and thinner. Falling asleep is like fleeing into a friendly, hopeful world of shadows, one of which might be able to provide her with the key out of her prison. But when she wakes up, she realizes she has failed. Her dreams were empty and sterile. No blue window, just a black screen. She puts her glasses back on and picks up the flashlight. She's beginning to sweat, either because it's so warm in the rock's womb or because she's afraid of dying. For she will surely die, from hunger, from thirst, from lack of oxygen, from lassitude. Her legs aren't broken like Almodius's were, and she feels no physical pain, just the disgraceful fear that has followed her panic. No longer is it the violent anguish washing over her like a wave, throwing her screaming against the conduit's rock walls when Simon began blocking it. Now it's a slow, silent, insidious terror, the fear dripping over her, dampening her hair and skin, wiping out any rebellious feelings and all will, all desire, to live. And then, too, there's the silence that comes before death, the voice of nothingness that's already spoken to her. For the first time, Johanna is ready to give up.

"My life has just been a waste of effort, a mass of illusions and lies," she thinks.

Confusion. She thinks about Pierrot, the twin brother whom she doesn't remember and whom she'll soon see again.

"Three months," she thinks. "That's not much time to live, just enough to disappear. August 15, the day we were born. This year we would both have turned thirty-four. I would have turned thirty-four, but he stopped aging the night of November 14 during our first year on earth. In any case, my parents would have sadly wished me another 'happy birthday.' It's hard for them to accept that time has been accumulating on one side only. Only on my side. 'Sudden infant death.' A strange phenomenon. Only when the victim dies are we aware of it. When it's all over."

The only trace of her twin brother left in her mind is a photo showing an eternal baby living in his little marble tomb and making sand pies with underground friends who come through tunnels to play with him. That's what she thought when she was a child. Since then, she's never thought about her brother, as she really has no memories of him. Never, until tonight. Apparently she had been sleeping beside him when he died. She probably hadn't even realized he was gone. And now that it's her turn to leave, she hopes that he'll see her coming. That he won't be sleeping. That he will greet her.

"How ridiculous. Because there's nothing after life. Nothing!" she thinks angrily. "And yet I'm going to die because I wanted to reunite two dead people. One who died in 1023 and the other in 1063! How ironic! How absurd!"

She feels like destroying everything in the grotto, breaking up the grotesque skeletons, dashing the little statue of the Mother Goddess to the ground, and then throwing herself against the stone wall to end it all! But then she sees Roman's skull lying near her. There's really nothing to distinguish it from the cranium she put back on Almodius's body with the baptismal cross around its neck. Will her own skull be just like theirs when her flesh is gone? She picks up Roman's skull and, following the beam of her flashlight, crawls over to the two primitive altars. Rubbing the skull with her hands as if it were Aladdin's lamp, she calls once more on magical spirits.

"Roman," she murmurs, looking at the goddess on horseback. "Perhaps you've misled me. Now that I'm about to die, I find that hard to accept. Simon took advantage of me. I'm locked up in here with his ancestors whom he's never seen, but he's a prisoner of their ghosts. I pity him. I find his actions odious, but I can't condemn him completely. He's sending me to my death, but he is already a corpse, a man without freedom, and I was not able to set him free. Maybe everything I've ever done has been in vain. Your body is lost, and I can't set you free either. And I, too, am lost, imprisoned. I couldn't see what I needed to see; I moved ahead thoughtlessly, without considering the people around me. Like you, I came to that realization too late! I was already in this prison with no way out! But you at least had prayer to enlighten you. And your contrition and suffering; the time you spent in your own purgatory made you clairvoyant. I don't even know how to pray, but I know that you can hear me. I hold you in my hands today, I'm touching part of you, the part that produces dreams, stone castles, and escape plans! Grant me the gift of your light, don't let me die like Almodius, who, like Simon, kills because he thinks he loves but is able to love only after he's killed. Save me. Everything I've done, I've done it out of love for you."

Roman died almost a thousand years ago. He's dead, and there's nothing left of him. The stones are deaf. Still, Johanna rises to her feet and begins to run her hands over them, inch by inch, in the beam of her flashlight. She can hardly breathe, even though she's taken off her jacket and blouse. Her tank top is drenched with sweat, and her long hair hangs down like frayed strings. She'd give her life, what little is left of it, for a drink of water. Water . . . the enemy the monks feared, on their island, in their isolation; water that at this time of day must be completely surrounding the rock. She'd drink even salt water. The rock. Look carefully at the rock, perhaps there is a way out.

"Impossible, but I have to try. How absurd death is for those without faith. Foolish and incoherent. Acedia, daughter of sadness, the grievous flagging of the soul. Quiet! Just look at the walls, Johanna! Stop thinking! You've spent your life looking at walls while others were looking for ways to get to the other side as best they could. Tonight the roles are reversed. Try to find a way out. Try! You can't just watch yourself die. The 'precious moment,' as the Benedictine monks used to call death. Precious, indeed. More like the dirty, hideous moment!"

She sweeps her light over the rock as if to wash away any hidden monsters. She rubs the granite with her fingers. Her eyes begin to ache. Her shoulders, too. She brushes against the rock wall as if she were dancing close with someone more powerful than she.

Beneath Notre-Dame-sous-Terre, Johanna is alone with bones from the past and eternal rock. Bare rock, and no way out. Nothing anywhere except some little marks engraved on the walls by the Celts. They are barely visible, and she hadn't even noticed them before her physical union with the grotto. Four ogams at each of the cavern's four cardinal points. They must surely indicate north, south, west, and east, so as to enable the druids to situate themselves in relation to the sun even down here in the depths of the rock. Johanna comes back to where Almodius is still leaning against the wall. She has to give up. This is her place. Her final resting place.

"*Ad accedendum ad caelum, terram fodere opportet*: You must dig in the earth to reach heaven," she says aloud, and then bursts out laughing. "Ah, Roman, that was a nice touch after all. And it sure fits me! I've certainly rooted around in the earth, and soon I'll see heaven's face! *Ad accedendum ad caelum, terram fodere opportet*! Nice little formula, right? It seems to have three meanings, and they all three have to be considered together. That's what I've done for you, Roman. I've literally dug in the earth so that you might reach your symbolic heaven, and with what results? I'm the one who'll end up in Paradise! Paradise, sure. That doesn't mean anything to me, I don't believe in Paradise. I'd prefer the literal heavens, the literal blue sky. Or even a leaden sky would be fine! So, Roman, how about inversing the meanings? Could you find some symbolic ground for me to dig in so I could reach the literal heavens?"

She bursts out laughing again, this time slapping her skeletal companion on the shoulder—his bones rattle.

"Sorry, Almodius," she mutters, replacing the skeleton against the wall.

She adjusts the cross hanging at the abbot's side. She stares at the crucifix, then slaps her forehead in amazement.

"Of course! I've got a symbol of the earth right here, an important symbol!"

With the nervousness that excitement brings at critical moments, she hurries over to her jacket rolled up in a corner. She drops to her hands and knees, digs into her pockets, and pulls out Moira's necklace, the one Simon threw down.

"Look, Almodius," she says, shining her light on the jewelry, "this is what he gave me. The symbols of the four elements. That must bring back some memories for you!"

She stops. Excitedly, she studies the Celtic necklace, then stands up quickly and shines her light on each of the four engravings on the grotto's rock walls.

"I'll be damned! How about that! The ogams! It's not the four cardinal points; it's the four elements! Just like the ones on Moira's druidic cross! Why were they carved into the wall?"

Johanna checks the three olams, all of whom are wearing Celtic crosses around their necks, but the crosses bear no inscriptions.

"Air, water, earth, fire," she murmurs, rubbing her fingers over Moira's necklace as if it were a rosary. "By the Archangel, might it be possible?" she shouts. "I have to try! Yes, I must try right away. Which of these symbols represents the earth? Simon told me. What did he say?"

Like a wild animal she rushes over to study the four ogams on the rock walls. One by one, she examines them. Which one of them is the earth?

"*Ad accedendum ad caelum, terram fodere opportet,*" she repeats as if it were a cabalistic prayer as she spins around. "If there's a solution, that's where it lies. But where? Roman, you must help me! What did Simon say? He said something important! Think," she begs, holding the jewelry up in the air.

She closes her eyes to commune with Roman.

"I must remember. I was over there, by the shaft. 'Moira's cross was the most precious thing I had, except for you. It dates from the beginning of the world. Brewen removed it from her body. The symbols, the four elements, Moira's executioners.' Roman, try again. 'Water below,' yes, water below. The other world of the Sidhe, for it is always beneath the water, at the bottom of lakes and seas, so it's below."

She looks at the cross's lower arm. Water is represented by three vertical lines cut by four horizontal lines. She looks up at the granite. There, she sees the same ogam on the wall. That must be water. Logically, fire should be the cross's upper arm. Let's see, there, a diamond shape. Fire must be diamond-shaped; lightning, thunder, fire. Now air. On the right or the left? She thinks he may have said on the right. She's not sure. Four horizontal lines. Is that it? In that case, earth is on the left. There are three horizontal lines on the left arm. Three horizontal lines. Johanna looks, and sees the same mark on the rock. And beneath it, on the grotto floor, there are the corpses of the three olams, laid out as if they, too, formed the three lines of the same symbol!

"Of course. The Celts were people of the earth!" she thinks, beginning to understand as she stuffs Moira's cross back in her pocket and hurries over to the stone emblem. "You must dig in the earth to reach heaven. Symbolic earth. I must dig in the Celtic symbol of the earth to reach the firmament, to get out of here!"

She digs desperately at the granite.

"Keep looking, Johanna! Keep looking!" she says aloud. "Dig into the earth's symbol. Because back in those days everything was symbolic, and this mountain has become mythical, the mythical meeting place of heaven and earth! Yes, the meeting place of heaven and earth, as the sea and lightning watch. This rock is the point of junction where all four elements meet!"

Her fingers begin to bleed as she scrapes away at the three lines. Probing here and there, she hopes to find some secret mechanism, but nothing happens. Her fingers are too thick. The narrow lines are deep and she can't slip her fingers into the depressions. She turns around. A tool! She needs a tool. Something very sharp and hard. What? A bone? Too thick! There's nothing, just her flashlight, and swinging it around she hopes against hope to find something to use. Then she trains the light back on it—a little tool—and it brings to her lips a cry of relief. Almodius's stylus! The stylus he used to write his testament on the wax tablet. She grabs it and digs its sharp metal point into the deep engraving on the stone wall. The top line. The middle line. The bottom one. Crack! There's a mechanical noise, a sound breaking the silence! And a piece of the rock pivots, opens up a few inches . . . then jams and stops. It hasn't moved for far too long.

With all her strength Johanna leans on the little stone door, but it won't budge. She pushes. Rubbing her shoulders raw, concentrating all her strength in a superhuman effort, she pushes She's no longer breathing, only pushing her own being toward life. The granite door trembles and loosens a little. She stands back up, out of breath, and leans down to look into the twenty-centimeter opening. There's a passageway, a secret passage dug by human hands through the rock, just like the one she used to come down into the grotto, except that this one is horizontal, and totally black. Johanna laughs and cries at the same time. It's a way out, it must be a way out!

"Roman!" she shouts. "Thank you, Roman! And thank you, Almodius

. . . Simon. I salute you, Moira, queen of the dead," she says, pulling out Moira's cross and kissing it. "I am the fruit of your womb blessed by the Archangel."

Around her sweaty neck she hangs the gold cross with inset bone. Time to flee! Get away through the walls. Reunite past and present! But don't forget anything. She puts Almodius's stylus in her jacket pocket, with the abbot's permission. She throws her jacket and sweater into the tunnel, and with them she carefully places Roman's skull. She bows down before Almodius to say good-bye, touches the baptismal cross hanging against his sternum, crosses herself, glances over at the three olams, at Epona, at her circular prison. Finally then she picks up her flashlight and places it, too, in the tunnel. She exhales, pulls in her chest as much as possible and, thankful that she's so thin, slides sideways into the opening. As soon as she's in the antechamber to the tunnel, she gets down on all fours. She slips her jacket back on, then wraps Roman's skull in her sweater and ties it around her back as if it were a baby. Holding her flashlight between her teeth, she starts down the mysterious tunnel.

In the mountain's viscera. June 3, 4:51 A.M. Johanna is crawling through the narrow tunnel. Still nothing but rock. The heat is oppressive. Her sweat is thick like the blood on her hands and shoulders. Her back scrapes against the tunnel, but Roman's skull is protected. Johanna can no longer stay on her hands and knees. Now she must inch forward on her elbows. She's panting like a beast of burden. The flashlight between her teeth makes it difficult to breathe. The exhilaration of her discovery past, anxiety is now overtaking her. Claustrophobia. The fear that in the end she'll find herself in another natural cave with no exit or, worse, up against solid rock. In which event, she won't be able to turn around and work her way back to the Celtic sanctuary. She'll die trapped in this corridor, married like a foreign body to the rock. Don't think. Just move forward. Inch ahead. Never has she felt so heavy. Or so big. She feels like she wants to vomit again. No time. No. Keep moving. Roman has guided her thus far. All of her companions are escorting her in their thoughts. She's not alone, she'll never be alone. Keep going. History. Tonight, she herself is making history. She has no notion of time except for the urgency of the present moment and a fervid hope for the future. A fresh, pure breath sweeps over her forehead. Air! Is it real? She hurries a little, her nose leading her. Something moves ahead of her. Some animal? No, quick, the flashlight. It doesn't look like granite. It's green, dark green. It's vegetation! She cries out like a wild beast. A curtain of grass and plants is waving before her. Natural light, so the sun is not far away! She lets out a raucous groan, and the moisture from her breath fogs up her glasses. She stops, tries to calm down, wipes her glasses as best she can on her soaking tank top, then starts inching forward again. Stones bruise her stomach; piles of rocks slow her down. She digs through them like a mole. It seems to her that the colors are changing, growing lighter. Now she's reached the natural curtain. She pushes it aside and, joyfully running thorns through her fingers, stares at the window she's just opened.

The most beautiful window in the world, both gentle and violent, without blemish, without stars, filled with melodious chirping, and she tells herself that the songs are surely the songs of all the earth's dead welcoming her back to life. She turns off her flashlight. The heavens above. She has dug into the earth and now has reached the heavens. Dawn hangs above her like a communion wafer.

22

A T 5:13 A.M., JOHANNA PULLS HERSELF OUT OF THE TUNNEL, GETS
shakily to her feet; the sky, she hopes, can heal her stigmata. Her
eyes have trouble adjusting to the dawning light. She looks at her watch.
Time is beginning to make its way back into her brain, as are the birds'
songs. The morning calls of the gulls and terns strike a welcome contrast
to the stark silence that was her companion in the shadows. Dawn: It's
time for the office of Lauds. *Laudare.* Praise. *De Angelis . . . Michael archangele*
veni in adjutorium . . . In excelsis angeli laudant te. In conspectu. The grave timbre of
medieval monks chanting resonates inside Johanna. Not in her head, but
in her body. The air makes her shiver. She looks around. Up above her
rises the church. Just beneath her lies Saint Aubert's spring, the only
source of fresh water available to the monks, water that was said to heal
demonic fevers. Johanna is facing north; she's arrived on the neglected
side of the monastery, among the briars, rocks, and prevailing winds,
halfway up the mountain. Off in the distance, Tombelaine Island is surrounded by moving water. The path . . . she's facing the path the early pilgrims used to take at low tide—they'd walk past Genêts and Tombelaine
to reach the abbey from the west, while carefully trying to avoid the
quicksand that frequently swallowed up the imprudent. This side, too,
faces the water passage, the path taken by those who hauled stone to the
abbey. The north and the west were one and the same for the Celts. They
called it the dark side, for from its direction came calamities and apoca-
lypses, whereas Christians climbed the path to lead them toward their
destination to the southeast, the choir of the abbey church, toward the

light and the resurrection. Johanna is standing at the very spot where the first village stood, long since gone. The gulls greet her noisily, and the north wind tickles her hair. She lets her hair fall free. She unties the sweater on her back and takes out Roman's skull, which she places back in the secret tunnel, just behind the thorny curtain that hides the entrance. Carefully she climbs down to the rising tide and kneels to wash off the dirt and blood. The air stings her wounds as it dries them. She's cold, hungry, and thirsty. She watches the circle of fire appearing in the east, near the choir, like the promise of new life. The first hour. She stands up, eyes sparkling, and starts toward the sleeping village.

She walks past the ramp leading up to the treadmill, past the back of her house without even glancing at the bathroom window. There's nobody in the streets, just a few cats digging through garbage cans. She doesn't know that her team and the police were searching for her until a half hour earlier. The watchman's walk along the ramparts takes her to Simon's house. On the wall, near the roof, the stone gargoyle threatens her, but she no longer feels fear and smiles at the monster. Above the door, the rusty lamp seems to be awaiting a hangman's rope, and the threshold to be waiting for the mandrake root to awaken. The gate in front of the entrance is open. She climbs the steps lined with wisteria and puts her nose close to the fading mauve flowers. The smell of heaven, powdery and captivating. She rings the doorbell, then pounds on the red door. No answer. She turns the knob, and the door opens.

"Simon!" she calls. "Simon, are you here?"

The key is still in the door, inside. There seems to be no life in the house, except the old grandfather clock generously spending time. Johanna inspects the lower rooms. She's very pale, and her heart is bursting with hope of finding him. She no longer fears for herself, but she is worried about him. His last words seemed to be shaded with the color of death. She decides to go up to the second floor. Still nobody, though the old furniture seems to be waiting for someone. Supporting herself on the banister, she climbs slowly up to the third floor. That's where Simon has his bedroom and office, his office with exposed beams on the ceiling and his bedroom with linen sheets that smell like linden blossoms. The bed is not unmade. Simon hasn't slept there. Johanna's hand shakes when she places it on the office door. In her memory persists the image of someone hanging. Finally she goes in. She breathes a sigh of relief when she sees the room is empty. On the medieval chest Simon used as a study table there's a letter addressed to Christian Brard. Johanna opens it.

> *My friend,*
>
> *Stop searching for Johanna. The woman I loved is dead, by my hand, just like Dimitri Portnoï and Jacques Lucas. Don't try to understand why I did it. My reasons will disappear along with me and with Johanna's body. On this the morning of June 4, I'm taking it to the far reaches of the sea.*
>
> *Don't follow us. Try to live!*
>
> *Adieu,*
>
> *Simon Le Meur*

"His boat in Saint-Malo!" she thinks. "Simon took his little sailboat out during the night and fled to the sea to escape this cursed earth. Water, the land of the Sidhe, the otherworld of the Celts, reachable by tunnels in the hearts of mountains, at the bottom of lakes and ponds, or at the ends of the sea, toward the west, beyond Brittany, out on the Atlantic's vast reaches! Simon has taken the legend to its logical conclusion. He probably threw himself into the ocean to join me in the kingdom of immortals, and I was supposed to reach it by going through the depths of the earth. Simon must be dead! They'll probably find his boat, but never his body."

Hot tears course down her cheeks.

"Simon, poor Simon," she whispers. "Angel of heaven, allow his soul to reach an island where it can rest in calm serenity!"

She lights a match and burns Simon's letter in an ashtray. Then she runs down the stairs, locks the front door, hurries down into the wine cellar, locks the door behind her, and puts the keys in her pocket. It's a nice wine cellar with a vaulted stone ceiling. There are rows of bottles with mildewed corks, an earthen floor, and a small window with a rusty grating. Johanna can hear the waves saying they carried Simon away. And now they, too, will leave, their mission accomplished. She grabs the grating and pulls with all her strength. Her wounded hands had stopped bleeding when she washed them in salt water, but now they begin to bleed again. So much the better; more evidence for the police. Pull, Johanna, pull! The old metal bars are worn, corroded by the salt air. Here the air nibbles away voraciously at everything, slowly but surely. Even human hearts. Johanna hopes that it has eaten away enough of the metal grating. She breathes deeply and keeps trying. Finally, a half hour later, the left side gives way. She pulls the grating away from the wall and, leaving her sweater on the ground, climbs out through the opening into the garden. The barbed wire on the garden fence rips some pieces out of her jacket. Good. More material evidence to confirm the story she'll be serving up to Commissioner Bontemps. Once outside, she makes sure there's nobody else in the street, wipes her fingerprints off Simon's keys, and tosses them across the ramparts into the water. It's six thirty. She looks back one last time at Simon's house, the sun, and then runs toward her own house.

JUNE 3, 3:15 P.M. Johanna is in Brittany, her car speeding toward the Plénée-Jugon retirement home and Father Placide. She has carefully cleaned and bandaged her hands and smells like soap after her long bath. Her head is still ringing with the tale she told everyone: Simon was crazy; he couldn't accept their breaking up, was jealous of everyone and everything around her, even Notre-Dame-sous-Terre. To get revenge, he killed Jacques and Dimitri; they were crimes of passion. Finally, he kidnapped Johanna while she was alone in the crypt the evening before and forced her to leave through the passage above the Trinity altar. Then he locked her up in his cellar with the intention of killing her, too. But he couldn't bring himself to harm her and ran away; he was planning to take his boat out and kill himself on the open sea. Johanna escaped by ripping out the bars on the cellar window. So far, the police haven't doubted her version of the story. Bontemps and his men broke down Simon's front door and inspected the cellar. In Saint-Malo, the port authorities confirmed that the antique dealer's boat had sailed out that morning. Out of respect for Simon and Moira's memory, Johanna decided that nobody should know about the Celtic grotto. She would make sure that the people François was calling in to restore the crypt sealed the Trinity altar back up carefully.

"By this time the new guardian must have learned that the torch has been passed to him," she guesses. "Simon surely alerted him somehow before he disappeared. Perhaps some day I'll try to find out who it is."

At the moment she's talking to Roman, whose skull is in a bag beside her on the passenger's seat. She can't bear to give up what's been keeping her alive all these years. While she was lying to her colleagues and to the police about her unusual adventures, Florence, taking care of her like a mother, had bandaged her wounds. Before Johanna's tired eyes flashed images of Epona on horseback, the skeletons of the three olams, and Almodius's wax tablet. The Archangel's sword was raised above Roman's head in the tomb the abbot had prepared for him. And then the monk was moving toward a blue window. That reminded her of her latest dream, the one she had in the church, in her mother's chapel. Since then she hadn't dreamed, but it was that particular dream that had led her to the Trinity altar, the hidden grotto, Roman's head, and finally the opening to the sky.

Might the dream still be useful? This morning she had thought about Father Placide lifting up a square blue communion wafer, and Brother Roman had appeared, free and young. She had to talk to Father Placide! That meant slipping away from police interrogations, from Florence and Sebastian's support, from Patrick's mistrust, from Brard's unspoken fears—because she hadn't linked Simon to the anonymous letter—and from François, who was to arrive later that afternoon. It seemed inconceivable to her that she could even see François. Now an abyss separated them. A mirror, and Johanna was on the other side. Alone. She needed to elude the commissioner and find some time to go see the monk in the old people's home. She refused to see a doctor and to go back to Simon's house with Bontemps. And she was careful not to push herself too far. The tension of the last few hours had been overwhelming, and the pressure of the hours to come was so palpable that she could no longer speak. She was completely exhausted, completely prostrate, and the image of the headless monk was hard to distinguish from the faces of the people she was talking to.

Strangely, it was Patrick who finally made everyone leave her alone, and Bontemps agreed to wait until the next day to take her deposition. Between searching for Simon and scouring his houses in Saint-Malo and at the Mount, the police had plenty to do. Patrick lay his hand on her aching shoulder and led her silently to her room. Although she was exhausted, she couldn't fall asleep. It had been far too long since she had slept. Not a single new dream could come to her until she had solved the one possessing her, perhaps a hoax, since she was a child. Water could perhaps restore her aching body. After a long hot bath, she had eaten with Sebastian and Florence looking pityingly at her and Patrick staring at her as if she were some archeological dig still hiding its secrets. The table wine they drank was like a magic elixir, a concentrate of life, the precious fruit of the timeless harmony of men and the earth under God's eyes. After lunch she said she needed to go out for fresh air, that she needed to be alone. Nobody dared disagree. It wasn't easy to go back to the tunnel to get Roman's head. At that time of day, tourists were king, and they were swarming all over the mountain. Finally, at three P.M., she was able to climb up the north slope and get her treasure.

PLÉNÉE-JUGON. 4:18 P.M. Johanna enters the old people's home with its monks dressed in a variety of colors. The watchdog nurse is at her post.

"Father Placide isn't doing well at all," says the nun. "We're waiting for an ambulance to take him to the hospital in Saint-Brieuc. You can't see him now."

"It's important, Sister," Johanna says. "It won't take long. If he's leaving, I . . . I've got to say good-bye to him. Five minutes, just five minutes, please!"

"I'm sorry, mademoiselle. Rules are rules."

Johanna walks out into the garden. She must find a way of getting into the building and talking to Father Placide before he leaves. She hides behind a tree, then slips back toward the building. There's a fat Franciscan, dressed in brown, watching her expressionlessly from a bench. She walks around behind the building and into the emergency exit. She runs up the stairs. Fifth floor, piglet-pink doors. Finally, there's his room. She knocks and goes in. The old monk is lying on his back and staring at the engraving of Mont-Saint-Michel. There's a tube in his nose, and his beard is hidden by an oxygen mask.

"Father!" she shouts. "Father, how happy I am to see you again!"

His only answer is to close his eyes. She sits down on the bed and squeezes his bony hand in hers.

"Dear Father," she continues more calmly. "I know . . . I know you're very weak. But I wanted to say good-bye before you leave for Saint-Brieuc. And I wanted to show you something."

He opens his eyes. His eyes are the color of storms. Each breath demands an enormous effort, and the apparatus magnifies the sound. This time, it's her turn to give him a gift. She opens the bag and shows him Roman's skull; she places it under the old man's yellowed fingers. He turns feebly toward her with a questioning look, and that gives Johanna the courage to speak.

"Thanks to you, I penetrated the secret of Notre-Dame-sous-Terre," she says, bending down. "Everything Dom Rose said in his notebook was true, Father. People were killed to keep them from finding a Celtic sanctuary hidden under the crypt. But I found it, and I'm still alive. Inside, I found a sculpture of Epona, some druids' graves, and this skull without a body. The skull belongs to the headless monk who was haunting the crypt, Brother Roman. In 1063 he was killed and decapitated by Abbot Almodius, whose bones also lie in the hidden grotto. Roman's head was thrown into the cave, but his headless body remained in Notre-Dame-sous-Terre. The monks mistook it for the remains of their abbot, so Roman's body must be in Almodius's grave! Father, tell me, must I give up and leave Mont-Saint-Michel? Or is there still a minute chance that the abbot's grave has not been destroyed? Perhaps the body has been exhumed. Where should I look? Should I start digging again in the crypt, in what was Saint Martin's Chapel?"

The old man squeezes her hand and shakes his head.

"No?" she wonders. "No, not there in the chapel. But what should I do? Please, Father."

She carefully raises the oxygen mask and leans down toward his mouth.

"M . . . Montfort," he rasps.

"Montfort?" asks Johanna. "What's that? Someone's name? Or is that where Almodius's grave is?"

"Montfort," he repeats, exhaling. "Montfort, the one in the middle."

And then his head drops over, and he loses his grip on her fingers. She puts his oxygen mask back on, but he no longer seems to be breathing. He must have drifted off to sleep or into a coma, or even worse. Johanna begins to panic. My God, she's killed him! She must call someone. But no need. The door suddenly opens and the nun appears, along with two lay nurses carrying a stretcher.

"What are you doing here?" the nun asks angrily. "Good heavens!" she cries when she checks Father Placide's heart and sees what condition he's in. "Help me," she says to the nurses. "Hurry, he's unconscious!"

Johanna slips Roman's cranium back into her bag and hurries out.

"Poor Father Placide," she whispers to herself. "It's my fault. If only he doesn't die. Montfort, the one in the middle. What could he have meant?"

Back in her car, she unfolds a road map and looks at the names of the nearby villages. Nothing nearby. Nothing to the east in Normandy. Nothing to the west, either. She moves her fingers down toward the south in Brittany. There! A little town named Montfort on the road to Rennes!

"That may not be it," she thinks. "But perhaps it is. I'm looking for a grave, so we're talking about a cemetery. I've got to check out the cemetery in Montfort right away. But how could Almodius's grave be there? The one in the middle? No matter. . . . "

As she starts the car, she looks at her watch. It shouldn't take her more than forty-five minutes to get there.

THE MONTFORT CEMETERY. 5:11 P.M. Johanna is walking up and down through the cemetery; she's concentrating on the path in the middle. But the tombs don't mean anything to her. Unknown names. Cold, modern stones, just like anywhere else.

"What are you doing here?" she asks herself. "How could Almodius's casket have ended up here? An abbot from Mont-Saint-Michel who died in 1063. That's ridiculous! I must be wrong. Evidently I should be looking for someone whose name is Montfort. Montfort is an old medieval name. Of course I won't find anything among all these new graves. I need a telephone book for the area, for Brittany and Normandy. And damn it, I've left my cell phone back at the Mount! At the post office, yes, there I can find a phone book if they are still open. . . . "

As she's about to leave the cemetery, she notices an old man with a wooden cane reverently carrying an armload of daisies toward a white tomb. She goes over to him.

"Excuse me, sir. I'm looking for . . . a very old grave . . . one of my ancestors. On her deathbed, my grandmother pronounced the name Montfort, but I can't find the grave here. I was wondering if there could be another older, cemetery somewhere in town."

The old man stares directly into her eyes and then, seeking who knows what, looks her up and down. She feels uncomfortable.

"Well, there's just the town cemetery, right here," he answers gruffly. "But what was your ancestor's name? Was he noble?"

"Yes, he was a nobleman from the region," she quickly answers, though she knows Almodius was Norman rather than Breton. "An aristocrat; yes, he was!"

"Well then, not here!" he says, thinking how difficult it is these days to know who's an aristocrat. "This cemetery is for ordinary people. The others wouldn't be here. Noblemen never leave their own land, and that's where their graves are."

"Where? Could you please tell me, sir?" she asks excitedly.

"I just told you, on the land belonging to the de Montfort family, of course! At their castle."

"De Montfort. I've heard that name before," she thinks. "But that wasn't Almodius's name. Oh well, I'll worry about that later. Quick, I must go to the castle and find the private tombs of the de Montfort family."

MONTFORT-EN-BRETAGNE. The de Montfort family castle, 6:00 P.M. It's not a medieval castle, but still, it must have been built during the Renaissance. Very run-down. As is often the case with old homes and old families. The grounds seem to be huge and are quite overgrown. It must be a struggle to keep up the family property. Its former splendor isn't much more than a memory slowly going to ruin. By now the family must be living on mostly boiled potatoes and memories of the past. They've surely been here for centuries. Johanna looks through the massive gate in the hope of finding the chapel, but she doesn't see it anywhere. She rings the bell. Well, how about that! There's an intercom.

"Yes?" a woman's voice answers.

"I . . . I'd like to speak to the owners," says Johanna.

"The castle is not for sale," the voice retorts.

"No, I know. That's not why I'm here. It's something personal, family business, related to the past, to history. I'm an archeologist, and I—"

"The countess never receives visitors after four P.M.," the voice answers. "Leave your card. Then call tomorrow morning and explain what you want if you'd like to see her. She'll decide if she'll see you or not."

Johanna is surprised at how old-fashioned the servant is. And the servant seems to have hung up the intercom.

"Wait!" Johanna shouts. "Please, I must see the countess immediately. It's extremely important. Father Placide sent me! Do you understand? Father Placide!"

Silence. Johanna clings to the gate as if it's her last chance. Then she hears gravel crunching in the lane and a dog barking. Someone's coming. She sees a plump little woman, perhaps sixty, or a little older, dressed in gray from head to toe and followed by an ugly orange poodle that's barking incessantly. The woman looks at Johanna's jeans, her sloppy jacket, her sallow skin, the bag, her unkempt hair, and then opens the gate with a huge key.

"The countess is waiting for you," the servant announces disapprovingly. "Don't tire her out; she's not well."

Johanna nods. The dog with a perm keeps barking. The castle guard! She would like to give him a good kick. Johanna is led into a room with a high ceiling and numerous traces of its former glory—seventeenth-century paneling on the walls, a huge stone fireplace with its escutcheon and porcelain knickknacks everywhere. The woman dressed in gray disappears with the poodle. Johanna doesn't dare sit down on the Voltaire-style chairs. She looks over at a showcase filled with little crystal cats. True kitsch. She spots the animal who surely inspired the collection: enthroned with truly feline grace on a marquetry cabinet, she's licking her paw—a Chartreux with yellow eyes and gray fur just like the servant's clothing.

"Hello, mademoiselle. Mademoiselle?" says an old woman's voice.

She whirls around to introduce herself. She had been expecting to see a woman in a wig and a seventeenth-century gown, with a beauty spot on her powdered face, a woman she would need to curtsy to, but the woman standing before her doesn't look anything like her commoner's fantasy. She appears to be about as old as Father Placide. Bent over a black cane with a silver knob, she's dressed in a very simple jade-green jersey wool suit, too warm for the season. She holds her head up proudly; her dark eyes are bright under drooping eyelids, and her white hair is cut short. No real sense of style, but she is discreetly elegant. She's not arrogant and doesn't try to act superior. Clearly, she's not intent on showing off her nobility, though her long lineage gives her an air of confidence and self-assurance.

"Hortense de Montfort," she announces, her hands still on her cane. "Please sit down. So, how is my dear Father Placide?"

"Not well at all, madame," Johanna answers timidly, sitting down at the edge of one of the Voltaire chairs. "That's why I'm here without calling ahead. He's just been rushed to the hospital in Saint-Brieuc."

The old woman makes herself comfortable in a chair across from Johanna. The news has clearly affected her.

"I'm sorry to hear that, for Father Placide is a friend dear to my heart. However, his greatest wish is to meet Our Lord. That's been the purpose of his entire life, but I hope he tarries as long as possible. Tea time is past, but would you like some port?"

"No, thank you, madame. In fact, I . . ." Johanna stutters, awed by the woman. "He wanted me to come see you. Before he left the retirement home, he asked me to say a prayer for him beside the grave of Abbot Almodius, eighth Benedictine abbot of Mont-Saint-Michel, who died in 1063," she whispers.

"May I ask who you are?"

Her voice is curt and shows her mistrust.

"I'm an archeologist at the Mount, madame, and I specialize in Romanesque art. That's how I met Father Placide not long ago in Plénée-Jugon. I needed information about some medieval manuscripts, and nobody knows manuscripts better than he does. I grew fond of him and have gone back to see him as a friend. I was there a short time ago when he felt faint."

"Did he tell you about it?"

"Yes, just before leaving for the hospital," she says, bluffing. "Oh, he didn't tell me everything, just bits and pieces, the poor man, he could hardly speak. But I promised never to repeat anything he said to anyone! He asked me to go pray on the tomb. That was his wish, something he couldn't do himself," she lies. "I won't say anything about it. I owe him that much, and I'm not here as an archeologist but rather as Father Placide's friend."

"Like the executrix of his will?"

Johanna smiles. She'll hold nothing back. Ever since this morning, since she pulled herself out of the shadowy grotto and away from her own death, she has done nothing but lie, dupe and trick other people. But she has no choice if she expects to discover the truth and show respect for those who have died or who will die. Life itself requires that much of her! The old countess hesitates, as if seeking an answer in her cat's eyes. Johanna clings tightly to the bag with Roman's skull in it. "Roman," she says to him in silence, "you also deceived people in order to preserve your love for Moira."

"Fine," the old woman finally says, though Johanna can't tell if she's really been fooled or not. "Since he told you, and especially since it's his last wish. But tell me. Why Almodius and not the others? All of them are here, you know!"

Ouch. How can she get out of this delicate situation? The countess has to stop asking questions and tell her where the tomb is!

"Well," Johanna begins. "Almodius, before he was abbot, was a famous copyist and later the head of the scriptorium at Mont-Saint-Michel. Father Placide loves his manuscripts, some of which are in Avranches, and we talk about them often."

"Oh, I didn't realize. You know, at my age, you lose your memory and

I'm not sure I'll be able to remember all their names. Let's see," she says, starting to count on her fingers, "Maynard I, Maynard II, his nephew, I believe, Hildebert, Thierry de Jumièges, then Almodius, and Ranulphe de Bayeux. That's right, six of them, the first six Benedictine abbots who died at the Mount—the founding fathers of the abbey!"

Johanna is flabbergasted. Her mind starts to wander. "Is it possible that with so little emotion, this woman is telling me that these castle grounds house the tombs of all the men she's just named? No, that would be amazing!"

"All six of them are right here?" she asks, pretending disinterest.

"Of course!" Hortense de Montfort answers. "If I remember correctly, only three abbots are missing: Aumode, Suppo, and Raoul de Beaumont, who also lived in the eleventh century but weren't buried at the Mount for some reason. Eloi de Montfort, my husband's ancestor, would have been willing to take more of them, some of the great abbots who came later, but they had to work quickly and without attracting attention. Some of them were in the choir, in stone tombs too difficult to open up. As for Aubert's skull, the revolutionaries had already carried it off and were going to destroy it. But Eloi persuaded one of his physician friends to let him keep it as a medical curiosity. And that's how it was preserved until they could start worship services again. That night, in the abbey church and in the cemetery, Eloi stood there before the apostles and all the saints, and he chose the apostles, the first ones, the founding fathers! When I think about it, what an epic tableau! It was in 1791, and the monks were chased out of the abbey by the riffraff, Mont-Saint-Michel became a commune called the Free Mountain, and the medieval manuscripts were rushed away along the shore to Avranches. And Eloi de Montfort, a nobleman educated in the ideas of the Enlightenment and the Revolution, by night, like a brigand or a desecrater, stole the remains of the first six abbots from the graves. He kept them wrapped in their shrouds and, hiding them inside empty wine barrels, brought them by cart here to the chateau and our family vault to save them from the destructive fury of the revolutionaries who were pillaging religious buildings and cemeteries!"

Johanna's mouth hangs open in disbelief.

"The legend of the stolen abbots," she murmurs, thinking about the olams.

"What are you saying?"

"That's a strange story. And now I know where I had heard your name before," Johanna suddenly exclaims. "During the Hundred Years' War, among the knights defending Mont-Saint-Michel against the English, was there not a Montfort?"

"That's right! Raoul de Montfort fought valiantly alongside Louis d'Estouville and was decorated Knight of Saint Michel, in 1470, posthumously. Our family has always been closely linked to the Mount in every era. Some members of our family were monks. For us, the Mount has always been and will always be Breton, and it was our duty to protect its apostles!"

Johanna feels like laughing aloud.

"What extraordinary news!" she thinks. "The mountain has aroused such passion over the years. Celts martyred by Christians, Benedictines martyred during the Revolution. And what secrets! Placide knew the family Montfort had been watching over the abbots' tombs since 1791. The Benedictines still know. Why didn't they ever say so? Why has no historian, no book, no employee of Historical Monuments, ever mentioned it?"

"Madame, why weren't the relics returned to the Mount once times were not so troubled?"

"After Eloi hid the six abbots, he was horrified to see that the revolutionaries were indeed carrying out their horrors. There was nothing left to save in the graves of the other abbots. The revolutionaries had also opened ossuaries belonging to ordinary monks, and they attacked even the living. In Paris, in 1792, they massacred the superior general of the Benedictine congregation at Saint-Maur, and in 1794 they guillotined the father superior of Cluny, among others. Eloi had accepted the new ideas, but surreptitiously he helped priests who hadn't and any monks who were in danger, including some Benedictines from Mont-Saint-Michel, to escape to England. Under the Terror he was denounced for his activities and guillotined in public. Before mounting the scaffold, he asked his sons not to reveal anything and to give the abbots' relics back only when true faith was reestablished, only when there was a new Benedictine community on the mountain. The Benedictines were the only ones to be trusted, because the abbots were their fathers, and the holy relics belonged to them. We were simply the secret guardians! So Eloi was beheaded and the secret of the abbots' tomb was passed in his memory from generation to generation of our family, while the abbey, empty of the faithful, was being transformed into a state prison and while the treadmill took the place of the ravaged religious cemetery."

"And Benedictines didn't come back until 1966!" Johanna exclaims.

"Yes," she answers thoughtfully. "For the celebration of one thousand years of monasticism, but it was only in 1969 that they restored a permanent community in the abbey. I thought Father Placide would have told you that, for that's about the time we met him, my late husband and I. We were so happy the black monks were coming back. We thought that as the true owners of Mont-Saint-Michel, the ones who had constructed its legend, the Benedictines would never leave, alas. In short, in 1969, in keeping with the last will of our ancestor Eloi, my late husband went to see the prior, who was fulfilling the role of the father abbot, and told him the whole story. You can imagine the man's surprise! And that's when the prior and Father Placide came themselves to see the relics in our family vault. The prior thought about it at length, consulted the community, and finally, to our great surprise, refused to take the holy relics back, preferring to let us keep protecting both the relics and their secret."

"But why?" Johanna wonders.

"Because, my dear girl, contrary to what my husband and I thought, things had greatly changed on the rock and in the monks' hearts! The Benedictines were no longer the same people. Except for dear Placide, none of them still wore the habit. They dressed in civilian clothes like lay brothers and led the prayers in French. They were no longer masters of their domain or of their glorious past. Now they were just renters. The government, Historical Monuments, and the administrator of the Mount were now the sole owners of the abbey. They opened it up to mass tourism, and in that museum décor, unchanging and atheistic, the monks were only puppets. When I think about it all, I tell myself that in the best of cases the prior was afraid that the precious relics, instead of being reburied and venerated in peace, would be studied, analyzed by historians, scientists, people like you, and then displayed to ungodly eyes in one of the monastery rooms like vulgar knickknacks. In the worst-case scenario, I'm afraid that modern Benedictines strayed away from their eternal history to get with the times. Yes, the black monks abandoned the Archangel. That's probably the sad truth."

Johanna drops her eyes. Simon felt the same way about his own relics. "If ever the Benedictines had discovered the grotto, they would have destroyed it because of their faith. And if people in the modern world had found it, they would have turned it into a museum, because of lack of faith," Simon had said.

"I'm not qualified to judge the attitude of present-day Benedictines," Johanna answers gently. "But about the government's role on the Mount, I don't have the same opinion, for after all, the government has saved and restored it."

"After devastating it for a whole century!" the old countess objects.

"If I step out of my archeologist's role and consult only my heart, I can understand the abbot's reaction," Johanna says.

"I think I understand it, too," Hortense de Montfort answers. "However, my husband and I have never regretted what we did. It allowed us to meet Father Placide, a monk who's proud of the past and ready to protect it ably. In fact, once a year since 1969 he's been coming here to say a mass for the founding fathers and pray in the chapel. And then, in 2001 the Benedictines left the holy mountain, and my husband died the same year. Father Placide kept coming until old age and disease finally caught up with him."

"Today I've come in his name," says Johanna, choking with emotion, "and I'll never betray the secret he has respected for so long."

"I believe you," answers the old woman, looking carefully at Johanna. "Eglantine will show you the way, at the back of the grounds. My legs can no longer take me there. Stay as long as you want. Pray for him, and for us. That's what he always did."

"Then so will I."

Under the bright sun, Johanna follows the servant across the castle grounds, where plants now grow in profusion. Behind some Scotch broom, a Gothic chapel looms up. Without a word, Eglantine unlocks the door, leaves the key in the lock, and starts back toward the house. Johanna clings to her bag. This is it, Roman, this is it! She walks into the mausoleum with some trepidation. On a marble altar are two white candles. On the wall is a crucifix. Three royal blue stained-glass windows allow some light to filter through. In the middle window, above the altar, Christ is shown in glory, rising from the dead. The left window shows the Virgin sitting on a throne. On the right, Saint Michael is striking down the dragon with his long sword. The Archangel's blue window. Johanna smiles at her angel. The chapel walls are covered with brass plaques commemorating those buried there, giving their names, their deeds, dates of their birth and death, and sometimes a loving word. The oldest are from the fourteenth century; the most recent is in memory of Hortense's husband. Johanna notices that the countess has already had her own plaque engraved and placed near her husband's. All that's missing is the date of her death. So she's ready and waiting to join her beloved. Naturally, nowhere are any abbots mentioned. Johanna examines the floor. There are three large stone slabs with bronze rings allowing access to underground tombs divided among three vaults. In which vault do the abbots lie? Hortense de Montfort didn't make it clear. Johanna drops to her knees, carefully studying the stone. There's not the slightest inscription that might be of help. Just three stone slabs, one on the left, one in the middle, one on the right.

"'The middle one!' Those were Father Placide's last words! 'Montfort, the middle one!'" Johanna gives a cheer. "Thank you, Father Placide."

She rubs her fingers over the middle slab. Underneath lies Roman's body. She can feel it, she's sure!

"Almodius," she thinks, "you kept Roman and Moira apart. You killed them both, but in death you did help your former rival. I thank you!"

Johanna tries to think. After he put the remains of the six abbots in the center vault, to preserve his secret, Eloi surely didn't let other people be buried there. That's why they prepared a third crypt beside the others. So, nobody would have opened the vault since 1791, except for the prior and Father Placide in 1969. Perhaps, but then how can she enter the vault now? In spite of the ring, Johanna isn't strong enough to raise the stone with her bare hands. She needs some tools. She can't imagine that the countess would give her permission to go down into the underground crypt or lend her a crowbar, so she has to act secretly and all alone. All her archeological tools are back in Notre-Dame-sous-Terre! What should she do? She looks around her and comes up with an idea. She lays down Roman's skull on a corner of the altar and goes back with the empty bag to the castle. She says she left Father Placide's missal in her car, and thus gains the opportunity to dig through her trunk. A few minutes later she returns to the chapel triumphantly. She locks herself inside before she digs in her bag and pulls out a flashlight, a stone, and her jack.

It's light outside, so there's no reason to light the candles. Still, Johanna climbs up on the altar. On her knees, her legs between the candles, she looks up at the blue stained-glass window and the crucifix hanging on the wall. It's a lovely bronze cross, but a little strange. Jesus is exalting his suffering. His open wounds are bleeding and his face is twisted in pain. Pure Sulpician style. The cross's vertical arm must be about a hundred and twenty centimeters long, and the horizontal arm eighty. Johanna reaches up toward the sacred object and finally dares to touch it. Then she grabs it with both hands and rips it from the wall, though she almost drops it because it's so heavy. She pulls it to her and places a kiss on the thorn-crowned forehead.

"Forgive me, Jesus," she murmurs, "but I need your help."

She lays the cross on the altar beside Roman's cranium, then jumps down and carries it with much difficulty over to the three stone slabs. Placing one end of the crucifix in the middle ring and putting the other end in a crack between two paving stones, she uses it like a crowbar. The slab moves slightly. Quickly, she places a small stone under it. Then she pushes the jack in, attaches the crank, and starts turning. The jack begins to unfold and lifts up the stone. A few more centimeters. There! The opening is wide enough for her to slip through. She turns on her little flashlight and starts down the vault steps.

Everything is dark, and the cold air is stale. The entrails of the earth are colder than the rock's entrails at Mont-Saint-Michel. There's the strong smell of aged game, the smell of dozens of corpses that have rotted away in the confines of what appears to be a small rectangular chamber. On all the walls are recesses containing wooden caskets. The mausoleum is not a womb, but a trench overcrowded with piled-up bodies and a heavy, sickening atmosphere. Instinctively, Johanna looks back and shines her light up on the stone slab. Everything looks fine. The jack will hold it in place. She tells herself that if she had to choose, she'd rather die in the round Celtic cavern with Epona, the olams, and Almodius than in this temple with its hidden bodies so neatly aligned.

"Roman, poor Roman, where are you?" she asks silently. "Have you also felt uncomfortable far from your rock and your abbey stones, even with these founding fathers at your side? Fortunately, your eternal soul has stayed in Notre-Dame-sous-Terre. And this prison has protected your body. For more than two centuries. And now the time has come for you to leave the earth."

It's freezing cold in the vault, and Johanna is unsettled as she looks for the six abbots' remains. All the coffins display the names of their occupants, and just as she thought, they are all noblemen from before 1791. From the seventeenth and eighteenth centuries only. Those who died before the seventeenth century must be in one of the other vaults. Both public and private history passes before her eyes. But there's no trace of the abbots from Mont-Saint-Michel.

"Eloi de Montfort would surely not have mixed their bones with others in the same coffin!" she thinks. "No, his faith would never have allowed him to do that. An abbot's bones are holy. They were the founding fathers, the six apostles of Mont-Saint-Michel. But where could he have hidden them?"

She shines her light around feverishly, and suddenly pauses. A wave of nausea overwhelms her. Part of one wall is covered with baby coffins. She thinks about Pierrot, her twin brother, and moves closer to the little coffins. It's disturbing to see how many there are—twenty-one, she counts—stacked up two by two along the wall. Twenty-one little Pierres gathered together in the same place. They can't make sand pies or dig tunnels, but they are together, and perhaps they can talk with each other. Or maybe together they can mourn their mothers who can no longer feed them. Sick to her stomach, Johanna, trembling, leans over one of the little coffins to see if there's a name on it, and drops her lamp in surprise. From behind the little wooden box an adult skull is smiling at her.

"How ingenious!" she thinks. "Eloi de Montfort hid the abbots' bones behind these infant coffins! The coffins are short, but also quite narrow, and the founding fathers of Mont-Saint-Michel, wrapped only in their shrouds, didn't need a lot of space. Aside from the practical considerations, there may also be spiritual significance to their location. The old venerable ancestors with their long, productive lives are protected by those whose lives were interrupted before they grew to be adults. The newborns' souls were without sin, and so as humans pure from birth they can watch over these sages who've been purified by experience. And at the same time the venerable saints ensure that the innocents rest in peace. Maynard I, Maynard II, Hildebert, Thierry de Jumièges, Ranulphe de Bayeux, and before Ranulphe, there's Roman, in place of Almodius."

Johanna feels like she's in a trance, she's so excited. She can scarcely breathe and has to move away from the wall to get control of her emotions. The moment of truth has arrived. She forces herself to breathe deeply and picks up her flashlight. Now she hardly feels the cold. She leans against the little wooden coffins and examines their fabulous treasure. Time has eaten away at the shrouds. She can see the abbots' crosses on their chests. She can't tell who's who, because there are no inscriptions. She would have liked to be able to identify Hildebert, but the person she's looking for should be easily recognizable. A few minutes later she finds him, on the third row from the bottom. Lying there on fragments of his shroud, he has a cross on his chest, a ring on his finger, but no head.

Johanna climbs back up into the chapel to get Roman's head. For a long time she studies the stained-glass window representing the Archangel. She lights two torches beside the stairs to the crypt and a large candle that she takes from the altar. An electric light wouldn't be appropriate for the ceremony. Back in the necropolis, facing the wall lined with little coffins, she carefully pulls out the two tiny sarcophagi that hide Roman's remains. She lays them on the crypt floor. Then she turns off her flashlight and moves the candle closer. The lack of oxygen makes the flame stand up tall and vigorous like a highway to heaven. The flame casts a golden circle like a sunflower, enveloping Roman's body as if it were the first dawn. Johanna kneels down beside the broken skeleton. She picks up the skull in her warm hands and places it between her legs. Emotion holds all words within her and clamps shut her white lips. Staring at the abbot's cross on the fleshless chest, she caresses Roman's forehead. Celestial love flows from her eyes, inundates her pale cheeks with tears like transparent salty veins, their warm flow a surrogate for her immobile blood. Silence is her prayer, her hope, and her melancholy. The gesture she is about to undertake is like passion in mourning, closure for her dreams. But for him, the blue window will finally open. She closes her eyes. Nearly a thousand years. A thousand years of reprieve, of suffering, of hopelessness. *Acedia* . . . She removes Moira's cross from around her neck and lays it on Roman's ribs. The Celtic cross slips down between the ribs. It'll be like his heart, so that Moira can gather his soul to her in the heavenly fields. Johanna shivers at the thought of their reunion. For her it will be separation. She lowers her head and her long black hair covers Roman's skull like a veil of parting. Parting forever. She picks up the skull, raises it like a communion wafer, kisses it, and slowly reunites it with its long-lost body.

JUNE 3, 10:47 P.M. Back on the road to Mont-Saint-Michel. The town of Pontorson. Pontorson, with its pink neon signs in the night, just a few kilometers from the Mount. Johanna speeds through the intersection. She must see it. See it as if it were the first and the last time. There, there it is, the "fairy castle set in the sea." There it is, at the end of her dreams, the end of the shadows, rising up alone in its everlasting glory, Jerusalem, the New Jerusalem. The city of God, the rock of the end of time, where Johanna hopes Roman awaits her. The fortress of his reunited body remained mute back in the chapel of the dead, beneath foreign soil.

"You couldn't appear in Montfort because your heart is with your soul," Johanna thinks. "And your soul is on the eternal mountain, in the granite womb of Notre-Dame-sous-Terre. I'm coming back, I want to bid you adieu before you leave the mountain as I soon will, too. I long to see you and finally contemplate your face. You must be waiting above the Trinity altar, on the stairway to heaven. The Archangel is golden; he'll relinquish his sword and scales and extend his hand to you. He'll keep his thousand-year promise. Time is nothing, it unites the angels as it reunites men."

She accelerates.

She gets to Beauvoir, a town that used to be called Astériac until the year 709, when a blind woman regained her sight at the moment she faced the Mount. Johanna drives through Beauvoir. The night is dark for the month of June. The tide is high. The abbey's stones are whispering, singing, screaming. Johanna is pure joy, sadness, and fatigue. Her head and body feel as heavy as an anvil. Her eyelids begin to droop, to close, and everything grows dark. The car skids off the road.

Suddenly, the night sky grows bright. A long, thin shape appears, dark and ominous. Then the specter grows clearer and takes on a human form. A dark, homespun frock, a hooded scapular, a crown of dark hair beneath the tonsure, and a face . . . what a face! The face of a young, handsome man, so handsome! Delicate lips, an aquiline nose, a high forehead, fine, light skin, and such eyes . . . big eyes, like two smoky gray signs, like mystery's black vapor. He opens his mouth.

"*Deo gratias*," he murmurs, his voice like a caress. "Merci!"

Moving through the sky as over clear waters, he draws closer. He raises one arm and extends his hand. His fingers are long, pale, soft, and thin, the fingers of someone whose hands have not known hard labor. Johanna's body grows as light as a cloud, and her spirit is as peaceful as the choir in a church.

"Johanna," he whispers. "You've unchained me from the earth. I was sentenced by the Archangel to wander like my heart, between earth and sky. Here on earth my heart was a vagabond, homeless, torn between the Almighty and Moira. When I appeared before the weigher of souls, the first among the angels, he told me that if they are true, human and divine love are not opposites but mutually beneficial. I could have loved Moira and consecrated myself to God or loved God while giving myself to Moira. But by refusing to choose, by separating my head from my body, by refusing to give myself fully to either or to renounce one or the other,

I wasn't able to truly love either one. '*Thou art neither cold nor hot. Why art thou not one or the other? Since thou art lukewarm, I shall spew thee out of my mouth,*' the Messiah says to the Angel of Laodicea in John's Book of Revelations, our Holy Book. That was me, neither cold nor hot, and Saint Michael spewed me out of his mouth.

"And yet the Archangel showed me people whom I could ask for help. But for centuries, alas, nobody could break the curse. When I saw my poor body leave the rock while my head remained beneath the crypt Notre-Dame-sous-Terre, I despaired of ever being delivered. Much later, the master of the holy mountain led me to a little girl. And I was afraid. When monks and warriors had failed, how could a child, a female child, succeed? Where monks and warriors had perished, how could you survive? I looked at you from the depths of time, Johanna, and I realized why he had chosen you. Your soul, as powerful as the souls of monks and warriors, loved me. Love is what saved me, and perhaps my love one day can save you. But tonight, when thanks to you I can leave my exile, all I can do is help you understand yourself. Part of your soul is like mine, Johanna, more inclined to love people's actions than the people themselves. Since Pierre's death, you've been hesitating, vacillating between life and death. You are still alive, but you've abandoned your heart. It's imprisoned by your brother's ghost, hidden away in the crypt of your memory. You, too, remain between earth and heaven, belonging to neither. This evening, Johanna, you need to choose. If you choose to leave the earth, the Archangel will lead you to the heavens. If you prefer life, you'll need to become flesh and quell your fear of loving, your fear of giving your heart to someone who might abandon you. You were able to connect with me. Don't forget: You must dig in the earth to reach heaven. Be your own earth, live in the shadows of your own wounds, where you will find light. But only you can decide, Johanna. Your story's end has not yet been written. It is never complete. You are free, and your job will be to write it yourself. Adieu, my good friend."

Roman pulls away his pale hand, and slowly he fades away until even his smile disappears. The firmament has lost its color, and darkness enshrouds Mont-Saint-Michel. Near Beauvoir, the night is brighter. The pale moonlight is lit up with flashing red and blue lights, and screaming sirens speed toward a car resting upside down, rear wheels still spinning. The front of the car is embedded in a muddy salt-grass ravine overlooking the moving sea.

At the gates of heaven, near the Archangel's feet, Roman passes through a white cloud and time's hidden face appears. Finally, he is able to decipher the invisible web of his own destiny and the destiny of those he holds dear. His heart burning with gratitude, he turns to look one last time at Johanna lying there unconscious between two worlds.